4.64

P197

Beeville Elem
Discarded

Beeville Elementary Schools
Discarded Materials

D0734888

The Fireside Book of
CHRISTMAS STORIES

THE
FIRESIDE BOOK
OF
CHRISTMAS
STORIES

Edited by EDWARD WAGENKNECHT

Illustrated by Wallace Morgan

NEW YORK *Grosset & Dunlap* PUBLISHERS

Copyright 1945 by The Bobbs-Merrill Company

PRINTED IN THE UNITED STATES OF AMERICA

TO

Julia Marlowe Sothern

FOR A CHRISTMAS CARD

R. A. HALL SCHOOL LIBRARY
Beeville, Texas

Contents

CONTENTS

III: CHRISTMAS IS DICKENS

IV: CHRISTMAS IS HOME

CONTENTS

Introduction

I suppose that "The Fireside Book of Christmas Stories" began the day I first read "The Other Wise Man." Perhaps it began even earlier than that, say on Christmas Day in the year 1912, when, at a little theater on Ogden Avenue in Chicago, I saw Florence LaBadie's radiant young Madonna in the Thanhouser film production of "The Star of Bethlehem," or at the Bijou Dream on State Street, where, younger still, I witnessed the old Pathé "Passion Play." I am sure the Star itself traveled upon wires in that prehistoric masterpiece, but the production had the naïve charm which distinguished early mystery plays and early cinema drama alike; and it thrilled me far more than any of the blasé and mechanically marvelous contrivances that Hollywood is capable of turning out nowadays.

My purpose in this book has been very simple. I have tried to bring together as many of the best Christmas stories as I could manage to crowd between a single pair of covers. There are, to be sure, a few essays in the book—in Section II the full exposition of my theme could hardly have been managed without them—but essentially I have made, as my title implies, a book of stories. A glance at the Table of Contents will quickly show, however, that the volume is not a miscellany. It does not include any and all types of Christmas story. On the contrary, its material has been arranged according to a definite plan.

It goes without saying, I take it, that most Christmas stories are bad. With the single exception of "Home and Mother," no subject is more likely than Christmas to bring out all the worst faults of the mawkishly inclined, especially when they are so inclined for a consideration. Yet I have been surprised to see how much good literature, written by good writers, I have been able to get into this book. I do not claim that every story I have reprinted here is a masterpiece; I certainly do not claim that there is no "sentimentality" in the volume. To bring out a collection of Christmas stories that completely avoided the sentimental would, indeed, strike me as rather quaint. Chesterton used to remind us that as a bad man was still a man, so a bad poet was still a poet. By the same token, I suppose we may say that even the sentimentalist has his right to a share in Christmas. I have, it is true, omitted a fair number of well-known purveyors of Christmas cheer—gulp as I might, I could not quite get them down—but I have not tried to make a "highbrow" book, as "An Anthology of Christmas Prose and Verse," edited by D. L. Kelleher, and "A Christmas Book, An Anthology for Moderns," edited by D. B. Wyndham Lewis and G. C. Haseltine, for example, are "highbrow" books. After all, Christmas belongs to the people. In this book the reader will find what it means to the people and what the people have made of it. The audience I have in mind is made up of adult "general readers" who are neither morons nor super-cynics, the people of good but not austere tastes who compose the great body of the book-buying public in North America.

Much of the material included in this volume has not, to the best of my knowledge, appeared in a Christmas anthology before. But I have not excluded any story I really wanted simply because another anthologist had wanted it before me.

The first, the distinctively religious, section of my book centers around the idea of the First Christmas. It opens, inevitably, with the two New Testament accounts of the birth and infancy of Jesus; I have named Saint Matthew and Saint Luke as the authors of these with no desire to enter into any of the controversial questions of Biblical scholarship which may be involved. Here, in Luke's account especially, we have the idyl of Christendom. Renan was surely right when he called Luke's Gospel the most beautiful book ever written; and surely no part of it is more beautiful than the Christmas story.

Naturally I have given these stories in the King James version. The old lady who rejected all modern translations of the Bible on the ground that if the King James version was good enough for Saint Paul it was good enough for her, was weak in history, but her literary taste was excellent.

Introduction

It is an amazing fact that the two greatest books ever published in England—the two books worth all the other books ever published in England put together—should have appeared within a dozen years of each other: the King James Bible in 1611 and the First Folio Shakespeare in 1623.

The Wise Men with their camels stand side by side with the shepherds whenever we set up our crèche: it is to be noted that the distinguished visitors are peculiar to Matthew's account. According to Matthew the infant Jesus was visited by "magoi," Wise Men from the East, who had been led by a star, and who did homage to him and presented him with gifts of gold and frankincense and myrrh.

Matthew does not tell us who these men were, how many they were, or where they came from. Herodotus speaks of magi as Medians and soothsayers; Plato connects them with Zoroaster. Tradition has taught us to think of the Wise Men as three in number; we call them Melchior, Caspar, and Balthasar. We get these names from the Armenian Gospel of the Infancy. Sometimes we call them Three Kings. That comes from medieval legend, possibly to fulfill the saying of Isaiah 49:7—"Kings shall see and arise, princes also shall worship." Christian commentators found a symbolical significance in the gifts of the Wise Men. Gold, they said, symbolized Christ's royalty, incense his priesthood, and the myrrh was brought for his entombment.

In Luke the only visitors who come to see the poor baby in the manger are humble shepherds from the hills of Judea. (Luke's interest in humble folk is never-failing.) But if the shepherds are humble in themselves, they come under high auspices, for the angel of the Lord appeared to them, while they were keeping watch over their flocks, to tell them that the Saviour had been born.

The whole story of Herod's interest in the newborn child, which involves the Slaughter of the Innocents and the flight of the Holy Family into Egypt, is peculiar to Matthew.

In addition to all these matters, there is one rather more subtle difference between Luke and Matthew. In Matthew, the whole story of the birth of Jesus is told from a man's point of view, from Joseph's point of view. Luke tells the story from a woman's point of view. This circumstance has led some scholars to suggest that Luke may have derived his account of the birth of Jesus from Mary. Luke tells us that Mary kept all these things and pondered them in her heart. Perhaps he had good reason to know how thoroughly, how profoundly she had pondered them.

The insight of the poet is not circumscribed by all the considerations which rightly constrain the historian. So, in the half story, half essay, called "Even Unto Bethlehem," Henry van Dyke enters imaginatively into the heart of the Mother of God, and frees us from the bondage of evidenced fact. Here is a "just suppose" speculation, a study in "what might have been." In some such way as this, a pious mother might have chosen that Bethlehem should have the honor of giving her offspring life. And so "Even Unto Bethlehem" makes a good introduction to the more elaborate literary embroidery upon the story of the First Christmas in the narratives which follow.

"The Other Wise Man," beloved now for fifty years, has become almost the type-tale for this kind of literature, but I think "The Man at the Gate of the World," by the British writer, W. E. Cule, quite as appealing. It is often supposed that Cule wrote in imitation of van Dyke; this is not the case. His story is much less known in America than it ought to be; I hope that this reprint may contribute in some way to bringing it before its potential audience.

Frances Hodgson Burnett tells the old story from a fresh point of view in "The Little Hunchback Zia"; the John Evans piece appealed to me because of its fresh and novel manner of presentation. Elizabeth Hart's short novel, "The Husband of Mary," takes its point of departure from an aspect of the story of the birth of Jesus which unbelievers made an occasion of scandal from the first century on down; it is interesting to compare this with T. F. Powys' much less conventional treatment of the matter in his Christmas story "in modern dress" (one might say), which is included in Section III. At the end of Section I, I have extended the theme of the First Christmas sufficiently to permit F. K. Foraandh to take a look at the baby a year later.

In a Pacific Coast city, some Christmases ago, we witnessed a shocking manifestation of our contemporary ignorance and paganism when a woman, passing a department-store window in which the Manger Scene had been set up as a holiday offering, was heard to exclaim, "Can you beat that? There's the Church trying to horn in on Christmas!"

The darkies in Roark Bradford's delightful skit are much concerned over who comed fust, ole Sandy Claus or de little Lawd Jesus; and the solution of the problem which they finally evolve for themselves ought to entertain us as much as it satisfies them. But the confusion they manifest is not theirs alone, nor yet that of the stupid woman at the department store. To lose Christ is no doubt to lose Christmas; but the festival has other than its strictly religious aspects, and most Christians believe that some of them have developed under the providence of God. So, in this book, Section II must follow Section I.

John Macy's account of the development of the Santa Claus legend is both lucid and scholarly; and Gamaliel Bradford was as warmly human and sympathetic as ever when he playfully applied his own distinctive method of character portraiture to the study of the children's saint. Coningsby Dawson mingles old traditions with fresh imagination in "When Father Christmas Was Young"; and Henry van Dyke comes back into the book to give us a wholly imaginative account of the origin of the Christmas tree. Other aspects of the Christmas legend are considered by Katharine Lee Bates, in her fine essay, and by James Lane Allen, in two easily detachable chapters from his novel, "The Doctor's Christmas Eve."

Section III is green with holly and smells strongly of plum pudding. Dickens dominates this section, but Dickens did not create the British Christmas out of hand; it is fitting, I think, that the old customs should be described first by Addison (who saw them in the eighteenth century) and by Washington Irving. Irving is the only American in Section III, an American writing on a British theme toward which, as sometimes happens, his attitude was more British than that of the British themselves.

Dickens has been called "The Man Who Discovered Christmas," and A. Edward Newton used to be fond of calling the "Carol" "The Greatest Little Book in the World." Well, Dickens rediscovered Christmas at any rate, and it is impossible to think of Christmas without thinking of him. The story of Mr. Pickwick's adventures at Dingley Dell is in the eighteenth-century manner, and "The Story of the Goblins and the Sexton" which is a part of it represents a ruder and probably more indigenous form of British Christmas tale than the later work. As for the "Carol" itself, I could not quite bring myself to omit it. Even an anthology must pay some attention to symmetry, to the fitness of things; and a "Fireside Book" of Christmas stories without the "Carol" would be rather like a production of "Hamlet" with the Prince of Denmark on an American tour. I have saved space, however, and at the same time avoided merely duplicating a book which all my readers must already have in their libraries by reprinting not the complete, familiar 1843 version, but the later abbreviated "Carol" which Dickens used as a reading.

Mrs. Gaskell is here too, as one more eminent Victorian and a member of the Dickens school; and both E. F. Bozman and that wonderful teller of tales, Marjorie Bowen (Joseph Shearing), whose amazing fecundity is surely one of the great blessings of life in our time, carry on the old British habit of telling ghost stories at Christmas, a habit which Dickens did not originate but which he certainly did much to encourage. (Vincent Starrett's "Snow for Christmas" in Section IV is a rare American example of the Christmas ghost story.)

The other stories in Section III are different. Mr. de la Mare's distinguished narrative—the adjective is superfluous, for "Mr. de la Mare's narrative" would mean the same thing—is a story which has a Christmas setting rather than a Christmas story in the narrower sense of the term; its astringency may be relished by those who find too many Christmas comfits cloying. There is astringency also in the

Introduction

T. F. Powys story, and astringency turns to bitterness in Daphne du Maurier's powerful tale, which gives the Jew his share in the Christmas festival.

Impudence, not astringency, is the word for "Oh, What a Horrid Tale!" by P. S. (John Hadfield), which I have included for the simple reason that I found it irresistible. It is like no other story I have ever read.

I have included one essay in Section III because here again I was quite unable to help myself. The Old World charm of the paper from Alexander Smith's "Dreamthorp" is as potent today as it was in the sixties.

In Section IV, the American section, the "Home for Christmas" motive dominates; we find it, for example, in Louisa May Alcott, Zona Gale (with a slightly wry turn), Archibald Rutledge, and Alice Van Leer Carrick. Zona Gale, like Elsie Singmaster, wrote so many good Christmas stories that it was difficult to make a choice. "The Birds' Christmas Carol" is the most famous of all American Christmas stories; here, if anywhere in the collection, we have Victorian tearfulness; but age has its privileges, and Americans have wept too often over this tale to decline to weep once again.

At the other extreme, we have Christopher Morley's "Worst Christmas Story," quite in the modern idiom. Langston Hughes' Negro story carries much the same kind of rebuke for racial snobbery that we have already found in Miss du Maurier's contribution in the British section; and "I Gotta Idee!" by Elsie Singmaster also falls under the head of social criticism.

Persons who remember how many American Christmases have been brightened by the genius of Howard Pyle will not like this book less, I think, for resurrecting a narrative first read in "Harper's Magazine," more than thirty-five Christmases ago; a very different item, Hamlin Garland's fine autobiographical piece, has not been reprinted, so far as either his daughters or I know, since it appeared in "The Ladies' Home Journal" in December 1911.

I have included the stories by Margaret Carpenter and Margery Williams Bianco because though this is not a book for children, I could see no reason why it should not be, in part, a book about them. Finally I bring down the curtain with two heart-warming pieces by Jake Falstaff and Bill Adams because if anything better in kind has been written about Christmas I do not know what it is.

And so, a Merry Christmas! And, as Tiny Tim observed . . .

EDWARD WAGENKNECHT

Evanston, Illinois

The Fireside Book of
CHRISTMAS STORIES

I

Christmas Is Christ

STORIES OF THE BABE OF BETHLEHEM

AND THE FIRST CHRISTMAS

That glorious form, that light unsufferable,
And that far-beaming blaze of majesty,
Wherewith he wont at Heaven's high council-table
To sit the midst of Trinal Unity,
He laid aside; and here with us to be,
   Forsook the courts of everlasting day,
And chose with us a darksome house of mortal clay.

JOHN MILTON : ODE ON THE MORNING
OF CHRIST'S NATIVITY

SAINT MATTHEW

The Birth of Jesus Christ...

NOW the birth of Jesus Christ was on this wise: when as his mother Mary was espoused to Joseph, before they came together, she was found with child of the Holy Ghost. Then Joseph her husband, being a just man, and not willing to make her a public example, was minded to put her away privily. But while he thought on these things, behold the angel of the Lord appeared unto him in a dream, saying, "Joseph, thou son of David, fear not to take unto thee Mary thy wife: for that which is conceived in her is of the Holy Ghost. And she shall bring forth a son, and thou shalt call his name JESUS: for he shall save his people from their sins."

Now all this was done, that it might be fulfilled which was spoken of the Lord by the prophet, saying, "Behold, a virgin shall

3

be with child, and shall bring forth a son, and they shall call his name Emmanuel, which being interpreted is, God with us."

Then Joseph being raised from sleep did as the angel of the Lord had bidden him, and took unto him his wife: and knew her not till she had brought forth her first-born son: and he called his name JESUS.

Now when Jesus was born in Bethlehem of Judea in the days of Herod the king, behold, there came wise men from the east to Jerusalem, saying, "Where is he that is born King of the Jews? for we have seen his star in the east, and are come to worship him." When Herod the king had heard these things, he was troubled, and all Jerusalem with him. And when he had gathered all the chief priests and scribes of the people together, he demanded of them where Christ should be born. And they said unto him, "In Bethlehem of Judea, for thus it is written by the prophet: 'And thou, Bethlehem, in the land of Judah, art not the least among the princes of Judah, for out of thee shall come a governor that shall rule my people Israel.' "

Then Herod, when he had privily called the wise men, inquired of them diligently what time the star appeared. And he sent them to Bethlehem, and said, "Go and search diligently for the young child; and when ye have found him, bring me word again, that I may come and worship him also."

When they had heard the king, they departed; and, lo, the star, which they saw in the east, went before them, till it came and stood over where the young child was. When they saw the star, they rejoiced with exceeding great joy.

And when they were come into the house, they saw the young child with Mary his mother, and fell down, and worshiped him; and when they had opened their treasures, they presented unto him gifts: gold, and frankincense, and myrrh. And being warned of God in a dream that they should not return to Herod, they departed into their own country another way.

And when they were departed, behold, the angel of the Lord appeared to Joseph in a dream, saying, "Arise, and take the young child and his mother, and flee into Egypt, and be thou there until I bring thee word; for Herod will seek the young child to destroy him." When he arose, he took the young child and his mother by night, and departed into Egypt, and was there until the death of Herod, that it might be fulfilled which was spoken of the Lord by the prophet, saying, "Out of Egypt have I called my son."

Then Herod, when he saw that he was mocked of the wise men, was exceeding wroth, and sent forth, and slew all the children that were in Bethlehem, and in all the coasts thereof, from two years old and under, according to the time which he had diligently inquired of the wise men. Then was fulfilled that which was spoken by Jeremy the prophet, saying, "In Rama was there a voice heard, lamentation, and weeping, and great mourning, Rachel weeping for her children, and would not be comforted, because they are not."

But when Herod was dead, behold, an angel of the Lord appeareth in a dream to Joseph in Egypt, saying, "Arise, and take the young child and his mother, and go into the land of Israel; for they are dead which sought the young child's life." And he arose, and took the young child and his mother, and came into the land of Israel. But when he heard that Archelaus did reign in Judea in the room of his father Herod, he was afraid to go thither. Notwithstanding, being warned of God in a dream, he turned aside into the parts of Galilee; and he came and dwelt in a city called Nazareth, that it might be fulfilled which was spoken by the prophets, "He shall be called a Nazarene."

SAINT LUKE

And It Came To Pass...

AND it came to pass in those days, that there went out a decree from Caesar Augustus, that all the world should be taxed. (And this taxing was first made when Cyrenius was governor of Syria.) And all went to be taxed, every one into his own city. And Joseph also went up from Galilee, out of the city of Nazareth, into Judea, unto the city of David, which is called Bethlehem (because he was of the house and lineage of David), to be taxed with Mary his espoused wife, being great with child.

And so it was, that, while they were there, the days were accomplished that she should be delivered. And she brought forth her first-born son, and wrapped him in swaddling clothes, and laid him in a manger; because there was no room for them in the inn.

And there were in the same country shepherds abiding in the field, keeping watch over their flock by night. And, lo, the angel of the Lord came upon them, and the glory of the Lord shone round about them: and they were sore afraid. And the angel said unto them, "Fear not: for, behold, I bring you good tidings of great joy, which shall be to all people. For unto you is born this day in the city of David a Saviour, which is Christ the Lord. And this shall be a sign unto you: Ye shall find the babe wrapped in swaddling clothes, lying in a manger." And suddenly there was with the angel a multitude of the heavenly host praising God, and saying, "Glory to God in the highest, and on earth peace, good will toward men."

And it came to pass, as the angels were gone away from them into heaven, the shepherds said one to another, "Let us now go even unto Bethlehem, and see this thing which is come to pass, which the Lord hath made known unto us." And they came with haste, and found Mary and Joseph, and the babe lying in a manger. And when they had seen it, they made known abroad the saying which was told them concerning this child. And all they that heard it wondered at those things which were told them by the shepherds. But Mary kept all these things, and pondered them in her heart. And the shepherds returned, glorifying and praising God for all the things that they had heard and seen, as it was told unto them.

And the shepherds returned, glorifying and praising God for all the things that they had heard and seen, just as it was told unto them.

HENRY VAN DYKE

Even Unto Bethlehem

THE STORY OF CHRISTMAS

I: *On the Hill Above Nazareth*

ON the high rondure of the hill above Nazareth the village carpenter, Joseph the son of Jacob, was resting in the evening hour with his young wife Mary. She was very fair and lovely in the habitual dress of a maid of Bethlehem—dark-red bodice, blue skirt and long blue cloak, a white veil covering her light golden hair but not her deep blue eyes and thoughtful face. Her husband was a man of middle age, brown-eyed, brown-bearded, wearing his working-clothes and carpenter's apron.

The grass beneath them was dry and warm, for it was October; the drouth of summer had left the fields parched; the early rains had not yet fallen. The wide rolling world around them was golden-brown, like the pale color of a topaz. Valley and plain and mountain-side lay bathed in the long radiance of the sinking sun.

It was a favorite time and place with these new-wedded lovers. The solitude and silence brought them closer to each other. The glorious view opened their hearts to the large and tranquil thoughts in which our little life expands to a nobler meaning, faith seems easier, and love more rich and pure—a pulse of the very heart of nature.

Northward, snowy Hermon, great Sheikh of Mountains, towered in rosy gold. Eastward, the rolling hills of Moab were a long bulwark beyond Jordan. Southward, across the Plain of Esdraelon, Samaria was a tumbled sea of crests and ridges. Westward, the wide open waters of the Mediterranean flashed in the sunlight or darkened in the shadow of a passing cloud.

The man repeated a verse from the Psalter in his deep drawling Galilean voice.

"I will lift up mine eyes unto the hills, from whence cometh my help."

The woman answered, in the clearer accent of the Judean folk.

"My help cometh from the Lord, who made heaven and earth."

Her blue eyes grew misty with tears—not tears of grief, but of that mysterious inquietude known only to a woman when she thinks of her time of supreme trial in bringing a new life into the world.

"Help?" she murmured. "God knows I shall need help, if the words the angel spoke to me in my dream are true. I am only a country girl. Why should I be chosen to bear the hope of Israel, the seed of David, the son of the Most High? And the time comes on so fast! Here it is, long past the second harvest; and by the turn of winter my baby must be born. How can I wait for it? How can I face it, husband?"

The bearded man, grown heavy and slow in his life of hard manual toil, laid his big brown hand, calloused and roughened by the use of saw and plane, mallet and chisel, very gently on the slender hand of his girl wife as if to comfort her. He was slow in speech as well as in thought.

"Be not afraid, my Mary," he said; "it is all right."

Then he tried to turn her mind away from herself. He pointed down to the great Roman highway which wound among the hills far below them—the road from Damascus to Acca where the white-sailed ships lay waiting in the harbor to carry the commerce of the East across the blue Mediterranean.

"Look, wife," he said, "there goes the third long caravan since we have been sitting here. Busy times!"

The great world distantly went by in a rich parade before the eyes of this rustic couple.

Roman soldiers in glittering ranks, armored and helmeted, with bright eagle-standards shining above their serried spears. Proud horsemen on their Arab stallions. Rich merchants and noblemen in their cushioned litters. Rumbling chariots of brass and gilded wood. Gaily-decorated mules, their collars studded with turquoises and their pack-saddles heaped with crates and boxes. Pattering asses moving under their huge loads like patient curious insects. Scornful, ungainly camels swaying silently along on their padded feet, fastened one to another by ropes or jingling chains, like lines of barges in a tow, laden with corn from the Hauran, silks and swords from Damascus, spices and fragrant woods from Arabia, sweet fruits from the orchards and gardens of Galilee, ornaments and jewels and carven-work from the Greek cities of the Dekapolis. All the wealth and splendor of earth poured along that paved road with its three tracks, each twelve feet wide, divided by upright stones.

On the southern track the eastward flow was scanty just now, mostly of unladen beasts and their drivers, going back to fetch another load, and perhaps one or two convoys of gold or silver money, heavily guarded by soldiers. On the central track, riders and foot-travelers met and passed, going and coming. On the northern track, the westward tide was in full flood. The ancient Orient, mother of luxury and proud indulgence, poured her varied riches toward the bright highway of the sea, that swift ships might bear her merchandise to the eager new markets of Greece and Italy, Gaul and Spain.

Yet on the very edge of all this gleaming, foaming turbulence of world-trade—on the edge of it and above it—the hills and valleys of fair Galilee lay peaceful and secluded. A fertile land and happy; a rustic land and old-fashioned; inhabited by a simple, warm-hearted people who cultivated their gardens and orchards, reaped their crops of wheat and barley, fed their flocks in green pastures, and caught fish in the still waters of the Lake-that-is-shaped-like-a-Harp.

From father to son the village crafts of the carpenter, the smith, the weaver, the potter, were handed down. From mother to daughter the household arts of spinning and sewing, butter-making and bread-baking were transmitted.

The teachers spoke a plainer doctrine. In the synagogues a simpler truth was preached. There was more poetry and faith in Galilee than in all Jerusalem and the rich cities of Judah.

Of this plain, hard-working, high-thoughted folk were Joseph and Mary. They were content in poverty, since they were enriched in soul by the promises made of old to the people of Israel. They were happy in obscurity and not cast down, since they knew that they were of the house and lineage of David from whose royal seed the Messiah was to come. They could let the pomp and vanity of the world stream by below them without an envious thought.

So they watched the amethyst colors deepening on the far mountains of Samaria and Moab, and listened to the larks rising and falling on their fountains of song in the last glow of sunset, and saw the gold and lilac crocuses of autumn blossoming sparsely in the short grass.This provision of beauty was enough for them.With their love, their peace, their great secret hope, they were well-content.

"Come," said Joseph, "the air grows colder. Let us go down to our house. You must not take a chill."

"Yes," answered Mary, "it is time to go home. I will light a fire on the hearth. I hope we can live there quietly until my son is born. It is a friendly house, though it is so small; I can wait patiently there.

I am the handmaid of the Lord; be it unto me according to his word."

So they went down the hill, not by the short steep path, but by a longer easier one. They came to their home on the outskirts of the village, a low cottage of gray stone with the workshop beside it, in a little garden of silvery olive-trees.

The small Egyptian windows toward the street were dark; the wooden door was fastened on the inside with bolts of wood. Joseph drew them back with his check key. They crossed the threshold. Mary kindled a fagot on the hearthstone, and lit a lamp of oil on the table. The whole house was full of light. From the open door of the workshop came a pleasant smell of fresh-hewn planks and wood-shavings. The carpenter and his wife were at home.

II: In the Carpenter's House

OF all the handicrafts in the world there is none cleaner, pleasanter, and more fragrant than that of the carpenter. He works in friendly stuff. If he knows it well enough and can feel its qualities, it yields readily to his working and takes the outward shape of his thought —chair or table or bed, window-frame or shelf or beam.

Well-seasoned lumber he wants, that it may not warp. Knots and cross-grains trouble him, like original sin in man; but he takes note carefully, and avoids or conquers them. He judges his material with his eye before he measures it with square and foot-rule. His mind guides his fingers; his fingers fit his tools; his tools work his will in wood.

What good odors rise around him as he labors! From each tree its own fragrance: the resinous smell of the terebinth and the cypress; the delicate scent of the wild-olive with its smooth, curly texture; the faint, dry sweetness of the orange-yellow acacia with its darker heart; the clean odor of the oak with its hard, solid grain; and on rare days, the aromatic perfume of some precious piece of the cedar of Lebanon, king of trees.

Joseph, the carpenter of Nazareth, was proud of his trade. He loved it. At the beginning of December, on a cloudy morning, he was in his shop making a wedding-chest for the daughter of a rich neighbor. The long box of durable shittim-wood was well smoothed with the plane and firmly mortised with pins of oak; and now on the lid Joseph was working an ornament. With gouge and chisel and file he wrought his design; not of birds or beasts or human figures, for that would have been against the Jewish tradition; but a graceful pattern of a vine with curving branches, broad leaves, and rich clusters of grapes. That was permitted by the law. Was it not even a sacred sign and emblem? Joseph hummed an old song as he carved.

> *"Blessed is every one that feareth the Lord,*
> *And walketh in his ways.*
> *Thou shalt eat the labor of thy hands;*
> *Happy shalt thou be.*
> *Thy wife shall be as a fruitful vine,*
> *Planted within thy house."*

He stood ankle-deep in shavings, absorbed in his task. From the doorway Mary called to him. He looked up.

"Husband, I am going to the village fountain to fill our water-jar. It is empty. There are curious rumors going about among the neighbors. All the other women will be at the fountain. They will tell me the news."

"They surely will," answered the man. "They always know all that is going on,—and sometimes more! But go carefully, beloved. Do not strain to lift the heavy jar."

Gathered around the clear flowing spring, beneath its arch of stone beyond the market-place, Mary found a little crowd of women and girls, filling their jars and pitchers, and talking volubly together. From them she gathered all the gossip. At last came the bit of news which she had feared.

They looked at her curiously and with those sidelong glances which women always wear when they have been talking about you before you came. But they were kind to her. There was even a shade of pity in their look as they told the news which had a special meaning for her. They helped her to lift her jar of water and balance it on her shoulder. Then she walked home with faltering steps under her burden.

Joseph met her at the door. He took the jar from her shoulder and set it within the house.

"What is it?" he asked. "Why are you so sad?"

"It is bad news, Joseph," she answered, "and it must be true, because it was the wife of the teacher who told me. A decree has gone out from the great heathen man at Rome—the one they call Caesar—that all the world must be enrolled for the payment of a new tax. The governor of Syria has proclaimed it, and that vile king, Herod the Idumean, has ordered it to be done. All the people must be written down in the lists in their own cities, according to Jewish law, by tribes and families. Oh, Joseph, do you see what that means for us? We must go to Bethlehem, the city of the family of David. I am terribly afraid of that long, hard journey now, with my time so near. What if we should run into some danger? What if an accident should befall me? What if I should lose the child I carry, the hope of Israel? I could not bear it. Ah, woe is me! Woe is me!"

She was shaken with grief as she sank upon the bench. The tears rolled down her cheeks, splashing on her dark-red bodice and long blue cloak. The white veil which covered her hair was thrown back in disorder. She was the picture of dismay and sorrow.

Joseph kneeled beside her, distressed and bewildered so that he could hardly speak.

"Listen, dear heart," he stammered, "it may not be so bad. You speak of Jewish law—but this decree is Roman law. Perhaps there is a way out! Our names might be enrolled here in Nazareth—I was born in Galilee—then we could send them to Bethlehem to be registered. What do you think? My friend Matthew in Capernaum is an officer for the Romans—a tax-gatherer—I will go and ask him about it. It is not far to Capernaum! I shall be back soon. Don't be afraid, my wife."

So Mary was a little comforted, and dried her tears. Joseph took his staff and a loaf of bread, and set out for the Lake-that-is-shaped-like-a-Harp.

Even Unto Bethlehem

In his absence Mary was at first very restless and anxious about the result of his journey. On the second day she went into the synagogue and took her place with the women behind the lattice, in the enclosure assigned to them. The speaker for that day was a stranger, a rabbi from Jerusalem. Standing, according to the custom, he read from the book of Prophet Micah.

"But thou, Bethlehem Ephrathah, which art little among the thousands of Judah, out of thee shall One come forth that is to be Ruler in Israel; whose goings forth are from of old, from eternity. Therefore will he give them up until the time that she who travaileth hath brought forth; ten the residue of his brethren shall return unto the children of Israel."

Strange words, thought Mary; could they have any special meaning for her? "Bethlehem"? "She who travaileth"? The "Ruler in Israel"? Here was matter that touched her closely.

She listened intently while the preacher, taking his seat now on the bema as was the custom, began to explain the scripture that he had read.

"Bethlehem was David's city. Nowhere else than in this little town can the Messiah, who is to be the son of David, come into the world. 'She who travaileth' is not named. But even now some unknown daughter of Israel may be carrying the Redeemer of God's people hidden under her breast. Wait then, ye faithful, wait patiently, and look with hope to Bethlehem. To Bethlehem first, to Bethlehem only!"

Mary, standing quietly among the women, with her veil drawn down to hide her face, was thrilled to the heart, uplifted, transfigured with a strong joy. Her prayer in time of trouble had been heard. A word direct from heaven had come to her. She herself was the "unknown daughter of Israel."

Her fear vanished. Her path shone clear before her. She lifted her veil from her face, and walked home full of courage and vigor, determined in her duty.

Late that evening Joseph returned from Capernaum, dusty and weary.

"Good news," he cried, "Matthew can arrange it. You can be enrolled here. I may have to go to Bethlehem, but you will stay here, dearest!"

"No, my husband," she answered quietly. "My mind has been changed. A message has come to me straight from heaven. All my fears are gone. My son shall be born in the place where the prophet has foretold his coming. For me, even more than for you, this journey is necessary. You shall never leave me nor forsake me. No harm will come to me. The power of the Most High has overshadowed me. Let us go even unto Bethlehem. To-morrow I will send a letter to my cousin Elizabeth to meet us there. In Bethlehem it must be."

III: *The Long Long Way to Bethlehem*

THE preparations for the journey were simple, but it took some time to make them. The affairs of Joseph must be put in order; his promised work delivered, his few debts paid, his small dues collected. With part of his savings he bought an ass, very small and old and thin, and therefore cheap.

"He is not much to look at," said Joseph, "poor old Thistles! But he is patient and tough; and he picks his living along the road. He can carry you over the rough places. The whole way on foot would wear you out."

The aged man who sold the donkey to Joseph had been a peddler, travelling around the country with earthenware for sale. For these journeys in all kinds of weather he had provided himself with a big mantle of goat's-hair, so closely woven that it was waterproof. This also he wished to sell, since his travelling days were done.

"This will be the very thing for my wife," thought Joseph. "It is not pretty; but the cold winter rains are coming on, and we may have to sleep out at night before we get to Bethlehem. This will be like a little tent for her."

So Joseph bought it with two of the few silver coins that were left in his purse. Mary laughed when she tried it on over her pretty blue cloak.

16

"It makes me look like an Edomite woman," she said.

"Little matter how it looks," said her husband, "if it only keeps you dry and warm."

Other clothing too would be needed, particularly some long linen bands for swaddling a baby. These Mary prepared with her own fingers, taking great pains with them and embroidering Hebrew letters on them in red and blue threads.

Joseph fastened a sharp iron spike on the end of his heaviest staff, so that it would serve as a weapon if any wild beast attacked them. Last of all a supply of bread must be baked, some thin strips of meat dried and salted, a bag full of lentils provided, and a small earthen pot to cook them in—also a cup and a water-bottle. So the outfit was completed and the time of their departure was at hand: the third week in December.

There were three ways from Galilee to the high lands of Judea. One went by the west along the sea-coast and the plain of Sharon. But that was frequented by rowdy foreigners and led through rich heathen seaports, full of abominations. The straightest and shortest road crossed the plain of Esdraelon into the mountains of Samaria, and so by Shechem and Bethel to Jerusalem. But it was a steep road and the Samaritans who lived along that line were rude and churlish folk and the Jews had no dealings with them. The third route descended into the Jordan Valley, followed the east bank of the river, and went up from Jericho into the hills. Perhaps it was a bit round-about, but it was fairly level and for a good part of the way it was the warmest of the three routes. This was their choice.

So they shut their small stone house and left it in charge of a neighbor; said good-bye to peaceful Nazareth nestling in its green hollow among the hills; and went down the open road to their great adventure.

There were no angelic wings to bear them up and carry them over the rough places, lest Mary should bruise her foot against a stone. No rich traveller rolling by offered them a lift in his chariot; they were too humble and poor for that courtesy. Nor was there any miracle to remove the hardships or shorten the weary miles of

17

the long, long way. It was plain plodding. Step after step they must measure the hundred miles, with only poor little Thistles to carry the scanty luggage and to let Mary ride on his back now and then, when she was too tired to put one foot before the other.

Past the village of Endor below Mount Tabor where Saul's witch once lived, past Shunem where Elisha's generous hostess built a room for him on the wall of her house and called it the prophet's chamber, the pilgrims trudged along until they came to a quiet nook on the lower slope of Little Hermon. Here they ate their mid-day meal.

All around them lay the ancient scenes of battle, murder and sudden death. Opposite was the dark bulk of Mount Gilboa, where Gideon sifted out his chosen band to attack the host of Midian, and where desperate Saul killed himself with his own sword because he had lost a battle to the Philistines. Not far away the savage Jael drove her tent-pin through the temples of the sleeping Sisera. In Jezreel on a spur of Mount Gilboa, the painted hag, Queen Jezebel, looked from her palace window to see Captain Jehu, the killer of her son and other kings, driving boldly up the street. "Is it peace," she cried, "thou Zimri, thy master's murderer?" So Jehu called out to two or three of her servants, and they threw the raddled royal harridan down from the high window, and her blood splashed on the wall, and Jehu's horses trod her under foot. "Bury her decently," he said, "for she was a king's daughter."

Little thought our lowly travellers of these by-gone strifes and cruelties. Mary and Joseph belonged to another kingdom. She was chosen to be the mother of the Prince of Peace, and she was going on foot, very quietly, to Bethlehem, in order that the words of the angel and the prophet might be fulfilled. This obedient resolve made her firm and fearless. On this purpose her whole being was centered.

Through the green vale of Jezreel they passed easily, for the going was nearly level. But when they came beyond the spurs of Mount Gilboa on the south, there was an abrupt drop of three hundred feet, down which the trail went in steep zig-zags, so that Mary dared not ride, but must go carefully afoot. Before them on its high mound in the long Jordan Valley rose the old city of Bethshan, now called Scythopolis, a heathen town and fortress.

"Not there," said Mary, "we can not lodge there! The very ground on which the idolaters build their houses is unclean. The Gentiles carry the taint of the wickedness by which the serpent corrupted Eve. Only the Jewish people have been cleansed from it. I am very tired; but let us go on till we come to a village of our own folk. A cottage there is better than a palace among the pagans."

So they trudged on to Bethabara, a poor hamlet beside the murmuring fords of the river Jordan. Here they were received into a humble house with that open hospitality which was practised among the Jews, and rested well until the morning.

The river was swollen by the rains. The fords were greatly deepened and the muddy water was foaming over them. But Mary rode on Thistles, with her feet tucked up, and Joseph waded the stream below, with his strong left arm around her and his sturdy body pressing up against the little shivering beast to keep him from being swept down by the swift current.

On the eastern side the descent of the Jordan Valley was not hard, though the road was miry, for the rain fell in sheets, and Mary was thankful for the big goat's-hair cloak. All day long they journeyed, but night fell before they could reach the village of Succoth, where they had hoped to find lodging. So they camped on a rising ground above the deep trench in which the Jordan raged through its matted jungle towards the Dead Sea. The night was not very cold, for they were below the level of the Mediterranean; and though a few drops of rain were falling, still the air of the Ghôr was soft and humid.

Mary was a poet by nature. In her heart the spring of song rose constant and flowed clear. Before she slept she sang again that lyric she had made more than six months ago when she visited her cousin Elizabeth beside the crystal fount of Ain Karim.

> "*My soul doth magnify the Lord;*
> *My spirit hath rejoiced in God my Savior,*

For he hath regarded the low estate of his handmaid;
Hereafter all the generations shall call me blessed."

The next day was heavier and more oppressive. The rain held off; but the path dropped steadily below the sea-level, eight hundred, nine hundred feet. These hill-people, accustomed to the pure, light air of Galilee, found exertion more difficult.

But Mary's resolution did not fail. Step after step she plodded on. They passed Succoth where Jacob had built him a house and made shelters for his cattle after his wrestling with the angel by the Brook Jabbok. That same little river was now pouring down in flood and Joseph had to go a long way up and around before he could find a safe ford through its turbid, bluish waters.

Down the broadening Ghôr the pilgrims held their way. There were few villages or human dwellings. On the evening of the third day, Mary's strength being almost spent, they were forced to camp again. This time they were nearer to the thick jungle of the river-bed, where savage beasts lurked—lions and leopards, jackals and wild boars. Joseph encircled the camp with a fire of thorn-bushes, which crackled and sent up sparks.

"They won't pass this," he said. "Don't be afraid, Mary."

"I'm afraid of nothing," she answered. "I will both lay me down in peace and sleep, for the Lord will watch over his Son whom I carry."

It was sprinkling rain, so she rolled herself in her big mantle and slept. But Joseph kept his fires going.

Once when the yapping of the jackals came nearer he heard also the fierce whine of a leopard, close to the fire, and saw a pair of green gleaming eyes in the darkness beyond. He hurled his heavy iron-pointed staff at them. There was a terrible cry of angry pain, a swift pattering of feet in the dark. Then silence. Mary slept on, for she was dead-tired.

The fourth day they reached Beth-Haran, very weary, and found a kindly shelter with poor folks. On the fifth morning they crossed the swollen ford with the aid of the villagers, passed around the stately city of Jericho with its palm-groves and rich gardens soaked in perpetual summer, and took the steep road south-west into the Judean hills.

Here the going was harder for Mary, heavy with child. Fleeting pains troubled her as she walked, and when she tried to ride it was worse. The Brook Kedron, in summer a bare bed of stones, was now a foaming torrent. They got over it with difficulty. Poor Thistles trembled and slipped among the rocks. Once Mary would have been thrown into the water if Joseph had not caught her in his arms. She suffered more and more. But she was not to be conquered in her purpose.

At noon they rested and took food in a lonely gulch among the red rocks. Wearied by her pains, Mary fell into a brief, troubled sleep. A vision of sudden death came to her. She saw herself as a woman walking alone over a crimson plain, which rolled and tossed under her feet like a stormy sea. There was a roaring sound about her as of many waters. Then the red ground split open and she sank down, down into death; but even as she sank, she lifted her child above her into safety. She woke with a little cry of pain. Joseph ran to comfort her.

"I am not afraid," she said. "I can go through the gates of death to bring forth my son and my Lord."

Towards nightfall they came over the last rugged hill into the little town of Bethlehem.

The inn was full, crowded with people who had come up to be registered; the courtyard swarmed with men and animals in noisy confusion, there was not a single vacant place in the alcoves which opened around it.

But Elizabeth, Mary's cousin, the wife of Zacharias the priest, was there to welcome them. Being forewarned by the letter from Mary that they were coming, she had climbed on foot ten miles across the hills from Bethcar where she lived, carrying her six-months-old son John, to meet the travellers from Nazareth.

She was gray-haired, over fifty years old, but a strong and hearty woman. She remembered well the day when young Mary had come to visit her in Bethcar more than six months ago, and the

21

R. A. HALL SCHOOL LIBRARY
Beeville, Texas

child within her had leaped in greeting to the mother of his coming Lord. That unconscious prophecy was now very near to its fulfilment. Elizabeth was a woman of experience, and she knew.

"Come with me," she said, "come quickly, beloved! I have a place for you. It is a dry grotto in the face of the cliff behind the inn. It has been used as a stable. It has two stalls. In the further part there is nothing but an old ox; the other part is empty and clean, and there is plenty of dry straw for a bed, and there is also a clean manger for a cradle. It is all ready, come quickly!"

Elizabeth took command like a general. Mary clung to her, weeping half in pain and half in joy. Joseph followed, leading Thistles. The weary old ass was put into the stall with the ox. Elizabeth spread the straw for Mary's bed, with a deft hand. The baby John was sound asleep in another corner. Joseph looked in and went away, closing the rough wooden door behind him. Elizabeth the good was left alone with Mary, whose days were fulfilled that she should now bring forth the Saviour in Bethlehem of Judea.

IV: *Curtains of Holy Night*

PART not the curtains of the night, friend of my soul. They are the wings of mystery brooding over the hidden things of life. They are the reserve of the Eternal.

Within that darkness are the sharpest pains and the deepest joys that mortal flesh can feel—interwoven grief and gladness of spirit that words can never tell—fears and hopes so sacred that they should be kept secret save from God, who knoweth all.

If you part the curtains these things are changed; they vanish into thin air. If you try to tell all, you lose part.

All things are lawful to speak of, but all things are not expedient. Reality is precious, but in the deepest depth of reality there is a mystery beyond utterance. Silence and shade lie round about it to guard it from profanation.

We like a man who tells the truth, and nothing but the truth. But the whole truth is more than man can tell.

How a life leaves this world we know not, except that the heart of flesh left behind ceases to beat. How a life enters this world we know not, except that the heart nourished by the mother's heart begins its own beating.

Let the curtains fall.

Leave the wise Elizabeth and her own sleeping babe alone with the pure Mary and her son Jesus coming into the world to save sinners.

It is Holy Night.

V: *Joy Cometh in the Morning*

In the gray light before sunrise Elizabeth talked with Mary, who was watching her baby asleep in the manger. Joseph was listening, silent and content.

"He is a splendid boy," said Elizabeth.

"Yes," said Mary.

"But not quite so big and strong as my baby John was," said Elizabeth.

"No?" said Mary.

"Yet he will be greater than my John," said Elizabeth. "There is a look of heaven on his face, as if he came from there."

"Yes," said Mary.

"What are you going to call him?" asked Elizabeth. "He surely must have a noble Jewish name."

"His name is Jesus," spoke up Joseph. "The angel I saw in my dream told me that long ago. For it is he that shall save his people from their sins."

"Yes," said Mary.

At this moment steps and voices were heard outside. There was a soft knocking on the door. Joseph opened it. Four men were standing there. They were simple peasants with sun-burned faces and rough clothes, but their manners were gentle. The eldest spoke for the others.

"Sir," he said, "we are the shepherds of the sheep which are kept near-by for the Temple sacrifices. Our names are Zadok, Jotham,

Shama and Nathan; poor men, sir, but honest and well known in the neighborhood. We were watching our flocks last night by the tower of Migdal Eder, where one of the prophets foretold that the Messiah should first be made known. A wonderful strange thing happened to us there. May we come in and tell it—that is, if perchance there is a new-born child here, wrapped in swaddling-bands and lying in a manger?"

"He is here," said Joseph. Then after a glance at Elizabeth, who smiled, he added, "Come in, shepherds, but speak softly."

They entered, stepping as lightly as they could, and looked with wonder on the young child in his quaint bed. Kneeling, they told of their vision of the first angel, with his glad tidings that the Messiah was born in the city of David, and then of the flock of many angels singing glory to God, peace on earth, good will among men. The child John looked at the shepherds with wide eyes. The baby Jesus slept. Joseph and Elizabeth were amazed at the tale of the shepherds. But Mary, still and happy, kept all these sayings, pondering them in her heart. That is a mother's way.

When the shepherds had gone, Elizabeth rose up and nursed her own child. Then she made ready to go out.

"You must have a better lodging than this," she said. "It will be days and days before you can travel. I have two cousins here who have good houses. Their guest-chambers were full last night because of the crowd in Bethlehem. But to-day one of them will surely have room for you. I will go and see."

While she was away there came another stranger to the grotto— a young shepherd, a wanderer in ragged clothes, with a worn and weary face of many troubles. He also desired to see the mother and her wondrous babe of whom his fellows had told him. Of this visit and of its ending the record is written in the story of "The Sad Shepherd." Perhaps there were also other visitors.

Elizabeth came back before noon, with joy in her face.

"Lemuel-bar-Zillai is making his guest-room ready. Come, let us go quickly. He will be glad to entertain us."

The house was a little larger than their own in Nazareth. Master and mistress were happy to receive them with the ancient Jewish kindness; for they were not mere strangers, they were kinsfolk. Three days later the good Elizabeth, remembering that her husband was lonely in Bethcar, tramped over the hills again to her home beside the beautiful flowing fountain of Ain Karim. Joseph and Mary with the young child Jesus stayed on in the house of Lemuel, welcome guests—welcome as angels.

VI: *Old Rites with New Meaning*

THERE were certain forms and ceremonies which they had to observe according to the Jewish law. First of all, after eight days, there was the formal naming of the child and his sealing as a son of Israel by the rite handed down from the times of Abraham. Then, after thirty-one days more, Joseph and Mary must go up to the Temple at Jerusalem, for the purification of the mother and her first-born son.

It was not a long journey—only five miles—and it was a happy one. They were poor, but they had money enough for the offering of the humble—a pair of turtle-doves or two young pigeons. So Mary dropped her eight pence into the third of the trumpet-shaped openings of the treasure chests which stood in the Court of the Women. The pair of doves was offered and the priest declared that the ransom of the first-born was paid.

An old praying man named Simeon, who frequented the Temple, and an ancient prophetess named Anna, a widow who spent all her time there, saw the infant Jesus with his parents and something told them that the Messiah for whom they had long waited had come at last.

> "Now lettest thou thy servant depart, Lord,
> According to thy word, in peace—"

quavered Simeon, holding the infant in his arms. Anna gave thanks to God, in her thin cracked voice, and spoke of the child to all her friends.

On their joyful way back to Bethlehem, Joseph and Mary passed

25

the tomb of Rachel with its low white dome standing beside the road. A dim foreboding of sorrow came over Mary's mind. She recalled the words of old Simeon in the Temple, about the sword which was to pierce through her own soul.

"I remember," she said, "there is a word in one of the prophets concerning Rachel; something about 'a voice heard in a high place, mourning and lamenting. Rachel weeping for her children because they are not.' Can this be an omen of grief for us and death for our Jesus? He is so little, and the world is so big and blind and cruel. He may perish in its ignorant crush."

"We must take good care of him; that is all," said Joseph. "He has been trusted to us. He cannot perish until his great task is done. God has promised. We are all in God's hand. We do not know how it will be worked out. We must do our part."

VII: *Visitors from Afar*

THE very next day there was a strange event which brought great cheer to the anxious parents, and amazement to the neighbors in Bethlehem. Down the narrow street swayed three tall richly harnessed camels carrying three strangers in costly raiment. They halted in front of the house of Lemuel and dismounted.

They were wise men of the East, Magians from the mountains of Persia. They said that a sign in the sky had led them to do homage to a heavenly King whose coming was foretold by the books of Zoroaster, as well as by the Jewish prophets. So they let down their corded bales and brought out gifts of gold and frankincense and myrrh. Kneeling in the house, they presented their tribute to the child Jesus.

Then they returned to the country from which they came; not by way of Jerusalem, for a dream had warned them against going back to the fierce and suspicious King Herod; but by the same road which Joseph and Mary had travelled—past Jericho and up the Jordan Valley towards Babylon and the Persian highlands.

Whether the infant Jesus knew anything of this visit of the

Magi, except perhaps the glitter of their gold and the sweet smell of their incense, who can tell? But doubtless his parents spoke to him about it in later years.

It was Mary's habit to hold things in memory and ponder their meaning. What might not this coming of the disciples of Zoroaster, princes from a far land, mean for her son Jesus? Was he indeed to be a light for revelation to the Gentiles, as well as the glory of his people Israel?

Mary, devout and strict Jewess that she was, could hardly understand this idea. Yet because she was of a generous nature and loved giving, the thought entered her heart and stayed there. So it was mingled with the very food of life which her son drew from her breasts.

VIII: *Home Again to Nazareth*

NEVER in his life had Joseph the carpenter been so well-off for money as he was after the visit of the Wise Men. It was not vast wealth that they brought him, but it was enough to make him easy in mind and hopeful for the future.

First, there were the rare and precious gums of frankincense and myrrh, the surplus of which could be sold for a considerable sum. Second, there was the gold, not a huge quantity, but at least a tribute worthy to be presented by princes to the Prince. With this small capital in hand Joseph could easily reward Lemuel for the generous entertainment he had provided, and perhaps set himself up in his trade and stay on as a carpenter in Bethlehem.

This idea appealed to him strongly, for Bethlehem was a pleasant place in a fertile region. He had made friends there, and it was near the Temple. Lemuel favored the plan.

"There are two carpenters here already," said he, "but there is room and need for another. The town is growing. We are right on the road from Jerusalem to Egypt, where the caravans pass. They give a lot of work in repairs on pack-saddles and chariots. I know of a good place for a work-shop. You will do well to stay here."

"I think so too," said Joseph; "there will be plenty for me to do

27

here. And though the pleasure-palace of that vile fox Herod is on the mountain top just before us, and Jerusalem is full of heathen, after all it is the center of Israel, the holy city where the true King must be lifted up and crowned."

While the two men were busy talking, Mary was silent. She was thinking of the dear, gray little house in Nazareth, the silvery olive-trees in the small garden, the flowing spring under its stone arch, the friendly peace of the hills and vales of Galilee.

Did not the old rabbis say that Galilee was a better place than Judea to bring up a child? Was not that her first and dearest duty, the holy charge given to her hands? Yet of course she would do what her husband wanted; stay with him here in Bethlehem, or go with him anywhere in the wide world.

Joseph slept at noon that day, and another dream came to him — a strange sudden dream, disquieting, full of alarm. They were great dreamers in those times, and they paid attention to their visions.

This new dream was terrifying.

An angel told of Herod's crazy design to have all the infant boys in Bethlehem killed by his soldiers, hoping thus to destroy the young child whom he feared and hated as his predicted rival for the throne. It was a madman's idea, unspeakably cruel. But what was that to a crafty lunatic who had already killed his wife, his mother-in-law, his uncle, and his own sons, Alexander, Aristobulus, and Antipater? The Jews knew Herod too well to doubt his readiness for any bloody villainy. Joseph was numb with the terror of his dream.

"Get up," said the angel, "and take the young child and his mother, and flee into Egypt, and stay there until I tell thee."

So Joseph rose quickly, and told Mary and their kind hosts the strange message that had come to him.

With part of his gold he bought a strong white ass of the famous breed of the Nile, and plenty of gear for the journey. Hasty were the preparations and the farewells.

Dark was the night when the holy family took the great south road for the distant land of the Sphinx and the Pyramids, the land where the children of Israel were once in bondage and where the ancient idols still throned in their crumbling temples.

The young child who was born to overthrow them had no throne but his mother's breast. There he reigned, in peace and joy, while the strong ass bore them through the darkness towards exile and safety.

It was the longest journey that Jesus ever took on earth.

What befell them in Egypt, and what they saw there, we do not know and can not guess.

What is certain is that the holy family stayed there until the wicked Herod died of a loathsome disease, and his son Archelaus reigned in his stead over Judea. Then Joseph made up his mind that it would be safe to go back to Judea and set up that new carpenter-shop which he had planned with his friend Lemuel.

But it was not to be so. Another dream came to him in which he was warned not to return to Bethlehem, but to go straight on to his old home in Galilee.

So Mary came again to the little gray house that she loved and the carpenter-shop in Nazareth.

There it was that the thought of Jesus had first entered Mary's heart.

So there it was that the boy lived, and was obedient to his parents and grew strong, filled with wisdom. The grace of God was upon him; and in due time he came forth from that little hill-town on his great mission to serve and save the world.

HENRY VAN DYKE

The Other Wise Man

YOU know the story of the Three Wise Men of the East, and
how they traveled from far away to offer their gifts at the
manger cradle in Bethlehem. But have you ever heard the
story of the Other Wise Man, who also saw the star in its rising,
and set out to follow it, yet did not arrive with his brethren in the
presence of the young child Jesus? Of the great desire of this fourth
pilgrim, and how it was denied, yet accomplished in the denial; of
his many wanderings and the probations of his soul; of the long way
of his seeking and the strange way of his finding the One whom he
sought—I would tell the tale as I have heard fragments of it in
the Hall of Dreams, in the palace of the Heart of Man.

The Other Wise Man

I

In the days when Augustus Caesar was master of many kings and Herod reigned in Jerusalem, there lived in the city of Ecbatana, among the mountains of Persia, a certain man named Artaban. His house stood close to the outermost of the walls which encircled the royal treasury. From his roof he could look over the sevenfold battlements of black and white and crimson and blue and red and silver and gold, to the hill where the summer palace of the Parthian emperors glittered like a jewel in a crown.

Around the dwelling of Artaban spread a fair garden, a tangle of flowers and fruit trees, watered by a score of streams descending from the slopes of Mount Orontes, and made musical by innumerable birds. But all color was lost in the soft and odorous darkness of the late September night, and all sounds were hushed in the deep charm of its silence, save the plashing of the water, like a voice half sobbing and half laughing under the shadows. High above the trees a dim glow of light shone through the curtained arches of the upper chamber, where the master of the house was holding council with his friends.

He stood by the doorway to greet his guests — a tall, dark man of about forty years, with brilliant eyes set near together under his broad brow, and firm lines graven around his fine, thin lips; the brow of a dreamer and the mouth of a soldier, a man of sensitive feeling but inflexible will — one of those who, in whatever age they may live, are born for inward conflict and a life of quest.

His robe was of pure white wool, thrown over a tunic of silk; and a white, pointed cap, with long lapels at the sides, rested on his flowing black hair. It was the dress of the ancient priesthood of the Magi, called the fire worshipers.

"Welcome!" he said, in his low, pleasant voice, as one after another entered the room — "welcome, Abdus; peace be with you, Rhodaspes and Tigranes, and with you, my father, Abgarus. You are all welcome. This house grows bright with the joy of your presence."

There were nine of the men, differing widely in age, but alike in the richness of their dress of many-colored silks, and in the massive golden collars around their necks, marking them as Parthian nobles, and in the winged circles of gold resting upon their breasts, the sign of the followers of Zoroaster.

They took their places around a small black altar at the end of the room, where a tiny flame was burning. Artaban, standing beside it, and waving a barsom of thin tamarisk branches above the fire, fed it with dry sticks of pine and fragrant oils. Then he began the ancient chant of the Yasna, and the voices of his companions joined in the hymn to Ahura-Mazda:

> *We worship the Spirit Divine,*
> *all wisdom and goodness possessing,*
> *Surrounded by Holy Immortals,*
> *the givers of bounty and blessing;*
> *We joy in the work of His hands,*
> *His truth and His power confessing.*
>
> *We praise all the things that are pure,*
> *for these are His only Creation;*
> *The thoughts that are true and the words*
> *and the deeds that have won approbation;*
> *These are supported by Him,*
> *and for these we make adoration.*
>
> *Hear us, O Mazda! Thou livest*
> *in truth and in heavenly gladness;*
> *Cleanse us from falsehood, and keep us*
> *from evil and bondage to badness;*
> *Pour out the light and the joy of Thy life*
> *on our darkness and sadness.*
>
> *Shine on our gardens and fields,*
> *shine on our working and weaving;*
> *Shine on the whole race of man,*
> *believing and unbelieving;*

The Other Wise Man

Shine on us now through the night,
Shine on us now in Thy might,
The flame of our holy love
and the song of our worship receiving.

The fire rose with the chant, throbbing as if the flame responded to the music, until it cast a bright illumination through the whole apartment, revealing its simplicity and splendor.

The floor was laid with tiles of dark blue veined with white; pilasters of twisted silver stood out against the blue walls; the clere-story of round-arched windows above them was hung with azure silk; the vaulted ceiling was a pavement of blue stones, like the body of heaven in its clearness, sown with silver stars. From the four corners of the roof hung four golden magic wheels, called the tongues of the gods. At the eastern end, behind the altar, there were two dark-red pillars of porphyry; above them a lintel of the same stone, on which was carved the figure of a winged archer, with his arrow set to the string and his bow drawn.

The doorway between the pillars, which opened upon the terrace of the roof, was covered with a heavy curtain of the color of a ripe pomegranate, embroidered with innumerable golden rays shooting upward from the floor. In effect the room was like a quiet, starry night, all azure and silver, flushed in the east with rosy promise of the dawn. It was, as the house of a man should be, an expression of the character and spirit of the master.

He turned to his friends when the song was ended, and invited them to be seated on the divan at the western end of the room.

"You have come tonight," said he, looking around the circle, "at my call, as the faithful scholars of Zoroaster, to renew your worship and rekindle your faith in the God of Purity, even as this fire has been rekindled on the altar. We worship not the fire, but Him of whom it is the chosen symbol, because it is the purest of all created things. It speaks to us of one who is Light and Truth. Is it not so, my father?"

"It is well said, my son," answered the venerable Abgarus. "The enlightened are never idolaters. They lift the veil of form and go in to the shrine of reality, and new light and truth are coming to them continually through the old symbols."

"Hear me, then, my father and my friends," said Artaban, "while I tell you of the new light and truth that have come to me through the most ancient of all signs. We have searched the secrets of Nature together, and studied the healing virtues of water and fire and the plants. We have read also the books of prophecy in which the future is dimly foretold in words that are hard to understand. But the highest of all learning is the knowledge of the stars. To trace their course is to untangle the threads of the mystery of life from the beginning to the end. If we could follow them perfectly, nothing would be hidden from us. But is not our knowledge of them still incomplete? Are there not many stars still beyond our horizon— lights that are known only to the dwellers in the far southland, among the spice trees of Punt and the gold mines of Ophir?"

There was a murmur of assent among the listeners.

"The stars," said Tigranes, "are the thoughts of the Eternal. They are numberless. But the thoughts of man can be counted, like the years of his life. The wisdom of the Magi is the greatest of all wisdoms on earth, because it knows its own ignorance. And that is the secret of power. We keep men always looking and waiting for a new sunrise. But we ourselves understand that the darkness is equal to the light, and that the conflict between them will never be ended."

"That does not satisfy me," answered Artaban, "for, if the waiting must be endless, if there could be no fulfillment of it, then it would not be wisdom to look and wait. We should become like those new teachers of the Greeks, who say that there is no truth, and that the only wise men are those who spend their lives in discovering and exposing the lies that have been believed in the world. But the new sunrise will certainly appear in the appointed time. Do not our own books tell us that this will come to pass, and that men will see the brightness of a great light?"

"That is true," said the voice of Abgarus; "every faithful disciple of Zoroaster knows the prophecy of the Avesta, and carries the word in his heart. 'In that day Sosiosh the Victorious shall arise out of the number of the prophets in the east country. Around him shall shine a mighty brightness, and he shall make life everlasting, incorruptible, and immortal, and the dead shall rise again.' "

"This is a dark saying," said Tigranes, "and it may be that we shall never understand it. It is better to consider the things that are near at hand, and to increase the influence of the Magi in their own country, rather than to look for one who may be a stranger, and to whom we must resign our power."

The others seemed to approve these words. There was a silent feeling of agreement manifest among them; their looks responded with that indefinable expression which always follows when a speaker has uttered the thought that has been slumbering in the hearts of his listeners. But Artaban turned to Abgarus with a glow on his face, and said:

"My father, I have kept this prophecy in the secret place of my soul. Religion without a great hope would be like an altar without a living fire. And now the flame has burned more brightly, and by the light of it I have read other words which also have come from the fountain of Truth, and speak yet more clearly of the rising of the Victorious One in his brightness."

He drew from the breast of his tunic two small rolls of fine parchment, with writing upon them, and unfolded them carefully upon his knee.

"In the years that are lost in the past, long before our fathers came into the land of Babylon, there were wise men in Chaldea, from whom the first of the Magi learned the secret of the heavens. And of these Balaam the son of Beor was one of the mightiest. Hear the words of his prophecy: 'There shall come a star out of Jacob, and a scepter shall arise out of Israel.' "

The lips of Tigranes drew downward with contempt, as he said:

"Judah was a captive by the waters of Babylon, and the sons of Jacob were in bondage to our kings. The tribes of Israel are scattered through the mountains like lost sheep, and from the remnant that dwells in Judea under the yoke of Rome neither star nor scepter shall arise."

35

"And yet," answered Artaban, "it was the Hebrew Daniel, the mighty searcher of dreams, the counselor of kings, the wise Belteshazzar, who was most honored and beloved of our great King Cyrus. A prophet of sure things and a reader of the thoughts of the Eternal, Daniel proved himself to our people. And these are the words that he wrote." (Artaban read from the second roll:) " 'Know, therefore, and understand that from the going forth of the commandment to restore Jerusalem, unto the Anointed One, the Prince, the time shall be seven and threescore and two weeks.' "

"But, my son," said Abgarus, doubtfully, "these are mystical numbers. Who can interpret them, or who can find the key that shall unlock their meaning?"

Artaban answered: "It has been shown to me and to my three companions among the Magi—Caspar, Melchior and Balthasar. We have searched the ancient tablets of Chaldea and computed the time. It falls in this year. We have studied the sky, and in the spring of the year we saw two of the greatest planets draw near together in the sign of the Fish, which is the house of the Hebrews. We also saw a new star there, which shone for one night and then vanished. Now again the two great planets are meeting. This night is their conjunction. My three brothers are watching by the ancient Temple of the Seven Spheres, at Borsippa, in Babylonia, and I am watching here. If the star shines again, they will wait ten days for me at the temple, and then we will set out together for Jerusalem, to see and worship the promised one who shall be born King of Israel. I believe the sign will come. I have made ready for the journey. I have sold my possessions, and bought these three jewels—a sapphire, a ruby and a pearl—to carry them as tribute to the King. And I ask you to go with me on the pilgrimage, that we may have joy together in finding the Prince who is worthy to be served."

While he was speaking he thrust his hand into the inmost fold of his girdle and drew out three great gems—one blue as a fragment of the night sky, one redder than a ray of sunrise, and one as pure as the peak of a snow mountain at twilight—and laid them on the outspread scrolls before him.

But his friends looked on with strange and alien eyes. A veil of doubt and mistrust came over their faces, like a fog creeping up from the marshes to hide the hills. They glanced at each other with looks of wonder and pity, as those who have listened to incredible sayings, the story of a wild vision, or the proposal of an impossible enterprise.

At last Tigranes said: "Artaban, this is a vain dream. It comes from too much looking upon the stars and the cherishing of lofty thoughts. It would be wiser to spend the time in gathering money for the new fire temple at Chala. No king will ever rise from the broken race of Israel, and no end will ever come to the eternal strife of light and darkness. He who looks for it is a chaser of shadows. Farewell."

And another said: "Artaban, I have no knowledge of these things, and my office as guardian of the royal treasure binds me here. The quest is not for me. But if thou must follow it, fare thee well."

And another said: "In my house there sleeps a new bride, and I cannot leave her nor take her with me on this strange journey. This quest is not for me. But may thy steps be prospered wherever thou goest. So, farewell."

And another said: "I am ill and unfit for hardship, but there is a man among my servants whom I will send with thee when thou goest, to bring me word how thou farest."

So, one by one, they left the house of Artaban. But Abgarus, the oldest and the one who loved him the best, lingered after the others had gone, and said, gravely: "My son, it may be that the light of truth is in this sign that has appeared in the skies, and then it will surely lead to the Prince and the mighty brightness. Or it may be that it is only a shadow of the light, as Tigranes has said, and then he who follows it will have a long pilgrimage and a fruitless search. But it is better to follow even the shadow of the best than to remain content with the worst. And those who would see wonderful things must often be ready to travel alone. I am too old for this journey, but my heart shall be a companion of thy pilgrimage day and night, and I shall know the end of thy quest. Go in peace."

Then Abgarus went out of the azure chamber with its silver stars, and Artaban was left in solitude.

He gathered up the jewels and replaced them in his girdle. For a long time he stood and watched the flame that flickered and sank upon the altar. Then he crossed the hall, lifted the heavy curtain, and passed out between the pillars of porphyry to the terrace on the roof.

The shiver that runs through the earth ere she rouses from her night sleep had already begun, and the cool wind that heralds the daybreak was drawing downward from the lofty, snow-traced ravines of Mount Orontes. Birds, half-awakened, crept and chirped among the rustling leaves, and the smell of ripened grapes came in brief wafts from the arbors.

Far over the eastern plain a white mist stretched like a lake. But where the distant peaks of Zagros serrated the western horizon the sky was clear. Jupiter and Saturn rolled together like drops of lambent flame about to blend in one.

As Artaban watched them, a steel-blue spark was born out of the darkness beneath, rounding itself with purple splendors to a crimson sphere, and spiring upward through rays of saffron and orange into a point of white radiance. Tiny and infinitely remote, yet perfect in every part, it pulsated in the enormous vault as if the three jewels in the Magian's girdle had mingled and been transformed into a living heart of light.

He bowed his head. He covered his brow with his hands.

"It is the sign," he said. "The King is coming, and I will go to meet him."

II

ALL night long, Vasda, the swiftest of Artaban's horses, had been waiting, saddled and bridled, in her stall, pawing the ground impatiently and shaking her bit as if she shared the eagerness of her master's purpose, though she knew not its meaning.

Before the birds had fully roused to their strong, high, joyful chant of morning song, before the white mist had begun to lift lazily from the plain, the Other Wise Man was in the saddle, riding swiftly along the highroad, which skirted the base of Mount Orontes, westward.

How close, how intimate is the comradeship between a man and his favorite horse on a long journey. It is a silent, comprehensive friendship, an intercourse beyond the need of words.

They drink at the same wayside springs, and sleep under the same guardian stars. They are conscious together of the subduing spell of nightfall and the quickening joy of daybreak. The master shares his evening meal with his hungry companion, and feels the soft, moist lips caressing the palm of his hand as they close over the morsel of bread. In the gray dawn he is roused from his bivouac by the gentle stir of a warm, sweet breath over his sleeping face, and looks up into the eyes of his faithful fellow traveler, ready and waiting for the toil of the day. Surely, unless he is a pagan and an unbeliever, by whatever name he calls upon his God, he will thank Him for this voiceless sympathy, this dumb affection, and his morning prayer will embrace a double blessing—God bless us both, the horse and the rider, and keep our feet from falling and our souls from death!

Then, through the keen morning air, the swift hoofs beat their tattoo along the road, keeping time to the pulsing of two hearts that are moved with the same eager desire—to conquer space, to devour the distance, to attain the goal of the journey.

Artaban must indeed ride wisely and well if he would keep the appointed hour with the other Magi; for the route was a hundred and fifty parasangs, and fifteen was the utmost that he could travel in a day. But he knew Vasda's strength, and pushed forward without anxiety, making the fixed distance every day, though he must travel late into the night, and in the morning long before sunrise.

He passed along the brown slopes of Mount Orontes, furrowed by the rocky courses of a hundred torrents.

He crossed the level plains of the Nicaeans, where the famous herds of horses, feeding in the wide pastures, tossed their heads at Vasda's approach, and galloped away with a thunder of many hoofs, and flocks of wild birds rose suddenly from the swampy meadows, wheeling in great circles with a shining flutter of innumerable wings and shrill cries of surprise.

He traversed the fertile fields of Concabar, where the dust from the threshing floors filled the air with a golden mist, half hiding the huge temple of Astarte with its four hundred pillars.

At Baghistan, among the rich gardens watered by fountains from the rock, he looked up at the mountain thrusting its immense rugged brow out over the road, and saw the figure of King Darius trampling upon his fallen foes, and the proud list of his wars and conquests graven high upon the face of the eternal cliff.

Over many a cold and desolate pass, crawling painfully across the wind-swept shoulders of the hills; down many a black mountain gorge, where the river roared and raced before him like a savage guide; across many a smiling vale, with terraces of yellow limestone full of vines and fruit trees; through the oak groves of Carine and the dark Gates of Zagros, walled in by precipices; into the ancient city of Chala, where the people of Samaria had been kept in captivity long ago; and out again by the mighty portal, riven through the encircling hills, where he saw the image of the High Priest of the Magi sculptured on the wall of rock, with hand uplifted as if to bless the centuries of pilgrims; past the entrance of the narrow defile, filled from end to end with orchards of peaches and figs, through which the river Gyndes foamed down to meet him; over the broad rice fields, where the autumnal vapors spread their deathly mists; following along the course of the river, under tremulous shadows of poplar and tamarind, among the lower hills; and out upon the flat plain, where the road ran straight as an arrow through the stubble fields and parched meadows; past the city of Ctesiphon, where the Parthian emperors reigned, and the vast metropolis of Seleucia which Alexander built; across the swirling floods of Tigris and the many channels of Euphrates, flowing yellow through the cornlands—Artaban pressed onward until he arrived, at nightfall on the tenth day, beneath the shattered walls of populous Babylon.

Vasda was almost spent, and Artaban would gladly have turned into the city to find rest and refreshment for himself and for her. But he knew that it was three hours' journey yet to the Temple of the Seven Spheres, and he must reach the place by midnight if he would find his comrades waiting. So he did not halt, but rode steadily across the stubble fields.

A grove of date palms made an island of gloom in the pale yellow sea. As she passed into the shadow Vasda slackened her pace, and began to pick her way more carefully.

Near the farther end of the darkness an access of caution seemed to fall upon her. She scented some danger or difficulty; it was not in her heart to fly from it—only to be prepared for it, and to meet it wisely, as a good horse should do. The grove was close and silent as the tomb; not a leaf rustled, not a bird sang.

She felt her steps before her delicately, carrying her head low, and sighing now and then with apprehension. At last she gave a quick breath of anxiety and dismay, and stood stock-still, quivering in every muscle, before a dark object in the shadow of the last palm tree.

Artaban dismounted. The dim starlight revealed the form of a man lying across the road. His humble dress and the outline of his haggard face showed that he was probably one of the Hebrews who still dwelt in great numbers around the city. His pallid skin, dry and yellow as parchment, bore the mark of the deadly fever which ravaged the marshlands in autumn. The chill of death was in his lean hand, and, as Artaban released it, the arm fell back inertly upon the motionless breast.

He turned away with a thought of pity, leaving the body to that strange burial which the Magians deemed most fitting—the funeral of the desert, from which the kites and vultures rise on dark wings, and the beasts of prey slink furtively away. When they are gone there is only a heap of white bones on the sand.

But, as he turned, a long, faint, ghostly sigh came from the man's lips. The bony fingers gripped the hem of the Magian's robe and held him fast.

Artaban's heart leaped to his throat, not with fear, but with a dumb resentment at the importunity of this blind delay.

How could he stay here in the darkness to minister to a dying stranger? What claim had this unknown fragment of human life upon his compassion or his service? If he lingered but for an hour he could hardly reach Borsippa at the appointed time. His companions would think he had given up the journey. They would go without him. He would lose his quest.

But if he went on now, the man would surely die. If Artaban stayed, life might be restored. His spirit throbbed and fluttered with the urgency of the crisis. Should he risk the great reward of his faith for the sake of a single deed of charity? Should he turn aside, if only for a moment, from the following of the star, to give a cup of cold water to a poor, perishing Hebrew?

"God of truth and purity," he prayed, "direct me in the holy path, the way of wisdom which Thou only knowest."

Then he turned back to the sick man. Loosening the grasp of his hand, he carried him to a little mound at the foot of the palm tree.

He unbound the thick folds of the turban and opened the garment above the sunken breast. He brought water from one of the small canals near by, and moistened the sufferer's brow and mouth. He mingled a draught of one of those simple but potent remedies which he carried always in his girdle—for the Magians were physicians as well as astrologers—and poured it slowly between the colorless lips. Hour after hour he labored as only a skillful healer of disease can do. At last the man's strength returned; he sat up and looked about him.

"Who art thou?" he said, in the rude dialect of the country, "and why hast thou sought me here to bring back my life?"

"I am Artaban the Magian, of the city of Ecbatana, and I am going to Jerusalem in search of one who is to be born King of the Jews, a great Prince and Deliverer of all men. I dare not delay any longer upon my journey, for the caravan that has waited for me may depart without me. But see, here is all that I have left of bread and wine, and here is a potion of healing herbs. When thy strength is restored thou canst find the dwellings of the Hebrews among the houses of Babylon."

The Jew raised his trembling hand solemnly to heaven.

"Now may the God of Abraham and Isaac and Jacob bless and

prosper the journey of the merciful, and bring him in peace to his desired haven. Stay! I have nothing to give thee in return—only this: that I can tell thee where the Messiah must be sought. For our prophets have said that he should be born not in Jerusalem, but in Bethlehem of Judah. May the Lord bring thee in safety to that place, because thou hast had pity upon the sick."

It was already long past midnight. Artaban rode in haste, and Vasda, restored by the brief rest, ran eagerly through the silent plain and swam the channels of the river. She put forth the remnant of her strength and fled over the ground like a gazelle.

But the first beam of the rising sun sent a long shadow before her as she entered upon the final stadium of the journey, and the eyes of Artaban, anxiously scanning the great mound of Nimrod and the Temple of the Seven Spheres, could discern no trace of his friends.

The many-colored terraces of black and orange and red and yellow and green and blue and white, shattered by the convulsions of nature, and crumbling under the repeated blows of human violence, still glittered like a ruined rainbow in the morning light.

Artaban rode swiftly around the hill. He dismounted and climbed to the highest terrace, looking out toward the west.

The huge desolation of the marshes stretched away to the horizon and the border of the desert. Bitterns stood by the stagnant pools and jackals skulked through the low bushes; but there was no sign of the caravan of the Wise Men, far or near.

At the edge of the terrace he saw a little cairn of broken bricks, and under them a piece of papyrus. He caught it up and read: "We have waited past the midnight, and can delay no longer. We go to find the King. Follow us across the desert."

Artaban sat down upon the ground and covered his head in despair.

"How can I cross the desert," said he, "with no food and with a spent horse? I must return to Babylon, sell my sapphire, and buy a train of camels, and provision for the journey. I may never overtake my friends. Only God the merciful knows whether I shall not lose the sight of the King because I tarried to show mercy."

43

III

THERE was a silence in the Hall of Dreams, where I was listening to the story of the Other Wise Man. Through this silence I saw, but very dimly, his figure passing over the dreary undulations of the desert, high upon the back of his camel, rocking steadily onward like a ship over the waves.

The land of death spread its cruel net around him. The stony waste bore no fruit but briers and thorns. The dark ledges of rock thrust themselves above the surface here and there, like the bones of perished monsters. Arid and inhospitable mountain ranges rose before him, furrowed with dry channels of ancient torrents, white and ghastly as scars on the face of nature. Shifting hills of treacherous sand were heaped like tombs along the horizon. By day the fierce heat pressed its intolerable burden on the quivering air. No living creature moved on the dumb, swooning earth, but tiny jerboas scuttling through the parched bushes, or lizards vanishing in the clefts of the rock. By night the jackals prowled and barked in the distance, and the lion made the black ravines echo with his hollow roaring, while a bitter, blighting chill followed the fever of the day. Through heat and cold, the Magian moved steadily onward.

Then I saw the gardens and orchards of Damascus, watered by the streams of Abana and Pharpar, with their sloping swards inlaid with bloom, and their thickets of myrrh and roses. I saw the long, snowy ridge of Hermon, and the dark groves of cedars, and the valley of the Jordan, and the blue waters of the Lake of Galilee, and the fertile plain of Esdraelon, and the hills of Ephraim, and the highlands of Judah. Through all these I followed the figure of Artaban moving steadily onward, until he arrived at Bethlehem. And it was the third day after the three Wise Men had come to that place and had found Mary and Joseph, with the young child, Jesus, and had laid their gifts of gold and frankincense and myrrh at his feet.

Then the Other Wise Man drew near, weary, but full of hope, bearing his ruby and his pearl to offer to the King. "For now at last," he said, "I shall surely find him, though I be alone, and later than my brethren. This is the place of which the Hebrew exile told me that the prophets had spoken, and here I shall behold the rising of the great light. But I must inquire about the visit of my brethren, and to what house the star directed them, and to whom they presented their tribute."

The streets of the village seemed to be deserted, and Artaban wondered whether the men had all gone up to the hill pastures to bring down their sheep. From the open door of a cottage he heard the sound of a woman's voice singing softly. He entered and found a young mother hushing her baby to rest. She told him of the strangers from the far East who had appeared in the village three days ago, and how they said that a star had guided them to the place where Joseph of Nazareth was lodging with his wife and her new born child, and how they had paid reverence to the child and given him many rich gifts.

"But the travelers disappeared again," she continued, "as suddenly as they had come. We were afraid at the strangeness of their visit. We could not understand it. The man of Nazareth took the child and his mother, and fled away that same night secretly, and it was whispered that they were going to Egypt. Ever since, there has been a spell upon the village; something evil hangs over it. They say that the Roman soldiers are coming from Jerusalem to force a new tax from us, and the men have driven the flocks and herds far back among the hills, and hidden themselves to escape it."

Artaban listened to her gentle, timid speech, and the child in her arms looked up in his face and smiled, stretching out its rosy hands to grasp at the winged circle of gold on his breast. His heart warmed to the touch. It seemed like a greeting of love and trust to one who had journeyed long in loneliness and perplexity, fighting with his own doubts and fears, and following a light that was veiled in clouds.

"Why might not this child have been the promised Prince?" he asked within himself, as he touched its soft cheek. "Kings have been born ere now in lowlier houses than this, and the favorite of the stars may rise even from a cottage. But it has not seemed good

45

to the God of wisdom to reward my search so soon and so easily. The one whom I seek has gone before me; and now I must follow the King to Egypt."

The young mother laid the baby in its cradle, and rose to minister to the wants of the strange guest that fate had brought into her house. She set food before him, the plain fare of peasants, but willingly offered, and therefore full of refreshment for the soul as well as for the body. Artaban accepted it gratefully; and, as he ate, the child fell into a happy slumber, and murmured sweetly in its dreams, and a great peace filled the room.

But suddenly there came the noise of a wild confusion in the streets of the village, a shrieking and wailing of women's voices, a clangor of brazen trumpets and a clashing of swords, and a desperate cry: "The soldiers! The soldiers of Herod! They are killing our children."

The young mother's face grew white with terror. She clasped her child to her bosom, and crouched motionless in the darkest corner of the room, covering him with the folds of her robe, lest he should wake and cry.

But Artaban went quickly and stood in the doorway of the house. His broad shoulders filled the portal from side to side, and the peak of his white cap all but touched the lintel.

The soldiers came hurrying down the street with bloody hands and dripping swords. At the sight of the stranger in his imposing dress they hesitated with surprise. The captain of the band approached the threshold to thrust him aside. But Artaban did not stir. His face was as calm as though he were watching the stars, and in his eyes there burned that steady radiance before which even the half-tamed hunting leopard shrinks, and the bloodhound pauses in his leap. He held the soldier silently for an instant, and then said in a low voice:

"I am all alone in this place, and I am waiting to give this jewel to the prudent captain who will leave me in peace."

He showed the ruby, glistening in the hollow of his hand like a great drop of blood.

46

The captain was amazed at the splendor of the gem. The pupils of his eyes expanded with desire, and the hard lines of greed wrinkled around his lips. He stretched out his hand and took the ruby.

"March on!" he cried to his men; "there is no child here. The house is empty."

The clamor and the clang of arms passed down the street as the headlong fury of the chase sweeps by the secret covert where the trembling deer is hidden. Artaban re-entered the cottage. He turned his face to the east and prayed:

"God of truth, forgive my sin! I have said the thing that is not, to save the life of a child. And two of my gifts are gone. I have spent for man that which was meant for God. Shall I ever be worthy to see the face of the King?"

But the voice of the woman, weeping for joy in the shadow behind him, said very gently:

"Because thou hast saved the life of my little one, may the Lord bless thee and keep thee; the Lord make His face to shine upon thee and be gracious unto thee; the Lord lift up His countenance upon thee and give thee peace."

IV

AGAIN there was a silence in the Hall of Dreams, deeper and more mysterious than the first interval, and I understood that the years of Artaban were flowing very swiftly under the stillness, and I caught only a glimpse, here and there, of the river of his life shining through the mist that concealed its course.

I saw him moving among the throngs of men in populous Egypt, seeking everywhere for traces of the household that had come down from Bethlehem, and finding them under the spreading sycamore trees of Heliopolis, and beneath the walls of the Roman fortress of New Babylon beside the Nile—traces so faint and dim that they vanished before him continually, as footprints on the wet river sand glisten for a moment with moisture and then disappear.

I saw him again at the foot of the pyramids, which lifted their sharp points into the intense saffron glow of the sunset sky, change-less monuments of the perishable glory and the imperishable hope of man. He looked up into the face of the crouching Sphinx and vainly tried to read the meaning of the calm eyes and smiling mouth. Was it, indeed, the mockery of all effort and all aspiration, as Tigranes had said—the cruel jest of a riddle that has no answer, a search that never can succeed? Or was there a touch of pity and encouragement in that inscrutable smile—a promise that even the defeated should attain a victory, and the disappointed should dis-cover a prize, and the ignorant should be made wise, and the blind should see, and the wandering should come into the haven at last?

I saw him again in an obscure house of Alexandria, taking coun-sel with a Hebrew rabbi. The venerable man, bending over the rolls of parchment on which the prophecies of Israel were written, read aloud the pathetic words which foretold the sufferings of the promised Messiah—the despised and rejected of men, the man of sorrows and acquainted with grief.

"And remember, my son," said he, fixing his eyes upon the face of Artaban, "the King whom thou seekest is not to be found in a palace, nor among the rich and powerful. If the light of the world and the glory of Israel had been appointed to come with the great-ness of earthly splendor, it must have appeared long ago. For no son of Abraham will ever again rival the power which Joseph had in the palaces of Egypt, or the magnificence of Solomon throned be-tween the lions in Jerusalem. But the light for which the world is waiting is a new light, the glory that shall rise out of patient and triumphant suffering. And the kingdom which is to be established forever is a new kingdom, the royalty of unconquerable love.

"I do not know how this shall come to pass, nor how the turbulent kings and peoples of earth shall be brought to acknowledge the Messiah and pay homage to him. But this I know. Those who seek him will do well to look among the poor and the lowly, the sorrow-ful and the oppressed."

So I saw the Other Wise Man again and again, traveling from place to place, and searching among the people of the Dispersion, with whom the little family from Bethlehem might, perhaps, have found a refuge. He passed through countries where famine lay heavy upon the land, and the poor were crying for bread. He made his dwelling in plague-stricken cities where the sick were languishing in the bitter companionship of helpless misery. He visited the oppressed and the afflicted in the gloom of subterranean prisons, and the crowded wretchedness of slave markets, and the weary toil of galley ships. In all this populous and intricate world of anguish, though he found none to worship, he found many to help. He fed the hungry, and clothed the naked, and healed the sick, and comforted the captive; and his years passed more swiftly than the weaver's shuttle that flashes back and forth through the loom while the web grows and the pattern is completed.

It seemed almost as if he had forgotten his quest. But once I saw him for a moment as he stood alone at sunrise, waiting at the gate of a Roman prison. He had taken from a secret resting place in his bosom the pearl, the last of his jewels. As he looked at it, a mellower luster, a soft and iridescent light, full of shifting gleams of azure and rose, trembled upon its surface. It seemed to have absorbed some reflection of the lost sapphire and ruby. So the secret purpose of a noble life draws into itself the memories of past joy and past sorrow. All that has helped it, all that has hindered it, is transfused by a subtle magic into its very essence. It becomes more luminous and precious the longer it is carried close to the warmth of the beating heart.

Then, at last, while I was thinking of this pearl, and of its meaning, I heard the end of the story of the Other Wise Man.

V

THREE-AND-THIRTY years of the life of Artaban had passed away, and he was still a pilgrim and a seeker after light. His hair, once darker than the cliffs of Zagros, was now white as the wintry snow that covered them. His eyes, that once flashed like flames of fire, were dull as embers smoldering among the ashes.

Worn and weary and ready to die, but still looking for the King, he had come for the last time to Jerusalem. He had often visited the Holy City before, and had searched all its lanes and crowded hovels and black prisons without finding any trace of the family of Nazarenes who had fled from Bethlehem long ago. But now it seemed as if he must make one more effort, and something whispered in his heart that, at last, he might succeed.

It was the season of the Passover. The city was thronged with strangers. The children of Israel, scattered in far lands, had returned to the Temple for the great feast, and there had been a confusion of tongues in the narrow streets for many days.

But on this day a singular agitation was visible in the multitude. The sky was veiled with a portentous gloom. Currents of excitement seemed to flash through the crowd. A secret tide was sweeping them all one way. The clatter of sandals and the soft, thick sound of thousands of bare feet shuffling over the stones, flowed unceasingly along the street that leads to the Damascus gate.

Artaban joined a group of people from his own country, Parthian Jews who had come up to keep the Passover, and inquired of them the cause of the tumult, and where they were going.

"We are going," they answered, "to the place called Golgotha, outside the city walls, where there is to be an execution. Have you not heard what has happened? Two famous robbers are to be crucified, and with them another, called Jesus of Nazareth, a man who has done many wonderful works among the people, so that they love him greatly. But the priests and elders have said that he must die, because he gave himself out to be the Son of God. And Pilate has sent him to the cross because he said that he was the 'King of the Jews.'"

How strangely these familiar words fell upon the tired heart of Artaban! They had led him for a lifetime over land and sea. And now they came to him mysteriously, like a message of despair. The King had arisen, but he had been denied and cast out. He was about to perish. Perhaps he was already dying. Could it be the same who had been born in Bethlehem thirty-three years ago, at whose birth the star had appeared in heaven, and of whose coming the prophets had spoken?

Artaban's heart beat unsteadily with that troubled, doubtful apprehension which is the excitement of old age. But he said within himself: "The ways of God are stranger than the thoughts of men, and it may be that I shall find the King, at last, in the hands of his enemies, and shall come in time to offer my pearl for his ransom before he dies."

So the old man followed the multitude with slow and painful steps toward the Damascus gate of the city. Just beyond the entrance of the guardhouse a troop of Macedonian soldiers came down the street, dragging a young girl with torn dress and disheveled hair. As the Magian paused to look at her with compassion, she broke suddenly from the hands of her tormentors, and threw herself at his feet, clasping him around the knees. She had seen his white cap and the winged circle on his breast.

"Have pity on me," she cried, "and save me, for the sake of the God of Purity! I also am a daughter of the true religion which is taught by the Magi. My father was a merchant of Parthia, but he is dead, and I am seized for his debts to be sold as a slave. Save me from worse than death!"

Artaban trembled.

It was the old conflict in his soul, which had come to him in the palm grove of Babylon and in the cottage at Bethlehem—the conflict between the expectation of faith and the impulse of love. Twice the gift which he had consecrated to the worship of religion had been drawn to the service of humanity. This was the third trial, the ultimate probation, the final and irrevocable choice.

Was it his great opportunity, or his last temptation? He could not tell. One thing only was clear in the darkness of his mind —it was inevitable. And does not the inevitable come from God?

One thing only was sure to his divided heart—to rescue this helpless girl would be a true deed of love. And is not love the light of the soul?

He took the pearl from his bosom. Never had it seemed so luminous, so radiant, so full of tender, living luster. He laid it in the hand of the slave.

"This is thy ransom, daughter! It is the last of my treasures which I kept for the King."

While he spoke, the darkness of the sky deepened, and shuddering tremors ran through the earth heaving convulsively like the breast of one who struggles with mighty grief.

The walls of the houses rocked to and fro. Stones were loosened and crashed into the street. Dust clouds filled the air. The soldiers fled in terror, reeling like drunken men. But Artaban and the girl whom he had ransomed crouched helpless beneath the wall of the Praetorium.

What had he to fear? What had he to hope? He had given away the last remnant of his tribute for the King. He had parted with the last hope of finding him. The quest was over, and it had failed. But even in that thought, accepted and embraced, there was peace. It was not resignation. It was not submission. It was something more profound and searching. He knew that all was well, because he had done the best that he could from day to day. He had been true to the light that had been given to him. He had looked for more. And if he had not found it, if a failure was all that came out of his life, doubtless that was the best that was possible. He had not seen the revelation of "life everlasting, incorruptible and immortal." But he knew that even if he could live his earthly life over again, it could not be otherwise than it had been.

One more lingering pulsation of the earthquake quivered through the ground. A heavy tile, shaken from the roof, fell and struck the old man on the temple. He lay breathless and pale, with his gray head resting on the young girl's shoulder, and the blood trickling from the wound. As she bent over him, fearing that he was dead, there came a voice through the twilight, very small and still, like music sounding from a distance, in which the notes are clear but the words are lost. The girl turned to see if someone had spoken from the window above them, but she saw no one.

Then the old man's lips began to move, as if in answer, and she heard him say in the Parthian tongue:

"Not so, my Lord! For when saw I thee an hungered and fed thee? Or thirsty, and gave thee drink? When saw I thee a stranger, and took thee in? Or naked, and clothed thee? When saw I thee sick or in prison, and came unto thee? Three-and-thirty years have I looked for thee; but I have never seen thy face, nor ministered to thee, my King."

He ceased, and the sweet voice came again. And again the maid heard it, very faint and far away. But now it seemed as though she understood the words:

"Verily I say unto thee, Inasmuch as thou hast done it unto one of the least of these my brethren, thou hast done it unto me."

A calm radiance of wonder and joy lighted the pale face of Artaban like the first ray of dawn on a snowy mountain peak. A long breath of relief exhaled gently from his lips.

His journey was ended. His treasures were accepted. The Other Wise Man had found the King.

W. E. CULE

The Man at the Gate of the World

A STORY OF THE STAR

I: In a Lowly Room They Found Him

WHEN the Star came, wonder stirred upon the golden plains of Iran, and among those Chaldean mountains which had seen the birth of human story. Everywhere the tale was the same, for the sign might not be mistaken. Such a star had last appeared to tell the world of Alexander's coming; and it must be that at last, moved by pity, the gods were sending a new Deliverer for mankind.

Nor was this all, for the new Star came with a greater glory that held a brighter promise. The star of Alexander had foretold failure as well as triumph, for after a few nights its uncertain light had been quenched in storm. The new Star shone with unclouded radiance, as though it claimed a place with those eternal planets which rule the destinies of men. Therefore, said the sages of the Magi, this prince should be greater than the Greek, a King of Kings, perchance the long-awaited Saviour of the world.

The Magi watched and wondered, and recorded their hope by the light of altar fires that were never allowed to die. But there were three in Susa who were not content to watch and wonder, for to them the light was a beckoning light. For many days they had had all things ready for a journey, even to the world's end: and now they set out over the plains and through the mountains westward, bearing great gifts and eager to be first at the cradle of the world's hope.

Melchior was old, yet full of faith and venture, for the assurance had been given to him that he should see a surpassing marvel before he must pass on. He was of the inner conclave of the Magi, skilled in the lore of stars, a guardian of princes. Balthasar was in the prime of his strength, a pillar of the throne of Iran, but eager to stand beside a brighter throne and to give the flower of his life to a great leader. Yet the chief secret of their journey lay with Caspar, the youth whom they guarded with the jealous watchfulness of love. He was of their blood, the last of a splendid line, but he was also of that kinship which is more than blood, the kinship of the spirit. Heir to the best gifts of this world, he was rich also in the more precious gifts which no wealth can buy, no love can command. Joyfully they led him forth, for they knew him worthy of the place foretold for him, a place at the right hand of the Deliverer.

When they had followed the sign from Persia to Palestine, they perceived that the Prince of the Star must be of the Hebrew people. Therefore they rejoiced, remembering the conquests of David and the wisdom of Solomon. So they came to the royal city of the Hebrews, where their eagerness outran their guide. Surely this palace of marble and cedar, set upon its noble hill, should be their journey's end. But they found no rejoicing there, but gloom and hate and fear, with an evil king who heard their tale with secret laughter. "There is indeed a prophecy of such a Prince," he said. "Moreover, in the prophet's words he is called a Star. But this is not to be his birth-place. Another city is your goal, the home of one of our early kings. Thus and thus shall ye find it. And if the Prince is there, come back and tell me, so that I may be a pilgrim also." And when they had gone he laughed aloud that men should still be pilgrims of the stars.

From that hour their ardor was strangely chilled, for that evil voice from the throne had stained the beauty of their faith and hope; but still the Star seemed to call them, and there was no lessening of its radiance when it looked down upon that ancient city of Judah. Moreover, its meaning seemed clear, for as they entered the gate it vanished from its place and they saw it no more. But they found no Prince there to receive their homage, for the only child newly born in that city was a poor man's babe, with a shadow upon his birth. In a lowly room they found him with a lowly mother, and with toil and poverty his heritage.

In doubt and sadness they looked upon the child, in doubt and wonder upon one another. Then Melchior took the father aside and questioned him, winning with gentle touch the ramparts of doubt and suspicion. When he had learned all, his heart sank, though there was no shadow upon his princely courtesy, his patience and pity. This newborn child was the son of poverty and toil, but there was more than this. There was a shadow upon his birth, the shadow of a mystery whose other name was shame.

Hope was stricken and wounded, but the old man said nothing. The strange Star had spoken, and he could still hope until the heavens denied its message. So they went away, and he set himself to cast the horoscope of this poor traveler's newborn son. Then hope died, for the heavens told them plainly that their journey had been in vain. This child would never fill a ruler's throne, for his earthly lot was pain and poverty, hate and scorn. Moreover, ere his star had reached its zenith it passed blood-red into the House of Death.

Further he would not read. The elder men were men of silence, and would not have spent words upon their vanished hopes: but Caspar pleaded, for his was the spirit of youth.

The Man at the Gate of the World

"But we saw the Star. Surely the stars cannot lie?"

Melchior answered him with compassion. "What is there that is impossible? Moreover, the stars speak here!" And he laid his hand upon the parchment of the horoscope.

"We misread the signs, or the signs have mocked us," said Balthasar. "We are but shadows, flitting for a moment between the Two Darknesses, yet we dream that we are considered by the gods. If they remember us it is to mock us, as the world was mocked when Alexander came. Now this dream is over, and I go home. I have much to do, and we have lost many days."

"I also go home," said Melchior. "My last long journey has failed."

Caspar could not gainsay them, for their words were wise; moreover, they loved him, and had suffered the ardor of his youth without rebuke. Yet his heart still whispered, "We saw the Star," and at last it overbore their counsel, despite the pain that must be given. He went back with them to Damascus, but there told them that he would not return to the East for yet a little while. "Suffer me to stay," he said. "And I will follow you when the time is come."

They saw that their love had met a stronger power, and it was not the custom of the Magi to set words against the call of the heart. So, standing among the ruins of their shattered world, they masked their sorrow and gave no glance of wonder or reproach. "Stay," said Melchior, "and the gods be with thee." And on the morrow, when they parted at the east gate, the old man blessed the boy again, and prayed for him once more. The other prayer had failed, so now he sought for his beloved the glory of a pure heart and open hands. Then the two turned their faces to their own land.

"It is youth, my father," said Balthasar, as they rode away. "Even in the noblest, youth is cruel as steel. But remembrance will come, and then he will follow us home."

At that time the old man gave no answer, but when they came to rest from the heat of the day he uttered his last judgment concerning Caspar. Heavily he spoke, his heart troubled by conflicting words of hope and sorrow.

57

"He will not follow us. In him I discern now the heart of the seeker, most wretched of the sons of men. Foredoomed to the road and the desert, the seeker has no home or kin. He has only a Star."

"And that but a mocking light!" muttered Balthasar: but the old man did not hear.

"Oft have I told thee, Balthasar, what the stars said at the birth of Caspar—that he should serve a King of Kings, and keep for Him a mighty citadel. Therefore did I prepare him to move among princes, and rejoiced when he showed royalty in mind and spirit. Then the Star came, and we would have helped the prophecy to fulfillment. This must be the promised King of Kings, the Deliverer. First to greet Him and to proclaim His destiny, we should have asked for our boy a place beside the throne. But there is no De- liverer, all is confusion, and our boy is gone. Naught is left but life—and prayer."

"Aye, if there are gods to hear."

"If there are no gods, my son, still greater is the need to pray."

Balthasar was silent in pity. Ere they slept the old man spoke again:

"It is good to be still, Balthasar, and to find content in the things near at hand. So much I know, though I have not followed that wisdom. Yet what can be greater in this dream of ours than the pursuit of the unattainable?"

"As thou sayest, my father."

"And if there are gods, Balthasar, they must surely have com- passion upon the spirit that knows no peace but is ever tracing their footprints in the world. So it may be that our boy shall arrive at length."

"As thou sayest, my father."

So they journeyed on to their home in Persia: and because Balthasar was patient and pitiful, they did not go so swiftly that a youthful rider might not overtake them. But the evening came and darkened without a sign upon the passionless horizon.

That night Caspar walked on the walls of the city, and sought that Star of mystery among the steadfast legions of the skies. He sought in vain, and resolved to forget that lost light forever; for his friends had gone, and he was solitary in the multitude. Yet in the morning, when they brought his camel, it was to the south that he went, back to that ancient city in Judah. For still his heart whispered, "We saw the Star!"

Only a few days had passed, but already the one hope had vanished. The poor man had left the city with his woman and the babe, and it was said that they had gone into Egypt, though they had come from Galilee. Caspar paused upon the verge of this further folly, but at last went down into Egypt, a half-hearted pursuer of the shadow of a dream.

But in Egypt the poor man and his babe were as grains of sand in a desert, so each evening he could only rebuke his folly for another wasted day. In a while he came to the burial places of the great kings whose matchless power and vanity were now but empty tombs upon the desert's edge. Here he called his pride to aid his reason, and resolved to follow the shadow no more.

"But we saw the Star!" said his heart, "and the stars are the beacons of the gods."

"It was a dream," he answered. "If there are gods they are pitiless, and will send no Prince to save the world. In mockery they watch these empty tombs; in mockery they led us to the cradle of a poor man's babe. But nay, they did not lead us. That also was a dream. Today I am awake, and shall begin to live."

He would not go back to Persia, for the kindness of his friends would have been hard to bear. Moreover, in Egypt the tide of life surged high around the crumbling tombs and temples, and life can be very sweet for youth. "And if the world cannot be saved," he said, "shall I not live for today?"

Faintly in answer came a whisper: "We saw the Star." But he would not hear, and for a time the voice died away.

II: "I Will Remember Caspar the Persian"

CASPAR found no home in Egypt, though the land offered him all the fairest fruits of life. He followed wonder and pleasure from place to place, but found no joy in wonder, no peace in pleasure: for still he took with him the heart of the seeker, and it found ghostly allies everywhere. Beyond the glowing cities on every side lay the silent desert, and in his dreams it called him with the music of camels' bells. In Alexandria the very streets tormented him, for they spoke of One who should be greater than the Greek, the One who had not come. Love and laughter and song could not drown those echoes of a fruitless quest.

He left Egypt, and passed at will from city to city of the East, everywhere welcomed for his youth and wealth, but hearing everywhere at the end of days the haunting whisper: "We saw the Star." "Nay, fool," he said to that troubled heart, "must I ever be slave to a dream!" But the voice would not be silenced, and in the end he was constrained to turn his face once more to the land of the Hebrews. Then he laughed in mockery of himself while yet he marveled, for he saw that an aimless pilgrimage of ten years was to find its goal at that old city where the Star had vanished long ago.

Yet this old city was to him as barren as before. After ten years there was still a memory of the Great Census, but there was no memory of a poor man and his child. He came to the stable of the khan, but found only cattle there: he sought the house where the babe had lain, but heard no whisper of a Prince. Then he passed on, tormented by the knowledge that his second quest was a greater folly than his first: and since he had no will save to wander, he journeyed on into the hill country of the Northern Kingdom. For among his memories of that first quest he found the name of Galilee, and took it as his guide.

In that region he wandered for many days, days that were always fruitless, and often bitter with mockery and loneliness; for there was no friend with whom he could share the secret of his folly. But in the end, one day at eventide, he came to the gate of a certain old city, and stood aside to watch the people pass in. He was worn and travel-stained, but his face had other marks than those of the sun and the road. From his eyes looked the heart of the seeker, weary with its own hunger, aching with the pain of silence and the desert.

While he stood thus, a child, a boy, came from among those playing by the gate. He looked at Caspar, and came nearer to look again. Then he spoke to him, gently yet urgently:

"Come, sir, to my mother's house, near at hand. There is water there for thy feet, and food also."

Caspar turned, and saw a boy gracious of manner, eager-eyed and very beautiful. "What is this, child?" he said. "What have I to do with thy mother's house?"

"There is water for thy feet," said the boy again. "I pray thee, come." And he took Caspar by the hand, anxious to lead him. Then Caspar thrust his wonder aside, supposing that the house must be an inn, and that it was the boy's custom to seek guests for his mother. So they went together, and ever and anon as they went the child looked up and smiled, as though well pleased; and it seemed to Caspar that there was a marvelous tenderness in the smile.

At last they came to a house within a courtyard, and the boy showed him a seat. He looked round him in wonder, for it was not an inn, but a small, poor house with a carpenter's workshop beside it. The boy went swiftly away, saying that he would bring water; and when he had gone a moment there came out of the house his mother, troubled yet smiling.

"I supposed it to be an inn," said Caspar. "Why did he bring me here to vex thee?"

"It vexes me not," she answered. "May we not give water for the feet, and bread and wine, and yet be untroubled? Daily my strange son goes to the gate, seeking any who seem weary and lacking so that he may bring them home; and so gentle is his spirit, so eager to deeds of compassion, that I dare not rebuke him, even though he make my poor house an inn."

Her smile was a mingling of joy and doubt and wonder, and so sweet was her joy, so patient her wonder, that Caspar's vexation passed like a shadow. "Here is a thing I have never seen before," he said within his heart; so as the boy came back, bearing water and a towel, he whispered: "Let it be. A good heart is not a matter for disquiet." And smiling again she went in to bring him bread and wine.

The boy set down the water and removed the sandals. Caspar, smiling, dipped his hands and dried them, and the child laved his feet. As he did this Caspar watched him closely, marveling; and now he saw that the beauty of the child was in his eyes, bright with a light that could not be named. "It is his soul," he thought. "Surely never before has the world seen such a spirit as this." So presently he spoke:

"Why dost thou these things, child?"

The boy shook his head. "So many have asked, but I cannot tell," he said.

"But surely there is some thought that governs thy deed, some purpose before thee? Look at me and answer."

For a space the boy pondered; then he raised his head, and Caspar looked into his eyes again. But now the light in those eyes was deepened, as though glorified by a passion beyond all human measure, a passion transcendent, a passion that glowed and burned like the sublime glory of a great star. As this look reached his heart he was strangely moved, for it seemed to him that unawares he had touched a power triumphant, a force so kingly that it might establish lordship over a whole world, and even that deep, dark world, the heart of man. . . . Yet this was the flashing thought of but a moment, and when he came to himself he sat in the courtyard of the carpenter's house, and it was but a boy that knelt before him, with down-bent head. And Caspar, somewhat amazed that a child's look should have done this, said only: "Speak on."

"Nay, sir," answered the boy, "I cannot tell thee what compels me, for I do not know. But someday I shall know. Till then I do what I must do. When I see men weary and travel-worn I feel that I must give them rest. And that is all."

The Man at the Gate of the World

There was something of sadness in his voice, for though he spoke with words beyond his years, he lacked the power to declare his heart. He took up the towel and rose, and Caspar prepared to go. They would take no payment for that gentle deed, but led him to the gate, and showed him the inn door and bade him farewell. And while the boy stood apart, looking eagerly for his playmates in the street, the mother whispered:

"I ask thy pardon for my boy. He seeks always the poor and needy, but today he mistook his guest. He knows so little of the world."

"Nay," said Caspar, sadly. "He made no mistake. I needed him more than any other man." And with that he passed on to the inn.

But his heart was stirred, and all through the night the thought of the Boy was with him. In the darkness he resolved to seek the lad again, but when day came he was ashamed of his longing of the night, and made ready to leave for the north without going to the carpenter's house. But when he came to the north gate, lo, the Boy stood there, fair and eager as yesterday, watching the stream that flowed out to the Damascus road. Then Caspar's heart leaped, and there was eager pleasure in his cry: "Is it thou, my lord of the bread and wine! Art thou to be found ever at the busiest gate?"

The Boy turned and knew his guest. Then he laughed, as though something in Caspar's face gave him joy. He seemed to see that the bitterness was gone, and the hunger of the unsatisfied heart.

"But thou hast no camel, master," he said, "nor yet an ass. Dost thou journey on foot?"

"I like it better so."

The Boy pondered. "I also will go on foot," he said. "But what is it that thou art seeking?"

Caspar wondered at the swiftness of his reasoning. It came to his mind to answer, "A star," but prudence checked the word.

"Naught that thou couldst help me to find," he said. "But I go to Damascus, and I would that I might bear thee with me."

"Gladly would I go," said the Boy. "In a while I shall go to our own great city, where the Temple stands; and after that, someday,

63

to Damascus. There are so many people there that some call it the Gate of the World. And I would love to stand at the Gate of the World."

As he spoke he looked northward, through the gate, and Caspar saw in his eyes some glow of the passion which had moved him yesterday. When he saw it he knew that he loved this lad, and a wild thought came: "Let me stay with him." But this also, with a man's wisdom, he thrust aside, and taking the Boy's hand led him out to a little hill by the way. There he gave him a coin of gold.

"A gift from Caspar the Persian," he said. "For thy pleasure now or for Damascus in the days to come."

The Boy looked at the gold. "Oh, sir," he said, "it will buy much bread and wine. Now my mother will not be vexed if I bring her a poor guest every day."

"There is naught else in thy heart!" said Caspar, his love and wonder deepening; and the child looked up with a look which paid him for the gold a thousandfold. Nay, when he met that look he knew that no gold in the world might be set in the balances against it: but he knew not how he knew, and even in that moment of knowledge felt that his knowledge must be folly. Then the Boy took his hand in his own, and kissed it.

"I will ever love Caspar the Persian," he said. "And ever when I need a friend I will remember him."

Caspar laughed, well pleased that his gift should have won love from such a heart as this. "All through my days," he thought, "I have given more for less." But in the next moment he was ashamed of the thought, and in that shame bade the Boy farewell, and turned to take the road to the north.

Once he looked back. The Boy still stood upon the hillock, holding the gift in his hand, gazing after the giver; and when he saw Caspar turn, he waved his hand in farewell. Then Caspar went on, looking back no more; but he went with heaviness, for to have stayed with the Boy or to have had his companionship upon the road would have been joy indeed. Moreover, there came to his mind the strange conceit that the child's hand raised in that last farewell had been a beckoning hand. Yet when he had gone a little way he found that some spirit of content had fallen upon his journey, so that he drew pleasure from hillside and stream, from the glory of the sunshine and the faces of his fellow men. "It is the gentle deed of that child," he said. "It was a thing so fair that it has lightened my way."

That night he spent at a roadside khan, and remembered that he had passed this house before, with Melchior and Balthasar. But now there was no bitterness in the memory, and when he lay down to rest his troubled heart gave him no torment. For when it would have spoken of unhappy things a Boy's voice came in gentle words: "I will ever love Caspar the Persian, and ever when I need a friend I will remember him." And when it heard those words the seeker's heart forgot to say: "We saw the Star."

III: *"The Boy Was Born at Bethlehem"*

CASPAR went back from the quiet hills to the world of men, and after a time took the glory of his manhood to the Mistress of the World. Rome gave him ready welcome, for he had wisdom and wealth, and his people had been princes before Rome was born. Seeking to forget the Star, he set before him the prizes sought by other men, the star that glows in the eyes of woman, the star that gleams upon the scepter of a king. He drank deeply of the wine of life, and found joy in the heat of the pursuit and in the glow of conquest.

Even in those years of power he could not forget, and often heard in the silences the murmur of the ancient quest, the camels' bells in the desert; but now he had a refuge, for out of the land of the Hebrews he had brought a healing memory. "There was a Star," murmured his heart of discontent. "See, the years fly fast, and still the riddle is unread." But then the Boy came into the garden of remembrance, his face full of eagerness, his hands full of kindness. "Come, sir, with me," he said. "I have water for thy feet, and bread and wine." And at that voice the heart of the man was quieted.

But that gracious memory was more than a solace. In that world of naked and mighty sins the Boy passed unsoiled, and the man was fain to keep his own garments clean to walk with him. Often in the streets and gardens he felt that little hand in his, and it led him always to the sunny open places where the children live and play. Nay, it led him also into a great compassion, for it was on that road that the Boy had found him. "His wealth must be great!" said the Romans. "See how he gives to the poor." But when he looked upon a piece of gold he judged it by a secret standard. "It will buy much bread and wine. Now my mother will not be vexed if I bring her a poor guest every day." Thus the clean heart and the open hands were his, Melchior's prayer finding its answer through the Boy of the Gate.

Often in those years the thought came that he would go back to the land of the Hebrews, and seek the Boy once more; but the Child was a child no longer, and wisdom told him that no reality could be so fair as this fair memory. Nor was there leisure, if he would hold his place by the throne of Caesar. So in the night he thought wearily that he would go tomorrow, to find rest, perchance, with the one who had given him rest before; but in the morning the world called him, and the strong man strode out to answer the call. So the battle for his soul swayed back and forth, the Boy defeated daily, yet returning forever undefeated through the shadowy paths of memory and love.

The end came when he had lived twenty years in Rome, and when he thought that it might never come. Suddenly the old voices rose again, and his heart was stirred anew to recall the dreams of his youth, the lore and legends of his fathers. He was bewildered, for at this time he knew no bitterness; and he was troubled to find that now even the thought of the Boy failed to bring him peace. The Boy came, but it seemed to Caspar that his eyes were filled with longing and reproach. "I should have gone to seek him," he said. "Often he must have wondered why I did not come. And now it is too late."

But though wisdom said "Too late," it could not give him peace.

The Man at the Gate of the World

Day by day the voices grew more urgent, until he heard them above the laughter of the feast, above the music of flattery. Nay, he heard them at last above the very tones of Caesar, when he stood beside the throne of the Master of the World. For on that day Caesar began to speak of Persia, asking many questions with the skill that seeks its end by tortuous ways. And suddenly he said, his watchful eyes searching the Persian's soul: "I have done nothing for thee, most loyal of strangers. Now it is in my mind to make thee Governor of Alexandria, a reward for thy love and to pleasure thy people."

Caspar's heart leaped, for he remembered Melchior's dream for him: but in that moment of wondrous promise he heard another king speak, in a voice of evil mockery: "Another city is your goal, the home of one of our early kings." And as he stood dumb in amazement, Caesar smiled, well pleased.

"It is a great charge," he said. "Go, weigh it well, and tell me if it is equal to thy merit. Not in vain shall any man be known as Caesar's friend."

But still Caspar stood dumb, for clear through the confusion of the moment came another voice, urgent and appealing: "I will ever love Caspar the Persian, and when I need a friend I will remember him." At that cry his heart leaped again, for it knew its master; and suddenly the fire of love flamed and soared upon its altar, never again to fail. So he knew that he must go, and on the morrow another man stepped into his place beside the throne.

He came again to the hills of Galilee, and followed in the footprints of his earlier journeying; but now he had a simpler purpose, for the love in the eyes of the Boy had become the Star which he would seek first. "I will find him," he said, "for in him I shall find a noble man. It may be that he will understand, and then we will go together to read the riddle of that mocking light." And it was with something of the joy and eagerness of the first quest that he drew near that mean city in the hills.

So one day at dusk he stood again in the gate where the child had found him, and passed on to the house of the carpenter. Stern was his face and proud his bearing, so that none might guess the tumult of his heart as he reached that lowly house. "This is strange indeed," he thought. "I have not been so moved since that night of wonder long ago, when the mystic Star came to rest over the gate at Bethlehem." So he went into the courtyard of the Boy.

But the Boy was gone. The carpenter who came to meet him was an old man, bent and gray, slow of speech and sullen.

"It is twenty years since I came to this city," said Caspar. "In those days a boy dwelt here, with his mother, and they gave me hospitality. Know you anything of them?"

The face of the carpenter darkened. "Many ask me that question," he said. "It might seem that I came here but to answer it."

Caspar waited, grave and still: and the man's harshness melted before his dignity.

"Thy pardon, sir. Questions concerning the Boy have been so many that they have tried my patience. He is not here now. He is dead."

Caspar stood dumb. Moved by his look the old man told him more.

"I tell thee what I know, as I tell others. A strange lad, he left this place and set himself up as a Rabbi, with a few friends who became his followers. He went to Jerusalem, and opposed the priests of the Temple, who will suffer no teacher but themselves. So they laid a charge of sedition against him, and slew him there."

Still Caspar could not speak, for he was stricken by wonder and sorrow and pain, and the carpenter told him more, for the stranger's pain had touched his heart.

"But his friends declare that his death was not the end. They claim that after he was slain he rose again. . . . But if he rose again he did not come here. I have not seen him."

Caspar heard here the mockery of the unbeliever who is almost persuaded to believe; but above all was his wonder at so strange a story. Swiftly was hope reborn in his heart, for there is nothing too hard for love to hope and believe.

"Tell me all that is known of him," he said. "Nor shall thy time be lost, for I will reward thee. Speak."

The Man at the Gate of the World

And the carpenter told him, gathering one by one the tales which had come upon the winds of mockery and chance to find harborage in the room where the Boy had lived his hidden youth. Nor could his undertone of mockery spoil the tale, for it is the noblest that the world has heard. And as the old man told what he knew, the Persian stood apart in his white robe, with gold upon his girdle and his hands, but with a fire in his eyes that was more steady than the gleam of gold, the fire of a strong heart startled and awake.

"Such are the tales," said the carpenter at last. "Strange tales, yet not so strange that they shall not find credit. For his friends have come to see the place where he lived, and there is no tale too strange for them. Now they weave wonder tales about his birth, but tales so wild that no man may believe them. But for thy patience I had not dared to speak of them."

"His birth?" said the Persian. "What tales are those?"

"Hear them, sir, as I have heard them. He was not born here, but in the southland, at Bethlehem, the City of David, when his parents were there for the Census of Augustus. Ever in some other province are the wonders too strange to be true! He was born in a stable, for there was no room in the inn; but it is declared by these people that angels proclaimed his birth with hymns in the sky, calling him Saviour and Lord. But I have never found a man who heard those hymns."

The man paused, and silence fell. In that silence Caspar's world recled and swayed; and as in a mist, he saw three tall camels sweep over the desert with a star to guide. But the carpenter spoke again, with a little shame at his own tale.

"There is another story, still more marvelous, of three men from the East, Magian astrologers, who came, led by a star, to hail him as royal and a Deliverer. But if they came they did not pass my door."

And again the silence, this time so long that the man thought: "I have wearied him with these wonders." He was startled when a question came, so moving was its tone.

"Born at Bethlehem—in a stable—in the days of the Census of Augustus! Is this very truth?"

"Aye, very truth. All men here know it."

"And that poor man's babe at Bethlehem became the Boy who dwelt here?"

"Even so. This was his home."

In vain Caspar tried to order his thoughts, while the carpenter waited in doubt and wonder. It might not be done till he was alone, nor could he bare his heart by further questions. But in the tumult he saw one step clearly:

"Those friends and followers of his—where shall I find them?"

"They are scattered in many cities," said the carpenter. "But they are strongest in Jerusalem, where he was slain, and in Damascus, where they have found refuge. Of those in Damascus some are Greeks and Syrians." For he saw that Caspar was of foreign race. "They are good and friendly people, and will greet thee gently. For that was their Master's way."

"It was his way," said Caspar.

The shadows had gathered, and he stood white in the shadows. In his slow and measured tones there was dignity and power, and after that day the carpenter had troubled thoughts concerning him. Was he not like unto one of those great angels who had visited men in earlier ages, but now came no more? For Caspar spoke thus out of the shadows, in fellowship and compassion born of his grief:

"As I consider him, carpenter, it comes to my heart that he sent me here, but not for my own good only. He remembers also the man who toils where he toiled."

"Nay," cried the carpenter, amazed: "He never knew me!"

"Nevertheless he considers thee. For thou also art a seeker, despite thy stubborn heart. And he would give thee water for thy feet, and bread and wine."

"Nay," cried the carpenter, "who said that I sought anything?"

But Caspar heeded not his words. Solemnly he spoke, passing the vain barrier of denial.

"I may not refuse thee what I can give. Know, then, that those wonder stories of his birth are not stories only. If he was the poor man's son born at Bethlehem in the days of the Census, I was one of three Magians who came from Persia to Bethlehem led by a star which promised us a world's Deliverer, a greater Alexander. When it brought us to the cradle of a poor man's child, born to shame and despair, we could not believe. But the tale is a true tale."

The carpenter stood by his bench, trembling and dumfounded. Caspar took a ring from his finger and laid it before him.

"It is a pearl," he said, "worth five years of thy labor. Let it be the reward of thy story and a sign that my tale is true. But hear this, carpenter, for I give counsel with my gift. Twice I saw the Star and did not know it for mine. Do not thou likewise, but seek on to the uttermost. So shall I do from this hour." And he passed out into the dusk of the city of memories.

Left alone, the carpenter gazed upon the ring. He trembled as though he feared something that dwelt in the shadows of the lowly room where the Boy had toiled. He sought his lamp, and set himself to light it; and as he moved here and there, the pearl in the ring lay upon the bench, a point of pale radiance like a distant star shrouded in mist.

IV: *"This Wondrous Thing Our Master Did"*

It was only a little after dawn when the Persian rode north, to travel for the third time that remembered road. He would seek light in Damascus, for he could not go to that hateful city where they had slain the Boy. His heart was hot and his eyes were eager, for a great hope had fanned the smoldering embers of a great love. He set out as though the mystic Star once more gleamed before him.

He drew rein by the little hill where he had left the Boy, and looked before and back while his wild thoughts ranged the years. Those thoughts would have seemed madness yesterday, but now all things were possible. For the carpenter had said that He had risen from the dead.

"We refused the witness of the Star. . . . Our proud hearts could not stoop to the cradle of a poor man's babe . . . and because our hearts failed, we could not read the horoscope aright. Ah, we did wrong! The stars do not lie, and we despaired too soon.

Yet who shall rebuke thee, Melchior, that thy dim eyes could not look beyond the River of Death. . . . Because a little faith lingered in my heart it was given to me to meet Him here. . . . I was warned to stay with Him, but I thought the impulse folly. Oh, fool, fool, to be so wise! . . . Aye, they slew Him, but He rose again — and if He could conquer death He must be indeed the world's Deliverer. . . . Melchior is dead, but I will send a letter to Balthasar. . . . Nay, the stars cannot lie, but we misread them . . . and always, always, we despair too soon. . . . Here I left Thee, Beloved, though my heart bade me stay. . . . But now I have found Thee again, and I follow, even to the world's end."

At Damascus he found helpers who had authority, and soon gained knowledge of the Nazarenes. They were poor people who met in secret, for the shadow of persecution was upon them; but they were friendly to all, and eager to tell of their lost Leader. Caspar was filled with wonder by what they told him, for already the Crucified Carpenter was their Messiah and a God: but with steadfast purpose he asked all and pondered all, and presently joined them when they met for comfort and remembrance.

He came again and yet again, a man solitary and apart. Silent and gray he sat, his heart a hidden fire of memory and yearning: but none so eager to hear the tales of the Nazarene, none so watchful for the remembered words of that lost Leader. So it was that he drew nearer to his goal; for as the days passed he perceived among these people a power which was a new thing in that world of sword and scepter, a power fugitive and mysterious, yet not to be denied. Sometimes it spoke in the light of their eyes, a light that seemed to be a faint reflection of a greater light; sometimes he caught it in the cadence of a voice, like a chord of wondrous and compelling music. Then he remembered what the old carpenter had said, of angels singing in the night, and would watch and listen with burning eyes till those humble men would wonder what had stirred him. But he could not tell them, for this new mystery was mingled in his memory with the cadences of the Boy's voice, the light in the Boy's eyes. And those were the treasures of a love too sacred to be told even if the tongue had words wherewith to tell it.

So he watched and waited, unaware that Balthasar followed Melchior into the unknown, careless that the Caesar who had been his friend had left him friendless. The Star and the Boy, the secret that lay with Him, were more than Caesar's favor, more than home or kin. Anon the thought came that he might go to Jerusalem, if only for a little time, to seek light where the Master had lived His last troubled days: but always that thought found its answer in his stubborn loyalty and hope. "He is risen from the dead—and He said He would come to Damascus. I must be here when He comes." So as the days passed he won to clearer vision of the power that moved among these people, and saw that it was a power imperfect. Here it came and there, in glance or word or gesture, but it had no free play and no abiding place. It came and fled, it shone and failed; anon it stirred their assembly like a wind, but like a wind was gone; anon it was a star which sought in vain to pierce a veil of cloud. It was a power frustrate and shorn, a voice that spoke indeed, but in an unknown tongue.

For many days he marveled, but at last he seemed to understand; and when he began to understand his heart was sore with a new sorrow. For it seemed to him that he saw the Boy come to that place of assembly, to stand with dumb beseeching among His friends, having no interpreter. He turned to Caspar sitting among the shadows, and held out pleading hands as though He said: "Long ago I saw love in thy eyes, so I called thee hither. Is there no help in thee now?" And Caspar sat with his heart torn, knowing that the vision had a message which he could not read.

But the hour came, and the path was made clear. To him one night came the leader of the Damascus Nazarenes.

"Though a stranger, thou art a friend," he said. "Therefore would we have thee share our joy. Tomorrow we greet as guest the disciple who is called Beloved. He was ever at the Master's side, and knew His inmost heart. He was with Him first and last."

"And I may come and hear him?" asked Caspar: and no man could have divined the fire that lay behind that question. If he had

73

dared to leave Damascus he would have tracked this man to the world's end.

"Tomorrow at this hour."

"Tomorrow at this hour I will come."

The gray Persian rose and went his way, but on the morrow he was first among the company, sitting in the shadow of the wall, his stern face a mask for the tumult of his heart. Then came the Apostle whom they called the Beloved, envied of all because he had lain upon the Master's bosom. He stood before them with the torches' glow upon his face, but when he spoke his eyes had a deeper glow, the glory that made his days magnificent. Tonight he told the old stories once more, but with such authority and fervor that women sat with streaming eyes and men with swelling hearts. Their lost one moved among them in the love of him who remembered, they heard and saw Him, matchless, wonderful; and suddenly Caspar was aware of that mysterious power once more, filling the hall, stirring all hearts, compelling, irresistible. "At last! at last!" he said; yet on the words came some doubt that bade him wait. "Not yet— not yet! There must be more than this!"

So the Beloved told of the night before the Cross, when the Master had supped with His friends for the last time: and in his tale they saw the Upper Room, and the bread and wine, heard the gracious words which are their heritage forever. He told how one of the company had sold the Master to His foes, a miracle of sin that no human heart might understand. Then he told a thing which they had not heard before, a mystery to all, but amazement and revelation indeed to the listening Persian in the shadow of the wall:

"Now after Supper our beloved Master rose, and laid aside His robe, and took a towel, and girded Himself; and He poured water into a basin, and came to wash the feet of His friends. And He dried their feet with the towel.

"When He had done this strange thing He looked upon them and said: 'Do you know why I have done this? If you know, you have my secret in your hearts.

"'You call me "Master," and you say well, for I am your

The Man at the Gate of the World

Master; and if I, your Master, wash your feet, what shall ye do? Is the servant greater than his Master, that he shall not do what his Master did?'

"This wondrous thing, my brothers, our Master did, even when the gloom of the Cross lay upon His spirit. To all of us He did it, even to him whom we call the Son of Perdition. He was ever hard and sullen, but surely that deed might have saved him. Nay, ever and anon I deem that it was done for his sake. But alas! he was captive to his sin, and would not be released."

When this was told the people wondered, but did not understand; but one man's heart was singing with sudden joy. The face of the Boy rose before him, not troubled now, but radiant. Such is the light upon the prophet's face when he has found one soul to receive his message. Moreover, in that flash of revelation he saw what he had seen in the eyes of the Boy of Nazareth, he heard the stir and murmur of a power which should save the world, even the dark world of the human heart. The murmur grew, till it filled the air as with a voice of many waters: and the unknown power swept through fast-closed city gates, thundered in forum and market, glowed upon the thrones of kings, flamed to the sky from the altars of ten thousand temples. Men looked up, and lo, there was music in the breeze, a splendor of purity in the light, a new hope in every face: and when evening came there was no darkness, for the heavens held a star which waxed in glory till night was day. Then men said with quivering lips and bounding hearts: "It is the Star of the Deliverer, and it shall not set until the end of time. For He is come, the long-awaited Saviour of the world."

The vision passed, leaving him filled with joy and certainty, though even in his joy he marveled that no others saw what he saw in that story. He waited till the throng had gone, and then he sought the leaders where they were gathered about their guest. In amazement they heard the gray stranger's question.

"He said that we should do as He did, even to washing the feet of the poor. Are there any who obey Him?"

A hush fell upon their rejoicing.

75

"Nay," said one at last, "surely, that was a symbol. The command is to be obeyed in spirit."

"For He spoke often in symbols and parables," said another. And all of them agreed. "Yea, it was His way to speak in symbols and parables."

Yet again he questioned, not sternly, but as with a wondering compassion, his joy subdued and chastened.

"Sirs, I knew Him as a boy, and even then He did this thing. In His last hours, and as His last command, He bade His friends do the same deed if they would be His friends. Is it not so?"

Again a silence fell, a silence of surprise and doubt: but in the silence doubt reared a wall between them and this man, and jealousy became as a coiled serpent ready to strike.

"Yes, but it was still a symbol," said their leader at last. "He would not command the impossible." And others whispered: "Who is this man, that he should claim to interpret the mind of the Master?" For they were His people, and this man was a stranger.

But the Persian waited, turning to the Beloved for his answer. They stood face to face, one face intent with question, the other radiant with assurance; but after that long moment Caspar turned away. He saw that the Apostle had no answer to give, and wearily spoke his heart through those contending voices: "They are very near, for His glory touches them; this man nearest, for it shines in his every word. Yet the secret is not with them. They will not do as He did, they will not go out as He would. What a marvel of men's hearts, that they should call Him God yet not obey Him! Nay, that they would die for Him yet not obey Him! But surely, now, the Boy has spoken clearly."

Down the hall he passed, till he was lost in the shadows at the door. The Beloved stood among his friends with trouble in his eyes.

"Who is this man?"

"Not of our company, but friendly," said the leader of the Nazarenes. "None so eager as he to hear the words of the Master, but silent and apart, and burdened with secret thought. He came first dressed as a Persian."

The gentle face darkened in bewilderment.

"There are no Persians in our company in any town," said the leader. "Proud in their ancient faith, they seek no new gods."

"Nay," said the Beloved. "Yet there is that strange story of the three who came to Bethlehem. Surely they were Persians."

There was silence till another spoke again:

"How should he claim to interpret the mind of the Master?" "Ah, no, he could not know," said their guest. "It is too difficult even for those who knew Him best, so godlike was His vision." Then the chorus of love and worship rose about him, and he put the mystery aside. Tonight he was here, tomorrow he must pass on with his tale of worship and wonder. How should he burden himself with the questions of a nameless Gentile?

But he lived in two worlds, and the echoes of a well-loved voice beset him at every turn of the way. Now it spoke once more in a fragment of a saying, sad, compassionate and wistful: "They shall come from the East and from the West, and shall sit down in the Kingdom. But the children of the Kingdom——"

Yet in the chorus of friendship and worship it was overwhelmed, and he heard it no more.

V: *So They Came from East and West*

CASPAR OF SUSA was of the proud Magian race, and had been a friend of princes; but above all he was a seeker, a pilgrim of the stars. Still in his clouded firmament shone the Star of mystery which had called him out of Persia; but in Galilee he had seen another star, the love of the Boy of the Gate. Now the two stars had come together, for the Boy of his love was the Child of Bethlehem, the Child of Melchior's troubled horoscope. Could it be that he was also the Prince greater than Iskander, the Prince of Promise, the long-awaited Saviour of the world? Could it be that this carpenter's son held the key to that new order which had been the dream of the Magi for a thousand years? And those questions his love and his knowledge answered now in triumphant unison. In that dear hour

77

at Nazareth he had seen the first gleam of a new and glorious day, and here among the people of the carpenter the promise had come once more with tenfold power.

But how should it come to pass? The Boy had spoken clearly, but the road He showed was a strange and lowly road. Moreover, His most faithful followers did not read His meaning so. Thus it was that the Persian spent troubled days in thought, walking in the gardens where the matchless fountains played, pacing at night those city walls from which he had sought that lost light long ago.

"Clearly hast Thou spoken, Child of my heart," he said, "nor could I fail again. Thine the power, indeed, for I saw it; and Thine would have been the glory, but they slew Thee too soon, before Thy sun was high. Oh, that I had stayed with Thee in Nazareth, for then I might have saved Thee and the world also! Yet Thy power hast Thou left in the world, for I have seen and touched it. It may be that it waits for one who will dare to tread Thy way. But how shall the world be saved by such a deed as this?"

On that question came an echo from afar, the echo of a gentle voice in doubt and wonder: "I know not why I do it, but someday I shall know." "No, He did not know, but He obeyed," said Caspar. "Then He came to know, and at the end gave this command. Words had failed to save the world, and wonders had failed, though He could call men back from the dead; and at the end He saw that the only way was that which the gods had shown Him in His childhood. So by word and deed He taught them His secret, and then sealed His command by the terrors of the Cross."

The hours passed heavily while he fought, but there was an end at last: for to the gardens and to the city wall came the Boy, with the light of a new hope upon His brows. His words were the remembered words, but now they had a new meaning. "There are many people here," He said.

"They call it the Gate of the World. I would love to stand at the Gate of the World." But anon He spoke in other tones, now eager and urgent, now wistful and sad: "You call me Master, and I am your Master. Is the servant greater than his Master, that he should not do as his Master does?" And when Caspar heard these things his heart grew hot with love that was stronger than life or death, love that feared no path however lowly, love that could not be less than true to its trust. "Twice have I lost the Star," he said. "O heart of mine, shall I lose it again! Nay, He said it, and I obey. I know not how it shall be, but I obey."

So it was that Caspar of Susa laid aside forever the girdle and chaplet which told his race and rank, laid aside the jewels and silk and linen which told his wealth, and did the thing which no man in Susa could have foretold of him. He took a humble house by the east gate, and found a boy to tend the house; and after that he went and stood by the gate, clad in a slave's apron, his gray face set in iron resolve, his heart filled with doubt and shame and love and wonder. There he watched for any who were wayworn and lacking, and came to them, and asked them to be his guests; and if they heeded this strange asking, he took them to his house, and with his own hands laved their feet and brought them food and wine. As surely as the sun rose he was there for the opening of the gates, and he held his place through the endless hours till sunset saw them closed. To those who questioned him he said that a certain vow constrained him, so that some thought him mad, and others supposed him to be a sinner making an amazing atonement; and if they asked his name he said that it was Servus; for he was truly slave to an unseen Master and His strange command.

The gatemen wondered, and questioned him, and mocked at first; but they came to bear with him and to pity, for he sought their good will because without it he could not obey his Lord's command. Then the Captain came, but would not deign to question, for he could not see in this man a friend of Caesar; but he told a comrade who had dwelt in Jerusalem, and that comrade smiled. "It is nothing," he said. "He is one of those Nazarenes, and all the Nazarenes are mad." So after that he was left in peace save for laughter that had a little pity in it.

To the Gate of the World came the people of the world, from farthest East and farthest West; for in those days the tide of life

moved East and West, and this was the Gate through which it must pass. And all through those days, a man stood in the shelter of the gatehouse, watching the tide of life, serving in his own mad way, but ever seeking in the tide a face that he should know. He sought it in the morning, in the stream that passed out eastward, he watched for it all through the day in the stream that flowed in to the noble street called Straight; he sought it most hopefully in the multitudes that crowded to the Gate at sunset. Ever and anon he must leave the Gate to tend a needy guest, for this was his duty here; but ever he came back with eager seeking, fearing lest the one he sought should pass while he was away. Yet from that fear even his own doubting heart would fain protect him. "That could not be," it said. "Thou shalt not lose His face by doing His will. Perhaps tomorrow He will come."

He did not come on any morrow, and through all those succeeding days the watcher's heart was the battleground of tormenting doubt and hope that would not die. "Tomorrow!" said the hope that would not die: and ever as it spoke there came the mocking echo, "Tomorrow." Wisdom joined the battle, always on the side of doubt. "O fool, fool, canst thou seek that face among these faces? Is there any likeness here to the face that smiled at thee at Nazareth? Nay, fool, only once has such a spirit walked the earth, and it will not come again." But Hope called Faith to her side to answer with the words that never failed to come: "But He said that He would love to stand at the Gate of the World. And He is risen from the dead."

So the days fled till a year was measured, and then the years fled, heaping snow upon the Persian's head but leaving his madness unhealed. He became one of the signs by which men spoke of Damascus in many lands, for this was the only city where such a marvel might be found. "As ye enter by the east gate ye shall see there an old gray man who gives to the poorest water for the feet, and bread and wine." So men looked to see him, and went away bewildered; some, supposing him to be afflicted, durst not question him, and did not pause to wonder what tumult of the heart might be hidden by that gray face and those eyes so eager to mark the signs of sorrow and sin; others, less kind or more curious, questioned him, and heard his story, and went away and told it, so that in the course of years it passed to farthest East and farthest West; and ever and anon its marvel would take lodging in some heart that was soil for it, to bring forth fruit in thought and deed—"I must go and see."

So they began to come from East and West, drawn out of many an uttermost wilderness by the lodestar of that amazing folly; and when they came, Caspar would take them, and tend them, and wash their wounded feet and give them bread and wine. Then they would ask him his secret, searching his heart with eyes that had looked unashamed upon unutterable evil. He would tell them gladly, for that story was his pride and joy; and they would ask and listen, till wonder overcame the evil in those shameless eyes, and a seed of hope found place in hearts that had hitherto been stone. Then the evil guest would go, to seek once more his uttermost wilderness, but with a star in the sky that had been black with doom; and Caspar would go back to the Gate, to wait for another guest, and to watch for the Guest who never came.

In those long years the whole world passed through the Gate and saw him: youth and age, wealth and want, greed and kindness, love and laughter, toil and idleness, pride and pomp and power and vanity, with hope and joy and fear and wretchedness; and loudest of all the might and majesty of Rome, in the tread of marching legions, the chariot of the Governor, the swift hoof stroke of the courier on his way to some distant frontier. But Rome did not pause to mark the old gray man at the Gate, for she could not deem that he was there to save the world. The world was hers, for she was heir to Alexander, and would save it by his sword and scepter. But as he stood he saw it all, and saw it many times; and ever and anon he stood as it were in a dream, while the life of the world surged through the city gate like a dark flood in which men were being swept away, and cried out feebly as they sank. Then there came into his heart a great pity and compassion, rising like a tide until it covered everything that was the Caspar of other years, so that he knew nothing but that great compassion, and yearned over that flood as if that stream of mankind had been his only child, the idol of his soul. Ever and anon he caught the hand of one who was being swept away, and saved him; but it was little that he could do, and pitilessly the flood rolled on. But when he spoke with men after such a vision as this they saw in his eyes a light which filled them with wonder. Some said that it was the sign of his madness, but it did not make them afraid.

The Nazarenes of Damascus heard of his deed, and were amazed: but when they had considered it they held it folly, or pride that was worse than folly. "Who is this man," they said, "that he should claim to interpret the mind of the Master?" Then they passed by daily, some with pity and wonder, some with doubt, and some with blame. At this time they were looking for their Lord's return, when He would answer all questions and reign in power; and there was no man to tell them that perchance He had already come, to stand day by day at the Gate of Damascus.

VI: "Here Must I Stay and Save the World"

Is there any will so strong that time and the world may not break it? It is written that after ten years Caspar's heart failed, his spirit sinking beneath the load of its own pain and the world's pain, the bitterness of disappointment and despair. One morning at this time he saw three Persians in a caravan that passed out eastward, and he remembered with searing grief the wise and gentle Melchior, the strong and patient Balthasar. It was here that he had parted from them forever, it was here that Melchior had given him an old man's blessing, and with his eyes to heaven had whispered a secret prayer. Surely he had prayed that his boy might come home at last, even after many years; and at this thought his loneliness and his sorrow overcame him, and he bowed beneath the load. "Tomorrow I will go," he said. "This dream is done, and I must die among my own people and under my own stars." And at that resolve the flame of life flickered anew in his heart, and he went home to make ready.

The Man at the Gate of the World

When all was done he slept the sleep of an old man's weariness, and in his sleeping, dreamed. He dreamed that morning was come, and that in the bright sunshine of the opening day he went joyfully to the Gate which should now be the gate of release. But when he came to the Gate his heart ceased its song, for in the place where he was wont to stand he saw another. It was the Boy of Nazareth, slender and sweet as He had been of old, but now with sadness and pain in the face once so radiant. Caspar looked again, and knew that it must be a dream; yet eagerly he spoke, from the depths of his wonder and his love.

"O my Son, my Son! What dost Thou here?"

The Boy looked up, love and remembrance in His marvelous eyes. "Hast thou forgotten, Caspar?" he said. "I told thee I must come to Damascus, for it is the Gate of the World."

"How should I forget?" cried the old man. "But this is no place for Thee, with the press and the heat and the harshness of men. Come to my house. For many years I have longed to have Thee for my own. Come!"

But the Boy answered sadly, while the glory of His eyes was dimmed by tears: "I cannot come to any house today. Here must I stay, for thus I save the world. And no man will stay for Me. O Caspar, the World, the World . . . I must save the World!"

Through the sadness of the answer came a music of sorrow and pity, as though He said: "Thou hast waited long, but the task is too great for thee." Then Caspar gave a cry, and he was awake in the dawn, with tears upon his furrowed cheeks and pain and penitence and joy surging in his heart.

"Again hast Thou spoken, Star of my Life," he said. "By this I know that I am not forgotten; by this I know that it is by Thy remembrance that I am set here. Still the way is dark, but now I know Thy will. And here I stay, for I am Thine to the uttermost."

So again the years were measured out in love and loyalty, though the task became a toil and the toil a travail. At last he could go no farther than from his house to the Gate and from the Gate to his house, often with halting steps and eyes half blind. And as his days drew nearer to their close, more and more the old man, waiting at the wall with bowed head and beard upon his breast, lost his present pain in dreams of other times. Now his great camel bore him swiftly over plain and hill, the mystic Star before, Melchior and Balthasar on either hand, silent in the doubt that mocked their hope; now he stood before the mighty tombs of nameless kings in Egypt, and uttered the last despair of an embittered heart: "The stars are pitiless. In mockery they watch these empty tombs, in mockery they show us the cradle of a poor man's babe!" Yet again he came at eventide to a lesser city in the hills of Galilee, and lo, a Boy within the gate, slender and eager, beautiful with childhood, with a wondrous light in His eyes and music in His voice. "Come, sir, with me, for I have water for thy feet, and bread and wine." So he walked up the city street to the house of the carpenter, and as they walked the Boy's hand was placed in his; but at the touch his heart swelled to bursting, so that his dream was shattered. And in the next vision the years had fled, and he heard another voice, laden with doom: "He is not here. He went to Jerusalem, and they slew Him there."

The last of these dreams came on the day before the last day, when his weakness was such that he could scarce keep his post by the Gate. The sun pursued him with lances of flame, scorching arms and hands and breast through the frail folds of linen: the pavement blistered his shrunken feet, and the wall burned like a wall of heated brass. Yet he would not go, for still the stream of life trickled through the open gate, seeking shelter from the greater heat of the dusty roads without; and when it was noon, the torments of that day and of all the other days were gathered up in one last anguish that transcended all. Then the wall behind him became a narrow shaft of wood whose touch was fiery pain, his hands were outstretched on either side, each a core of agony unspeakable. In the same moment the torture of his burning feet was multiplied a thousandfold, for they were nailed by iron nails to the wood on which he swooned in torment. But when his parched and swollen tongue sought words of agonized surrender—"It is finished," the effort died, for clear through the storm came a whisper: "I know this too. But the hour will come, and I must not fail." And when he heard that word the old man smiled, and sank swooning beside the wall.

A giant gateman, touched with pity, gathered him up and bore him to his house. His boy came, and they looked down upon him together; then the man turned and went out, a little scorn mingled with the pity in his farewell. "That is the end," he said. "He will come out no more." But on the next day he saw the old man, upheld by that sullen lad, limping down to the Gate as of old, there to keep his watch from hour to hour, the flame of purpose burning steadily amid his frailty and his pain. And when they reasoned with him in their mercy, his answer was an echo of a voice which only he had heard.

"I must not fail."

VII: *"What Shall Ye Do for One Another?"*

It was within an hour of sunset, and the east gate was a tumult of traffic. Horses, camels and men streamed in, and after them a thin following of travelers on foot who had gathered to the caravan for the protection of its guards. Among these were some who were evil and hopeless driftage upon the river of fate.

Caspar stood in the shelter of the gatehouse looking with anxious eyes for the thing he sought, but now too frail to enter the press. At last it seemed that a fragment from the stream drifted to his side, for a man lame, crooked and evil of face stood before him, regarding him with a rude mingling of mockery and greed. Then strangely the heart of Caspar misgave him, for in this creature there seemed to be some spirit of evil that bade even mercy to beware. Here sin reigned unchallenged, with Despair and Defiance twin keepers of the Gate. So he stood uncertain, till he saw the vision of Him who scorned not the vilest of men, and at once the flame of his love burned away his doubt. Timidly he put out his hand to the stranger.

"Art thou weary?" he said. "Come, then, with me, to my house close at hand. I have water for thy feet, and bread and wine."

The man laughed, a laugh of evil mockery. "Here is indeed a

welcome to Damascus!" he said. "But what shall I pay thee for this?"

"Nay," said the old man. "I take no payment. All is freely given. Come thou with me."

The gatemen had gathered to see and mock. "Answer gently, Rose of the Desert," said one. "He that speaketh with thee is the Wonder of Damascus, the giver of bread and wine."

"And the Washer of Feet," said another. "Thou hast need of him!"

The stranger heeded the mockery little, for he met it in every city; but he looked at Caspar searchingly, and it seemed that the old man's gentleness called forth the bitter anger of a black heart. Suddently he began to revile him, with foul words in many tongues; and as he poured forth his gall the gatemen laughed to provoke him further. And when Caspar answered nothing the beggar spat upon him:

"That for thy aid," he screamed. "Now go, seek some easier soil for thy folly."

There was a hush, and Caspar was shaken to the inmost heart; and somewhere in that inmost heart dwelt the shadow of one who had been the friend of Caesar: but immediately he saw the judgment hall of Pilate, and One there who wore a crown of thorns, and had been mocked and scourged and spat upon.

"Nay, let it pass," he said. "Thou art weary and in pain. I pray thee come with me."

"Will naught rid me of this pestilence?" raved the beggar; and he struck at the old man with his staff, so that he bled from the blow. Again he would have struck him, but the gatemen seized his staff and held it. "O fool," they cried to Caspar, "let this viper go, lest he sting thee to death." For though he was ever to them a fount of bewilderment, his goodness had reached them all.

Then Caspar was tempted to let the creature go, for surely it was enough. Not pride spoke now, but gentle reason and the wisdom that is almost divine. Yet one thing still constrained him, the vision of Him who in His direst agony could say: "Father, forgive them."

86

So he answered with an old man's pleading: "Nay, it is nothing. Let him come with me."

As he spoke he looked again at the beggar, his eyes living wells of compassion: and suddenly and strangely the mood of the creature changed, moving from bitter wrath to bitter derision. "Aye," he said, with an evil laugh. "Let me grant his prayer. Let me go with him. Let us see whether he will truly fill my belly! Why should I spare him? Come, fool, and show me the way."

So amid the scorn and wonder of the guards and gossips they went up the street together, the beggar filling the brief journey with the poison of his mockery and scorn.

"So this is the Wonder of Damascus," he said. "Nay, it is the Wonder of the World, for I have not seen thy fellow in any other city. Yet the Wonder is only a madman, for only a madman would do it. Is it not so, Whitebeard?"

Caspar answered nothing. "Words are precious with thee," mocked the stranger. "Yet what are words when there is food and wine! I would see thy bounty, for I have heard of it in many cities. Nay, but for this I should not be here today. It was the tale of thy folly that drew me, for I have been hungry many times; and since no other city desired me, I came to see it. Doth not that please thee, fool?"

"Surely, it pleases me," said Caspar, gently. "Shall I not welcome what the Spirit of God hath sent?" And at that saying his guest's laughter rang loud in the busy street.

"So it was God that sent me! But I said that thy madness had called me. Then thy God is madness. Oh, fool of fools! And what am I, the gift of thy God? Little dost thou know, but a mad gift indeed. But I must hold my tongue till I am filled, or I may still go away empty. The food, the food! And the wine, fool, the wine!"

So they came to the house, and food and wine were brought. He ate and drank like a beast of the field, greed mingling with mockery and wonder in every glance. But as Caspar watched and served this appalling guest, it came to his heart that never was his compassion so greatly needed as now, so utter was the sin and loss. Then he rejoiced, for it seemed to him that he understood more the heart of his Master, who had not shrunk even from the touch of the leper, and had found pardon possible in the agony of the nails. So he bore all with patience and pity.

"Let us cast him out, master," whispered the boy who served the house. "Surely thou shalt not wash the feet of such as this!" But Caspar had already conquered that thought in his own soul, and gently rebuked him for his words. Then he girded himself, and brought the basin and the towel, and knelt at the feet of his doomful guest. As his Lord had done so he did, and in the same manner.

"I would wash thy feet," he said. "Suffer it to be so, for it is my custom. And thou hast come far today."

The stranger looked, and for a moment a shadow as of terror overcame the evil in his glance. Though his question was fiercely spoken, his hoarse voice quivered:

"So it is true!" he said. "What is this madness, fool? I had heard of it and wondered. Tell me—who art thou?"

"My name is Caspar, and I was a Persian," said the old man. "Here I am Servus, a slave to give aid to the weary and travel-stained. Therefore would I wash thy feet."

"A Persian?" muttered the guest. "Then this is some madness of the Persians." And he spoke aloud, defiance once more upon his lips and scorn in his eyes. "Fool, fool, why should I forbid thy folly! Wash these feet of mine, and do it well."

So Caspar took the filthy feet and laved them, thinking always of the Master and desiring only that he might learn more of the love that could do such mighty deeds. So it was that he drew ever nearer to the Secret of the Star. But as he laved the feet the beggar mocked him still, for his brief terror had left shame behind it.

"Are they not beautiful, my fool? Nay, sayest thou? But consider, fool. These feet of mine have had a heavy task, for they sought to bear me to some place where I might find peace. And there was no peace. But in the seeking they have borne me into many dark places where the road was rough and stony. If they have lost their beauty it was there that they lost it."

Caspar answered nothing, but stinted not his care. And the beggar derided him again.

"Should I love thee for this, thou fool? Is that thy hope? Nay, I hate thee for it. I hate all men, and all men hate me; but such folly as thine wins my deepest hate. Nay, once I saw the best and hated it; and if I hated the best, what shall I have for a fool's shadow of the best? Can I give less than my hate?"

Still Caspar answered nothing, for what answer might there be? Only golden silence and tender care. But the beggar raved the more, as though to provoke an answer.

"Aye, I hated the best, poor fool. Nay, I did more, for I slew a god! Aye, now I have told thee my secret. O fool, is there any other man who hath slain a god? And if I could slay a god, how can I spare any other living thing? Nay, I would slay all, all, all, to the last fool who stands by a city gate!"

But Caspar answered nothing, for now he saw that the man was mad; but when he saw it he did not fear, but rather gloried in the new peril and its call upon his pity. He remembered how his Master had dared the evil spirits, and in His compassion had cast them out. He might not cast out evil spirits, but he could show the same compassion; so tenderly he laved those hideous feet, and called to mind the toil of the homeless and unfriendly roads, the pitiless stones, the burning, blinding dust. And suddenly he stooped and kissed the feet of that loathsome one.

The man was stricken with amazement. "Oh, fool, fool!" he cried. "What dost thou now?"

"Nay," said Caspar, trembling before his anger. "Be not wroth with me. I did this thing for the sake of One greatly beloved, who would most surely have me do it."

A silence fell. Had Caspar looked up then he would have seen terror once more upon that evil face. But he did not lift his eyes, and the man hardened his heart.

"What is this?" he said at last. "Some mad story to cover thy folly?"

"Let me tell thee," pleaded Caspar. "For this story is my joy. And the world has no tale so marvelous."

89

For a time there was silence, heavy and dread. The guest could not have desired that story, but perchance was constrained by the secret power that dwelt in that humble chamber.

"Speak on, my fool," he said. "Since I have been fed I will be gracious, and hear thee. But keep thy eyes from my face. There can be no pleasure in the regard of a fool!"

So Caspar began his story, sitting at his guest's feet, and never looking up into his face. Nay, when he told this tale he looked always into the past and into his own heart. He told first of his home in Susa, where the priest princes of an ancient faith had waited for the greater than Iskander, for the World's Deliverer: of how the Star had come, and of the three who had abandoned their quest at the manger cradle of a poor man's babe. But after that came the joy of his story, for he told how he had found the Boy at the gate of Nazareth, with the gentle deed which to him had become another star. And as he told these things the stranger laughed mockingly at first, and then was silent for a time, as though weary of his own scorn. Anon he muttered, "Hasten! hasten!" and again he seemed to curse the old man for his waste of words and time. Once he made as if to rise, and that was when Caspar told of the glory of the Boy's look, and its power to stir a strong man's heart. But when the listener moved, the old man laid a trembling hand upon him, and pleaded with him by a touch. So he sank into his seat again to hear to the end.

So Caspar came to those tales which he had gathered from the old carpenter and the Nazarenes, and he told them not as he had heard them but with the fire of his own love. Then the stream of mocking ceased, and there was silence in the room save for his own voice and the echoing sounds of the street; but once the guest seemed to shudder in his rags, as though some chill wind had found him through the warmth of the dusk. For now sunset had come, and the city gates were closed, and the thunder of the streets had died down into the restless murmur which only ceases when darkness deepens.

So Caspar came to the story of the end. Briefly he told it, for every word pierced his own heart. Still in silence the listener heard him, and once he sat tense in his listening, as though he knew what must come. But it did not come, for Caspar had no evil word for any man. Eagerly he passed on from the scene of sorrow to the morning of joy, to the riven tomb and the risen Lord: and still in silence the listener heard him, his face half hidden upon his arms, as though he were greatly weary, worn into helpless patience. And when he had told of the wonder of Easter morning, Caspar turned in his story and came back to the night of the Supper. For here was the cause for all that he did.

"And now, O guest of mine, I tell thee of a deed of His on the night before His death, when He supped with His friends. At the end of the Supper He took a basin and a towel, and washed the feet of His company, though they were poor and lowly men. They resisted Him, but He persuaded them to bear His deed. And when He had done this He said: 'You call me Master, and I am your Master; but if your Master wash your feet, what shall ye do for one another? Is the servant greater than his Master, that he should not do as his Master does?' And they marveled, for they did not understand. For so deep was His love that it was beyond their understanding. Nay, no man hath measured it to this day."

Again the guest seemed to shudder; but he gave no sign, and Caspar ended his tale in a hush that seemed as deep as the hush of death. Then he said:

"Thus it is, my brother, that I stand at the Gate of Damascus, with water for the feet of the wayfarer, and bread and wine. As a Boy He did it; as a man He bade me do it, sealing His command by the terrors of the Cross. Can I do less in my love for Him, though the world pass by in scorn, and even His friends disown my deed? Nay, I have naught to do but obey, though still His purpose is dark."

The silent guest answered not by word or sign. The old man ended his tale with a strain of triumph in his quavering voice.

"Now for five-and-twenty years have I done this, and spent all the wealth of my fathers on the needy and the outcast. But my heart is glad, for the only thing I desire is to be worthy of His love; and I rejoice greatly that at last I have learned something of His heart. So was I able to kiss thy feet today. Yet verily it was He that did it, and not I."

At that saying the guest stirred again, but he did not raise his head. Then a hand, hot and quivering, was laid upon Caspar's shoulder.

"Fool, I have heard something of this tale from other lips. Was there not one of His company who betrayed Him?"

"Alas; it was so!" answered the old man. "But should I dwell upon that sin when I had so great a tale to tell?"

"Thou art the first to hide it, fool. But was that evil one there at the Supper, and the deed that followed it? Aye, sayest thou? And did he suffer it too?"

"He suffered it," said Caspar. "Some hold that it was done for his sake only. But his heart was hardened, so that he might not be saved."

"He might not be saved? Then thy Master failed, poor fool, thy Master failed!"

For a moment Caspar was silent. The taunt had pierced him now, as the doubt had tormented him ever. It was his faith that answered:

"So it seemed, my guest, but so it cannot be. My heart tells me that He had the one power in the world that could not fail."

The quivering hand gripped the old man's shoulder. The evil guest panted as he spoke.

"But the memory of that deed! O fool, the memory of it! It would be a hell to the traitor through all the years after."

"Nay," said Caspar pitifully. "It was not so. In a few days he died, self-slain in his despair."

Again a silence fell. In that silence great forces gathered to battle in that bare room.

"Fool! fool!" groaned the guest. "That was a tale they told to save him from the doom of Cain. They had learned a little of their Master's way of mercy, as thou hast learned it all. He could not die. How could he go to meet his Lord?"

Caspar heard, but at first could not believe that he heard. Then he crouched on the floor, trembling, transfixed with wonder and horror. His heart leapt to the incredible truth, and recoiled in shuddering fear. That was the hand that had taken the price of blood; these were the feet that had led the soldiers to the garden on the night of shame. And after fear came anger, the wrath of age and weakness, but the wrath of a measureless love that bears measureless wrong. It swept through him like a flame.

But it did not overwhelm him. Instantly he knew that it was not of his Lord, and drove it out, and closed and sealed his heart against it. In that instant, too, his eyes were opened to the hour and its purpose. Sin and despair had their legions in array, never so sure of triumph, their trophy and their citadel this loneliest soul in the universe. And this man had slain the God who would have saved him.

But the God had not forsaken him. Through the agony of despair and the darkness of the grave, through the bitter pain of barren years, He had watched and waited, with the terrible patience of the love that is divine. Now He was at the Gate to claim His own, though this frail old man was the only soul who obeyed His summons to the battle.

The old man shook. He was too frail to meet the hour, and the issue trembled in the balance. Then came a whisper in a voice beloved: "The World, the World! O Caspar, I must save the World!" and at that cry his fainting heart rallied as it had ever done. In a moment it was flooded by that love of many days, that star of many a desert year; and as it glowed once more with the old passion, he found power to pardon the unpardonable, to seek the unutterably lost, to shelter the soul for which there was no other shelter in the world. He raised his head to seek the face of his awful guest.

That face was the face of a hunted soul, terrible with the horror and despair of a sin that cannot be forgiven; but then the beggar gave a cry, for he had looked into Caspar's face. "His eyes!" he cried. "It is He! It is He! And He loves me still!" Before the glory of that look Despair and Defiance, twin keepers of the citadel, trembled and fled, for even in the black heart of man there is no power that shall withstand it. So, torn by an anguish no other had ever known, he sank to the floor and clasped the old man's feet. And there he lay, moaning in his agony: "Master, Master, I fled Thee far, but Thou hast found me! But how can I be forgiven? Never! Never!"

But at that word Caspar placed his arms about him, tender as a mother with her child, tender as the Master Himself. "Nay," he said, triumphantly, "there is no Never in His love. Long has He sought thee, my brother, for He could not be the World's Deliverer without delivering thee. It was He that set me by the Gate and bade me stay; and it was for thee that He waited there with me. Today hath He washed thy feet again, and by that sign of pardon and of love hath claimed thee for His own."

When he heard those words the man wept as no man had wept before in all the story of the world: for he did not hear the voice of Caspar, but that other voice, lost but unforgotten, rich now with the harmonies of love triumphant, the voice of the Deliverer. "Nay, my brother Judas, there is no Never in my love. Long have I sought thee, my brother, for I could not be the World's Deliverer without delivering thee." So he wept, and in that storm of tears gave his heart forever to the Lord who had sought it so long. Then save for his sobs the room was so still that it was as though some sweet Presence had come in, silently bringing peace. And Caspar said to that silent Presence:

"Now I know Thee, O Matchless One, Prince of the Star, the Deliverer for whom the world has waited. Thine the power indeed, and Thine the glory, for here is Thy Sign."

Then the sobbing died away, for that torn heart rested at last with the Lord who would give rest to all; and there stole into the room the noises of the street, the murmur of the unresting flood of toil and pain. But Caspar knelt, his face uplifted and a light upon his face; for over that unresting flood shone the love of the Carpenter's Son, a mighty Star that would not set until the end of time.

ELIZABETH HART

The Husband of Mary

I

WHEN they came into the plain of Esdraelon, it seemed to the Nazarenes that the great rippling expanse smiled a gentle welcome. They saw the yellow fields of grain, the poppies stirring lightly in the breeze, the low, familiar outlines of the hills behind which their village lay hidden, and a change was wrought in their little band. Those who had lagged in the rear from weariness urged their mules and camels to a brisker pace. Women loosened their veils, taking deep breaths of the evening freshness; the strains of pipes and timbrels ceased as youths put their instruments away. Scattered family groups merged, brother drawing nearer to sister, husband to wife, and the talk that arose was of the flock and the threshing floor, the supply of oil that must be replenished, the roof that could wait no longer for mending.

Forgotten now was the Passover, its solemn ecstasy of sacrifice and its joyful feasting. The splendors of the Temple receded into the back of the travelers' minds. They were filled to the exclusion of all other thoughts with the sweet importance of coming home.

To Joseph, the village carpenter, this sudden tightening of family bonds was something that thrust him apart from his companions. He was surrounded by small knots of people who were talking intimately of domestic matters in which he had no concern. Instinctively he sought the side of the only other man who, like himself, had no ties in the company.

"Matthew," he said, "the figs are very fine this year, aren't they? You won't find fig groves like these, the length and breadth of Judea." He gazed proudly at the sturdy trees with their burden of dark blue fruit and his eyes passed on to where clusters of new grapes gleamed on the vine. "Nor such vineyards," he added. He would have liked to speak also of the peace and simplicity of Nazareth, whose flat white roof tops were now visible among the cradling hills, but the deep refreshment and content that these things brought him, he was unable to express in words.

Matthew did not reply. His face was turned eagerly toward Nazareth and suddenly he dug both heels into his mule and pressed forward until he was in the front ranks of the caravan.

Jehiel, the physician, who had been jostled by Matthew's hasty passage, smiled with that mixture of good-humored envy and contempt, which is so often in the eyes of the old when they look at the young.

"If one has a young wife and a child scarce a year old at home," he said to Joseph, "the last league seems longer than the world itself."

Joseph nodded silently. He reflected that it must be pleasanter to return to a house where a woman stood in the doorway, eagerly awaiting one, than to an empty dwelling like his own. He pictured the welcome of Matthew: his wife's embraces, the babe put in his arm to hold, the evening repast shared together, the questions asked and answered after the child slept and the woman had filled the lamp with oil, against the dark.

"And you, my friend," said Jehiel. "By the next Passover, you will be hastening back for a similar cause, I hope?"

"Let us hope so indeed," Joseph replied in a voice that expressed nothing.

"I have often marveled that you remain unwed," Jehiel pursued. "It has distressed me—and there are a score of maidens in Nazareth, whom I daresay it has distressed likewise."

Joseph paid no heed to the physician's levity. He was putting to himself the question that Jehiel had hinted at. Always he had considered wedlock as essential, as inevitable, as the gaining of bread. Always he had known that to beget strong sons and daughters was at once the duty and the crowning felicity of a man's life. Yet he was past thirty years, and among his people it was customary for a man to take a wife at eighteen. Why had he waited so long?

"There was my mother to care for at first." He spoke aloud, half forgetting the presence of Jehiel. "And after her death—I don't know—my work at the bench and the bit of land with olive trees I've tried to tend, and the society of friends, and the Synagogue on the Sabbath——" He paused, disturbed by the physician's attentive gaze. For he could not explain to Jehiel that these things had filled his life so that the years had passed as minutes, and that now he was no longer a youth and these things were no longer enough.

"Of course, of course," said Jehiel heartily, "but you don't want to be thinking backward now, you want to be thinking of the future." He lowered his voice. "Now there's Esau's daughter, Sara —a fine, healthy girl—look how straight and firmly she walks yonder! And Malachi's eldest—I forget how she is called—not so comely, I grant, but Malachi means to give a hundred kine as her wedding portion. That is something to be thought of, you know, with kine so scarce."

Jehiel's wife drew near, her eyes brightening with interest.

"Pay no heed to him," she told Joseph. "My brother's girl,

Deborah, brings the largest vineyard in these parts to the man she weds, and what's more important, she is the fairest and most sensible virgin in Nazareth."

Jehiel laughed. "Observe," he said, "Naomi desires you as a kinsman. If our children were daughters instead of sons, she would try to find you a wife among them. And I would aid her."

They were coming into Nazareth now, and Joseph's way lay in an opposite direction to that of the physician. As he turned to take leave of them, Naomi whispered in his ear:

"Lose no time in going to my brother, Samuel, if you wish Deborah. Her hand is greatly sought after."

Joseph smiled on her amiably. It was a good thing, a warming thing, that these friends should desire him as a husband for their niece; Naomi even persisted urgently, "Could you not go to Samuel tonight? Delay never served a purpose yet."

"I cannot go tonight," said Joseph. "I have promised my cousin, Ioachim, that I would sup with him on my return from Jerusalem. It's five years since he was able to attend the Passover, and he takes comfort in hearing about it."

"He's failing fast," said Jehiel with a sigh. "It's unlikely that he will live to hear about another Passover."

"Things have never gone rightly for Ioachim since Anna's death," said Naomi. "First his sheep were stolen—then this sickness. He has little left now but the conversation of friends—and his daughter."

There was a tinge of contempt, Joseph thought, in the way she spoke the last word. He said sharply:

"As devoted a daughter as a man could wish for. She has been everything to him since he fell ill—his hands, his feet, his eyes——"

Naomi held up her hand as though Joseph's praise wearied her.

"Doubtless she is dutiful," she said. "There is nothing uncommon in looking after a father who is ill and stricken in years. I know of no single maid in Nazareth who would not do the same."

"You speak as though you disliked Mary," said Joseph. His voice was quiet but it was chill. Naomi hastened to deny his charge.

"But," she added, "were I Ioachim, I would not be at ease with such a daughter."

Joseph stiffened. He felt a strong distaste for the physician's wife rising within him.

"What is your meaning?" he asked bluntly.

"It's hard to put in proper words. She's so—so unlike other girls. She seems to prefer her own company to that of friends. That's not natural when you're young—and although she is gently spoken with everyone, you feel she isn't listening or caring greatly when you talk to her. She fills her jar at the fountain and straightway goes home— never stays to chat a bit, like everyone else."

"Naturally," said Joseph. "She is anxious to get back to her father."

"Yes," said Naomi, "but Ioachim passes a great part of the time in sleep—he has no need of her then. The women of my age have often gone to sit with him so that Mary could get out for a little while. She does not visit with a friend or take her spinning to my sister's where all the other girls like to meet and work together— she is fonder of climbing into the hills by herself to pick flowers and sing parts of the Hallel aloud or sit in the grass doing nothing, just mooning out over the valleys. This I know, for my son Hezekiah often comes on her there when he is out with his flocks. Scrambling about the hills is all very well for a boy but for a young woman!"

"Young woman!" Joseph repeated with a laugh. "Why, Mary is a child!"

Naomi gave him a curious glance. "Mary is sixteen," she said shortly, "though there's not an ounce of flesh on her bones to spare —not an ounce!"

"Come! Come!" cried Jehiel. "We've stood here long enough gossiping about the girl! It's only in the last year that she's taken to these odd ways—she was friendly and spirited enough once and will be again. We all behave foolishly at her age. It's a disorder of the blood."

They bade Joseph a very cordial farewell. But as they rode away, Naomi's voice drifted back to the carpenter.

"Well, I would rather have my daughter casting soft eyes at the young men. That sort of foolishness is at least natural."

Joseph frowned. Naomi's tongue was sharp, and much she had said was sheer unreason. Yet it would perhaps do no harm to offer Mary a little friendly counsel. The child had need of hearing laughter and women's prattle, shut up constantly as she was with an ailing old man. He would tell her this when he saw her tonight, and he would caution her against letting her thoughts stray when others were speaking. He himself had never found her inattentive, but she must take care to offend no one.

He reached his own dwelling and Mary passed from his mind as he surveyed the bolted door and the empty threshold. He must lose no time in finding a wife—he had had enough of solitude.

While he loosed the tether of his mule and led it to water, he considered the maidens of whom Jehiel and Naomi had spoken; while he washed away the dust of the journey, he considered other maidens. He must choose prudently. Undue comeliness he would not demand but his wife should be healthy and of honest parentage, she should bring a goodly wedding portion, she should possess an even temper and show no inclination to sloth or shiftlessness.

He was so deep in these considerations that he set out for the house of Ioachim with bent head and eyes fixed on the ground. He took no notice of the distance he covered but strode on until he was arrested by a light peal of laughter. A voice called to him gaily: "Have you forgotten your promise to sup with us, cousin?"

Joseph turned and walked back to a small house where a girl leaned in the doorway and looked at him with mirthful eyes.

"I am sorry, Mary," he said, a flush mounting to his face. "I was even now on my way here but——" He paused for there was something in her appearance that made him forget what he wished to say. He gazed at her with a dawning wonder. For a change had come over Mary. He had seen her less than a month past, and she had been a child. And now, behold, she was a woman. The soul of Joseph marveled, while his eyes hesitated to believe in the mysterious transformation.

Mary returned his gaze quietly, and some of the mischief left her smile.

"I know how it was with you," she said. "When inner visions blind the eyes, it is easy to pass one's own doorstep without knowing it."

"Yes," said Joseph, "but one should not permit one's self visions, when bound for a destination. There is no order in a life that confuses dreaming with action."

He spoke austerely because he was vexed with himself for having first walked past Mary like a man in his sleep, and then gaped at her like an unmannerly urchin. The girl stooped and set about unlacing his sandals.

"You speak truly," she said, then looking up at him, added with a laugh, "I fear, though, that I am often beset with that confusion."

Her words made him remember his intention of chiding her. To his surprise he found the thought distasteful. She motioned him to precede her into the house and he did so, without uttering another syllable.

As Joseph crossed the threshold, Ioachim struggled vainly to raise himself from the mat upon which he reclined. He peered eagerly through the dusk with his almost sightless eyes, and in a voice that, still resonant and full-timbred, seemed to triumph over his wasted body, spoke ceremonious words of welcome. Joseph replied by inquiring for his cousin's health, an empty courtesy, since it was evident that death alone could alter Ioachim's malady. The old man then bade Mary complete her preparations for the meal. He longed to ask Joseph to speak of the Passover but hospitality forbade that a guest should be questioned before he had eaten.

Joseph for his part could think of little to say. He was still bemused by the sudden unfolding of Mary's womanhood. He watched her spread a cloth on the low dining table, watched her bring the bowls of *libban* and cooked fruit from the oven, watched her fill and light the clay lamp, half expecting when its revealing beams fell upon her that the great change would prove nothing more than a trick of the failing light outside. Yet how oddly Naomi had looked at him when he had said Mary was but a child! Perhaps others had observed this new Mary and he alone had remained blind.

Now she approached and asked him if he would not eat. She assisted Ioachim into a more upright position and remained, supporting him with her shoulder, while he blessed the food. This accomplished, she let him down gently upon his cushions.

"Father has already supped," she said to Joseph. Then as though to divert attention from Ioachim's infirmity she skillfully drew her cousin on to speak of the Passover. Presently Joseph found himself describing the changes that had taken place in the Temple since last year: the three new gates, one overlaid with gold, one with silver, and one with solid Corinthian brass; the double cloisters of red and white marble; the clusters of golden grapes, each cluster as large as a man, that twined about the doors; the elevated seats in the Court of Women, finely carven of the best cedarwood from the Lebanons. At first Ioachim and Mary listened with wide eyes and parted lips, but as Joseph's eloquence increased, the face of the old man fell into lines of sadness, and his voice rang forth in a sorrowful wail:

"Yet these things of which you speak were given us by an infidel whose hands are red with the blood of his own kindred. Yea, our very Holy of Holies is the gift of Herod, most accursed of men in sight of the Lord. And fixed above our gates are the eagles of Rome, the symbol of our subjection. What do marble and gold and votive jewels profit us when we must endure such shame?"

Mary stretched out a hand and stroked her father's head which had fallen on his breast. Joseph cleared his throat and said slowly:

"There is the coming of the Messiah."

"Yes, there is the coming of the Messiah," cried Mary. She gave Joseph a swift glance that dazzled him, it was so radiant with the intimate delight that seems to say, "We share the same feelings, you and I!"

Joseph had spoken as the common man of his time spoke, of an assured but somewhat vague event of the future that would make everything right and establish Israel's supremacy over the rest of the world. He was glad that this was to be so, it was pacification for just such a dark and bitter mood as Ioachim was suffering, yet it had never seemed to come close to his personal life. He had heard an occasional priest or prophet predict that the blessed hour was near, but he had never before heard the note of clear joy that was in Mary's voice.

"Surely he will come soon," she said to Ioachim and there was a look in her eyes, as though she spoke of some dearly cherished friend who was arriving on the morrow.

Ioachim gazed at her fondly, but melancholy still shadowed his features.

"You are young, Mary, and therefore see all things brightly," he said. "Well, poor child, you have need of your happy vision. Jehovah has forsaken Israel and our poor Galilee is the scorn and mock of all. Tell me, Joseph," he turned to the carpenter, "is the feeling against us as strong as formerly in Jerusalem?"

"I fear so," Joseph replied reluctantly. "Of course, I know that our raiment is plain and our speech hasn't the polish of the city—the Scribes and Pharisees think we lack learning and to the rich Sadducees our simple ways seem uncouth. But—" his voice grew vexed—"the Judeans from the small villages, not a whit bigger than Nazareth—they aren't treated with such contempt. Even the money-changers don't cheat them as they do us. And what makes my blood hot is to see them imitating the learned and powerful ones and flinging rude jests and insults at us. I can endure that sort of treatment from a priest or a sage—but from another carpenter—because he happens to live in Judea——"

"It is unfair," interrupted Ioachim, stretching himself wearily upon the mat. "But it has not always been so. Our forefathers should not have allowed the Greeks and Phoenicians to settle in our land. The Judeans think we are lax. They accuse us of intermarriage with the Gentiles—they say that our blood is tainted with infidel strains. It is too late to remove the odium from our country's name. Truly, Galilee is accursed!"

While Ioachim and Joseph were conversing, Mary had been busy clearing away the remains of the supper. She now approached with the brazen ewer, freshly filled. A silence fell as she poured the contents over the hands of the two men and over her own. Joseph was oppressed by Ioachim's gloom and strove for words to protest against his black view of things. He began to say that Galilee was the fairest and most fruitful country in the world, that the people were honest and happy and lived at peace among themselves and worshiped Jehovah devoutly, and that he for his part asked no more of the Lord than his present lot, save only a wife and sons to carry on his name.

"You are right," said Mary, and again there was in her look that sympathy which seemed to make them the sharers of a secret conviction. "I don't believe it matters what others think of us, so long as we can honestly think well of ourselves."

But Ioachim lay prone on his pallet staring out into the night with woe in his eyes and a murmur of lamentation on his tongue. Mary went to where he lay and knelt beside him silently for a moment. Then, with a sudden clearing of her features, she said:

"Come, father, there's no reason to despair of our country. Have you not read the words of the holy Isaiah who tells that the Lord afflicted Zebulon and Napthali and afterward more grievously afflicted Galilee? But he says that the dimness is not as great as it was at first." She pressed his hand and quoted softly:

" 'The people that walked in darkness have seen a great light; they that dwell in the land of the shadow of death, upon them hath the light shined.' "

Her tender young voice vibrated with overtones and depths, as though the music of the words had struck an answering chord of music in her throat. Joseph was unfamiliar with the passage, but from that night he would always remember it with a stirring of the heart. He sat quite still gazing at the slant of lamplight on Mary's smooth dark head, as she bent over Ioachim. He was profoundly moved and filled with a nameless excitement. Ioachim, on the other hand, seemed to be soothed and tranquilized by his daughter's recitation. He caressed her and fell to talking with some degree of cheer on village matters. Joseph listened respectfully but his attention wavered. He remembered that Naomi's son had overheard Mary chanting parts of the Hallel aloud and he was wondering if she knew his favorite verses and thinking he would like to hear her repeat them.

"I am sorry, my cousin," he said with a start. "I didn't hear what you said."

"I asked you if you were well acquainted with Saul, the son of Ephraim, the blacksmith—and what opinion you had formed of his character."

"Why, yes, I know him," Joseph began. "He is much younger than I and not one of my close friends, but he seems to be a good youth—he is certainly a handsome one."

"So Mary tells me. But I'm not interested in his appearance. Is he honest, is he stable, is he well thought of in Nazareth?"

Before Joseph could reply, Mary arose and asked if they would excuse her from the room—the heat making her head ache and she wished to go up on the housetop for a breath of the night air.

Ioachim peered after her as she hastened out, her cheeks flushed, an air of slight confusion about her.

"She should have waited and heard what you thought of young Saul," he said fretfully. "After all, the matter concerns her more than anybody else. He was here before he left for the Passover, asking me for her—I told him I'd give him my answer when he got back. He'll come to see me tomorrow most likely, and my mind's not made up yet."

"Does Mary—want him?" Joseph hardly understood why he asked this. The question fell from his lips without volition.

"Mary will naturally abide by my decision," Ioachim replied. "But it's been a long time since I was able to get around the village. And the men as young as Saul have grown up since my sickness. That's why I want you to tell me frankly what you think of him. All that you say will be held in confidence."

Joseph opened his mouth, started to speak, and closed it again. He was dismayed at the impulse that had prompted him to say things both mean and false. What had he against Saul, the son of Ephraim, that he should seek to discredit that amiable and worthy young man in the eyes of Ioachim? He wet his lips and spoke with painstaking justice. When he had finished, Ioachim nodded his head in satisfaction.

"Well, from your account he seems to be a good-enough lad," he said. "I suppose I shall have to let him have her."

There arose before Joseph a picture of young Saul's flashing black eyes and full, red mouth parted in a smile that revealed all his splendid teeth. A reasonless wrath took possession of him.

"Why are you in such haste to have Mary wed?" he asked.

Ioachim sighed. "Is it not plain?" he demanded. "You know as well as I that the days of my life are numbered. I could not die in peace if I left my daughter alone, without protection. She'd have other suitors, if she didn't take Saul, I know that. But I may not live to see the others—I must know her safe before I die."

"Your feeling is natural," said Joseph reluctantly. He tried to utter some expressions of good will but his strange newborn dislike of Saul stifled the words in his throat. "It is because I am tired," he told himself, "that my mind takes such wayward turnings." He rose and asked Ioachim's permission to bid him good night. "Today's journey was long," he said, "and my limbs are heavy."

"You will sleep well," said Ioachim. "It is full recompense for bodily fatigue—deep, dreamless sleep." He sighed. "I envy you."

"Yes, I shall sleep," said Joseph, and he too sighed, from content. Yet when he lay upon his bed at last, his mind swirled giddily with a thousand images that he was powerless to drive away, and a restlessness seized him so that he desired, weary as he was, to get up and walk alone through the honey-smelling night. Dayspring was on the hills when he fell into slumber. The sun swung high in the heavens when he awakened.

"I am a shameful sluggard," he thought, "to lie abed like this and all the tasks awaiting me in my workshop." He hastened into the shed where his bench and his tools were kept. Great was the energy with which he fell to work. The chips flew furiously beneath the adze, the saw whined, the hammer rose and fell in a storm of blows. Joseph, however, was ill content. His hand seemed to have lost its skill; twice it slipped and spoiled good pieces of pine wood; twice it bungled a simple task of dovetailing.

A shadow fell across the wall and he looked up to find Ephraim the blacksmith, standing at his side.

"I've spoken to you three times," said Ephraim testily. "Have you grown deaf from the clatter you make at your work?"

Joseph made a sign of apology. "Though indeed, Ephraim," he said mildly, "I knew not that noise was a stranger to your forge." The second time he had left his senses in the clouds, he thought with concern! Today he could not hear, yesterday he could not see. How Mary had laughed at him! Her laughter was a pleasant sound —kindly and gay. And her eyes had sparkled as bright as——

"I vow," cried Ephraim, staring at him, "you have the same witless smirk on your face that my son Saul wears when he sees the maid his fancy dwells on. Why, friend——"

"Enough of jesting," Joseph broke in rudely. It was hateful to be likened to Saul. "Have you come about the new bolt for the door of your shop? I'll not be able to attend to it till after the Sabbath. My tasks are like the sands of the sea."

Ephraim, however, was in a mood for talk and lingered on after he had dispatched his business. He spoke again of his son and told the carpenter that Saul had injured his foot in Jerusalem. He was tarrying an extra day with kindred there, thinking it prudent to let the healing get well under way before he commenced his homeward journey.

"That is *his* tale," Ephraim concluded, with a wink. "But it's plain to me that he doesn't want to show himself with a limp before Ioachim's daughter."

He laughed loudly and Joseph joined him, glad to disguise his guilty delight in Saul's injury as innocent mirth. He hoped that the blacksmith's son would be delayed many weeks in Jerusalem.

"What is wrong with me?" he muttered, when Ephraim had gone. "This unkind joy in another's misfortune, this malicious spite toward one who has never done me an ill turn—I must be possessed of a demon."

His throat was parched, and taking a gourd he went out to slake his thirst. It was the hour of sundown, when the women of Nazareth made their second daily journey to the fountain. As Joseph approached, he heard a light twittering of female voices and coming into the square was surrounded by women of every age. To and fro they went, each with her tall clay jar balanced gracefully on one shoulder; they gathered in little clusters, their dark heads swaying eagerly together; they leaned indolently against trees and walls, calling out sweet, high-pitched greetings to one another. There was a gentle gaiety about the scene that lightened Joseph's troubled spirits.

"Good evening, Deborah," he said to a handsome girl who smiled at him. This was the niece whom Naomi had pressed him to wed. He watched her saunter across the square, accompanied by four other comely maidens. Then his eye brightened as it fell on the figure of his cousin. It was a figure that possessed—Naomi had been right—no spare ounce of flesh. Yet there was a fine and delicate beauty in this slenderness that the other women seemed to lack. Beside Mary, the rich curves, the soft plumpness, of Deborah and her companions appeared coarse and heavy, their profiles blurred. Joseph was filled with a curious pride in this contrast, and he wished that he could walk at Mary's side and carry her water jug. It looked a burden for her slight shoulders.

Forgetting his thirst and the gourd that was still unfilled, he hastened to overtake her. He had gone only a few steps, when he halted. Mary passed from sight around a bend in the street and Joseph stood quite still, his heart in tumult, his mind blinking in the sudden light of truth. It was Mary he wanted for his wife. It was Mary he had wanted long. If he could not wed her, he would wed no one. If he could not gain her love his life would be a poor, thin thing without meaning or purpose.

Again evening found him on his way to Ioachim's dwelling. This time the old man was alone. Joseph did not delay in idle talk, but spoke at once what was in his heart.

The Husband of Mary

When he had finished, he looked anxiously at the countenance of his listener. Ioachim was smiling as though he were well content.

"Joseph," he said, "your father and mother were dear to me, and you whom I have known since you were a babe are close to my heart. Yet had I seen but little of you, I could judge what manner of man you are from your carpentry. You give full value for the silver you receive—your timbers fit together as they should, your nails hold. You do not press the wages due you, when your debtors have fallen on lean days." He laid his weightless hand on Joseph's shoulder. "My son, I give you my blessing and I pray that you may also receive the blessing of the Lord. He has looked with mercy and loving-kindness on His servant, and has eased my heart of its anxiety. For out of all Galilee, I would have chosen you, had I the power, as the husband of my daughter."

Joseph was so greatly moved by these words that he could only stammer the pride and gratitude he felt.

"Say no more," Ioachim bade him kindly. "Let us speak of Mary's wedding portion. It is a meager one, alas, as you know. There is a strip of farming land though, that with tending can be made to yield something. It has fallen into neglect since my sickness but it was once fine soil for melons——" He sensed that Joseph was not listening. "You will find Mary on the housetop," he said, smiling a little. "She's planted flowers there. A thriftless thing to do, isn't it? The fields are full of flowers and we could have used the space for grapes. But she sets such store by her lilies and oleanders that I haven't the heart to chide her. She's most likely giving them water now."

Joseph's breathing grew less controlled with every step of the outside stairway to the roof. At the top he was obliged to halt and summon composure. The night was moonless, but in the deep sky the stars shone with a brilliance and a tranquil propinquity, uncommon even for this land where the glory of the heavens was never remote and cold. In the faint glimmer Joseph was just able to make out Mary, standing among tall lilies, whose whiteness made her gown seem a gray mist. She did not move, save to incline her head in a questioning movement.

"Who is it?" she asked.

"It is I, Joseph," he replied.

"Oh! I thought—I did not know you in the dimness, cousin."

There was both surprise and pleasure in her voice but Joseph heard only the surprise. Jealousy wrung words from him that he did not intend.

"You were expecting Saul."

Mary did not trouble to deny this.

"I am glad that it was you instead," she said with a kind of hushed gaiety. "Come over here, I want to show you my flowers. They are loveliest at night, I think. They seem to hoard their perfume for the stars."

But Joseph did not stir. "What is it, cousin?" asked Mary, drawing closer to him. "I cannot see your face but you stand there so silent, so rigid—is something amiss with my father?"

"No, no." Her alarm released his speech. "I—I have been talking with your father, Mary. I have been telling him that I want you as my wife."

He heard her draw in her breath with a quick, startled sound. "What answer did he make you?" she whispered.

"He was willing. But it matters more what you feel, Mary. That's what I'm here to ask you. I've heard of—of Saul's suit. I wouldn't want you to take me if you love him."

"I do not love Saul." Her voice was so low that he could barely catch the words, but they fell on his heart like fresh spring water.

"Then," he said, trembling, "will you wed me, Mary?" He stretched out a hand and timidly touched her hair where it lay on her shoulder. She did not draw back and he continued earnestly. "Remember, you must speak from your heart. I am speaking from mine."

He continued to caress her hair and now he bent his head and brought his eyes on a level with hers, as though to make her see all the things he had not said, could not say. For it is upon the hands and the eyes that man depends at such times for communication, realizing with unconscious wisdom that the poor, stumbling tongue will only maim or travesty the song in the soul.

The Husband of Mary

Mary gazed back at Joseph until the darkness grew familiar and no longer veiled their faces from one another. Then she slipped her hand into his.

"I speak from my heart," she said. "I will be your wife and I am glad—so glad!"

He drew her into his arms and kissed her mouth, as though he set a reverent seal upon the words it had uttered. And Mary lifted her arms and put them around his neck. He kissed her again, with a great surge of tenderness and desire. And she laid her cheek against his, and they stood together with no sound to break the stillness but the rustling sigh of the night breeze in a distant grove of palms.

Presently Joseph noticed that her head was uncovered. He said in a tone of concern:

"You came out without a veil. That was very imprudent. The night air is unhealthy—you might take a chill."

Mary smiled and moved toward the staircase. "Take my hand," he cried, "lest you stumble on those narrow stairs."

She took his hand and pressed it tightly in her own. "I will try not to forget the veil at night again," she murmured, "but you must remind me—you must keep me from doing many imprudent things."

When they had descended, she clung to him a moment, and looked up into his face strangely.

"You are steadfast, are you not, Joseph? And loyal? Yes, I've felt that about you long. It is a comforting thing to feel."

"What do you mean, Mary?" He was a little puzzled. "You speak as though you were afraid."

"No," she shook her head. "Only sometimes I——" She broke off, her own face bewildered. "It's a fancy," she said quickly. "Too unformed to put in words. Come, let us go in and tell my father."

Joseph's eyes glowed. "Yes," he echoed eagerly, "let us tell your father." As he followed Mary into the house he would have liked to tell all Israel of his happiness.

II

RUMOR ran as swiftly through the tranquil lanes of Nazareth as through the greatest city in Judea, and was as welcome a guest. But when word went about that Ioachim's daughter was to wed Joseph, the carpenter, the wagging of tongues took the form of a general denial.

There was good reason for the Nazarenes' incredulity. No one had seen a sign of Joseph's wooing; almost everyone knew of young Saul's. Several were prepared to take oath that the suit of the black-smith's son had been accepted by Ioachim. The matter appeared settled when the physician's wife, Naomi, confided to several close companions, who in turn confided to others, that Joseph (she had it from his own lips) looked with longing on her niece, Deborah, and was awaiting a suitable opportunity to ask for her hand.

By sundown, however, disbelief had vanished. The chief of the synagogue, the rosh-hak-keneseth himself, had verified the tale. He had that day gone to the house of Ioachim and heard the pair exchange their solemn vows before Mary's father. The wedding date was set for three and a half months hence, in accordance with the Oral Law, which required a fixed period between the betrothal and the nuptial ceremonies.

In the excited babble that followed this announcement, not a little of the talk was spiced with malice. Said the mother of Saul: "For my part, I'm glad of the turn matters have taken. The girl had no wedding portion worth mentioning and—well, of course she's been brought up without a mother's care—her nature is too heedless, too unstable to make the kind of wife I would want for my son. Just the same she's treated him ill—and so has Ioachim, which surprises me more. Mary encouraged him with her soft looks and the old man gave him reason to think his suit would be accepted."

Naomi was free with equally tart comment on the behavior of Joseph. He had willfully made sport of her husband and herself, she declared. "He told us he was thinking of marriage; he plainly said that if we could assure him his chances were good he would ask for Deborah. And all the time he had his eye fixed on his cousin."

Deborah herself, who had been privately informed that Joseph wished to make her his bride, tossed her head and declared she did not think much of Mary's choice, but then when a girl had so little attention it was not surprising she should take the second man who offered himself.

Several maidens who secretly pined after Saul's lustrous eyes, whispered to one another that Mary loved the blacksmith's son but had consented to marry the carpenter out of obedience to her father's wishes.

For several days the chatter continued in full spate. Then its temper was altered by the death of Ioachim.

The old man had clung to life with a tenacity which astonished those who knew that by all natural laws, he should be dead. And then, without a visible portent, the end had come. Mary, going to rouse her father one morning, found him dead. The expression he wore was peaceful and contented. Almost it seemed that he had intentionally relaxed his vigil against death.

Mary spoke to Joseph of this sudden yielding.

"He would not let himself die," she said, "until he was assured that I would not be left alone."

She turned away her head, that she might hide her tears. Joseph caressed her hand, cursing his tongue that would never say what he wished it to. He had come with her to the narrow cave in the cliffs that was Ioachim's tomb, in the hope that he might find some means to assuage her grief. Now, as they stood outside on the steep path, an idea came to him.

"Mary," he said, "wouldn't you like to take a walk farther up in the hills instead of going back to the village? You've told me about the fine views one can get from a spot you know of, but you've never shown them to me."

He was pleased to see that her face brightened, even while she hesitated.

"Yes—I would like that very much," she said. "It's thoughtful of you to suggest it."

113

Joseph girded up his long gown.

"You won't find me as nimble of foot as I might be," he said, "but I'm anxious to see the places that mean much to you."

She smiled and brushed his cheek with her finger tips, and Joseph's heart rejoiced that she understood his desire to share the things that were dear to her. He watched her as she ascended the steep slope before him, graceful and sure, balancing herself easily on loose ground, leaping as though on wings over small hollows. At one of these she paused and bade him listen. She lifted her voice and called his name, and after a long breathing space the echo flooded around them, deep and plangent. It was like standing inside a bell.

Joseph grasped the low-hanging branch of a sycamore and swung himself like a frolicking boy. They skirted a flock of snowy sheep, grazing on a lush stretch of mountain pasture, and he was pricked by the foolish impulse to pelt them with the oval, golden fruit of a lemon tree. Within him there was a bubbling, a lightness that made him feel as though he were a child released from study. He told himself that it was the effect of the high air, with its cool, tingling stimulation and its fused perfume of sun-soaked grass and pines and flowers and distant snows. But when Mary turned a laughing face and, shaking a tall oleander bush, drenched him with cool petals, he knew that it was more than this—and knowing, was doubly intoxicated.

They came suddenly onto level ground that was thickly carpeted with poppies and anemones. Mary clapped her hands in delight. "It is like the veil I am weaving for the rabbi," she cried. "Scarlet and purple! The very colors!"

Joseph slipped his arm through hers.

"You are weaving a veil for the rabbi?" he inquired. "I did not know that."

"It happened before—" she threw him a teasing glance— "before you cared overmuch about my doings. It was the rabbi's idea that the virgins of Nazareth should make a ceremonial veil to send as a present from our village to the priests of the Temple. The one which hangs in the Holy Place is worn and faded, a disgrace to the magnificence of its surroundings. So he chose me and four others and we drew lots to see who should weave the different portions. The scarlet and purple fell to me."

"What were the other colors?" asked Joseph.

"Blue, gold and white—mine are interwoven, you see, and therefore count as one."

Joseph frowned. "I wish you had drawn something else," he said. "I don't like purple and scarlet." He scanned the gorgeous field with unfriendly eyes.

"Why——" Mary was staring at him, astounded. He laughed uneasily, plucked at the hem of his gown, dug the toe of one sandal into the ground.

"Purple is the color of royalty, scarlet of blood," he said. "That means unrest, violence, grandeur—such things disgust me, Mary. I have simple tastes and I like peace—a color like blue suits me best."

Mary looked at him smilingly. "It is unlike you to have such fancies," she said.

"I don't as a rule." He pondered a moment. "And when I do," he went on, "I never think of expressing them. When I'm with you it's different. I seem to say whatever comes into my head."

All his life he had been talking to people from a familiar central space in his mind. But with Mary he found himself reaching into the corners and recesses as well. He did it poorly, haltingly enough; he could never find the proper words, but in the attempt there was a sense of fulfillment.

"Ah," said Mary softly, "you must go on doing that. I shall be unhappy if you don't."

He put both his arms around her and turned up her face to his.

"Will you do likewise with me?" he asked.

"Yes," said Mary.

He caught her to him and kissed her, trembling a little at the look he had surprised in her eyes, at the scent of her hair, at the knowledge that she belonged in his arms. His emotion flowed into her and they clung together, shaken and quickened by an ecstasy in which all the springtime about them seemed to enter.

Mary drew away a little. Her cheeks were flushed and her smooth hair tumbled. She lowered her eyes but he could catch the light in them through the veil of her lashes.

"Oh!" she said, "there are shepherds in yonder pasture. What will they think?"

Joseph caught her to him again and tilted her chin upward so she must meet his eyes. "I do not believe you care overmuch for anyone's opinion," he said laughingly. "Is that not true, my beloved?"

Mary shook her head. "But that is an ill thing to say of me, Joseph," she objected. "You make me sound like an Arab outlaw."

"Oh, no," he said, "but confess now it does not disturb you if the villagers gossip a bit at the fountain. And once you told me yourself 'it does not matter what others think of us so long as we can honestly think well of ourselves.' "

"But in your heart you didn't agree with me, did you, Joseph?"

She spoke gravely but before the carpenter could answer, her manner altered again and she smiled at him. "There is one villager at least whose opinion means much to me," she whispered. "You'll not deny that."

They walked onward, his arm around her waist, her head against his shoulder. Mary led him onto a flat shelf of rock that jutted out sharply from the mountainside and was spongy with pale moss. They sat down and he knew without asking that this was the place she came to oftenest, the spot she had made her own.

He followed her gaze, drawing a deep breath of delight. By turning his head he could glimpse almost the entire land of Canaan, which was to him almost the entire world. There to the east was the plain of Esdraelon tilting gently upward to the hills of Samaria, each hill a varying tint of hazy blue, and the chasm of the Jordan like a dark scar. Farther east still, was the rounded bosom of Tabor and a faint gleam from the marble temples of Galeara, the Greek city. Northward was the white tip of Hermon, southward the long, low range of Carmel, rising emerald-hued from an apple-green plain. And to the west the land ran out into a spur and plunged into the glittering sea.

The Husband of Mary

Mary was the first to break the spell of silence that held them.

"It is impossible to be troubled here," she said. "One is too close to God." She encircled her knees with her arms and leaned back against a twisted shrub. "Fear!" she cried in a low, passionate voice. "If we could only learn to cast it out of our hearts—if we could only cease to rack ourselves with the vexatious details of life! Children have a measure of serenity—they can submit—accept—trust. What is it that happens to us when we leave childhood behind, Joseph? Why do we begin to fill our existence with unimportant cares? Why do we grow so afraid of what the morrow will bring?"

Joseph was something taken aback by this outburst.

"I don't know," he said slowly. "I had never thought of it in just that way, Mary. I suppose there is truth in what you say, but—" he hesitated—"the cares you speak of—I don't think of them as irksome burdens. There's pleasure in getting a certain amount of work done and doing it well, of seeing that the ones you care for are happy and well——"

"Of course," she interrupted, "I didn't mean that. But think of my poor father. He was ready for death long ago. Yet he fought it because he feared for what might become of me alone. He tortured himself, he lived in constant anxiety for years. If only he could have spared himself that! If only he could have had faith in God to provide for me. Think of the peace he would have found!"

"But," said Joseph, "he loved you too much to abstain from anxiety. I should be just the same."

"Love for God should come first," said Mary. She continued in a quieter tone. "It's very hard, though—very hard. Look at me, now. I have known from the hour I found my father dead, that it was for the best. Yet I could not bring myself to bow before the wisdom of my Lord. I wept and refused to take comfort and went about with a heavy heart. I could think only that my father was no longer at my side, and that the house seemed cold and empty——"

Joseph gently sought her hand.

"You will not be long in an empty house," he said. "Oh, Mary, doesn't the thought of our marriage make you a little happier?"

She wheeled at the pleading in his voice.

"Dear one—yes," she murmured. "Surely you do not doubt that."

He answered her by drawing closer and slipping his arm around her waist. After a little pause he said eagerly: "I have commenced to make a new chest for us. My own is not large enough to hold both our possessions and I have noticed that yours is badly chipped and scratched. This will be very handsome—scrollwork all around the lid—and perhaps a double division inside."

"It will be beautiful," cried Mary. "And what color will you paint it?" she added slyly. "A simple peaceful color like blue?"

"I like blue," said Joseph, unruffled by her teasing. "It is a color that suits you, Mary." He looked at her soft robes with pleasure.

She laughed and rested her head against him. "Perhaps our children will have blue eyes," she said.

"No," said Joseph firmly. "Then they would look like Greeks or some other Gentile race. I should want our eldest son—our eldest son," he repeated for the joy and pride that the mere saying of the words gave him, "to resemble you, Mary. Except his stature of course." And he glanced down with innocent satisfaction at his own broad shoulders, and powerful, heavy arms.

"Oh, and he must have a brow like yours too, Joseph, and when he grows older he must have your silky black beard. And I hope that he will have your good sense."

So they continued to talk and to dream on the future that they would share together. It was close to twilight when they returned to Nazareth, laved in a warm tranquil tide of anticipation, filled with a new sense of strength and security. They drew aside into the shadow of a wall and exchanged a kiss that to Joseph was a promise of the deep sweet kisses they would exchange all their lifetime. They bade one another good night.

"I shall have to work by the light of my lamp this evening," the carpenter said with a guilty smile. "Matthew expects a new plow tomorrow, and I have spent this afternoon when I should have been making it, in idling with you."

Yet despite the pressure of his duties, he lingered at Mary's doorstep. "Isn't that the Greek merchant, Philo?" he asked, point-ing down the street to the retreating figure of a man.

Mary said that it was. "He has been here all day, in the market place with all sorts of strange new ointments and philters and clear amber and cream-smooth ivory and fine, lovely stuff for garments brought back from his last journey to Alexandria. Tomorrow he is going to Jerusalem with his wife and his two young children. He believes he can open a little shop there and do well. He is tired of wandering from place to place."

"How did you learn all this?" Joseph asked in surprise.

"I talked to him. I always do when he comes to town. I like Philo. He is wise and gentle and I think that he has suffered greatly. From what he tells me his race were once a great people who have fallen on evil days—like ourselves."

It was on the tip of Joseph's tongue to chide her. Such intimate talk with one who belonged to an infidel race was not seemly. A sudden impulse, however, had come into his head and in order to gratify it, he would have no time to deliver rebukes. Once more he bade Mary good night. When a backward glance told him that she had gone into the house, he quickened his pace, and shouted to the Greek merchant to wait for him.

Philo was willing and eager to display those wares that he had with him. He regretted that the supply was scanty, owing to the day's commerce in the market place. If his patron would consent to walk a little way with him—he was encamped just below the village —he could show him all manner of marvelous things that he had not even unpacked as yet.

Joseph's eye, however, was caught by a box of carved alabaster. The box when opened disclosed a deliciously fragrant spikenard, which Philo declared was one of the rarest and most delicate in existence. It had been perfected by a secret formula, the treasured possession of a certain Alexandrian family for countless generations. After some haggling, the box and its precious contents passed into the hands of the carpenter. He was ashamed of the price he had paid, but there was a triumphant smile on his lips as he carefully wrapped the box in a fragment of old cloth and placed it at the bottom of the new chest.

"A wedding gift," he murmured. "And it will surely please her, for it has the perfume of the flowers that she loves so well." He would tell her when he gave it to her, that he had bought it on the happiest day of his life. Then he smiled and the blood ran quicker in his veins.

"That won't be true after tonight," he said to himself, "for there will be many other days like this one."

*   *   *   *   *

The knocking was insistent. Joseph went to open the door, wondering drowsily why anyone should come to his house at so early an hour. He had not yet commenced his frugal breakfast. He tugged at the bolt and it yielded so suddenly that he lost his balance and was obliged to catch for support at the shoulder of the girl who stood without.

"Good morning," she said. "I fear I've wakened you."

"Why, Mary!" His face shone with delight. "No—I had risen. I was just about to breakfast." He took her hand, then observing something distraught about her, asked anxiously: "Is anything the matter?"

Mary withdrew her hand and leaned against the lintel for a moment, without replying. When she spoke, her voice was calm but there was an unconcealable intensity in her manner, and the color rose and ebbed in her face.

"Do not be alarmed. After we parted last eve, I received tidings—" she hesitated; her eyes left Joseph and fixed themselves upon a burgeoning almond tree—"tidings of our cousin Elizabeth at Juttah," she continued. "She has conceived a child."

"What!" exclaimed Joseph. "But Elizabeth is almost sixty, isn't she? And you say she is with child! Surely that is foolish gossip!"

Mary shook her head. A glow came into her eyes.

"It is true. With the Lord, nothing is impossible."

She looked at him suddenly, as though to watch the effect of her words. For a second, despite her shining eyes, he felt that she was anxious, that she was pleading with him for something.

"Well," he said, "I'm very glad to hear it. A woman of her age — yes, she is indeed blessed. I've heard of these things, but they are rare."

Some of the light left Mary's face. She bit her lip and looked away again.

"Elizabeth and I were always very close to one another," she said. "I used to visit there before my father's illness, and after he was unable to travel she came here once with her husband Zacharias. She was without children and looked on me as her daughter. I, who had lost my mother, felt for her a daughter's love. I would like to be with her at this time. I want to go to Juttah, Joseph — at once."

"You want to leave here — to go to Juttah?" Joseph repeated stupidly.

"Yes — yes." Her words tripped one another in their impatience to be said. "I want to leave at once — this morning." She touched his arm beseechingly. "It is hard for you to understand. But I need Elizabeth — I need to be for a time with another woman. And there is no one here in the village that I feel close to."

Joseph remembered what she had told him of the desolate emptiness of the house since her father's death.

"I know it is very lonely for you," he said. "I see that you would like to be with someone who is of your blood and dear to you — someone who could console you for your loss. That's what you mean, isn't it?" He thought she nodded and he continued with a rush of remorse. "I — I know I haven't been much comfort to you. I wanted to be, but I am dull. I don't know how to ease suffering as some do——"

She gave a quick little cry of reproach.

"That is not true — you have lifted the weight of my sorrow — I have leaned on you, and you have never failed me. But there are times when no man——"

"I think I understand," said Joseph. "But you said you wanted to leave this morning, Mary. You can't go alone. It's a long journey, a hard journey. And if there's anyone from the village traveling in that direction, I haven't heard of it. In fact, there's almost no traveling in any direction at this time of year, with the Passover just done."

"I know that," said Mary. "That is why I'm so eager to start now. It may be months before I have another chance to find companions. I can travel with Philo and his wife if I leave this morning. They will make room for me, I know. They have a large tent and they are kindly people." She picked up a bundle that Joseph had not noticed. "See, I have what I need here. I must make haste, for they will be setting out soon."

He grasped her arm.

"Mary—" he cried, "have you taken leave of your senses? Are you jesting?"

"No," said Mary gently. "Surely you do not think that Philo would let me come to harm? He has been bringing his wares to our village since I was a child. You have done business with him—you know he is honest. His wife is as good as he. Both are experienced in travel and——"

"It isn't that," Joseph interrupted. "So far as I can judge, the man is honest enough—yes, and he seems to have a kindly disposition. His knowledge of the country, too, I don't question. But Mary, he is a Greek. You, a daughter of Israel, cannot travel in company with a family of infidels."

"I do not see why not." Her glance was gentle but unyielding. "My faith is secure and Philo respects it, though he does not share it; certainly I would not offend him by denouncing his. Why should we not travel together in amity?"

Joseph spread his hands in a gesture of thwarted protest.

"I cannot argue with you," he said. "I can only beg you not to do this thing. Perhaps it isn't wrong—but it certainly is not wise, not— not fit. I have never thought very much about the laws and customs that I obey. I suppose that I could ignore many of them without becoming a sinful man. But I should not be a good citizen. I don't think a people can hold together without a certain strictness of behavior. Life that isn't regulated is unprotected against all manner of ills. Please don't go, Mary—there'll be a caravan along soon enough that you can join."

"No, Joseph," she said. "You have said yourself that no one travels at this time of year. I must go this morning, or not at all."

"Our wedding feast is set for little more than three months distant," said Joseph. "Had you forgotten that?"

"Ah, no," she said. Again the blood flamed in her face. "I shall be gone only a short while, Joseph. Suffer my wish, this once, I beg you. Hereafter, I swear it, I shall bow to your judgment in all things." There was supplication in her look. "You are my betrothed and it is your right to forbid me to stir from Nazareth."

Joseph shook his head slowly.

"It is my right, yes, but I cannot forbid you. There is something in me that cannot keep you here against your will." He took her bundle from her and closed the door behind him. "Come, I will walk with you to the tent of the Greek."

Mary pressed his hands fervently. She poured out warm words of gratitude as they walked through the village together. Joseph did not reply. He was too disturbed for speech. It was very early and the streets of Nazareth were empty. The sky was clotted with dark clouds, which pressed close around the sickly sun. The air was moist and lifeless, and the western horizon streaked with rain.

"Is the mantle you are wearing a warm one?" asked Joseph. "Rainfall is sure to overtake you before you have gone far."

"I am warmly clad," said Mary. A smile lay on her mouth; a secret excitement flickered in her eyes.

"There's the Greek now, saddling his mules. I'll go ahead and speak to him."

He handed her the bundle and ran down the slope to where Philo stood, his children frolicking at his feet. Joseph's greeting was brief. He wasted no time in stating the purpose of his visit.

"You understand," he said, "that she is my betrothed. I am loath to part with her, and I shall hold you responsible for her safety and well-being."

123

"Rest assured that I shall guard her as though she were my own," said the merchant stiffly. His face softened into a smile as Mary approached, and he bowed deeply to her.

"It is a day's journey from Jerusalem to Juttah, where her kindred dwell," Joseph continued. "See that you find a suitable escort for her before you let her leave you." He held out a handful of coins. The other waved it back.

"That is not needed. I myself will conduct her to Juttah. It is but a step farther than my destination and I have always done good business in the neighboring town of Hebron." He turned to Mary. "When you return," he said, "come to me in Jerusalem and I will find some trustworthy persons who are going to and fro."

Philo's wife, heavily swathed in veils, came out of the tent and beckoned to him. With a word of apology he hurried away. Joseph patted the head of the mule nearest him and said in a troubled voice, "I forgot to ask him will there be room for you to ride."

"Yes—I can ride on a cushion behind one of the children."

"You will not be very comfortable. I had best go back and get my mule for you. Then you will be sure of a mount on your return."

Mary drew him back as he turned to leave.

"No, Joseph, no. I cannot take your only mule from you. Don't you think I know that you are often summoned to Nian and other villages to do a piece of work? Do not worry—there is always someone with an extra donkey or camel in the caravan. Zacharias is old and cannot ride about much. Perhaps he will let me have one of his beasts as a wedding gift!" She leaned closer to him, brushed his forehead with her lips. "And now, go back to your breakfast. See, Philo is taking down the tent. We shall be gone shortly."

Joseph kissed her cheek.

"Do not stay long." he said unsteadily. "There are preparations that we must make for our wedding."

"Joseph—" there was a strange wildness in her voice. Tears welled in her eyes— "you may not wish to marry me when the time comes— You may change when——"

"What are you saying?" Joseph cried sharply. "You are overwrought." He patted her shoulder awkwardly. "I love you, Mary," he said. "It will be lonely without you. It's only in planning and working for our life together that I shall find consolation."

He saw that Philo was folding up the tent and that Philo's wife had already mounted.

"Go with God," he said, turning away.

"Go with God," Mary repeated softly.

III

SUMMER that year came upon Galilee like a wasting fever. The white, fiery sunlight beat down pitilessly on the green fields and they turned sallow and withered; on the flowers, and they shriveled up and died; on the streams, and they dwindled away to threads of water feebly trickling through wide beds of burning stones and baked mud. Trees hung limp and dejected, as though aware that their shade was of small comfort on such torrid days; goats sickened and gave little milk; sturdy rams and bullocks that had been the pride of their owners' hearts, grew lean and listless. The hyacinth-breasted doves no longer cooed on the roof tops and in the square. The very water in the fountain had a warm, brackish taste.

Naked, save for a loincloth, Joseph plied his adze in the grateful dimness of his shop. Sweat ran down his face in rivulets but he worked with zeal and his expression was cheerful. Almost three months had passed since Mary's departure. A Phoenician peddler of dyes, bound for the port of Tyre, had stopped in Nazareth and eased Joseph's anxiety by giving him word of his betrothed's safe arrival in Jerusalem. Since then, as he had promised her, he had sought solace for her absence in preparations for the future.

Until lately his carpentry had been neglected, while he worked on the strip of land that she had brought him as her dowry. Scant as was Joseph's knowledge of husbandry, he could look back on these labors with satisfaction. The weeds were gone, the soil was ready for sowing, the pomegranate trees were pruned, and their

fruit gathered and drying in a barrel, just inside his door. Next year
Mary and he would have melons and beans and barley. And his
own olive crop had been better than ever before this spring. He had
pressed enough oil to last for several years. He could sell the olives
next season if the crop were equally abundant.

He watched the shavings fall in clean, yellow curls. His olive
grove and Mary's strip were very near one another. If he could
purchase the narrow meadow between, they would have a piece of
land which could be made into a solid inheritance for their sons.

He laid down the plow he was shaping and went to the back
of the room. The new chest stood there, complete even to its coating
of soft, blue paint. He regarded it, his head poised to one side,
opened and shut the lid, ran a finger along the inner grooves.

"It is good work," he said aloud. Then he returned to the yoke
with renewed energy. If he finished quickly he would have time to
put up a new railing on the outside stairway before nightfall. Mary
was fond of sitting on the roof top and would doubtless plant flowers
there. He must make it safe for her.

At any time, now, she should be home. Their wedding was less
than three weeks distant and she had promised to return a good
interval before.

"I wonder in what company she will come back," he thought. He
had told the meddlesome, that "friends" had accompanied her on
her journey to Juttah, and although he knew that in certain quarters
the identity of these "friends" was suspected, he did not allow this
to trouble him overmuch. Nor was he any longer disturbed by Mary's
strange behavior on the morning of her departure. She had over-
ridden his wishes and she had spoken wildly and foolishly to him,
but how could the memory of these things darken a heart that her
love had illuminated? Faster and faster beat Joseph's heart, until
it seemed to mark the time of a joyous refrain—tomorrow, she may
be back tomorrow!

But Mary came back that night.

At first he was aware of nothing but the need to hold her in his
arms. He did not even desire to kiss her, simply to feel her there,

close to him and let her love flow out to him and fill him with the great and blissful peace that she alone could give.

"My well-beloved," he murmured. And again, "My well-beloved."

Mary said nothing. She had barely uttered a word since he had come rushing into her house. Suddenly Joseph perceived that she was holding him away from her, that her face was averted from his.

"What is wrong?" he stammered.

She raised her eyes and he saw that they were darkly circled.

"I rose early this morning," she said, "and I have been riding in the dreadful heat all day. You must forgive me if I am dull. I am so weary."

"I will go," cried Joseph contritely. "It was thoughtless of me not to see that you were in need of rest." He looked at her more closely. "You are pale," he said. "It's only fatigue, isn't it? You're feeling quite well?"

"Quite well," she said, with a faint smile. "A night's repose and I shall have color in my cheeks again."

Joseph kissed her gently. "Good night," he said. "I am happier than I have been since you left here, Mary." He hesitated and then asked shyly, "Are—are you glad to be back too?"

"Of course." How hollow her voice was! Yet as he moved toward the door, she flung out a hand to detain him and cried, "Don't go, Joseph—not yet," in such agitated tones that he halted, amazed.

"I've something to tell you—I must tell you now. Come and sit down here, won't you? It—it will take me a little while."

Her lips trembled, and her voice was strained. A tremor of foreboding ran through him.

"Can you not wait till morning," he suggested, "when you are less fatigued?"

"No, no," she cried. "I should have told you long before—I should have told you the morning that I left for Juttah. But, Joseph, I was too dazed that day to think rightly. I was selfish and cowardly. My sole wish was to fly to the protection of someone whom I knew would believe me and understand."

Joseph could make nothing of what she said, but his alarm

was increased by the glint of tears on her lashes and the rapid rise and fall of her breast. He sat down beside her and tried to take her hand in his. All at once her voice grew controlled, her expression calm.

"What I am going to tell you will tax your faith heavily," she said. "But you must try—oh, you must try to believe that I speak the truth." She gazed at him as though she would send this belief from her soul into his by the channel of their eyes. "If you cannot have faith you will suffer sorely, you will blacken the whole world for yourself." She clasped her hands beseechingly. "Promise me that you will try to cast out doubt from your heart!"

"I promise you that, Mary," said Joseph quietly. "What do you wish to tell me?"

She released his hand and leaned back against a cushion. There was something in the way she did this that reminded Joseph of another woman; something slow and careful, unlike Mary's free, swift motions.

"After we came down from the hills that afternoon," she began, "I was very happy. I have felt that way before, Joseph, but never quite like this time. It was as though—as though all the music in the world were in my ears—the sad and the joyful, so close to one another, that I could hardly tell which was which and both so beautiful—oh, so beautiful that I was in pain—I say I was happy, Joseph, but also I was near to weeping. When I took my jar and went to the fountain, it seemed to me that the Lord had flung open once more the gates of the Garden from which our forefathers were driven long ago. The air was so sweet and the doves with their purple breasts and bright little eyes and the sky so radiant— all dyed with pale gold. I wanted to embrace everyone I saw, and to dance and to chant hymns of thanksgiving to the Lord."

Her voice soared to a note of ecstasy that struck a quivering response in Joseph.

"I lit my lamp and I sat down at my loom to finish the scarlet and purple for the veil that will hang in my Father's Holy Temple. When the last thread was woven into the woof, a great stillness seemed to settle over the world, so that even the little voices of the insects were hushed. And suddenly I was afraid.

"And then the light from my lamp was magnified until the whole room shone with a brightness greater than the sun—and I looked up from the loom——"

She made an effort to continue, her lips moved, but no sound came. One hand went to her head in a wavering gesture and with the other she clutched at Joseph's shoulder. He flung out an arm and she fell across it heavily. Her face was waxen.

"Mary, Mary," he cried, as he chafed her cold hands and sprinkled water on her brow. "Speak to me—open your eyes!"

He laid his ear to her heart and heard the fluttering with a rush of relief. Her eyelids lifted. Joseph let her gently down on the cushions and ran to get a wineskin that hung on the wall.

"Drink some of this," he said, trickling it between her pale lips.

After a little she whispered, with a sigh: "I am sorry. A faintness came over me suddenly that I could not control."

Joseph smoothed her hair away from her eyes and arranged a cushion beneath her head.

"You must lie still until I come back," he commanded. "I shall be away only a second. I am going to Simon across the way and bid him fetch Jehiel for me."

"No—no," she cried vehemently, "I do not want Jehiel here. I am not ill, Joseph. It would be folly to bring him—I beseech you not to."

She struggled to rise, she caught at his gown and pulled him back. Joseph sought to quiet her.

"I cannot leave you, I cannot go back to my house and sleep, don't you see, Mary, until I am sure that nothing is wrong with you? What if you were to swoon like that when you are alone? It may be that you are sickening of a fever, or that the night air, after the heat of the valley all day, has chilled you. At all events, Jehiel will know the malady and he will be able to——"

"But, Joseph, Joseph, do you not understand—I do not want Jehiel to tell what ails me!"

"But why?" Joseph asked obstinately. "Please lie back. Mary— it must be bad for you to excite yourself so. Why do you not want Jehiel here?"

"Because, Joseph," her voice was weary. "Because when Jehiel looks at me he will tell you what I prefer to have you learn from my own lips. He will tell you that you should not take alarm at my swooning—because—" how her body tautened, how her breath labored!—"because it is the natural thing for a woman who rides all day in the heat when she is—with child."

"What do you mean?"

His eyes were like those of a child begging to be told that this was only an elder's strange conception of a jest. Mary winced and looked away.

"You're not speaking of yourself?"

She began to say something—something about being sorry— "I did not mean to speak so bluntly—I was trying to tell you the whole story when I grew faint—now you must let me continue— you must listen to me, Joseph!"

Listen? No, he must speak himself. If he put this thing into words, heard himself speaking them he would know—he would realize——He rose from his knees beside her. He said very slowly, very carefully: "You have been untrue to me. You have betrayed my love."

"No, no." Mary, too, was standing now. "I swear that I have been faithful to our love—by the sacred Ark, I swear it."

Joseph stared at her. Her face was wrung with compassion. For him? Then it was he who had swooned, not she? And in his swoon had he been visited by terrible visions? And called out terrible things? He seized her by the shoulders.

"You aren't with child? You aren't with child?" he cried. "Bring me back to reason," his eyes implored.

"Yes, Joseph."

She moved closer to him. That slow, careful movement again. He remembered now where he had seen it before. His sister in Capernaum—when she was great with her first-born——

"It is not what you think, Joseph—oh, won't you let me tell you how——"

She was clinging to him, trying to force him to sit down. He tore her hands away.

"I am going," he said. "Why should I tarry with you?" He heard her running after him and turned, blindly threatening her with an uplraised fist. "Stay back!" Then he slammed the door shut after him.

A desperate desire for solitude propelled him away from the street. He could not meet anyone—he could not bear that a living soul should look upon his face. Down a tortuous lane, stumbling and slipping, bruising himself against sharp stones, up again and onward—*Mary, my love is wanton*—through a vineyard—*Mary, my bride is unfaithful*—up a steep embankment—*Mary has sinned; has sinned*——

The street again. Someone was coming toward him—a man, a friend—"And it's true that your betrothed is back? Well, no need to ask if you're pleased, is there?" He could hear the words as plainly as though they were already said. He made himself flat against a doorway. The man passed by. His grief and his shame were still his own.

As he turned to leave the doorway where he had sought shelter he saw that it was the synagogue. Three weeks hence, Mary and he—a groan was wrenched from his throat and he sank down upon the ground, his body rocking to and fro in anguish.

"Ah, Mary, how can it be, how can it be, that you who held my head against your breast and kissed me with your sweet, young mouth, have lain in another's arms and yielded yourself to his embrace? You poured into my ears those things that lay closest to your heart and yet you have betrayed me! You were that which made my soul like a strong runner who reaches his goal, and now you are that which makes it like a wretched slave who is flogged in the public place.

"I remember your smile, Mary, your smile that was as grave and as beautiful as the chanting of a psalm, when we exchanged our vows of betrothal. How is it possible that you have broken those vows, as binding, as holy, as the ceremony of marriage itself? And once, Mary, once you looked into my eyes and spoke with me of our children—our children——"

Thus lamented the soul of Joseph while his tongue uttered wordless moans.

After a time he got up and began walking, in the direction of his own dwelling. A thin mist, blown down from the mountain, was grateful against his burning face. The wild whirring in his head lessened. When he came to his doorway, he did not enter but sat down on a low, stone bench outside and leaned his head against the smooth bark of his favorite almond tree. The blossoms had fallen off long ago and the almonds had crisped to powder on the boughs under the relentless sun, but it had been a pretty sight once —in its tender first foliage, with all its little fruit swelling in their green sheaths it had somehow made him think of a young girl— of Mary. It was on this tree too, that Mary had kept her eyes fixed the morning she had come to tell him she was leaving for Juttah.

Her heart had been full of guilt and treachery that morning. She had lied to him, she had not met his eyes, her good-by kiss had been a kiss of betrayal. It was to meet her lover that she had journeyed away. And she had chosen the Greek's company rather than that of a neighbor or friend because a Greek can be bribed to silence.

Why had she not remained with her lover? Why had she come back to him? Was she so cruel that she had wished to see with her own eyes his terrible suffering? No, it could not be that. She had found it difficult to tell him—she had wept, she had clung to him and implored him to listen to—what were the words she had used? "the whole tale." She had even—he remembered now—sworn that she had been faithful to their love, and for a moment he had believed that he had imagined those other terrible words of hers. Yet she did not deny them—she said again that she was with child. How could she insist that she had not betrayed him—how could she have added that mockery—unless—unless——

Into his pain-racked mind darted a new thought. It was dark and ugly enough, yet he seized on it with pitiful eagerness. He had refused to lend an ear to something she had tried to tell him, and he had threatened to strike her when she had run after him, still pleading that he must listen. Now, trembling all over, the suspicion in his mind kindling to a blaze of wrath and pity, he sprang up and sped back with desperate haste to her house.

"Mary!" he cried, as he pushed open the door.

"Yes, Joseph, I am here." She rose and came toward him. "I hoped that you would return."

Her gaze rested compassionately on his disheveled hair, his gown wet and torn from his stumbling flight, his haggard eyes. "My poor Joseph," she said.

He grasped her wrist roughly in his excitement and the question burst from his lips. "If this is the case," he cried, "forgive me for the hard things I said. I was maddened with grief, Mary—and tell me his name that I may take suitable vengeance on him."

"No," said Mary, "it is not the case."

After a moment she asked pityingly, "You would be happier then, had I been defiled?"

Joseph answered in a voice as lifeless and heavy as the thickly gathering fog without: "I would know then, at least, that you did not willingly profane our love."

He did not move when Mary's arms went around him. He suffered her tears upon his cheek without protest. After a time she began to speak and he knew that she was continuing the tale she had begun with such earnestness, a long time ago, so it seemed. He did not interrupt her, for what did it matter now, what she said? And besides, he was too weary, too utterly spent, to stir from the corner in which he had flung himself.

"He shall be great and shall be called the Son of the Highest; and the Lord God shall give unto him the throne of his father David."

Her hushed voice was like the string of a lute touched by unseen fingers. But Joseph heard her only with his ears, for his heart and his mind were stricken with deafness.

133

"The Holy Ghost shall come upon thee and the power of the Highest shall overshadow thee: therefore also that holy thing which shall be born of thee shall be called the Son of God."

Her face was all alight with a look that was mysterious and tender. But Joseph did not see her for he did not raise his head from the shelter of his arms.

"For with God nothing is impossible."

For a little space she was silent, seeming to forget the presence of Joseph. Then slowly she drew his hands away and scanned his countenance. The rapture that still lingered in her own features gave way to melancholy.

"You do not believe me," she said.

Joseph stumbled to his feet.

"Did you expect that I would? I don't know why you take refuge in such abominable lies—such blasphemies. I had thought of you as the most pious of women. I have been blind to everything about you, it seems." He gazed at her a moment. "It's strange you look as you do," he said. "Your face is as kind and fair as it was before——" He turned away: "I'll be leaving now. We can talk about what's to be done some other time."

"But what is there to talk about, Joseph? You will procure a permission from the council at the next Sabbath service to dissolve our betrothal bonds, won't you?"

He thought of a Sabbath many years ago when he had been a stripling—the rabbi's words rapping hard and pitiless as hail, the congregation, every face set in lines of contempt or hatred, and a girl no more than Mary in years, standing before them all with drooping head and heavy, ceaseless tears. Then there was that tale he had heard a fortnight ago—how in a certain village in Judea, they had stoned a woman whose betrothed had set her aside publicly because she was unchaste. Blood had run from her eyes and mouth, she had tried to throw herself down a well—no, he could not demand a public divorce from Mary.

"I shall tell you what I have decided tomorrow," he said.

IV

THE new chest stood forth pridefully in Joseph's workshop. It was the first thing his eye alighted on when he opened the door and walked slowly toward his deserted bench. Its fresh smooth coat of paint seemed to jeer at him, deriding the loving care he had put into its fashioning. He seized his ax and advanced to destroy the hateful object. A weakness came over him and his hand dropped to his side. The ax slipped from his fingers. He fell upon his knees and dropped his head upon the polished lid, tears aching in his throat and scalding his eyes.

Fiercely he wiped his eyes with the sleeve of his gown. Ah, he had been shamefully weak and as full of weeping as a woman of late! He had slunk out of sight like a thief; he had utterly neglected his work; worst of all he had delayed putting an end to the mockery of his betrothal.

"Tomorrow" he had told her—but tomorrow had come and the next day and the next and he had not spoken to her or looked upon her face. And now a week had passed, and though his decision was made, still he tarried and did not inform her of it.

Well, he must conquer this craven shrinking from a meeting with the woman who had brought him woe and dishonor. Now—now— while his resolution was strong upon him, he would go to her.

Many glances were turned Joseph's way as he walked through the village. But his appearance was so unkempt, his speech so taciturn, his eye so cold and unfriendly that few approached him. It was the first time for many days they noted, that he had shown himself on the streets before nightfall. Nor had he admitted anyone into his house, telling all who sought entrance that he was too busy to spare the time for a minute's chat. Yet men had passed his workshop at all hours and heard no sound issuing thence.

Jehiel, the physician, had had even more disturbing things to tell. Returning one night from Nian where he had gone to attend a husbandman, stricken with fever, he had come unexpectedly upon Joseph, walking alone on an unfrequented path, the tears streaming down his face, his voice lifted in strange curses and lamentations. He had called out to him but Joseph had plunged off into the wilderness like a hart pursued by wolves.

And, meanwhile, as all her neighbors knew well, his betrothed, Mary, sat alone in her house, waiting for the carpenter, who had not come near her but once since her return to Nazareth. This when the wedding date was but a fortnight distant.

Joseph was unaware of the whispers, the shaking of heads that arose as he passed by. As he drew nearer and nearer to the familiar dwelling, his thoughts grew confused, a weakness beset his limbs. Suddenly he saw Mary coming from the opposite direction. There was a basket laden with fruit on her arm, and her hair blew about her face in a dark cloud.

Several paces behind Mary rode the aged Widow Leah, on the donkey which conveyed her to the market place since her legs had become too feeble for use. Neither the old woman nor the girl noticed Joseph who had halted, partially concealing himself behind a palm tree. As Mary was on the point of turning into her doorway, the Widow came abreast of her and roughly crowded her against the wall.

"It would be well for daughters of the accursed Jezebel to seek other towns where the way is not so narrow," Joseph heard the old woman cry out in a shrill spiteful voice. Mary entered the house without replying and he followed her in haste.

"How is this?" he began, without a greeting. "What did that toothless hag mean?"

Mary was very pale and the hollows of sleeplessness were deeper beneath her eyes, but her smile was still untroubled.

"The Widow has had twenty children," she said. "It is not strange that she should divine a secret hidden from the rest of the world. She has been watching me closely for several days. Now, it seems, she has made up her mind."

Joseph frowned. "She is the worst talebearer in the village," he said.

"I know." A shadow crossed her face. He said abruptly:

"I have come to tell you of a plan for dissolving our betrothal. We can go to Jerusalem and apply to the Sanhedrin for a private divorce. It is often granted when the wedding vows have not been taken. Afterward I will return here and you—you can go again to Elizabeth at Juttah?"

"Yes. It is kind of you, Joseph, to make a long journey that you may spare me mortification." Her voice was unsteady.

He did not look at her. "That is settled then," he said. "We will set out in about three days. I have some tasks to finish here first and I must get together some money."

"I shall be ready," she said. "I am grateful—very grateful."

Joseph hesitated. "Mary," he said, "you were happy at Juttah, were you not? Our cousin made you welcome?" She nodded. "And she—believed you?" Again Mary made a sign of confirmation.

"Then why did you come back to Nazareth? You must have known that you would find many like the Widow Leah."

"I was betrothed to you," she answered simply. "It was your right to hear what had befallen me, and to act according to what you thought best after you had heard."

"You do not lack courage," Joseph muttered. He turned to her a face of the most agonized supplication. "Will you not repent of your sin, Mary? Will you not ask forgiveness of God?"

"Why should I ask forgiveness of God for having accepted His divine will?" Her eyes met Joseph's unwaveringly.

"You still persist in that vile blasphemy?"

"No, Joseph, it is you who blaspheme by your doubt. Why do you punish yourself so? Is it not difficult for you to think of the woman you once loved as a wanton, and a wicked liar?"

"I love you still," he groaned. "And to believe you guilty of these abominations has almost cost me my reason."

"Yet nevertheless you believe me guilty. Ah, why is it easier for you to credit the blackest evil than the supreme good?"

"Woman, what are you saying?" he cried. "A virgin cannot bear a child! You spoke to me of the Son of God—who can that mean but Emmanuel, but the Messiah? Will the Messiah come to us

137

through mortal birth? Will a humble Galilean maiden be the mother of the Lord of the Earth? No, no, it is wicked even to think such things—it is an insult to Jehovah!"

"The ways of Jehovah——" she began, but he cut her short.

"Be silent!" shouted Joseph. The veins in his neck stood out like hempen cords. "You have offended enough in the sight of the Lord—do not tempt his wrath further. Mary, you have read much of the sayings of holy men, and you have listened to the Scribes and prophets in Jerusalem and you have talked often with the good rabbi of our village. Don't you remember what they have taught you? The Divine Redeemer before whom all kingdoms shall perish save Israel——" He spoke slowly and patiently now, as though he were bringing a wayward child to reason. "The King who shall be greater than all kings, yea, even than David—when he comes the gates of heaven will open and the waters of the earth will stand still and he will descend to us down a stairway of fire, wrapped in a cloud of light, and every living creature will fall down prone before his awful majesty."

"I know that is what men believe," said Mary. "And yet the Lord has singled out a humble maiden from the despised country of Galilee——"

"You have gone mad!" he cried fearfully, and because he could bear no longer to look at her face with the terrible light of madness upon it, he left her. He desired now to work that he might forget his torture in bodily toil. He sought Simon, the wealthiest man in Nazareth, and agreed to put up a gate for his sheepfold if Simon would pay him as soon as the task was completed.

He fell to labor, sparing himself little rest, and by noon of the next day, the tall gate stood finished and in his pouch jingled new silver coins. There was nothing now to prevent him from setting out for Jerusalem with Mary. The Sanhedrin would be swift in granting him divorce. Very soon he would be free.

"And then?" he asked himself. But he knew the answer too well. Then Mary would go to Juttah and he would return here and try to take up the threads of his life as though he had never met her.

Such dull, slack threads they had been before she made them golden and aquiver with song! She had put honey in his mouth, who knew only the taste of dry bread, and though that honey had turned to gall he could never forget its brief sweetness.

"And even now," he thought, as he stretched himself upon the ground and stared up into the burning, glass-clear sky, "even now my heart turns to water when I see her and I long to take her in my arms. Surely, surely she has gone mad! She was always strangely devout—she pondered overmuch on the coming of the Messiah and perhaps, being alone so much with such thoughts has turned her wits. But the other—the other man? If I could but find out who he is, he would marry her or perish by my hand. But she will not say—she is shielding him. Yet when she swears that there is no other man, I cannot help but feel that she believes her own wild words."

He pressed his hands to his temples, as though he would squeeze the torment of his perplexity out of his mind.

"It may be," he reasoned painfully, "that she has not been truly sane for a long while. There was a woman in Bethany whose own kin did not know that anything ailed her, until they found her in a sort of crazed trance—yet the handmaiden said that she had often before been seized thusly. Perhaps Mary suffered one of these trances—and some infamous fellow chanced to come on her—and while she knew nothing of what was happening——"

He beat the ground with his clenched fist, he twisted his body in the fury of thwarted vengeance. But his thoughts ran on and on.

"What will become of her when the babe is born? Zacharias and Elizabeth are old. They will die and then who will give her shelter? A woman with a child who bears no man's name——"

He started and then lay flatter in the tall grass at the sound of approaching voices. He had no wish for speech with anyone at this moment.

"Here is a good piece of work." Joseph recognized that it was Jehiel who spoke. The physician shook the gate and tested its firmness with a kick of the foot. "There is no better carpenter in the land than Joseph," he declared with admiration.

The other person laughed and revealed himself as Jehiel's son Asa. "'Tis fortunate he has more skill in choosing his woods than in choosing a wife."

Joseph half sat up. Jehiel's next words checked him.

"What do you say, my son? It is not the part of a man to repeat women's gossip."

"Well," protested Asa sullenly, "everybody in the village has seen that Joseph is like another man since she came back—a man near out of his senses. You yourself saw him weeping, you said, and he hasn't gone near her but once—is that the natural conduct for a man to take toward the woman he is pledged to marry any day now? And I heard the wife of Ephraim tell Mother yesterday that there was very little doubt of Mary's condition. Women don't err on matters of that kind, you will admit, Father——"

Joseph rose to his feet. The other two had their backs to him and were too absorbed in argument to hear him as he drew closer.

"I will admit nothing," said Jehiel severely. "As to the night I found Joseph so distraught, that may have been due to any number of causes."

"Ephraim's wife thinks that it is someone in Jerusalem," Asa continued, unheedingly, "but Mother says it is far more likely to be Saul. He wanted to marry Mary once, you know. Likely he found that he could get her favors more easily—Saul's a handsome fellow." He laughed meaningly. The laugh broke abruptly as Joseph placed a hand on his shoulder and spun him around. For a moment the boy looked full in the carpenter's eyes. Then Joseph struck him heavily across the mouth.

Asa screamed and blood rose between his lips. Joseph gave him a savage push which sent him stumbling backward to fall upon the ground.

"If you do not think this a deserved punishment, Jehiel, I will be glad to fight with you also."

Jehiel helped Asa to his feet and bade him go home, and have his mother bind up his injured mouth.

"He deserved it, Joseph," he said sadly, "but he meant no harm.

He is that age when the gossip of idle women is as exciting as a feast."

"That may be," said Joseph, "but I can't let him go about basely slandering my future wife. Wait!" he called sharply, as Asa commenced to slink away, holding a fold of his garment to his mouth. "Tell your mother that I have heard of her lies and if she mentions my betrothed again except in terms of respect, I shall have her publicly rebuked in the synagogue."

He then bid Jehiel a curt farewell and strode off in an opposite direction. Straight he went to the blacksmith's forge and marched up to Ephraim who sat there alone.

"It has come to my ears," he said, "that your wife occupies herself these days in wicked slander of my betrothed wife, Mary. She is a woman, therefore I can't punish her with the sound flogging she deserves. But if you are unable to make her hold her tongue, you can answer for its utterances with your fists. Let me hear of another hateful lie from her and I'll be here to call you to account."

He noted that several women were passing the open doorway in a leisurely fashion, and he added loudly, so they could not fail to hear: "We are to be married tomorrow at the customary hour. There won't be much of a celebration—Mary has no heart for it with her father so recently laid in his tomb. But if you'll assist in bringing home the bride, I'll be glad to have you drink a little wine with us in honor of our happiness."

He departed without waiting for a reply. As he passed the women, he saw that their heads were close together and they were whispering excitedly.

"Yes," he muttered, "you have something else to sharpen your teeth on now, haven't you? The beasts of the wilderness are more clement than you."

He made two more visits that day—one to the synagogue, and the last to Mary herself. She did not answer his knock and he found her crouched at the back of the room on the little sleeping platform, her shoulders shaking with the sobs she strove to suppress. He cleared his throat and she sprang up, hastily wiping her eyes.

"It is foolish of me to give way like this," she said, and tried to smile at him. Joseph felt his whole heart flow toward her in a melting stream of pity. "Someone has been taunting you," he said gruffly.

"I—I—don't mind that so much, but today some children—oh, they were only shouting at me what they had heard their parents say—they had no idea what their words meant—but it hurt. They were such pretty children and they said such ugly things."

She seemed no more than a child herself, with her mouth screwed into a tight knot to keep the sobs back, and her faltering voice and the bewildered pain in her eyes. And suddenly he was holding her to his breast, and stroking her cheek with a comforting hand, while he told her that she must waste no more time in moping, for there was much for her to do.

"We leave tomorrow, is that it?" she asked, and added, under her breath, "I am glad."

"No," said Joseph. "We are to be married tomorrow." He felt her start tremendously; she drew back from his arms and looked at him unbelievingly. "And now," he continued in as matter-of-fact tones as he could muster, "do you take your jar and go down to the fountain and bid all whom you meet to come to the ceremony and to drink a toast to us afterward at our home. Tomorrow you must spend in baking, so that we can offer our guests something with their wine. It will be a simple wedding, but it must be attended with some amount of celebration—we can dispense with the dancing and singing, out of respect to your father's memory."

"Joseph," she said, "Joseph, you truly want to do this? You mustn't think that, because you found me weeping—you have been kind enough, God knows."

"Yes, Mary—I want it." He saw that she was still unsatisfied and he began to talk about the guests.

"You need not ask the Widow Leah if you don't want to," he said, "but I think it would be better if you did. Otherwise, it will look as though we had paid too much heed to her evil tongue. Do you understand?"

She nodded, her eyes fixed on him with such emotion that he looked away, embarrassed.

"I must go now and purchase some wine," he said. "I will return in the morning and bring some woman to help you with the baking."

"No, you must not trouble to do that. I can manage alone." She paused, and then asked hesitantly, "Are—are you going to leave me after the ceremony to be conducted by the others to your house?"

"To my house where I shall await you with some of my close friends," he amended. "Our marriage will be simple, but we must be careful to do things properly. It is more important for us to be careful than for——"

He left the thought unvoiced, but she finished it for him in a sad little voice.

"Than for people whose marriage is not under the cloud of scandal. Oh, my poor Joseph, and you had looked forward to a joyful wedding!"

Her words came back to him that night when he lay on his couch in the darkness, sorely tired from the events of the day. Yes, he had looked forward to a joyful wedding, the kind he had often attended, where the bridegroom went with reverence and honor in his heart to claim his bride; where afterward he waited for her in his doorway, triumphant and eager, and watched her approach through the village, like a queen, garlanded with flowers, surrounded by a singing throng, lighted by a hundred candles, the bright unstained treasure that was to be delivered to him for his cherishing and safekeeping. A thousand times he had pictured this supreme moment. A thousand times he had pictured the honest merrymaking to follow, the hearty good wishes, the embraces and tears and laughter of the good people he had been brought up with and understood and loved. And now it was his bridal eve. The smile he wore tomorrow would be a lie, and the merrymaking would be a mockery and back of every wish, every embrace there would be curiosity or doubt or scorn or pity. And his bride would be watched by greedy, piercing eyes. And he and she and everyone else would be pretending that this was a wedding like any other.

Yet it had been sweet to hold her in his arms again and dry her tears and to feel her small, frightened hands hold his so trustingly, so gratefully. All the bitter wrath he had felt toward her was gone —what the flame of his anger toward her persecutors had not burned away, her helplessness had melted. There was left only his love and his pity and his sorrow.

Joseph raised himself to his knees and clasped his hands. Through his door, half ajar on account of the night's closeness, he could see a patch of luminous sky and toward this he turned his face.

His prayer was brief. He told the Lord that he had that day been rash and hasty, that he had acted on an impulse without meditation, that he had failed to ask for the divine guidance of Jehovah in his perplexities.

"Tomorrow I take unto me as wife, the woman Mary whom I know to be unchaste and unfaithful to our solemn vows of betrothal and blasphemous in her denial of her guilt. I have promised to provide for and protect her all the days of my life and also the child that is in her womb. I know not whether I am wrong and sinful to do this thing or not. If I transgress thy laws, O Lord, forgive me. And forgive also, her whom I love, my betrothed, Mary."

He breathed his amen with a heart already lighter and sank back on his couch. Very shortly he was asleep. And in his sleep he dreamed. . . .

The last guest had gone, the last drop of wine had been drunk, and Joseph was alone with the woman he had made his wife. She, abandoning the forced sprightliness which she had assumed for so many hours, sank down upon a heap of cushions and closed her eyes. For a moment she remained thus, motionless and spent. Then, with an effort, she opened her eyes again and commenced to say something. She halted, stricken mute at what she saw. Her husband was on his knees before her, and in his upturned face was reverence and remorse.

"Mary," he said, "forgive me!"

She did not understand; she drew back from him as though she feared some cruel mockery.

144

"I have wronged you," he said brokenly. "I have wronged you by my words and in my heart. I looked into your holy face, I listened to your sacred words and I saw only sin and heard only lies. I have doubted the word of God and He has been more merciful to me than I deserve and has not punished me for my wickedness. But you, Mary, will you be also merciful? For if you cannot pardon me I do not want to live."

While he spoke Mary's lassitude vanished. She leaned forward and seizing his bowed head in her hands she turned his face toward hers, searching it with eager eyes.

Then she cried, "Tell me, tell me, how did you come to believe?"

Slowly, stumblingly, he described his bridal eve. He told her how he had gone to bed, distraught in mind and conscience and how he had begged the Lord to condone his actions of the morrow, which he knew not were right or wrong. And how he had dreamed that a messenger of Jehovah stood beside his bed, an angel of almost terrible beauty and bade him listen to Jehovah's wish. And how this holy visitor had then told him that he must grieve no longer, that he must fear no more to take Mary for his wife, for all that she had said was true.

"Surely the Lord heard my supplication, and this dream was His answer. And, Mary, He did not bid His Angel chide me for my doubts! Truly His mercy and loving-kindness are boundless!"

Mary laid her cheek against her husband's and her voice when she spoke was low and wondering.

"Not until last night was the truth revealed to you," she said. "Yet you came to me before sundown and said that you would marry me." She let her head fall back and regarded him. "Why did you do that, Joseph? You could have saved me from disgrace by a private divorce. To marry a woman who has been unfaithful to the sacred vows of betrothal is a sin against the Lord; doesn't the Pentateuch say it?"

"I suppose so," he answered, without meeting her gaze. "But I loved you so, Mary—even then, and—and——"

"Once we talked of that, you and I," she said musingly, "and I said that love for God should come first. Do you remember? It was on the mountainside that afternoon. I still think so, Joseph. But you —but you, my beloved——" and suddenly she threw her arms around him and strained him to her close, and her kisses fell upon his face and her tears also, for she was weeping.

When she spoke of the afternoon on the hillside, Joseph was reminded of the alabaster box of spikenard. After a while he went to a low shelf where he had placed it the night before and took it in his hand. He well remembered how he had purchased this pretty trinket, meaning to give it to Mary as a wedding gift. He had thought that he would slip it into her hand and tell her between kisses when and why he had bought it, and they would smile with pleasure together over the memory of that shining afternoon. Then had come those black days when any remembrance of the happiness he had lost was like thorns against the flesh, and he had come near smashing the little box to bits. But he had not done so, and on his wedding eve, with his heart full of the desire to comfort his shamed, unhappy bride, he had determined to give it to her as a token of his forgiveness.

And now another great change had been wrought in his soul. He approached Mary and knelt before her. In his outstretched hand he tendered her his gift, and on his face was the look that was to be seen on the faces of all devout Israelites when they brought their frankincense and myrrh to burn at the altars of the Holy Temple.

V

"Mary—it's time to rise. We leave in an hour." Joseph stooped and gently repeated the words in his wife's ear. When she stirred he stepped back, waiting patiently for her eyes to open.

Mary sat up, hugging her coverings about her, with a slight shiver. She looked from Joseph who was fully clad in fresh, clean raiment, to the low table in the center of the room which was set for the morning repast.

"You should have awakened me before," she chided with a smile. "You indulge me too much, Joseph."

For answer he brought her garments, a bowl of water and a linen cloth.

"I must go now and saddle the mule," he said. "I'll be back by the time you're dressed and we can eat then."

He went outside, closing the door carefully behind him, for it was chill and damp. The sky was bleak and the clouds were lower than the hills. When he returned he regarded Mary anxiously.

"How do you feel this morning?" he asked her.

"In the best of health. I had a fine sleep—as you know."

"Mary," he said, "do you think it's wise for you to make this journey with me? The weather's unhealthy today—and it's a long, tedious way to Bethlehem, with maybe snow and sleet before we get there. It's not necessary for you to go, you know. The tax proclamation stated that a man could register for his wife."

"I know," Mary replied, "but I want to go with you. Joseph, He will be born in Bethlehem, as it was prophesied in the Scriptures. Do you not see that this command of Caesar's is the Lord's device for fulfilling that prophecy? Where else but in David's birthplace should the heir to David's throne be born?"

Joseph bowed his head in reverent acquiescence. But after they had commenced their meal, he asked: "You will wear the new cloak I bought you yesterday? It is thick and warm."

She nodded and smiled. Joseph saw that her thoughts were far away from the warm cloak and from him, so he spoke no more, but busied himself in serving her. At first, they had contested this matter of serving. Mary had been obstinate in her refusal to allow him to wait on her at table, to fetch the brazen ewer and clear away the dishes. These were the wife's accepted duties in an Israelite home, and she would not shirk them. So, for a while he had been forced to undergo the torment of being waited upon by her, of sitting while she stood, of watching her work while he was idle.

"Can you not understand," he had longed to cry to her, "that you are not my wife as most women are wives? Do you not see that you have been exalted above men and above all living beings as the stars are exalted above the earth? Were an archangel to sup with us, would you let him bring you bread and pour water over your hands? It is no more fitting that I should accept such things from you."

But he had said nothing of this, for ever since his dream, a shyness had fallen on the tongue of Joseph when he spoke to Mary. When the child began to press heavily upon her and she moved about with a slower step, he had declared that she must spare herself, and begun gradually to take more and more of the household cares on himself. Mary, as she grew more languid with the approaching of her time, had wrapped herself in long meditations, had paid less and less heed to what went on around her, until now she accepted his care and ceased to protest when he performed the duties of the repast.

He looked at her rather wistfully, as she sat there, her food almost untouched before her, her chin cupped in her hand, a secret smile on her face. He knew that she was in some mysterious, visionary world where he could not follow, and not for anything would he have intruded on her thoughts—but it was cheerless, somehow, to eat a meal in silence when there were two at table. He arose and commenced to set the room to rights. Mary roused herself with a guilty start, and asked if she could help him.

"No," he said, "there's nothing more to be done. The sack of food is ready, the blankets are strapped to the mule. Put this on and let us start."

He held out a long cloak of brilliantly hued wool. Mary slipped into it, caressing the soft folds admiringly.

"It's a beautiful garment," she said. "Far too fine for traveling. I am a little surprised at the colors, though. Purple and scarlet! I thought you did not like them."

Joseph did not respond to her levity and she added, coaxingly, "Do not be so grave and solemn, my Joseph. You have not smiled for a long time and I like to see you smile."

Thus urged, the carpenter allowed his features to relax in a momentary semblance of mirth.

"That is better," said Mary. "Oh, you were right about the weather. I'm glad this cloak is as warm as it is resplendent."

Joseph lifted her in his arms and swung her carefully onto the pillion he had prepared for her. He adjusted the sack of food on his own back and picked up the leading rope.

"You are secure—comfortable?" he asked, looking back at Mary.

"Indeed, yes. Lead on!" she replied gaily.

He was glad that she was in such high spirits. And how beautiful she looked this morning, wrapped in the sumptuous cloak, perched upon the humble little mule like a great queen. Purple and scarlet—no, he did not like those colors, but they were royal hues and therefore suitable for her, the mother of the King of earth. As for himself, he wore his customary sober brown. And that, too, was suitable.

The little band of Nazarenes awaiting them in the square, watched their approach curiously. The mystery of this marriage was still gossiped about in every home, but with more discretion than hitherto, for Joseph's punishment of Asa and his warning to Ephraim were known to all, and as the carpenter was a man of great strength there were few who relished the prospect of an encounter with him.

It was apparent to everyone that Mary's full time was near at hand, and that the child could not have been begotten in wedlock, but most people now held that Joseph, himself, had been responsible for this, and that his stricken aspect before his marriage had been due to self-reproach. Certainly, they admitted, no man could be more devoted to his wife, than was the carpenter. There was something unmanly almost, about the way he indulged her. They would never have thought that the sensible Joseph could behave so dotingly, but then he had changed much in every way. They no longer felt at ease with him, he was so guarded in his manner, so short of speech and so eternally solemn. As for Mary, she had been queer and hard to know since she grew into young womanhood. No, the carpenter and his wife weren't a pair you cared to drop in on for a friendly visit, and the village had let them alone. A pity, too, for Joseph had been such a sociable man once, and such a well-liked one.

Joseph and Mary halted on the edge of the group. Joseph was aware that his friends greeted them in a constrained, awkward fashion and this wounded him. Looking about, he realized that he had not seen many of these good people for a month, except to nod at in passing. He exchanged some comment on the weather with the men near and tightened the strings in the mouth of his food sack. He was uncomfortable and restlessly wished that the caravan would start.

"What are we waiting for?" he asked of no one in particular.

Several voices answered him eagerly. It was Matthew they attended, and a very good reason he had for delay, too, his wife having given birth to a second son at the dawn of this very day. While they were speaking, Matthew himself came riding into their midst, looking so proud and jubilant that Jehiel proposed they should drink the health of the newborn.

A jug of wine was passed around, everyone taking a sip and amidst much laughter and well-wishing, the company set out. Joseph walked slowly in the rear, glancing from time to time at Matthew who was smiling and talking merrily in the center of an attentive group. Each time he looked, it was as though he had added a dry twig to the fire of envy that smoldered within him. At length he dropped his eyes, fearful that Matthew might turn around and read his thoughts in them.

"It is unfair," he thought bitterly. "Two sons in two years' time, while I——" He checked himself, aghast, and stole a look of mingled guilt and awe at Mary. Had he truly forgotten for a moment that supreme life that she carried within her, a life more precious than ever mortal womb had held before? Had he insulted his Lord Jehovah by envying a common man his common son? Jehovah, who had stooped to bestow the mightiest of honors—"on my wife." Something in his brain that he could not control, finished the sentence and added, "What has the Son of God to do with me?"

Joseph's hand tightened on the leading rope, until the coarse fibers bit into his flesh. He said to himself indignantly:

"The Lord has informed me of the wondrous thing that shall come to pass. I am the Lord's servant and I am the husband of Mary, mother of His Son." And he held his head higher and walked proudly for a little space. Then another thought shaped itself and accused him thusly:

"Yet I would change places with Matthew whose wife's sons are also his own.

"That is not true! The devil has entered my mind," and Joseph forced himself to think of practical things—of how far they could travel that day and whether the changing wind meant snow. He was soon to discover that it did. As they came into the plain of Esdraelon they were met by a flurry of great, soft flakes, and before long the earth was covered as far as eye could reach with a thin white veil through which grass and soil showed with an odd effect of nakedness. Joseph pulled his cloak about him and bade Mary cover her head. Jehiel heard his admonition and nodded approvingly.

"That's right—you should run no risks of growing chilled. There's nothing that could be worse for the little one." His tone was kindly. Presently he drew closer to the pair and began to advise them of the precautions Mary should take on the journey.

"You must eat heartily and drink a little wine with every repast— that keeps up the strength. And you must not ride too many miles in a day—though if this snowfall continues there will be small danger of that." He looked at the great, white plain which the wind was ruffling into eddies and ripples, until it resembled a sea composed entirely of foam. "Do you remember the last time that you and I traveled this path together, Joseph? It looked somewhat different then, eh?"

"Yes," said Joseph, "I remember—coming home from the Passover. There were as many flowers then as there are snowflakes now —I don't know that I've ever seen a fairer spring."

He had envied Matthew then, also. How well he recalled the loneliness he had felt at watching the other men with their wives at their sides, and his determination to marry. Many of the same men were in the present company, but this time most of them traveled alone, for he was one of the few whose wife had accompanied him. And yet he was lonelier now than he had been that long-past day in the springtime. Ah, much, much lonelier, though his wife sat on the mule and he walked beside her. He could not understand this thing, yet it was so.

They broke their first day's journey at a wayside khan near the foot of Mount Hermon. It grew colder that night and the next morning the snow had ceased to fall, but the earth was covered with a hard crust, as slippery as glass. They were forced to travel very slowly and the second night found them on the banks of the Jordan, a Jordan filmed with blue-gleaming ice, far from any village, without even an abandoned hillside cave to seek refuge in.

The erection of little booths of twigs covered with leaves, the ordinary shelter of Israelites on journey, was impossible in such weather and such surroundings. Three or four of the party, however, had been prudent enough to provide themselves with tents and one of them was Jehiel. Fires were lighted to melt the snow, and the frail walls of skins were set up around the damp, bare ground which was covered as well as possible with other skins. Into these tents the entire company crowded with their mules and camels, and fortifying themselves with food and wine warmed over the fires, they huddled beneath their cloaks for a night's sleep.

It happened that among those who sought the protection of the physician's tent were Joseph and Mary and also a youthful couple who had been wed but a short time ago. The girl had come on the journey with her husband for the reason, which she frankly stated, that she could not endure to be separated from him and since leaving Nazareth they had scarcely taken their eyes off one another. Joseph had insisted on laying his own cloak, doubled for extra warmth, over Mary that night and he awoke early the next morning, unable to sleep longer from the cold that clung to his cramped limbs. Glancing about at the slumbering occupants of the tent, his eye fell on the youth, Daniel, and his bride. The girl lay with her head on her husband's breast, her lips parted as though for a kiss, one arm wound loosely about his neck. Under the wolfskin which covered them both, Joseph could divine the outline of his arms clasping her waist in an embrace which sleep had only slightly relaxed. His cheek was sunk in her outspread hair. While Joseph looked, Daniel stirred a little and without opening his eyes murmured an endearment. His unconscious words must have penetrated into the girl's dreams, for a tender smile came over her face and she crept closer to him.

Joseph turned away, an ache in his breast. He gazed down at the calm lovely face of the woman beside him but he did not see Mary the holy, Mary the exalted, whom he worshiped with love and devotion. He saw the girl whose voice had broken when she cried, "I am glad—so glad," the night he asked her to be his wife. He saw the girl who had clung to him on the mountainside above Nazareth, warm and loving and close—so close he could feel her heart beat—no different from other women—how happy he had been with that girl——

Mary moved and opened her eyes. He sprang up in haste, having but one thought now and that to build a fire so he could thaw out the frozen food for her. But he did not glance in the direction of Daniel and his wife again. When the young pair parted from the caravan at Jericho, two days later, Joseph was astounded at the relief with which he saw them leave.

They left four others also at Jericho and before noon of the sixth day, Jehiel and his sons quit the Jerusalem road to go eastward toward Bethany. Joseph watched the physician ride away with regret. Jehiel was kind and friendly, his conversation was cheerful, and helped to disperse the misgivings and loneliness that weighed on the carpenter's soul. In the depleted band that was left, there was no one else who could do this and Joseph felt his spirits sink to lower and lower levels.

The country through which they were passing served to increase his dolor. Stern and frowning, the cliffs leaned over them, without even a tuft of withered grass or a stunted evergreen to soften their austerity. Ravens flew overhead, uttering their harsh and dismal cries. There was no snow now, but the Brook Cherith, swollen by recent rainfalls, muttered angrily in its deep bed. Joseph felt a shiver pass over him; and he was seized with a panic of unreasoning dread.

"Mary," he cried, and turned toward her, with his hands outstretched imploringly. He longed to have her bend down and put her arms around him, to feel her mouth against his in a kiss like those of their early betrothal days, to hold her close to him until he heard the quickened beat of her heart, to take refuge in the warm security of her love.

But though his heart cried out her name, his lips whispered it and Mary did not hear. She was, he saw, deep in one of her fathomless dreams. Joseph's hands fell to his sides and he drew back.

Late that night the caravan reached Jerusalem and disbanded. Mary and Joseph were the only two for whom the end of the journey had not been reached. They alone must go on tomorrow.

Joseph had friends in Jerusalem and it was to their home that he took Mary, who was beginning to show the strain of the arduous traveling. He was fatigued himself, and would have preferred to retire with his wife, but Aaron, his host, brought out some wineskins and seemed so eager for company that Joseph, in all civility, could not insist on bed.

"Well, my friend," said Aaron, after they had discussed the annoyance of the tax and the unusual inclemency of the weather, "you are a lucky man, aren't you? A pretty young wife and a child already on the way—when do you expect it to arrive?"

"He will be born very shortly," replied Joseph.

"He? As sure as that, are you?" laughed Aaron.

Joseph looked down in confusion.

"Yes—that is——" he began.

Aaron laughed again and clapped him on the back.

"Of course! Of course! We all hope the first-born will be a son. But if yours isn't, you mustn't be disappointed. They say that if the first's a daughter, all the rest will be sons—and it's better that way than to have the eldest a boy and the rest all girls."

Joseph did not reply.

"Don't you agree with me?" asked Aaron. "Or are you loath to have even one girl in your family? A girl's needed, you know, to help her mother about the house. However, may your first three be sons!"

He tipped his wineskin above his mouth and drank lustily to emphasize his wish. Joseph did not drink with him.

"I shall never have children," he said in a dull voice. His eyes were fastened on the wall. He did not realize that he had spoken aloud until he heard Aaron gasp and saw his expression of amazement.

"Don't pay any heed to what I say," he cried. "I—I am in a bad mood—Mary is not strong, you see, and sometimes I let myself fear that both she and the child——" He did not finish. He was tired, so very tired, and suddenly it did not matter to him what Aaron thought.

Aaron, however, appeared to accept the explanation, though he scoffed at it vigorously.

"Nonsense!" he exclaimed several times. "Your wife is hearty and strong. You are going far afield, indeed, my friend, to find something to worry you. It's your health that must be bad, you're so gloomy. Better turn in and get some sleep. You'll see things differently in the morning."

But for Joseph sleep was impossible. Aaron's talk of future sons and daughters had jerked open a door in his mind and now he lay staring at what he saw beyond that portal. It was very clear. When he had spoken aloud unconsciously, he had spoken from an innermost conviction. Mary's son would be born but never would she bear a child to Joseph. Never would she bear a child to Joseph, because—

"But what if she herself wishes to go back with you to Nazareth as your wife and no more? What if the Lord has no further use for her after she has borne His Son? What if He has selected others to bring up the Holy Child—the priests of the Temple, for instance? Why should you not have children of your own and live the sort of life that you had expected to live before this miracle occurred—the happy simple life that all your friends pursue? Whatever happens, why should Mary not bear you children? She is your wife—you love her—she loves you."

Sensible words, logical words. Joseph's mind heard them with approval, his heart with wild upspringing of hope. Yet, something stronger than mind or heart rose within him and groaned: "I cannot — I cannot. She whom the Holy Spirit of Jehovah has entered into, she who has conceived the Son of God is not as other women and never will be. Were I to take her unto me as men take their wives, I would be profane in my own eyes. She is set apart from my love by a barrier that I could not bring myself to cross. Whatever happens, whether she wishes it or not, I can never know her, I can never ask her to bear me sons."

And Joseph turned his face from the sleeping woman whom he so greatly loved and wept silently for a long time.

The following morning they set out from Jerusalem on the road that led to Bethlehem, the City of David. And while they were passing through the Valley of Hinnom, Joseph heard Mary utter a little sob and looking up, he saw that the tears were in her eyes and that her face was set in lines of suffering. Fearful that her labor had begun, he stopped the mule and made to lift her off. But Mary shook her head and bade him proceed. And when he glanced at her anxiously, less than a moment later, he saw that her tears had dried and that she was smiling as though all the happiness of the world was in her heart.

"How is this?" he asked, astonished. "One second you are sad, the next——"

"I seem to see two persons," replied Mary, "the one weeping and the other smiling."

Joseph did not understand her words and he asked her no more questions. He slackened the mule's pace and led it as carefully as possible, avoiding the rough places in the road, of which there were many, as much as he could. After a while they came to a spring and Mary asked for a drink of water. He made her dismount and rest while she drank, then seeing that she had grown very pale, he climbed up behind her, caught the reins in one hand and encircled her firmly with his free arm so as to brace her against the jolts.

"She will not need me much longer," he thought. "When her son is born, all Canaan will be eager to serve her."

They jogged on and Mary leaned her head wearily against his shoulder.

"When the Messiah is born, the world will come to do Him honor," thought Joseph, "and likewise, His mother—but I? There will be no place for me—there will be no need for me. I am her husband but she is the bride of Jehovah and the mother of the King of Earth. What have I, a simple Galilean carpenter, to do with such grandeur? Surely, the Lord will not blame me, surely He will understand and approve if I go back quietly to Nazareth. It is better for everyone that I do. I shall not be missed and—ah, surely God will not expect me to linger by her side, knowing what is in my heart! When He is born—when they come to bow down before Him and do Him honor—then I shall steal out and go back to Nazareth. It is better so for all. They will not need me and perhaps someday I shall find another wife and some small measure of happiness."

Mary moaned faintly and he tightened his clasp.

"We have not very much farther to go," he said soothingly. "Lean against me more—so—and close your eyes—that makes the time pass faster. We are almost at the hills now—soon we will be in Bethlehem and you shall have a soft bed to rest on."

"You are so good," murmured Mary. "So good and loyal and steadfast. Do you remember I said these same things on the night you asked me to be your wife?"

"Yes, Mary, I remember."

"I said that it was a comforting thing to know you were thus—it is a comforting thing now. You will not leave me, Joseph? You will stay by my side?"

"Of course, Mary."

"Always?" She twisted her head so that she could look full into his eyes. Her voice took on a fevered note. "For all the years that lie ahead? Give me your promise, Joseph, your solemn promise that you will never leave me."

At midnight Joseph was wakened by the sound of many voices

and the strains of music. He opened his eyes to a radiance that pervaded every corner of the stable yard wherein he lay, a little apart from Mary and the newborn infant. The gateway was filled with men in shepherd dress and their gaze was fixed as a single pair of eyes upon his wife and the child she held to her breast.

Joseph rose as he saw these men surge into the stable yard and advance with timid, hesitating steps. And then Mary smiled upon them and held up the babe for them to see. And pressing closer still, they went down upon their knees before her.

Others were arriving and their number filled full the small enclosure.

"I shall be just outside, Mary, when you need me," Joseph whispered.

He threaded an unobtrusive way through the kneeling ranks of shepherds and crept out of the stable yard unnoticed, as their voices rose and swelled in a chant of adoration. He lifted his eyes and for an instant looked into the blazing heavens. Then, slowly, he settled himself upon the ground to wait for Mary's call.

JOHN EVANS

Strange Story of a Traveler to Bethlehem

This story was printed as a news dispatch in the first column of page one in the "Chicago Tribune," on Christmas Day, 1943. It was presented as having been written "BY CORNELIUS [As envisioned by the Rev. John Evans, Tribune Religious Editor]." The date line read: "BETHLEHEM, Judea, Dec. 25—In the 36th Year of the Reign of Herod—[Special]." The story has since been published in Dr. Evans' book, "I Saw His Glory" (Willett, Clark & Company, 1945).

OUR caravan was rerouted at Gaza as it proceeded northward to accommodate my employer, Eleazar, a rich Jewish glass merchant of Alexandria, who had to deliver some luxury merchandise to customers in the new Zion district of Jerusalem in time for a winter festival.

But here we are, stalled in this miserable village of Bethlehem. Eleazar thinks the crowds which held us up will slacken so that we can proceed tomorrow. Seldom do caravans travel northward along this route. Usually they travel the coastal plain, but despite nasty weather here in this rock pile of a country there is fascination in this historic land, even for a Roman.

Ostensibly, the crowds stalling us here are en route to a Roman census taking, but Eleazar, with a wink, spoke of today's anniversary of the country's liberation a century and a half ago from the tyranny of Syrian-Greek despotism. Even my tolerant country does not like any of its mandated peoples to remember their past victories too well.

Since we left the coastal route our troubles mostly were this incessant drizzle, chill winds, fog. The cold penetrates to the marrow, but last night's strange incident, together with Eleazar's stories about his peculiar people, has made up for some of the discomfort.

Eleazar, now on what he calls his last pilgrimage to the city of his fathers, warned against expectation of hospitality by his people here in Judea. They will be distant and aloof, he said, but he told me of their traditions in a way which made one feel a kindly sympathy for those who remained here in this desolate and unproductive land in order to conserve a rich cultural and religious tradition reaching back more than a thousand years.

Here, off all main trade routes, and by holding firm against all outside influences, the garden of tradition blooms where nothing else will grow. Eleazar said the temple at Jerusalem really supports the whole of Judea. In addition to being a religious center it is virtually a bank with its own coinage, a very rich institution that conquerors would like to plunder. Part of its wealth comes from exchange fees, for sacrificial animals must be purchased in temple coins.

But Eleazar explained with a shrug that our caravan would be as comfortable in the open as in these leaky, mud-roofed houses. He added that Jerusalem will hang out no welcome sign to me, a Roman on unofficial business. You see, he said, the sphere of influence of Rome is constantly widening just as that of Macedonian Greece did a couple of centuries ago. A bitter war and incredible feats of heroism by a few followers of a man they called "The Hammerer" were necessary to the freedom of this tiny religious commonwealth.

Now another conflict looms as the people on today's festival recall "The Hammerer's" exploits and look to the dynasty he established. Even though the Roman senate set up Herod's present throne in part to end that dynasty, the wily Herod married into "The Hammerer's" line. Herod is a sort of naturalized Jew, but is really a descendant of the hated Edomites.

How Judea hates this "Edomite slave" who rules over it! But he has kept the land peaceful and reasonably prosperous. Did he not keep Judea out of the hands of Cleopatra, and did he not quell the rebellion in Galilee with an iron hand? And did he not rebuild the temple and fortify Jerusalem impregnably against any possible attack?

Yes, but did he not rebuild Samaria into a hated Greek city, and help build pagan temples elsewhere? But his wickedness and pagan spirit are now catching up with him. He spends more and more time each year at Callirrhoe Hot Springs and is sick most of the time. His jealousies are becoming furious.

Recently he became suspicious of the ambitions of his sons, who, through their mother, are members of "The Hammerer's" dynasty and he is not. He summarily recalled them from Rome and executed his own sons, as he put their mother to death twenty-two years ago. Herod strikes instantly and ruthlessly when he thinks his power is threatened.

A few days ago he was unbelievably cruel. He sentenced some tiny infants to death because he had heard mere rumors from eastern travelers that the foretold time had come for a son to be born in the great David's dynasty. Tradition said this king would be God's anointed and would set up universal reign, even over Rome! But with all his violent tempers and cruelty, the people are worried about what will happen when he dies. From accounts of his sickness, that time is not far off. Will the country then suffer partition and resulting civil violence leading to further intervention by Rome? A large section of the people, particularly in Galilee, want to attack now, just as "The Hammerer" did. But that means war, and the loss of temple revenue from pilgrims. Ruination would ensue.

Here in Bethlehem the main business is sheep raising. The sheep are certified by the priests for temple sacrifices and economic conditions are good. What they want more than anything else is peace, so they tolerate Herod but worry about the state of his health.

These worries were accentuated last night by a strange incident. Drivers heard a commotion in stables where our caravan animals are kept. We did not want to run into further trouble and delay so Eleazar and I went out, despite the late night chill, to see if something else would stall us longer.

To our amazement, the sky was clear, and a brilliant star not known to these people seemed to shine directly into one of the stables. On approaching we learned that a young woman from Galilee had become a mother in the stable, where the young woman and her husband had been forced to go because the village was crowded. Eleazar explained that a new and brilliant star would be one of the sure signs of the birth of David's divinely anointed descendant.

Then frightened shepherds began arriving in the village. They told of hearing heavenly songs in the sky telling of peace to men of good will. While still terror-struck, they saw an angel who bade them be unafraid; that good news was breaking on the world. . . .

"For unto you is born this day in the city of David a Saviour, which is the anointed of the Lord. And this shall be a sign unto you; ye shall find the babe wrapped in swaddling clothes, lying in a manger," the angel said.

In an awe-stricken voice, Eleazar whispered to me that Bethlehem is David's city; that here the great king would be born. He turned back to the stable, and I, following him, entered. The loveliness of the scene was unforgettable; the light of the star on two beautiful faces, mother and babe, with the glow forming a crown around the baby's head. The husband knelt before the manger as in adoration.

Before parting with Eleazar for the short remainder of the night, I asked him if there should be anything to these strange things. His moist eye glistened in the star's light.

"I think there is," he said. "I am sure of it."

FRANCES HODGSON BURNETT

The Little Hunchback Zia

THE little hunchback Zia toiled slowly up the steep road, keeping in the deepest shadows, even though the night had long fallen. Sometimes he staggered with weariness or struck his foot against a stone and smothered his involuntary cry of pain. He was so full of terror that he was afraid to utter a sound which might cause any traveler to glance toward him. This he feared more than any other thing—that some man or woman might look at him too closely. If such a one knew much and had keen eyes, he or she might in some way guess even at what they might not yet see.

Since he had fled from the village in which his wretched short life had been spent he had hidden himself in thickets and behind walls or rocks or bushes during the day, and had only come forth at night to stagger along his way in the darkness. If he had not managed to steal some food before he began his journey and if he had not found in one place some beans dropped from a camel's feeding bag, he would have starved. For five nights he had been wandering on, but in his desperate fear he had lost count of time. When he had left the place he had called his home he had not known where he was going or where he might hide himself in the end. The old woman with whom he had lived and for whom he had begged and labored had driven him out with a terror as great as his own.

"Begone!" she had cried in a smothered shriek. "Get you gone, accursed! Even now thou mayest have brought the curse upon me also. A creature born a hunchback comes on earth with the blight of Jehovah's wrath upon him. Go far! Go as far as thy limbs will carry thee! Let no man come near enough to thee to see it! If you go far away before it is known, it will be forgotten that I have harbored you."

He had stood and looked at her in the silence of the dead, his immense, black Syrian eyes growing wider and wider with childish horror. He had always regarded her with slavish fear. What he was to her he did not know; neither did he know how he had fallen into her hands. He knew only that he was not of her blood or of her country and that he yet seemed to have always belonged to her. In his first memory of his existence, a little deformed creature rolling about on the littered floor of her uncleanly hovel, he had trembled at the sound of her voice and had obeyed it like a beaten spaniel puppy. When he had grown older he had seen that she lived upon alms and thievery and witchlike evil doings that made all decent folk avoid her. She had no kinsfolk or friends, and only such visitors as came to her in the dark hours of night and seemed to consult with her as she sat and mumbled strange incantations while she stirred a boiling pot. Zia had heard of soothsayers and dealers with evil spirits, and at such hours was either asleep on his pallet in a far corner or, if he lay awake, hid his face under his wretched covering and stopped his ears. Once when she had drawn near and found his large eyes open and staring at her in spellbound terror, she had beaten him horribly and cast him into the storm raging outside.

A strange passion in her seemed her hatred of his eyes. She

could not endure that he should look at her as if he were thinking. He must not let his eyes rest on her for more than a moment when he spoke. He must keep them fixed on the ground or look away from her. From his babyhood this had been so. A hundred times she had struck him when he was too young to understand her reason. The first strange lesson he had learned was that she hated his eyes and was driven to fury when she found them resting innocently upon her. Before he was three years old he had learned this thing and had formed the habit of looking down upon the earth as he limped about. For long he thought that his eyes were as hideous as his body was distorted. In her frenzies she told him that evil spirits looked out from them and that he was possessed of devils. Without thought of rebellion or resentment he accepted with timorous humility, as part of his existence, her taunts at his twisted limbs. What use in rebellion or anger? With the fatalism of the East he resigned himself to that which was. He had been born a deformity, and even his glance carried evil. This was life. He knew no other. Of his origin he knew nothing except that from the old woman's rambling outbursts he had gathered that he was of Syrian blood and a homeless outcast.

But though he had so long trained himself to look downward that it had at last become an effort to lift his heavily lashed eyelids, there came a time when he learned that his eyes were not so hideously evil as his taskmistress had convinced him that they were. When he was only seven years old she sent him out to beg alms for her, and on the first day of his going forth she said a strange thing, the meaning of which he could not understand.

"Go not forth with thine eyes bent downward on the dust. Lift them, and look long at those from whom thou askest alms. Lift them and look as I see thee look at the sky when thou knowest not I am near thee. I have seen thee, hunchback. Gaze at the passers-by as if thou sawest their souls and asked help of them."

She said it with a fierce laugh of derision, but when in his astonishment he involuntarily lifted his gaze to hers, she struck at him, her harsh laugh broken in two.

"Not at me, hunchback! Not at me! At those who are ready to give!" she cried out.

He had gone out stunned with amazement. He wondered so greatly that when he at last sat down by the roadside under a fig tree he sat in a dream. He looked up at the blueness above him as he always did when he was alone. His eyelids did not seem heavy when he lifted them to look at the sky. The blueness and the billows of white clouds brought rest to him, and made him forget what he was. The floating clouds were his only friends. There was something—yes, there was something, he did not know what. He wished he were a cloud himself, and could lose himself at last in the blueness as the clouds did when they melted away. Surely the blueness was the something.

The soft, dull pad of camel's feet approached upon the road without his hearing them. He was not roused from his absorption until the camel stopped its tread so near him that he started and looked up. It was necessary that he should look up a long way. He was a deformed little child, and the camel was a tall and splendid one, with rich trappings and golden bells. The man it carried was dressed richly, and the expression of his dark face was at once restless and curious. He was bending down and staring at Zia as if he were something strange.

"What dost thou see, child?" he said at last, and he spoke almost in a breathless whisper. "What art thou waiting for?"

Zia stumbled to his feet and held out his bag, frightened, because he had never begged before and did not know how, and if he did not carry back money and food, he would be horribly beaten again.

"Alms! alms!" he stammered. "Master—Lord—I beg for—for her who keeps me. She is poor and old. Alms, great lord, for a woman who is old!"

The man with the restless face still stared. He spoke as if unaware that he uttered words and as if he were afraid.

"The child's eyes!" he said. "I cannot pass him by! What is it? I must not be held back. But the unearthly beauty of his eyes!" He caught his breath as he spoke. And then he seemed to awaken as one struggling against a spell.

"What is thy name?" he asked.

Zia also had lost his breath. What had the man meant when he spoke of his eyes?

He told his name, but he could answer no further questions. He did not know whose son he was; he had no home; of his mistress he knew only that her name was Judith and that she lived on alms.

Even while he related these things he remembered his lesson, and, dropping his eyelids, fixed his gaze on the camel's feet.

"Why dost thou cast thine eyes downward?" the man asked in a troubled and intense voice.

Zia could not speak, being stricken with fear and the dumbness of bewilderment. He stood quite silent, and as he lifted his eyes and let them rest on the stranger's own, they became large with tears —big, piteous tears.

"Why?" persisted the man, anxiously. "Is it because thou seest evil in my soul?"

"No! no!" sobbed Zia. "One taught me to look away because I am hideous and—my eyes—are evil."

"Evil!" said the stranger. "They have lied to thee." He was trembling as he spoke. "A man who has been pondering on sin dare not pass their beauty by. They draw him, and show him his own soul. Having seen them, I must turn my camel's feet backward and go no farther on this road which was to lead me to a black deed." He bent down, and dropped a purse into the child's alms bag, still staring at him and breathing hard. "They have the look," he muttered, "of eyes that might behold the Messiah. Who knows? Who knows?" And he turned his camel's head, still shuddering a little, and he rode away back toward the place from which he had come.

There was gold in the purse he had given, and when Zia carried it back to Judith, she snatched it from him and asked him many questions. She made him repeat word for word all that had passed.

After that he was sent out to beg day after day, and in time he vaguely understood that the old woman had spoken falsely when she had said that evil spirits looked forth hideously from his eyes. People often said that they were beautiful, and gave him money because something in his gaze drew them near to him. But this was not all. At times there were those who spoke under their breath to one another of some wonder of light in them, some strange luminousness which was not earthly.

"He surely sees that which we cannot. Perhaps when he is a man he will be a great soothsayer and reader of the stars," he heard a woman whisper to a companion one day.

Those who were evil were afraid to meet his gaze, and hated it as old Judith did, though, as he was not their servant, they dared not strike him when he lifted his soft, heavy eyelids.

But Zia could not understand what people meant when they whispered about him or turned away fiercely. A weight was lifted from his soul when he realized that he was not as revolting as he had believed. And when people spoke kindly to him he began to know something like happiness for the first time in his life. He brought home so much in his alms bag that the old woman ceased to beat him and gave him more liberty. He was allowed to go out at night and sleep under the stars. At such times he used to lie and look up at the jeweled myriads until he felt himself drawn upward and floating nearer and nearer to that unknown something which he felt also in the high blueness of the day.

When he first began to feel as if some mysterious ailment was creeping upon him he kept himself out of Judith's way as much as possible. He dared not tell her that sometimes he could scarcely crawl from one place to another. A miserable fevered weakness became his secret. As the old woman took no notice of him except when he brought back his day's earnings, it was easy to evade her. One morning, however, she fixed her eyes on him suddenly and keenly.

"Why art thou so white?" she said, and caught him by the arm, whirling him toward the light. "Art thou ailing?"

"No! no!" cried Zia.

She held him still for a few seconds, still staring.

"Thou art too white," she said. "I will have no such whiteness. It is the whiteness of—of an accursed thing. Get thee gone!"

He went away, feeling cold and shaken. He knew he was white. One or two almsgivers had spoken of it, and had looked at him a little fearfully. He himself could see that the flesh of his thin body was becoming an unearthly color. Now and then he had shuddered as he looked at it because—because—— There was one curse so horrible beyond all others that the strongest man would have quailed in his dread of its drawing near him. And he was a child, a twelve-year-old boy, a helpless little hunchback mendicant.

When he saw the first white-and-red spot upon his flesh he stood still and stared at it, gasping, and the sweat started out upon him and rolled down in great drops.

"Jehovah!" he whispered, "God of Israel! Thy servant is but a child!"

But there broke out upon him other spots, and every time he found a new one his flesh quaked, and he could not help looking at it in secret again and again. Every time he looked it was because he hoped it might have faded away. But no spot faded away, and the skin on the palms of his hands began to be rough and cracked and to show spots also.

In a cave on a hillside near the road where he sat and begged there lived a deathly being who, with face swathed in linen and with bandaged stumps of limbs, hobbled forth now and then, and came down to beg also, but always keeping at a distance from all human creatures, and, as he approached the pitiful, rattled loudly his wooden clappers, wailing out: "Unclean! Unclean!"

It was the leper Berias, whose hopeless tale of awful days was almost done. Zia himself had sometimes limped up the hillside and laid some of his own poor food upon a stone near his cave so that he might find it. One day he had also taken a branch of almond blossom in full flower, and had laid it by the food. And when he had gone away and stood at some distance watching to see the poor ghost come forth to take what he had given, he had seen him first clutch at the blossoming branch and fall upon his face, holding it to his breast, a white, bound, shapeless thing, sobbing, and uttering hoarse, croaking, unhuman cries. No almsgiver but Zia had ever dreamed of bringing a flower to him who was forever cut off from all bloom and loveliness.

It was this white, shuddering creature that Zia remembered with the sick chill of horror when he saw the spots.

"Unclean! Unclean!" he heard the cracked voice cry to the sound of the wooden clappers. "Unclean! Unclean!"

Judith was standing at the door of her hovel one morning when Zia was going forth for the day. He had fearfully been aware that for days she had been watching him as he had never known her to watch him before. This morning she had followed him to the door, and had held him there a few moments in the light with some harsh speech, keeping her eyes fixed on him the while.

Even as they so stood there fell upon the clear air of the morning a hollow, far-off sound—the sound of wooden clappers rattled together, and the hopeless crying of two words, "Unclean! Unclean!"

Then silence fell. Upon Zia descended a fear beyond all power of words to utter. In his quaking young torment he lifted his eyes and met the gaze of the old woman as it flamed down upon him.

"Go within!" she commanded suddenly, and pointed to the wretched room inside. He obeyed her, and she followed him, closing the door behind them.

"Tear off thy garment!" she ordered. "Strip thyself to thy skin— to thy skin!"

He shook from head to foot, his trembling hands almost refusing to obey him. She did not touch him, but stood apart, glaring. His garments fell from him and lay in a heap at his feet, and he stood among them naked.

One look, and she broke forth, shaking with fear herself, into a breathless storm of fury.

"Thou hast known this thing and hidden it!" she raved. "Leper! Leper! Accursed hunchback thing!"

As he stood in his nakedness and sobbed great, heavy, childish sobs, she did not dare to strike him, and raged the more.

If it were known that she had harbored him, the priests would be upon her, and all that she had would be taken from her and burned. She would not even let him put his clothes on in her house.

"Take thy rags and begone in thy nakedness! Clothe thyself on the hillside! Let none see thee until thou art far away! Rot as thou wilt, but dare not to name me! Begone! Begone! Begone!"

And with his rags he fled naked through the doorway, and hid himself in the little wood beyond.

Later, as he went on his way, he had hidden himself in the daytime behind bushes by the wayside or off the road; he had crouched behind rocks and boulders; he had slept in caves when he had found them; he had shrunk away from all human sight. He knew it could not be long before he would be discovered, and then he would be shut up; and afterward he would be as Berias until he died alone. Like unto Berias! To him it seemed as though surely never child had sobbed before as he sobbed, lying hidden behind his boulders, among his bushes, on the bare hill among the rocks.

For the first four nights of his wandering he had not known where he was going, but on this fifth night he discovered. He was on the way to Bethlehem—beautiful little Bethlehem curving on the crest of the Judean mountains and smiling down upon the fairness of the fairest of sweet valleys, rich with vines and figs and olives and almond trees. He dimly recalled stories he had overheard of its loveliness, and when he found that he had wandered unknowingly toward it, he was aware of a faint sense of peace. He had seen nothing of any other part of the world than the poor village outside which the hovel of his bond-mistress had clung to a low hill. Since he was near it, he vaguely desired to see Bethlehem.

He had learned of its nearness as he lay hidden in the undergrowth on the mountainside that he had begun to climb the night before. Awakening from sleep, he had heard many feet passing up the climbing road—the feet of men and women and children, of camels and asses, and all had seemed to be of a procession ascending the mountainside. Lying flat upon the earth, he had parted the bushes cautiously, and watched, and listened to the shouts, cries, laughter, and talk of those who were near enough to be heard. So bit by bit he had heard the story of the passing throng. The great Emperor Augustus, who to the common herd seemed some strange omnipotent in his remote and sumptuous paradise of Rome, had issued a decree that all the world of his subjects should be enrolled, and every man, woman, and child must enroll himself in his own city. And to the little town of Bethlehem all these travelers were wending their way to the place of their nativity, in obedience to the great Caesar's command.

All through the day he watched them—men and women and children who belonged to one another, who rode together on their beasts, or walked together hand in hand. Women on camels or asses held their little ones in their arms, or walked with the youngest slung on their backs. He heard boys laugh and talk with their fathers— boys of his own age, who trudged merrily along, and now and again ran forward, shouting with glee. He saw more than one strong man swing his child up to his shoulder and bear him along as if he found joy in his burden. Boy and girl companions played as they went and made holiday of their journey; young men or women who were friends, lovers, or brothers and sisters bore one another company.

"No one is alone," said Zia, twisting his thin fingers together, "no one! no one! And there are no lepers. The great Caesar would not count a leper. Perhaps, if he saw one, he would command him to be put to death."

And then he writhed upon the grass and sobbed again, his bent chest almost bursting with his efforts to make no sound. He had always been alone—always, always; but this loneliness was such as no young human thing could bear. He was no longer alive; he was no longer a human being. Unclean! Unclean! Unclean!

At last he slept, exhausted, and past his piteous, prostrate childhood and helplessness the slow procession wound its way up the mountain road toward the crescent of Bethlehem, knowing nothing of his nearness to its unburdened comfort and simple peace.

When he awakened, the night had fallen, and he opened his eyes upon a high vault of blue-velvet darkness strewn with great stars. He saw this at the first moment of his consciousness; then he realized that there was no longer to be heard the sound either of passing hoofs or treading feet. The travelers who had gone by during the day had probably reached their journey's end, and gone to rest in their tents, or had found refuge in the inclosing khan that gave shelter to wayfarers and their beasts of burden.

But though there was no human creature near, and no sound of human voice or human tread, a strange change had taken place in him. His loneliness had passed away, and left him lying still and calm as though it had never existed, as though the crushed and broken child who had plunged from a precipice of woe into deadly, exhausted sleep was only a vague memory of a creature in a dark past dream.

Had it been himself? Lying upon his back, seeing only the immensity of the deep blue above him and the greatness of the stars, he scarcely dared to draw breath lest he should arouse himself to new anguish. It had not been he who had so suffered; surely it had been another Zia. What had come upon him, what had come upon the world? All was so still that it was as if the earth waited—as if it waited to hear some word that would be spoken out of the great space in which it hung. He was not hungry or cold or tired. It was as if he had never staggered and stumbled up the mountain path and dropped shuddering, to hide behind the bushes before the daylight came and men could see his white face. Surely he had rested long. He had never felt like this before, and he had never seen so wonderful a night. The stars had never been so many and so large. What made them so soft and brilliant that each one was almost like a sun? And he strangely felt that each looked down at him as if it said the word, though he did not know what the word was. Why had he been so terror-stricken? Why had he been so wretched? There were no lepers; there were no hunchbacks. There was only Zia, and he was at peace, and akin to the stars that looked down.

How heavenly still the waiting world was, how heavenly still! He lay and smiled and smiled; perhaps he lay so for an hour. Then high, high above he saw, or thought he saw, in the remoteness of the vault of blue a brilliant whiteness float. Was it a strange, snowy cloud or was he dreaming? It seemed to grow whiter, more brilliant. His breath came fast, and his heart beat trembling in his breast, because he had never seen clouds so strangely, purely brilliant. There was another, higher, farther distant, and yet more dazzling still. Another and another showed its radiance until at last an arch of splendor seemed to stream across the sky.

"It is like the glory of the ark of the covenant," he gasped, and threw his arm across his blinded eyes, shuddering with rapture.

He could not uncover his face, and it was as he lay quaking with an unearthly joy that he first thought he heard sounds of music as remotely distant as the lights.

"Is it on earth?" he panted. "Is it on earth?"

He struggled to his knees. He had heard of miracles and wonders of old, and of the past ages when the sons of God visited the earth.

"Glory to God in the highest!" he stammered again and again and again. "Glory to the great Jehovah!" and he touched his forehead seven times to the earth.

Then he beheld a singular thing. When he had gone to sleep a flock of sheep had been lying near him on the grass. The flock was still there, but something seemed to be happening to it. The creatures were awakening from their sleep as if they had heard something. First one head was raised, and then another and another and another, until every head was lifted, and every one was turned toward a certain point as if listening. What were they listening for? Zia could see nothing, though he turned his own face toward the climbing road and listened with them. The floating radiance was so increasing in the sky that at this point of the mountainside it seemed no longer to be night, and the far-away paeans held him breathless with mysterious awe. Was the sound on earth? Where did it come from? Where?

"Praised be Jehovah!" he heard his weak and shaking young voice quaver.

Some belated travelers were coming slowly up the road. He heard an ass's feet and low voices.

The sheep heard them also. Had they been waiting for them? They rose one by one—the whole flock—to their feet, and turned in a body toward the approaching sounds.

Zia stood up with them. He waited also, and it was as if at this moment his soul so lifted itself that it almost broke away from his body—almost.

Around the curve an ass came slowly bearing a woman, and led by a man who walked by its side. He was a man of sober years and walked wearily. Zia's eyes grew wide with awe and wondering as he gazed, scarce breathing.

The light upon the hillside was so softly radiant and so clear that he could see that the woman's robe was blue and that she lifted her face to the stars as she rode. It was a young face, and pale with the pallor of lilies, and her eyes were as stars of the morning. But this was not all. A radiance shone from her pure pallor, and bordering her blue robe and veil was a faint, steady glow of light. And as she passed the standing and waiting sheep, they slowly bowed themselves upon their knees before her, and so knelt until she had passed by and was out of sight. Then they returned to their places, and slept as before.

When she was gone, Zia found that he also was kneeling. He did not know when his knees had bent. He was faint with ecstasy.

"She goes to Bethlehem," he heard himself say as he had heard himself speak before. "I, too; I, too."

He stood a moment listening to the sound of the ass's retreating feet as it grew fainter in the distance. His breath came quick and soft. The light had died away from the hillside, but the high-floating radiance seemed to pass to and fro in the heavens, and now and again he thought he heard the faint, far sound that was like music so distant that it was as a thing heard in a dream.

"Perhaps I behold visions," he murmured. "It may be that I shall awake."

But he found himself making his way through the bushes and

setting his feet upon the road. He must follow, he must follow. Howsoever steep the hill, he must climb to Bethlehem. But as he went on his way it did not seem steep, and he did not waver or toil as he usually did when walking. He felt no weariness or ache in his limbs, and the high radiance gently lighted the path and dimly revealed that many white flowers he had never seen before seemed to have sprung up by the roadside and to wave softly to and fro, giving forth a fragrance so remote and faint, yet so clear, that it did not seem of earth. It was perhaps part of the vision.

Of the distance he climbed his thought took no cognizance. There was in this vision neither distance nor time. There was only faint radiance, far, strange sounds, and the breathing of air which made him feel an ecstasy of lightness as he moved. The other Zia had traveled painfully, had stumbled and struck his feet against wayside stones. He seemed ten thousand miles, ten thousand years away. It was not he who went to Bethlehem, led as if by some power invisible. To Bethlehem! To Bethlehem, where went the woman whose blue robe was bordered with a glow of fair luminousness and whose face, like an uplifted lily, softly shone. It was she he followed, knowing no reason but that his soul was called.

When he reached the little town and stood at last near the gateway of the khan in which the day-long procession of wayfarers had crowded to take refuge for the night, he knew that he would find no place among the multitude within its walls. Too many of the great Caesar's subjects had been born in Bethlehem and had come back for their enrolment. The khan was crowded to its utmost, and outside lingered many who had not been able to gain admission and who consulted plaintively with one another as to where they might find a place to sleep, and to eat the food they carried with them.

Zia had made his way to the entrance gate only because he knew the travelers he had followed would seek shelter there, and that he might chance to hear of them.

He stood a little apart from the gate and waited. Something would tell him what he must do. Almost as this thought entered his mind he heard voices speaking near him. Two women were talking together, and soon he began to hear their words.

"Joseph of Nazareth and Mary his wife," one said. "Both of the line of David. There was no room for them, even as there was no room for others not of royal lineage. To the mangers in the cave they have gone, seeing the woman had sore need of rest. She, thou knowest—"

Zia heard no more. He did not ask where the cave lay. He had not needed to ask his way to Bethlehem. That which had led him again directed his feet away from the entrance gate of the khan, past the crowded court and the long, low wall of stone within the inclosure of which the camels and asses browsed and slept, on at last to a pathway leading to the gray of rising rocks. Beneath them was the cave, he knew, though none had told him so. Only a short distance, and he saw what drew him trembling nearer. At the open entrance, through which he could see the rough mangers of stone, the heaps of fodder, and the ass munching slowly in a corner, the woman who wore the blue robe stood leaning wearily against the heavy wooden post. And the soft light bordering her garments set her in a frame of faint radiance and glowed in a halo about her head.

"The light! The light!" cried Zia in a breathless whisper. And he crossed his hands upon his breast.

Her husband surely could not see it. He moved soberly about, unpacking the burden the ass had carried and seeming to see naught else. He heaped straw in a corner with care, and threw his mantle upon it.

"Come," he said. "Here thou canst rest, and I can watch by thy side. The angels of the Lord be with thee!" The woman turned from the door and went toward him, walking with slow steps. He gazed at her with mild, unillumined eyes.

"Does he not see the light!" panted Zia. "Does he not see the light!"

Soon he himself no longer saw it. Joseph of Nazareth came to the wooden doors and drew them together, and the boy stood alone on the mountainside, trembling still, and wet with the dew of the night; but not weary, not hungered, not athirst or afraid, only quaking with wonder and joy—he, the little hunchback Zia, who had known no joy before since the hour of his birth.

He sank upon the earth slowly in an exquisite peace—a peace that thrilled his whole being as it stole over his limbs, deepening moment by moment. His head drooped softly upon a cushion of moss. As his eyelids fell, he saw the splendor of whiteness floating in the height of the purple vault above him.

The dawn was breaking, and yet the stars had not faded away. This was his thought when his eyes first opened on a great one, greater than any other in the sky, and of so pure a brilliance that it seemed as if even the sun would not be bright enough to put it out. It hung high in the paling blue, high as the white radiance; and as he lay and gazed, he thought it surely moved. What new star was it that in that one night had been born? He had watched the stars through so many desolate hours that he knew each great one as a friend, and this one he had never seen before.

The morning was cold, and his clothes were wet with dew, but he felt no chill. He remembered; yes, he remembered. If he had lived in a vision the day before, he was surely living in one yet. The Zia who had been starved and beaten and driven out naked into the world, who had clutched his thin breast and sobbed, writhing upon the earth, where was he? He looked down upon his hands and saw the cracked and scaling palms, and it was as though they were not. He thrust back the covering from his chest and saw the spots there. But there were no lepers, there were no hunchbacks; there were only Zia and the light. He knelt and turned himself toward the cave and prayed, and as he so knelt and prayed the man Joseph rolled open the heavy wooden door.

Then Zia, still kneeling, beat himself softly upon the breast and prayed again, not as before to Jehovah, but to that which he beheld.

The light was there, fair, radiant, wonderful. The cave was

bathed in it. The woman in the blue robe sat upon the straw, and in her arms she held a newborn child. Zia touched his forehead to the earth again, again, again, unknowing that he did so. The child was the light itself!

He must rise and draw near. That which had drawn him up the mountainside drew him again. The child was the light itself! As he crept near the cave's entrance, the woman's eyes rested upon him soft and wonderful.

She spoke to him—she spoke!

"Be not afraid," she said. "Draw nigh and behold!"

Her voice was not as the voice of other women; it was like her eyes, soft and wonderful. It could not be withstood even by awe such as his. He could not remain outside, but entered trembling, and trembling drew near.

The child lying upon His mother's breast opened His eyes and smiled. Zia fell upon his knees before Him. He held out his piteous hands, remembering for one moment the Zia who had sobbed on the mountainside alone.

"I am a leper!" he cried. "I may not touch Him! Unclean! Unclean!"

"Draw nigh," the woman said, "and let His hand rest upon thee!"

Zia crouched upon his knees. The newborn hand fell softly upon his shoulder and rested there. Through his body, through his blood, through every limb and fleshly atom of him, he felt it steal—new life, warming, thrilling, wakening in his veins new life! As he felt it, he knelt quaking with rapture even as he had stood the night before gazing at the light. The newborn hand lay still.

He did not know how long he knelt. He did not know that the woman leaned toward him, scarce drawing breath, her wondrous eyes resting upon him as if she waited for a sign. Even as she so gazed she beheld it, and spoke, whispering as in awed prayer:

"Go forth and cleanse thy flesh in running water," she said. "Go forth."

He moved, he rose, he stood upright—the hunchback Zia who had never stood upright before! His body was straight, his limbs were strong. He looked upon his hands, and there was no blemish or spot to be seen!

"I am made whole!" he cried in ecstasy so wild that his boy's voice rang and echoed in the cave's hollowed roof. "I am made whole!"

"Go forth," she said softly. "Go forth and give praise."

He turned and went into the dawning day. He stood swaying, and heard himself sob forth a rapturous cry of prayer. His flesh was fresh and pure; he stood erect and tall. He was as others whom God had not cursed. The light! the light! He stretched forth his arms to the morning sky.

Some shepherds roughly clothed in the skins of lambs and kids were climbing the hill toward the cave. They carried their crooks, and they talked eagerly as though in wonderment at some strange thing which had befallen them, looking up at the heavens, and one pointed with his crook.

"Surely it draws nearer, the star!" he said. "Look!"

As they passed a thicket where a brook flowed through the trees a fair boy came forth, cleansed, fresh, and radiant as if he had but just bathed in its clear waters. It was the boy Zia.

"Who is this one?" said the oldest shepherd.

"How beautiful he is! How the light shines on him. He looks like a king's son."

And as they passed, they made obeisance to him.

F. K. FORAANDH
The Second Christmas

THE reign of unconsciousness slowly gave way to the dim stirrings of intelligence. Little Jesus, one year old, was waking up. Black obscurity—darkness—then a faint glimmer of light. Nothing radiant, glistening, or with form; simply the preface to a shapeful glow. But enough to excite curiosity.

From the outer room Mary the mother could hear if anything were wrong, which was unlikely. Jesus was a peaceful sleeper. But now little Jesus was waking up; waking up in a three-room cabin; a three-room cabin in the darkness of passionless Palestine. He began to recognize the light without much bustle on his part, which is not unusual for an infant of twelve months. Unless alarmed by some sudden interference from without, the senses of a child ascend silently through stratum and ever-lighter stratum of unknowingness till finally they bubble gently to the surface of the conscious. Aroused, no doubt, by some abstruse jerk in the machinery of his tiny middle, Baby Jesus moved gently in his little crib—the crib made by the industrious Joseph. With a stifled, imperceptible yawn, he pulled his right arm out from under his chest and rolled over on his back. This demanded another yawn, then his eyes opened.

Immensity! A vast universe! Without floor, without ceiling, without walls. Only tremendous distances in every direction. A dreadful, unknown, terrifying world without even a line of horizon. Alone in space—unknown space—eclipsed, yet not altogether black.

Joseph was insistent on leaving him a night lamp. But any baby knows that a night lamp, especially a flickering oil burner, can bring to life more intimidating apparitions than the nothingness of unaided night. Then, suddenly the lonely universe was filled with silent beings. Even by so small, so immature an intelligence as Baby Jesus' these beings were perceived, apprehended. And is it little wonder, for are we not born in the clutch of racial consciousness? And do we not in those waking splinters of time, relive, reinhabit the lives of men dead these thousands of years?

Little Jesus, heir on this planet to a life heavily endowed by the shortcomings, errors and sins of all his myriad forefathers, lay awake in the outskirts of darkness. And though he could not, as yet, be held accountable for the fact, he was also the inheritor of that strong cord of wisdom, beauty and love which had needled its way down through the ages.

There he lay, in the terror of loneliness peopled with shapes. It was hardly possible for him really to know the shapes; but in his little undeveloped mind he was aware that they were there. In that delicate undermind handed down from the past, he felt them.

All was stillness—save for an indistinct purr from the night lamp. Then a sudden flicker of light and all the shadows hiding in the corners bounced to life. Something approached, came close. It couldn't be seen; nothing tangible moved, but those shapes were there. They not only lingered over him, next to his delicate cheek, but were at the same time at a great distance, far away, which roused a wild terror in Baby Jesus' poor little unarmed soul.

Flight was the only answer. Nothing but fleeing into the darkness could stamp out those feelings. And turning away, seeking cover, was the only flight possible to a baby. He must put a stop to seeing, and so be no longer there. With a stunted cry that uttered his soul's alarm, little Jesus rolled sharply over and buried his face in warm, soft obscurity. In the fleecy softness of the new birthday pillow (purchased that afternoon by the never-forgetting Joseph) the baby buried his whole being. He was not. Nothing could seize him now. Those strange shapes could not reach him in that consoling, warm, soft obscurity. No wonder that Joseph had commented on the luxurious quality of the new pillow. It certainly was seducing in its softness. Surely the child must have been uncomfortable on that hard straw bolster of a thing!

Out in the front room the two parents were intent on their usual evening occupation. That is to say, Mary was weaving at her loom, and Joseph sat motionless save for his rhythmic strokes with the file on the saw he was sharpening. Mary was, at the moment, endeavoring to count out the required twenty-five threads necessary for one weave. And except for an occasional secret recollection of the events of "that day" of the preceding year, she was silently filled with an enlightenment of which few women are gifted. Suddenly she looked up. "Did you hear anything, Joseph?" she turned to ask her husband.

"Uh . . . did you say something, Mary?" he inquired, a little peevishly, detaching his mind with reluctance from the beautiful chair he was planning to start carving in the morning.

"I thought I heard the baby."

"I didn't," mumbled Joseph, his thoughts already back on the chair.

Mary paused, finished the weave, which, she having miscounted, contained only twenty-four threads. Then she got up from her loom. "I don't suppose there's anything wrong," she said to herself, "but . . ." She went into the sleeping room.

A couple of minutes passed before she returned. Her face was quite pale. "Nothing wrong, is there?" inquired Joseph, who had sensed her departure from the room.

"He's all right now," was her brief answer. She was a quiet, prayerful woman, never known to make a fuss. Adjusting her stool, she continued her weaving. But it must not go by unnoticed that she was, however, shaken up a bit. She realized, and certainly would never forget, what a close call it had been. It is altogether conceivable that she might have merely noted with calm satisfaction the way the child pressed his tiny face into the soft pillow. She might have walked out without realizing that the new possession in which he appeared to take such comfort was actually smothering him! But a flash of intuition had led her to turn his head. Then she had replaced the soft pillow with the hard one, and added this episode to the many ponderings of her heart.

II

Christmas Is Santa Claus

STORIES OF THE CHILDREN'S SAINT,
THE CHRISTMAS TREE, AND OTHER ASPECTS
OF THE CHRISTMAS LEGEND

*"Sure, there's a heap o' sense in some nonsense,
mind that! And never be so foolish, just because
ye grow up and get a little book knowledge, as to
turn up your nose and mock at the things ye loved
and believed in when ye were a little lad. Them
that do, lose one of the biggest cures for heartache
there is in the world, mind that!"*

RUTH SAWYER : THIS WAY TO CHRISTMAS

ROARK BRADFORD

How Come Christmas?

SCENE: *Corner in rural Negro church by the stove. The stove is old, and the pipe is held approximately erect by guy wires, but a cheerful fire is evident through cracks in the stove, and the wood box is well filled. Six children sit on a bench which has been shifted to face the stove, and the Reverend stands between them and the stove. A hatrack on the wall supports sprigs of holly and one "plug" hat. A window is festooned with holly, long strips of red paper, and strings of popcorn. A small Christmas bell and a tiny American flag are the only "store bought" decorations.*

REVEREND: Well, hyar we is, chilluns, and hyar hit is Christmas. Now we all knows we's hyar 'cause hit's Christmas, don't we? But what I want to know is, who gonter tell me how come hit's Christmas?

WILLIE: 'Cause old Sandy Claus come around about dis time er de year, clawin' all de good chilluns wid presents.

CHRISTINE: Dat ain't right, is hit, Revund? Hit's Christmas 'cause de Poor Little Jesus was bawned on Christmas, ain't hit, Revund?

REVEREND: Well, bofe er dem is mighty good answers. Old Sandy Claus do happen around about dis time er de year wid presents, and de Poor Little Jesus sho was bawned on Christmas Day. Now, de question is, did old Sandy Claus start clawin' chilluns wid presents before de Poor Little Jesus got bawned, or did de Little Jesus git bawned before old Sandy Claus started gittin' around?

WILLIE: I bet old Sandy Claus was clawin' chilluns before de Poor Little Jesus started studdin' about gittin' bawned.

CHRISTINE: Naw, suh. De Little Jesus comed first, didn't he, Revund?

WILLIE: Old Sandy Claus is de oldest. I seed his pitchers and I seed Jesus' pitchers and old Sandy Claus is a heap de oldest. His whiskers mighty nigh tetch de ground.

DELIA: Dat ain't right. Old Methuselah is de oldest, ain't he, Revund? 'Cause de Bible say

> Methuselah was de oldest man of his time.
> He lived nine hund'ed and sixty-nine.
> And he died and went to heaven in due time.

REVEREND: Methuselah was powerful old, all right.

WILLIE: He wa'n't no older den old Sandy Claus, I bet. Old Sandy Claus got a heap er whiskers.

CHRISTINE: But de Poor Little Jesus come first. He was hyar before old man Methuselah, wa'n't he, Revund?

REVEREND: He been hyar a powerful long time, all right.

WILLIE: So has old Sandy Claus. He got powerful long whiskers.

DELIA: Moses got a heap er whiskers too.

REVEREND: Yeah, Moses was a mighty old man, too, but de p'int is, how come Christmas git started bein' Christmas? Now who gonter tell me? 'Cause hyar hit is Christmas Day, wid ev'ybody happy and rejoicin' about, and hyar is us, settin' by de stove in de wa'm churchhouse, tawkin' about hit. But ain't nobody got no idee how come hit start bein' Christmas?

WILLIE: You can't fool old Sandy Claus about Christmas. He know, don't he, Revund? He jest lay around and watch and see how de chilluns mind dey maw, and den de fust thing you know he got his mind make up about who been good and who been bad, and den he just hauls off and has hisse'f a Christmas.

CHRISTINE: Yeah, but how come he know hit's time to haul off and have hisse'f a Christmas?

WILLIE: 'Cause any time old Sandy Claus make up his mind to have Christmas, well, who gonter stop him?

CHRISTINE: Den how come he don't never make up his mind ontwell de middle er winter? How come he don't make up his mind on de Fou'th er July? Ev'ybody git good around de Fou'th er July, jest like Christmas, so's dey kin go to de picnic. But Sandy Claus ain't payin' no mind to dat cause hit ain't time for Christmas, is hit, Revund?

WILLIE: Cou'se he don't have Christmas on de Fou'th er July. 'Cause hit ain't no p'int in Sandy Claus clawin' ev'ybody when ev'ybody's goin' to de picnic, anyhow. Sandy Claus b'lieve in scatterin' de good stuff out, don't he, Revund? He say, "Well, hit ain't no p'int in me clawin' fo'ks when dey already havin' a good time goin' to de picnic. Maybe I better wait to de dead er winter when hit's too cold for de picnic." Ain't dat right, Revund?

REVEREND: Sandy Claus do b'lieve in scatterin' de good stuff about de seasons, Willie, and hit sho ain't no p'int in havin' Christmas on de Fou'th er July. 'Cause de Fou'th er July is got hit's own p'int. And who gonter tell me what de p'int er de Fou'th er July is?

CHORUS:

> *Old Gawge Wash'n'ton whupped de kaing,*
> *And de eagle squalled, Let Freedom raing.*

REVEREND: Dat's right. And dat was in de summertime, so ev'y-body went out and had a picnic 'cause dey was so glad dat Gawge Wash'n'ton whupped dat kaing. Now what's de p'int er Christmas?

WILLIE: Old Sandy Claus . . .

CHRISTINE: De Poor Little Jesus . . .

REVEREND: Well, hit seem like old Sandy Claus and de Poor Little Jesus bofe is mixed up in dis thing, f'm de way y'all chilluns looks at hit. And I reckon y'all is just about 'zackly right too. 'Cause dat's how hit is. Bofe of 'em is so mixed up in hit I can't tell which is which, hardly.

DELIA: Was dat before de Fou'th er July?

CHRISTINE: Cou'se hit was. Don't Christmas always come before de Fou'th er July?

WILLIE: Naw, suh. Hit's de Fou'th er July fust, and den hit's Christmas. Ain't dat right, Revund?

REVEREND: I b'lieve Christine got you dat time, Willie. Christmas do come before de Fou'th er July. 'Cause you see hit was at Christ-mas when old Gawge Wash'n'ton got mad at de kaing 'cause de kaing was gonter kill de Poor Little Jesus. And him and de kaing fit f'm Christmas to de Fou'th er July before old Gawge Wash'n'ton finally done dat kaing up.

WILLIE: And Gawge Wash'n'ton whupped dat kaing, didn't he?

REVEREND: He whupped de stuffin' outn him. He whupped him f'm Balmoral to Belial and den back again. He jest done dat kaing up so bad dat he jest natchally put kaingin' outn style, and ev'y since den, hit ain't been no more kaings to 'mount to much.

You see, kaings was bad fo'ks. Dey was mean. Dey'd druther kill you den leave you alone. You see a kaing wawkin' down de road, and you better light out across de field, 'cause de kaing would wawk up and chop yo' haid off. And de law couldn't tetch him, 'cause he was de kaing.

So all de fo'ks got skeered er de kaing, 'cause dey didn't know how to do nothin' about hit. So ev'ybody went around, tryin' to stay on de good side of him. And all er dat is how come de Poor

Little Jesus and Old Sandy Claus got mixed up wid gittin' Christmas goin'.

You see, one time hit was a little baby bawned name' de Poor Little Jesus, but didn't nobody know dat was his name yit. Dey knew he was a powerful smart and powerful purty little baby, but dey didn't know his name was de Poor Little Jesus. So, 'cause he was so smart and so purty, ev'ybody thought he was gonter grow up and be de kaing. So quick as dat news got spread around, ev'ybody jest about bust to git on de good side er de baby, 'cause dey figure efn dey start soon enough he'd grow up likin' 'em and not chop dey haids off.

So old Moses went over and give him a hund'ed dollars in gold. And old Methuselah went over and give him a diamond ring. And old Peter give him a fine white silk robe. And ev'ybody was runnin' in wid fine presents so de Poor Little Jesus wouldn't grow up and chop de haids off.

Ev'ybody but old Sandy Claus. Old Sandy Claus was kind er old and didn't git around much, and he didn't hyar de news dat de Poor Little Jesus was gonter grow up and be de kaing. So him and de old lady was settin' back by de fire one night, toastin' dey shins and tawkin' about dis and dat, when old Miz Sandy Claus up and remark, she say, "Sandy, I hyars Miss Mary got a brand new baby over at her house."

"Is dat a fack?" says Sandy Claus. "Well, well, hit's a mighty cold night to do anything like dat, ain't hit? But on de yuther hand, he'll be a heap er pleasure and fun for her next summer I reckon."

So de tawk went on, and finally old Sandy Claus remark dat hit was powerful lonesome around de house since all er de chilluns growed up and married off.

"Dey all married well," say Miz Sandy Claus, "and so I say, 'Good ruddance.' You ain't never had to git up and cyore dey colic and mend dey clothes, so you gittin' lonesome. Me, I love 'em all, but I'm glad dey's married and doin' well."

So de tawk run on like dat for a while, and den old Sandy Claus got up and got his hat. "I b'lieve," he say, "I'll drap over and see how dat baby's gittin' along. I ain't seed no chilluns in so long I'm pyore hongry to lean my eyes up agin a baby."

"You ain't goin' out on a night like dis, is you?" say Miz Sandy Claus.

"Sho I'm goin' out on a night like dis," say Sandy Claus. "I'm pyore cravin' to see some chilluns."

"But hit's snowin' and goin' on," say Miz Sandy Claus. "You know yo' phthisic been devilin' you, anyhow, and you'll git de chawley mawbuses sloppin' around in dis weather."

"No mind de tawk," say Sandy Claus. "Git me my umbrella and my overshoes. And you better git me a little somethin' to take along for a cradle gift, too, I reckon."

"You know hit ain't nothin' in de house for no cradle gift," say Miz Sandy Claus.

"Git somethin'," say Sandy Claus. "You got to give a new baby somethin', or else you got bad luck. Get me one er dem big red apples outn de kitchen."

"What kind er cradle gift is an apple?" say Miz Sandy Claus. "Don't you reckon dat baby git all de apples he want?"

"Git me de apple," say Sandy Claus. "Hit ain't much, one way you looks at hit. But f'm de way dat baby gonter look at de apple, hit'll be a heap."

So Sandy Claus got de apple and he lit out.

Well, when he got to Miss Mary's house ev'ybody was standin' around givin' de Poor Little Jesus presents. Fine presents. Made outn gold and silver and diamonds and silk, and all like dat. Dey had de presents stacked around dat baby so high you couldn't hardly see over 'em. So when ev'ybody seed old Sandy Claus come in dey looked to see what he brang. And when dey seed he didn't brang nothin' but a red apple, dey all laughed.

"Quick as dat boy grows up and gits to be de kaing," dey told him, "he gonter chop yo' haid off."

"No mind dat," say Sandy Claus. "Y'all jest stand back." And so he went up to de crib and he pushed away a handful er gold and silver and diamonds and stuff, and handed de Poor Little Jesus dat red apple. "Hyar, son," he say, "take dis old apple. See how she shines?"

And de Poor Little Jesus reached up and grabbed dat apple in bofe hands, and laughed jest as brash as you please!

Den Sandy Claus tuck and tickled him under de chin wid his before finger, and say, "Goodly-goodly-goodly." And de Poor Little Jesus laughed some more and he reached up and grabbed a fist full er old Sandy Claus' whiskers, and him and old Sandy Claus went round and round!

So about dat time, up stepped de Lawd. "I swear, old Sandy Claus," say de Lawd. "Betwixt dat apple and dem whiskers, de Poor Little Jesus ain't had so much fun since he been bawn."

So Sandy Claus stepped back and bowed low and give de Lawd hy-dy, and say, "I didn't know ev'ybody was chiv-areein', or else I'd a stayed at home. I didn't had nothin' much to bring dis time, 'cause you see how hit's been dis year. De dry weather and de bull weevils got mighty nigh all de cotton, and de old lady been kind er puny——"

"Dat's all right, Sandy," say de Lawd. "Gold and silver have I a heap of. But verily you sho do know how to handle yo'se't around de chilluns."

"Well, Lawd," say Sandy Claus, "I don't know much about chilluns. Me and de old lady raised up fou'teen. But she done most er de work. Me, I jest likes 'em and I manages to git along wid 'em."

"You sho do git along wid 'em good," say de Lawd.

"Hit's easy to do what you likes to do," say Sandy Claus.

"Well," say de Lawd, "hit might be somethin' in dat, too. But de trouble wid my world is, hit ain't enough people which likes to do de right thing. But you likes to do wid chilluns, and dat's what I needs. So stand still and shet yo' eyes whilst I passes a miracle on you."

So Sandy Claus stood still and shet his eyes, and de Lawd r'ared back and passed a miracle on him and say, "Old Sandy Claus, live forever, and make my chilluns happy."

So Sandy Claus opened his eyes and say, "Thank you kindly,

Lawd. But do I got to keep 'em happy all de time? Dat's a purty big job. Hit'd be a heap er fun, but still and at de same time——"

"Yeah, I knows about chilluns, too," say de Lawd. "Chilluns got to fret and git in devilment ev'y now and den and git a whuppin' f'm dey maw, or else dey skin won't git loose so's dey kin grow. But you jest keep yo' eyes on 'em and make 'em all happy about once a year. How's dat?"

"Dat's fine," say Sandy Claus. "Hit'll be a heap er fun, too. What time er de year you speck I better make 'em happy, Lawd?"

"Christmas suit me," say de Lawd, "efn hit's all O.K. wid you."

"Hit's jest about right for me," say old Sandy Claus.

So ev'y since dat day and time old Sandy Claus been clawin' de chilluns on Christmas, and dat's on de same day dat de Poor Little Jesus got bawned. 'Cause dat's de way de Lawd runs things. O' cou'se de Lawd knowed hit wa'n't gonter be long before de Poor Little Jesus growed up and got to be a man. And when he done dat, all de grown fo'ks had him so's dey c'd moan they sins away and lay they burdens down on him, and git happy in they hearts. De Lawd made Jesus for de grown fo'ks. But de Lawd know de chilluns got to have some fun, too, so dat's how come hit's Sandy Claus and Christmas and all.

CLEMENT C. MOORE

A Visit from St. Nicholas

'TWAS the night before Christmas, when all through
the house
Not a creature was stirring, not even a mouse;
The stockings were hung by the chimney with care,
In hopes that St. Nicholas soon would be there;
The children were nestled all snug in their beds,
While visions of sugar-plums danced in their heads;
And Mamma in her kerchief, and I in my cap,
Had just settled our brains for a long winter's nap—
When out on the lawn there rose such a clatter,
I sprang from my bed to see what was the matter.
Away to the window I flew like a flash,
Tore open the shutters and threw up the sash.

The moon, on the breast of the new-fallen snow,
Gave a luster of mid-day to objects below;
When, what to my wondering eyes should appear,
But a miniature sleigh, and eight tiny reindeer,
With a little old driver, so lively and quick,
I knew in a moment it must be St. Nick.
More rapid than eagles his coursers they came,
And he whistled, and shouted, and called them by name:
  "Now, Dasher! now, Dancer! now, Prancer and Vixen!
On! Comet, on! Cupid, on! Dunder and Blitzen—
To the top of the porch, to the top of the wall!
Now, dash away, dash away, dash away all!"
  As dry leaves that before the wild hurricane fly,
When they meet with an obstacle, mount to the sky,
So, up to the house-top the coursers they flew,
With a sleigh full of toys—and St. Nicholas too.
And then in a twinkling I heard on the roof,
The prancing and pawing of each little hoof.
  As I drew in my head, and was turning around,
Down the chimney St. Nicholas came with a bound.
He was dressed all in fur from his head to his foot,
And his clothes were all tarnished with ashes and soot;
A bundle of toys he had flung on his back,
And he looked like a peddler just opening his pack.
His eyes how they twinkled! his dimples how merry!
His cheeks were like roses, his nose like a cherry;
His droll little mouth was drawn up like a bow,
And the beard on his chin was as white as the snow;
The stump of a pipe he held tight in his teeth,
And the smoke, it encircled his head like a wreath.
He had a broad face, and a little round belly,
That shook when he laughed, like a bowl full of jelly.
He was chubby and plump—a right jolly old elf;
And I laughed when I saw him, in spite of myself.

A Visit from St. Nicholas

A wink of his eye, and a twist of his head,
Soon gave me to know I had nothing to dread.
He spoke not a word, but went straight to his work,
And filled all the stockings; then turned with a jerk,
And laying his finger aside of his nose,
And giving a nod, up the chimney he rose.
He sprang to his sleigh, to his team gave a whistle,
And away they all flew like the down of a thistle;
But I heard him exclaim, ere he drove out of sight,

"HAPPY CHRISTMAS TO ALL,

AND TO ALL A GOOD-NIGHT!"

JOHN MACY

The True Story of Santy Claus

IF we should wake on the sixth of December and find our stockings full of candy and toys we should think that the ruddy old fellow who comes down the chimney had lost his wits and arrived about three weeks too soon. But his arrival would seem exactly on time to children in other parts of the world. For the feast of Saint Nicholas is the sixth of December, and how he became the patron saint of the day of the Saint of saints, the Christ child, is a story.

It is the story of a story. And when we say that it is true we shall remember that truth lives in the region of dreams. We shall be true to a glorious legend and to the way that legend has come down to us. Truth here consists in knowing that Santy Claus does come down the chimney and fill our stockings. If we do not believe that truth, we are lost souls and beauty and poetry, the only real truth, mean nothing.

Nicholas was an actual person. Though he is the most popular saint in the calendar, not excepting St. Christopher and St. Francis, we know little about the man to whom so many lovely deeds, human and miraculous, have been ascribed. He was bishop of Myra, in Lycia, Asia Minor, in the first part of the fourth century of the Christian Era. Asia Minor is far away from reindeer and Santy Claus, but the world of faith and fable is small and ideas travel far if they have centuries of time for their journey round the world. And Asia Minor is the cradle of all Christian ideas.

From the day of his birth Nicholas revealed his piety and grace. He refused on fast days to take the natural nourishment of a child. He was the youngest bishop in the history of the church. He was persecuted and imprisoned with many other Christians during the reign of the Roman emperor Diocletian, and was released and honored when Constantine the Great established the Christian Church as the official religion, or at least recognized and encouraged it. Under Constantine, in 325, was held the first general council of the Christians at Nicaea, where many important matters were decided. These matters belong to theology and are not in our picture, but Nicholas may have had a hand, a vigorous hand, in them. One of the arguers who seemed to Nicholas, and to the later orthodox church, a dangerous heretic, so roused the righteous ire of the saint that Nicholas smote him in the jaw. This is one of the first episodes in militant Christianity.

About two hundred years after his death Nicholas was a great figure in Christian legend, and Justinian, the last powerful Roman emperor in the East, built a church in honor of St. Nicholas in Constantinople. But the bones of the saint were not allowed to rest in peace in his home town, Myra, where he was probably buried. About seven hundred years after his death, in the eleventh century, what remained of the earthly Nicholas was dug up and moved to the city of Bari, in Italy. In its day it was one of many important seaports that dominated Mediterranean traffic. The merchants of Bari organized a predatory expedition to the burial place of Nicholas, stole the bones, reburied them in Bari and built a church which was long an objective for religious pilgrims and is still worth the travel of a lover of art and architecture. The city of Venice, not to be outdone by a rival maritime town, also claims to enshrine the bones of the saint. So the curious tourist may take his choice. The bones are dust, wherever they lie. The churches in Bari and in many cities of Europe still stand; there are more than four hundred dedicated to Nicholas in England. More important, the spirit of the saint is alive throughout the Christian world.

Nicholas was not a barefoot recluse vowed to poverty. His father was a wealthy merchant, and his riches, inherited or created by the magic wand which fairy godfathers wield, enabled him to be a dispenser of the good things of life, an earthly representative of the Supreme Giver of gifts.

The most famous episode in his long career of benevolence is his rescue of the three dowerless maidens. An impoverished nobleman had three daughters whom he was about to send forth into a life of shame. Nicholas heard of the tragic situation and at night threw a purse of gold into the house. This furnished the dowry for the eldest daughter, and she was married.

After a little while, says the *Golden Legend*, which is the great medieval story of the saints, after a little while this holy hermit of God "threw in another mass of gold" and that provided a dowry for the second daughter. "And after a few days Nicholas doubled the mass of gold and cast it into the house." So the third daughter was endowed. The happy father, wishing to know his benefactor, ran after Nicholas and recognized him, but the holy man "required him not to tell nor discover this thing as long as he lived."

Thus Nicholas became not only the generous giver but the special patron saint of maidenhood and was so known and celebrated throughout the Middle Ages. Dante speaks in three short lines, as if he assumed that everybody already knew the story, of the generosity of Nicholas to maidens, "to lead their youth to honor." The Italian painters made much of this story. A fine pictorial representation of it is in the Metropolitan Art Museum in New York City. It is one of those dramatic paintings in which the old artists told a really moving tale long before the days of the camera and the moving picture. Inside the house you see the three distressed daughters and the still more dejected and ragged father. Outside is Nicholas climbing up at the door in the act of throwing the purse through a little window.

The story takes what seems an almost humorous turn. Let us imagine three purses or "masses" of gold. We recognize them, in conventional form, in the three gold balls over the pawnbroker's shop. Thus the holy man of the early Christian Church presides symbolically over a business which throughout Europe during the Middle Ages was conducted largely though not exclusively by members of the older Jewish Church. Pawnbroking included all forms of banking and moneylending with personal movable property as security. At first glance it does not seem quite appropriate that the charitable benevolent saint should become associated with a business, long notorious for exaction and usury, which the Mosaic law forbade and which the derivative Christian morality condemned. One of the earliest acts of Christ was the expulsion of moneylenders from the temple; he "overthrew the tables of the money-changers" and scourged forth others who bought and sold.

But it may well be that the bankers and brokers wished to give sanctity and dignity to their business and so adopted the generous Nicholas as their heavenly protector. Every profession, guild, trade, craft, had its favorite saint and was free to choose from the calendar; or, more likely, there was not much deliberate choice, these assimilations of legend to fact simply happened, nobody knows just how. Nicholas was adopted not only by the more or less respectable brokers but by thieves and pirates. The sinner as well as the honest man had his heavenly benefactor. And it is no more strange in the history of mythology that Nicholas should have been invoked by thieves than that the Greek-Roman god Mercury should have been the tutelary deity of robbers and tricksters.

Nicholas was the patron of all who went down to the sea in ships, whether bound on a predatory cruise or a military expedition or an errand of peaceful trade. The distinctions were not always clear in fact or theory. There are many stories of his having rescued sailors from shipwreck. It is written in the Roman Breviary, which is the "official account," that "in his youth on a sea voyage he saved the ship from a fearful storm." Greek and Russian sailors appeal to him for protection and carry in the cabin of the ships an image of the saint with a perpetually burning lamp. It is in accordance with the spirit of Christianity and other religions that a drowning man needs help, no matter what the moral purpose of his voyage through life may have been up to the hour of disaster.

Nicholas, however, was a dispenser of justice, according to the ideas of justice that prevailed when the stories about him grew up and took shape. One curious story of his judgment as patron of moneylending and trade reveals the attitude of those who made the story; it shows the somewhat confused relations between Jew and Gentile, relations familiarized for us by the story of Shylock. The tale is told in the *Golden Legend*, translated by Caxton, the father of English printing and a tireless interpreter of foreign books into our English tongue. I change a little Caxton's words, which are not quite modern in form and construction:

"There was a man who had borrowed of a Jew a sum of money and swore upon the altar of St. Nicholas that he would pay it back, as soon as he could, and gave no other pledge. The man kept the money so long that the Jew demanded payment. And the man said that he had paid. Then the Jew summoned the debtor into court. The debtor brought a hollow staff in which he had put the money in gold. While he was taking oath he gave the staff to the Jew to hold. Then he swore that he had given the Jew more than he owed and asked the Jew to give him back the staff. The Jew, not suspecting the trickery, gave the staff back to the debtor, who took it and went away. Sleep overcame him and he lay down in the road. A cart ran over him and killed him and broke the staff so that the gold rolled out. When the Jew heard this he came and saw the fraud. Many people said to him that he should take the gold. But he refused saying that if the dead man were brought to life again by the power of St. Nicholas, he would take the money and become a Christian. So the dead man arose, and the Jew was christened."

Thus the ends of justice were served and everybody was happy.

The most important role of Nicholas to us at the present time is his patronage of schoolboys, for this brings him close to us as Santy Claus, the bearer of gifts and the special saint of childhood. He was himself the Boy Bishop. A famous story of him is that of his bringing to life three boys. On their way home, the tale runs, the boys stopped at a farmhouse. The farmer and his wife murdered them, cut their bodies in pieces and put them into casks used for pickling meat. St. Nicholas arrived, charged the murderers with their crime and caused the boys to rise from the casks fully restored. That is one reason, so far as there is any reason in fable, why schoolboys celebrated the feast of St. Nicholas on December sixth.

Intimately connected with the feast of Nicholas was the custom of electing a Boy Bishop for a limited number of days extending just over Christmas. To get something of the spirit of this ceremony and celebration we have only to think of a modern game played in New York and other American cities in which a boy is elected mayor for a day with a full staff of subordinate juvenile officials. The motive of the modern custom is to teach youths civic virtue, public service and patriotism. The motive underlying the Boy Bishop was partly religious, partly childish love of pranks and parody, and partly a sort of democratic rebellion, tolerated for a short period each year, against constituted authority.

The Boy Bishop was dressed in handsome robes like a real bishop, and he and his companions led a mock solemn parade and in some cities actually took possession of the churches. There was much feasting, the way to a boy's heart being through his stomach as well as through gaudy garments; and there was on the part of elder participants a good deal of drinking. On the whole it was a charming and innocent affair. The boys took it seriously enough, especially the supper which concluded the performance. As early as the first part of the tenth century Conrad I, king of Germany, described a visit to a monastery when the revels were at their height. He was amused especially by the procession of the children, so grave and sedate that even when Conrad ordered his followers to throw apples down the aisle, the children did not lose their gravity. But these high jinks so near to sacred things met with opposition and censure. Ecclesiastical and civil authority shut down on the Boy Bishops and parades and ceremonies in one country after another. Grown people are not always profoundly wise about either the fooling or the intense seriousness of children. The Roman Catholic Church in the middle of the fifteenth century tried to suppress by edict the Boy Bishop and all the customs relating to him. In England, where this childish festival prevailed not only in the cathedral cities but in the small towns, the Protestant Reformation applied a depressing hand, and Queen Elizabeth, whose own court was gay with revelries, masques, interludes, finally abolished the Boy Bishop.

Childhood, however, has its revenges upon the interfering adult, with the aid of the conniving adult who refuses to grow up. Nicholas remained the saint of children. In some countries his festival was taken over, assimilated to Christmas, partly because St. Nicholas Day is so near to Christmas and partly because in some parts of the world there arose a sort of Protestant hostility to the worship of saints. But custom and amusement prevail even when religion and history are forgotten or ignored. To cite another example as familiar as Christmas, on the evening of the last day of October children bob apples, make pumpkin jack-o'-lanterns, and play all kinds of tricks to pester innocent neighbors. They call the occasion Halloween, but few of them or their neighbors know that "hallow" means saint, and that the first of November is All Saints' Day.

So it is with Nicholas. He is honored and accepted with a kind of childish ignorance. Professor George H. McKnight of Ohio State University, who has given us the best account in English of the good St. Nicholas, begins his book by saying that strangely little is known of him in America. But he belongs to us by a very special inheritance. Our Dutch ancestors in New York—ancestry is a matter of tradition, not of blood—brought St. Nicholas over to New Amsterdam. The English colonists borrowed him from their Dutch neighbors. The Dutch form is San Nicolaas. If we say that rather fast with a stress on the broad double-A of the last syllable, a D or a T slips in after the N and we get "Sandyclaus" or "Santy Claus." And our American children are probably the only ones in the world who say it just that way; indeed the learned, and very British, *Encyclopaedia Britannica* calls our familiar form "an American corruption" of the Dutch. I suspect, however, that we should hear something very like it from the lips of children in Holland and Germany; in parts of southern Germany the word in sound, and I think in spelling, is "Santiklos."

However that may be, America owes the cheery saint of Christmas to Holland and Germany. In Belgium and Holland the festival of the saint is still observed on his birthday, December sixth, and the jollities and excitements are much the same as those that we enjoy at Christmas, with some charming local variations. Saint Nicholas is not the merry fellow with a chubby face and twinkling eye, but retains the gravity appropriate to a venerable bishop. He rides a horse or an ass instead of driving a team of reindeer. He leaves his gifts in stockings, shoes or baskets. And for children who have been very naughty, and whose parents cannot give him a good account of them, he leaves a rod by way of admonition, for he is a highly moral saint, though kind and forgiving. If the parents are too poor to buy gifts, the children say ruefully that the saint's horse has glass legs and has fallen down and broken his foot. The horse or ass of St. Nicholas is not forgotten; the children leave a wisp of hay for him, and in the morning it is gone.

As with us, the older people have their own festivities, suppers, exchange of gifts, surprises. But also as with our Christmas, the feast of Nicholas is primarily a day for children.

Where did Santy Claus get his reindeer? And how did the grave saint become that gnomelike fat fellow, with nothing ecclesiastic about him, so vividly described in Clement Moore's famous poem, " 'Twas the night before Christmas"? The answers to these questions are only provisional, matters of conjecture.

Notice that in Moore's poem, the form Santy Claus does not appear. The title of the poem is "A Visit from St. Nicholas," and in the verses the visitor is St. Nicholas and "Saint Nick." The verses were written in the first half of the last century. The author was a distinguished Biblical scholar and professor in the General Theological Seminary in New York. In these verses he was writing not as a scholar but as a jolly human being, the father of a family taking a day off from his serious studies. His verses must represent the idea of Santy Claus that prevailed in his time, and long before his time in New York and far outside New York, for they spread all over the country, are still reprinted every year.

Now in this delightful jingling poem there is not a touch of religion. The "jolly old elf" has not the slightest resemblance to a reverend saint. And there is no suggestion, except in the word Christmas, of any connection in thought or spirit with what is, excepting possibly Easter, the most sacred day in the whole Christian year. And similarly we may observe in our time many a gay Christmas party run its course without any of the participants giving a thought to a birth in a manger from which our year is dated. So Santy Claus is strangely different from his pious namesake and also in some places and among some people estranged from the very religious occasion to which he is attached!

But in some parts of America where the people are of Dutch or German descent there is a charming alliance between Santy Claus and the Christ child. It came about in this way: In some parts of Germany after the feast of St. Nicholas had been moved forward and identified with Christmas it was felt that the real patron of the day, the true giver of gifts, should be Christ Himself. This feeling probably arose from the Protestant objection to the worship of saints. So St. Nicholas was deposed from power; gradually, not by any sudden revolution, he disappeared in some places, from the customs long associated with him. But the customs remained. On Christmas Eve there were gifts of sweets and toys for good children. Or they put bowls in the window, and behold, in the morning they found that the windowpane had been taken out during the night and gifts laid in the bowls. The bringer of these gifts was not St. Nicholas but the Christ child, in popular German, Kriss Kringle.

The True Story of Santy Claus

But among the German people in America the legend of Santy Claus still survived, and so Kriss Kringle is a combination of Santy Claus and the Christ child.

This combination gives us an inkling of what happened in the whole story of Christmas from earliest times. Santy Claus, the merry elf, is not Christian at all, but pagan, coming down from times earlier than the Christian Era or at least earlier than the times when the Teutonic people were Christianized. He belongs to popular fairyland, the land of elves, gnomes, sprites, hobgoblins. In countless fairy tales there are good spirits and evil spirits. The evil spirits haunt the woods and molest innocent people. The good spirits aid the poor, bring gifts in the night, rescue princes in distress and so on.

These stories are not originally of Christian origin. They may not be definitely part of any of the religions which Christianity supplanted. Associated with them are popular festivals and ceremonies. It may well be that the apples in our Christmas stockings are the descendants of apples that grew on very old trees, trees older than history; perhaps there was a late harvest festival, or a kind of pagan Thanksgiving, presided over by a beneficent elf, and accompanied by dancing and feasting. We do not know.

But we do know that as Christianity developed, the Church encouraged all the popular customs, or many of them, took them over and associated them with Christian holidays. This may have been a deliberate attempt of the priests to win the favor of the people and make the new religion really popular, or the people may have made the transfer themselves by the vague and untraceable but very real process of folk poetry.

Now where did Santy Claus get his reindeer? There are no reindeer in Germany and probably never were, certainly not the kind that are broken to harness like horses. And oddly enough the reindeer does not appear in any of the surviving Christmas legends and customs in old Germany. The reindeer first paws the roofs of American houses. But of course he cannot be an American animal. The explanation, one explanation, is this:

There are reindeer in northern Scandinavia where they have been domesticated from time immemorial. Scandinavian and German legend and mythology are closely related. The old German gods came from the north and many German folk tales are of Scandinavian origin. The reindeer of our Santy Claus certainly came from Lapland, and Santy is an arctic explorer, exploring the other way! Dr. Moore, with true poetic imagination, describes him as "dressed all in fur, from his head to his foot"—not in the red flannel with which we are accustomed to clothe him. Among the Germans or Dutch who came to this country there must have been a legend of a Scandinavian Santy, and in Germany the reindeer inexplicably got lost. Perhaps their bones will be found in a German forest by one of the literary archaeologists who dig into such matters. But no, the bones will never be found, for the reindeer are still alive and fly over the housetops.

The career of Santy Claus through the ages is as mysterious as his annual flight. One might suppose that he would have gone directly from Germany or Holland to their near neighbor England, as the Christmas tree was transplanted to England after the shortest possible journey. But there is every likelihood that Santy Claus, having become a good American colonist, recrossed the Atlantic in an English ship—or perhaps as the first transatlantic flier. He has long been a well-established figure in the Christmas customs not only of the mother country but in all parts of the British Empire. The allegiance of English children, however, is divided. Some believe that Santy Claus brings them their presents. Others believe in Father Christmas, a more recent creation, whom English artists represent as an old gentleman in what seems to be a sort of eighteenth-century costume with gaitered legs, a tail coat and a squarish beaver hat.

It is rather strange that English Christmas customs are not more closely imitated by American. We know nothing of the yule log, even in houses that have open fireplaces. Perhaps the reason that we borrowed little from the English Christmas is that the English who came to America, especially to New England, were not of the merrymaking kind; they would have abhorred the idea of making Christmas an occasion for mirth and happiness. They would have groaned at one pretty custom, which is inherited directly from England and which their less godly descendants indulge in on Beacon Hill in Boston—the singing of carols in the streets on Christmas Eve. In all New England literature of the classical period there is scarcely a reference in prose or verse to Christmas, and that was the time when Dickens and Thackeray and other English writers, eagerly read in America, were giving the holiday new spirit and brightness in England.

Customs differ in different countries. A Russian coming from the country of which Nicholas is the chief saint would not at first sight understand our Santy Claus. He would see no relation between his saint before whose icon he bows and the figure in a red suit with a long white beard standing in front of a department store and doing his bit to keep a spirit of good cheer in that enormous American institution—Christmas trade. An American tourist brought up as a Protestant finding himself in an Italian city would look up in his guidebook an ornate Italian painting of St. Nicholas miraculously answering a prayer for help, and that tourist unless he had historical imagination might not realize the connection between this beautiful painting, the angel on his last Christmas tree at home and the letter that he wrote as a boy asking Santy Claus to bring him a new sled.

Yet these connections do exist, and they are very important, for they are bonds that hold the world together and help to give its disparate parts and antagonistic faiths a human unification. No other saint and few other men embrace such a wide variety of benevolent ideas as Nicholas, with such duration in time and such extent throughout the Christian world. And he is probably the only serious figure in religious history in any way associated with humor, with the spirit of fun. For he is the patron of giving. And it is fun to give.

CONINGSBY DAWSON

When Father Christmas Was Young

SOMEONE had hinted that there wasn't a Santa Claus. If there wasn't, who brought Christmas presents? For weeks, when Mac had been put to bed and was supposed to be asleep, he had lain awake puzzling. He had reached the point at which suspense ached like a guilty conscience. He simply had to share his secret with a wiser person.

He had postponed and postponed till at last it was Christmas Eve. All day Daddy had been finishing a story. Daddy could be so inconvenient. When he was finishing a story, he turned the key in his lock and everybody went on tiptoe.

Mac had returned from his afternoon's walk with Nannie. Streets and stores had been gay with excited preparations. To make things perfect, snow was falling. Mac had prayed for snow. He'd set himself a task, which was nothing less than to prove that Santa Claus existed. If there was snow on housetops, it would be impossible for old Santa to tether his reindeer to chimneys without leaving tracks.

And now to take Daddy into his confidence. Having escaped from the nursery, he twisted the handle of the study door. It wasn't locked. An instant later a jolly voice invited him to enter. Across the threshold he halted, his fat legs astride, a worried expression on his cherubic countenance.

"I've been thinking, Daddy."

"You don't say, old son! Climb on my knee and tell me."

The red lacquer room with the fire shining afforded a friendly setting. Yet Mac couldn't blurt out the wicked heresy he had overheard. Instead he cuddled against the smoky jacket and asked:

"Who was Santa when he was young? He's terribly old now, but he must have been little as me once. Who taught him to be fond of reindeer and to come down chimbleys and to leave presents? Was he the first to do things like that or did he have a mummy and daddy who did them before him?"

His father filled and lit a pipe. He was playing for time. He hated to disappoint his son; he hated still more to deceive him. He said:

"I'm afraid you'll consider me a most ignorant parent. I don't know the answer to a single one of your questions. I ought to. I've no excuse. With your help, I propose to educate myself. Do you see all those books—the tall ones? They're books of reference, which means that they can answer anything. All you have to do is to open them and turn to the word 'potato,' for instance; every fact about a potato is recorded. Let's make a game of it and go on a hunt. . . . What shall we look for?" Daddy prompted.

"Santa Claus."

Daddy ran his eyes along the shelves.

" 'Who's Who in America.' We shan't find him mentioned there; he's international. Let's try the encyclopedia."

But the encyclopedia proved stodgy. As soon as you'd hit on

what you thought you wanted, it referred you to another volume. Having looked up Santa Claus, you were at once informed that you ought to have looked up Saint Nicholas. When you looked up Saint Nicholas you were told that he had lived in a funny place called Myra in Lycia. In fact he'd been a bishop who had been tortured to death. He had gained the reputation of being fond of children. In England alone four hundred churches had been dedicated to his memory, each of them containing a stained-glass window representing him pulling three little boys out of a tub.

"That's silly, Daddy. Why a tub?"

"Goodness knows. But listen, Doodles; this is interesting. He's the Russian Santa Claus and the greatest saint in Russia; that brings him close to reindeer. Reindeer live up north in Lapland. And here's something else; after he'd been dead for hundreds of years, some people from another city stole his bones, made a huge procession and built an enormous church over him. After which all the world started to make pilgrimages to his sepulcher. He worked miracles, especially for children."

"Go on, Daddy. Read more."

"It ends there." Daddy frowned. "Darn the idiots; they always dry up when you're hoping to learn something. Tell you what—the last volume is an index; we'll look up Christmas."

The items recorded about Christmas were even more confusing. The origin of the yule log was traced and the prerogatives of the Lord of Misrule. In olden days, it appeared, the Lord of Misrule— a sort of clown—was appointed to direct the Christmas festivities. He was king for a day, who did whatever he pleased while the season lasted. In still older days he'd been the king of the Roman Saturnalia and had been killed at the end of the revels for having made himself a nuisance.

"Very enlightening!" Daddy banged the volume back on its shelf. "That helps a lot."

Taking down another volume he struck luck and grew good-humored. He had run across the name Befana.

"By Jove, that's a new one!"

The little boy peered above his shoulder. The words were too long for him to spell.

"Is it about reindeer, Daddy?"

"It isn't. It's about stockings. According to what's printed here, this Befana was a fairy. The Three Wise Men on their journey to Bethlehem passed by her cottage. She was too busy or too disagreeable to look out of her window—said she'd see them when they came back. Of course they didn't come back, on account of Herod. Her punishment was to gaze in vain from her window for them always."

"Is she still gazing, Dad?"

"I expect so. But that's not all. She was given a second punishment; on the anniversary of the night when she'd been too busy to see the Wise Men pass, she was ordered to fill children's stockings. But the angel who ordered her punishment was careless. What he'd meant was that she must fill children's stockings with presents. He didn't say with presents; he forgot. As she was spiteful, what do you suppose she did? She filled the children's stockings with ashes."

"She doesn't now. I never found no ashes in my stocking," Mac objected.

"Neither did I," Daddy agreed. "Something that these stupid books don't relate must have happened."

"Then look up stockings," Mac suggested. "We'll find the rest of the story."

"Afraid not." Daddy shoved the books back on the shelves disgustedly. "The trouble with the fellows who write all this learned rot is that they aren't poets. If we're going to discover the truth about when Father Christmas was young, we'll have to make it up."

"Are we poets?" The little boy blushed at the compliment.

"You bet—at least you are. All children are poets—they're much wiser than these encyclopedia fellows. We believe in Santa Claus, you and I, Doodles; they don't and didn't. They were like Befana, who might have ridden with the Wise Men to Bethlehem if only she hadn't been too busy to have faith."

"Can't one be busy if one has faith?" the little boy inquired.

"Not often. Being busy kills faith, as a rule. I've been busy lately —too busy. That's why I'm appealing to you. You're not busy because you're young. That's the reason you ought to believe in almost everything. If you try, I'm certain you can tell me about Santa's boyhood."

They shifted the lamp, so that it spilled a pool of illumination over the deep armchair. Minutes ticked by. They sat as though merged into one.

"I'm waiting," Daddy urged.

"Don't know where to start."

"That's obvious—with Befana. She lived in a forest so dark that she hardly ever saw the sun. A highroad ran through it along which camels plodded with their tinkling bells. You see, even I know that."

"I know more." Mac wagged a finger, imitating one of his father's gestures.

"Then, for the love of Mike, prove it."

"Befana was like you, Daddy, when you're finishing a story; she was cross, but she wasn't bad."

"Is that so?" Daddy chuckled. "Thanks for your frankness."

"Yes, that's so, Daddy. If she wasn't finishing something, she was hurrying to begin something."

"What sort of things, Doodles?"

"Don't 'zactly know. But yes, I do," Mac corrected himself. "She was a writer of fairy stories. She lived in the dark forest 'cause she simply had to be quiet, same as you lock your door. She never could find time to do her housework, so she was very glad one morning when she opened her door and saw Santa on her step."

"What on earth was he doing there?"

"He wasn't doing nuffing; he'd been left. Someone passing with the camels had dropped him. He was as tiny as a doll. He couldn't even talk and the bottle beside him was empty. Befana took him in and stared. She twiddled his toes, and he laughed. She thought, 'He's an orphling. I can keep him. I'll learn him to do my housework.'"

"Teach, Mackie—not learn."

216

"All right, teach," Mac conceded, "but it don't make no difference. Not till evening, when she was putting him to bed, did she learn what he was called. A piece of paper had been pinned to his frock with 'Nick' written on it. That was what he was called first; the Santa name came after."

"Did he have a beard?" Daddy questioned.

"Course not; nor no hair. He was a baby." Mac cuddled closer. "Befana washed his bottles and pushed his pram through the forest. She was sorry for him, but he was an awful bother."

"I'm surprised to hear that she was sorry for him," Daddy attempted to guide the story. "A fairy who could be so cruel as to put ashes into children's stockings——"

"But listen," Mac seized his father's chin. "She wasn't married. She didn't know about chillen; she spoiled him and upset his stomick. She let him sit up late, the way you let me on Christmas. She did it every night and she gave him candies before breakfast."

"Extremely foolish!" Daddy looked shocked. "Why did she?"

"To keep him quiet so she could do her fairy stories. As he growed bigger, he learned to talk. She couldn't write when people talked. To get rid of him, she ordered him to do all the housework, which was hard for a little boy. And he cooked the meals and he swept and dusted."

"Befana must have been a great lazy lump," Daddy interrupted. "Didn't she help him?"

"She was always writing. Jack-and-the-Beanstalk was one of hers. So was Cinderella. Oh, almost all of them."

"I believe you are inventing." Daddy squinted down his nose.

"Trufe and honor I'm not," Mac asserted. "Her fingers was inky. Nick would call to her to come and play. She would shake her head. He was most awful lonely. When he'd dusted the cottage, he'd go out and sit by the road to watch the camels pass. He would wonder where the camels were going and wish he could follow them. Sometimes he'd wonder whether they was driven by people what had dropped him. He was about as big as me, when one day coming terrible fast——"

"How fast would you say, Mackie?"

"As fast as when we ride in a taxi. They was three racing camels, each with a man sitting on him. The men wore crowns and was all dressed up. He knowed they must be kings. A great white star floated over them just above the branches. It made the forest, which was always dark, quite bright. Nacherly he guessed something wonderful was going to happen."

"Naturally," Daddy nodded.

"Well, little Nick, who was no bigger than me, thought they were going to rush past him. But they saw him in time and they pulled up.

" 'Little boy,' one of them asked, 'where is Bethlehem?' "

"He said more than that." Daddy wished to be helpful. "He said, 'Where is He that is born King of the Jews? For we have seen His star in the East and are come to worship Him.' "

"P'raps he did," Mac grudgingly agreed. "Nick was so little he'd never heard of Bethlehem. He asked the Wise Men to wait a minute while he runned in and asked Aunt Befana. He was breathless with climbing the stairs to her study. The door was locked. When he tapped, she didn't answer. Then he started to explain, the way I do to you, Daddy, through the keyhole.

" 'Go 'way,' she grunted.

"The Wise Men was in a hurry, so Nick didn't dare stop longer. He had to go back and say that Aunt Befana was too busy even to answer their question.

"They rode away very sad, the star sailing over them. Soon the forest growed dark, like it always was.

"That night at supper Nick told Aunt Befana how they'd rode on racing camels, wearing crowns, so that he was sure they was kings.

" 'Kings don't wear crowns when they ride camels. You're fibbing,' she said.

"She didn't want to believe that he was telling the trufe, so she spanked him.

"Next day she couldn't write fairy tales for fancying what she'd

218

missed. She'd never seen three kings all together. She made Nick come to her study and promised not to spank him if he'd tell her over again what had happened."

"But you're forgetting, Mackie." Daddy caressed the bare knees. "I didn't halt you before because I hoped you might remember. Two of the kings were old; but the third was young. The young one had told Nick why they were in such a hurry to reach Bethlehem. A baby was to be born who would be King of all the world. When He grew up He would be King, especially of children. He would take them in His arms and play with them. Nick had never been properly loved and he'd never been played with at all. He wished he'd been born later, so he could have played with the King of children. As it was, he'd be a man by the time the King was grown up, so he'd be too big for the King to take him in His arms. Most of this he said to Befana. The more he talked about the Wise Men, the more sorry she became that she hadn't taken the time off to see them.

" 'But I haven't missed much,' she pretended; 'they'll be coming back.'

"As you know, Doodles, they didn't."

" 'Cause of Herod."

"Precisely. They were warned in a dream that Herod would seek the child to slay Him, so they went back to the East secretly by a different route."

"But Befana didn't know they'd been warned." Mac seized the telling of the story. "Every day she sat by her study window watching. She hid behind her curtains ashamed, so Nick wouldn't see her and would think she was writing. And, Daddy, I forgot to tell you. She kept the table spread for five instead of two. You see why, don't you?"

"So as to be ready to invite the Three Kings to eat a meal with her, whatever hour they returned," Daddy conjectured. "Do you know that's very interesting? People still do it in Russia. They bake King's Cake and put it outside the door on Christmas Eve to let the Three Kings know they're welcome."

"Befana did the same," Mac nodded like a turtle. "She called it King's Cake, too. But don't you think, Daddy, that you could tell a little of the story?"

"With pleasure." Daddy stroked the narrow shoulders. "As the news began to spread about the wonder-child who had been born at Bethlehem she regretted everything most dreadfully. One day when she was watching the road she saw a man who looked like a man yet wasn't, approaching through the forest. She saw him stop little Nick to pat his head; the next moment he was tapping at her cottage."

"He wore wings, didn't he, Daddy?"

"He may have."

"But if he wore wings, Daddy, even though his coat was over them, they'd be humpy."

"I expect they were; but the humps aren't important. The important thing is that he'd been sent to punish her. Long after the angel had gone away, she stayed locked up in her study. When she came down to supper, little Nick could see by the redness of her eyes that she'd been crying. Of course you and I know what the angel had told her: that she must watch forever for the Wise Men and that once a year she must fill children's stockings."

"But why had she been crying, Daddy?"

"Because as long as she lived she'd never have time to write any more fairy stories. Don't forget, Mackie, that till now she'd been a most distinguished authoress. Little Nick didn't know why she'd been crying and he didn't dare ask. The first hint he got was next morning. Having swept out the fireplace, he was throwing away the ashes.

" 'Don't do that,' she snapped. 'Take them back. We're going to save them.'

"Overnight she'd been thinking hard with what she was to fill the children's stockings; she'd decided on ashes. According to you, when first she saw Nick on her doorstep she was rather sorry for him. She wasn't any longer. She grew crankier and crankier. Because of her punishment, she grew to hate children. Little Nick was the child who came handiest; she was perfectly horrid to him. She kept him always working at dirty jobs. She complained of the meals he prepared for her and, because he was dirty, refused to sit down with him."

"As it came near Christmas," Mac took up the running, "she growed nervouser and nervouser. She'd been counting her ashes and was certain there wasn't enough to fill all the stockings. So what did she do? She thought of soot. There wasn't much difference between soot and ashes. She made poor Nick climb her chimbley to shake the soot down."

"You're probably correct," Daddy said, "but it doesn't sound sensible."

"It wasn't." Mac clapped his hands gleefully. "It wasn't his fault. Befana made him. That was how he learned the habit. When he was young he climbed up them; now he's old he climbs down them."

"I see," Daddy smiled, "at what you're driving."

"When the first Christmas Eve came round after the Wise Men had passed," Mac continued, "Nick was awful tired. All day he'd been tying up ashes in sacks. About four o'clock in the afternoon Befana surprised him. She said she'd be gone for the whole night and he must hang up his stocking. He asked why his stocking; she told him that next morning if he looked in it, he'd find something. So he went to bed early and closed his eyes tight. He was so 'cited he wanted morning to come quicker. He thought his Aunt Befana had gone to town to buy a wonderful present."

"And instead, when he woke and looked in his stocking, Doodles, we know what he found. It was cruel of her."

"And there she was back for breakfast, as though nothing had happened, Daddy, and all the sacks was disappeared."

"How had she carried them?"

"She was a fairy. By magic. Every Christmas after that she always did the same and Nick was always hoping that instead of ashes he'd find a present."

"He never did, of course?"

Mac shook his head dolefully.

"That's why he's kind to boys and girls. He remembers how sad he was. When he growed up, he ran away from Befana and became a saint for chillen. He washed them."

Again his father was astounded.

"Washed them! Who told you that?"

"Those tall books; they said there was hundreds of churches with picture windows, showing Santa pulling three little boys out of a tub. He was washing them, 'cause when he was young, he'd hated to be dirty. That was how he got killed and became a saint, 'cause people was so angry with him for washing their chillen. He never asked if he might; he just did it."

"Perhaps there's another mystery you can clear up." Daddy rubbed his chin thoughtfully. "Being a saint through having been martyred, he went straight to Heaven. On earth for many years he was forgotten. Then the people from another town stole his body, honored him by building a huge church over him and were rewarded by finding that his tomb worked miracles. According to the encyclopedia, the miracles started pilgrimages. Sick little children were brought to touch his tomb and were instantly cured. Now, as everybody knows, the sickness children usually have is the tummy-ache. Why should he have been so good at curing that?"

The reply came promptly.

" 'Cause he'd always had a tummy-ache himself. He sat up too late—I've told you that—and Befana, knowing nuffin' about chillen, allowed him to eat candy before breakfast."

"Your explanation sounds reasonable, Doodles. But for the life of me I don't see how our story goes on."

"It's only begun, Daddy. Santa wasn't happy in Heaven. 'Cause why? 'Cause he kept on thinking how Befana was still filling chillen's stockings with ashes. He went to God and told him how miser'ble he'd been every Christmas morning when he'd been little. He said: ' 'Tisn't right to be miser'ble Christmas morning. Chillen will always be miser'ble so long as they find ashes. If no one else wants to do it, I'm going to give them presents.' "

"And God thought the idea splendid." Daddy's tone was delighted. "In order that Santa might get to all the stockings before Befana filled them with ashes, he lent him the Three Wise Men's camels. They were racing camels."

"But he uses reindeer, Daddy."

"So he docs." Daddy hung his head.

"You're right." The little boy took compassion on his father. "At first he did use camels. On earth he'd lived in hot countries. Everyone did in those days. It was nacheral for him to choose camels. But presently the world growed larger. People went to live in cold places like Russia. The camels weren't so good on snow."

"Excuse my interrupting." Daddy's recent blunder had made him humble. "It's a fact this that you're telling me. Russian children still believe that Christmas presents are brought on camels. They believe that the Three Wise Men ride out from the East every Christmas Eve just as they did when they sought the Christ child——"

"They don't now," the little boy broke in hurriedly. "Santa doesn't deliver presents that way any longer. Camels wasn't quick on ice. One Christmas in Lapland he got stuck. 'Never again,' he said, and changed to reindeer."

"I think he was very wise," Daddy nodded gravely. "A camel's such a big animal to go prancing over roofs and chimneys."

"And that was why, too, Daddy. So now we know, don't we?"

"You know everything, Doodles. Poets do. You're a poet."

Suddenly Mackie hugged his father, crushing his face against the smoky jacket.

"Somebody told me," he almost sobbed; "somebody said there wasn't no Santa Claus."

"But there is. That's ridiculous. If there isn't a Santa Claus, how did he get into the encyclopedia? Encyclopedias print nothing but facts. They do really, I assure you, Doodles. Everything we've found out about Santa Claus's boyhood is set down there in those large volumes. All about Befana. All about the ashes in stockings. All about——"

A tear-stained face glanced up.

223

"Then tomorrow let's prove it. Promise?"

"If you know how to prove it, Doodles, I promise."

A tap fell on the study door. Nannie's voice was heard announcing that Mac's bath was ready.

"Don't come in. One minute," Daddy implored. He bent over his little boy. "I promise. But how to prove it?"

The child's voice sank to a whisper.

"It's snowing. Tomorrow we'll go on the roof. If Santa truly *is*, we'll find marks of reindeer and sleigh runners."

Daddy had promised—and a promise is a promise.

Next morning after breakfast—Christmas morning—having evaded Mummy and Nannie, father and son climbed the stairs to the attic, placed a ladder against the trap door solemnly and peered out. Not a sign of a reindeer's hoof or a sleigh runner.

"But he's been, 'cause he's left the presents," Mackie whispered. For a moment he looked worried; then his expression cleared. "How silly of us, Daddy! They wouldn't be here. We'll have to wait till next Christmas. A new lot of snow has fallen."

So it had. Even in the many streets, which could be seen from so high up, there was scarcely a track noticeable.

Mummy's voice calling:

"What on earth are you two lunatics doing, catching cold up there?"

Daddy closed the trap hurriedly. As they scuttled down the ladder he whispered, "You're right again, Doodles. The new snow has fooled us. If you're still a poet, we'll try again next Christmas."

JAMES LANE ALLEN

The Realm of Midnight

A QUARTER of a century ago or more the German Christmas Tree—the diffusion of which throughout the world was begun soon after the close of the Napoleonic wars— had not made its way into general use throughout the rural districts of central Kentucky. The older Dutch and English festivals which had blended their features into the American holiday was the current form celebrated in bluegrass homes. The German forest idea had been adopted in the towns for churches and other public festivities and in private houses also that were in the van of the world movement. But out in the country the evergreen had not yet enriched the great winter drama of Nature with its fresh note of the immortal drawn from a dead world: the evergreen was to eyes there the evergreen still, as the primrose to other eyes had been the primrose and nothing more.

From *The Doctor's Christmas Eve* by James Lane Allen. By permission of The Macmillan Company, publishers.

Thus there was no Christmas Tree; and Christmas Eve brought no joy to children except that of waiting for Christmas morning. Not until they went to sleep or feigned slumber; not until fires died down in chimney corners where socks and stockings hung from a mantelpiece or from the backs of maternal and paternal chairs—not till then did the Sleigh of the White World draw near across the landscape of darkness. Out of its realm of silence and snow it was suddenly there!—outside the house, laden with gifts, drawn by tireless reindeer and driven by its indefatigable forest god. He was no longer young, the driver, as was shown in his case, quite as it is shown in the case of commoner men, by his white beard and round ruddy middle-aged face; but his twinkling eyes and fresh good humor showed that the core of him was still boyish; and apparently the one great lesson he had learned from half a lifetime was that the best service he could render the whole world consisted in giving it one night of innocent happiness and kindness. Not until well on toward midnight was he there at the house, without sound or signal, the Sleigh perhaps halted at the front gate or drawn up behind aged cedar trees in the yard; or for all that anyone knew to the contrary, resting lightly on the roof of the house itself, or remaining poised up in the air.

At least on the roof he was: he peeked down the chimney to see whether the fire were out (and he never by any mistake went to the wrong chimney); then he scrambled hurriedly down. If any children were in bed in the room, he tickled the soles of their feet to prove if they were asleep; then crammed socks and stockings; dispersed other gifts around on the tops of furniture; left his smile on everything to last a year—the smile of old forgiveness and of new affection—and was up the chimney again—back in the Sleigh—gone! Gone to the next house, then to the next, and on from house to house over the neighborhood, over the nation, over the world: the first to operate without accidental breakdown the heavier-than-air machine, unless it were possibly a remote American kinswoman of his, the New England witch on her broomstick airplane; which, however, she was never able to travel on outside New England. In this belting of the globe with a sleigh in a single night he must often have come to rivers and mountain ranges where passage was impossible; and then it is certain that the Sleigh was driven up to the roadway of the clouds and traveled across the lonely stretches of the snow before it fell.

Why he should come near midnight—who ever asked such a question? Has not that hour always been the natural locality and resort for the supernatural? What things merry or sorry could ever have come to pass but for the stroke of midnight? How could Shakespeare have written certain dramas without the mere aid of twelve o'clock? What considerable part of English literature would drop out of existence but for the fact that Big Ben struck twelve!

The children stood at the head of the stairs; and the Great Night which was to climb so high began for them low down—with the furniture. Standing there, they listened for the sound of any movement in the house: there was none, and they began to descend. Stairways in homesteads built as solid as that did not give way with any creaking of timbers under the pressure of feet, and they were thickly carpeted. Halfway down the children leaned over the banisters and listened again.

Here at the turning of the stairway, directly below, there lived in his pointed weather house the old Time Sentinel of the family, who with his one remaining arm saluted evermore backward and forward in front of his stiff form; and at every swing of this limb you could hear his muscle crack in his ancient shoulder joint. A metallic salute which the children had been accustomed to all their lives was one of the only two sounds that now reached them.

The other sound came from near him: sitting on the hall carpet on a square rug of tin especially provided for her was the winter companion of the timepiece—a large, round, mica-plated, anthracite stove—middle-aged, designing and corpulent. This seeming stove, whose puffed, flushed cheeks now reflected an unusual excitement, gave out little comfortable wooing sounds, all confidential and traveling in a soft volley toward the sentinel, backed gaunt and taciturn against the wall.

The children of the house had long ago named this pair the Cornered Soldier and the Marrying Stove; and they explained the positions of the two as indicating that the stove had backed the veteran into the corner and had sat largely down before him with the determination to remain there until she had warmed him up to the proper response. The veteran however devoted his existence to moving his arm back and forth to ward off her infatuation, and meanwhile he persisted in muttering in his loudest possible monotone: Go away—keep off! Go away—keep off! Go away—keep off! There were seasons of course when the stove became less ardent, for even with the fiber of iron such pursuits must relax sometimes; but the veteran never permitted his arm to stop waving, trusting her least when she was cold—rightly enough!

At the foot of the stairway they encountered a pair of objects that were genuinely alive. Two aged setters with gentle eyes and gentle ears and gentle dispositions rose from where they lay near the stove, came around, and, putting their feet on the lowest step, stretched themselves backward with a low bow, and then, leaning forward with softly wagging tails, they pushed their noses against the two children of the house, inquiring why they were out of bed at that unheard-of hour; they offered their services. But being shoved aside, they returned to their places and threw themselves down again—not curled inward with chilliness, but flat on the side with noses pointed outward: they were not wholly reassured, and the ear of one was thrown half back, leaving the auditory channel uncurtained; they had no fear, but they felt solicitude.

The children made their way on tiptoe along the hall toward the door of the library. Having paused there and listened, they entered and groped their way to the far end where the doors connected this room with the parlor. As they strained their ears against these barriers, low sounds reached them from the other side: smothered laughter; the noise of things being taken out of papers; the sound of feet moving on a stepladder; the sagging of a laden bough as it touched other laden boughs. Through the keyhole there streamed into the darkness of the library a little shaft of light.

"They are in there! There is a light in the room! They're hanging the presents on! We've caught them!"

The leader of the group was about to insert the key when suddenly upon the intense stillness there broke a sound; and following upon that sound what a chorus of noises!

For at that moment the old house sentinel struck twelve—the Christmas-Night Twelve. The children had never heard such startling strokes—for the natural reason that never before had they been awake and alone at that hour. As those twelve loud clear chimes rang out, the two other guardians of the house drowsing by the clock, apprehensive after all regarding the children straying about in the darkness—these expressed their uneasiness by a few low gruff barks, and one followed with a long questioning howl—a real Christmas ululation! Then out in the henhouse a superannuated rooster drew his long-barreled single-shooter out of its feather and leather case, cocked it and fired a volley point-blank at the rafters: the sound seemed made up of drowsiness, a sore throat, general gallantry, and a notice that he kept an eye on the sun even when he had no idea where it was—the early Christmas clarion! Farther away in the barn a motherly cow, kept awake by the swayings and totterings of an infant calf apparently intoxicated on new milk, stood up on her hind feet and then on her fore feet and mooed—quite a Christmas moo! In a near-by stall an aged horse who now seemed to recognize what was expected of him on the occasion struggled to his fore feet and then to his hind feet, and squaring himself nickered— his best Christmas nicker! Under some straw in a shed a litter of pigs, disposed with heads and tails as is the packing of sardines— except that for the sardines the oil is poured on the general outside, but for the pigs it still remained on the individual inside—these pigs slept on—the proper Christmas indifference! For there had never been any holy art for them; nor miracles of their manger; they had merely been good enough to be eaten, never good enough to be painted! They slept on while they could!—mindful of the peril of ancestral boar's head and of the modern peril of brains for break-fast and sausage for supper. Then on the hearthstone of the library itself not far from where the children were huddled the American mouse which is always found there on Christmas Eve—this mouse, coming out and seeing the children, shrieked and scampered—a fine Christmas shriek! Whereat on the opposite side of the hearth a cricket stopped chirping and dodged over the edge of the brick—a clever Christmas dodge!

All these leaving what a stillness!

As noiselessly as possible the key was now inserted, the lock turned, and the door thrown quickly open; and there on the thresh-old of the forbidden room, the children gasped—baffled—gazing into total darkness! The coals of mystery forever glow even under the ashes in the human soul; and these coals now sent up in faint wavering flashes of a burnt-out faith: they were like the strange, delicate, wavering, northern lights above a frozen horizon: after all—in the darkness—amid the hush of the house—at the hour of midnight—with the perfume of wonderful things wafted thickly to their sense—after all, was there not some truth in the Legend?

Then out of that perfumed darkness a voice sounded: "Come in if you wish to come in!"

And the voice was wonderful, big, deep, merry, kind—as though it had but one meaning, the love of the earth's children; it betokened almighty justice and impartiality to children. And it betrayed no surprise or resentment at being intruded upon. After a while it invited more persuasively: "Come in if you wish to come in."

And this time it seemed not so much to proceed from near the Tree as to emanate from the Tree itself—to be the Tree speaking!

The children of the house at once understood that the nature of their irruption had shifted. Their father in that disguised voice was issuing instructions that they were not to dare question the ancient Christmas rites of the house, nor attack his sacred office in them. For this hour he was still to be the Santa Claus of childish faith. Since they did not believe, they must make believe! The scene had instantly been turned into a house miracle drama, and they were as in a theater; and they were to witness a play! And the voice did not hesitate an instant in its exaction of obedience, but at once entered upon the role of a supernatural personage:

"Was I mistaken? Were not children heard whispering on the other side of a door, and was not the door unlocked and thrown open? They must be there! If they are gone, I am sorry. If they are still there—you children! I'm glad to see you. Though of course I don't see you!"

"We're glad to see you—though we don't see you!"

"You came just in time. I was about going. What delayed me—but strange things have happened tonight! As I drove up to this house, suddenly the life seemed to go out of me. It was never so before. And as I stepped out of the Sleigh, I felt weary and old. And the moment I left the reins on the dashboard, my reindeer, which were trembling with fright of a new kind, fled with the Sleigh. And now I am left without knowing when and how I shall get away. But on a night like this wonderful things happen; and I may get some signal from them. A frightened horse will run away from its dismounted master and then come back to him. And they may come for me. I may get a signal. I shall wait. But as I said, I feel strangely lifeless; and I think I shall sit down. Will you sit down, please? Where you are, since you cannot see any chairs," he said with the sweetest gaiety.

In the darkness there were the sounds of laughing delighted children, grouping themselves on the floor.

"Now," said the voice, "I think I'll come around to your side of the Tree so that there'll be nothing between us!"

He was coming—coming as the white-haired Winter God, Forest Spirit, of the earth's children! They heard him advance around from behind the Tree, moving to the right; and one of them who possessed the most sensitive hearing felt sure that another personage advanced more softly around from behind the Tree, on the left side. However this may be, all heard *him* sit down, heard the boughs rustle about him as he worked his thick jolly figure back under them until they must have hung about his neck and down over his eyes: then he laughed out as though he had taken his seat on his true Forest Throne.

"When I am at home in my own country," he said, "I am accustomed to sleep with my back against an evergreen. I believe in your lands you prefer pine furniture; I like the whole tree."

A tender voice put forth an unexpected question:

"Are you sure that there is not someone with you?"

"Is not that a strange question?"

"Ah yes, but in the old story when St. Nicholas arrived, an angel came with him; are you right sure there's not an angel in the room with you now?"

"I certainly see no angel, though I think I hear the voice of one! Do you see any angel?"

"With my mind's eye."

"That must be the very best eye with which to see an angel!"

"But if there were a light in the room——"

"Pardon me! If there were a light, I might not be here myself. If you changed the world at all, you would change it altogether."

A bolder voice broke in:

"You're a very mysterious person, are you not?"

"Not more mysterious than you, I should say. Is there anything more mysterious than one of you children?"

"Oh, but that's a different kind of mysterious. We don't pretend to be mysterious; you do!"

"Oh, do I! You seem to know more about me than I know about myself. When you have lived longer, you may not feel so certain about understanding other people. But then I'm not people," he added joyously, and they heard him push his way farther back under the boughs of the Tree—withdrawing more deeply into its mystery.

"Now then, while I wait, what shall we do?"

A hurried whispering began among the children, and the result was quickly announced:

"We should like to ask you some questions." Evidently the intention was that questions should riddle him—make reasonable daylight shine through his mysterious pretensions: on the stage of his own theater he was to be stripped.

"I treat all children alike," he replied with immediate insistence on his divine rights. "And if any could ask, all should ask. But suppose every living child asked me a question. That would be at least a million to every hair on my head; don't you think that would make any head a little heavy? Besides, I've always gotten along so well all over the world because I have done what I had to do and have never stopped to talk. As soon as you begin to talk, don't you get into trouble—with somebody? Who has ever forced a word out of me!"

How alert he was, nimble, brisk, alive! A marvelous kind of mental arctic light from him began to spread through the pitchiness of the room as from a sun hidden below the horizon.

"But everything seems going to pieces tonight," he continued; "and maybe I might let my silence go to pieces also. Your request is granted—but—remember, one question apiece—the first each thinks of—and not quarrelsome: this is no night for quarrelsome questions!"

The lot of asking the first fell naturally to Elsie, and her question had her history back of it; the question of each had life history.

When Elsie first came to know about the mysterious Gift Bringer from the North, she promptly noticed in her sharp way that he was already old; nor thereafter did he grow older. She found pictures of him taken generations before she was born—and there he was just as old! She judged him to be about fifty-five years or sixty as compared with middle-aged Kentucky farmers, some of whom were heavy-set men like him with florid complexions, and with snow on their beards and hair, and mischievous eyes and the same high spirits. Only, there was one who had no spirits at all except the very lowest. This was a deacon of the country church, who instead of giving presents to the children once a year pushed a long-handled box at them every Sunday and tried to force them to make presents to him! One hot morning of early summer—he had so annoyed her—when the box again paused tantalizingly in front of her, she had shot out a plump little hand and dropped into it a frantic, indignant June bug which presently raised a hymn for the whole congregation. She hated the deacon furthermore because he resembled Santa Claus, and she disliked Santa Claus because he resembled the deacon: she held them responsible for resembling each other. All this was long ago in her short life, but the ancient grudge was still lodged in her mind, and it now came out in her question:

"Why did you wait to get old before you began to bring presents to children; why didn't you bestir yourself earlier; and what were you doing all the years when you were young?"

If you could have believed that trees laughed, you would have said that the Christmas Fir was laughing now.

"That is a very good question, but it is not very simple, I am sorry to say; and by my word I am bound not to answer it; you were told that the question must be simple! However, I am willing to make you a promise: I do not know where I may be next year, but wherever you are, you will receive, I hope, a little book called *Santa Claus in the Days of his Youth.* I hope you will find your question answered there to your satisfaction. And now—for the next."

During the years of Elizabeth's belief in the great Legend of the North, second to her delight in the coming of the gifts was sorrow at the going of them. Every year an avalanche of beautiful things flowed downward over the world, across mountain ranges, across valleys and rivers; and each house chimney received its share from the one vast avalanche. Every year! And for all she knew these avalanches had been in motion thousands of years. But where were the gifts? Gone, melted away; so that there were now no more at the end of time than there had been at the beginning. The fate of the vanished lay tenderly over the landscape of the world for her.

"You say that one night of every winter you drive round the earth in your sleigh, carrying presents. Every summer don't you disguise yourself and drive over the same track in an old cart and gather them up again? Many a summer day I have watched you without your knowing it!"

The Realm of Midnight

This time you could have believed that if evergreens are sensitive, the Fir now stood with its boughs lowered a little pensively and very still.

"I am sorry! The question violates the same mischief-making rule, and by my word I am bound not to answer it. But it is as easy to give a promise to two as to one; next year I hope you will receive a little book called *Santa Claus with the Wounded and the Lost*. And I wish you joy in that story. Now then!"

"Father told me not to ask any questions while I was over here: to wait and ask *him*."

The little theater of make-believe almost crumbled to its foundations beneath that one touch of reality! The great personage of the drama lost control of his resources for a moment. Then the little miracle play was successfully resumed:

"Well, then, I won't have to answer any questions for you!"

"But I can tell you what I was *going* to ask! I was going to ask you if you are married. And if you are, why you travel always without your wife. I was wondering whether you didn't like your wife!"

The answer came like a blinding flash—like a flash meant to extinguish another flash.

"A book, a book! Another book! There will have to be another book! Look out for one next Christmas, dropped down the chimney especially for you: and I hope it won't fall into the fire or into the soot—*Santa Claus and his Wife*. Now then—time flies!"

During the infantile years when the heir of the house had been a believer in the figure beside the Tree, there had always been one point he jealously weighed: whether children of white complexion were not entitled to a larger share of Christmas bounty than those of red or yellow or brown or black faces; and in particular whether among all white children those native to the United States ought not to receive highest consideration. The old question now rang out:

"What do you think of the immigrants?"

The Tree did not exactly laugh aloud, but it certainly laughed all over—with hearty, wholesome, approving laughter.

"That question is the worst offender of all; it is quarrelsome! It is the most quarrelsome question that could be asked. What are immigrants to me? But next year look out for a book called *Santa Claus on Immigrants*."

"Put plenty of gore in it!"

"Gore! Gore on Christmas Eve! But if there was gore, since it is in a book, it would have to be dry gore. But wouldn't salve be better—salve for old wounds?"

"If you're going to put salve in, you might use my Waterloo salve!"

"Don't be peculiar, Herbert—especially away from home!"

Certainly the Tree was shaken with laughter this time.

"See what things grow to when once started; here were four questions, and now they fill four books. But time flies. Now I must make haste! My reindeer!"

His ingenuity was evidently at work upon this pretext as perhaps furnishing him later on a way through which he might effect his escape: in this little theater of thin illusion there must be some rear exit; and through this he hoped to retire from the stage without losing his dignity and the illusion of his role.

"My reindeer," he insisted, holding fast to that clew for whatsoever it might lead him to. "If they should rush by for me, I must be ready. A faint distant signal—and I'm gone! So before I go, in return for your questions I am going to ask you one. But first there is a little story—my last story; and I beg you to listen to it."

After a pause he began:

"Listen, you children! You children of this house, you children of the world!

"You love the snow. You play in it, you hunt in it; it brings the melody of sleigh bells; it gives white wings to the trees and new robes to the earth. Whenever it falls on the roof of this house and in the yard and upon the farm, sooner or later it vanishes; it is forever rising and falling, forming and melting—on and on through the ages.

236

The Realm of Midnight

"If you should start from your home tonight and travel north-ward, after a while you would find everything steadily changing: the atmosphere growing colder, living creatures beginning to be left behind, those that remain beginning to look white, the voices of the earth beginning to die out: color fading, song failing. As you journeyed on always you would be traveling toward the silent, the white, the dead. And at last you would come to a land of no sun and of all silence except the noise of wind and ice; you would have entered the kingdom of eternal snow.

"If from your home you should start southward, as you crossed land after land in the same way, you would begin to see that life was failing and the harmonies of the planet replaced by the discord of lifeless forces—storming, crushing, grinding. And at last you would reach the threshold of another world that you dared not enter and that nothing alive ever faces: the home of perpetual frost.

"If you should rise straight into the air from your housetop as though you were climbing the side of a mountain, you would find at last that you had ascended to a height where the mountain would be capped forever with snow. For all round the earth wherever its mountains are high enough, their summits are capped with the one same snow; above us all everywhere lies the upper land of eternal cold.

"Sometime in the future—we do not know when—the spirit of cold at the north will move southward; the spirit of cold at the south will move northward; the spirit of cold in the upper air will move downward; and the three will meet, and for the earth there will be one whiteness and silence—rest.

"Little children, the earth is burning out like a bedroom candle. The great sun is but a longer candle that burns out also. All the stars are but candles that one by one go out in the darkness of the universe. Now tell me, you children of this house, you children of the earth, for I make no difference among you and ask each the same question: when the earth and the sun and the stars are burnt out like your bedroom candles, where in that darkness will you be? Where will all the children of the earth be then?"

237

And now at last the Great Solemn Night drew apart its curtains of mystery and revealed its spiritual summit.

Out of these ordinary American children had all but died the last vestiges of the superstitions of their time and of earlier ages. They were new children of a new land in a new time; and they were the voices of fresh millions — voices that rose and floated far and wide as a revelation of the spirit of man stripped of worn-out rags and standing forth in its divine nakedness — winged and immortal.

"I know where I shall be," said the lad whose ideal of this life turned toward strength that would not fail and truth that could not waver.

"I know where I shall be," said the little soul whose earthly ideal was selfishness, who had within herself humanity's ideal that hereafter somewhere in the universe all desires will be gratified.

"I know where I shall be," said the little soul whose earthly ideal was the quieting of the world's pain, who had vague notions of a land where none would be sick and none suffer.

"I know where I shall be," said the little soul whose ideal of life was the gathering and keeping of all beautiful things that none should be lost and that none should change.

Then in the same spirit in which the group of them had carried on their drama of the night they now asked him:

"Where will you be?"

For a while there was no answer, and when at length the answer came it was low indeed:

"Wherever the earth's children are, may I be there with them!"

As the vast, modern, cathedral organ can be traced back through centuries to the throat of a dry reed shaken with its fellows by the wind on the banks of some ancient river, so out of the throats of these children began once more the chant of ages — that deep, majestical organ roll of humanity.

The darkened parlor of the Kentucky farmhouse became the plain where shepherds watched their flocks — it became the Mount of Transfiguration — it became Calvary — it became the Apocalypse.

The Realm of Midnight

It became the chorus out of all lands, out of all ages:

"And there were shepherds—The Lord is my shepherd—Unto us a child is born—I know that my Redeemer liveth—I know in whom I have believed—In my Father's house are many mansions—I go to prepare a place for you—Where I am you may be also—The earth shall pass away, but my word will not pass away—Now is Christ risen from the dead—Trailing clouds of glory do we come from God Who is our home—Thou wilt not leave us in the dust—Sunset and evening Star, and one clear call for me—My Pilot face to face when I have crossed the bar——"

In the room was the spiritual hymn of the whole earth from the beginning until now: that somewhere in the universe there is a Father and a Fatherland; that on a dying planet under a dying sun amid myriads of dying stars there is something that does not die—the Youth of Man. In that youth all that had been best in him will come to fullest life; all that was worst will have dropped away.

The room was very still awhile.

Then upon its intense stillness there broke a sound—faint, far away through the snow-thickened air—a melody of coming sleigh bells. All heard, all listened.

"Hark, hark! Do you hear! Listen! They are coming for me! They're coming!"

The Tree shook as he who was sitting under its branches rose to his feet with these words.

"That is father's sleigh: I know those bells: those are our sleigh bells. That is father!" said a grave boy excitedly.

"Ah! Is that what you think I hear! Then indeed it is time for me to be going!"

There was a rustling of the boughs of the Christmas Tree as though the guest were leaving.

Nearer, nearer, nearer, along the turnpike came the sound of the bells. At the front gate the sound suddenly ceased.

"They're waiting for me!" said a voice from behind the Tree as it moved away in the direction of the chimney.

Then all heard something more startling still.

The sleigh was approaching the house. Out of the silence and the darkness of Christmas Eve there was traveling toward the house another story—the drama of a man's life.

At the distance of a few hundred yards the sound of the sleigh bells, borne softly into the room and to the rapt listeners, showed that the driver had turned out of the main drive and begun to encircle the house by that path which enclosed it as within a ring— within the symbol of the eternal.

Under old trees now snow-laden, past the flower beds of summer, past the long branches of flowering shrubs and of roses that no longer scattered their petals, but now dropped the flowers of the sky, past thoughts and memories, it made its way, as for one who doubles back upon the track of experience with a new purpose and revisits the past as he turns away from it toward another future. Through the darkness, across the fresh snow, on this night of the anniversary of home life, there and on this final Christmas Eve after which all would soon vanish, he drew this band—binding together all the lives there grouped—putting about them the ring of oneness.

That mournful melody of secrecy and darkness began to die out. Fainter and fainter it pulsed through the air. At the gate it was barely heard and then it was not heard: was it gone or was it waiting there?

By the chimney side there were faint noises.

"He is gone!" whispered Elizabeth with one intense breath.

KATHARINE LEE BATES

A Marchpane for Christmas

IN what season was Christ born? Milton makes positive reply:

> *It was the winter wild*
> *While the Heaven-born Child*
> *All meanly wrapt in the rude manger lies.*

But the second century of the Christian Era would have answered that Christ was born in the spring, the season when the earth was created; for of course it would have been created in the hour of its perfect beauty and equally of course it would have worn its loveliest aspect to welcome its divine guest. Favorite dates were March 28, April 19, April 20 and May 20. As for the day of the week, some theologians claimed that the Light of the World first shone forth on a Wednesday, because on the fourth day God created the sun, moon and stars, while others felt it more seemly that Christ should have been born on Sunday and baptized the following Wednesday.

In the absence of record, scholars in the fields of primitive life and myth have been searching out the reasons that determined such a wintry date for the world's blithest festival. These wise men tell

241

us that the year, for the fighting pastoral tribes of Aryan stock that had possessed themselves of Europe, knew but two seasons: winter, beginning about mid-November, when the rough weather drove warriors and herders back from the open to the comfort of their own villages, and summer, reckoned from about mid-March when the river ice was breaking up and the fresh life of nature was, in Chaucer's phrase, pricking men in their hearts, so that they longed to be up and away. The home-coming at the close of summer was naturally the occasion for a festival, a Thanksgiving, with prodigious eating and drinking. Such a Winter Feast is the scene of Charles Rann Kennedy's drama of that name, but as the action takes place in Iceland, where summers are short, the time is mid-October. Farther south November was the "blood-month," so called from the general slaughtering of cattle, for there was not enough fodder to feed all the herd till spring. But in course of the centuries these forest dwellers became interested in agriculture, felled trees and tamed the lands about their settlements to the bearing of crops. To the great trenchers of meat were added "bakes of griddles" and there was fodder enough to keep the kine longer. So the Winter Feast, as it moved south, gradually advanced in date to December. It had always had the double quality of family affection and religion. Forest wood, heaped high on the hearth for the "new fire," blazed cheerily, lighting the eager faces of children as they leaned shyly against the fathers and big brothers, almost strangers after the summer of absence, while the maidens passed the mead cup and the mother saw to it that goodly portions for the household dead were set outside the door. There were sacrifices to the gods, whose healths were drunk in even deeper draughts than those of the family ancestors. Our Christmas merrymaking is not far removed from the home joys and simple pieties of those primeval reunions around the yule log, whose name, at least, is of the North.

It was under the Roman Empire that the exact and permanent date for Christmas was established, not through Church tradition but by way of compromise with paganism. It is believed that the mother of the Emperor Aurelian (270-275) had been a priestess of the Syrian sun-god Baal and brought his cult to Rome, where his birthday was celebrated on December 25, incorrectly fixed by the Julian calendar as the winter solstice. It is then, when the days are at their shortest, that the sun manifests himself as Sol Novus, Sol Invictus, and proceeds to lengthen his course. The Romans were already accustomed to revel on this date as it marked the close of the Bruma (brevissima), a solar feast borrowed from Thrace, which began November 24 and kept the sun lively company through his diminishing period to December 25. Later emperors, notably Diocletian and, even after his conversion to Christianity, Constantine the Great, maintained the worship of Sol Invictus, by that time identified in the Empire with Mithra. This was a solar deity so ancient that he had been adored by the Aryans in Central Asia before the Persians had parted from the Hindoos. It was by way of Persia that he came to Europe about 70 B. C. A fierce, bull-slaughtering figure, the Greeks would have none of him, but he made strong appeal to the Roman legions. The intellectual circles, too, as well as the court and aristocracy, were won to the worship of this foreign god, this Sol Invictus interpreted by the philosophers, in his winter waning and waxing, as symbolic of death and resurrection. By the third century Mithra was the most formidable rival to Christianity, but he had made the fatal mistake of excluding women from his Mysteries. Not even the fervent devotion of Julian the Apostate, who in the fourth century brought the cult of Mithra to Constantinople, could impose upon humanity an exclusively masculine religion.

To the people at large the two religions would not have seemed much unlike. Both were democratic and fraternal in spirit and, to some degree, in organization; both kept Sunday, used bell and candle and holy water, had sacraments of baptism and of a Last Supper with consecrated bread and wine; both taught a Heaven above, a Hell below, and a Day of Judgment to come; both urged self-control and self-denial. How, then, were young Christians to be kept out of the fun of the feast held in honor of Mithra's birthday on December 25? This high festival was sandwiched in between two still more riotous revels, the Saturnalia, beginning December

17, and the Kalends, properly covering the three days January 1-3, but in fact these two folk jubilees ran to meet each other, forming a continuous Carnival. In the midst of the merrymaking came the impressive ceremonies of December 25, honoring the birth of Mithra. The Fathers of the Church, apparently before the middle of the fourth century, met the situation by proclaiming the Feast of the Nativity on this same date. Our Christmas joy still holds not only the far-off echoes of the Northern Winter Feast but many features ingrafted from these Roman holidays. From the Saturnalia, when the world went topsy-turvy, masters carousing with their slaves and even waiting upon them, came the Lord of Misrule, who, in the old English Christmas, carried on the tradition of license and disorder. Presents were given, too, chiefly of little clay images. From the many representations of Mithra in art still found all over the extent of the Roman Empire, it may be assumed that these festival gifts figured him in various guises, as sun-god, soldier god, and especially in his miraculous birth, leaping forth in the full force of young manhood from the Generative Rock, in the view only of shepherds, who hastened to kneel before him and lay at his feet their rustic offerings. While the disciples of Mithra exchanged these gifts, what more natural than that the Christians, their neighbors and fellow artisans, should fashion for one another those Nativity groups which still, in the Catholic countries of Latin blood or influence, are the distinctive Christmas tokens? In Spain, for instance, one sees the *Nacimiento* everywhere, life-size and giant-size in the churches and cathedrals, richly wrought by sculptors, manufactured for sale in almost all substances from bronze to paste; often, as proudly displayed in household windows, the product of family skill. In collecting a group to bring home, we enjoyed capping a selection of costly Magi from a studio and moderately priced Holy Family from the shops, with angels, three for a penny, from a peasant's stall by the Guadalquivir. While waiting for customers to bargain for his onions and peppers this laughing Andalusian would scoop up a handful of wet clay from the riverbank, mold it deftly into winged cherubs with chubby legs crossed and with tambourines, fiddles, or castanets in hand, and set them in the sun to dry. Then a few touches of his cheap pigments would adorn them with gay caps and gaiters, with flyaway coats in the Madonna blue and, above all, with toper-red, jovial faces. If he wanted to be an angel, that was the kind of angel he wanted to be.

Often these Christmas craftsmen carry on their moldings or carvings into scores of kindred scenes—the journey into Egypt, an angel leading the ass which bears Mary and the Holy Child, while Joseph, a staff tall as himself in hand, trudges behind; the home at Nazareth, Mary busy with her basket of sewing, while the Christ child fondles his pet lamb; the carpenter's shop, Joseph planing a board, while a rosy little Jesus is picking up the shavings. We visited at Seville in Christmas week a Refuge for the Aged Poor and found the old men and old women laboring in emulous pride on *Nacimientos* that covered the east walls of their respective sitting rooms—walls hidden behind cork mountains, plaster rocks, troops of clay mules and donkeys laden with wee water jars, tiny bundles of firewood and bales of elfin merchandise. The *ancianos* had the more varied and spirited panorama, including an isinglass river on which sailed ships and swans of equal size; but the *ancianas* scored in composition, the manger scene being the center of their representation, while the old men had crowded the Holy Family to one side, in order to make room for an encounter between smugglers and the Civil Guard. The only battle scene portrayed by the women claimed to be Scriptural in that a black-bearded Herod, thrusting his head over a gilt balcony, watched his soldiers running away from the brooms of the Rachels.

At the Kalends, too, presents were given, not after our lavish, indiscriminate fashion but as emblems of good wishes for the New Year—sugared cakes, pots of honey, flasks of wine, that the year might be full of sweetness; candles or lamps that it might abound in light. Originally the New Year's gift in Rome was a twig from the sacred grove of Strenia, so that a popular feaster would come home with his arms piled with greenery. At the Kalends, too, the doors of the houses were crowned with laurels. As we hang pine wreaths on our own doors and trim our rooms with holly and mistletoe, ghostly hands are helping us. The bands of revelers that went through the Roman streets singing, and often pausing at one of the branch-bedecked, window-lighted houses for hospitality, have their descendants in the Christmas carolers.

In the midst of these festivities Christmas was kept, by human necessity forcing ecclesiastical decree, on December 25 at Rome. Thence it slowly made its way over Christendom, reaching Antioch about 375 and Alexandria about 430. It was not before the sixth century that it won recognition at Jerusalem. It probably came to the British Isles with St. Augustine and his procession of chanting monks in 592, for the ten thousand British converts of 598 were baptized on Christmas Day. Germany did not adopt it until 813, and Norway not until the middle of the tenth century. The date of Christmas was by this time held to be the literal date of the birthday—a belief that has had popular acceptance ever since.

By the middle of the eighth century, Christmas, Epiphany and Easter were generally recognized as the three main feasts of the Church. Epiphany antedated Christmas, being established in the East during the second century as the anniversary of Christ's baptism in the Jordan. By a grudging exchange, Rome in the fifth century accepted Epiphany, and the Greek Church Christmas. Their ceremonies, with pagan admixture in both, were naturally somewhat confused. Greek peasants still look upon the twelve days from Christmas to Epiphany as peculiarly open to the invasion of goblins, especially the Lame Needles, whose dreaded name has a rheumatic suggestion, while Shakespeare, spokesman for western Europe, maintains quite the opposite view:

> Some say that ever 'gainst that season comes
> Wherein our Saviour's birth is celebrated,
> The bird of dawning singeth all night long:
> And then, they say, no spirit dares stir abroad;
> The nights are wholesome; then no planets strike,
> No fairy takes, nor witch hath power to charm,
> So hallow'd and so gracious is the time.

A Marchpane for Christmas

Heathen superstition and Christian love, working together in the childlike heart of the folk, have woven the Christmas story into a curious tapestry. If the devotees of Mithra worshiped the stars, Christianity claims the Star of Bethlehem for its own. The *Golden Legend* depicts it as "a right fair child, which had a cross in his forehead." If shepherds brought their gifts to the newborn Mithra, Christianity has made its own three shepherds such familiar friends that it knows the names even of their dogs. Many a sheep dog of Spain and Portugal and South America will never go mad because it answers to the name Melampo, Cubilon or Lobina. Of course the Three Kings are everywhere known by name, Melchior and Gaspar and Balthasar, and in Provence perhaps known by sight, since for generations the boys of that Land of Song, running out on Epiphany just before the falling of the dusk, have glimpsed them riding in their splendor on white camels through the sunset. On many a balcony in both hemispheres and in the far islands of the sea the camels will find a row of little sandals holding for their refreshment wisps of hay. In the morning there will be found, in place of the hay, some simple token of gratitude—a few figs wrapped in a green leaf, a diminutive donkey in marchpane, a handful of almonds in a twist of gay paper. In other countries there are strange stories told of those who have heard the Magi riding by and followed them on to various adventures. Sweetest of these stories is that of old Babushka, the little peasant grandmother of Russia, who, drawn to the window of her forest hut at night, saw the glistening cavalcade and heard the call to come and worship the Christ child. Fearing the dark, she waited for dawn, when—alas!—the camel tracks were blurred with fresh-fallen snow. All in vain was her wild search for the manger, but ever since, on Epiphany, she catches a far-off sound of bells and hurries forth through forest and over plain, bearing on her arm a basket of tiny warm garments that she has knitted for the Babe of Bethlehem—garments that she gives away to the babies of the poor; for never, never may she overtake those stately riders.

The scene of Mithra's birth was savage. The Prince of War, most often represented as the fierce slayer of the sacrificial bull, his heart may well have been as hard as the Rock from which he was born; but upon the Bethlehem manger has been poured out the tenderness of human imagination. Paintings, carols, miracle plays, artists and poets of many lands and ages have elaborated its every feature. The Prince of Peace, over whose first slumber star-choirs of angels sing, is warmed by the breath of horses and kine, one kneeling on either side. His birth was made known to the animals so long ago that barnyards still talked Latin. "Christus natus est," crowed the cock. "Quando?" croaked the raven. "Hac nocte," brayed the donkey. "Ubi?" lowed the ox. "In Bethlehem," bleated the lamb. . . .

The ass has his own part in the legend. It is this very ass that brought the weary Mary to Bethlehem and thence carried her and the Holy Child to Egypt, this very ass that comes, silvery as moonlight, shining through the mists of death, to poor little donkeys, worn out by blows and burdens, the world over, and guides them to the clover pastures of Paradise.

The Holy Family are great wanderers. In any clime there may be met, especially at the Christmas season, that tired little group, the Madonna, with the starry child in her arms, seated on the gray donkey, with old Saint Joseph trudging alongside. Hospitality to these travelers is often rewarded by the fairy gift of three wishes, as notably in the case of Smetse Smee of Flanders, the cunning smith who was thus enabled to trick the devils out of his soul which, like a less learned but more resourceful Faustus, he had signed away to hell. But sometimes the Madonna comes alone, a drooping but smiling lady in a blue mantle with the rose of Jericho in her hair. In Italy Il Santissimo Bambino goes roaming by himself, while in the North he knocks at your door as a young boy with a bundle of evergreen across his shoulders. In the course of time he has drawn to himself a queer retinue of Christmas saints, Bishop Nicholas, beloved as jolly St. Nick, Santa Claus, Kriss Kringle, Père Noël, Frau Holle, Kolyada of the Golden Hair, all on the friendliest terms with such pagan brownies as Knecht Clobes of Holland and old Jule-Nissen of Denmark.

There are plants, as the Glastonbury thorn, cherry trees and apple trees, that are said to blossom at Christmas; even the pennyroyal that Sicilian children tuck into their shoes knows the blessed date; but the Christmas tree is a comparatively new feature of the celebration, traced back in its homeland, Germany, only to the beginning of the seventeenth century. That its ornaments are symbolic of Norse mythology is but one more instance of the Christmas welcome to old heathen faiths and practices. To bear in mind the relation of our December festival to the Winter Feast of the North and the Sun Feast of the South, those immemorial jubilees in which home fondness and neighborhood friendliness, with worship of the highest divinities then known, were the main elements, only binds God's children into a closer circle. Who can doubt that His blessing rested on those anticipatory revels of joy and good will? Whatever the name given to the yule log, the hearth glowed with the glory of fire. Southwell's Wassail Song carries the mirth of a million ancestral voices:

> Wassail, wassail, all over the town!
> Our toast it is white and our ale it is brown;
> Our bowl is made of a maplin tree;
> We be good fellows all—I drink to thee.

Here and there a special survival of hoary usage, as in Queen's College, Oxford, where a boar's head, wreathed with greens, is borne in to the Christmas banquet with song in which the feasters join, takes the race memory back over uncharted centuries. As William Morris has it:

> E'en so the world of men may turn
> At even of some hurried day
> And see the ancient glimmer burn
> Across the waste that hath no way.

The three Magi kneeling before the Lord of Love and tendering him their best of gifts—are they not the Past, the Present and the Future?

HENRY VAN DYKE

The First Christmas Tree

I

THE day before Christmas, in the year of our Lord 722.
Broad snow-meadows glistening white along the banks of
the river Moselle; steep hill-sides blooming with mystic for-
get-me-not where the glow of the setting sun cast long shadows
down their eastern slope; an arch of clearest, deepest gentian bending overhead; in the centre of the aerial garden the walls of the
cloister of Pfalzel, steel-blue to the east, violet to the west; silence
over all,—a gentle, eager, conscious stillness, diffused through the
air, as if earth and sky were hushing themselves to hear the voice of
the river faintly murmuring down the valley.

In the cloister, too, there was silence at the sunset hour. All day
long there had been a strange and joyful stir among the nuns. A

breeze of curiosity and excitement had swept along the corridors and through every quiet cell. A famous visitor had come to the convent.

It was Winfried of England, whose name in the Roman tongue was Boniface, and whom men called the Apostle of Germany. A great preacher; a wonderful scholar; but, more than all, a daring traveller, a venturesome pilgrim, a priest of romance.

He had left his home and his fair estate in Wessex; he would not stay in the rich monastery of Nutescelle, even though they had chosen him as the abbot; he had refused a bishopric at the court of King Karl. Nothing would content him but to go out into the wild woods and preach to the heathen.

Through the forests of Hesse and Thuringia, and along the borders of Saxony, he had wandered for years, with a handful of companions, sleeping under the trees, crossing mountains and marshes, now here, now there, never satisfied with ease and comfort, always in love with hardship and danger.

What a man he was! Fair and slight, but straight as a spear and strong as an oaken staff. His face was still young; the smooth skin was bronzed by wind and sun. His gray eyes, clean and kind, flashed like fire when he spoke of his adventures, and of the evil deeds of the false priests with whom he contended.

What tales he had told that day! Not of miracles wrought by sacred relics; not of courts and councils and splendid cathedrals; though he knew much of these things. But to-day he had spoken of long journeyings by sea and land; of perils by fire and flood; of wolves and bears, and fierce snowstorms, and black nights in the lonely forest; of dark altars of heathen gods, and weird, bloody sacrifices, and narrow escapes from murderous bands of wandering savages.

The little novices had gathered around him, and their faces had grown pale and their eyes bright as they listened with parted lips, entranced in admiration, twining their arms about one another's shoulders and holding closely together, half in fear, half in delight. The older nuns had turned from their tasks and paused, in passing by, to hear the pilgrim's story. Too well they knew the truth of what he spoke. Many a one among them had seen the smoke rising from the ruins of her father's roof. Many a one had a brother far away in the wild country to whom her heart went out night and day, wondering if he were still among the living.

But now the excitements of that wonderful day were over; the hour of the evening meal had come; the inmates of the cloister were assembled in the refectory.

On the daïs sat the stately Abbess Addula, daughter of King Dagobert, looking a princess indeed, in her purple tunic, with the hood and cuffs of her long white robe trimmed with ermine, and a snowy veil resting like a crown on her silver hair. At her right hand was the honoured guest, and at her left hand her grandson, the young Prince Gregor, a big, manly boy, just returned from school.

The long, shadowy hall, with its dark-brown rafters and beams; the double row of nuns, with their pure veils and fair faces; the ruddy glow of the slanting sunbeams striking upward through the tops of the windows and painting a pink glow high up on the walls,—it was all as beautiful as a picture, and as silent. For this was the rule of the cloister, that at the table all should sit in stillness for a little while, and then one should read aloud, while the rest listened.

"It is the turn of my grandson to read to-day," said the abbess to Winfried; "we shall see how much he has learned in the school. Read, Gregor; the place in the book is marked."

The lad rose from his seat and turned the pages of the manuscript. It was a copy of Jerome's version of the Scriptures in Latin, and the marked place was in the letter of St. Paul to the Ephesians, —the passage where he describes the preparation of the Christian as a warrior arming for battle. The young voice rang out clearly, rolling the sonorous words, without slip or stumbling, to the end of the chapter.

Winfried listened, smiling. "That was bravely read, my son," said he, as the reader paused. "Understandest thou what thou readest?"

"Surely, father," answered the boy; "it was taught me by the masters at Treves; and we have read this epistle from beginning to end, so that I almost know it by heart."

Then he began to repeat the passage, turning away from the page as if to show his skill.

But Winfried stopped him with a friendly lifting of the hand.

"Not so, my son; that was not my meaning. When we pray, we speak to God. When we read, God speaks to us. I ask whether thou hast heard what He has said to thee in the common speech. Come, give us again the message of the warrior and his armour and his battle, in the mother-tongue, so that all can understand it."

The boy hesitated, blushed, stammered; then he came around to Winfried's seat, bringing the book. "Take the book, my father," he cried, "and read it for me. I cannot see the meaning plain, though I love the sound of the words. Religion I know, and the doctrines of our faith, and the life of priests and nuns in the cloister, for which my grandmother designs me, though it likes me little. And fighting I know, and the life of warriors and heroes, for I have read of it in Virgil and the ancients, and heard a bit from the soldiers at Treves; and I would fain taste more of it, for it likes me much. But how the two lives fit together, or what need there is of armour for a clerk in holy orders, I can never see. Tell me the meaning, for if there is a man in all the world that knows it, I am sure it is thou."

So Winfried took the book and closed it, clasping the boy's hand with his own.

"Let us first dismiss the others to their vespers," said he, "lest they should be weary."

A sign from the abbess; a chanted benediction; a murmuring of sweet voices and a soft rustling of many feet over the rushes on the floor; the gentle tide of noise flowed out through the doors and ebbed away down the corridors; the three at the head of the table were left alone in the darkening room.

Then Winfried began to translate the parable of the soldier into the realities of life.

At every turn he knew how to flash a new light into the picture out of his own experience. He spoke of the combat with self, and of the wrestling with dark spirits in solitude. He spoke of the demons that men had worshipped for centuries in the wilderness, and whose malice they invoked against the stranger who ventured into the gloomy forest. Gods, they called them, and told weird tales of their dwelling among the impenetrable branches of the oldest trees and in the caverns of the shaggy hills; of their riding on the wind-horses and hurling spears of lightning against their foes. Gods they were not, but foul spirits of the air, rulers of the darkness. Was there not glory and honour in fighting them, in daring their anger under the shield of faith, in putting them to flight with the sword of truth? What better adventure could a brave man ask than to go forth against them, and wrestle with them, and conquer them?

"Look you, my friends," said Winfried, "how sweet and peaceful is this convent to-night! It is a garden full of flowers in the heart of winter; a nest among the branches of a great tree shaken by the winds; a still haven on the edge of a tempestuous sea. And this is what religion means for those who are chosen and called to quietude and prayer and meditation.

"But out yonder in the wide forest, who knows what storms are raving to-night in the hearts of men, though all the woods are still? who knows what haunts of wrath and cruelty are closed to-night against the advent of the Prince of Peace? And shall I tell you what religion means to those who are called and chosen to dare, and to fight, and to conquer the world for Christ? It means to go against the strongholds of the adversary. It means to struggle to win an entrance for the Master everywhere. What helmet is strong enough for this strife save the helmet of salvation? What breastplate can guard a man against these fiery darts but the breastplate of righteousness? What shoes can stand the wear of these journeys but the preparation of the gospel of peace?"

"Shoes?" he cried again, and laughed as if a sudden thought had struck him. He thrust out his foot, covered with a heavy cowhide boot, laced high about his leg with thongs of skin.

"Look here,—how a fighting man of the cross is shod! I have seen the boots of the Bishop of Tours.—white kid, broidered with silk;

a day in the bogs would tear them to shreds. I have seen the sandals that the monks use on the highroads,—yes, and worn them; ten pair of them have I worn out and thrown away in a single journey. Now I shoe my feet with the toughest hides, hard as iron; no rock can cut them, no branches can tear them. Yet more than one pair of these have I outworn, and many more shall I outwear ere my journeys are ended. And I think, if God is gracious to me, that I shall die wearing them. Better so than in a soft bed with silken coverings. The boots of a warrior, a hunter, a woodsman,—these are my preparation of the gospel of peace.

"Come, Gregor," he said, laying his brown hand on the youth's shoulder, "come, wear the forester's boots with me. This is the life to which we are called. Be strong in the Lord, a hunter of the demons, a subduer of the wilderness, a woodsman of the faith. Come."

The boy's eyes sparkled. He turned to his grandmother. She shook her head vigorously.

"Nay, father," she said, "draw not the lad away from my side with these wild words. I need him to help me with my labours, to cheer my old age."

"Do you need him more than the Master does?" asked Winfried; "and will you take the wood that is fit for a bow to make a distaff?"

"But I fear for the child. Thy life is too hard for him. He will perish with hunger in the woods."

"Once," said Winfried, smiling, "we were camped on the bank of the river Ohru. The table was set for the morning meal, but my comrades cried that it was empty; the provisions were exhausted; we must go without breakfast, and perhaps starve before we could escape from the wilderness. While they complained, a fish-hawk flew up from the river with flapping wings, and let fall a great pike in the midst of the camp. There was food enough and to spare! Never have I seen the righteous forsaken, nor his seed begging bread."

"But the fierce pagans of the forest," cried the abbess,—"they may pierce the boy with their arrows, or dash out his brains with their axes. He is but a child, too young for the danger and the strife."

"A child in years," replied Winfried, "but a man in spirit. And if the hero fall early in the battle, he wears the brighter crown, not a leaf withered, not a flower fallen."

The aged princess trembled a little. She drew Gregor close to her side, and laid her hand gently on his brown hair.

"I am not sure that he wants to leave me yet. Besides, there is no horse in the stable to give him, now, and he cannot go as befits the grandson of a king."

Gregor looked straight into her eyes.

"Grandmother," said he, "dear grandmother, if thou wilt not give me a horse to ride with this man of God, I will go with him afoot."

II

Two years had passed since that Christmas-eve in the cloister of Pfalzel. A little company of pilgrims, less than a score of men, were travelling slowly northward through the wide forest that rolled over the hills of central Germany.

At the head of the band marched Winfried, clad in a tunic of fur, with his long black robe girt high above his waist, so that it might not hinder his stride. His hunter's boots were crusted with snow. Drops of ice sparkled like jewels along the thongs that bound his legs. There were no other ornaments on his dress except the bishop's cross hanging on his breast, and the silver clasp that fastened his cloak about his neck. He carried a strong, tall staff in his hand, fashioned at the top into the form of a cross.

Close beside him, keeping step like a familiar comrade, was the young Prince Gregor. Long marches through the wilderness had stretched his legs and broadened his back, and made a man of him in stature as well as in spirit. His jacket and cap were of wolf-skin, and on his shoulder he carried an axe, with broad, shining blade. He was a mighty woodsman now, and could make a spray of chips fly around him as he hewed his way through the trunk of a pine-tree.

Behind these leaders followed a pair of teamsters, guiding a rude sledge, loaded with food and the equipage of the camp, and drawn by two big, shaggy horses, blowing thick clouds of steam from their frosty nostrils. Tiny icicles hung from the hairs on their lips. Their flanks were smoking. They sank above the fetlocks at every step in the soft snow.

Last of all came the rear guard, armed with bows and javelins. It was no child's play, in those days, to cross Europe afoot.

The weird woodland, sombre and illimitable, covered hill and vale, table-land and mountain-peak. There were wide moors where the wolves hunted in packs as if the devil drove them, and tangled thickets where the lynx and the boar made their lairs. Fierce bears lurked among the rocky passes, and had not yet learned to fear the face of man. The gloomy recesses of the forest gave shelter to inhabitants who were still more cruel and dangerous than beasts of prey,—outlaws and sturdy robbers and mad were-wolves and bands of wandering pillagers.

The pilgrim who would pass from the mouth of the Tiber to the mouth of the Rhine must trust in God and keep his arrows loose in the quiver.

The travellers were surrounded by an ocean of trees, so vast, so full of endless billows, that it seemed to be pressing on every side to overwhelm them. Gnarled oaks, with branches twisted and knotted as if in rage, rose in groves like tidal waves. Smooth forests of beech-trees, round and gray, swept over the knolls and slopes of land in a mighty ground-swell. But most of all, the multitude of pines and firs, innumerable and monotonous, with straight, stark trunks, and branches woven together in an unbroken flood of darkest green, crowded through the valleys and over the hills, rising on the highest ridges into ragged crests, like the foaming edge of breakers.

Through this sea of shadows ran a narrow stream of shining whiteness,—an ancient Roman road, covered with snow. It was as if some great ship had ploughed through the green ocean long ago, and left behind it a thick, smooth wake of foam. Along this open track the travellers held their way,—heavily, for the drifts were deep;

warily, for the hard winter had driven many packs of wolves down from the moors.

The steps of the pilgrims were noiseless; but the sledges creaked over the dry snow, and the panting of the horses throbbed through the still air. The pale-blue shadows on the western side of the road grew longer. The sun, declining through its shallow arch, dropped behind the tree-tops. Darkness followed swiftly, as if it had been a bird of prey waiting for this sign to swoop down upon the world.

"Father," said Gregor to the leader, "surely this day's march is done. It is time to rest, and eat, and sleep. If we press onward now, we cannot see our steps; and will not that be against the word of the psalmist David, who bids us not to put confidence in the legs of a man?"

Winfried laughed. "Nay, my son Gregor," said he, "thou hast tripped, even now, upon thy text. For David said only, 'I take no pleasure in the legs of a man.' And so say I, for I am not minded to spare thy legs or mine, until we come farther on our way, and do what must be done this night. Draw thy belt tighter, my son, and hew me out this tree that is fallen across the road, for our camp-ground is not here."

The youth obeyed; two of the foresters sprang to help him; and while the soft fir-wood yielded to the stroke of the axes, and the snow flew from the bending branches, Winfried turned and spoke to his followers in a cheerful voice, that refreshed them like wine.

"Courage, brothers, and forward yet a little! The moon will light us presently, and the path is plain. Well know I that the journey is weary; and my own heart wearies also for the home in England, where those I love are keeping feast this Christmas-eve. But we have work to do before we feast to-night. For this is the Yuletide, and the heathen people of the forest are gathered at the thunder-oak of Geismar to worship their god, Thor. Strange things will be seen there, and deeds which make the soul black. But we are sent to lighten their darkness; and we will teach our kinsmen to keep a Christmas with us such as the woodland has never known. Forward, then, and stiffen up the feeble knees!"

A murmur of assent came from the men. Even the horses seemed to take fresh heart. They flattened their backs to draw the heavy loads, and blew the frost from their nostrils as they pushed ahead.

The night grew broader and less oppressive. A gate of brightness was opened secretly somewhere in the sky. Higher and higher swelled the clear moon-flood, until it poured over the eastern wall of forest into the road. A drove of wolves howled faintly in the distance, but they were receding, and the sound soon died away. The stars sparkled merrily through the stringent air; the small, round moon shone like silver; little breaths of dreaming wind wandered across the pointed fir-tops, as the pilgrims toiled bravely onward, following their clew of light through a labyrinth of darkness.

After a while the road began to open out a little. There were spaces of meadow-land, fringed with alders, behind which a boisterous river ran clashing through spears of ice.

Rude houses of hewn logs appeared in the openings, each one casting a patch of inky shadow upon the snow. Then the travellers passed a larger group of dwellings, all silent and unlighted; and beyond, they saw a great house, with many outbuildings and inclosed courtyards, from which the hounds bayed furiously, and a noise of stamping horses came from the stalls. But there was no other sound of life. The fields around lay naked to the moon. They saw no man, except that once, on a path that skirted the farther edge of a meadow, three dark figures passed them, running very swiftly.

Then the road plunged again into a dense thicket, traversed it, and climbing to the left, emerged suddenly upon a glade, round and level except at the northern side, where a hillock was crowned with a huge oak-tree. It towered above the heath, a giant with contorted arms, beckoning to the host of lesser trees. "Here," cried Winfried, as his eyes flashed and his hand lifted his heavy staff, "here is the Thunder-oak; and here the cross of Christ shall break the hammer of the false god Thor."

III

WITHERED leaves still clung to the branches of the oak: torn and faded banners of the departed summer. The bright crimson of autumn had long since disappeared, bleached away by the storms and the cold. But to-night these tattered remnants of glory were red again: ancient bloodstains against the dark-blue sky. For an immense fire had been kindled in front of the tree. Tongues of ruddy flame, fountains of ruby sparks, ascended through the spreading limbs and flung a fierce illumination upward and around. The pale, pure moonlight that bathed the surrounding forests was quenched and eclipsed here. Not a beam of it sifted through the branches of the oak. It stood like a pillar of cloud between the still light of heaven and the crackling, flashing fire of earth.

But the fire itself was invisible to Winfried and his companions. A great throng of people were gathered around it in a half-circle, their backs to the open glade, their faces toward the oak. Seen against that glowing background, it was but the silhouette of a crowd, vague, black, formless, mysterious.

The travellers paused for a moment at the edge of the thicket, and took counsel together.

"It is the assembly of the tribe," said one of the foresters, "the great night of the council. I heard of it three days ago, as we passed through one of the villages. All who swear by the old gods have been summoned. They will sacrifice a steed to the god of war, and drink blood, and eat horse-flesh to make them strong. It will be at the peril of our lives if we approach them. At least we must hide the cross, if we would escape death."

"Hide me no cross," cried Winfried, lifting his staff, "for I have come to show it, and to make these blind folks see its power. There is more to be done here to-night than the slaying of a steed, and a greater evil to be stayed than the shameful eating of meat sacrificed to idols. I have seen it in a dream. Here the cross must stand and be our rede."

At his command the sledge was left in the border of the wood, with two of the men to guard it, and the rest of the company moved forward across the open ground. They approached unnoticed, for all the multitude were looking intently toward the fire at the foot of the oak.

Then Winfried's voice rang out, "Hail, ye sons of the forest! A stranger claims the warmth of your fire in the winter night."

Swiftly, and as with a single motion, a thousand eyes were bent upon the speaker. The semicircle opened silently in the middle; Winfried entered with his followers; it closed again behind them.

Then, as they looked round the curving ranks, they saw that the hue of the assemblage was not black, but white,—dazzling, radiant, solemn. White, the robes of the women clustered together at the points of the wide crescent; white, the glittering byrnies of the warriors standing in close ranks; white, the fur mantles of the aged men who held the central palace in the circle; white, with the shimmer of silver ornaments and the purity of lamb's-wool, the raiment of a little group of children who stood close by the fire; white, with awe and fear, the faces of all who looked at them; and over all the flickering, dancing radiance of the flames played and glimmered like a faint, vanishing tinge of blood on snow.

The only figure untouched by the glow was the old priest, Hunrad, with his long, spectral robe, flowing hair and beard, and dead-pale face, who stood with his back to the fire and advanced slowly to meet the strangers.

"Who are you? Whence come you, and what seek you here?"

"Your kinsman am I, of the German brotherhood," answered Winfried, "and from England, beyond the sea, have I come to bring you a greeting from that land, and a message from the All-Father, whose servant I am."

"Welcome, then," said Hunrad, "welcome, kinsman, and be silent; for what passes here is too high to wait, and must be done before the moon crosses the middle heaven, unless, indeed, thou hast some sign or token from the gods. Canst thou work miracles?"

The question came sharply, as if a sudden gleam of hope had flashed through the tangle of the old priest's mind. But Winfried's voice sank lower and a cloud of disappointment passed over his face as he replied: "Nay, miracles have I never wrought, though I have heard of many; but the All-Father has given no power to my hands save such as belongs to common man."

"Stand still, then, thou common man," said Hunrad, scornfully, "and behold what the gods have called us hither to do. This night is the death-night of the sun-god, Baldur the Beautiful, beloved of gods and men. This night is the hour of darkness and the power of winter, of sacrifice and mighty fear. This night the great Thor, the god of thunder and war, to whom this oak is sacred, is grieved for the death of Baldur, and angry with this people because they have forsaken his worship. Long is it since an offering has been laid upon his altar, long since the roots of his holy tree have been fed with blood. Therefore its leaves have withered before the time, and its boughs are heavy with death. Therefore the Slavs and the Wends have beaten us in battle. Therefore the harvests have failed, and the wolf-hordes have ravaged the folds, and the strength has departed from the bow, and the wood of the spear has broken, and the wild boar has slain the huntsman. Therefore the plague has fallen on our dwellings, and the dead are more than the living in all our villages. Answer me, ye people, are not these things true?"

A hoarse sound of approval ran through the circle. A chant, in which the voices of the men and women blended, like the shrill wind in the pine-trees above the rumbling thunder of a waterfall, rose and fell in rude cadences.

> *O Thor, the Thunderer,*
> *Mighty and merciless,*
> *Spare us from smiting!*
> *Heave not thy hammer,*
> *Angry, against us;*
> *Plague not thy people.*
> *Take from our treasure*
> *Richest of ransom.*
> *Silver we send thee,*
> *Jewels and javelins,*

Goodliest garments,
All our possessions,
Priceless, we proffer.
Sheep will we slaughter,
Steeds will we sacrifice;
Bright blood shall bathe thee,
O tree of Thunder,
Life-floods shall lave thee,
Strong wood of wonder.
Mighty, have mercy,
Smite us no more,
Spare us and save us,
Spare us, Thor! Thor!

With two great shouts the song ended, and a stillness followed so intense that the crackling of the fire was heard distinctly. The old priest stood silent for a moment. His shaggy brows swept down over his eyes like ashes quenching flame. Then he lifted his face and spoke.

"None of these things will please the god. More costly is the offering that shall cleanse your sin, more precious the crimson dew that shall send new life into this holy tree of blood. Thor claims your dearest and your noblest gift."

Hunrad moved nearer to the group of children who stood watching the fire and the swarms of spark-serpents darting upward. They had heeded none of the priest's words, and did not notice now that he approached them, so eager were they to see which fiery snake would go highest among the oak branches. Foremost among them, and most intent on the pretty game, was a boy like a sunbeam, slender and quick, with blithe brown eyes and laughing lips. The priest's hand was laid upon his shoulder. The boy turned and looked up in his face.

"Here," said the old man, with his voice vibrating as when a thick rope is strained by a ship swinging from her moorings, "here is the chosen one, the eldest son of the Chief, the darling of the people. Hearken, Bernhard, wilt thou go to Valhalla, where the heroes dwell with the gods, to bear a message to Thor?"

The boy answered, swift and clear:

"Yes, priest, I will go if my father bids me. Is it far away? Shall I run quickly? Must I take my bow and arrows for the wolves?"

The boy's father, the Chieftain Gundhar, standing among his bearded warriors, drew his breath deep, and leaned so heavily on the handle of his spear that the wood cracked. And his wife, Irma, bending forward from the ranks of women, pushed the golden hair from her forehead with one hand. The other dragged at the silver chain about her neck until the rough links pierced her flesh, and the red drops fell unheeded on her breast.

A sigh passed through the crowd, like the murmur of the forest before the storm breaks. Yet no one spoke save Hunrad:

"Yes, my Prince, both bow and spear shalt thou have, for the way is long, and thou art a brave huntsman. But in darkness thou must journey for a little space, and with eyes blindfolded. Fearest thou?"

"Naught fear I," said the boy, "neither darkness, nor the great bear, nor the were-wolf. For I am Gundhar's son, and the defender of my folk."

Then the priest led the child in his raiment of lamb's-wool to a broad stone in front of the fire. He gave him his little bow tipped with silver, and his spear with shining head of steel. He bound the child's eyes with a white cloth, and bade him kneel beside the stone with his face to the east. Unconsciously the wide arc of spectators drew inward toward the centre, as the ends of the bow draw together when the cord is stretched. Winfried moved noiselessly until he stood close behind the priest.

The old man stooped to lift a black hammer of stone from the ground,—the sacred hammer of the god Thor. Summoning all the strength of his withered arms, he swung it high in the air. It poised for an instant above the child's fair head—then turned to fall.

One keen cry shrilled out from where the women stood: "Me! take me! not Bernhard!"

The flight of the mother toward her child was swift as the falcon's swoop. But swifter still was the hand of the deliverer.

Winfried's heavy staff thrust mightily against the hammer's handle as it fell. Sideways it glanced from the old man's grasp, and the black stone, striking on the altar's edge, split in twain. A shout of awe and joy rolled along the living circle. The branches of the oak shivered. The flames leaped higher. As the shout died away the people saw the lady Irma, with her arms clasped round her child, and above them, on the altar-stone, Winfried, his face shining like the face of an angel.

IV

A SWIFT mountain-flood rolling down its channel; a huge rock tumbling from the hill-side and falling in mid-stream: the baffled waters broken and confused, pausing in their flow, dash high against the rock, foaming and murmuring, with divided impulse, uncertain whether to turn to the right or the left.

Even so Winfried's bold deed fell into the midst of the thoughts and passions of the council. They were at a standstill. Anger and wonder, reverence and joy and confusion surged through the crowd. They knew not which way to move: to resent the intrusion of the stranger as an insult to their gods, or to welcome him as the rescuer of their prince.

The old priest crouched by the altar, silent. Conflicting counsels troubled the air. Let the sacrifice go forward; the gods must be appeased. Nay, the boy must not die; bring the chieftain's best horse and slay it in his stead; it will be enough; the holy tree loves the blood of horses. Not so, there is a better counsel yet; seize the stranger whom the gods have led hither as a victim and make his life pay the forfeit of his daring.

The withered leaves on the oak rustled and whispered overhead. The fire flared and sank again. The angry voices clashed against each other and fell like opposing waves. Then the chieftain Gundhar struck the earth with his spear and gave his decision.

"All have spoken, but none are agreed. There is no voice of the council. Keep silence now, and let the stranger speak. His words shall give us judgment, whether he is to live or to die."

Winfried lifted himself high upon the altar, drew a roll of parchment from his bosom, and began to read.

"A letter from the great Bishop of Rome, who sits on a golden throne, to the people of the forest, Hessians and Thuringians, Franks and Saxons. *In nomin Domini, sanctae et individuae Trinitatis, amen!*"

A murmur of awe ran through the crowd. "It is the sacred tongue of the Romans; the tongue that is heard and understood by the wise men of every land. There is magic in it. Listen!"

Winfried went on to read the letter, translating it into the speech of the people.

"We have sent unto you our Brother Boniface, and appointed him your bishop, that he may teach you the only true faith, and baptise you, and lead you back from the ways of error to the path of salvation. Hearken to him in all things like a father. Bow your hearts to his teaching. He comes not for earthly gain, but for the gain of your souls. Depart from evil works. Worship not the false gods, for they are devils. Offer no more bloody sacrifices, nor eat the flesh of horses, but do as our Brother Boniface commands you. Build a house for him that he may dwell among you, and a church where you may offer your prayers to the only living God, the Almighty King of Heaven."

It was a splendid message: proud, strong, peaceful, loving. The dignity of the words imposed mightily upon the hearts of the people. They were quieted as men who have listened to a lofty strain of music.

"Tell us, then," said Gundhar, "what is the word that thou bringest to us from the Almighty? What is thy counsel for the tribes of the woodland on this night of sacrifice?"

"This is the word, and this is the counsel," answered Winfried. "Not a drop of blood shall fall to-night, save that which pity has drawn from the breast of your princess, in love for her child. Not a life shall be blotted out in the darkness to-night; but the great shadow of the tree which hides you from the light of heaven shall be swept away. For this is the birth-night of the white Christ, son of the All-Father, and Saviour of mankind. Fairer is He than Baldur the Beautiful, greater than Odin the Wise, kinder than Freya the Good. Since He has come to earth the bloody sacrifice must cease. The dark Thor, on whom you vainly call, is dead. Deep in the shades of Niffelheim he is lost forever. His power in the world is broken. Will you serve a helpless god? See, my brothers, you call this tree his oak. Does he dwell here? Does he protect it?"

A troubled voice of assent rose from the throng. The people stirred uneasily. Women covered their eyes. Hunrad lifted his head and muttered hoarsely, "Thor! take vengeance! Thor!"

Winfried beckoned to Gregor. "Bring the axes, thine and one for me. Now, young woodsman, show thy craft! The king-tree of the forest must fall, and swiftly, or all is lost!"

The two men took their places facing each other, one on each side of the oak. Their cloaks were flung aside, their heads bare. Carefully they felt the ground with their feet, seeking a firm grip of the earth. Firmly they grasped the axe-helves and swung the shining blades.

"Tree-god!" cried Winfried, "art thou angry? Thus we smite thee!"

"Tree-god!" answered Gregor, "art thou mighty? Thus we fight thee!"

Clang! clang! the alternate strokes beat time upon the hard, ringing wood. The axe-heads glittered in their rhythmic flight, like fierce eagles circling about their quarry.

The broad flakes of wood flew from the deepening gashes in the sides of the oak. The huge trunk quivered. There was a shuddering in the branches. Then the great wonder of Winfried's life came to pass.

Out of the stillness of the winter night, a mighty rushing noise sounded overhead.

Was it the ancient gods on their white battle-steeds, with their black hounds of wrath and their arrows of lightning, sweeping through the air to destroy their foes?

A strong, whirling wind passed over the tree-tops. It gripped the oak by its branches and tore it from the roots. Backward it fell, like a ruined tower, groaning and crashing as it split asunder in four great pieces.

Winfried let his axe drop, and bowed his head for a moment in the presence of almighty power.

Then he turned to the people, "Here is the timber," he cried, "already felled and split for your new building. On this spot shall rise a chapel to the true God and his servant St. Peter.

"And here," said he, as his eyes fell on a young fir-tree, standing straight and green, with its top pointing toward the stars, amid the divided ruins of the fallen oak, "here is the living tree, with no stain of blood upon it, that shall be the sign of your new worship. See how it points to the sky. Call it the tree of the Christ-child. Take it up and carry it to the chieftain's hall. You shall go no more into the shadows of the forest to keep your feasts with secret rites of shame. You shall keep them at home, with laughter and songs and rites of love. The thunder-oak has fallen, and I think the day is coming when there shall not be a home in all Germany where the children are not gathered around the green fir-tree to rejoice in the birth-night of Christ."

So they took the little fir from its place, and carried it in joyous procession to the edge of the glade, and laid it on the sledge. The horses tossed their heads and drew their load bravely, as if the new burden had made it lighter.

When they came to the house of Gundhar, he bade them throw open the doors of the hall and set the tree in the midst of it. They kindled lights among the branches until it seemed to be tangled full of fire-flies. The children encircled it, wondering, and the sweet odour of the balsam filled the house.

Then Winfried stood beside the chair of Gundhar, on the daïs at the end of the hall, and told the story of Bethlehem; of the babe in the manger, of the shepherds on the hills, of the host of angels and their midnight song. All the people listened, charmed into stillness.

But the boy Bernhard, on Irma's knee, folded in her soft arms, grew restless as the story lengthened, and began to prattle softly at his mother's ear.

"Mother," whispered the child, "why did you cry out so loud, when the priest was going to send me to Valhalla?"

"Oh, hush, my child," answered the mother, and pressed him closer to her side.

"Mother," whispered the boy again, laying his finger on the stains upon her breast, "see, your dress is red! What are these stains? Did some one hurt you?"

The mother closed his mouth with a kiss. "Dear, be still, and listen!"

The boy obeyed. His eyes were heavy with sleep. But he heard the last words of Winfried as he spoke of the angelic messengers, flying over the hills of Judea and singing as they flew. The child wondered and dreamed and listened. Suddenly his face grew bright. He put his lips close to Irma's cheek again.

"Oh, mother!" he whispered very low, "do not speak. Do you hear them? Those angels have come back again. They are singing now behind the tree."

And some say that it was true; but others say that it was only Gregor and his companions at the lower end of the hall, chanting their Christmas-hymn:

> *All glory be to God on high,*
> *And on the earth be peace!*
> *Good-will henceforth, from heaven to men*
> *Begin and never cease.*

GAMALIEL BRADFORD

Santa Claus: A Psychograph

THE first thing a psychographer must do is to look for material, facts on which to base his deductions and guesses as to the development and workings of a character. Now in the case of Santa Claus the facts are deplorably scanty. Fortunately what charms us most in saints is what we do not know about them.

The real, original Saint Nicholas celebrates his *festa* on the sixth of December, and in some countries that date is still the one appropriated to his observances, though they have more generally been transferred to December twenty-fifth. It appears that there was a Bishop of Myra, which in itself has a delightfully mythical sound, named Nicholas, who worked his way into the calendar by various marvels, the general characteristic of which was an attractive aptitude for giving. This same Saint Nicholas established himself as the patron of more or less generous and lavish persons, sailors, school-boys, and even thieves. It will be remembered that in *Ivanhoe* Gurth is eased of his financial burden by a parcel of Saint Nicholas' clerks. All these somewhat thoughtless worshipers seem to proceed on the principle that it is more blessed to give than to receive, at least that the source of supply is of comparatively little consequence, and even should not be too closely subjected to scrutiny, so long as it corresponds sufficiently to the large necessities of outlay. In the Saint Nicholas legend, as in so many stories of the early saints, we find traces of something elemental, of a profound naturalism, closely connected with the pagan sources which got themselves intimately intertwined in the origins of Christian thought and worship.

But a much more charming and more concrete source of information about the most popular of saints than all the old documents is the poem by Clement Moore, which may safely be said to be as well known as Gray's "Elegy," though the American poem has somewhat less pretension to literary finish and elegance. We get from it at least a vividly satisfactory presentation of the saint, as he has appeared on millions of Christmas cards and will appear on millions more:

> He was dressed all in fur from his head to his foot,
> And his clothes were all tarnished with ashes and soot;
> A bundle of toys he had flung on his back,
> And he looked like a peddler just opening his pack.
> His eyes how they twinkled! His dimples how merry!
> His cheeks were like roses, his nose like a cherry;
> His droll little mouth was drawn up like a bow,
> And the beard on his chin was as white as the snow;
> The stump of a pipe he held tight in his teeth,
> And the smoke, it encircled his head like a wreath.
> He had a broad face and a little round belly,
> That shook when he laughed, like a bowl full of jelly.
> He was chubby and plump—a right jolly old elf;
> And I laughed when I saw him, in spite of myself.

At first sight it may seem inappropriate that the saint of jollity, of wild revels and Christmas gambols, should be so old. One thinks of other types that might perhaps have been more suitable, more fit and ready to take a boisterous or a sympathetic part in rounds of physical and spiritual gaiety. Should we not have had a god of Christmas like the young Apollo, a creature of rounded and flawless beauty and tireless vigor, who would have been able not only to dispense joy and merriment, but to partake of them without limit? Or one thinks again of some light, diaphanous fairy, who would hover over the Christmas festivity, showering light and grace and loving-kindness with dim, incalculable charm. Or might not the presiding spirit of Christmas perhaps have been a child, since he deals so much with children, a cherub, or a cupid, clapping his hands himself in dancing glee and forgetful ecstasy over the broad munificence which he scatters about the world?

But the more one thinks of it, the more one concludes that the immortal age of Santa is symbolically best. The essence of the type that he embodies is the pure delight of giving, the absolute disregard of self and selfish enjoyment in the exhaustless pleasure of seeing and making others happy. And surely age is the time of life which best knows and develops this delight. There is, to be sure, a hard and meager age, which stints itself and others, which is so impressed by the fear of dependence and misery that it has nothing to spare for giving and no pleasure in it. But there is also, let us hope much more often, an ample and sunny and generous age which, having reached the limit of personal enjoyment, is ready and anxious to impart to others what it can no longer taste itself. Young vigorous gods and diaphanous fairies are all very well; but they are apt to be youthfully busy about their own concerns. Children are delightful in their expansive generosity when the whim seizes them; but they are without the broad experience which disposes to the sympathetic touch. Sweet and sunny age has no concerns of its own, or none that are pressing enough to bother about, and it has the full knowledge of all the charm of life that can be given to others and of all of others' misery that may be so easily relieved.

Santa Claus: A Psychograph

Moreover, age is tolerant as youth is not. Age is not exacting in its requirements, does not too nicely discriminate in the objects of its bounty, does not demand a pure perfection in the recipient as an indispensable preliminary to gifts and kindly help. Age, if it is wise and venerable, has learned the beautiful precept of the old physician of King Louis XIV, "*Il faut beaucoup pardonner à la nature,*" and expresses itself in the lovely words of the old lady in the French comedy: "*Je suis trop vieille pour ne pas pardonner.*" And age, after all, is the period that best understands and most loves children. It has the patience to study them and the leisure to enjoy them. Perhaps second childhood, with all its drawbacks, has at least this golden privilege.

Then, too, it must be remembered that the age of Santa Claus is not a withered, haggard, misshapen age. It is hearty, robust, vigorous and well nourished. It has the aspect and the essence of immortal youth. Those rosy cheeks and that dancing belly are not the equipment of an ascetic who grudges to others the gaiety of life because he has long since lost his share in it. The saint has made merry through his thousand years and he proposes to keep it up with all the wisdom and all the variety of long experience. Let silly youth and callow infancy think to outdo him: they will find themselves mistaken. And he rushes his gay and riotous movement through the wide, sparkling progress of the winter night, without cessation and without fatigue. And then it occurs to me to wonder what Santa Claus does in summer. Does he spend month after month piling up the wonderful stores of varied richness which he is to dispense in one tremendous nocturnal outburst of world-wide beneficence? Or does he assume some other shape and brighten and gladden summer days and hours by a continued splendor of giving which we know nothing about? Or does he sleep, sleep, and renew his exhausted forces for the resumption of his eternal winter task? Since we cannot say he hibernates, shall we say he estivates, through the long hot months when his services are not required? Also, there is the further doubt: how does Santa appear in the Southern Hemisphere, when Christmas flares up with all the blazing intensity of ending June? What becomes then of the reindeer and the fur coat and the glittering icicles hanging from the snowy beard? But one must not vex the reverend sanctity of these ancient legends with impertinent questions.

One thing is certain, that being a saint and so in a sense divine, Santa Claus does not know the drawbacks that affect and impair the perfection of mere earthly Christmas giving. First of all, he does not stay to watch the imperfect working of many of his gifts. All is gay and lovely on Christmas Eve and Christmas Day, or ought to be. But afterward, there is apt to be discontent and complaints: Why did I get this, and not that? Why did Mary have the lovely doll, while only this stupid picture book has come to me? These things the saint is not aware of, sweeping in his joyous progress round the world. Then for the parent of this earth there is the unspeakable fatigue. Oh, yes, it is delightful to make the children happy, if they are; but one goes to bed, if one is lucky enough to get there, with every limb aching, and one's chief consciousness is of relief that Christmas cannot come again till three-hundred-and-sixty-four common days have come between. And Santa Claus apparently does not have to bother about expense. He puts his hand into his pocket or his sack, and draws out illimitably. Not for nothing is he the patron of Saint Nicholas' clerks. Easy come, easy go. It is a fine thing to be generous and lavish when you draw upon an inexhaustible store. But when you are worried about where the dollars are to come from to provide all the gifts that the children are expecting, you think with a little envy of a saint who has only to lift his hand, and everything desirable will drop from it with prolific and unfailing splendor.

So the legend of Saint Nicholas is a lovely and delectable myth, the last living relic of the vanishing world of dreams. The fairies are gone. No little children or innocent maidens watch any longer through the ardent summer nights to catch some echo of the songs and dances of tiny people, footing it daintily over the dewy turf. The witches are gone. Unpleasant old ladies can look about them ill-favoredly and purvey gossip without the danger of being burned at the stake. Nobody pays heed to them and nobody fears what they do. The ghosts are gone. Solitary graveyards are far more comfortable and agreeable sojourning places in the summer evenings than crowded streets where one has to be constantly on the watch against becoming a ghost oneself. Santa Claus alone still lingers with us. For Heaven's sake, let us keep him as long as we can. There are some excellent people who are scrupulous about deceiving their children with such legendary nonsense. They are mistaken. The children learn to see soon enough, too clearly and too well, or to think they do. Ah, leave them at least one thrill of passionate mystery that may linger with them when the years begin to grow too plain and dull and bare. After all, in this universe of ignorance, anything may be true, even our dreams.

And there is a still deeper value in the preservation of the Santa Claus legend, even by those who have no faith in that or any other legend whatever. For such preservation typifies the profound principle that, sacred as both are, the law of love is higher than the law of truth. For this there is a perfectly simple and unassailable reason, that truth at its best is deceiving, but love is never. We toil and tire ourselves and sacrifice our lives for the dim goddess Truth. Then she eludes us, slips away from us, mocks at us. But love grows firmer and surer and more prevailing as the years pass by.

Therefore, why should not old and young alike, in the brilliant, deceptive Christmas moonlight, hearken for the tinkling bells and the pawing reindeer and echo the merry greeting of the saint, broadcast to the whole wide world:

"Merry Christmas to all and to all a good-night."

III

Christmas Is Dickens

BRITISH STORIES OF THE HOLLY AND PLUM PUDDING
TRADITION, GHOST STORIES OF CHRISTMAS,
AND SOME TALES IN THE MODERN IDIOM

*. . . apart from the veneration due to its sacred
name and origin, if anything belonging to it can be
apart from that . . .*

CHARLES DICKENS : A CHRISTMAS CAROL

II

Christmas Stories

BEING STORIES OF THE HOLLY AND THE MISTLETOE
UPON GHOST-STORIES OF CHRISTMAS
AND SOME TALE IN THE MODERN IDIOM

... apart from the sentiment due to its sacred
name and origin if anything belonging to it can be
apart from that.

CHARLES DICKENS: A CHRISTMAS TREE

JOSEPH ADDISON

Christmas with Sir Roger

(*The Spectator*, No. 269)

I WAS this morning surprised with a great knocking at the door, when my landlady's daughter came up to me and told me there was a man below desired to speak with me. Upon my asking who it was, she told me it was a very grave elderly person, but that she did not know his name. I immediately went down to him, and found him to be the coachman of my worthy friend, Sir Roger de Coverley. He told me that his master came to town last night, and would be glad to take a turn with me in Gray's-Inn walks. As I was wondering in myself what had brought Sir Roger to town, not having lately received any letter from him, he told me that his master was come up to get a sight of Prince Eugene, and that he desired I would immediately meet him.

I was not a little pleased with the curiosity of the old knight, though I did not much wonder at it, having heard him say more than once in private discourse, that he looked upon Prince Eugenio (for so the knight always calls him) to be a greater man than Scanderbeg.

I was no sooner come into Gray's-Inn walks, but I heard my friend upon the terrace hemming twice or thrice to himself with great vigor, for he loves to clear his pipes in good air (to make use of his own phrase), and is not a little pleased with anyone who takes notice of the strength which he still exerts in his morning hems.

I was touched with a secret joy at the sight of the good old man, who before he saw me was engaged in conversation with a beggar-man that had asked an alms of him. I could hear my friend chide him for not finding out some work; but at the same time saw him put his hand in his pocket and give him sixpence.

Our salutations were very hearty on both sides, consisting of many kind shakes of the hand, and several affectionate looks which we cast upon one another. After which the knight told me my good friend his chaplain was very well, and much at my service, and that the Sunday before he had made a most incomparable sermon out of Dr. Barrow. "I have left," says he, "all my affairs in his hands, and being willing to lay an obligation upon him, have deposited with him thirty marks, to be distributed among his poor parishioners."

He then proceeded to acquaint me with the welfare of Will Wimble. Upon which he put his hand into his fob and presented me in his name with a tobacco-stopper, telling me that Will had been busy all the beginning of the winter in turning great quantities of them; and that he made a present of one to every gentleman in the country who has good principles, and smokes. He added that poor Will was at present under great tribulation, for that Tom Touchy had taken the law of him for cutting some hazel sticks out of one of his hedges.

Among other pieces of news which the knight brought from his country-seat, he informed me that Moll White was dead, and that about a month after her death the wind was so very high that it blew down the end of one of his barns. "But for my own part," says Sir Roger, "I do not think that the old woman had any hand in it."

He afterward fell into an account of the diversions which had passed in his house during the holidays; for Sir Roger, after the laudable custom of his ancestors, always keeps open house at Christmas. I learned from him that he had killed eight fat hogs for the season, that he had dealt about his chines very liberally among his neighbors, and that in particular he had sent a string of hog's-puddings with a pack of cards to every poor family in the parish. "I have often thought," says Sir Roger, "it happens very well that Christmas should fall out in the middle of the winter. It is the most dead uncomfortable time of the year, when the poor people would suffer very much from their poverty and cold, if they had not good cheer, warm fires, and Christmas gambols to support them. I love to rejoice their poor hearts at this season, and to see the whole village merry in my great hall. I allow a double quantity of malt to my smallbeer, and set it a-running for twelve days to everyone that calls for it. I have always a piece of cold beef and a mince pie upon the table, and am wonderfully pleased to see my tenants pass away a whole evening in playing their innocent tricks and smutting one another. Our friend Will Wimble is as merry as any of them, and shows a thousand roguish tricks upon these occasions."

I was very much delighted with the reflection of my old friend, which carried so much goodness in it. He then launched out into the praise of the late act of Parliament for securing the Church of England, and told me with great satisfaction that he believed it already began to take effect, for that a rigid dissenter who chanced to dine at his house on Christmas Day had been observed to eat very plentifully of his plum porridge.

After having dispatched all our country matters, Sir Roger made several inquiries concerning the club, and particularly of his old antagonist, Sir Andrew Freeport. He asked me with a kind of smile whether Sir Andrew had not taken advantage of his absence to vent among them some of his republican doctrines; but soon after gathering up his countenance into a more than ordinary seriousness, "Tell me truly," says he, "don't you think Sir Andrew had a hand in the pope's procession?"— But without giving me time to answer him, "Well, well," says he, "I know you are a wary man, and do not care to talk of public matters."

The knight then asked me if I had seen Prince Eugenio, and made me promise to get him a stand in some convenient place where he might have a full sight of that extraordinary man, whose presence does so much honor to the British nation. He dwelt very long on the praises of this great general, and I found that since I was with him in the country he had drawn many observations together out of his reading in Baker's Chronicle, and other authors, who always lie in his hall window, which very much redound to the honor of the prince.

Having passed away the greatest part of the morning in hearing the knight's reflections, which were partly private and partly political, he asked me if I would smoke a pipe with him over a dish of coffee at Squire's? As I love the old man, I take delight in complying with everything that is agreeable to him, and accordingly waited on him to the coffeehouse, where his venerable figure drew upon us the eyes of the whole room. He had no sooner seated himself at the upper end of the high table, but he called for a clean pipe, a paper of tobacco, a dish of coffee, a wax candle, and the Supplement, with such an air of cheerfulness and good humor, that all the boys in the coffeeroom (who seemed to take pleasure in serving him) were at once employed on his several errands, insomuch that nobody else could come at a dish of tea, until the knight had got all his conveniences about him.

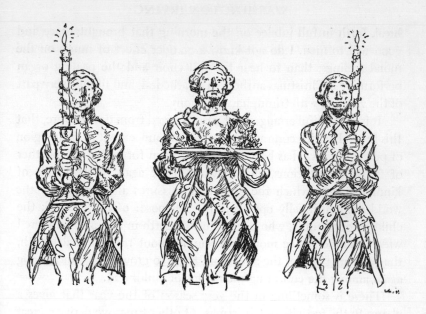

WASHINGTON IRVING

Christmas Papers

CHRISTMAS

NOTHING in England exercises a more delightful spell over my imagination, than the lingerings of the holiday customs and rural games of former times. . . .

Of all the old festivals, however, that of Christmas awakens the strongest and most heartfelt associations. There is a tone of solemn and sacred feeling that blends with our conviviality, and lifts the spirit to a state of hallowed and elevated enjoyment. The services of the church about this season are extremely tender and inspiring. They dwell on the beautiful story of the origin of our faith, and the pastoral scenes that accompanied its announcement. They gradually increase in fervor and pathos during the season of Advent, until they break forth in full jubilee on the morning that brought peace and good will to men. I do not know a grander effect of music on the moral feelings, than to hear the full choir and the pealing organ performing a Christmas anthem in a cathedral, and filling every part of the vast pile with triumphant harmony.

It is a beautiful arrangement, also, derived from days of yore, that this festival, which commemorates the announcement of the religion of peace and love, has been made the season for gathering together of family connections, and drawing closer again those bands of kindred hearts, which the cares and pleasures and sorrows of the world are continually operating to cast loose: of calling back the children of a family, who have launched forth in life, and wandered widely asunder, once more to assemble about the paternal hearth, that rallying-place of the affections, there to grow young and loving again among the endearing mementos of childhood.

There is something in the very season of the year that gives a charm to the festivity of Christmas. At other times we derive a great portion of our pleasures from the mere beauties of nature. . . . But in the depth of winter, when nature lies despoiled of every charm, and wrapped in her shroud of sheeted snow, we turn for our gratifications to moral sources. The dreariness and desolation of the landscape, the short gloomy days and darksome nights, while they circumscribe our wanderings, shut in our feelings also from rambling abroad, and make us more keenly disposed for the pleasure of the social circle. Our thoughts are more concentrated, our friendly sympathies more aroused. We feel more sensibly the charm of each other's society, and are brought more closely together by dependence on each other for enjoyment. Heart calleth unto heart; and we draw our pleasures from the deep wells of loving-kindness, which lie in the quiet recesses of our bosoms; and which, when resorted to, furnish forth the pure element of domestic felicity. . . .

The English, from the great prevalence of rural habit throughout every class of society, have always been fond of those festivals and holidays which agreeably interrupt the stillness of country life; and they were, in former days, particularly observant of the religious and social rites of Christmas. It is inspiring to read even the dry details which some antiquaries have given of the quaint humors, the burlesque pageants, the complete abandonment to mirth and good-fellowship, with which this festival was celebrated. It seemed to throw open every door, and unlock every heart. It brought the peasant and the peer together, and blended all ranks in one warm generous flow of joy and kindness. The old halls of castles and manor houses resounded with the harp and the Christmas carol, and their ample boards groaned under the weight of hospitality. Even the poorest cottage welcomed the festive season with green decorations of bay and holly—the cheerful fire glanced its rays through the lattice, inviting the passengers to raise the latch, and join the gossip knot huddled round the hearth, beguiling the long evening with legendary jokes and oft-told Christmas tales.

One of the least pleasing effects of modern refinement is the havoc it has made among the hearty old holiday customs. It has completely taken off the sharp touchings and spirited reliefs of these embellishments of life, and has worn down society into a more smooth and polished, but certainly a less characteristic surface. Many of the games and ceremonials of Christmas have entirely disappeared, and, like the sherris sack of old Falstaff, are become matters of speculation and dispute among commentators. They flourished in times full of spirit and lustihood, when men enjoyed life roughly, but heartily and vigorously; times wild and picturesque, which have furnished poetry with its richest materials, and the drama with its most attractive variety of characters and manners. . . .

Shorn, however, as it is, of its ancient and festive honors, Christmas is still a period of delightful excitement in England. It is gratifying to see that home feeling completely aroused which holds so powerful a place in every English bosom. The preparations making on every side for the social board that is again to unite friends and kindred; the presents of good cheer passing and repassing, those tokens of regard, and quickeners of kind feelings; the evergreens distributed about houses and churches, emblems of peace and gladness; all these have the most pleasing effect in producing fond associations, and kindling benevolent sympathies. Even the sound of the Waits, rude as may be their minstrelsy, breaks upon the midwatches of a winter night with the effect of perfect harmony. As I have been awakened by them in that still and solemn hour, "when deep sleep falleth upon man," I have listened with a hushed delight, and, connecting them with the sacred and joyous occasion, have almost fancied them into another celestial choir, announcing peace and good will to mankind.

How delightfully the imagination, when wrought upon by these moral influences, turns everything to melody and beauty! The very crowing of the cock, heard sometimes in the profound repose of the country, "telling the night watches to his feathery dames," was thought by the common people to announce the approach of this sacred festival:

> Some say that ever 'gainst that season comes
> Wherein our Saviour's birth is celebrated,
> The bird of dawning singeth all night long:
> And then, they say, no spirit dares stir abroad;
> The nights are wholesome; then no planets strike,
> No fairy takes, nor witch hath power to charm;
> So hallow'd and so gracious is the time.

Stranger and sojourner as I am in the land—though for me no social hearth may blaze, no hospitable roof throw open its doors, nor the warm grasp of friendship welcome me at the threshold—yet I feel the influence of the season beaming into my soul from the happy looks of those around me. Surely happiness is reflective, like the light of heaven; and every countenance, bright with smiles, and glowing with innocent enjoyment, is a mirror transmitting to others the rays of a supreme and ever-shining benevolence. He who can turn churlishly away from contemplating the felicity of his fellow beings, and can sit down darkling and repining in his loneliness when all around is joyful, may have his moments of strong excitement and selfish gratification, but he wants the genial and social sympathies which constitute the charm of a merry Christmas.

CHRISTMAS EVE

It was a brilliant moonlight night, but extremely cold; our chaise whirled rapidly over the frozen ground; the postboy smacked his whip incessantly, and a part of the time his horses were on a gallop. "He knows where he is going," said my companion, laughing, "and is eager to arrive in time for some of the merriment and good cheer of the servants' hall. My father, you must know, is a bigoted devotee of the old school, and prides himself upon keeping up something of old English hospitality. He is a tolerable specimen of what you will rarely meet with nowadays in its purity, the old English country gentleman; for our men of fortune spend so much of their time in town, and fashion is carried so much into the country, that the strong rich peculiarities of ancient rural life are almost polished away. . . . Being representative of the oldest family in the neighborhood, and a great part of the peasantry being his tenants, he is much looked up to, and, in general, is known simply by the appellation of 'The Squire,' a title which has been accorded to the head of the family since time immemorial. I think it best to give you these hints about my worthy old father, to prepare you for any eccentricities that might otherwise appear absurd."

We had passed for some time along the wall of a park, and at length the chaise stopped at the gate. It was in a heavy magnificent old style, of iron bars, fancifully wrought at top into flourishes and flowers. The huge square columns that supported the gate were surmounted by the family crest. Close adjoining was the porter's lodge, sheltered under dark fir trees, and almost buried in shrubbery.

The postboy rang a large porter's bell, which resounded through the still frosty air, and was answered by the distant barking of dogs, with which the mansion house seemed garrisoned. An old woman immediately appeared at the gate. As the moonlight fell strongly upon her, I had a full view of a little primitive dame, dressed very much in the antique taste, with a neat kerchief and stomacher, and her silver hair peeping from under a cap of snowy whiteness. She came curtseying forth, with many expressions of simple joy at seeing her young master. Her husband, it seemed, was up at the house keeping Christmas Eve in the servants' hall; they could not do without him, as he was the best hand at a song and story in the household.

My friend proposed that we should alight and walk through the park to the hall, which was at no great distance, while the chaise should follow on. Our road wound through a noble avenue of trees, among the naked branches of which the moon glittered as she rolled through the deep vault of a cloudless sky. The lawn beyond was sheeted with a slight covering of snow, which here and there sparkled as the moonbeams caught a frosty crystal; and at a distance might be seen a thin transparent vapor, stealing up from the low grounds and threatening gradually to shroud the landscape. . . .

As we approached the house, we heard the sound of music, and now and then a burst of laughter, from one end of the building. This, Bracebridge said, must proceed from the servants' hall, where a great deal of revelry was permitted, and even encouraged, by the squire, throughout the twelve days of Christmas, provided everything was done conformably to ancient usage. Here were kept up the old games of hoodman blind, shoe the wild mare, hot cockles, steal the white loaf, bob apple, and snap dragon: the yule clog and Christmas candle were regularly burnt, and the mistletoe, with its white berries, hung up, to the imminent peril of all the pretty housemaids.*

So intent were the servants upon their sports, that we had to ring repeatedly before we could make ourselves heard. On our arrival being announced, the squire came out to receive us, accompanied by his two other sons; one a young officer in the army, home on leave of absence; the other an Oxonian, just from the University. The squire was a fine healthy-looking old gentleman, with silver hair curling lightly round an open florid countenance; in which the physiognomist, with the advantage, like myself, of a previous hint

* The mistletoe is still hung up in farmhouses and kitchens at Christmas, and the young men have the privilege of kissing the girls under it, plucking each time a berry from the bush. When the berries are all plucked, the privilege ceases. [Irving's note.]

or two, might discover a singular mixture of whim and benevolence.

The family meeting was warm and affectionate; as the evening was far advanced, the squire would not permit us to change our traveling dresses, but ushered us at once to the company, which was assembled in a large old-fashioned hall. It was composed of different branches of a numerous family connection, where there were the usual proportion of old uncles and aunts, comfortable married dames, superannuated spinsters, blooming country cousins, half-fledged striplings, and bright-eyed boarding-school hoydens. They were variously occupied: some at a round game of cards, others conversing around the fireplace; at one end of the hall was a group of the young folks, some nearly grown up, others of a more tender and budding age, fully engrossed by a merry game; and a profusion of wooden horses, penny trumpets, and tattered dolls, about the floor, showed traces of a troop of little fairy beings, who, having frolicked through a happy day, had been carried off to slumber through a peaceful night.

While the mutual greetings were going on between young Brace-bridge and his relatives, I had time to scan the apartment. I have called it a hall, for so it had certainly been in old times, and the squire had evidently endeavored to restore it to something of its primitive state. Over the heavy projecting fireplace was suspended a picture of a warrior in armor, standing by a white horse, and on the opposite wall hung a helmet, buckler and lance. At one end an enormous pair of antlers were inserted in the wall, the branches serving as hooks on which to suspend hats, whips, and spurs; and in the corners of the apartment were fowling pieces, fishing rods, and other sporting implements. The furniture was of the cumbrous workmanship of former days, though some articles of modern convenience had been added, and the oaken floor had been carpeted; so that the whole presented an odd mixture of parlor and hall.

The grate had been removed from the wide overwhelming fireplace, to make way for a fire of wood, in the midst of which was an enormous log glowing and blazing, and sending forth a vast volume of light and heat; this I understood was the yule clog, which the squire was particular in having brought in and illumined on a Christmas Eve, according to ancient custom. . . .*

Supper was announced shortly after our arrival. It was served up in a spacious oaken chamber, the panels of which shone with wax, and around which were several family portraits decorated with holly and ivy. Besides the accustomed lights, two great wax tapers, called Christmas candles, wreathed with greens, were placed on a highly polished beaufet among the family plate. The table was abundantly spread with substantial fare; but the squire made his supper of frumenty, a dish made of wheat cakes boiled in milk, with rich spices, being a standing dish in old times for Christmas Eve. I was happy to find my old friend, mince pie, in the retinue of the feast; and finding him to be perfectly orthodox, and that I need not be ashamed of my predilection, I greeted him with all the warmth wherewith we usually greet an old and very genteel acquaintance. . . .

The supper had disposed everyone to gaiety, and an old harper was summoned from the servants' hall, where he had been strumming all the evening, and to all appearance comforting himself with some of the squire's home-brewed. He was a kind of hanger-on, I

---

* The *yule clog* is a great log of wood, sometimes the root of a tree, brought into the house with great ceremony, on Christmas Eve, laid in the fireplace, and lighted with the brand of last year's clog. While it lasted, there was great drinking, singing, and telling of tales. Sometimes it was accompanied by Christmas candles; but in the cottages the only light was from the ruddy blaze of the great wood fire. The yule clog was to burn all night; if it went out, it was considered a sign of ill-luck. Herrick mentions it in one of his songs—

> Come, bring with a noise
> My merrie, merrie boyes,
> The Christmas log to the firing;
> While my good dame, she
> Bids ye all be free,
> And drink to your hearts' desiring.

The yule clog is still burnt in many farmhouses and kitchens in England, particularly in the north, and there are several superstitions connected with it among the peasantry. If a squinting person come to the house while it is burning, or a person barefooted, it is considered an ill omen. The brand remaining from the yule clog is carefully put away to light the next year's Christmas fire. [Irving's note.]

was told, of the establishment, and, though ostensibly a resident of the village, was oftener to be found in the squire's kitchen than his own home, the old gentleman being fond of the sound of "harp in hall."

The dance, like most dances after supper, was a merry one; some of the older folks joined in it, and the squire himself figured down several couple with a partner, with whom he affirmed he had danced at every Christmas for nearly half a century. . . .

The party now broke up for the night with the kind-hearted old custom of shaking hands. As I passed through the hall, on my way to my chamber, the dying embers of the yule clog still sent forth a dusky glow, and had it not been the season when "no spirit dares stir abroad," I should have been half tempted to steal from my room at midnight, and peep whether the fairies might not be at their revels about the hearth.

My chamber was in the old part of the mansion, the ponderous furniture of which might have been fabricated in the days of the giants. The room was paneled, with cornices of heavy carved work, in which flowers and grotesque faces were strangely intermingled; and a row of black-looking portraits stared mournfully at me from the walls. The bed was of rich though faded damask, with a lofty tester, and stood in a niche opposite a bow window. I had scarcely got into bed when a strain of music seemed to break forth in the air just below the window. I listened, and found it proceeded from a band, which I concluded to be the Waits from some neighboring village. They went round the house, playing under the windows. I drew aside the curtains to hear them more distinctly. The moonbeams fell through the upper part of the casement, partially lighting up the antiquated apartment. The sounds, as they receded, became more soft and aerial, and seemed to accord with the quiet and moonlight. I listened and listened—they became more and more tender and remote, and, as they gradually died away, my head sunk upon the pillow, and I fell asleep.

CHRISTMAS DAY

WHEN I woke the next morning, it seemed as if all the events of the preceding evening had been a dream, and nothing but the identity of the ancient chamber convinced me of their reality. While I lay musing on my pillow, I heard the sound of little feet pattering outside of the door, and a whispering consultation. Presently a choir of small voices chanted forth an old Christmas carol, the burden of which was —

> *Rejoice, our Saviour he was born*
> *On Christmas Day in the morning.*

I rose softly, slipped on my clothes, opened the door suddenly, and beheld one of the most beautiful little fairy groups that a painter could imagine. It consisted of a boy and two girls, the eldest not more than six, and lovely as seraphs. They were going the rounds of the house, and singing at every chamber door; but my sudden appearance frightened them into mute bashfulness. They remained for a moment playing on their lips with their fingers, and now and then stealing a shy glance, from under their eyebrows, until, as if by one impulse, they scampered away, and as they turned an angle of the gallery, I heard them laughing in triumph at their escape. . . .

I had scarcely dressed myself, when a servant appeared to invite me to family prayers. He showed me the way to a small chapel in the old wing of the house, where I found the principal part of the family already assembled in a kind of gallery, furnished with cushions, hassocks, and large prayer books; the servants were seated on benches below. The old gentleman read prayers from a desk in front of the gallery, and Master Simon acted as clerk, and made the responses; and I must do him the justice to say that he acquitted himself with great gravity and decorum.

The service was followed by a Christmas carol, which Mr. Brace-bridge himself had constructed from a poem of his favorite author, Herrick; and it had been adapted to an old church melody by Master Simon. As there were several good voices among the household, the effect was extremely pleasing; but I was particularly gratified by the exaltation of heart, and sudden sally of grateful feeling, with which the worthy squire delivered one stanza: his eye glistening, and his voice rambling out of all the bounds of time and tune.

> *'Tis thou that crown'st my glittering hearth*
> > *With guiltlesse mirth,*
> *And givest me Wassaile bowles to drink*
> > *Spiced to the brink:*
> *Lord, 'tis thy plenty-dropping hand*
> > *That soiles my land:*
> *And giv'st me for by bushell sowne,*
> > *Twice ten for one.*

Our breakfast consisted of what the squire denominated true old English fare. He indulged in some bitter lamentations over modern breakfasts of tea and toast, which he censured as among the causes of modern effeminacy and weak nerves, and the decline of old English heartiness; and though he admitted them to his table to suit the palates of his guests, yet there was a brave display of cold meats, wine, and ale on the sideboard.

After breakfast I walked about the grounds with Frank Bracebridge and Master Simon, or Mr. Simon, as he was called by everybody but the squire. We were escorted by a number of gentlemanlike dogs, that seemed loungers about the establishment; from the frisking spaniel to the steady old staghound; the last of which was of a race that had been in the family time out of mind; they were all obedient to a dog whistle which hung to Master Simon's buttonhole, and in the midst of their gambols would glance an eye occasionally upon a small switch he carried in his hand. . . .

While we were talking, we heard the distant toll of the village bell, and I was told that the squire was a little particular in having his household at church on a Christmas morning; considering it a day of pouring out of thanks and rejoicing; for, as old Tusser observed,

> *At Christmas be merry, and thankful withal,*
> *And feast thy poor neighbours, the great with the small.*

As the morning, though frosty, was remarkably fine and clear, the most of the family walked to the church, which was a very old building of gray stone, and stood near a village, about half a mile from the park gate. Adjoining it was a low snug parsonage, which seemed coeval with the church. The front of it was perfectly matted with a yew tree that had been trained against its walls, through the dense foliage of which apertures had been formed to admit light into the small antique lattices. As we passed this sheltered nest, the parson issued forth and preceded us.

I had expected to see a sleek well-conditioned pastor, such as is often found in a snug living in the vicinity of a rich patron's table, but I was disappointed. The parson was a little, meager, black-looking man, with a grizzled wig that was too wide, and stood off from each ear, so that his head seemed to have shrunk away within it, like a dried filbert in its shell. He wore a rusty coat, with great skirts, and pockets that would have held the church Bible and prayer book; and his small legs seemed still smaller, from being planted in large shoes, decorated with enormous buckles.

I was informed by Frank Bracebridge that the parson had been a chum of his father's at Oxford, and had received this living shortly after the latter had come to his estate. He was a complete black-letter hunter, and would scarcely read a work printed in the Roman character. The editions of Caxton and Wynkyn de Worde were his delight; and he was indefatigable in his researches after such old English writers as have fallen into oblivion from their worthlessness.

In deference, perhaps to the notions of Mr. Bracebridge, he had made diligent investigations into the festive rites and holiday customs of former times, and had been as zealous in the inquiry as if he had been a boon companion, but it was merely with that plodding spirit with which men of adust temperament follow up any track of study merely because it is denominated learning, indifferent to its intrinsic nature, whether it be the illustration of the wisdom or of the ribaldry and obscenity of antiquity. He had pored over these old volumes so intensely that they seemed to have been reflected into his countenance, which, if the face be indeed an index of the mind, might be compared to a title page of black letter.

On reaching the church porch, we found the parson rebuking the gray-headed sexton for having used mistletoe among the greens with which the church was decorated. It was, he observed, an unholy plant, profaned by having been used by the Druids in their mystic ceremonies; and though it might be innocently employed in the festive ornamenting of halls and kitchens, yet it had been deemed by the Fathers of the Church as unhallowed, and totally unfit for sacred purposes. So tenacious was he on this point, that the poor sexton was obliged to strip down a great part of the humble trophies of his taste, before the parson would consent to enter upon the service of the day. . . .

The orchestra was in a small gallery, and presented a most whimsical grouping of heads, piled one above the other, among which I particularly noticed that of the village tailor, a pale fellow with a retreating forehead and chin, who played on the clarinet, and seemed to have blown his face to a point; and there was another, a short pursy man, stooping and laboring at a bass viol, so as to show nothing but the top of a round bald head, like the egg of an ostrich. There were two or three pretty faces among the female singers, to which the keen air of a frosty morning had given a bright rosy tint; but the gentlemen choristers had evidently been chosen, like old Cremona fiddles, more for tone than looks; and as several had to sing from the same book, there were clusterings of odd physiognomies, not unlike those groups of cherubs we sometimes see on country tombstones.

The usual services of the choir were managed tolerably well, the vocal parts generally lagging a little behind the instrumental, and some loitering fiddler now and then making up for lost time by traveling over a passage with prodigious celerity, and clearing more bars than the keenest fox hunter to be in at the death. But the great trial was an anthem that had been prepared and arranged by Master Simon, and on which he had founded great expectation. Unluckily there was a blunder at the very onset; the musicians became flurried;

Master Simon was in a fever; everything went on lamely and irregularly until they came to a chorus beginning "Now let us sing with one accord," which seemed to be a signal for parting company: all became discord and confusion; each shifted for himself, and got to the end as well, or rather, as soon as he could, excepting one old chorister in a pair of horn spectacles bestriding and pinching a long sonorous nose, who happened to stand a little apart, and, being wrapped up in his own melody, kept on a quavering course, wriggling his head, ogling his book, and winding all up by a nasal solo of at least three bars' duration.

The parson gave us a most erudite sermon on the rites and ceremonies of Christmas, and the propriety of observing it not merely as a day of thanksgiving, but of rejoicing; supporting the correctness of his opinions by the earliest usages of the church, and enforcing them by the authorities of Theophilus of Caesarea, St. Cyprian, St. Chrysostom, St. Augustine, and a cloud more of saints and fathers, from whom he made copious quotations. I was a little at a loss to perceive the necessity of such a mighty array of forces to maintain a point which no one present seemed inclined to dispute; but I soon found that the good man had a legion of ideal adversaries to contend with; having, in the course of his researches on the subject of Christmas, got completely embroiled in the sectarian controversies of the Revolution, when the Puritans made such a fierce assault upon the ceremonies of the church, and poor old Christmas was driven out of the land by proclamation of Parliament. The worthy parson lived but with times past, and knew but little of the present. . . .

I have seldom known a sermon attended apparently with more immediate effects; for on leaving the church the congregation seemed one and all possessed with the gaiety of spirit so earnestly enjoined by their pastor. The elder folks gathered in knots in the churchyard, greeting and shaking hands; and the children ran about crying "Ule! Ule!" and repeating some uncouth rhymes which the parson, who had joined us, informed me had been handed down from days of yore. The villagers doffed their hats to the squire as he passed, giving him the good wishes of the season with every appearance of heartfelt sincerity, and were invited by him to the hall, to take something to keep out the cold of the weather; and I heard blessings uttered by several of the poor, which convinced me that, in the midst of his enjoyments, the worthy old cavalier had not forgotten the true Christmas virtue of charity. . . .

We had not been long home when the sound of music was heard from a distance. A band of country lads, without coats, their shirt sleeves fancifully tied with ribands, their hats decorated with greens, and clubs in their hands, were seen advancing up the avenue, followed by a large number of villagers and peasantry. They stopped before the hall door, where the music struck up a peculiar air, and the lads performed a curious and intricate dance, advancing, retreating, and striking their clubs together, keeping exact time to the music; while one, whimsically crowned with a fox's skin, the tail of which flaunted down his back, kept capering round the skirts of the dance, and rattling a Christmas box, with many antic gesticulations.

The squire eyed this fanciful exhibition with great interest and delight, and gave me a full account of its origin, which he traced to the times when the Romans held possession of the island, plainly proving that this was a lineal descendant of the sword dance of the ancients. "It was now," he said, "nearly extinct, but he had accidentally met with traces of it in the neighborhood, and had encouraged its revival; though, to tell the truth, it was too apt to be followed up by the rough cudgel-play and broken heads in the evening."

After the dance was concluded, the whole party was entertained with brawn and beef, and stout home-brewed. The squire himself mingled among the rustics, and was received with awkward demonstrations of deference and regard. It is true, I perceived two or three of the younger peasants, as they were raising their tankards to their mouths, when the squire's back was turned, making something of a grimace, and giving each other the wink, but the moment they caught my eye, they pulled grave faces, and were exceedingly demure. . . .

The bashfulness of the guests soon gave way before good cheer and affability. There is something genuine and affectionate in the gaiety of the lower orders, when it is excited by the bounty and familiarity of those above them; the warm glow of gratitude enters into their mirth, and a kind word or a small pleasantry frankly uttered by a patron, gladdens the heart of the dependent more than oil and wine. When the squire had retired, the merriment increased, and there was much joking and laughter, particularly between Master Simon and a hale, ruddy-faced, white-headed farmer, who appeared to be the wit of the village; for I observed all his companions to wait with open mouths for his retorts, and burst into a gratuitous laugh before they could well understand them.

The whole house, indeed, seemed abandoned to merriment; as I passed to my room to dress for dinner, I heard the sound of music in a small court, and looking through a window that commanded it, I perceived a band of wandering musicians, with pandean pipes and tambourine; a pretty, coquettish housemaid was dancing a jig with a smart country lad, while several of the other servants were looking on. In the midst of her sport, the girl caught a glimpse of my face at the window, and, coloring up, ran off with an air of roguish affected confusion.

THE CHRISTMAS DINNER

I HAD finished my toilet, and was loitering with Frank Bracebridge in the library, when we heard a distinct thwacking sound, which he informed me was a signal for the serving up of the dinner. The squire kept up old customs in kitchen as well as hall; and the rolling pin, struck upon the dresser by the cook, summoned the servants to carry in the meats.

> Just in this nick the cook knock'd thrice,
> And all the waiters in a trice
>   His summons did obey;
> Each serving man, with dish in hand,
> March'd boldly up, like our train band,
>   Presented and away.*

* Sir John Suckling. [Irving's note.]

The dinner was served up in the great hall, where the squire always held his Christmas banquet. A blazing crackling fire of logs had been heaped on to warm the spacious apartment, and the flame went sparkling and wreathing up the wide-mouthed chimney. The great picture of the crusader and his white horse had been profusely decorated with greens for the occasion; and holly and ivy had likewise been wreathed round the helmet and weapons on the opposite wall, which I understood were the arms of the same warrior. . . .

We were ushered into this banqueting scene with the sound of minstrelsy, the old harper being seated on a stool beside the fireplace, and twanging his instrument with a vast deal more power than melody. Never did Christmas board display a more goodly and gracious assemblage of countenances; those who were not handsome were, at least, happy; and happiness is a rare improver of your hardfavored visage. . . .

The parson said grace, which was not a short familiar one, such as is commonly addressed to the Deity in these unceremonious days; but a long, courtly, well-worded one of the ancient school. There was now a pause, as if something was expected, when suddenly the butler entered the hall with some degree of bustle; he was attended by a servant on each side with a large waxlight, and bore a silver dish, on which was an enormous pig's head, decorated with rosemary, with a lemon in its mouth, which was placed with great formality at the head of the table. The moment this pageant made its appearance, the harper struck up a flourish; at the conclusion of which the young Oxonian, on receiving a hint from the squire, gave, with an air of the most comic gravity, an old carol, the first verse of which was as follows:

> *Caput apri defero,*
> *Reddens laudes Domino.*
> *The boar's head in hand bring I,*
> *With garlands gay and rosemary.*
> *I pray you all synge merily*
> *Qui estis in convivio.*

Though prepared to witness many of these little eccentricities, from being apprised of the peculiar hobby of mine host; yet, I confess, the parade with which so odd a dish was introduced somewhat perplexed me, until I gathered from the conversation of the squire and the parson, that it was meant to represent the bringing in of the boar's head; a dish formerly served up with much ceremony and the sound of minstrelsy and song, at great tables, on Christmas Day. "I like the old custom," said the squire, "not merely because it is stately and pleasing in itself, but because it was observed at the college at Oxford at which I was educated. When I hear the old song chanted, it brings to mind the time when I was young and gamesome—and the noble old college hall—and my fellow students loitering about in their black gowns; many of whom, poor lads, are now in their graves!" . . .

The table was literally loaded with good cheer, and presented an epitome of country abundance, in this season of overflowing larders. A distinguished post was allotted to "ancient sirloin," as mine host termed it; being, as he added, "the standard of old English hospitality, and a joint of goodly presence, and full of expectation." There were several dishes quaintly decorated, and which had evidently something traditional in their embellishments; but about which, as I did not like to appear overcurious, I asked no questions.

I could not, however, but notice a pie, magnificently decorated with peacock's feathers, in imitation of the tail of that bird, which overshadowed a considerable tract of the table. This, the squire confessed, with some little hesitation, was a pheasant pie, though a peacock pie was certainly the most authentical; but there had been such a mortality among the peacocks this season, that he could not prevail upon himself to have one killed. . . .

When the cloth was removed, the butler brought in a huge silver vessel of rare and curious workmanship, which he placed before the squire. Its appearance was hailed with acclamation, being the Wassail Bowl, so renowned in Christmas festivity. The contents had been prepared by the squire himself; for it was a beverage in the skillful mixture of which he particularly prided himself;

alleging that it was too abstruse and complex for the comprehension of an ordinary servant. It was a potation, indeed, that might well make the heart of a toper leap within him; being composed of the richest and raciest wines, highly spiced and sweetened, with roasted apples bobbing about the surface. The old gentleman's whole countenance beamed with a serene look of indwelling delight, as he stirred this mighty bowl. Having raised it to his lips, with a hearty wish of a merry Christmas to all present, he sent it brimming round the board, for everyone to follow his example, according to the primitive style; pronouncing it "the ancient fountain of good-feeling, where all hearts met together." . . .

The dinnertime passed away in this flow of innocent hilarity; and, though the old hall may have resounded in its time with many a scene of broader rout and revel, yet I doubt whether it ever witnessed more honest and genuine enjoyment. . . .

When the ladies had retired, the conversation, as usual, became still more animated; many good things were broached which had been thought of during dinner, but which would not exactly do for a lady's ear; and though I cannot positively affirm that there was much wit uttered, yet I have certainly heard many contests of rare wit produce much less laughter. . . .

After the dinner table was removed, the hall was given up to the younger members of the family, who, prompted to all kind of noisy mirth by the Oxonian and Master Simon, made its old walls ring with their merriment, as they played at romping games. I delight in witnessing the gambols of children, and particularly at this happy holiday season, and could not help stealing out of the drawing room on hearing one of their peals of laughter. I found them at the game of blindman's buff. Master Simon, who was the leader of their revels, and seemed on all occasions to fulfill the office of that ancient potentate, the Lord of Misrule,* was blinded in the midst

* At Christmasse there was in the Kinge's house, wheresoever hee was lodged, a lorde of misrule, or mayster of merie disportes, and the like had ye in the house of every nobleman of honour, or good worshippe, were he spirituall or temporall. Stowe. [Irving's note.]

of the hall. The little beings were as busy about him as the mock fairies about Falstaff; pinching him, plucking at the skirts of his coat, and tickling him with straws. One fine blue-eyed girl of about thirteen, with her flaxen hair all in beautiful confusion, her frolic face in a glow, her frock half torn off her shoulders, a complete picture of a romp, was the chief tormentor; and, from the slyness with which Master Simon avoided the smaller game, and hemmed this wild little nymph in corners, and obliged her to jump shrieking over chairs, I suspected the rogue of being not a whit more blinded than was convenient.

When I returned to the drawing room, I found the company seated round the fire listening to the parson, who was deeply ensconced in a high-backed oaken chair, the work of some cunning artificer of yore, which had been brought from the library for his particular accommodation. From this venerable piece of furniture, with which his shadowy figure and dark weazen face so admirably accorded, he was dealing out strange accounts of the popular superstitions and legends of the surrounding country, with which he had become acquainted in the course of his antiquarian researches. I am half inclined to think that the old gentleman was himself somewhat tinctured with superstition, as men are very apt to be who live a recluse and studious life in a sequestered part of the country, and pore over black-letter tracts, so often filled with the marvelous and supernatural. He gave us several anecdotes of the fancies of the neighboring peasantry, concerning the effigy of the crusader, which lay on the tomb by the church altar. As it was the only monument of the kind in that part of the country it had always been regarded with feelings of superstition by the good wives of the village. It was said to get up from the tomb and walk the rounds of the churchyard in stormy nights, particularly when it thundered; and one old woman, whose cottage bordered on the churchyard, had seen it through the windows of the church, when the moon shone, slowly pacing up and down the aisles. It was the belief that some wrong had been left unredressed by the deceased, or some treasure hidden, which kept the spirit in a state of trouble and restlessness. Some talked of gold and jewels buried in the tomb, over which the specter kept watch; and there was a story current of a sexton in old times who endeavored to break his way to the coffin at night, but, just as he reached it, received a violent blow from the marble hand of the effigy, which stretched him senseless on the pavement. These tales were often laughed at by some of the sturdier among the rustics, yet when night came on, there were many of the stoutest unbelievers that were shy of venturing alone in the footpath that led across the churchyard.

From these and other anecdotes that followed, the crusader appeared to be the favorite hero of ghost stories throughout the vicinity. His picture which hung up in the hall, was thought by the servants to have something supernatural about it; for they remarked that, in whatever part of the hall you went, the eyes of the warrior were still fixed on you. The old porter's wife too, at the lodge, who had been born and brought up in the family, and was a great gossip among the maidservants, affirmed that in her young days she had often heard say, that on Midsummer Eve, when it was well known all kinds of ghosts, goblins, and fairies become visible and walk abroad, the crusader used to mount his horse, come down from his picture, ride about the house, down the avenue, and so to the church to visit the tomb; on which occasion the church door most civilly swung open of itself; not that he needed it; for he rode through closed gates and even stone walls, and had been seen by one of the dairymaids to pass between two bars of the great park gate, making himself as thin as a sheet of paper. . . .

Whilst we were all attention to the parson's stories, our ears were suddenly assailed by a burst of heterogeneous sounds from the hall, in which were mingled something like the clang of rude minstrelsy, with the uproar of many small voices and girlish laughter. The door suddenly flew open, and a train came trooping into the room, that might almost have been mistaken for the breaking-up of the court of Fairy. That indefatigable spirit, Master Simon, in the faithful discharge of his duties as Lord of Misrule, had conceived the idea of a Christmas mummery or masking; and having called in to his assistance the Oxonian and the young officer, who were equally ripe for anything that should occasion romping and merriment, they had carried it into instant effect. The old housekeeper had been consulted; the antique clothespresses and wardrobes rummaged, and made to yield up the relics of finery that had not seen the light for several generations; the younger part of the company had been privately convened from the parlor and hall, and the whole had been bedizened out, into a burlesque imitation of an antique mask.

Master Simon led the van, as "Ancient Christmas," quaintly appareled in a ruff, a short cloak, which had very much the aspect of one of the old housekeeper's petticoats, and a hat that might have served for a village steeple, and must indubitably have figured in the days of the Covenanters. From under this his nose curved boldly forth, flushed with a frost-bitten bloom, that seemed the very trophy of a December blast. He was accompanied by the blue-eyed romp, dished up as "Dame Mince Pie," in the venerable magnificence of a faded brocade, long stomacher, peaked hat, and high-heeled shoes. The young officer appeared as Robin Hood, in a sporting dress of Kendal green, and a foraging cap with a gold tassel.

The costume, to be sure, did not bear testimony to deep research, and there was an evident eye to the picturesque, natural to a young gallant in the presence of his mistress. The fair Julia hung on his arm in a pretty rustic dress, as "Maid Marian." The rest of the train had been metamorphosed in various ways; the girls trussed up in the finery of the ancient belles of the Bracebridge line, and the striplings bewhiskered with burnt cork, and gravely clad in broad skirts, hanging sleeves, and full-bottomed wigs, to represent the character of Roast Beef, Plum Pudding and other worthies celebrated in ancient maskings. The whole was under the control of the Oxonian, in the appropriate character of Misrule; and I observed that he exercised rather a mischievous sway with his wand over the smaller personages of the pageant.

The irruption of this motley crew, with beat of drum, according to ancient custom, was the consummation of uproar and merriment. Master Simon covered himself with glory by the stateliness with which, as Ancient Christmas, he walked a minuet with the peerless, though giggling, Dame Mince Pie. It was followed by a dance of all the characters, which, from its medley of costumes, seemed as though the old family portraits had skipped down from their frames to join in the sport. Different centuries were figuring at cross hands and right and left; the Dark Ages were cutting pirouettes and rigadoons; and the days of Queen Bess jiggling merrily down the middle, through a line of succeeding generations. . . .

But enough of Christmas and its gambols; it is time for me to pause in this garrulity. Methinks I hear the questions asked by my grave readers, "To what purpose is all this—how is the world to be made wiser by this talk?" Alas! is there not wisdom enough extant for the instruction of the world? And if not, are there not thousands of abler pens laboring for its improvement! It is so much pleasanter to please than to instruct—to play the companion rather than the preceptor.

What, after all, is the mite of wisdom that I could throw into the mass of knowledge; or how am I sure that my sagest deductions may be safe guides for the opinion of others? But in writing to amuse, if I fail, the only evil is in my own disappointment. If, however, I can by any lucky chance, in these days of evil, rub out one wrinkle from the brow of care, or beguile the heavy heart of one moment of sorrow; if I can now and then penetrate through the gathering film of misanthropy, prompt a benevolent view of human nature, and make my reader more in good humor with his fellow beings and himself, surely, surely, I shall not then have written entirely in vain.

CHARLES DICKENS

A Christmas Carol

IN FOUR STAVES

Stave One: Marley's Ghost

MARLEY was dead, to begin with. There is no doubt whatever about that. The register of his burial was signed by the clergyman, the clerk, the undertaker, and the chief mourner. Scrooge signed it. And Scrooge's name was good upon 'Change for anything he chose to put his hand to.

Old Marley was as dead as a door-nail.

EDITOR'S NOTE: As explained in the Introduction, this is the shortened version of the *Carol*, made by Dickens himself for use in his public readings.

Scrooge knew he was dead? Of course he did. How could it be otherwise? Scrooge and he were partners for I don't know how many years. Scrooge was his sole executor, his sole administrator, his sole assign, his sole residuary legatee, his sole friend, his sole mourner.

Scrooge never painted out old Marley's name, however. There it yet stood, years afterwards, above the warehouse door—Scrooge and Marley. The firm was known as Scrooge and Marley. Sometimes people new to the business called Scrooge Scrooge, and sometimes Marley. He answered to both names. It was all the same to him.

Oh! But he was a tight-fisted hand at the grindstone, was Scrooge! a squeezing, wrenching, grasping, scraping, clutching, covetous old sinner! External heat and cold had little influence on him. No warmth could warm, no cold could chill him. No wind that blew was bitterer than he, no falling snow was more intent upon its purpose, no pelting rain less open to entreaty. Foul weather didn't know where to have him. The heaviest rain and snow and hail and sleet could boast of the advantage over him in only one respect,—they often "came down" handsomely, and Scrooge never did.

Nobody ever stopped him in the street to say, with gladsome looks, "My dear Scrooge, how are you? When will you come to see me?" No beggars implored him to bestow a trifle, no children asked him what it was o'clock, no man or woman ever once in all his life inquired the way to such and such a place, of Scrooge. Even the blind men's dogs appeared to know him, and when they saw him coming on, would tug their owners into doorways and up courts; and then would wag their tails as though they said, "No eyes at all is better than an evil eye, dark master!"

But what did Scrooge care! It was the very thing he liked. To edge his way along the crowded paths of life, warning all human sympathy to keep its distance, was what the knowing ones call "nuts" to Scrooge.

Once upon a time—of all the good days in the year, upon a Christmas eve—old Scrooge sat busy in his counting-house. It was cold, bleak, biting, foggy weather; and the city clocks had only just gone three, but it was quite dark already.

The door of Scrooge's counting-house was open, that he might keep his eye upon his clerk, who, in a dismal little cell beyond, a sort of tank, was copying letters. Scrooge had a very small fire, but the clerk's fire was so very much smaller that it looked like one coal. But he couldn't replenish it, for Scrooge kept the coal-box in his own room; and so surely as the clerk came in with the shovel, the master predicted that it would be necessary for them to part. Wherefore the clerk put on his white comforter, and tried to warm himself at the candle; in which effort, not being a man of a strong imagination, he failed.

"A Merry Christmas, uncle! God save you!" cried a cheerful voice. It was the voice of Scrooge's nephew, who came upon him so quickly that this was the first intimation Scrooge had of his approach.

"Bah!" said Scrooge; "humbug!"

"Christmas a humbug, uncle! You don't mean that, I am sure?"

"I do. Out upon merry Christmas! What's Christmas time to you but a time for paying bills without money; a time for finding yourself a year older, and not an hour richer; a time for balancing your books and having every item in 'em through a round dozen of months presented dead against you? If I had my will, every idiot who goes about with 'Merry Christmas' on his lips should be boiled with his own pudding, and buried with a stake of holly through his heart. He should!"

"Uncle!"

"Nephew, keep Christmas in your own way, and let me keep it in mine."

"Keep it! But you don't keep it."

"Let me leave it alone, then. Much good may it do you! Much good it has ever done you!"

"There are many things from which I might have derived good, by which I have not profited, I dare say, Christmas among the rest. But I am sure I have always thought of Christmas time, when it has come round—apart from the veneration due to its sacred origin, if anything belonging to it can be apart from that—as a good time; a kind, forgiving, charitable, pleasant time; the only time I know of, in the long calendar of the year, when men and women seem by one consent to open their shut-up hearts freely, and to think of people below them as if they really were fellow-travellers to the grave, and not another race of creatures bound on other journeys. And therefore, uncle, though it has never put a scrap of gold or silver in my pocket, I believe that it *has* done me good, and *will* do me good; and I say, God bless it!"

The clerk in the tank involuntarily applauded.

"Let me hear another sound from you," said Scrooge, "and you'll keep your Christmas by losing your situation! You're quite a powerful speaker, sir," he added, turning to his nephew. "I wonder you don't go into Parliament."

"Don't be angry, uncle. Come! Dine with us to-morrow."

Scrooge said that he would see him—yes, indeed he did. He went the whole length of the expression, and said that he would see him in that extremity first.

"But why?" cried Scrooge's nephew. "Why?"

"Why did you get married?"

"Because I fell in love."

"Because you fell in love!" growled Scrooge, as if that were the only one thing in the world more ridiculous than a merry Christmas. "Good afternoon!"

"Nay, uncle, but you never came to see me before that happened. Why give it as a reason for not coming now?"

"Good afternoon."

"I want nothing from you; I ask nothing of you; why cannot we be friends?"

"Good afternoon."

"I am sorry, with all my heart, to find you so resolute. We have never had any quarrel, to which I have been a party. But I have made the trial in homage to Christmas, and I'll keep my Christmas humour to the last. So A Merry Christmas, uncle!"

"Good afternoon!"

"And A Happy New-Year!"

"Good afternoon!"

His nephew left the room without an angry word, notwithstanding. The clerk, in letting Scrooge's nephew out, had let two other people in. They were portly gentlemen, pleasant to behold, and now stood, with their hats off, in Scrooge's office. They had books and papers in their hands, and bowed to him.

"Scrooge and Marley's, I believe," said one of the gentlemen, referring to his list. "Have I the pleasure of addressing Mr. Scrooge or Mr. Marley?"

"Mr. Marley has been dead these seven years. He died seven years ago, this very night."

"At this festive season of the year, Mr. Scrooge," said the gentleman, taking up a pen, "it is more than usually desirable that we should make some slight provision for the poor and destitute, who suffer greatly at the present time. Many thousands are in want of common necessaries; hundreds of thousands are in want of common comforts, sir."

"Are there no prisons?"

"Plenty of prisons. But under the impression that they scarcely furnish Christian cheer of mind or body to the unoffending multitude, a few of us are endeavouring to raise a fund to buy the poor some meat and drink, and means of warmth. We choose this time, because it is a time, of all others, when Want is keenly felt, and Abundance rejoices. What shall I put you down for?"

"Nothing!"

"You wish to be anonymous?"

"I wish to be left alone. Since you ask me what I wish, gentlemen, that is my answer. I don't make merry myself at Christmas, and I can't afford to make idle people merry. I help to support the prisons and the workhouses,—they cost enough,—and those who are badly off must go there."

"Many can't go there; and many would rather die."

"If they would rather die, they had better do it, and decrease the surplus population."

At length the hour of shutting up the counting-house arrived. With an ill-will Scrooge, dismounting from his stool, tacitly admitted the fact to the expectant clerk in the tank, who instantly snuffed his candle out, and put on his hat.

"You want all day to-morrow, I suppose?"

"If quite convenient, sir."

"It's not convenient, and it's not fair. If I was to stop half a crown for it, you'd think yourself mightily ill-used, I'll be bound?"

"Yes, sir."

"And yet you don't think me ill-used, when I pay a day's wages for no work."

"It's only once a year, sir."

"A poor excuse for picking a man's pocket every twenty-fifth of December! But I suppose you must have the whole day. Be here all the earlier next morning."

The clerk promised that he would, and Scrooge walked out with a growl. The office was closed in a twinkling, and the clerk, with the long ends of his white comforter dangling below his waist (for he boasted no great-coat), went down a slide, at the end of a lane of boys, twenty times, in honour of its being Christmas eve, and then ran home as hard as he could pelt, to play at blindman's buff.

Scrooge took his melancholy dinner in his usual melancholy tavern; and having read all the newspapers, and beguiled the rest of the evening with his banker's book, went home to bed. He lived in chambers which had once belonged to his deceased partner. They were a gloomy suite of rooms, in a lowering pile of building up a yard. The building was old enough now, and dreary enough, for nobody lived in it but Scrooge, the other rooms being all let out as offices.

Now it is a fact, that there was nothing at all particular about the knocker on the door of this house, except that it was very large; also, that Scrooge had seen it, night and morning, during his whole residence in that place; also, that Scrooge had as little of what is called fancy about him as any man in the city of London. And yet Scrooge, having his key in the lock of the door, saw in the knocker, without its undergoing any intermediate process of change, not a knocker, but Marley's face.

Marley's face, with a dismal light about it, like a bad lobster in a dark cellar. It was not angry or ferocious, but it looked at Scrooge as Marley used to look,—ghostly spectacles turned up upon its ghostly forehead.

As Scrooge looked fixedly at this phenomenon, it was a knocker again. He said, "Pooh, pooh!" and closed the door with a bang.

The sound resounded through the house like thunder. Every room above, and every cask in the wine-merchant's cellars below, appeared to have a separate peal of echoes of its own. Scrooge was not a man to be frightened by echoes. He fastened the door, and walked across the hall, and up the stairs. Slowly too, trimming his candle as he went.

Up Scrooge went, not caring a button for its being very dark. Darkness is cheap, and Scrooge liked it. But before he shut his heavy door, he walked through his rooms to see that all was right. He had just enough recollection of the face to desire to do that.

Sitting-room, bedroom, lumber-room, all as they should be. Nobody under the table, nobody under the sofa; a small fire in the grate; spoon and basin ready; and the little saucepan of gruel (Scrooge had a cold in his head) upon the hob. Nobody under the bed; nobody in the closet; nobody in his dressing-gown, which was hanging up in a suspicious attitude against the wall. Lumber-room as usual. Old fire-guards, old shoes, two fish-baskets, washing-stand on three legs, and a poker.

Quite satisfied, he closed his door, and locked himself in; double-locked himself in, which was not his custom. Thus secured against surprise, he took off his cravat, put on his dressing-gown and slippers and his nightcap, and sat down before the very low fire to take his gruel.

As he threw his head back in the chair, his glance happened to rest upon a bell, a disused bell, that hung in the room, and communicated, for some purpose now forgotten, with a chamber in the highest story of the building. It was with great astonishment, and with a strange, inexplicable dread, that, as he looked, he saw this bell begin to swing. Soon it rang out loudly, and so did every bell in the house.

This was succeeded by a clanking noise, deep down below as if some person were dragging a heavy chain over the casks in the wine-merchant's cellar.

Then he heard the noise much louder, on the floors below; then coming up the stairs; then coming straight towards his door.

It came on through the heavy door, and a spectre passed into the room before his eyes. And upon its coming in, the dying flame leaped up, as though it cried, "I know him! Marley's ghost!"

The same face, the very same. Marley in his pigtail, usual waistcoat, tights, and boots. His body was transparent; so that Scrooge, observing him, and looking through his waistcoat, could see the two buttons on his coat behind.

Scrooge had often heard it said that Marley had no bowels, but he had never believed it until now.

No, nor did he believe it even now. Though he looked the phantom through and through, and saw it standing before him,—though he felt the chilling influence of its death-cold eyes, and noticed the very texture of the folded kerchief bound about its head and chin,—he was still incredulous.

"How now!" said Scrooge, caustic and cold as ever. "What do you want with me?"

"Much!"—Marley's voice, no doubt about it.

"Who are you?"

"Ask me who I was."

"Who were you then?"

"In life I was your partner, Jacob Marley."

"Can you—can you sit down?"

"I can."

"Do it, then."

Scrooge asked the question, because he didn't know whether a ghost so transparent might find himself in a condition to take a chair; and felt that, in the event of its being impossible, it might involve the necessity of an embarrassing explanation. But the ghost sat down on the opposite side of the fireplace, as if he were quite used to it.

"You don't believe in me."

"I don't."

"What evidence would you have of my reality beyond that of your senses?"

"I don't know."

"Why do you doubt your senses?"

"Because a little thing affects them. A slight disorder of the stomach makes them cheats. You may be an undigested bit of beef, a blot of mustard, a crumb of cheese, a fragment of an underdone potato. There's more of gravy than of grave about you, whatever you are!"

Scrooge was not much in the habit of cracking jokes, nor did he feel in his heart by any means waggish then. The truth is, that he tried to be smart, as a means of distracting his own attention, and keeping down his horror.

But how much greater was his horror when, the phantom taking off the bandage round its head, as if it were too warm to wear indoors, its lower jaw dropped down upon its breast!

"Mercy! Dreadful apparition, why do you trouble me? Why do spirits walk the earth, and why do they come to me?"

"It is required of every man that the spirit within him should walk abroad among his fellow-men, and travel far and wide; and if that spirit goes not forth in life, it is condemned to do so after death. I cannot tell you all I would. A very little more is permitted to me. I cannot rest, I cannot stay, I cannot linger anywhere. My spirit never walked beyond our counting-house—mark me!—in life my spirit never roved beyond the narrow limits of our money-changing hole; and weary journeys lie before me!"

"Seven years dead. And travelling all the time? You travel fast?"

"On the wings of the wind."

"You might have got over a great quantity of ground in seven years."

"O blind man, blind man! not to know that ages of incessant labour by immortal creatures for this earth must pass into eternity before the good of which it is susceptible is all developed. Not to know that any Christian spirit working kindly in its little sphere, whatever it may be, will find its mortal life too short for its vast means of usefulness. Not to know that no space of regret can make amends for one life's opportunities misused! Yet I was like this man; I once was like this man!"

"But you were always a good man of business, Jacob," faltered Scrooge, who now began to apply this to himself.

"Business!" cried the Ghost, wringing its hands again. "Mankind was my business. The common welfare was my business; charity, mercy, forbearance, benevolence, were all my business. The dealings of my trade were but a drop of water in the comprehensive ocean of my business!"

Scrooge was very much dismayed to hear the spectre going on at this rate, and began to quake exceedingly.

"Hear me! My time is nearly gone."

"I will. But don't be hard upon me! Don't be flowery, Jacob! Pray!"

"I am here to-night to warn you that you have yet a chance and hope of escaping my fate. A chance and hope of my procuring, Ebenezer."

"You were always a good friend to me. Thank'ee!"

"You will be haunted by Three Spirits."

"Is that the chance and hope you mentioned, Jacob? I—I think I'd rather not."

"Without their visits, you cannot hope to shun the path I tread. Expect the first to-morrow night, when the bell tolls One. Expect the second on the next night at the same hour. The third, upon the next night, when the last stroke of Twelve has ceased to vibrate. Look to see me no more; and look that, for your own sake, you remember what has passed between us!"

It walked backward from him; and at every step it took, the window raised itself a little, so that, when the apparition reached it, it was wide open.

Scrooge closed the window, and examined the door by which the Ghost had entered. It was double-locked, as he had locked it with his own hands, and the bolts were undisturbed. Scrooge tried to say, "Humbug!" but stopped at the first syllable. And being, from the emotion he had undergone, or the fatigues of the day, or his glimpse of the invisible world, or the dull conversation of the Ghost, or the lateness of the hour, much in need of repose, he went straight to bed, without undressing, and fell asleep on the instant.

Stave Two: The First of the Three Spirits

WHEN Scrooge awoke, it was so dark, that, looking out of bed, he could scarcely distinguish the transparent window from the opaque walls of his chamber, until suddenly the church clock tolled a deep, dull, hollow, melancholy ONE.

Light flashed up in the room upon the instant, and the curtains of his bed were drawn aside by a strange figure,—like a child; yet not so like a child as like an old man, viewed through some supernatural medium, which gave him the appearance of having receded from the view, and being diminished to a child's proportions. Its hair, which hung about its neck and down its back, was white as if with age; and yet the face had not a wrinkle in it, and the tenderest bloom was on the skin. It held a branch of fresh green holly in its hand; and, in singular contradiction of that wintry emblem, had its dress trimmed with summer flowers. But the strangest thing about it was, that from the crown of its head there sprung a bright clear jet of light, by which all this was visible; and which was doubtless the occasion of its using, in its duller moments, a great extinguisher for a cap, which it now held under its arm.

"Are you the Spirit, sir, whose coming was foretold to me?"

"I am!"

"Who and what are you?"

"I am the Ghost of Christmas Past."

"Long Past?"

"No. Your past. The things that you will see with me are shadows of the things that have been; they will have no consciousness of us."

Scrooge then made bold to inquire what business brought him there.

"Your welfare. Rise and walk with me!"

It would have been in vain for Scrooge to plead that the weather and the hour were not adapted to pedestrian purposes; that bed was warm, and the thermometer a long way below freezing; that he was clad but lightly in his slippers, dressing-gown, and night-cap; and that he had a cold upon him at that time. The grasp, though gentle as a woman's hand, was not to be resisted. He rose; but finding that the Spirit made towards the window, clasped its robe in supplication.

"I am a mortal, and liable to fall."

"Bear but a touch of my hand *there*," said the Spirit, laying it upon his heart, "and you shall be upheld in more than this!"

As the words were spoken, they passed through the wall, and stood in the busy thoroughfares of a city. It was made plain enough by the dressing of the shops that here, too, it was Christmas time. The Ghost stopped at a certain warehouse door, and asked Scrooge if he knew it.

"Know it! I was apprenticed here!"

They went in. At sight of an old gentleman in a Welsh wig, sitting behind such a high desk that, if he had been two inches taller, he must have knocked his head against the ceiling, Scrooge cried in great excitement: "Why, it's old Fezziwig! Bless his heart, it's Fezziwig, alive again!"

Old Fezziwig laid down his pen, and looked up at the clock, which pointed to the hour of seven. He rubbed his hands; adjusted his capacious waistcoat; laughed all over himself, from his shoes to his organ of benevolence; and called out in a comfortable, oily, rich, fat, jovial voice: "Yo ho, there! Ebenezer! Dick!"

A living and moving picture of Scrooge's former self, a young man, came briskly in, accompanied by his fellow-apprentice.

"Dick Wilkins, to be sure!" said Scrooge to the Ghost. "My old fellow-prentice, bless me, yes. There he is. He was very much attached to me, was Dick. Poor Dick! Dear, dear!"

"Yo ho, my boys!" said Fezziwig. "No more work to-night. Christmas eve, Dick. Christmas, Ebenezer! Let's have the shutters up, before a man can say Jack Robinson! Clear away, my lads, and let's have lots of room here!"

Clear away! There was nothing they wouldn't have cleared away, or couldn't have cleared away, with old Fezziwig looking on. It was done in a minute. Every movable was packed off, as if it were dismissed from public life for evermore; the floor was swept and watered, the lamps were trimmed, fuel was heaped upon the fire; and the warehouse was as snug and warm and dry and bright a ballroom as you would desire to see on a winter's night.

In came a fiddler with a music-book, and went up to the lofty desk, and made an orchestra of it, and tuned like fifty stomach-aches. In came Mrs. Fezziwig, one vast substantial smile. In came the three Miss Fezziwigs, beaming and lovable. In came the six young followers whose hearts they broke. In came all the young men and women employed in the business. In came the housemaid, with her cousin the baker. In came the cook, with her brother's particular friend the milkman. In they all came one after another; some shyly, some boldly, some gracefully, some awkwardly, some pushing, some pulling; in they all came, anyhow and everyhow. Away they all went, twenty couples at once; hands half round and back again the other way; down the middle and up again; round and round in various stages of affectionate grouping; old top couple always turning up in the wrong place; new top couple starting off again, as soon as they got there; all top couples at last, and not a bottom one to help them. When this result was brought about, old Fezziwig, clapping his hands to stop the dance, cried out, "Well done"; and the fiddler plunged his hot face into a pot of porter especially provided for that purpose.

There were more dances, and there were forfeits, and more dances, and there was cake, and there was negus, and there was a great piece of Cold Roast, and there was a great piece of Cold Boiled, and there were mince-pies, and plenty of beer. But the great effect of the evening came after the Roast and Boiled, when the fiddler struck up "Sir Roger de Coverley." Then old Fezziwig stood out to dance with Mrs. Fezziwig. Top couple, too; with a good stiff piece of work cut out for them; three or four and twenty pair of partners; people who were not to be trifled with; people who would dance, and had no notion of walking.

But if they had been twice as many—four times—old Fezziwig would have been a match for them, and so would Mrs. Fezziwig. As to her, she was worthy to be his partner in every sense of the term. A positive light appeared to issue from Fezziwig's calves. They shone in every part of the dance. You couldn't have predicted, at any given time, what would become of 'em next. And when old Fezziwig and Mrs. Fezziwig had gone all through the dance,—advance and retire, turn your partner, bow and courtesy, corkscrew, thread the needle, and back again to your place,—Fezziwig "cut,"—cut so deftly, that he appeared to wink with his legs.

When the clock struck eleven this domestic ball broke up. Mr. and Mrs. Fezziwig took their stations, one on either side the door, and, shaking hands with every person individually as he or she went out, wished him or her a Merry Christmas. When everybody had retired but the two 'prentices, they did the same to them; and thus the cheerful voices died away, and the lads were left to their beds, which were under a counter in the back shop.

"A small matter," said the Ghost, "to make these silly folks so full of gratitude. He has spent but a few pounds of your mortal money,—three or four perhaps. Is that so much that he deserves this praise?"

"It isn't that," said Scrooge, heated by the remark, and speaking unconsciously like his former, not his latter self,—"it isn't that, Spirit. He has the power to render us happy or unhappy; to make our service light or burdensome; a pleasure or a toil. Say that his power lies in words and looks; in things so slight and insignificant that it is impossible to add and count 'em up: what then? The happiness he gives is quite as great as if it cost a fortune."

He felt the Spirit's glance, and stopped.

"What is the matter?"

"Nothing particular."

"Something, I think?"

"No, no. I should like to be able to say a word or two to my clerk just now. That's all."

"My time grows short," observed the Spirit. "Quick!"

This was not addressed to Scrooge, or to any one whom he could see, but it produced an immediate effect. For again he saw himself. He was older now; a man in the prime of life.

He was not alone, but sat by the side of a fair young girl in a black dress, in whose eyes there were tears.

"It matters little," she said softly to Scrooge's former self. "To you very little. Another idol has displaced me; and if it can comfort you in time to come, as I would have tried to do, I have no just cause to grieve."

"What idol has displaced you?"

"A golden one. You fear the world too much. I have seen your nobler aspirations fall off one by one, until the master-passion, Gain, engrosses you. Have I not?"

"What then? Even if I have grown so much wiser, what then? I am not changed towards you. Have I ever sought release from our engagement?"

"In words, no. Never."

"In what, then?"

"In a changed nature; in an altered spirit; in another atmosphere of life; another Hope as its great end. If you were free to-day, to-morrow, yesterday, can even I believe that you would choose a dowerless girl; or, choosing her, do I not know that your repentance and regret would surely follow? I do; and I release you. With a full heart, for the love of him you once were."

"Spirit! remove me from this place."

"I told you these were shadows of the things that have been," said the Ghost. "That they are what they are, do not blame me!"

"Remove me!" Scrooge exclaimed. "I cannot bear it! Leave me! Take me back. Haunt me no longer!"

As he struggled with the Spirit he was conscious of being exhausted, and overcome by an irresistible drowsiness; and, further, of being in his own bedroom. He had barely time to reel to bed before he sank into a heavy sleep.

Stave Three: The Second of the Three Spirits

SCROOGE awoke in his own bedroom. There was no doubt about that. But it and his own adjoining sitting-room, into which he shuffled in his slippers, attracted by a great light there, had undergone a surprising transformation. The walls and ceiling were so hung with living green, that it looked a perfect grove. The leaves of holly, mistletoe, and ivy reflected back the light, as if so many little mirrors had been scattered there; and such a mighty blaze went roaring up the chimney, as that petrifaction of a hearth had never known in Scrooge's time, or Marley's, or for many and many a winter season gone. Heaped upon the floor, to form a kind of throne, were turkeys, geese, game, brawn, great joints of meat, sucking pigs, long wreaths of sausages, mince-pies, plum-puddings, barrels of oysters, red-hot chestnuts, cherry-cheeked apples, juicy oranges, luscious pears, immense twelfth-cakes, and great bowls of punch. In easy state upon this couch there sat a Giant glorious to see; who bore a glowing torch, in shape not unlike Plenty's horn, and who raised it high to shed its light on Scrooge, as he came peeping round the door.

"Come in,—come in! and know me better, man! I am the Ghost of Christmas Present. Look upon me! You have never seen the like of me before."

"Never."

"Have never walked forth with the younger members of my family; meaning (for I am very young) my elder brothers born in these later years?" pursued the Phantom.

"I don't think I have, I am afraid I have not. Have you had many brothers, Spirit?"

"More than eighteen hundred."

"A tremendous family to provide for! Spirit, conduct me where you will. I went forth last night on compulsion, and I learnt a lesson which is working now. To-night, if you have aught to teach me, let me profit by it."

"Touch my robe!"

Scrooge did as he was told, and held it fast.

The room and its contents all vanished instantly, and they stood in the city streets upon a snowy Christmas morning.

Scrooge and the Ghost passed on, invisible, straight to Scrooge's clerk's; and on the threshold of the door the Spirit smiled, and stopped to bless Bob Cratchit's dwelling with the sprinklings of his torch. Think of that! Bob had but fifteen "bob" a week himself; he pocketed on Saturdays but fifteen copies of his Christian name; and yet the Ghost of Christmas Present blessed his four-roomed house!

Then up rose Mrs. Cratchit, Cratchit's wife, dressed out but poorly in a twice-turned gown, but brave in ribbons, which are cheap and make a goodly show for sixpence; and she laid the cloth, assisted by Belinda Cratchit, second of her daughters, also brave in ribbons; while Master Peter Cratchit plunged a fork into the saucepan of potatoes, and, getting the corners of his monstrous shirt-collar (Bob's private property, conferred upon his son and heir in honour of the day) into his mouth, rejoiced to find himself so gallantly attired, and yearned to show his linen in the fashionable Parks. And now two smaller Cratchits, boy and girl, came tearing in, screaming that outside the baker's they had smelt the goose, and known it for their own; and, basking in luxurious thoughts of sage and onion, these young Cratchits danced about the table, and exalted Master Peter Cratchit to the skies, while he (not proud, although his collars nearly choked him) blew the fire, until the slow potatoes, bubbling up, knocked loudly at the saucepan-lid to be let out and peeled.

"What has ever got your precious father then?" said Mrs. Cratchit. "And your brother Tiny Tim! And Martha warn't as late last Christmas day by half an hour!"

"Here's Martha, mother!" said a girl, appearing as she spoke.

"Here's Martha, mother!" cried the two young Cratchits. "Hurrah! There's such a goose, Martha!"

"Why, bless your heart alive, my dear, how late you are!" said

Mrs. Cratchit, kissing her a dozen times, and taking off her shawl and bonnet for her.

"We'd a deal of work to finish up last night," replied the girl, "and had to clear away this morning, mother!"

"Well! Never mind so long as you are come," said Mrs. Cratchit. "Sit ye down before the fire, my dear, and have a warm, Lord bless ye!"

"No, no! There's father coming," cried the two young Cratchits, who were everywhere at once. "Hide, Martha, hide!"

So Martha hid herself, and in came little Bob, the father, with at least three feet of comforter, exclusive of the fringe, hanging down before him; and his threadbare clothes darned up and brushed, to look seasonable; and Tiny Tim upon his shoulder. Alas for Tiny Tim, he bore a little crutch, and had his limbs supported by an iron frame!

"Why, where's our Martha?" cried Bob Cratchit, looking round.

"Not coming," said Mrs. Cratchit.

"Not coming!" said Bob, with a sudden declension in his high spirits; for he had been Tim's blood-horse all the way from church, and had come home rampant,—"not coming upon Christmas day!"

Martha didn't like to see him disappointed, if it were only in joke; so she came out prematurely from behind the closet door, and ran into his arms, while the two young Cratchits hustled Tiny Tim, and bore him off into the wash-house, that he might hear the pudding singing in the copper.

"And how did little Tim behave?" asked Mrs. Cratchit, when she had rallied Bob on his credulity, and Bob had hugged his daughter to his heart's content.

"As good as gold," said Bob, "and better. Somehow he gets thoughtful, sitting by himself so much, and thinks the strangest things you ever heard. He told me, coming home, that he hoped the people saw him in the church, because he was a cripple, and it might be pleasant to them to remember, upon Christmas day, who made lame beggars walk and blind men see."

Bob's voice was tremulous when he told them this, and trembled more when he said that Tiny Tim was growing strong and hearty.

His active little crutch was heard upon the floor, and back came Tiny Tim before another word was spoken, escorted by his brother and sister to his stool beside the fire; and while Bob, turning up his cuffs,—as if, poor fellow, they were capable of being made more shabby,—compounded some hot mixture in a jug with gin and lemons, and stirred it round and round, and put it on the hob to simmer, Master Peter and the two ubiquitous young Cratchits went to fetch the goose, with which they soon returned in high procession.

Mrs. Cratchit made the gravy (ready beforehand in a little saucepan) hissing hot; Master Peter mashed the potatoes with incredible vigour; Miss Belinda sweetened up the apple-sauce; Martha dusted the hot plates; Bob took Tiny Tim beside him in a tiny corner at the table; the two young Cratchits set chairs for everybody, not forgetting themselves, and mounting guard upon their posts, crammed spoons into their mouths, lest they should shriek for goose before their turn came to be helped. At last the dishes were set on, and grace was said. It was succeeded by a breathless pause, as Mrs. Cratchit, looking slowly all along the carving-knife, prepared to plunge it in the breast; but when she did, and when the long-expected gush of stuffing issued forth, one murmur of delight arose all round the board, and even Tiny Tim, excited by the two young Cratchits, beat on the table with the handle of his knife, and feebly cried, Hurrah!

There never was such a goose. Bob said he didn't believe there ever was such a goose cooked. Its tenderness and flavour, size and cheapness, were the themes of universal admiration. Eked out by apple-sauce and mashed potatoes, it was a sufficient dinner for the whole family; indeed, as Mrs. Cratchit said with great delight (surveying one small atom of a bone upon the dish) they hadn't ate it all at last! Yet every one had had enough, and the youngest Cratchits in particular were steeped in sage and onion to the eyebrows! But now, the plates being changed by Miss Belinda, Mrs. Cratchit left the room alone,—too nervous to bear witnesses,—to take the pudding up, and bring it in.

Suppose it should not be done enough! Suppose it should break in turning out! Suppose somebody should have got over the wall of the back yard, and stolen it, while they were merry with the goose, —a supposition at which the two young Cratchits became livid! All sorts of horrors were supposed.

Hallo! A great deal of steam! The pudding was out of the copper. A smell like a washing-day! That was the cloth. A smell like an eating-house and a pastry-cook's next door to each other, with a laundress's next door to that! That was the pudding! In half a minute Mrs. Cratchit entered,—flushed but smiling proudly,—with the pudding, like a speckled cannon-ball, so hard and firm, blazing in half of half a quartern of ignited brandy, and bedight with Christmas holly stuck into the top.

Oh, a wonderful pudding! Bob Cratchit said, and calmly too, that he regarded it as the greatest success achieved by Mrs. Cratchit since their marriage. Mrs. Cratchit said that now the weight was off her mind, she would confess she had had her doubts about the quantity of flour. Everybody had something to say about it, but nobody said or thought it was at all a small pudding for a large family. Any Cratchit would have blushed to hint at such a thing.

At last the dinner was all done, the cloth was cleared, the hearth swept, and the fire made up. The compound in the jug being tasted, and considered perfect, apples and oranges were put upon the table, and a shovelful of chestnuts on the fire.

Then all the Cratchit family drew round the hearth, in what Bob Cratchit called a circle, and at Bob Cratchit's elbow stood the family display of glass,—two tumblers, and a custard-cup without a handle.

These held the hot stuff from the jug, however, as well as golden goblets would have done; and Bob served it out with beaming looks, while the chestnuts on the fire spluttered and crackled noisily. Then Bob proposed:—

"A Merry Christmas to us all, my dears. God bless us!"

Which all the family re-echoed.

"God bless us every one!" said Tiny Tim, the last of all.

He sat very close to his father's side, upon his little stool. Bob held his withered little hand in his, as if he loved the child, and wished to keep him by his side, and dreaded that he might be taken from him.

Scrooge raised his head speedily, on hearing his own name.

"Mr. Scrooge!" said Bob; "I'll give you Mr. Scrooge, the Founder of the Feast!"

"The Founder of the Feast indeed!" cried Mrs. Cratchit, reddening. "I wish I had him here. I'd give him a piece of my mind to feast upon, and I hope he'd have a good appetite for it."

"My dear," said Bob, "the children! Christmas day."

"It should be Christmas day, I am sure," said she, "on which one drinks the health of such an odious, stingy, hard, unfeeling man as Mr. Scrooge. You know he is, Robert! Nobody knows it better than you do, poor fellow!"

"My dear," was Bob's mild answer, "Christmas day."

"I'll drink his health for your sake and the day's," said Mrs. Cratchit, "not for his. Long life to him! A merry Christmas and a happy New Year! He'll be very merry and very happy, I have no doubt!"

The children drank the toast after her. It was the first of their proceedings which had no heartiness in it. Tiny Tim drank it last of all, but he didn't care twopence for it. Scrooge was the Ogre of the family. The mention of his name cast a dark shadow on the party, which was not dispelled for full five minutes.

After it had passed away, they were ten times merrier than before, from the mere relief of Scrooge the Baleful being done with. Bob Cratchit told them how he had a situation in his eye for Master Peter, which would bring him, if obtained, full five and sixpence weekly. The two young Cratchits laughed tremendously at the idea of Peter's being a man of business; and Peter himself looked thoughtfully at the fire from between his collars, as if he were deliberating what particular investments he should favour when he came into the receipt of that bewildering income. Martha, who was a poor apprentice at a milliner's, then told them what kind of work she had to do, and how many hours she worked at a stretch, and how she meant to lie abed to-morrow morning for a good long rest; to-morrow being a holiday she passed at home. Also how she had seen a countess and a lord some days before, and how the lord "was much about as tall as Peter;" at which Peter pulled up his collars so high that you couldn't have seen his head if you had been there. All this time the chestnuts and the jug went round and round; and by and by they had a song, about a lost child travelling in the snow, from Tiny Tim, who had a plaintive little voice, and sang it very well indeed.

There was nothing of high mark in this. They were not a handsome family; they were not well dressed; their shoes were far from being waterproof; their clothes were scanty; and Peter might have known, and very likely did, the inside of a pawnbroker's. But they were happy, grateful, pleased with one another, and contented with the time; and when they faded, and looked happier yet in the bright sprinklings of the Spirit's torch at parting, Scrooge had his eye upon them, and especially on Tiny Tim, until the last.

It was a great surprise to Scrooge, as this scene vanished, to hear a hearty laugh. It was a much greater surprise to Scrooge to recognize it as his own nephew's, and to find himself in a bright, dry, gleaming room, with the Spirit standing smiling by his side, and looking at that same nephew.

It is a fair, even-handed, noble adjustment of things, that while there is infection in disease and sorrow, there is nothing in the world so irresistibly contagious as laughter and good-humour. When Scrooge's nephew laughed, Scrooge's niece by marriage laughed as heartily as he. And their assembled friends, being not a bit behind-hand, laughed out lustily.

"He said that Christmas was a humbug, as I live!" cried Scrooge's nephew. "He believed it too!"

"More shame for him, Fred!" said Scrooge's niece, indignantly. Bless those women! they never do anything by halves. They are always in earnest.

She was very pretty; exceedingly pretty. With a dimpled, surprised-looking, capital face; a ripe little mouth that seemed made to be kissed,—as no doubt it was; all kinds of good little dots about her chin, that melted into one another when she laughed; and the sunniest pair of eyes you ever saw in any little creature's head. Altogether she was what you would have called provoking, but satisfactory, too. Oh, perfectly satisfactory.

"He's a comical old fellow," said Scrooge's nephew, "that's the truth; and not so pleasant as he might be. However, his offences carry their own punishment, and I have nothing to say against him. Who suffers by his ill whims? Himself, always. Here he takes it into his head to dislike us, and he won't come and dine with us. What's the consequence? He don't lose much of a dinner."

"Indeed, I think he loses a very good dinner," interrupted Scrooge's niece. Everybody else said the same, and they must be allowed to have been competent judges, because they had just had dinner; and, with the dessert upon the table, were clustered round the fire, by lamplight.

"Well, I am very glad to hear it," said Scrooge's nephew, "because I haven't any great faith in these young housekeepers. What do you say, Topper?"

Topper clearly had his eye on one of Scrooge's niece's sisters, for he answered that a bachelor was a wretched outcast, who had no right to express an opinion on the subject. Whereat Scrooge's niece's sister—the plump one with the lace tucker; not the one with the roses—blushed.

After tea they had some music. For they were a musical family, and knew what they were about, when they sung a Glee or Catch, I can assure you,—especially Topper, who could growl away in the bass like a good one, and never swell the large veins in his forehead, or get red in the face over it

But they didn't devote the whole evening to music. After a while they played at forfeits; for it is good to be children sometimes, and never better than at Christmas, when its mighty Founder was a child himself. There was first a game at blindman's buff though. And I no more believe Topper was really blinded than I believe he had eyes in his boots. Because the way in which he went after that plump sister in the lace tucker was an outrage on the credulity of human nature. Knocking down the fire-irons, tumbling over the chairs, bumping up against the piano, smothering himself among the curtains, wherever she went there went he! He always knew where the plump sister was. He wouldn't catch anybody else. If you had fallen up against him, as some of them did, and stood there, he would have made a feint of endeavouring to seize you, which would have been an affront to your understanding, and would instantly have sidled off in the direction of the plump sister.

"Here is a new game," said Scrooge. "One half-hour, Spirit, only one!"

It was a Game called Yes and No, where Scrooge's nephew had to think of something, and the rest must find out what; he only answering to their questions yes or no, as the case was. The fire of questioning to which he was exposed elicited from him that he was thinking of an animal, a live animal, rather a disagreeable animal, a savage animal, an animal that growled and grunted sometimes, and talked sometimes, and lived in London, and walked about the streets, and wasn't made a show of, and wasn't led by anybody, and didn't live in a menagerie, and was never killed in a market, and was not a horse, or an ass, or a cow, or a bull, or a tiger, or a dog, or a pig, or a cat, or a bear. At every new question put to him, this nephew burst into a fresh roar of laughter; and was so inexpressibly tickled, that he was obliged to get up off the sofa and stamp. At last the plump sister cried out: —

"I have found it out! I know what it is, Fred! I know what it is!"

"What is it?" cried Fred.

"It's your uncle Scro-o-o-o-oge!"

Which it certainly was. Admiration was the universal sentiment, though some objected that the reply to "Is it a bear?" ought to have been "Yes."

Uncle Scrooge had imperceptibly become so gay and light of heart, that he would have drank to the unconscious company in an inaudible speech. But the whole scene passed off in the breath of the last word spoken by his nephew; and he and the Spirit were again upon their travels.

Much they saw, and far they went, and many homes they visited, but always with a happy end. The Spirit stood beside sick-beds, and they were cheerful; on foreign lands, and they were close at home; by struggling men, and they were patient in their greater hope; by poverty, and it was rich. In almshouse, hospital, and jail, in misery's every refuge, where vain man in his little brief authority had not made fast the door, and barred the Spirit out, he left his blessing, and taught Scrooge his precepts. Suddenly, as they stood together in an open place, the bell struck twelve.

Scrooge looked about him for the Ghost, and saw it no more. As the last stroke ceased to vibrate, he remembered the prediction of old Jacob Marley, and, lifting up his eyes, beheld a solemn Phantom, draped and hooded, coming like a mist along the ground towards him.

Stave Four: The Last of the Spirits

THE Phantom slowly, gravely, silently approached. When it came near him, Scrooge bent down upon his knee; for in the air through which this Spirit moved it seemed to scatter gloom and mystery.

It was shrouded in a deep black garment, which concealed its head, its face, its form, and left nothing of it visible save one outstretched hand. He knew no more, for the Spirit neither spoke nor moved.

"I am in the presence of the Ghost of Christmas Yet to Come? Ghost of the Future! I fear you more than any spectre I have seen. But as I know your purpose is to do me good, and as I hope to live to be another man from what I was, I am prepared to bear you company, and do it with a thankful heart. Will you not speak to me?"

It gave him no reply. The hand was pointed straight before them.

"Lead on! Lead on! The night is waning fast, and it is precious time to me, I know. Lead on, Spirit!"

They scarcely seemed to enter the city; for the city rather seemed to spring up about them. But there they were in the heart of it; on 'Change, amongst the merchants.

The Spirit stopped beside one little knot of business men. Observing that the hand was pointed to them, Scrooge advanced to listen to their talk.

"No," said a great fat man with a monstrous chin. "I don't know much about it either way. I only know he's dead."

"When did he die?" inquired another.

"Last night, I believe."

"Why, what was the matter with him? I thought he'd never die."

"God knows," said the first, with a yawn.

"What has he done with his money?" asked a red-faced gentleman.

"I haven't heard," said the man with the large chin. "Company, perhaps. He hasn't left it to me. That's all I know. By, by."

Scrooge was at first inclined to be surprised that the Spirit should attach importance to conversation apparently so trivial; but feeling assured that it must have some hidden purpose, he set himself to consider what it was likely to be. It could scarcely be supposed to have any bearing on the death of Jacob, his old partner, for that was Past, and this Ghost's province was the Future.

He looked about in that very place for his own image; but another man stood in his accustomed corner, and though the clock pointed to his usual time of day for being there, he saw no likeness of himself amongst the multitudes that poured in through the Porch. It gave him little surprise, however; for he had been revolving in his mind a change of life, and he thought and hoped he saw his new-born resolutions carried out in this.

They left this busy scene, and went into an obscure part of the town, to a low shop where iron, old rags, bottles, bones, and greasy offal were bought. A grey-haired rascal, of great age, sat smoking his pipe. Scrooge and the Phantom came into the presence of this man, just as a woman with a heavy bundle slunk into the shop. But she had scarcely entered, when another woman, similarly laden, came in too; and she was closely followed by a man in faded black. After a short period of blank astonishment, in which the old man with the pipe had joined them, they all three burst into a laugh.

"Let the charwoman alone to be the first!" cried she who had entered first. "Let the laundress alone to be the second; and let the undertaker's man alone to be the third. Look here, old Joe, here's a chance! If we haven't all three met here without meaning it!"

"You couldn't have met in a better place. You were made free of it long ago, you know; and the other two ain't strangers. What have you got to sell? What have you got to sell?"

"Half a minute's patience, Joe, and you shall see."

"What odds then! What odds, Mrs. Dilber?" said the woman. "Every person has a right to take care of themselves. He always did! Who's the worse for the loss of a few things like these? Not a dead man, I suppose."

Mrs. Dilber, whose manner was remarkable for general propitiation, said, "No, indeed, ma'am."

"If he wanted to keep 'em after he was dead, a wicked old screw, why wasn't he natural in his lifetime? If he had been, he'd have had somebody to look after him when he was struck with Death, instead of lying gasping out his last there, alone by himself."

"It's the truest word that ever was spoke, it's a judgment on him."

"I wish it was a little heavier judgment, and it should have been, you may depend upon it, if I could have laid my hands on anything else. Open that bundle, old Joe, and let me know the value of it. Speak out plain. I'm not afraid to be the first, nor afraid for them to see it."

Joe went down on his knees for the greater convenience of opening the bundle, and dragged out a large and heavy roll of some dark stuff.

"What do you call this? Bed-curtains!"

"Ah! Bed-curtains! Don't drop that oil upon the blankets, now."

"*His* blankets?"

"Whose else's do you think? He isn't likely to take cold without 'em, I dare say. Ah! You may look through that shirt till your eyes ache; but you won't find a hole in it, nor a threadbare place. It's the best he had, and a fine one too. They'd have wasted it by dressing him up in it, if it hadn't been for me."

Scrooge listened to this dialogue in horror.

"Spirit! I see, I see. The case of this unhappy man might be my own. My life tends that way, now. Merciful Heaven, what is this!"

The scene had changed, and now he almost touched a bare, un-curtained bed. A pale light, rising in the outer air, fell straight upon this bed; and on it, unwatched, unwept, uncared for, was the body of this plundered unknown man.

"Spirit, let me see some tenderness connected with a death, or this dark chamber, Spirit, will be for ever present to me."

The Ghost conducted him to poor Bob Cratchit's house,—the dwelling he had visited before,—and found the mother and the children seated round the fire.

Quiet. Very quiet. The noisy little Cratchits were as still as statues in one corner, and sat looking up at Peter, who had a book before him. The mother and her daughters were engaged in needle-work. But surely they were very quiet!

" 'And he took a child, and set him in the midst of them.' "

Where had Scrooge heard those words? He had not dreamed them. The boy must have read them out, as he and the Spirit crossed the threshold. Why did he not go on?

The mother laid her work upon the table, and put her hand up to her face. "The colour hurts my eyes," she said.

The colour? Ah, poor Tiny Tim!

"They're better now again. It makes them weak by candle-light; and I wouldn't show weak eyes to your father when he comes home, for the world. It must be near his time."

"Past it rather," Peter answered, shutting up his book. "But I think he has walked a little slower than he used, these few last evenings, mother."

"I have known him walk with—I have known him walk with Tiny Tim upon his shoulder, very fast indeed."

"And so have I," cried Peter. "Often."

"And so have I," exclaimed another. So had all.

"But he was very light to carry, and his father loved him so, that it was no trouble,—no trouble. And there is your father at the door!"

She hurried out to meet him; and little Bob in his comforter—he had need of it, poor fellow—came in. His tea was ready for him on the hob, and they all tried who should help him to it most. Then the two young Cratchits got upon his knees and laid, each child, a little cheek against his face, as if they said, "Don't mind it, father. Don't be grieved!"

Bob was very cheerful with them, and spoke pleasantly to all the family. He looked at the work upon the table, and praised the industry and speed of Mrs. Cratchit and the girls. They would be done long before Sunday, he said.

"Sunday! You went to-day, then, Robert?"

"Yes, my dear," returned Bob. "I wish you could have gone. It would have done you good to see how green a place it is. But you'll see it often. I promised him that I would walk there on a Sunday. My little, little child! My little child!"

He broke down all at once. He couldn't help it. If he could have helped it, he and his child would have been farther apart, perhaps, than they were.

"Spectre," said Scrooge, "something informs me that our parting moment is at hand. I know it, but I know not how. Tell me what man that was, with the covered face, whom we saw lying dead?"

The Ghost of Christmas Yet to Come conveyed him to a dismal, wretched, ruinous churchyard.

The Spirit stood amongst the graves, and pointed down to One.

"Before I draw nearer to that stone to which you point, answer me one question. Are these the shadows of the things that Will be, or are they shadows of the things that May be only?"

Still the Ghost pointed downward to the grave by which it stood.

"Men's courses will foreshadow certain ends, to which, if persevered in, they must lead. But if the courses be departed from, the ends will change. Say it is thus with what you show me!"

The Spirit was immovable as ever.

Scrooge crept towards it, trembling as he went; and, following the finger, read upon the stone of the neglected grave his own name —Ebenezer Scrooge.

"Am *I* that man who lay upon the bed? No, Spirit! Oh no, no! Spirit! hear me! I am not the man I was. I will not be the man I must have been but for this intercourse. Why show me this, if I am past all hope? Assure me that I yet may change these shadows you have shown me by an altered life."

For the first time the kind hand faltered.

"I will honour Christmas in my heart, and try to keep it all the year. I will live in the Past, the Present, and the Future. The Spirits of all three shall strive within me. I will not shut out the lessons that they teach. Oh, tell me I may sponge away the writing on this stone!"

Holding up his hands in one last prayer to have his fate reversed, he saw an alteration in the Phantom's hood and dress. It shrunk, collapsed, and dwindled down into a bedpost.

Yes, and the bedpost was his own. The bed was his own, the room was his own. Best and happiest of all, the Time before him was his own, to make amends in!

He was checked in his transports by the churches ringing out the lustiest peals he had ever heard.

Running to the window, he opened it, and put out his head. No fog, no mist, no night; clear, bright, stirring, golden day.

"What's to-day?" cried Scrooge, calling downward to a boy in Sunday clothes, who perhaps had loitered in to look about him.

"Eh?"

"What's to-day, my fine fellow?"

"To-day! Why Christmas day."

"It's Christmas day! I haven't missed it. Hallo, my fine fellow!"

"Hallo!"

"Do you know the Poulterer's, in the next street but one, at the corner?"

"I should hope I did."

"An intelligent boy! A remarkable boy! Do you know whether they've sold the prize Turkey that was hanging up there? Not the little prize Turkey,—the big one?"

"What, the one as big as me?"

"What a delightful boy! It's a pleasure to talk to him. Yes, my buck!"

"It's hanging there now."

"Is it? Go and buy it."

"Walk-*er!*" exclaimed the boy.

"No, no, I am in earnest. Go and buy it, and tell 'em to bring it here, that I may give them the direction where to take it. Come back with the man, and I'll give you a shilling. Come back with him in less than five minutes, and I'll give you half a crown!"

The boy was off like a shot.

"I'll send it to Bob Cratchit's! He sha'n't know who sends it. It's twice the size of Tiny Tim. Joe Miller never made such a joke as sending it to Bob's will be!"

The hand in which he wrote the address was not a steady one; but write it he did, somehow, and went down stairs to open the street door, ready for the coming of the poulterer's man.

It *was* a Turkey! He never could have stood upon his legs, that bird. He would have snapped 'em short off in a minute, like sticks of sealing-wax.

Scrooge dressed himself "all in his best," and at last got out into the streets. The people were by this time pouring forth, as he had seen them with the Ghost of Christmas Present; and, walking with his hands behind him, Scrooge regarded every one with a delighted smile. He looked so irresistibly pleasant, in a word, that three or four good-humoured fellows said, "Good morning, sir! A merry Christmas to you!" And Scrooge said often afterwards, that, of all the blithe sounds he had ever heard, those were the blithest in his ears.

In the afternoon, he turned his steps towards his nephew's house.

He passed the door a dozen times, before he had the courage to go up and knock. But he made a dash, and did it.

"Is your master at home, my dear?" said Scrooge to the girl. Nice girl! Very.

"Yes, sir."

"Where is he, my love?"

"He's in the dining-room, sir, along with mistress."

"He knows me," said Scrooge, with his hand already on the dining-room lock. "I'll go in here, my dear."

"Fred!"

"Why, bless my soul!" cried Fred, "who's that?"

"It's I. Your uncle Scrooge. I have come to dinner. Will you let me in, Fred?"

Let him in! It is a mercy he didn't shake his arm off. He was at home in five minutes. Nothing could be heartier. His niece looked just the same. So did Topper when *he* came. So did the plump sister when *she* came. So did every one when *they* came. Wonderful party, wonderful games, wonderful unanimity, won-derful happiness!

But he was early at the office next morning. Oh, he was early there. If he could only be there first, and catch Bob Cratchit coming late! That was the thing he had set his heart upon.

And he did it. The clock struck nine. No Bob. A quarter past. No Bob. Bob was full eighteen minutes and a half behind his time. Scrooge sat with his door wide open, that he might see him come into the tank.

Bob's hat was off before he opened the door; his comforter too. He was on his stool in a jiffy; driving away with his pen, as if he were trying to overtake nine o'clock.

"Hallo!" growled Scrooge, in his accustomed voice, as near as he could feign it. "What do you mean by coming here at this time of day?"

"I am very sorry, sir. I am behind my time."

"You are? Yes. I think you are. Step this way if you please."

"It's only once a year, sir. It shall not be repeated. I was making rather merry yesterday, sir."

"Now, I'll tell you what, my friend. I am not going to stand this sort of thing any longer. And therefore," Scrooge continued, leaping from his stool, and giving Bob such a dig in the waistcoat that he staggered back into the tank again,—"and therefore I am about to raise your salary!"

Bob trembled, and got a little nearer to the ruler.

"A merry Christmas, Bob!" said Scrooge, with an earnestness that could not be mistaken, as he clapped him on the back. "A merrier Christmas, Bob, my good fellow, than I have given you for many a year! I'll raise your salary, and endeavour to assist your struggling family, and we will discuss your affairs this very afternoon, over a Christmas bowl of smoking bishop, Bob! Make up the fires, and buy a second coal-scuttle before you dot another *i*, Bob Cratchit!"

Scrooge was better than his word. He did it all, and infinitely more; and to Tiny Tim, who did NOT die, he was a second father. He became as good a friend, as good a master, and as good a man as the good old city knew, or any other good old city, town, or borough in the good old world. Some people laughed to see the alteration in him; but his own heart laughed, and that was quite enough for him.

He had no further intercourse with Spirits, but lived in that respect upon the Total Abstinence Principle ever afterwards; and it was always said of him that he knew how to keep Christmas well, if any man alive possessed the knowledge. May that be truly said of us, and all of us! And so, as Tiny Tim observed, God Bless Us, Every One!

CHARLES DICKENS

Christmas at Dingley Dell

FROM the centre of the ceiling of . . . [the] kitchen, old Wardle had . . . suspended, with his own hands, a huge branch of mistletoe, and this same branch of mistletoe instantaneously gave rise to a scene of general and delightful struggling and confusion; in the midst of which, Mr. Pickwick, with a gallantry that would have done honour to a descendant of Lady Tollimglower herself, took the old lady by the hand, led her beneath the mystic branch, and saluted her in all courtesy and decorum. The old lady submitted to this piece of practical politeness with all the dignity which befitted so important and serious a solemnity, but the younger ladies, not being so thoroughly imbued with a superstitious veneration for the custom; or imagining that the value of a salute is very much enhanced if it cost a little trouble to obtain it: screamed and

339

struggled, and ran into corners, and threatened and remonstrated, and did everything but leave the room, until some of the less adventurous gentlemen were on the point of desisting, when they all at once found it useless to resist any longer, and submitted to be kissed with a good grace. . . . Wardle stood with his back to the fire, surveying the whole scene, with the utmost satisfaction; and the fat boy took the opportunity of appropriating to his own use, and summarily devouring, a particularly fine mince-pie, that had been carefully put by for somebody else.

Now, the screaming had subsided, and faces were in a glow, and curls in a tangle, and Mr. Pickwick, after kissing the old lady as before mentioned, was standing under the mistletoe, looking with a very pleased countenance on all that was passing around him, when the young lady with the black eyes, after a little whispering with the other young ladies, made a sudden dart forward, and, putting her arm round Mr. Pickwick's neck, saluted him affectionately on the left cheek; and before Mr. Pickwick distinctly knew what was the matter, he was surrounded by the whole body, and kissed by every one of them.

It was a pleasant thing to see Mr. Pickwick in the centre of the group, now pulled this way, and then that, and first kissed on the chin, and then on the nose, and then on the spectacles: and to hear the peals of laughter which were raised on every side; but it was a still more pleasant thing to see Mr. Pickwick, blinded shortly afterwards with a silk handkerchief, falling up against the wall, and scrambling into corners, and going through all the mysteries of blind-man's buff, with the utmost relish for the game, until at last he caught one of the poor relations, and then had to evade the blind-man himself, which he did with a nimbleness and agility that elicited the admiration and applause of all beholders. The poor relations caught the people who they thought would like it, and, when the game flagged, got caught themselves. When they were all tired of blind-man's buff, there was a great game at snap-dragon, and when fingers enough were burned with that, and all the raisins were gone, they sat down by the huge fire of blazing logs to a substantial supper, and a mighty bowl of wassail, something smaller than an ordinary wash-house copper, in which the hot apples were hissing and bubbling with a rich look, and a jolly sound, that were perfectly irresistible.

"This," said Mr. Pickwick, looking around him, "this is, indeed, comfort."

"Our invariable custom," replied Mr. Wardle. "Everybody sits down with us on Christmas eve, as you see them now—servants and all; and here we wait, until the clock strikes twelve, to usher Christmas in, and beguile the time with forfeits and old stories. Trundle, my boy, rake up the fire."

Up flew the bright sparks in myriads as the logs were stirred. The deep red blaze sent forth a rich glow, that penetrated into the furthest corner of the room, and cast its cheerful tint on every face. . . .

"How it snows!" said one of the men, in a low tone.

"Snows, does it?" said Wardle.

"Rough, cold night, sir," replied the man; "and there's a wind got up, that drifts it across the fields, in a thick white cloud."

"What does Jem say?" inquired the old lady. "There ain't anything the matter, is there?"

"No, no, mother," replied Wardle; "he says there's a snowdrift, and a wind that's piercing cold. I should know that, by the way it rumbles in the chimney."

"Ah!" said the old lady, "there was just such a wind, and just such a fall of snow, a good many years back, I recollect—just five years before your poor father died. It was a Christmas eve, too; and I remember that on that very night he told us the story about the goblins that carried away old Gabriel Grub."

"The story about what?" said Mr. Pickwick.

"Oh, nothing, nothing," replied Wardle. "About an old sexton, that the good people down here suppose to have been carried away by goblins."

"Suppose!" ejaculated the old lady. "Is there anybody hardy enough to disbelieve it? Suppose! Haven't you heard ever since you were a child, that he *was* carried away by the goblins, and don't you know he was?"

"Very well, mother, he was, if you like," said Wardle, laughing. "He *was* carried away by goblins, Pickwick; and there's an end of the matter."

"No, no," said Mr. Pickwick, "not an end of it, I assure you; for I must hear how, and why, and all about it."

Wardle smiled, as every head was bent forward to hear; and filling out the wassail with no stinted hand, nodded a health to Mr. Pickwick, and began as follows:

THE STORY OF THE GOBLINS WHO STOLE A SEXTON

"In an old abbey town, down in this part of the country, a long, long while ago—so long, that the story must be a true one, because our great grandfathers implicitly believed it—there officiated as sexton and grave-digger in the churchyard, one Gabriel Grub. It by no means follows that because a man is a sexton, and constantly surrounded by the emblems of mortality, therefore he should be a morose and melancholy man; your undertakers are the merriest fellows in the world; and I once had the honour of being on intimate terms with a mute, who in private life, and off duty, was as comical and jocose a little fellow as ever chirped out a devil-may-care song, without a hitch in his memory, or drained off the contents of a good stiff glass without stopping for breath. But, notwithstanding these precedents to the contrary, Gabriel Grub was an ill-conditioned, cross-grained, surly fellow—a morose and lonely man, who consorted with nobody but himself, and an old wicker bottle which fitted into his large deep waistcoat pocket—and who eyed each merry face, as it passed him by, with such a deep scowl of malice and ill-humour, as it was difficult to meet, without feeling something the worse for.

"A little before twilight, one Christmas eve, Gabriel shouldered his spade, lighted his lantern, and betook himself towards the old churchyard; for he had got a grave to finish by next morning, and, feeling very low, he thought it might raise his spirits, perhaps, if he went on with his work at once. As he went his way, up the ancient street, he saw the cheerful light of the blazing fires gleam through the old casements, and heard the loud laugh and the cheerful shouts of those who were assembled around them; he marked the bustling preparations for next day's cheer, and smelt the numerous savoury odours consequent thereupon, as they steamed up from the kitchen windows in clouds. All this was gall and wormwood to the heart of Gabriel Grub; and when groups of children bounded out of the houses, tripped across the road, and were met, before they could knock at the opposite door, by half a dozen curly-headed little rascals who crowded round them as they flocked up-stairs to spend the evening in their Christmas games, Gabriel smiled grimly, and clutched the handle of his spade with a firmer grasp, as he thought of measles, scarlet-fever, thrush, whooping-cough, and a good many other sources of consolation besides.

"In this happy frame of mind, Gabriel strode along: returning a short, sullen growl to the good-humoured greetings of such of his neighbours as now and then passed him: until he turned into the dark lane which led to the churchyard. Now, Gabriel had been looking forward to reaching the dark lane, because it was, generally speaking, a nice, gloomy, mournful place, into which the towns-people did not much care to go, except in broad daylight, and when the sun was shining; consequently, he was not a little indignant to hear a young urchin roaring out some jolly song about a merry Christmas, in this very sanctuary, which had been called Coffin Lane ever since the days of the old abbey, and the time of the shaven-headed monks. As Gabriel walked on, and the voice drew nearer, he found it proceeded from a small boy, who was hurrying along, to join one of the little parties in the old street, and who, partly to keep himself company, and partly to prepare himself for the occasion, was shouting out the song at the highest pitch of his lungs. So Gabriel waited until the boy came up, and then dodged him into a corner, and rapped him over the head with his lantern five or six times, to teach him to modulate his voice. And as the boy hurried away with his hand to his head, singing quite a different sort of tune, Gabriel Grub chuckled very heartily to himself, and entered the churchyard: locking the gate behind him.

"He took off his coat, put down his lantern, and getting into the unfinished grave, worked at it for an hour or so, with right good will. But the earth was hardened with the frost, and it was no very easy matter to break it up, and shovel it out; and although there was a moon, it was a very young one, and shed little light upon the grave, which was in the shadow of the church. At any other time, these obstacles would have made Gabriel Grub very moody and miserable, but he was so well pleased with having stopped the small boy's singing, that he took little heed of the scanty progress he had made, and looked down into the grave, when he had finished work for the night, with grim satisfaction: murmuring as he gathered up his things:

> Brave lodgings for one, brave lodgings for one,
> A few feet of cold earth, when life is done;
> A stone at the head, a stone at the feet,
> A rich, juicy meal for the worms to eat;
> Rank grass overhead, and damp clay around,
> Brave lodgings for one, these, in holy ground!

" 'Ho! ho!' laughed Gabriel Grub, as he sat himself down on a flat tombstone which was a favourite resting-place of his; and drew forth his wicker bottle. 'A coffin at Christmas! A Christmas Box. Ho! ho! ho!'

" 'Ho! ho! ho!' repeated a voice which sounded close behind him.

"Gabriel paused in some alarm, in the act of raising the wicker bottle to his lips; and looked round. The bottom of the oldest grave about him, was not more still and quiet, than the churchyard in the pale moonlight. The cold hoarfrost glistened on the tombstones, and sparkled like rows of gems, among the stone carvings of the old church. The snow lay hard and crisp upon the ground; and spread over the thickly strewn mounds of earth so white and smooth a cover that it seemed as if corpses lay there, hidden only by their winding sheets. Not the faintest rustle broke the profound tranquillity of the solemn scene. Sound itself appeared to be frozen up, all was so cold and still.

" 'It was the echoes,' said Gabriel Grub, raising the bottle to his lips again.

" 'It was *not*,' said a deep voice.

"Gabriel started up, and stood rooted to the spot with astonishment and terror; for his eyes rested on a form that made his blood run cold.

"Scated on an upright tombstone, close to him, was a strange unearthly figure, whom Gabriel felt at once, was no being of this world. His long fantastic legs which might have reached the ground, were cocked up, and crossed after a quaint, fantastic fashion; his sinewy arms were bare; and his hands rested on his knees. On his short round body, he wore a close covering, ornamented with small slashes; a short cloak dangled at his back; the collar was cut into curious peaks, which served the goblin in lieu of ruff or neckerchief; and his shoes curled up at his toes into long points. On his head, he wore a broad-brimmed sugar-loaf hat, garnished with a single feather. The hat was covered with the white frost; and the goblin looked as if he had sat on the same tombstone very comfortably, for two or three hundred years. He was sitting perfectly still; his tongue was put out, as if in derision; and he was grinning at Gabriel Grub with such a grin as only a goblin could call up.

" 'It was *not* the echoes,' said the goblin.

"Gabriel Grub was paralysed, and could make no reply.

" 'What do you do here on Christmas eve?' said the goblin sternly.

" 'I came to dig a grave, sir,' stammered Gabriel Grub.

" 'What man wanders among graves and churchyards on such a night as this?' cried the goblin.

" 'Gabriel Grub! Gabriel Grub!' screamed a wild chorus of voices that seemed to fill the churchyard. Gabriel looked fearfully round— nothing was to be seen.

" 'What have you got in that bottle?' said the goblin.

" 'Hollands, sir,' replied the sexton, trembling more than ever;

for he had bought it of the smugglers, and he thought that perhaps his questioner might be in the excise department of the goblins.

" 'Who drinks Hollands alone, and in a churchyard, on such a night as this?' said the goblin.

" 'Gabriel Grub! Gabriel Grub!' exclaimed the wild voices again.

"The goblin leered maliciously at the terrified sexton, and then raising his voice, exclaimed:

" 'And who, then, is our fair and lawful prize?'

"To this inquiry the invisible chorus replied, in a strain that sounded like the voices of many choristers singing to the mighty swell of the old church organ—a strain that seemed borne to the sexton's ears upon a wild wind, and to die away as it passed onward; but the burden of the reply was still the same, 'Gabriel Grub! Gabriel Grub!'

"The goblin grinned a broader grin than before, as he said, 'Well, Gabriel, what do you say to this?'

"The sexton gasped for breath.

" 'What do you think of this, Gabriel?' said the goblin, kicking up his feet in the air on either side of the tombstone, and looking at the turned-up points with as much complacency as if he had been contemplating the most fashionable pair of Wellingtons in all Bond Street.

" 'It's—it's—very curious, sir,' replied the sexton, half dead with fright; 'very curious, and very pretty, but I think I'll go back and finish my work, sir, if you please.'

" 'Work!' said the goblin, 'what work?'

" 'The grave, sir; making the grave,' stammered the sexton.

" 'Oh, the grave, eh?' said the goblin; 'who makes graves at a time when all other men are merry, and takes a pleasure in it?'

"Again the mysterious voices replied, 'Gabriel Grub! Gabriel Grub!'

" 'I'm afraid my friends want you, Gabriel,' said the goblin, thrusting his tongue further into his cheek than ever—and a most astonishing tongue it was—'I'm afraid my friends want you, Gabriel,' said the goblin.

Christmas at Dingley Dell

" 'Under favour, sir,' replied the horror-stricken sexton, 'I don't think they can, sir; they don't know me, sir; I don't think the gentlemen have ever seen me, sir.'

" 'Oh yes, they have,' replied the goblin; 'we know the man with the sulky face and grim scowl, that came down the street to-night, throwing his evil looks at the children, and grasping his burying spade the tighter. We know the man who struck the boy in the envious malice of his heart, because the boy could be merry, and he could not. We know him, we know him.'

"Here, the goblin gave a loud shrill laugh, which the echoes returned twenty-fold: and throwing his legs up in the air, stood upon his head, or rather upon the very point of his sugar-loaf hat, on the narrow edge of the tombstone: whence he threw a somerset with extraordinary agility, right to the sexton's feet, at which he planted himself in the attitude in which tailors generally sit upon the shop-board.

" 'I—I—am afraid I must leave you, sir,' said the sexton, making an effort to move.

" 'Leave us!' said the goblin, 'Gabriel Grub going to leave us. Ho! ho! ho!'

"As the goblin laughed, the sexton observed, for one instant, a brilliant illumination within the windows of the church, as if the whole building were lighted up; it disappeared, the organ pealed forth a lively air, and whole troops of goblins, the very counterpart of the first one, poured into the churchyard, and began playing at leap-frog with the tombstones: never stopping for an instant to take breath, but 'overing' the highest among them, one after the other, with the most marvellous dexterity. The first goblin was a most astonishing leaper, and none of the others could come near him; even in the extremity of his terror the sexton could not help observing, that while his friends were content to leap over the common-sized gravestones, the first one took the family vaults, iron railings and all, with as much ease as if they had been so many street posts. At last the game reached to a most exciting pitch; the organ played quicker and quicker; and the goblins leaped faster and faster:

coiling themselves up, rolling head over heels upon the ground, and bounding over the tombstones like foot-balls. The sexton's brain whirled round with the rapidity of the motion he beheld, and his legs reeled beneath him, as the spirits flew before his eyes: when the goblin king, suddenly darting towards him, laid his hand upon his collar, and sank with him through the earth.

"When Gabriel Grub had had time to fetch his breath, which the rapidity of his descent had for the moment taken away, he found himself in what appeared to be a large cavern, surrounded on all sides by crowds of goblins, ugly and grim; in the centre of the room, on an elevated seat, was stationed his friend of the church-yard; and close beside him stood Gabriel Grub himself, without power of motion.

" 'Cold to-night,' said the king of goblins, 'very cold. A glass of something warm, here!'

"At this command, half a dozen officious goblins, with a perpetual smile upon their faces, whom Gabriel Grub imagined to be courtiers, on that account, hastily disappeared, and presently returned with a goblet of liquid fire, which they presented to the king.

" 'Ah!' cried the goblin, whose cheeks and throat were transparent, as he tossed down the flame, 'This warms one, indeed! Bring a bumper of the same for Mr. Grub.'

"It was in vain for the unfortunate sexton to protest that he was not in the habit of taking anything warm at night; one of the goblins held him while another poured the blazing liquid down his throat; the whole assembly screeched with laughter as he coughed and choked, and wiped away the tears which gushed plentifully from his eyes, after swallowing the burning draught.

" 'And now,' said the king, fantastically poking the taper corner of his sugar-loaf hat into the sexton's eyes, and thereby occasioning him the most exquisite pain: 'And now, show the man of misery and gloom, a few of the pictures from our own great storehouse!'

"As the goblin said this, a thick cloud which obscured the remoter end of the cavern, rolled gradually away, and disclosed, apparently at a great distance, a small and scantily furnished, but neat and clean apartment. A crowd of little children were gathered round a bright fire, clinging to their mother's gown, and gambolling around her chair. The mother occasionally rose, and drew aside the window-curtain, as if to look for some expected object; a frugal meal was ready spread upon the table, and an elbow chair was placed near the fire. A knock was heard at the door; the mother opened it, and the children crowded round her, and clapped their hands for joy, as their father entered. He was wet and weary, and shook the snow from his garments, as the children crowded round him, and seizing his cloak, hat, stick, and gloves, with busy zeal, ran with them from the room. Then, as he sat down to his meal before the fire, the children climbed about his knee, and the mother sat by his side, and all seemed happiness and comfort.

"But a change came upon the view, almost imperceptibly. The scene was altered to a small bed-room, where the fairest and youngest child lay dying; the roses had fled from his cheek, and the light from the eye; and even as the sexton looked upon him with an interest he had never felt or known before, he died. His young brothers and sisters crowded round his little bed, and seized his tiny hand, so cold and heavy; but they shrunk back from its touch, and looked with awe on his infant face; for calm and tranquil as it was and sleeping in rest and peace as the beautiful child seemed to be, they saw that he was dead, and they knew that he was an Angel looking down upon, and blessing them, from a bright and happy Heaven.

"Again the light cloud passed across the picture, and again the subject changed. The father and mother were old and helpless now, and the number of those about them was diminished more than half; but content and cheerfulness sat on every face, and beamed in every eye, as they crowded round the fireside, and told and listened to old stories of earlier and bygone days. Slowly and peacefully, the father sank into the grave, and, soon after, the sharer of all his cares and troubles followed him to a place of rest. The few, who yet survived them, knelt by their tomb, and watered the green turf which covered it, with their tears; then rose, and turned away: sadly and mournfully,

349

but not with bitter cries, or despairing lamentations, for they knew that they should one day meet again; and once more they mixed with the busy world, and their content and cheerfulness were restored. The cloud settled upon the picture, and concealed it from the sexton's view.

" 'What do you think of *that*?' said the goblin, turning his large face towards Gabriel Grub.

"Gabriel murmured out something about its being very pretty, and looked somewhat ashamed, as the goblin bent his fiery eyes upon him.

" 'You a miserable man!' said the goblin, in a tone of excessive contempt. 'You!' He appeared disposed to add more, but indignation choked his utterance, so he lifted up one of his very pliable legs, and flourishing it above his head a little, to insure his aim, administered a good sound kick to Gabriel Grub; immediately after which, all the goblins in waiting crowded round the wretched sexton, and kicked him without mercy: according to the established and invariable custom of courtiers upon earth, who kick whom royalty kicks, and hug whom royalty hugs.

" 'Show him some more!' said the king of the goblins.

"At these words, the cloud was dispelled, and a rich and beautiful landscape was disclosed to view—there is just such another, to this day, within half a mile of the old abbey town. The sun shone from out the clear blue sky, the water sparkled beneath its rays, and the trees looked greener, and the flowers more gay, beneath his cheering influence. The water rippled on, with a pleasant sound; the trees rustled in the light wind that murmured among their leaves; the birds sang upon the boughs; and the lark carolled on high her welcome to the morning. Yes, it was morning; the bright, balmy morning of summer; the minutest leaf, the smallest blade of grass, was instinct with life. The ant crept forth to her daily toil, the butterfly fluttered and basked in the warm rays of the sun; myriads of insects spread their transparent wings, and revelled in their brief but happy existence. Man walked forth, elated with the scene; and all was brightness and splendour.

" 'You a miserable man!' said the king of the goblins, in a more contemptuous tone than before. And again the king of the goblins gave his leg a flourish; again it descended on the shoulders of the sexton; and again the attendant goblins imitated the example of their chief.

"Many a time the cloud went and came, and many a lesson it taught to Gabriel Grub, who, although his shoulders smarted with pain from the frequent applications of the goblins' feet, looked on with an interest that nothing could diminish. He saw that men who worked hard, and earned their scanty bread with lives of labour, were cheerful and happy; and that to the most ignorant, the sweet face of nature was a never-failing source of cheerfulness and joy. He saw those who had been delicately nurtured, and tenderly brought up, cheerful under privations, and superior to suffering that would have crushed many of a rougher grain, because they bore within their own bosoms the materials of happiness, contentment, and peace. He saw that women, the tenderest and most fragile of all God's creatures, were the oftenest superior to sorrow, adversity, and distress; and he saw that it was because they bore, in their own hearts, an inexhaustible well-spring of affection and devotion. Above all, he saw that men like himself, who snarled at the mirth and cheerfulness of others, were the foulest weeds on the fair surface of the earth; and setting all the good of the world against the evil, he came to the conclusion that it was a very decent and respectable sort of world after all. No sooner had he formed it, than the cloud which closed over the last picture, seemed to settle on his senses, and lull him to repose. One by one, the goblins faded from his sight; and as the last one disappeared, he sunk to sleep.

"The day had broken when Gabriel Grub awoke, and found himself lying, at full length on the flat gravestone in the churchyard, with the wicker bottle lying empty by his side, and his coat, spade, and lantern, all well whitened by the last night's frost, scattered on the ground. The stone on which he had first seen the goblin seated stood bolt upright before him, and the grave at which he had worked, the night before, was not far off. At first, he began to doubt the reality of his adventures, but the acute pain in his shoulders when he attempted to rise assured him that the kicking of the goblins was certainly not ideal. He was staggered again by observing no traces of footsteps in the snow on which the goblins had played at leap-frog with the gravestones, but he speedily accounted for this circumstance when he remembered that, being spirits, they would leave no visible impression behind them. So, Gabriel Grub got on his feet as well as he could, for the pain in his back; and brushing the frost off his coat, put it on, and turned his face towards the town.

"But he was an altered man, and he could not bear the thought of returning to a place where his repentance would be scoffed at, and his reformation disbelieved. He hesitated for a few moments; and then turned away to wander where he might, and seek his bread elsewhere.

"The lantern, the spade, and the wicker bottle, were found, that day, in the churchyard. There were a great many speculations about the sexton's fate, at first, but it was speedily determined that he had been carried away by the goblins; and there were not wanting some very credible witnesses who had distinctly seen him whisked through the air on the back of a chestnut horse blind of one eye, with the hind-quarters of a lion, and the tail of a bear. At length all this was devoutly believed; and the new sexton used to exhibit to the curious, for a trifling emolument, a good-sized piece of the church weathercock which had been accidentally kicked off by the aforesaid horse in his aerial flight, and picked up by himself in the churchyard, a year or two afterwards.

"Unfortunately, these stories were somewhat disturbed by the un-looked-for re-appearance of Gabriel Grub himself, some ten years afterwards, a ragged, contented, rheumatic old man. He told his story to the clergyman, and also to the mayor; and in course of time it began to be received, as a matter of history, in which form it has continued down to this very day. The believers in the weather-cock tale, having misplaced their confidence once, were not easily prevailed upon to part with it again, so they looked as wise as they could, shrugged their shoulders, touched their foreheads, and murmured something about Gabriel Grub having drunk all the Hollands, and then fallen asleep on the flat tombstone; and they affected to explain what he supposed he had witnessed in the goblin's cavern, by saying that he had seen the world, and grown wiser. But this opinion, which was by no means a popular one at any time, gradually died off; and be the matter how it may, as Gabriel Grub was afflicted with rheumatism to the end of his days, this story has at least one moral, if it teach no better one—and that is, that if a man turn sulky and drink by himself at Christmas time, he may make up his mind to be not a bit the better for it: let the spirits be never so good, or let them be even as many degrees beyond proof, as those which Gabriel Grub saw in the goblin's cavern."

*   *   *   *   *

"WELL, Sam," said Mr. Pickwick as that favoured servitor entered his bed-chamber with his warm water, on the morning of Christmas day, "still frosty?"

"Water in the wash-hand basin's a mask o' ice, sir," responded Sam.

"Severe weather, Sam," observed Mr. Pickwick.

"Fine time for them as is well wropped up, as the Polar Bear said to himself, ven he was practising his skating," replied Mr. Weller.

"I shall be down in a quarter of an hour, Sam," said Mr. Pickwick, untying his nightcap.

"Wery good, sir," replied Sam. . . .

"Now," said Wardle, after a substantial lunch, with the agreeable items of strong beer and cherry-brandy, had been done ample justice to; "what say you to an hour on the ice? We shall have plenty of time."

"Capital!" said Mr. Benjamin Allen.

"Prime!" ejaculated Mr. Bob Sawyer.

"You skate, of course, Winkle?" said Wardle.

"Ye-es; oh, yes," replied Mr. Winkle. "I—I—am *rather* out of practice."

"Oh, *do* skate, Mr. Winkle," said Arabella. "I like to see it so much."

"Oh, it is so graceful," said another young lady.

A third young lady said it was elegant, and a fourth expressed her opinion that it was "swan-like."

"I should be very happy, I'm sure," said Mr. Winkle, reddening; "but I have no skates."

This objection was at once overruled. Trundle had a couple of pair, and the fat boy announced that there were half-a-dozen more down-stairs: whereat Mr. Winkle expressed exquisite delight, and looked exquisitely uncomfortable.

Old Wardle led the way to a pretty large sheet of ice; and the fat boy and Mr. Weller, having shovelled and swept away the snow which had fallen on it during the night, Mr. Bob Sawyer adjusted his skates with a dexterity which to Mr. Winkle was perfectly marvellous and described circles with his left leg, and cut figures of eight, and inscribed upon the ice, without once stopping for breath, a great many other pleasant and astonishing devices, to the excessive satisfaction of Mr. Pickwick, Mr. Tupman, and the ladies: which reached a pitch of positive enthusiasm, when old Wardle and Benjamin Allen, assisted by the aforesaid Bob Sawyer, performed some mystic evolutions, which they called a reel.

All this time, Mr. Winkle, with his face and hands blue with the cold, had been forcing a gimlet into the soles of his feet, and putting his skates on, with the points behind, and getting the straps into a very complicated and entangled state, with the assistance of Mr. Snodgrass, who knew rather less about skates than a Hindoo. At length, however, with the assistance of Mr. Weller, the unfortunate skates were firmly screwed and buckled on, and Mr. Winkle was raised to his feet.

"Now, then, sir," said Sam, in an encouraging tone; "off vith you, and show 'em how to do it."

"Stop, Sam, stop!" said Mr. Winkle, trembling violently, and clutching hold of Sam's arms with the grasp of a drowning man. "How slippery it is, Sam!"

"Not an uncommon thing upon ice, sir," replied Mr. Weller. "Hold up, sir!"

This last observation of Mr. Weller's bore reference to a demonstration Mr. Winkle made at the instant, of a frantic desire to throw his feet in the air, and dash the back of his head on the ice.

"These—these—are very awkward skates; ain't they, Sam?" inquired Mr. Winkle, staggering.

"I'm afeerd there's a orkard gen'l'm'n in 'em, sir," replied Sam.

"Now, Winkle," cried Mr. Pickwick, quite unconscious that there was anything the matter. "Come; the ladies are all anxiety."

"Yes, yes," replied Mr. Winkle, with a ghastly smile. "I'm coming."

"Just a goin' to begin," said Sam, endeavouring to disengage himself. "Now, sir, start off!"

"Stop an instant, Sam," gasped Mr. Winkle, clinging most affectionately to Mr. Weller. "I find I've got a couple of coats at home that I don't want, Sam. You may have them, Sam."

"Thank'ee, sir," replied Mr. Weller.

"Never mind touching your hat, Sam," said Mr. Winkle, hastily. "You needn't take your hand away to do that. I meant to have given you five shillings this morning for a Christmas-box, Sam. I'll give it you this afternoon, Sam."

"You're wery good, sir," replied Mr. Weller.

"Just hold me at first, Sam; will you?" said Mr. Winkle. "There—that's right. I shall soon get in the way of it, Sam. Not too fast, Sam; not too fast."

Mr. Winkle stooping forward, with his body half doubled up, was being assisted over the ice by Mr. Weller, in a very singular and un-swan-like manner, when Mr. Pickwick most innocently shouted from the opposite bank:

"Sam!"

"Sir?"

"Here. I want you."

"Let go, sir," said Sam. "Don't you hear the governor a callin'? Let go, sir."

With a violent effort, Mr. Weller disengaged himself from the grasp of the agonised Pickwickian, and, in so doing, administered a considerable impetus to the unhappy Mr. Winkle. With an accuracy which no degree of dexterity or practice could have insured, that unfortunate gentleman bore swiftly down into the centre of the reel, at the very moment when Mr. Bob Sawyer was performing a flourish of unparalleled beauty. Mr. Winkle struck wildly against him, and with a loud crash they both fell heavily down. Mr. Pickwick ran to the spot. Bob Sawyer had risen to his feet, but Mr. Winkle was far too wise to do anything of the kind, in skates. He was seated on the ice, making spasmodic efforts to smile; but anguish was depicted on every lineament of his countenance. . . .

"Lift him up," said Mr. Pickwick. Sam assisted him to rise.

Mr. Pickwick retired a few paces apart from the bystanders; and, beckoning his friend to approach, fixed a searching look upon him, and uttered in a low, but distinct and emphatic tone, these remarkable words: "You're a humbug, sir."

"A what?" said Mr. Winkle, starting.

"A humbug, sir. I will speak plainer, if you wish it. An impostor, sir."

With those words, Mr. Pickwick turned slowly on his heel, and rejoined his friends.

While Mr. Pickwick was delivering himself of the sentiment just recorded, Mr. Weller and the fat boy, having by their joint endeavours cut out a slide, were exercising themselves thereupon, in a very masterly and brilliant manner. Sam Weller, in particular, was displaying that beautiful feat of fancy-sliding which is currently denominated "knocking at the cobbler's door," and which is achieved by skimming over the ice on one foot, and occasionally giving a postman's knock upon it with the other. It was a good long slide, and there was something in the motion which Mr. Pickwick, who was very cold with standing still, could not help envying.

"It looks a nice warm exercise that, doesn't it?" he inquired of Wardle, when that gentleman was thoroughly out of breath, by reason of the indefatigable manner in which he had converted his legs into a pair of compasses, and drawn complicated problems on the ice.

"Ah, it does indeed," replied Wardle. "Do you slide?"

"I used to do so, on the gutters, when I was a boy," replied Mr. Pickwick.

"Try it now," said Wardle.

"Oh, do, please, Mr. Pickwick!" cried all the ladies.

"I should be very happy to afford you any amusement," replied Mr. Pickwick, "but I haven't done such a thing these thirty years."

"Pooh! Pooh! Nonsense!" said Wardle, dragging off his skates with the impetuosity which characterised all his proceedings. "Here; I'll keep you company; come along!" And away went the good-tempered old fellow down the slide, with a rapidity which came very close upon Mr. Weller, and beat the fat boy all to nothing.

Mr. Pickwick paused, considered, pulled off his gloves and put them in his hat: took two or three short runs, baulked himself as often, and at last took another run, and went slowly and gravely down the slide, with his feet about a yard and a quarter apart, amidst the gratified shouts of all the spectators.

"Keep the pot a bilin', sir!" said Sam; and down went Wardle again, and then Mr. Pickwick, and then Sam, and then Mr. Winkle, and then Mr. Bob Sawyer, and then the fat boy, and then Mr. Snodgrass, following closely upon each other's heels, and running after each other with as much eagerness as if all their future prospects in life depended on their expedition.

It was the most intensely interesting thing, to observe the manner in which Mr. Pickwick performed his share in the ceremony; to watch the torture of anxiety with which he viewed the person behind, gaining upon him at the imminent hazard of tripping him up; to see him gradually expend the painful force he had put on at first, and turn slowly round on the slide, with his face towards the point from which he had started; to contemplate the playful smile which mantled on his face when he had accomplished the distance, and the eagerness with which he turned round when he had done so, and ran after his predecessor: his black gaiters tripping pleasantly through the snow, and his eyes beaming cheerfulness and gladness through his spectacles. And when he was knocked down (which happened upon the average every third round), it was the most invigorating sight that can possibly be imagined, to behold him gather up his hat, gloves, and handkerchief, with a glowing countenance, and resume his station in the rank, with an ardour and enthusiasm that nothing could abate.

The sport was at its height, the sliding was at the quickest, the laughter was at the loudest, when a sharp smart crack was heard. There was a quick rush towards the bank, a wild scream from the ladies, and a shout from Mr. Tupman. A large mass of ice disappeared; the water bubbled up over it; Mr. Pickwick's hat, gloves, and handkerchief were floating on the surface; and this was all of Mr. Pickwick that anybody could see.

Dismay and anguish were depicted on every countenance, the males turned pale, and the females fainted. Mr. Snodgrass and Mr. Winkle grasped each other by the hand and gazed at the spot where their leader had gone down, with frenzied eagerness: while Mr. Tupman, by way of rendering the promptest assistance, and at the same time conveying to any persons who might be within hearing, the clearest possible notion of the catastrophe, ran off across the country at his utmost speed, screaming "Fire!" with all his might.

It was at this moment, when old Wardle and Sam Weller were approaching the hole with cautious steps, and Mr. Benjamin Allen was holding a hurried consultation with Mr. Bob Sawyer, on the advisability of bleeding the company generally, as an improving little bit of professional practice — it was at this very moment, that a face, head, and shoulders, emerged from beneath the water, and disclosed the features and spectacles of Mr. Pickwick.

"Keep yourself up for an instant — for only one instant!" bawled Mr. Snodgrass.

"Yes, do; let me implore you — for my sake!" roared Mr. Winkle, deeply affected. The adjuration was rather unnecessary; the probability being, that if Mr. Pickwick had declined to keep himself up for anybody else's sake, it would have occurred to him that he might as well do so, for his own.

"Do you feel the bottom there, old fellow?" said Wardle.

"Yes, certainly," replied Mr. Pickwick, wringing the water from his head and face, and gasping for breath. "I fell upon my back. I couldn't get on my feet at first."

The clay upon so much of Mr. Pickwick's coat as was yet visible, bore testimony to the accuracy of this statement; and as the fears of the spectators were still further relieved by the fat boy's suddenly recollecting that the water was nowhere more than five feet deep, prodigies of valour were performed to get him out. After a vast quantity of splashing, and cracking, and struggling, Mr. Pickwick was at length fairly extricated from his unpleasant position, and once more stood on dry land.

"Oh, he'll catch his death of cold," said Emily.

"Dear old thing!" said Arabella. "Let me wrap this shawl round you, Mr. Pickwick."

"Ah, that's the best thing you can do," said Wardle, "and when you've got it on, run home as fast as your legs can carry you, and jump into bed directly."

A dozen shawls were offered on the instant. Three or four of the thickest having been selected, Mr. Pickwick was wrapped up, and started off, under the guidance of Mr. Weller: presenting the singular phenomenon of an elderly gentleman, dripping wet, and without a hat, with his arms bound down to his sides, skimming over the ground, without any clearly defined purpose, at the rate of six good English miles an hour.

But Mr. Pickwick cared not for appearances in such an extreme case, and urged on by Sam Weller, he kept at the very top of his speed until he reached the door of Manor Farm, where Mr. Tupman had arrived some five minutes before, and had frightened the old lady into palpitations of the heart by impressing her with the unalterable conviction that the kitchen chimney was on fire—a calamity which always presented itself in glowing colours to the old lady's mind, when anybody about her evinced the smallest agitation.

Mr. Pickwick paused not an instant until he was snug in bed. Sam Weller lighted a blazing fire in the room, and took up his dinner; a bowl of punch was carried up afterwards, and a grand carouse held in honour of his safety. Old Wardle would not hear of his rising, so they made the bed the chair, and Mr. Pickwick presided. A second and a third bowl were ordered in; and when Mr. Pickwick awoke next morning, there was not a symptom of rheumatism about him: which proves, as Mr. Bob Sawyer very justly observed, that there is nothing like hot punch in such cases: and that if ever hot punch did fail to act as a preventive, it was merely because the patient fell into the vulgar error of not taking enough of it.

MRS. GASKELL

Christmas Storms and Sunshine

IN the town of——(no matter where) there circulated two local
newspapers (no matter when). Now the *Flying Post* was long
established and respectable—alias bigoted and Tory; the *Examiner* was spirited and intelligent—alias new-fangled and democratic. Every week these newspapers contained articles abusing each
other; as cross and peppery as articles could be, and evidently the
production of irritated minds, although they seemed to have one
stereotyped commencement—"Though the article appearing in last
week's *Post* (or *Examiner*) is below contempt, yet we have been
induced," &c., &c., and every Saturday the Radical shopkeepers shook
hands together, and agreed that the *Post* was done for, by the slash-
ing clever *Examiner*; while the more dignified Tories began by re-
gretting that Johnson should think that low paper, only read by a
few of the vulgar, worth wasting his wit upon; however, the *Examiner*
was at its last gasp.

It was not though. It lived and flourished; at least it paid its way, as one of the heroes of my story could tell. He was chief compositor, or whatever title may be given to the head-man of the mechanical part of a newspaper. He hardly confined himself to that department. Once or twice, unknown to the editor, when the manuscript had fallen short, he had filled up the vacant space by compositions of his own; announcements of a forthcoming crop of green peas in December; a grey thrush having been seen, or a white hare, or such interesting phenomena; invented for the occasion, I must confess; but what of that? His wife always knew when to expect a little specimen of her husband's literary talent by a peculiar cough, which served as prelude; and, judging from this encouraging sign, and the high-pitched and emphatic voice in which he read them, she was inclined to think, that an "Ode to an early Rose-bud," in the corner devoted to original poetry, and a letter in the correspondence department, signed "*Pro Bono Publico*," were her husband's writing, and to hold up her head accordingly.

I never could find out what it was that occasioned the Hodgsons to lodge in the same house as the Jenkinses. Jenkins held the same office in the Tory paper, as Hodgson did in the *Examiner*, and, as I said before, I leave you to give it a name. But Jenkins had a proper sense of his position, and a proper reverence for all in authority, from the king down to the editor, and sub-editor. He would as soon have thought of borrowing the king's crown for a nightcap, or the king's sceptre for a walking-stick, as he would have thought of filling up any spare corner with any production of his own; and I think it would have even added to his contempt of Hodgson (if that were possible), had he known of the "productions of his brain," as the latter fondly alluded to the paragraphs he inserted, when speaking to his wife.

Jenkins had his wife too. Wives were wanting to finish the completeness of the quarrel, which existed one memorable Christmas week, some dozen years ago, between the two neighbours, the two compositors. And with wives, it was a very pretty, a very complete quarrel. To make the opposing parties still more equal, still more well-matched, if the Hodgsons had a baby ("such a baby!—a poor puny little thing"), Mrs. Jenkins had a cat ("such a cat! a great, nasty, miowling tom-cat, that was always stealing the milk put by for little Angel's supper"). And now, having matched Greek with Greek, I must proceed to the tug of war. It was the day before Christmas; such a cold east wind! such an inky sky! such a blue-black look in people's faces, as they were driven out more than usual, to complete their purchases for the next day's festival.

Before leaving home that morning, Jenkins had given some money to his wife to buy the next day's dinner.

"My dear, I wish for turkey and sausages. It may be a weakness, but I own I am partial to sausages. My deceased mother was. Such tastes are hereditary. As to the sweets—whether plum-pudding or mince-pies—I leave such considerations to you; I only beg you not to mind expense. Christmas comes but once a year."

And again he had called out from the bottom of the first flight of stairs, just close to the Hodgsons' door ("Such ostentatiousness," as Mrs. Hodgson observed), "You will not forget the sausages, my dear?"

"I should have liked to have had something above common, Mary," said Hodgson, as they too made their plans for the next day, "but I think roast beef must do for us. You see, love, we've a family."

"Only one, Jem! I don't want more than roast beef, though, I'm sure. Before I went to service, mother and me would have thought roast beef a very fine dinner."

"Well, let's settle it then, roast beef and a plum-pudding; and now, good-bye. Mind and take care of little Tom. I thought he was a bit hoarse this morning."

And off he went to his work.

Now, it was a good while since Mrs. Jenkins and Mrs. Hodgson had spoken to each other, although they were quite as much in possession of the knowledge of events and opinions as though they did. Mary knew that Mrs. Jenkins despised her for not having a real lace cap, which Mrs. Jenkins had; and for having been a servant, which Mrs. Jenkins had not; and the little occasional pinchings

which the Hodgsons were obliged to resort to, to make both ends
meet, would have been very patiently endured by Mary, if she had
not winced under Mrs. Jenkins's knowledge of such economy. But
she had her revenge. She had a child, and Mrs. Jenkins had none. To
have had a child, even such a puny baby as little Tom, Mrs. Jenkins
would have worn commonest caps, and cleaned grates, and drudged
her fingers to the bone. The great unspoken disappointment of her
life soured her temper, and turned her thoughts inward, and made
her morbid and selfish.

"Hang that cat! He's been stealing again! He's gnawed the cold
mutton in his nasty mouth till it's not fit to set before a Christian;
and I've nothing else for Jem's dinner. But I'll give it him now I've
caught him, that I will!"

So saying, Mary Hodgson caught up her husband's Sunday cane,
and despite pussy's cries and scratches, she gave him such a beating
as she hoped might cure him of his thievish propensities; when lo!
and behold, Mrs. Jenkins stood at the door with a face of bitter
wrath.

"Aren't you ashamed of yourself, ma'am, to abuse a poor dumb
animal, ma'am, as knows no better than to take food when he sees
it, ma'am? He only follows the nature which God has given, ma'am;
and it's a pity your nature, ma'am, which I've heard is of the stingy
saving species, does not make you shut your cupboard-door a little
closer. There is such a thing as law for brute animals. I'll ask Mr.
Jenkins, but I don't think them Radicals has done away with that
law yet, for all their Reform Bill, ma'am. My poor precious love of
a Tommy, is he hurt? and is his leg broke for taking a mouthful of
scraps, as most people would give away to a beggar,—if he'd take
'em!" wound up Mrs. Jenkins, casting a contemptuous look on the
remnant of a scrag end of mutton.

Mary felt very angry and very guilty. For she really pitied the
poor limping animal as he crept up to his mistress, and there lay
down to bemoan himself; she wished she had not beaten him so
hard, for it certainly was her own careless way of never shutting the
cupboard-door that had tempted him to his fault. But the sneer at

Christmas Storms and Sunshine

her little bit of mutton turned her penitence to fresh wrath, and she shut the door in Mrs. Jenkins's face, as she stood caressing her cat in the lobby, with such a bang, that it wakened little Tom, and he began to cry.

Everything was to go wrong with Mary to-day. Now baby was awake, who was to take her husband's dinner to the office? She took the child in her arms, and tried to hush him off to sleep again, and as she sung she cried, she could hardly tell why—a sort of reaction from her violent angry feelings. She wished she had never beaten the poor cat; she wondered if his leg was really broken. What would her mother say if she knew how cross and cruel her little Mary was getting? If she should live to beat her child in one of her angry fits?

It was of no use lullabying while she sobbed so; it must be given up, and she must just carry her baby in her arms, and take him with her to the office, for it was long past dinner-time. So she pared the mutton carefully, although by so doing she reduced the meat to an infinitesimal quantity, and taking the baked potatoes out of the oven, she popped them piping hot into her basket with the et-cæteras of plate, butter, salt, and knife and fork.

It was, indeed, a bitter wind. She bent against it as she ran, and the flakes of snow were sharp and cutting as ice. Baby cried all the way, though she cuddled him up in her shawl. Then her husband had made his appetite up for a potato pie, and (literary man as he was) his body got so much the better of his mind, that he looked rather black at the cold mutton. Mary had no appetite for her own dinner when she arrived at home again. So, after she had tried to feed baby, and he had fretfully refused to take his bread and milk, she laid him down as usual on his quilt, surrounded by playthings, while she sided away, and chopped suet for the next day's pudding. Early in the afternoon a parcel came, done up first in brown paper, then in such a white, grass-bleached, sweet-smelling towel, and a note from her dear, dear mother; in which quaint writing she endeavoured to tell her daughter that she was not forgotten at Christmas time; but that learning that Farmer Burton was killing his pig, she had made interest for some of his famous pork, out of which she had manufactured some sausages, and flavoured them just as Mary used to like when she lived at home.

"Dear, dear mother!" said Mary to herself. "There never was any one like her for remembering other folk. What rare sausages she used to make! Home things have a smack with 'em, no bought things can ever have. Set them up with their sausages! I've a notion if Mrs. Jenkins had ever tasted mother's, she'd have no fancy for them town-made things Fanny took in just now."

And so she went on thinking about home, till the smiles and the dimples came out again at the remembrance of that pretty cottage, which would look green even now in the depth of winter, with its pyracanthus, and its holly-bushes, and the great Portugal laurel that was her mother's pride. And the back path through the orchard to Farmer Burton's; how well she remembered it. The bushels of unripe apples she had picked up there, and distributed among his pigs, till he had scolded her for giving them so much green trash.

She was interrupted—her baby (I call him a baby, because his father and mother did, and because he was so little of his age, but I rather think he was eighteen months old) had fallen asleep some time before among his playthings; an uneasy, restless sleep; but of which Mary had been thankful, as his morning's nap had been too short, and as she was so busy. But now he began to make such a strange crowing noise, just like a chair drawn heavily and gratingly along a kitchen-floor! His eyes were open, but expressive of nothing but pain.

"Mother's darling!" said Mary, in terror, lifting him up. "Baby, try not to make that noise. Hush—hush—darling; what hurts him?" But the noise came worse and worse.

"Fanny! Fanny!" Mary called in mortal fright, for her baby was almost black with his gasping breath, and she had no one to ask for aid or sympathy but her landlady's daughter, a little girl of twelve or thirteen, who attended to the house in her mother's absence, as daily cook in gentlemen's families. Fanny was more especially considered the attendant of the upstairs lodgers (who paid for the use of the kitchen, "for Jenkins could not abide the smell of meat cooking"), but just now she was fortunately sitting at her afternoon's work of darning stockings, and hearing Mrs. Hodgson's cry of terror, she ran to her sitting-room, and understood the case at a glance.

"He's got the croup! Oh, Mrs. Hodgson, he'll die as sure as fate. Little brother had it, and he died in no time. The doctor said he could do nothing for him, it had gone too far; he said if we'd put him in a warm bath at first, it might have saved him; but, bless you! he was never half so bad as your baby." Unconsciously there mingled in her statement some of a child's love of producing an effect; but the increasing danger was clear enough.

"Oh, my baby! my baby. Oh, love! love! don't look so ill; I cannot bear it. And my fire so low! There, I was thinking of home, and picking currants, and never minding the fire. Oh, Fanny! what is the fire like in the kitchen? Speak."

"Mother told me to screw it up, and throw some slack on as soon as Mrs. Jenkins had done with it, and so I did; it's very low and black. But oh, Mrs. Hodgson! let me run for the doctor—I cannot abear to hear him, it's so like little brother."

Through her streaming tears Mary motioned her to go; and trembling, sinking, sick at heart, she laid her boy in his cradle, and ran to fill her kettle.

Mrs. Jenkins having cooked her husband's snug little dinner, to which he came home; having told him her story of pussy's beating, at which he was justly and dignifiedly (?) indignant, saying it was all of a piece with that abusive *Examiner*; having received the sausages, and turkey, and mince-pies, which her husband had ordered; and cleaned up the room, and prepared everything for tea, and coaxed and duly bemoaned her cat (who had pretty nearly forgotten his beating, but very much enjoyed the petting)—having done all these and many other things, Mrs. Jenkins sate down to get up the real lace cap. Every thread was pulled out separately, and carefully stretched: when, what was that? Outside, in the street, a chorus of piping children's voices sang the old carol she had heard a hundred times in the days of her youth.

> "*As Joseph was a walking he heard an angel sing,*
> *'This night shall be born our heavenly King.*
> *He neither shall be born in housen nor in hall,*
> *Nor in the place of Paradise, but in an ox's stall.*
> *He neither shall be clothed in purple nor in pall,*
> *But all in fair linen, as were babies all:*
> *He neither shall be rocked in silver nor in gold,*
> *But in a wooden cradle that rocks on the mould,'* " &c.

She got up and went to the window. There, below, stood the group of grey black little figures, relieved against the snow, which now enveloped everything. "For old sake's sake," as she phrased it, she counted out a halfpenny apiece for the singers, out of the copper bag, and threw them down below.

The room had become chilly while she had been counting out and throwing down her money, so she stirred her already glowing fire, and sat down right before it—but not to stretch her lace; like Mary Hodgson, she began to think over long-past days—on softening remembrances of the dead and gone—on words long forgotten —on holy stories heard at her mother's knee.

"I cannot think what's come over me to-night," said she, half-aloud, recovering herself by the sound of her own voice from her train of thought; "my head goes wandering on them old times. I'm sure more texts have come into my head with thinking on my mother within this last half hour, than I've thought on for years and years. I hope I'm not going to die. Folks say, thinking too much on the dead betokens we're going to join 'em; I should be loth to go just yet—such a fine turkey as we've got for dinner to-morrow, too!"

Knock, knock, knock, at the door, as fast as knuckles could go. And then, as if the comer could not wait, the door was opened, and Mary Hodgson stood there as white as death. "Mrs. Jenkins!—oh, your kettle is boiling, thank God! Let me have the water for my baby, for the love of God!—he's got croup, and is dying!"

Christmas Storms and Sunshine

Mrs. Jenkins turned on her chair with a wooden inflexible look on her face, that (between ourselves) her husband knew and dreaded for all his pompous dignity.

"I'm sorry I can't oblige you, ma'am; my kettle is wanted for my husband's tea. Don't be afeared, Tommy, Mrs. Hodgson won't venture to intrude herself where she's not desired. You'd better send for the doctor, ma'am, instead of wasting your time in wringing your hands, ma'am—my kettle is engaged."

Mary clasped her hands together with passionate force, but spoke no word of entreaty to that wooden face—that sharp, determined voice; but, as she turned away, she prayed for strength to bear the coming trial, and strength to forgive Mrs. Jenkins.

Mrs. Jenkins watched her go away meekly, as one who has no hope, and then she turned upon herself as sharply as she ever did on any one else.

"What a brute I am, Lord forgive me! What's my husband's tea to a baby's life? In croup, too, where time is everything. You crabbed old vixen, you—any one may know you never had a child!"

She was downstairs (kettle in hand) before she had finished her self-upbraiding; and when in Mrs. Hodgson's room, she rejected all thanks (Mary had not the voice for many words), saying stiffly, "I do it for the poor baby's sake, ma'am, hoping he may live to have mercy to poor dumb beasts, if he does forget to lock his cupboards."

But she did everything, and more than Mary, with her young inexperience, could have thought of. She prepared the warm bath, and tried it with her husband's own thermometer (Mr. Jenkins was as punctual as clock-work in noting down the temperature of every day). She let his mother place her baby in the tub, still preserving the same rigid affronted aspect, and then she went upstairs without a word. Mary longed to ask her to stay, but dared not; though, when she left the room, the tears chased each other down her cheeks faster than ever. Poor young mother! How she counted the minutes till the doctor should come. But, before he came, down again stalked Mrs. Jenkins, with something in her hand.

"I've seen many of these croup-fits, which, I take it, you've not,

369

ma'am. Mustard plaisters is very sovereign put on the throat; I've been up and made one, ma'am, and, by your leave, I'll put it on the poor little fellow."

Mary could not speak, but she signed her grateful assent.

It began to smart while they still kept silence; and he looked up to his mother as if seeking courage from her looks to bear the stinging pain, but she was softly crying, to see him suffer, and her want of courage reacted upon him, and he began to sob aloud. Instantly Mrs. Jenkins's apron was up, hiding her face. "Peep bo, baby," said she, as merrily as she could. His little face brightened, and his mother having once got the cue, the two women kept the little fellow amused, until his plaister had taken effect.

"He's better,—oh, Mrs. Jenkins, look at his eyes! how different! And he breathes quite softly——" As Mary spoke thus, the doctor entered. He examined his patient. Baby was really better.

"It has been a sharp attack, but the remedies you have applied have been worth all the Pharmacopœia an hour later. I shall send a powder," &c., &c.

Mrs. Jenkins stayed to hear this opinion; and (her heart wonderfully more easy) was going to leave the room, when Mary seized her hand and kissed it; she could not speak her gratitude.

Mrs. Jenkins looked affronted and awkward, and as if she must go upstairs and wash her hand directly.

But, in spite of these sour looks, she came softly down an hour or so afterwards to see how baby was.

The little gentleman slept well after the fright he had given his friends; and on Christmas morning, when Mary awoke and looked at the sweet little pale face lying on her arm, she could hardly realize the danger he had been in.

When she came down (later than usual), she found the household in a commotion. What do you think had happened? Why, pussy had been a traitor to his best friend, and eaten up some of Mr. Jenkins's own especial sausages; and gnawed and tumbled the rest so, that they were not fit to be eaten! There were no bounds to that cat's appetite! he would have eaten his own father if he had been tender enough. And now Mrs. Jenkins stormed and cried—"Hang the cat!"

Christmas day, too! and all the shops shut! "What was turkey without sausages?" gruffly asked Mr. Jenkins.

"Oh, Jem!" whispered Mary. "Hearken, what a piece of work he's making about sausages,—I should like to take Mrs. Jenkins up some of mother's; they're twice as good as bought sausages."

"I see no objection, my dear. Sausages do not involve intimacies, else his politics are what I can no ways respect."

"But, O Jem, if you had seen her last night about baby! I'm sure she may scold me for ever, and I'll not answer. I'd even make her cat welcome to the sausages." The tears gathered to Mary's eyes as she kissed her boy.

"Better take 'em upstairs, my dear, and give them to the cat's mistress." And Jem chuckled at his saying.

Mary put them on a plate, but still she loitered.

"What must I say, Jem? I never know."

"Say—I hope you'll accept of these sausages, as my mother—no, that's not grammar,—say what comes uppermost, Mary, it will be sure to be right."

So Mary carried them upstairs and knocked at the door; and when told to "come in," she looked very red, but went up to Mrs. Jenkins, saying, "Please, take these. Mother made them." And was away before an answer could be given.

Just as Hodgson was ready to go to church, Mrs. Jenkins came downstairs, and called Fanny. In a minute the latter entered the Hodgsons' room, and delivered Mr. and Mrs. Jenkins's compliments, and they would be particular glad if Mr. and Mrs. Hodgson would eat their dinner with them.

"And carry baby upstairs in a shawl, be sure," added Mrs. Jenkins's voice in the passage, close to the door, whither she had followed her messenger. There was no discussing the matter, with the certainty of every word being overheard. Mary looked anxiously at her husband. She remembered his saying he did not approve of Mr. Jenkins's politics.

"Do you think it would do for baby?" asked he.

"Oh yes," answered she, eagerly; "I would wrap him up so warm."

"And I've got our room up to sixty-five already, for all it's so frosty," added the voice outside.

Now, how do you think they settled the matter? The very best way in the world. Mr. and Mrs. Jenkins came down into the Hodgsons' room, and dined there. Turkey at the top, roast beef at the bottom, sausages at one side, potatoes at the other. Second course, plum-pudding at the top, and mince-pies at the bottom.

And after dinner, Mrs. Jenkins would have baby on her knee; and he seemed quite to take to her; she declared he was admiring the real lace on her cap, but Mary thought (though she did not say so) that he was pleased by her kind looks, and coaxing words. Then he was wrapped up and carried carefully upstairs to tea, in Mrs. Jenkins's room. And after tea, Mrs. Jenkins, and Mary, and her husband, found out each other's mutual liking for music, and sat singing old glees and catches, till I don't know what o'clock, without one word of politics or newspapers.

Before they parted, Mary had coaxed pussy on to her knee; for Mrs. Jenkins would not part with baby, who was sleeping on her lap.

"When you're busy, bring him to me. Do, now, it will be a real favour. I know you must have a deal to do, with another coming; let him come up to me. I'll take the greatest of cares of him; pretty darling, how sweet he looks when he's asleep!"

When the couples were once more alone, the husbands unburdened their minds to their wives.

Mr. Jenkins said to his: "Do you know, Burgess tried to make me believe Hodgson was such a fool as to put paragraphs into the *Examiner* now and then; but I see he knows his place, and has got too much sense to do any such thing."

Hodgson said, "Mary, love, I almost fancy from Jenkins's way of speaking (so much civiller than I expected), he guesses I wrote that "*Pro Bono*" and the "*Rose-bud*"—at any rate, I've no objection to your naming it, if the subject should come uppermost; I should like him to know I'm a literary man."

Well! I've ended my tale; I hope you don't think it too long; but, before I go, just let me say one thing.

If any of you have any quarrels, or misunderstandings, or cool-nesses, or cold shoulders, or shynesses, or tiffs, or miffs, or huffs, with any one else, just make friends before Christmas,—you will be so much merrier if you do.

I ask it of you for the sake of that old angelic song, heard so many years ago by the shepherds, keeping watch by night, on Bethlehem Heights.

ALEXANDER SMITH

Christmas

OVER the dial face of the year, on which the hours are months, the apex resting in sunshine, the base in withered leaves and snows, the finger of time does not travel with the same rapidity. Slowly it creeps up from snow to sunshine; when it has gained the summit it seems almost to rest for a little; rapidly it rushes down from sunshine to the snow. Judging from my own feelings, the distance from January to June is greater than from June to January—the period from Christmas to Midsummer seems longer than the period from Midsummer to Christmas. This feeling arises, I should fancy, from the preponderance of *light* on that half of the dial on which the finger seems to be traveling upward, compared with the half on which it seems to be traveling downward. This light to the eye, the mind translates into time. Summer days are long, often wearisomely so. The long-lighted days are bracketed together by a little bar of twilight, in which but a star or two find time to twinkle. Usually one has less occupation in summer than in winter, and the surplusage of summer light, a stage too large for the play, wearies, oppresses, sometimes appalls. From the sense of time we can only shelter ourselves by occupation; and when occupation ceases while yet some three or four hours of light remain, the burden falls down, and is often greater than we can bear. Personally, I have a certain morbid fear of those endless summer twilights. A space of light stretching from half past two A.M. to eleven P.M. affects me with a sense of infinity, of horrid sameness, just as the sea or the desert would do. I feel that for too long a period I am under the eye of a taskmaster. Twilight is always in itself, or at least in its suggestions, melancholy; and these midsummer twilights are so long, they pass through such series of lovely change, they are throughout so mournfully beautiful, that in the brain they beget strange thoughts, and in the heart strange feelings. We see too much of the sky, and the long, lovely, pathetic, lingering evening light, with its suggestions of eternity and death, which one cannot for the soul of one put into words, is somewhat too much for the comfort of a sensitive human mortal. The day dies, and makes no apology for being such an unconscionable time in dying; and all the while it colors our thoughts with its own solemnity. There is no relief from this kind of thing at midsummer. You cannot close your shutters and light your candles; that in the tone of mind which circumstances superinduce would be brutality. You cannot take Pickwick to the window and read it by the dying light; that is profanation. If you have a friend with you, you can't talk; the hour makes you silent. You are driven in on your self-consciousness. The long light wearies the eye, a sense of time disturbs and saddens the spirit; and that is the reason, I think, that one half of the year seems so much longer than the other half; that on the dial plate whose hours are months, the restless finger seems to move more slowly when traveling upward from autumn leaves and snow to light, than when it is traveling downward from light to snow and withered leaves.

Of all the seasons of the year, I like winter best. The peculiar burden of time I have been speaking of does not affect me now. The day is short, and I can fill it with work; when evening comes, I have my lighted room and my books. Should black care haunt me, I throw it off the scent in Spenser's forests, or seek refuge from it among Shakespeare's men and women, who are by far the best company I have met with, or am like to meet with, on earth. I am sitting at this present moment with my curtains drawn; the cheerful fire is winking at all the furniture in the room, and from every leg and arm the furniture is winking to the fire in return. I put off the outer world with my greatcoat and boots, and put on contentment and idleness with my slippers. On the hearthrug, Pepper, coiled in a shaggy ball, is asleep in the ruddy light and heat. An imaginative sense of the cold outside increases my present comfort—just as one never hugs one's own good luck so affectionately as when listening to the relation of some horrible misfortune which has overtaken others. Winter has fallen on Dreamthorp, and it looks as pretty when covered with snow, as when covered with apple blossoms. Outside, the ground is hard as iron; and over the low dark hill, lo! the tender radiance that precedes the moon. Every window in the little village has its light, and to the traveler coming on, enveloped in his breath, the whole place shines like a congregation of glowworms. A pleasant enough sight to him if his home be there! At this present season, the canal is not such a pleasant promenade as it was in summer. The barges come and go as usual, but at this time I do not envy the bargemen quite so much. The horse comes smoking along; the tarpaulin which covers the merchandise is sprinkled with hoarfrost; and the helmsman, smoking his short pipe for the mere heat of it, cowers over a few red cinders contained in a framework of iron. The labor of the poor fellows will soon be over for a time; for if this frost continues, the canal will be sheathed in a night, and next day stones will be thrown upon it, and a daring urchin venturing upon it will go souse head over heels, and run home with his teeth in a chatter; and the day after, the lake beneath the old castle will be sheeted, and the next, the villagers will be sliding on its gleaming face from ruddy dawn at nine to ruddy eve at three; and hours later, skaters yet unsatisfied will be moving ghostlike in the gloom—now one, now another, shooting on sounding irons into a clear space of frosty light, chasing the moon, or the flying image of a star! Happy youths leaning against the frosty wind!

Christmas

I am a Christian, I hope, although far from a muscular one—consequently I cannot join the skaters on the lake. The floor of ice, with the people upon it, will be but a picture to me. And, in truth, it is in its pictorial aspect that I chiefly love the bleak season. As an artist, winter can match summer any day. The heavy, feathery flakes have been falling all the night through, we shall suppose, and when you get up in the morning the world is draped in white. What a sight it is! It is the world you knew, but yet a different one. The familiar look has gone, and another has taken its place; and a not unpleasant puzzlement arises in your mind, born of the patent and the remembered aspect. It reminds you of a friend who has been suddenly placed in new circumstances, in whom there is much that you recognize, and much that is entirely strange. How purely, divinely white when the last snowflake has just fallen! How exquisite and virginal the repose! It touches you like some perfection of music. And winter does not work only on a broad scale; he is careful in trifles. Pluck a single ivy leaf from the old wall, and see what a jeweler he is! How he has silvered over the dark-green reticulations with his frosts! The faggot which the Tramp gathers for his fire is thicklier incrusted with gems than ever was scepter of the Moguls. Go into the woods, and behold on the black boughs his glories of pearl and diamond—pendant splendors that, smitten by the noon ray, melt into tears and fall but to congeal into splendors again. Nor does he work in black and white alone. He has on his palette more gorgeous colors than those in which swim the summer setting suns; and with these, about three o'clock, he begins to adorn his west, sticking his red-hot ball of a sun in the very midst; and a couple of hours later, when the orb has fallen, and the flaming crimson has mellowed into liquid orange, you can see the black skeletons of trees scribbled upon the melancholy glory. Nor need I speak of the magnificence of a winter midnight, when space, somber blue, crowded with star and planet, "burnished by the frost," is glittering like the harness of an archangel full panoplied against a battle day.

For years and years now I have watched the seasons come and go around Dreamthorp, and each in its turn interests me as if I saw it for the first time. But the other week it seems that I saw the grain ripen; then by day a motley crew of reapers were in the fields, and at night a big red moon looked down upon the stooks of oats and barley; then in mighty wains the plenteous harvest came swaying home, leaving a largess on the roads for every bird; then the round, yellow, comfortable-looking stacks stood around the farmhouses, hiding them to the chimneys; then the woods reddened, the beech hedges became russet, and every puff of wind made rustle the withered leaves; then the sunset came before the early dark, and in the east lay banks of bleak pink vapor, which are ever a prophecy of cold; then out of a low dingy heaven came all day, thick and silent, the whirling snow; and so, by exquisite succession of sight and sound have I been taken from the top of the year to the bottom of it, from midsummer, with its unreaped harvests, to the night on which I am sitting here—Christmas 1862.

Sitting here, I incontinently find myself holding a levee of departed Christmas nights. Silently, and without special call, into my study of imagination come these apparitions, clad in snowy mantles, brooched and gemmed with frosts. Their numbers I do not care to count, for I know they are the numbers of my years. The visages of two or three are sad enough, but on the whole 'tis a congregation of jolly ghosts. The nostrils of my memory are assailed by a faint odor of plum pudding and burnt brandy. I hear a sound as of light music, a whisk of women's dresses whirled round in dance, a click as of glasses pledged by friends. Before one of these apparitions is a mound, as of a new-made grave, on which the snow is lying. I know, I know! Drape thyself not in white like the others, but in mourning stole of crape; and instead of dance music, let there haunt around thee the service for the dead! I know that sprig of Mistletoe, O Spirit in the midst! Under it I swung the girl I loved—girl no more now than I am boy—and kissed her spite of blush and pretty shriek. And thou, too, with fragrant trencher in hand, over which blue tongues of flame are playing, do I know—most ancient apparition of them all. I remember thy reigning night. Back to very days of childhood am I taken by thy ghostly raisins simmering in a ghostly brandy flame. Where now the merry boys and girls that thrust their fingers in thy blaze? And now, when I think of it, thee also would I drape in black raiment; around thee also would I make the burial service murmur.

Men hold the anniversaries of their birth, of their marriage, of the birth of their first-born, and they hold—although they spread no feast, and ask no friends to assist—many another anniversary besides. On many a day in every year does a man remember what took place on that self-same day in some former year, and chews the sweet or bitter herb of memory, as the case may be. Could I ever hope to write a decent Essay, I should like to write one "On the Revisiting of Places." It is strange how important the poorest human being is to himself! how he likes to double back on his experiences, to stand on the place he has stood before, to meet himself face to face as it were! I go to the great city in which my early life was spent, and I love to indulge myself in this whim. The only thing I care about is that portion of the city which is connected with myself. I don't think this passion of reminiscence is debased by the slightest taint of vanity. The lamppost, under the light of which in the winter rain there was a parting so many years ago, I contemplate with the most curious interest. I stare on the windows of the houses in which I once lived, with a feeling which I should find difficult to express in words. I think of the life I led there, of the good and the bad news that came, of the sister who died, of the brother who was born; and were it at all possible, I should like to knock at the once familiar door, and look at the old walls—which could speak to me so strangely—once again. To revisit that city is like walking away back with my yesterdays. I startle myself with myself at the corners of streets, I confront forgotten bits of myself at the entrance to houses. In windows which to another man would seem blank and meaningless, I find personal poems too deep to be ever turned into rhymes—more pathetic, mayhap, than I have ever found on printed page. The spot of ground on which a man has stood is forever interesting to him. Every experience is an anchor holding him the more firmly to existence. It is for this reason that we hold our sacred days, silent and solitary anniversaries of joy and bitterness, renewing ourselves thereby, going back upon ourselves, living over again the memorable experience. The full yellow moon of next September will gather into itself the light of the full yellow moons of Septembers long ago. In this Christmas night all the other Christmas nights of my life live. How warm, breathing, full of myself is the year 1862, now almost gone! How bare, cheerless, unknown, the year 1863, about to come in! It stretches before me in imagination like some great, gaunt, un-tenanted ruin of a Colosseum, in which no footstep falls, no voice is heard; and by this night year its naked chambers and windows, three hundred and sixty-five in number, will be clothed all over, and hidden by myself as if with covering ivies. Looking forward into an empty year strikes one with a certain awe, because one finds therein no recognition. The years behind have a friendly aspect, and they are warmed by the fires we have kindled, and all their echoes are the echoes of our own voices.

This, then, is Christmas 1862. Everything is silent in Dream-thorp. The smith's hammer reposes beside the anvil. The weaver's flying shuttle is at rest. Through the clear wintry sunshine the bells this morning rang from the gray church tower amid the leafless elms, and up the walk the villagers trooped in their best dresses and their best faces—the latter a little reddened by the sharp wind: mere red-ness in the middle-aged; in the maids, wonderful bloom to the eyes of their lovers—and took their places decently in the ancient pews. The clerk read the beautiful prayers of our Church, which seem more beautiful at Christmas than at any other period. For that very feeling which breaks down at this time the barriers which custom, birth, or wealth have erected between man and man, strikes down the barrier of time which intervenes between the worshiper of today and the great body of worshipers who are at rest in their graves. On such a day as this, hearing these prayers, we feel a kinship with the devout generations who heard them long ago. The devout lips of the Christian dead murmured the responses which we now murmur; along this road of prayer did their thoughts of our innumerable dead, our brothers and sisters in faith and hope, approach the Maker even as ours at present approach Him. Prayers over, the clergyman—who is no Boanerges, or Chrysostom, golden-mouthed, but a loving, genial-hearted, pious man, the whole extent of his life from boyhood until now, full of charity and kindly deeds, as autumn fields with heavy wheaten ears; the clergyman, I say—for the sentence is becoming unwieldy on my hands, and one must double back to secure connection—read out in that silvery voice of his, which is sweeter than any music to my ear, those chapters of the New Testament that deal with the birth of the Saviour. And the red-faced rustic congregation hung on the good man's voice as he spoke of the Infant brought forth in a manger, of the shining angels that appeared in mid-air to the shepherds, of the miraculous star that took its station in the sky, and of the wise men who came from afar and laid their gifts of frankincense and myrrh at the feet of the Child. With the story everyone was familiar, but on that day, and backed by the persuasive melody of the reader's voice, it seemed to all quite new—at least, they listened attentively as if it were. The discourse that followed possessed no remarkable thoughts; it dealt simply with the goodness of the Maker of heaven and earth, and the shortness of time, with the duties of thankfulness and charity to the poor; and I am persuaded that everyone who heard returned to his house in a better frame of mind. And so the service remitted us all to our own homes, to what roast beef and plum pudding slender means permitted, to gatherings around cheerful fires, to half-pleasant, half-sad remembrances of the dead and the absent.

From sermon I have returned like the others, and it is my purpose to hold Christmas alone. I have no one with me at table, and my own thoughts must be my Christmas guests. Sitting here, it is pleasant to think how much kindly feeling exists this present night in England. By imagination I can taste of every table, pledge every toast, silently join in every roar of merriment. I become a sort of universal guest. With what propriety is this jovial season placed amid dismal December rains and snows! How one pities the unhappy Australians, with whom everything is turned topsy-turvy, and who hold Christmas at midsummer! The face of Christmas glows all the brighter for the cold. The heart warms as the frost increases. Estrangements which have embittered the whole year melt in to-night's hospitable smile. There are warmer handshakings on this night than during the bypast twelve months. Friend lives in the mind of friend. There is more charity at this time than at any other. You get up at midnight and toss your spare coppers to the half-benumbed musicians whiffling beneath your windows, although at any other time you would consider their performance a nuisance, and call angrily for the police. Poverty and scanty clothing and fireless grates come home at this season to the bosoms of the rich, and they give of their abundance. The very redbreast of the woods enjoys his Christmas feast. Good feeling incarnates itself in plum pudding. The Master's words, "The poor ye have always with you," wear at this time a deep significance. For at least one night in each year over all Christendom there is brotherhood. And good men, sitting among their families, or by the solitary fire like me, when they remember the light that shone over the poor clowns huddling on the Bethlehem plains eighteen hundred years ago, the apparition of shining angels overhead, the song "Peace on earth and good will toward men," which for the first time hallowed the midnight air—pray for that strain's fulfillment, that battle and strife may vex the nations no more, that not only on Christmas Eve, but the whole year round, men shall be brethren, owning one Father in heaven.

Although suggested by the season, and by a solitary dinner, it is not my purpose to indulge in personal reminiscence and talk. Let all that pass. This is Christmas Day, the anniversary of the world's greatest event. To one day all the early world looked forward; to the same day the latter world looks back. That day holds time together. Isaiah, standing on the peaks of prophecy, looked across ruined empires and the desolations of many centuries, and saw on the horizon the new star arise, and was glad. On this night eighteen hundred years ago, Jove was discrowned, the pagan heaven emptied of its divinities, and Olympus left to the solitude of the snows. On this night, so many hundred years bygone, the despairing voice was heard shrieking on the Aegean, "Pan is dead, great Pan is dead!" On this night, according to the fine reverence of the poets, all things that blast and blight are powerless, disarmed by sweet influences:

> Some say that ever 'gainst the season comes
> Wherein our Saviour's birth is celebrated,
> The bird of dawning singeth all night long;
> And then, they say, no spirit dares stir abroad;
> The nights are wholesome; then no planets strike,
> No fairy takes, nor witch hath power to charm;
> So hallow'd and so gracious is the time.

The flight of the pagan mythology before the new faith has been a favorite subject with the poets; and it has been my custom for many seasons to read Milton's "Hymn to the Nativity" on the evening of Christmas Day. The bass of heaven's deep organ seems to blow in the lines, and slowly and with many echoes the strain melts into silence. To my ear the lines sound like the full-voiced choir and the rolling organ of a cathedral, when the afternoon light streaming through the painted windows fills the place with solemn colors and masses of gorgeous gloom. Tonight I shall float my lonely hours away on music:

> The oracles are dumb,
> No voice or hideous hum
> Runs through the archèd roof in words deceiving:
> Apollo from his shrine
> Can no more divine
> With hollow shriek the steep of Delphos leaving,
> No nightly trance or breathèd spell
> Inspires the pale-eyed priest from the prophetic cell.

> The lonely mountains o'er,
> And the resounding shore,
> A voice of weeping heard and loud lament:
> From haunted spring and dale
> Edged with poplars pale,
> The parting genius is with sighing sent:

With flower-enwoven tresses torn
The nymphs in twilight shades of tangled thickets mourn.

Peor and Baalim
Forsake their temples dim
With that twice-batter'd god of Palestine;
And moonèd Ashtaroth,
Heaven's queen and mother both,
Now sits not girt with tapers' holy shrine!
The Lybic Hammon shrinks his horn,
In vain the Tyrian maids their wounded Thammuz mourn.

And sullen Moloch, fled,
Hath left in shadows dread
His burning idol, all of blackest hue:
In vain with cymbals' ring
They call the grisly king
In dismal dance about the furnace blue:
The brutish gods of Nile as fast,
Isis, and Orus, and the dog Anubis haste.

He feels from Juda's land
The dreaded Infant's hand
The rays of Bethlehem blind his dusky eyne:
Nor all the gods beside
Dare longer there abide,
Not Typhon huge ending in snaky twine.
Our Babe to shew his Godhead true
Can in His swaddling bands control the damnèd crew.

These verses, as if loath to die, linger with a certain persistence
in mind and ear. This is the "mighty line" which critics talk about!
And just as in an infant's face you may discern the rudiments of the
future man, so in the glorious hymn may be traced the more majestic
lineaments of the "Paradise Lost."

Strangely enough, the next noblest dirge for the unrealmed

divinities which I can call to remembrance, and at the same time the most eloquent celebration of the new power and prophecy of its triumph, has been uttered by Shelley, who cannot in any sense be termed a Christian poet. It is one of the choruses in "Hellas," and perhaps had he lived longer among us, it would have been the prelude to higher strains. Of this I am certain, that before his death the mind of that brilliant genius was rapidly changing—that for him the Cross was gathering attractions round it—that the wall which he complained had been built up between his heart and his intellect was being broken down, and that rays of a strange splendor were already streaming upon him through the interstices. What a contrast between the darkened glory of "Queen Mab"—of which in afterlife he was ashamed, both as a literary work and as an expression of opinion—and the intense, clear, lyrical light of this triumphant poem!

> *A power from the unknown God,*
>> *A Promethean conqueror came:*
> *Like a triumphal path he trod*
>> *The thorns of death and shame.*
>> *A mortal shape to him*
>> *Was like the vapour dim*
> *Which the orient planet animates with light.*
>> *Hell, sin, and slavery came*
>> *Like bloodhounds mild and tame,*
> *Nor prey'd until their lord had taken flight.*
>> *The moon of Mahomet*
>> *Arose, and it shall set;*
> *While blazon'd, as on heaven's immortal noon,*
>> *The Cross leads generations on.*
> *Swift as the radiant shapes of sleep,*
>> *From one whose dreams are paradise,*
> *Fly, when the fond wretch wakes to weep,*
>> *And day peers forth with her blank eyes:*
>> *So fleet, so faint, so fair,*
>> *The powers of earth and air*

Fled from the folding-star of Bethlehem.
Apollo, Pan, and Love,
And even Olympian Jove,
Grew weak, for killing Truth had glared on them.
Our hills, and seas, and streams,
Dispeopled of their dreams,
Their waters turn'd to blood, their dew to tears,
Wail'd for the golden years.

For my own part, I cannot read these lines without emotion—not so much for their beauty as for the change in the writer's mind which they suggest. The self-sacrifice which lies at the center of Christianity should have touched this man more deeply than almost any other. That it was beginning to touch and mold him, I verily believe. He died and made *that* sign. Of what music did that storm in Spezia Bay rob the world!

"The Cross leads generations on." Believing as I do that my own personal decease is not more certain than that our religion will subdue the world, I own that it is with a somewhat saddened heart that I pass my thoughts around the globe, and consider how distant is yet that triumph. There are the realms on which the Crescent beams, the monstrous many-headed gods of India, the Chinaman's heathenism, the African's devil rites. These are, to a large extent, principalities and powers of darkness with which our religion has never been brought into collision, save at trivial and far-separated points, and in these cases the attack has never been made in strength. But what of our own Europe—the home of philosophy, of poetry, and painting? Europe, which has produced Greece and Rome and England's centuries of glory; which has been illumined by the fires of martyrdom; which has heard a Luther preach; which has listened to Dante's "mystic unfathomable song"; to which Milton has opened the door of heaven—what of it? And what, too, of that younger America, starting in its career with all our good things, and enfranchised of many of our evils? Did not the December sun now shining look down on thousands slaughtered at Fredericksburg, in a most mad, most incomprehensible quarrel? And is not the public air which European nations breathe at this moment, as it has been for several years back, charged with thunder? Despots are plotting, ships are building, man's ingenuity is bent, as it never was bent before, on the invention and improvement of instruments of death; Europe is bristling with five millions of bayonets: and this is the condition of a world for which the Son of God died eighteen hundred and sixty-two years ago! There is no mystery of Providence so inscrutable as this; and yet, is not the very sense of its mournfulness a proof that the spirit of Christianity is living in the minds of men? For, of a verity, military glory is becoming in our best thoughts a bloody rag, and conquest the first in the catalogue of mighty crimes, and a throned tyrant, with armies, and treasures, and the cheers of millions rising up like a cloud of incense around him, but a mark for the thunderbolt of Almighty God—in reality poorer than Lazarus stretched at the gate of Dives. Besides, all these things are getting themselves to some extent mitigated. Florence Nightingale —for the first time in the history of the world—walks through the Scutari hospitals, and "poor, noble, wounded, and sick men," to use her Majesty's tender phrases, kiss her shadow as it falls on them. The Emperor Napoleon does not make war to employ his armies, or to consolidate his power; he does so for the sake of an "idea" more or less generous and disinterested. The soul of mankind would revolt at the blunt, naked truth; and the taciturn emperor knows this, as he knows most things. This imperial hypocrisy, like every other hypocrisy, is a homage which vice pays to virtue. There cannot be a doubt that when the political crimes of kings and governments, the sores that fester in the heart of society, and all "the burden of the unintelligible world," weigh heaviest on the mind, we have to thank Christianity for it. That pure light makes visible the darkness. The Sermon on the Mount makes the morality of the nations ghastly. The Divine love makes human hate stand out in dark relief. This sadness, in the essence of it nobler than any joy, is the heritage of the Christian. An ancient Roman could not have felt so. Everything runs on smoothly enough so long as Jove wields the thunder. But Venus, Mars and Minerva are far behind us now; the Cross is before us; and self-denial and sorrow for sin, and the remembrance of the poor, and the cleansing of our own hearts, are duties incumbent upon every one of us. If the Christian is less happy than the pagan, and at times I think he is so, it arises from the reproach of the Christian's unreached ideal, and from the stings of his finer and more scrupulous conscience. His whole moral organization is finer, and he must pay the noble penalty of finer organizations.

Once again, for the purpose of taking away all solitariness in feeling, and of connecting myself, albeit only in fancy, with the proper gladness of the time, let me think of the comfortable family dinners now being drawn to a close, of the good wishes uttered, and the presents made, quite valueless in themselves, yet felt to be invaluable from the feelings from which they spring; of the little children, by sweetmeats lapped in Elysium; and of the pantomime, pleasantest Christmas sight of all, with the pit a sea of grinning delight, the boxes a tier of beaming juvenility, the galleries, piled up to the far-receding roof, a mass of happy laughter which a clown's joke brings down in mighty avalanches. In the pit, sober people relax themselves and suck oranges, and quaff ginger pop; in the boxes, Miss, gazing through her curls, thinks the Fairy Prince the prettiest creature she ever beheld, and Master, that to be a clown must be the pinnacle of human happiness; while up in the galleries the hard, literal world is for an hour sponged out and obliterated; the chimney sweep forgets, in his delight when the policeman comes to grief, the harsh call of his master, and Cinderella, when the demons are foiled, and the long-parted lovers meet and embrace in a paradise of light and pink gauze, the grates that must be scrubbed tomorrow. All bands and trappings of toil are for one hour loosened by the hands of imaginative sympathy. What happiness a single theater can contain! And those of maturer years, or of more meditative temperament, sitting at the pantomime, can extract out of the shifting scenes meanings suitable to themselves; for the pantomime is a symbol or adumbration of human life. Have we not all known Harlequin, who rules the roost, and has the pretty Columbine to himself? Do we not all know that rogue of a clown with his peculating fingers, who brazens out of every scrape, and who conquers the world by good humor and ready wit? And have we not seen Pantaloons not a few, whose fate it is to get all the kicks and lose all the halfpence, to fall through all the trap doors, break their shins over all the barrows, and be forever captured by the policeman, while the true pilferer, the clown, makes his escape with the booty in his possession? Methinks I know the realities of which these things are but the shadows; have met with them in business, have sat with them at dinner. But tonight no such notions as these intrude; and when the torrent of fun, and transformation, and practical joking which rushed out of the beautiful fairy world, is in the beautiful fairy world gathered up again, the high-heaped happiness of the theater will disperse itself, and the Christmas pantomime will be as a pleasant memory the whole year through. Thousands on thousands of people are having their midriffs tickled at this moment; in fancy I see their lighted faces, in memory I hear their mirth.

By this time I should think every Christmas dinner at Dreamthorp or elsewhere has come to an end. Even now in the great cities the theaters will be dispersing. The clown has wiped the paint off his face. Harlequin has laid aside his wand, and divested himself of his glittering raiment; Pantaloon, after refreshing himself with a pint of porter, is rubbing his aching joints; and Columbine, wrapped up in a shawl, and with sleepy eyelids, has gone home in a cab. Soon, in the great theater, the lights will be put out, and the empty stage will be left to ghosts. Hark! Midnight from the church tower vibrates through the frosty air. I look out on the brilliant heaven, and see a milky way of powdery splendor wandering through it, and clusters and knots of stars and planets shining serenely in the blue frosty spaces; and the armed apparition of Orion, his spear pointing away into immeasurable space, gleaming overhead; and the familiar constellation of the Plough dipping down into the west; and I think when I go in again that there is one Christmas the less between me and my grave.

WALTER DE LA MARE

The Almond Tree

My old friend, "the Count" as we used to call him, made very strange acquaintances at times. Let but a man have plausibility, a point of view, a crotchet, an enthusiasm, he would find in him an eager and exhilarating listener. And though he was often deceived and disappointed in his finds, the Count had a heart proof against lasting disillusionment. I confess, however, that these planetary cronies of his were rather disconcerting at times. And I own that meeting him one afternoon in the busy High Street, with a companion on his arm even more than usually voluble and odd— I own I crossed the road to avoid meeting the pair.

But the Count's eyes had been too sharp for me. He twitted me unmercifully with my snobbishness. "I am afraid we must have appeared to avoid you today," he said; and received my protestations with contemptuous indifference.

But the next afternoon we took a walk together over the heath; and perhaps the sunshine, something in the first freshness of the May weather, reminded him of bygone days.

"You remember that rather out-of-the-world friend of mine yesterday that so shocked your spruce proprieties, Richard? Well, I'll tell you a story."

As closely as I can recall this story of the Count's childhood I have here related it. I wish, though, I had my old friend's gift for such things; then perhaps his story might retain something of the charm in the reading which he gave to it in the telling. Perhaps that charm lies wholly in the memory of his voice, his companionship, his friendship. To revive these, what task would be a burden? . . .

"The house of my first remembrance, the house that to my last hour on earth will seem home to me, stood in a small green hollow on the verge of a wide heath. Its five upper windows faced far eastward toward the weather-cocked tower of a village which rambled down the steep inclination of a hill. And, walking in its green old garden—ah, Richard, the crocuses, the wallflowers, the violets!— you could see in the evening the standing fields of corn, and the dark furrows where the evening star was stationed; and a little to the south, upon a crest, a rambling wood of fir trees and bracken.

"The house, the garden, the deep quiet orchard, all had been a wedding gift to my mother from a great-aunt, a very old lady in a kind of turban, whose shrewd eyes used to watch me out of her picture, sitting in my high cane chair at mealtimes—with not a little keenness; sometimes, I fancied, with a faint derision. Here passed by, to the singing of the lark, and the lamentation of autumn wind and rain, the first long nine of all these heaped-up inextricable years. Even now, my heart leaps up with longing to see again with those untutored eyes the lofty clouds of evening; to hear again as then I heard it the two small notes of the yellowhammer piping from his green spray. I remember every room of the old house, the steep stairs, the cool apple-scented pantry; I remember the cobbles by the scullery, the well, my old dead raven, the bleak and whistling elms; but best of all I remember the unmeasured splendor of the heath, with its gorse, and its deep canopy of sunny air, the haven of every wild bird of the morning.

"Martha Rodd was a mere prim snippet of a maid then, pale and grave, with large contemplative, Puritan eyes. Mrs. Ryder, in her stiff blue martial print and twisted gold brooch, was cook. And besides these, there was only old Thomas the gardener (as out-of-doors, and as distantly seen a creature as a dryad); my mother; and that busy-minded little boy, agog in wits and stomach and spirit—myself. For my father seemed but a familiar guest in the house, a guest ever eagerly desired and welcome, but none too eager to remain. He was a dark man with gray eyes and a long chin; a face unusually impassive, unusually mobile. Just as his capricious mood suggested, our little household was dejected or wildly gay. I never shall forget the spirit of delight he could conjure up at a whim, when my mother would go singing up and down stairs, and in her tiny parlor; and Martha in perfect content would prattle endlessly on to the cook, basting the twirling sirloin, while I watched in the firelight. And the long summer evenings too, when my father would find a secret, a magic, a mystery in everything; and we would sit together in the orchard while he told me tales, with the small green apples overhead, and beyond contorted branches, the first golden twilight of the moon.

"It's an old picture now, Richard, but true to the time.

"My father's will, his word, his caprice, his frown, these were the tables of the law in that small household. To my mother he was the very meaning of her life. Only that little boy was in some wise independent, busy, inquisitive, docile, sedate; though urged to a bitterness of secret rebellion at times. In his childhood he experienced such hours of distress as the years do not in mercy bring again to a heart that may analyze as well as remember. Yet there also sank to rest the fountain of life's happiness. In among the gorse bushes were the green mansions of the fairies; along the furrows before his adventurous eyes stumbled crooked gnomes, hopped bewitched robins. Ariel trebled in the sunbeams and glanced from the dew-drops; and he heard the echo of distant and magic waters in the falling of the rain.

"But my father was never long at peace in the house. Nothing satisfied him; he must needs be at an extreme. And if he was compelled to conceal his discontent, there was something so bitter and imperious in his silence, so scornful a sarcasm in his speech, that we could scarcely bear it. And the knowledge of the influence he had over us served only at such times to sharpen his contempt.

"I remember one summer's evening we had been gathering strawberries. I carried a little wicker basket, and went rummaging under the aromatic leaves, calling ever and again my mother to see the 'tremenjous' berry I had found. Martha was busy beside me, vexed that her two hands could not serve her master quick enough. And in a wild race with my mother my father helped us pick. At every ripest one he took her in his arms to force it between her lips; and of all those pecked by the birds he made a rhymed offering to Pan. And when the sun had descended behind the hill, and the clamor of the rooks had begun to wane in the elm-tops, he took my mother on his arm, and we trooped all together up the long straggling path, and across the grass, carrying our spoil of fruit into the cool dusky corridor. As we passed into the gloaming I saw my mother stoop impulsively and kiss his arm. He brushed off her hand impatiently, and went into his study. I heard the door shut. A moment afterward he called for candles. And, looking on those two other faces in the twilight, I knew with the intuition of childhood that he was suddenly sick to death of us all; and I knew that my mother shared my intuition. She sat down, and I beside her, in her little parlor, and took up her sewing. But her face had lost again all its girlishness as she bent her head over the white linen.

"I think she was happier when my father was away; for then, free from anxiety to be forever pleasing his variable moods, she could entertain herself with hopes and preparations for his return. There was a little green summerhouse, or arbor, in the garden, where she would sit alone, while the swallows coursed in the evening air.

Sometimes, too, she would take me for a long walk, listening distantly to my chatter, only, I think, that she might entertain the pleasure of supposing that my father might have returned home unforeseen, and be even now waiting to greet us. But these fancies would forsake her. She would speak harshly and coldly to me, and scold Martha for her owlishness, and find nothing but vanity and mockery in all that but a little while since had been her daydream.

"I think she rarely knew where my father stayed in his long absences from home. He would remain with us for a week, and neglect us for a month. She was too proud, and when he was himself, too happy and hopeful to question him, and he seemed to delight in keeping his affairs secret from her. Indeed, he sometimes appeared to pretend a mystery where none was, and to endeavor in all things to make his character and conduct appear quixotic and inexplicable.

"So time went on. Yet, it seemed, as each month passed by, the house was not so merry and happy as before; something was fading and vanishing that would not return; estrangement had pierced a little deeper. I think care at last put out of my mother's mind even the semblance of her former gaiety. She sealed up her heart lest love should break forth anew into the bleakness.

"On Guy Fawkes' Day Martha told me at bedtime that a new household had moved into the village on the other side of the heath. After that my father stayed away from us but seldom.

"At first my mother showed her pleasure in a thousand ways, with dainties of her own fancy and cooking, with ribbons in her dark hair, with new songs (though she had but a small thin voice). She read to please him; and tired my legs out in useless errands in his service. And a word of praise sufficed her for many hours of difficulty. But by and by, when evening after evening was spent by my father away from home, she began to be uneasy and depressed; and though she made no complaint, her anxious face, the incessant interrogation of her eyes vexed and irritated him beyond measure.

" 'Where does my father go after dinner?' I asked Martha one night, when my mother was in my bedroom, folding my clothes.

" 'How dare you ask such a question?' said my mother, 'and how dare you talk to the child about your master's comings and goings?'

" 'But where does he?' I repeated to Martha, when my mother was gone out of the room.

" 'Ssh now, Master Nicholas,' she answered, 'didn't you hear what your mamma said? She's vexed, poor lady, at master's never spending a whole day at home, but nothing but them cards, cards, cards, every night at Mr. Grey's. Why, often it's twelve and one in the morning when I've heard his foot on the gravel beneath the window. But there, I'll be bound, she doesn't mean to speak unkindly. It's a terrible scourge is jealousy, Master Nicholas; and not generous or manly to give it cause. Mrs. Ryder was kept a widow all along of jealousy, and but a week before her wedding with her second.'

" 'But why is mother jealous of my father playing cards?'

"Martha slipped my nightgown over my head. 'Ssh, Master Nicholas, little boys mustn't ask so many questions. And I hope when you are grown up to be a man, my dear, you will be a comfort to your mother. She needs it, poor soul, and sakes alive, just now of all times!' I looked inquisitively into Martha's face; but she screened my eyes with her hand; and instead of further questions, I said my prayers to her.

"A few days after this I was sitting with my mother in her parlor, holding her gray worsted for her to wind, when my father entered the room and made me put on my hat and muffler. 'He is going to pay a call with me,' he explained curtly. As I went out of the room, I heard my mother's question, 'To your friends at the Grange, I suppose?'

" 'You may suppose whatever you please,' he answered. I heard my mother rise to leave the room, but he called her back and the door was shut. . . .

"The room in which the card-players sat was very low-ceiled. A piano stood near the window, a rosewood table with a fine dark crimson workbasket upon it by the fireside, and some little distance away, a green card table with candles burning. Mr. Grey was a slim,

elegant man, with a high, narrow forehead and long fingers. Major
Aubrey was a short, red-faced, rather taciturn man. There was also
a younger man with fair hair. They seemed to be on the best of
terms together; and I helped to pack the cards and to pile the silver
coins, sipping a glass of sherry with Mr. Grey. My father said little,
paying me no attention, but playing gravely with a very slight frown.

"After some little while the door opened, and a lady appeared.
This was Mr. Grey's sister, Jane, I learned. She seated herself at her
worktable, and drew me to her side.

" 'Well, so this is Nicholas!' she said. 'Or is it Nick?'

" 'Nicholas,' I said.

" 'Of course,' she said, smiling, 'and I like that, too, much the
best. How very kind of you to come to see me! It was to keep me
company, you know, because I am very stupid at games, but I love
talking. Do you?'

"I looked into her eyes, and knew we were friends. She smiled
again, with open lips, and touched my mouth with her thimble.
'Now, let me see, business first, and—me afterward. You see I have
three different kinds of cake, because, I thought, I cannot in the
least tell which kind he'll like best. Could I now? Come, you shall
choose.'

"She rose and opened the long door of a narrow cupboard, looking toward the cardplayers as she stooped. I remember the cakes
to this day; little oval shortbreads stamped with a beehive, custards
and mince pies; and a great glass jar of goodies which I carried in
both arms round the little square table. I took a mince pie, and sat
down on a footstool near by Miss Grey, and she talked to me
while she worked with slender hands at her lace embroidery. I told
her how old I was; about my great-aunt and her three cats. I told her
my dreams, and that I was very fond of Yorkshire pudding, 'from
under the meat, you know.' And I told her I thought my father the
handsomest man I had ever seen.

" 'What, handsomer than Mr. Spencer?' she said laughing, looking along her needle.

"I answered that I did not very much like clergymen.

" 'And why?' she said gravely.

" 'Because they do not talk like real,' I said.

"She laughed very gaily. 'Do men ever?' she said.

"And her voice was so quiet and so musical, her neck so graceful, I thought her a very beautiful lady, admiring especially her dark eyes when she smiled brightly and yet half sadly at me; I promised, moreover, that if she would meet me on the heath, I would show her the rabbit warren and the 'Miller's Pool.'

" 'Well, Jane, and what do you think of my son?' said my father when we were about to leave.

"She bent over me and squeezed a lucky fourpenny-piece into my hand. 'I love fourpence, pretty little fourpence, I love fourpence better than my life,' she whispered into my ear. 'But that's a secret,' she added, glancing up over her shoulder. She kissed lightly the top of my head. I was looking at my father while she was caressing me, and I fancied a faint sneer passed over his face. But when we had come out of the village on to the heath, in the bare keen night, as we walked along the path together between the gorse bushes, now on turf, and now on stony ground, never before had he seemed so wonderful a companion. He told me little stories; he began a hundred, and finished none; yet with the stars above us, they seemed a string of beads all of bright colors. We stood still in the vast darkness, while he whistled that strangest of old songs—'The Songs the Sirens Sang.' He pilfered my wits and talked like my double. But when—how much too quickly, I thought with sinking heart—we were come to the house gates, he suddenly fell silent, turned an instant, and stared far away over the windy heath.

" 'How weary, stale, flat——' he began, and broke off between uneasy laughter and a sigh. 'Listen to me, Nicholas,' he said, lifting my face to the starlight, 'you must grow up a man—a Man, you understand; no vaporings, no posings, no caprices; and above all, no sham. No sham. It's your one and only chance in this unfaltering Scheme.' He scanned my face long and closely. 'You have your mother's eyes,' he said musingly. 'And that,' he added under his breath, '*that's* no joke.' He pushed open the squealing gate, and we went in.

"My mother was sitting in a low chair before a dying and cheerless fire.

" 'Well, Nick,' she said very suavely, 'and how have you enjoyed your evening?'

"I stared at her without answer. 'Did you play cards with the gentlemen; or did you turn over the music?'

" 'I talked to Miss Grey,' I said.

" 'Really,' said my mother, raising her eyebrows, 'and who then is Miss Grey?' My father was smiling at us with sparkling eyes.

" 'Mr. Grey's sister,' I answered in a low voice.

" 'Not his wife, then?' said my mother, glancing furtively at the fire. I looked toward my father in doubt, but could lift my eyes no higher than his knees.

" 'You little fool!' he said to my mother with a laugh, 'what a sharpshooter! Never mind, Sir Nick; there, run off to bed, my man.'

"My mother caught me roughly by the sleeve as I was passing her chair. 'Aren't you going to kiss me good night, then,' she said furiously, her narrow underlip quivering, 'you, too!' I kissed her cheek. 'That's right, my dear,' she said scornfully, 'that's how little fishes kiss.' She rose and drew back her skirts. 'I refuse to stay in the room,' she said haughtily, and with a sob she hurried out.

"My father continued to smile, but only a smile it seemed gravity had forgotten to smooth away. He stood very still, so still that I grew afraid he must certainly hear me thinking. Then with a kind of sigh he sat down at my mother's writing table, and scribbled a few words with his pencil on a slip of paper.

" 'There, Nicholas, just tap at your mother's door with that. Good night, old fellow'; he took my hand and smiled down into my eyes with a kind of generous dark appeal that called me straight to his side. I hastened conceitedly upstairs and delivered my message. My mother was crying when she opened the door.

" 'Well?' she said in a low, trembling voice.

"But presently afterward, while I was still lingering in the dark corridor, I heard her run down quickly, and in a while my father and mother came upstairs together, arm in arm, and by her light talk and laughter you might suppose she had no knowledge of care or trouble at all.

"Never afterward did I see so much gaiety and youthfulness in my mother's face as when she sat next morning with us at breakfast. The honeycomb, the small bronze chrysanthemums, her yellow gown seemed dainty as a miniature. With every word her eyes would glance covertly at my father; her smile, as it were, hesitating between her lashes. She was so light and girlish and so versatile I should scarcely have recognized the weary and sallow face of the night before. My father seemed to find as much pleasure, or relief, in her good spirits as I did; and to delight in exercising his ingenuity to quicken her humor.

"It was but a transient morning of sunshine, however, and as the brief and somber day waned, its gloom pervaded the house. In the evening my father left us to our solitude as usual. And that night was very misty over the heath, with a small, warm rain falling.

"So it happened that I began to be left more and more to my own devices, and grew so inured at last to my own narrow company and small thoughts and cares, that I began to look on my mother's unhappiness almost with indifference, and learned to criticize almost before I had learned to pity. And so I do not think I enjoyed Christmas very much the less, although my father was away from home and all our little festivities were dispirited. I had plenty of good things to eat, and presents, and a picture book from Martha. I had a new rocking horse—how changeless and impassive its mottled battered face looks out at me across the years! It was brisk, clear weather, and on St. Stephen's Day I went to see if there was any ice yet on the Miller's Pool. I was stooping down at the extreme edge of the pool, snapping the brittle splinters of the ice with my finger, when I heard a voice calling me in the still air. It was Jane Grey, walking on the heath with my father, who had called me, having seen me from a distance stooping beside the water.

" 'So you see I have kept my promise,' she said, taking my hand.

" 'But you promised to come by yourself,' I said.

" 'Well, so I will then,' she answered, nodding her head. 'Good-by,' she added, turning to my father. 'It's three's none, you see. Nicholas shall take me home to tea, and you can call for him in the evening, if you will; that is, if you are coming.'

" 'Are you asking me to come?' he said moodily; 'do you care whether I come or not?'

"She lifted her face and spoke gravely. 'You are my friend,' she said, 'of course I care whether you are with me or not!' He scrutinized her through half-closed lids. His face was haggard, gloomy with ennui. 'How you harp on the word, you punctilious Jane. Do you suppose I am still in my teens? Twenty years ago, now—— It amuses me to hear you women talk. It's little you ever really feel.'

" 'I don't think I am quite without feeling,' she replied, 'you are a little difficult, you know.'

" 'Difficult,' he echoed in derision. He checked himself and shrugged his shoulders. 'You see, Jane, it's all on the surface; I boast of my indifference. It's the one rag of philosophy age denies no one. It is so easy to be heroic—debonair, iron-gray, fluent, dramatic— you know it's captivation, perhaps? But after all, life's comedy, when one stops smiling, is only the tepidest farce. Or the gilt wears off and the pinchbeck tragedy shows through. And so, as I say, we talk on, being past feeling. One by one our hopes come home to roost, our delusions find themselves out, and the mystery proves to be nothing but sleight of hand. It's age, my dear Jane—age; it turns one to stone. With you young people life's a dream; ask Nicholas here!' He shrugged his shoulders, adding under his breath, 'But one wakes on a devilish hard pallet.'

" 'Of course,' said Jane slowly, 'you are only talking cleverly, and then it does not matter whether it's true or not, I suppose. I can't say. I don't think you mean it, and so it comes to nothing. I can't and won't believe you feel so little—I can't.' She continued to smile, yet I fancied, with the brightness of tears in her eyes. 'It's all mockery and make-believe; we are not the miserable slaves of time you try to fancy. There must be some way to win through.' She turned away, then added slowly, 'You ask me to be fearless, sincere, to speak my heart; I wonder, do you?'

The Almond Tree

"My father did not look at her, appeared not to have seen the hand she had half held out to him, and as swiftly withdrawn. 'The truth is, Jane,' he said slowly, 'I am past sincerity now. And as for *heart* it is a quite discredited organ at forty. Life, thought, selfishness, egotism, call it what you will; they have all done their worst with me; and I really haven't the sentiment to pretend that they haven't. And when bright youth and sentiment are gone; why, go too, dear lady! Existence proves nothing but brazen inanity afterward. But there's always that turning left to the dullest and dustiest road—oblivion.' He remained silent a moment. Silence deep and strange lay all around us. The air was still, the wintry sky unalterably calm. And again that low dispassionate voice continued: 'It's only when right seems too easy a thing, too trivial, and not worth the doing; and wrong a foolish thing—too dull. . . . There, take care of her, Nicholas; take care of her, "snips and snails," you know. Au revoir, 'pon my word, I almost wish it was good-by.'

"Jane Grey regarded him attentively. 'So then do I,' she replied in a low voice, 'for I shall never understand you; perhaps I should hate to understand you.'

"My father turned with an affected laugh, and left us.

"Miss Grey and I walked slowly along beside the frosty bulrushes until we came to the wood. The bracken and heather were faded. The earth was dark and rich with autumnal rains. Fir cones lay on the moss beneath the dark green branches. It was all now utterly silent in the wintry afternoon. Far away rose tardily, and alighted, the hoarse rooks upon the plowed earth; high in the pale sky passed a few on ragged wing.

" 'What does my father mean by wishing it was good-by?' I said.

"But my companion did not answer me in words. She clasped my hand; she seemed very slim and gracious walking by my side on the hardened ground. My mother was small now and awkward beside her in my imagination. I questioned her about the ice, about the red sky, and if there was any mistletoe in the woods. Sometimes she, in turn, asked me questions too, and when I answered them we would look at each other and smile, and it seemed it was with her as it was with me—of the pure gladness I found in her company. In the middle of our walk to the Thorns she bent down in the cold twilight, and putting her hands on my shoulders, 'My dear, dear Nicholas,' she said, 'you must be a good son to your mother—brave and kind; will you?'

" 'He hardly ever speaks to mother now,' I answered instinctively.

"She pressed her lips to my cheek, and her cheek was cold against mine, and she clasped her arms about me. 'Kiss me,' she said. 'We must do our best, mustn't we?' she pleaded, still holding me. I looked mournfully into the gathering darkness. 'That's easy when you're grown up,' I said. She laughed and kissed me again, and then we took hands and ran till we were out of breath, toward the distant lights of the Thorns. . . .

"I had been some time in bed, lying awake in the warmth, when my mother came softly through the darkness into my room. She sat down at the bedside, breathing hurriedly. 'Where have you been all the evening?' she said.

" 'Miss Grey asked me to stay to tea,' I answered.

" 'Did I give you permission to go to tea with Miss Grey?'

"I made no answer.

" 'If you go to that house again, I shall beat you. You hear me, Nicholas? Alone, or with your father, if you go there again, without my permission, I shall beat you. You have not been whipped for a long time, have you?' I could not see her face, but her head was bent toward me in the dark, as she sat—almost crouched—on my bedside.

"I made no answer. But when my mother had gone, without kissing me, I cried noiselessly on into my pillow. Something had suddenly flown out of memory, never to sing again. Life had become a little colder and stranger. I had always been my own chief company; now another sentimental barrier had risen between the world and me, past its heedlessness, past my understanding to break down.

"Hardly a week passed now without some bitter quarrel. I seemed ever to be stealing out of sound of angry voices; ever fearful of being made the butt of my father's serene taunts, of my mother's passions and desperate remorse. He disdained to defend himself against her, never reasoned with her; he merely shrugged his shoulders, denied her charges, ignored her anger; coldly endeavoring only to show his indifference, to conceal by every means in his power his own inward weariness and vexation. I saw this, of course, only vaguely, yet with all a child's certainty of insight, though I rarely knew the cause of my misery; and I continued to love them both in my selfish fashion, not a whit the less.

"At last, on St. Valentine's Day, things came to a worse pass than before. It had always been my father's custom to hang my mother a valentine on the handle of her little parlor door, a string of pearls, a fan, a book of poetry, whatever it might be. She came down early this morning, and sat in the window seat, looking out at the falling snow. She said nothing at breakfast, only feigned to eat, lifting her eyes at intervals to glance at my father with a strange intensity, as if of hatred, tapping her foot on the floor. He took no notice of her, sat quiet and moody with his own thoughts. I think he had not really forgotten the day, for I found long afterward in his old bureau a bracelet purchased but a week before with her name written on a scrap of paper, inside the case. Yet it seemed to be the absence of this little gift that had driven my mother beyond reason.

"Toward evening, tired of the house, tired of being alone, I went out and played awhile listlessly in the snow. At nightfall I went in; and in the dark heard angry voices. My father came out of the dining room and looked at me in silence, standing in the gloom of the wintry dusk. My mother followed him. I can see her now, leaning in the doorway, white with rage, her eyes ringed and darkened with continuous trouble, her hand trembling.

" 'It shall learn to hate you,' she cried in a low, dull voice. 'I will teach it every moment to hate and despise you as I—— Oh, I hate and despise you.'

"My father looked at her calmly and profoundly before replying. He took up a cloth hat and brushed it with his hand. 'Very well then, you have chosen,' he said coldly. 'It has always lain with you.

You have exaggerated, you have raved, and now you have said what can never be recalled or forgotten. Here's Nicholas. Pray do not imagine, however, that I am defending myself. I have nothing to defend. I think of no one but myself—no one. Endeavor to understand me, no one. Perhaps, indeed, you yourself—no more than—— But words again—the dull old round!' He made a peculiar gesture with his hand. 'Well, life is . . . ach! I have done. So be it.' He stood looking out of the door. 'You see, it's snowing,' he said, as if to himself.

"All the long night before and all day long, snow had been falling continuously. The air was wintry and cold. I could discern nothing beyond the porch but a gloomy accumulation of cloud in the twilight air now darkened with the labyrinthine motion of the snow. My father glanced back for an instant into the house, and, as I fancy, regarded me with a kind of strange, close earnestness. But he went out and his footsteps were instantly silenced.

"My mother peered at me in terrible perplexity, her eyes wide with terror and remorse. 'What? What?' she said. I stared at her stupidly. Three snowflakes swiftly and airily floated together into the dim hall from the gloom without. She clasped her hand over her mouth. Overburdened her fingers seemed to be, so slender were they, with her many rings.

" 'Nicholas, Nicholas, tell me; what was I saying? What was I saying?' She stumbled hastily to the door. 'Arthur, Arthur,' she cried from the porch. 'It's St. Valentine's Day, that was all I meant; come back, come back!' But perhaps my father was already out of hearing; I do not think he made any reply.

"My mother came in doubtfully, resting her hand on the wall. And she walked very slowly and laboriously upstairs. While I was standing at the foot of the staircase, looking out across the hall into the evening, Martha climbed primly up from the kitchen with her lighted taper, shut-to the door and lit the hall lamp. Already the good smell of the feast cooking floated up from the kitchen, and gladdened my spirits. 'Will he come back?' Martha said, looking very scared in the light of her taper. 'It's such a fall of snow, already it's a hand's breadth on the window sill. Oh, Master Nicholas, it's a hard world for us women.' She followed my mother upstairs, carrying light to all the gloomy upper rooms.

"I sat down in the window seat of the dining room, and read in my picture book as well as I could by the flamelight. By and by, Martha returned to lay the table.

"As far back as brief memory carried me, it had been our custom to make a Valentine's feast on the Saint's day. This was my father's mother's birthday also. When she was alive I well remember her visiting us with her companion, Miss Schreiner, who talked in such good-humored English to me. This same anniversary had last year brought about a tender reconciliation between my father and mother, after a quarrel that meant how little then. And I remember on this day to have seen the first fast-sealed buds upon the almond tree. We would have a great spangled cake in the middle of the table, with marzipan and comfits, just as at Christmastide. And when Mrs. Merry lived in the village her little fair daughters used to come in a big carriage to spend the evening with us and to share my Valentine's feast. But all this was changed now. My wits were sharper, but I was none the less only the duller for that; my hopes and dreams had a little fallen and faded. I looked idly at my picture book, vaguely conscious that its colors pleased me less than once upon a time; that I was rather tired of seeing them, and they just as tired of seeing me. And yet I had nothing else to do, so I must go on with a hard face, turning listlessly the pictured pages.

"About seven o'clock my mother sent for me. I found her sitting in her bedroom. Candles were burning before the looking glass. She was already dressed in her handsome black silk gown, and wearing her pearl necklace. She began to brush my hair, curling its longer ends with her fingers, which she moistened in the pink bowl that was one of the first things I had set eyes on in this world. She put on me a clean blouse and my buckle shoes, talking to me the while, almost as if she were telling me a story. Then she looked at herself long and earnestly in the glass; throwing up her chin with a smile, as was a habit of hers in talk. I wandered about the room, fingering the little toilet-boxes and knickknacks on the table. By mischance I upset one of these, a scent bottle that held rose water. The water ran out and filled the warm air with its fragrance. 'You foolish, clumsy boy!' said my mother, and slapped my hand. More out of vexation and tiredness than because of the pain, I began to cry. And then, with infinite tenderness, she leaned her head on my shoulder. 'Mother can't think very well just now,' she said; and cried so bitterly in silence that I was only too ready to extricate myself and run away when her hold on me relaxed.

"I climbed slowly upstairs to Martha's bedroom, and kneeling on a cane chair looked out of the window. The flakes had ceased to fall now, although the snowy heath was encompassed in mist; above the snow the clouds had parted, drifting from beneath the stars, and these in their constellations were trembling very brightly, and here and there burned one of them in solitude larger and wilder in its shining than the rest. But though I did not tire of looking out of the window, my knees began to ache; and the little room was very cold and still so near the roof. So I went down to the dining room, with all its seven candlesticks kindled, seeming to my unaccustomed eyes a very splendid blaze out of the dark. My mother was kneeling on the rug by the fireside. She looked very small, even dwarfish, I thought. She was gazing into the flames; one shoe curved beneath the hem of her gown, her chin resting on her hand.

"I surveyed the table with its jellies and sweetmeats and glasses and fruit, and began to be very hungry, so savory was the smell of the turkey roasting downstairs. Martha knocked at the door when the clock had struck eight.

" 'Dinner is ready, Ma'am.'

"My mother glanced fleetingly at the clock. 'Just a little, only a very little while longer, tell Mrs. Ryder; your master will be home in a minute.' She rose and placed the claret in the hearth at some distance from the fire.

" 'Is it nicer warm, mother?' I said. She looked at me with startled eyes and nodded. 'Did you hear anything, Nicholas? Run to the door and listen; was that a sound of footsteps?'

"I opened the outer door and peered into the darkness; but it seemed the world ended here with the warmth and the light: beyond could extend only winter and silence, a region that, familiar though it was to me, seemed now to terrify me like an enormous sea.

" 'It's stopped snowing,' I said, 'but there isn't anybody there; nobody at all, mother.'

"The hours passed heavily from quarter on to quarter. The turkey, I grieved to hear, was to be taken out of the oven, and put away to cool in the pantry. I was bidden help myself to what I pleased of the trembling jellies, and delicious pink blancmange. Already midnight would be the next hour to be chimed. I felt sick, yet was still hungry and very tired. The candles began to burn low. 'Leave me a little light here, then,' my mother said at last to Martha, 'and go to bed. Perhaps your master has missed his way home in the snow.' But Mrs. Ryder had followed Martha into the room.

" 'You must pardon my interference, Ma'am, but it isn't right, it isn't really right of you to sit up longer. Master will not come back, maybe, before morning. And I shouldn't be doing my bounden duty, Ma'am, except I spoke my mind. Just now too, of all times.'

" 'Thank you very much, Mrs. Ryder,' my mother answered simply, 'but I would prefer not to go to bed yet. It's very lonely on the heath at night. But I shall not want anything else, thank you.'

" 'Well, Ma'am, I've had my say, and done my conscience' bidding. And I have brought you up this tumbler of mulled wine; else you'll be sinking away or something with fatigue.'

"My mother took the wine, sipped of it with a wan smile at Mrs. Ryder over the brim; and Mrs. Ryder retired with Martha. I don't think they had noticed me sitting close in the shadow on my stool beside the table. But all through that long night, I fancy, these good souls took it in turn to creep down stealthily and look in on us; and in the small hours of the morning, when the fire had fallen low, they must have wrapped us both warm in shawls. They left me then, I think, to be my mother's company. Indeed, I remember we spoke in the darkness, and she took my hand.

"My mother and I shared the steaming wine together when they were gone; our shadows looming faintly huge upon the ceiling. We said very little, but I looked softly into her gray childish eyes, and we kissed one another kneeling there together before the fire. And afterward, I jigged softly round the table, pilfering whatever sweet or savory mouthful took my fancy. But by and by in the silent house—a silence broken only by the fluttering of the flames, and the odd faraway stir of the frost, drowsiness vanquished me; I sat down by the fireside, leaning my head on a chair. And sitting thus, vaguely eying firelight and wavering shadow, I began to nod, and very soon dreams stalked in, mingling with reality.

"It was early morning when I awoke, dazed and cold and miserable in my uncomfortable resting place. The rare odor of frost was on the air. The ashes of the fire lay iron-gray upon the cold hearth. An intensely clear white ray of light leaned up through a cranny of the shutters to the cornice of the ceiling. I got up with difficulty. My mother was still asleep, breathing heavily, and as I stooped, regarding her curiously, I could almost watch her transient dreams fleeting over her face; and now she smiled faintly; and now she raised her eyebrows as if in some playful and happy talk with my father; then again utterly still darkness would descend on brow and lid and lip.

"I touched her sleeve, suddenly conscious of my loneliness in the large house. Her face clouded instantly; she sighed profoundly: 'What?' she said, 'nothing—nothing?' She stretched out her hand toward me; the lids drew back from eyes still blind from sleep. But gradually time regained its influence over her. She moistened her lips and turned to me, and suddenly, in a gush of agony, remembrance of the night returned to her. She hid her face in her hands, rocking her body gently to and fro; then rose and smoothed back her hair at the looking glass. I was surprised to see no trace of tears on her cheeks. Her lips moved, as if unconsciously a heart worn out with grief addressed that pale reflection of her sorrow in the glass. I took hold of the hand that hung down listlessly on her silk skirt, and fondled it, kissing punctiliously each loose ring in turn.

"But I do not think she heeded my kisses. So I returned to the table on which was still set out the mockery of our Valentine feast, strangely disenchanted in the chill dusk of daybreak. I put a handful of wine biscuits and a broken piece of cake in my pocket; for a determination had taken me to go out onto the heath. My heart beat thick and fast in imagination of the solitary snow and of myself wandering in loneliness across its untrampled surface. A project also was forming in my mind of walking over to the Thorns; for somehow I knew my mother would not scold or punish me that day. Perhaps, I thought, my father would be there. And I would tell Miss Grey all about my adventure of the night spent down in the dining room. So moving very stealthily, and betraying no eagerness, lest I should be forbidden to go, I stole at length unperceived from the room, and leaving the great hall door ajar, ran out joyously into the wintry morning.

"Already dawn was clear and high in the sky, already the first breezes were moving in the mists; and breathed chill, as if it were the lingering darkness itself on my cheeks. The air was cold, yet with a fresh faint sweetness. The snow lay crisp across its perfect surface, mounded softly over the gorse bushes, though here and there a spray of parched blossom yet protruded from its cowl. Flaky particles of ice floated invisible in the air. I called out with pleasure to see the little ponds where the snow had been blown away from the black ice. I saw on the bushes, too, the webs of spiders stretched from thorn to thorn, and festooned with crystals of hoarfrost. I turned and counted as far as I could my footsteps leading back to the house, which lay roofed in gloomy pallor, dim and obscured in the darkened west.

"A waning moon that had risen late in the night shone, it seemed, very near to the earth. But every moment light swept invincibly in, pouring its crystal like a river; and darkness sullenly withdrew into the north. And when at last the sun appeared, glittering along the rosy snow, I turned in an ecstasy and with my finger pointed him out, as if the house I had left behind me might view him with my own delight. Indeed, I saw its windows transmuted, and heard afar a thrush pealing in the bare branches of a pear tree; and a robin startled me, so suddenly shrill and sweet he broke into song from a snowy tuft of gorse.

"I was now come to the beginning of a gradual incline, from the summit of which I should presently descry in the distance the avenue of lindens that led toward the village from the margin of the heath. As I went on my way, munching my biscuits, looking gaily about me, I brooded deliciously on the breakfast which Miss Grey would doubtless sit me down to; and almost forgot the occasion of my errand, and the troubled house I had left behind me. At length I climbed to the top of the smooth ridge and looked down. At a little distance from me grew a crimson hawthorn tree that often in past Aprils I had used for a green tent from the showers: but now it was closely hooded, darkening with its faint shadow the long expanse of unshadowed whiteness. Not very far from this bush I perceived a figure lying stretched along the snow and knew instinctively that this was my father lying there.

"The sight did not then surprise or dismay me. It seemed but the lucid sequel to that long heavy night watch, to all the troubles and perplexities of the past. I felt no sorrow, but stood beside the body, regarding it only with deep wonder and a kind of earnest curiosity, yet perhaps with a remote pity too, that he could not see me in the beautiful morning. His gray hand lay arched in the snow, his darkened face, on which showed a smear of dried blood, was turned away a little as if out of the oblique sunshine. I understood that he was dead, was already loosely speculating on what changes it would make; how I should spend my time; what would happen in the house now that he was gone, his influence, his authority, his discord. I remembered, too, that I was alone, was master of this immense secret, that I must go home sedately, as if it were a Sunday, and in a low voice tell my mother, concealing any exultation I might feel in the office. I imagined the questions that would be asked me, and was considering the proper answers to make to them, when my morbid dreams were suddenly broken in on by Martha Rodd. She stood in my footsteps, looking down on me from the ridge from which I had but just now descended. She hastened toward me, stooping a little as if she carried a burden, her mouth ajar, her forehead wrinkled beneath its wispy light-brown hair.

" 'Look, Martha, look,' I cried, 'I found him in the snow; he's dead.' And suddenly a bond seemed to snap in my heart. The beauty and solitude of the morning, the perfect whiteness of the snow— it was all an uncouth mockery against me—a subtle and quiet treachery. The tears gushed into my eyes and in my fear and affliction I clung to the poor girl, sobbing bitterly, protesting my grief, hiding my eyes in terror from that still, inscrutable shape. She smoothed my hair with her hand again and again, her eyes fixed; and then at last, venturing cautiously nearer, she stooped over my father. 'O Master Nicholas,' she said, 'his poor dark hair! What will we do now? What will your poor mamma do now, and him gone?' She hid her face in her hands, and our tears gushed out anew.

"But my grief was speedily forgotten. The novelty of being left entirely alone, my own master; to go where I would; to do as I pleased; the experience of being pitied most when I least needed it, and then—when misery and solitariness came over me like a cloud—of being utterly ignored, turned my thoughts gradually away. My father's body was brought home and laid in my mother's little parlor that looked out onto the garden and the snowy orchard. The house was darkened. I took a secret pleasure in peeping on the sunless rooms, and stealing from door to door through corridors screened from the daylight. My mother was ill; and for some inexplicable reason I connected her illness with the bevy of gentlemen dressed in black who came one morning to the house and walked away together over the heath. Finally Mrs. Marshall drove up one afternoon from Islington, and by the bundles she had brought with her and her grained box with the iron handles I knew that she was come, as once before in my experience, to stay.

"I was playing on the morrow in the hall with my leaden soldiers when there came into my mind vaguely the voices of Mrs. Ryder and of Mrs. Marshall gossiping together on their tedious way upstairs from the kitchen.

" 'No, Mrs. Marshall, nothing,' I heard Mrs. Ryder saying, 'not one word, not one word. And now the poor dear lady left quite alone, and only the doctor to gainsay that fatherless mite from facing the idle inquisitive questions of all them strangers. It's neither for me nor you, Mrs. Marshall, to speak out just what comes into our heads here and now. The ways of the Almighty are past under-standing—but a kinder at *heart* never trod this earth.'

" 'Ah,' said Mrs. Marshall.

" 'I knew to my sorrow,' continued Mrs. Ryder, 'there was words in the house; but there, wheresoever you be there's that. Human beings ain't angels, married or single, and in every——'

" 'Wasn't there talk of some—?' insinuated Mrs. Marshall discreetly.

" 'Talk, Mrs. Marshall,' said Mrs. Ryder, coming to a standstill. 'I scorn the word! A pinch of truth in a hogshead of falsehood. I don't gainsay it even. I just shut my ears—there—with the dead.' Mrs. Marshall had opened her mouth to reply when I was discovered, crouched as small as possible at the foot of the stairs.

" 'Well, here's pitchers!' said Mrs. Marshall pleasantly. 'And this is the poor fatherless manikin, I suppose. It's hard on the innocent, Mrs. Ryder, and him grown such a sturdy child too, as I said from the first. Well, now, and don't you remember me, little man, don't you remember Mrs. Marshall? He ought to, now!"

" 'He's a very good boy in general,' said Mrs. Ryder, 'and I'm sure I hope and pray he'll grow up to be a comfort to his poor widowed mother, if so be——' They glanced earnestly at one an-other, and Mrs. Marshall stooped with a sigh of effort and drew a big leather purse from a big loose pocket under her skirt, and selected a bright ha'penny from among its silver and copper.

" 'I make no doubt he will, poor mite,' she said cheerfully; I took the ha'penny in silence and the two women passed slowly upstairs.

"In the afternoon, in order to be beyond call of Martha, I went out onto the heath with a shovel, intent on building a great tomb in the snow. Yet more snow had fallen during the night; it now

lay so deep as to cover my socks above my shoes. I labored
very busily, shoveling, beating, molding, stamping. So intent was
I that I did not see Miss Grey until she was close beside me.
I looked up from the snow and was surprised to find the sun already set and the low mists of evening approaching. Miss Grey was
veiled and dressed in furs to the throat. She drew her ungloved
hand from her muff.

" 'Nicholas,' she said in a low voice.

"I stood for some reason confused and ashamed without answering her. She sat down on my shapeless mound of snow, and took
me by the hand. Then she drew up her veil, and I saw her face
pale and darkened, and her dark eyes gravely looking into mine.

" 'My poor Nicholas,' she said, and continued to gaze at me with
her warm hand clasping mine. 'What can I say? What can I do?
Isn't it very, very lonely out here in the snow?'

" 'I didn't feel lonely much,' I answered, 'I was making a —
I was playing at building.'

" 'And I am sitting on your beautiful snowhouse, then?' she
said, smiling sadly, her hand trembling upon mine.

" 'It isn't a house,' I answered, turning away.

"She pressed my hand on the furs at her throat.

" 'Poor cold, blue hands,' she said. 'Do you like playing alone?'

" 'I like you being here,' I answered. 'I wish you would come
always, or at least sometimes.'

"She drew me close to her, smiling, and bent and kissed my
head.

" 'There,' she said, 'I am here now.'

" 'Mother's ill,' I said.

"She drew back and looked out over the heath toward the
house.

" 'They have put my father in the little parlor, in his coffin; of
course, you know he's dead, and Mrs. Marshall's come; she gave me
a ha'penny this morning. Dr. Graham gave me a whole crown,
though.' I took it out of my breeches pocket and showed it her.

" 'That's very, very nice,' she said. 'What lots of nice things you can buy with it! And, look, I am going to give you a little keepsake too, between just you and me.'

"It was a small silver box that she drew out of her muff, and embossed in the silver of the lid was a crucifix. 'I thought, perhaps, I should see you today, you know,' she continued softly. 'Now, who's given you this?' she said, putting the box into my hand.

" 'You,' I answered softly.

" 'And who am I?'

" 'Miss Grey,' I said.

" 'Your friend, Jane Grey,' she repeated, as if she were fond of her own name. 'Say it now—always my friend, Jane Grey.'

"I repeated it after her.

" 'And now,' she continued, 'tell me which room is—is the little parlor. Is it that small window at the corner under the ivy?'

"I shook my head.

" 'Which?' she said in a whisper, after a long pause.

"I twisted my shovel in the snow. 'Would you like to see my father?' I said. 'I am sure, you know, Martha would not mind; and mother's in bed.' She started, and looked with quiet, dark eyes into my face. 'Where?' she said, without stirring.

" 'It's at the back, a little window that comes out—if you were to come this evening, I would be playing in the hall; I always play in the hall, after tea, if I can; and now, always. Nobody would see you at all, you know.'

"She sighed. 'Oh, what are you saying?' she said, and stood up, drawing down her veil.

" 'But would you like to?' I repeated. She stooped suddenly, press-ing her veiled face to mine. 'I'll come, I'll come,' she said, her face utterly changed so close to my eyes. 'We can both still—still be loyal to him, can't we, Nicholas?'

"She walked away quickly, toward the pool and the little dark-ened wood. I looked after her and knew that she would be waiting there alone till evening. I looked at my silver box with great satis-faction, and after opening it, put it into my pocket with my crown piece and my ha'penny, and continued my building for a while.

"But now zest for it was gone; and I began to feel cold, the frost closing in keenly as darkness gathered. So I went home.

"My silence and suspicious avoidance of scrutiny and question passed unnoticed. Indeed, I ate my tea in solitude, except that now and again one or other of the women would come bustling in on some brief errand. A peculiar suppressed stir was in the house. I wondered what could be the cause of it; and felt a little timid and anxious of my project being discovered.

"None the less I was playing in the evening, as I had promised, close to the door, alert to catch the faintest sign of the coming of my visitor.

" 'Run down in the kitchen, dearie,' said Martha. Her cheeks were flushed. She was carrying a big can of steaming water. 'You must keep very, very quiet this evening, and go to bed like a good boy, and perhaps tomorrow morning I'll tell you a great, great secret.' She kissed me with hasty rapture. I was not especially inquisitive of her secret just then, and eagerly promised to be quite quiet if I might continue to play where I was.

" 'Well, very, very quiet then, and you mustn't let Mrs. Marshall,' she began, but hurried hastily away in answer to a peremptory summons from upstairs.

"Almost as soon as she was gone I heard a light rap on the door. It seemed that Jane Grey brought in with her the cold and freshness of the woods. I led the way on tiptoe down the narrow corridor and into the small silent room. The candles burned pure and steadfastly in their brightness. The air was still and languid with the perfume of flowers. Overhead passed light, heedful footsteps; but they seemed not a disturbing sound, only a rumor beyond the bounds of silence.

" 'I am very sorry,' I said, 'but they have nailed it down. Martha says the men came this afternoon.'

"Miss Grey took a little bunch of snowdrops from her bosom, and hid them in among the clustered wreaths of flowers; and she knelt down on the floor, with a little silver cross which she sometimes wore pressed tight to her lips. I felt ill at ease to see her praying, and wished I could go back to my soldiers. But while I watched her, seeing in marvelous brilliancy everything in the little room, and remembering dimly the snow lying beneath the stars in the darkness of the garden, I listened also to the quiet footsteps passing to and fro in the room above. Suddenly, the silence was broken by a small, continuous, angry crying.

"Miss Grey looked up. Her eyes were very clear and wonderful in the candlelight.

" 'What was that?' she said faintly, listening.

"I stared at her. The cry welled up anew, piteously, as if of a small remote helpless indignation.

" 'Why, it sounds just like—a little baby,' I said.

"She crossed herself hastily and arose. 'Nicholas!' she said in a strange, quiet, bewildered voice—yet her face was most curiously bright. She looked at me lovingly and yet so strangely I wished I had not let her come in.

"She went out as she had entered. I did not so much as peep into the darkness after her, but busy with a hundred thoughts returned to my play.

"Long past my usual bedtime, as I sat sipping a mug of hot milk before the glowing cinders of the kitchen fire, Martha told me her secret. . . .

"So my impossible companion in the High Street yesterday was own and only brother to your crazy old friend, Richard," said the Count. "His only brother," he added in a muse.

MARJORIE BOWEN

The Prescription

JOHN CUMING collected ghost stories; he always declared
that this was the best that he knew, although it was partially
secondhand and contained a mystery that had no reasonable
solution, while most really good ghost stories allow of a plausible
explanation, even if it is one as feeble as a dream, excusing all;
or a hallucination or a crude deception. Cuming told the story rather
well. The first part of it at least had come under his own observation
and been carefully noted by him in the flat green book which he
kept for the record of all curious cases of this sort. He was a shrewd
and trained observer; he honestly restrained his love of drama from
leading him into embellishing facts. Cuming told the story to us
all on the most suitable occasion—Christmas Eve—and prefaced
it with a little homily.

417

"You all know the good old saw—'The more it changes the more it is the same thing'—and I should like you to notice that this extremely up-to-date ultramodern ghost story is really almost exactly the same as one that might have puzzled Babylonian or Assyrian sages. I can give you the first start of the tale in my own words, but the second part will have to be in the words of someone else. They were, however, most carefully and scrupulously taken down. As for the conclusion, I must leave you to draw that for yourselves— each according to your own mood, fancy, and temperament; it may be that you will all think of the same solution, it may be that you will each think of a different one, and it may be that everyone will be left wondering."

Having thus enjoyed himself by whetting our curiosity, Cuming settled himself down comfortably in his deep armchair and unfolded his tale.

"It was about five years ago. I don't wish to be exact with time, and of course I shall alter names—that's one of the first rules of the game, isn't it? Well, whenever it was, I was the guest of a—Mrs. Janey we will call her—who was, to some extent, a friend of mine; an intelligent, lively, rather bustling sort of woman who had the knack of gathering interesting people about her. She had lately taken a new house in Buckinghamshire. It stood in the grounds of one of those large estates which are now so frequently being broken up. She was very pleased with the house, which was quite new and had only been finished a year, and seemed, according to her own rather excited imagination, in every way desirable. I don't want to emphasize anything about the house except that it was new and did stand on the verge, as it were, of this large old estate, which had belonged to one of those notable English families now extinct and completely forgotten. I am no antiquarian or connoisseur in architecture, and the rather blatant modernity of the house did not offend me. I was able to appreciate its comfort and to enjoy what Mrs. Janey rather maddeningly called 'the old-world gardens,' which were really a section of the larger gardens of the vanished mansion which had once commanded this domain. Mrs. Janey, I should tell you, knew nothing about the neighborhood nor anyone who lived there, except that for the first it was very convenient for town, and for the second she believed that they were all 'nice' people, not likely to bother one. I was slightly disappointed with the crowd she had gathered together at Christmas. They were all people whom either I knew too well or whom I didn't wish to know at all, and at first the party showed signs of being extremely flat. Mrs. Janey seemed to perceive this too, and with rather nervous haste produced, on Christmas Eve, a trump card in the way of amusement —a professional medium, called Mrs. Mahogany, because that could not possibly have been her name. Some of us 'believed in,' as the saying goes, mediums, and some didn't; but we were all willing to be diverted by the experiment. Mrs. Janey continually lamented that a certain Dr. Dilke would not be present. He was going to be one of the party, but had been detained in town and would not reach Verrall, which was the name of the house, until later, and the medium, it seemed, could not stay; for she, being a personage in great demand, must go on to a further engagement. I, of course, like everyone else possessed of an intelligent curiosity and a certain amount of leisure, had been to mediums before. I had been slightly impressed, slightly disgusted, and very much bewildered, and on the whole had decided to let the matter alone, considering that I really preferred the more direct and old-fashioned method of getting in touch with what we used to call 'The Unseen.' This sitting in the great new house seemed rather banal. I could understand in some haunted old manor that a clairvoyant, or a clairaudient, or a trance-medium might have found something interesting to say, but what was she going to get out of Mrs. Jancy's bright, brilliant, and comfortable dwelling?

"Mrs. Mahogany was a nondescript sort of woman—neither young nor old, neither clever nor stupid, neither dark nor fair, placid, and not in the least self-conscious. After an extremely good luncheon (it was a gloomy, stormy afternoon) we all sat down in a circle in the cheerful drawing room; the curtains were pulled across the dreary prospect of gray sky and gray landscape, and we had merely the light of the fire. We sat quite close together in order to increase 'the power,' as Mrs. Mahogany said, and the medium sat in the middle, with no special precautions against trickery; but we all knew that trickery would have been really impossible, and we were quite prepared to be tremendously impressed and startled if any manifestations took place. I think we all felt rather foolish, as we did not know each other very well, sitting round there, staring at this very ordinary, rather common, stout little woman, who kept nervously pulling a little tippet of gray wool over her shoulders, closing her eyes and muttering, while she twisted her fingers together. When we had sat silent for about ten minutes Mrs. Janey announced in a rather raw whisper that the medium had gone into a trance. 'Beautifully,' she added. I thought that Mrs. Mahogany did not look at all beautiful. Her communication began with a lot of rambling talk which had no point at all, and a good deal of generalization under which I think we all became a little restive. There was too much of various spirits who had all sorts of ordinary names, just regular Toms, Dicks, and Harrys of the spirit world, floating round behind us, their arms full of flowers and their mouths of good will, all rather pointless. And though, occasionally, a Tom, a Dick, or a Harry was identified by some of us, it wasn't very convincing, and, what was worse, not very interesting. We got, however, our surprise and our shock, because Mrs. Mahogany began suddenly to writhe into ugly contortions and called out in a loud voice, quite different from the one that she had hitherto used: 'Murder!'

"This word gave us all a little thrill, and we leaned forward eagerly to hear what further she had to say. With every sign of distress and horror Mrs. Mahogany began to speak:

" 'He's murdered her. Oh, how dreadful. Look at him! Can't somebody stop him? It's so near here, too. He tried to save her. He was sorry, you know. Oh, how dreadful! Look at him — he's borne it as long as he can, and now he's murdered her! I see him mixing it in a glass. Oh, isn't it awful that no one could have saved her — and he was so terribly remorseful afterward. Oh, how dreadful! How horrible!'

The Prescription

"She ended in a whimpering of fright and horror, and Mrs. Janey, who seemed an adept at this sort of thing, leaned forward and asked eagerly:

" 'Can't you get the name—can't you find out who it is? Why do you get that here?'

" 'I don't know,' muttered the medium, 'it's somewhere near here—a house, an old dark house, and there are curtains of mauve velvet—do you call it mauve? a kind of blue red—at the windows. There's a garden outside with a fishpond and you go through a low doorway and down stone steps.'

" 'It isn't near here,' said Mrs. Janey decidedly, 'all the houses are new.'

" 'The house is near here,' persisted the medium. 'I am walking through it now; I can see the room, I can see that poor, poor woman, and a glass of milk——'

" 'I wish you'd get the name,' insisted Mrs. Janey, and she cast a look, as I thought not without suspicion, round the circle. 'You can't be getting this from my house, you know, Mrs. Mahogany,' she added decidedly, 'it must be given out by someone here— something they've read or seen, you know,' she said, to reassure us that our characters were not in dispute.

"But the medium replied drowsily, 'No, it's somewhere near here. I see a light dress covered with small roses. If he could have got help he would have gone for it, but there was no one; so all his remorse was useless. . . .'

"No further urging would induce the medium to say more; soon afterward she came out of the trance, and all of us, I think, felt that she had made rather a stupid blunder by introducing this vague piece of melodrama, and if it was, as we suspected, a cheap attempt to give a ghostly and mysterious atmosphere to Christmas Eve, it was a failure.

"When Mrs. Mahogany, blinking round her, said brightly, 'Well, here I am again! I wonder if I said anything that interested you?' we all replied rather coldly, 'Of course it has been most interesting, but there hasn't been anything definite.' And I think that even

Mrs. Janey felt that the sitting had been rather a disappointment, and she suggested that if the weather was really too horrible to venture out of doors we should sit round the fire and tell old-fashioned ghost stories. 'The kind,' she said brightly, 'that are about bones and chairs and shrouds. I really think that is the most thrilling kind after all.' Then, with some embarrassment, and when Mrs. Mahogany had left the room, she suggested that not one of us should say anything about what the medium had said in her trance.

" 'It really was rather absurd,' said our hostess, 'and it would make me look a little foolish if it got about; you know some people think these mediums are absolute fakes, and anyhow, the whole thing, I am afraid, was quite stupid. She must have got her contacts mixed. There is no old house about here and never has been since the original Verrall was pulled down, and that's a good fifty years ago, I believe, from what the estate agent told me; and as for a murder, I never heard the shadow of any such story.'

"We all agreed not to mention what the medium had said, and did this with the more heartiness as we were, not any one of us, impressed. The feeling was rather that Mrs. Mahogany had been obliged to say something and had said that. . . .

"Well," said Cuming comfortably, "that is the first part of my story, and I daresay you'll think it's dull enough. Now we come to the second part.

"Latish that evening Dr. Dilke arrived. He was not in any way a remarkable man, just an ordinary successful physician, and I refuse to say that he was suffering from overwork or nervous strain; you know that is so often put into this kind of story as a sort of excuse for what happens afterward. On the contrary, Dr. Dilke seemed to be in the most robust of health and the most cheerful frame of mind, and quite prepared to make the most of his brief holiday. The car that fetched him from the station was taking Mrs. Mahogany away, and the doctor and the medium met for just a moment in the hall. Mrs. Janey did not trouble to introduce them, but without waiting for this Mrs. Mahogany turned to the doctor, and looking at him fixedly, said, 'You're very psychic, aren't you?'

And upon that Mrs. Janey was forced to say hastily: 'This is Mrs. Mahogany, Dr. Dilke, the famous medium.'

"The physician was indifferently impressed. 'I really don't know,' he answered, smiling, 'I have never gone in for that sort of thing. I shouldn't think I am what you call "psychic" really; I have had a hard, scientific training, and that rather knocks the bottom out of fantasies.'

" 'Well, you are, you know,' said Mrs. Mahogany; 'I felt it at once; I shouldn't be at all surprised if you had some strange experience one of these days.'

"Mrs. Mahogany left the house and was duly driven away to the station. I want to make the point very clear that she and Dr. Dilke did not meet again and that they held no communication except those few words in the hall spoken in the presence of Mrs. Janey. Of course Dr. Dilke got twitted a good deal about what the medium had said; it made quite a topic of conversation during dinner and after dinner, and we all had queer little ghost stories or incidents of what we considered 'psychic' experiences to trot out and discuss. Dr. Dilke remained civil, amused, but entirely unconvinced. He had what he called a material, or physical, or medical explanation for almost everything that we said, and, apart from all these explanations he added, with some justice, that human credulity was such that there was always someone who would accept and embellish anything, however wild, unlikely, or grotesque it was.

" 'I should rather like to hear what you would say if such an experience happened to you,' Mrs. Janey challenged him; 'whether you use the ancient terms of "ghost," "witches," "black magic," and so on, or whether you speak in modern terms like "medium," "clairvoyance," "psychic contacts," and all the rest of it; well, it seems one is in a bit of a tangle anyhow, and if any queer thing ever happens to you——'

"Dr. Dilke broke in pleasantly: 'Well, if it ever does I will let you all know about it, and I dare say I shall have an explanation to add at the end of the tale.'

"When we all met again the next morning we rather hoped that

Dr. Dilke would have something to tell us—some odd experience that might have befallen him in the night, new as the house was, and banal as was his bedroom. He told us, of course, that he had passed a perfectly good night.

"We most of us went to the morning service in the small church that had once been the chapel belonging to the demolished mansion, and which had some rather curious monuments inside and in the churchyard. As I went in I noticed a mortuary chapel with niches for the coffins to be stood upright, now whitewashed and used as a sacristy. The monuments and mural tablets were mostly to the memory of members of the family of Verrall—the Verralls of Verrall Hall, who appeared to have been people of little interest or distinction. Dr. Dilke sat beside me, and I, having nothing better to do through the more familiar and monotonous portions of the service, found myself idly looking at the mural tablet beyond him. This was a large slab of black marble deeply cut with a very worn Latin inscription which I found, unconsciously, I was spelling out. The stone, it seemed, commemorated a woman who had been, of course, the possessor of all the virtues; her name was Philadelphia Carwithen, and I rather pleasantly sampled the flavor of that ancient name—Philadelphia. Then I noticed a smaller inscription at the bottom of the slab, which indicated that the lady's husband also rested in the vault; he had died suddenly about six months after her—of grief at her loss, I thought, scenting out a pretty romance.

"As we walked home across the frost-bitten fields and icy lanes Dr. Dilke, who walked beside me, as he had sat beside me in church, began to complain of cold; he said he believed that he had caught a chill. I was rather amused to hear this old-womanish expression on the lips of so distinguished a physician, and I told him that I had been taught in my more enlightened days that there was no such thing as 'catching a chill.' To my surprise he did not laugh at this, but said:

" 'Oh, yes, there is, and I believe I've got it—I keep on shivering; I think it was that slab of black stone I was sitting next. It was as cold as ice, for I touched it, and it seemed to me exuding moisture

—some of that old stone does, you know; it's always, as it were, sweating; and I felt exactly as if I were sitting next a slab of ice from which a cold wind was blowing; it was really as if it penetrated my flesh.'

"He looked pale, and I thought how disagreeable it would be for us all, and particularly for Mrs. Janey, if the good man was to be taken ill in the midst of her already not-too-successful Christmas party. Dr. Dilke seemed, too, in that ill-humor which so often presages an illness; he was quite peevish about the church and the service, and the fact that he had been asked to go there.

" 'These places are nothing but charnel houses, after all,' he said fretfully; 'one sits there among all those rotting bones, with that damp marble at one's side. . . .'

" 'It is supposed to give you "atmosphere," ' I said. 'The atmosphere of an old-fashioned Christmas. . . . Did you notice who your black stone was erected "to the memory of"?' I asked, and the doctor replied that he had not.

" 'It was to a young woman—a young woman, I took it, and her husband: "Philadelphia Carwithen," I noticed that, and of course there was a long eulogy of her virtues, and then underneath it just said that he had died a few months afterward. As far as I could see it was the only example of that name in the church—all the rest were Verralls. I suppose they were strangers here.'

" 'What was the date?' asked the doctor, and I replied that really I had not been able to make it out, for where the Roman figures came the stone had been very worn.

"The day ambled along somehow, with games, diversions, and plenty of good food and drink, and toward the evening we began to feel a little more satisfied with each other and our hostess. Only Dr. Dilke remained a little peevish and apart, and this was remarkable in one who was obviously of a robust temperament and an even temper. He still continued to talk of a 'chill,' and I did notice that he shuddered once or twice, and continually sat near the large fire which Mrs. Janey had rather laboriously arranged in imitation of what she would call 'the good old times.'

"That evening, the evening of Christmas Day, there was no talk whatever of ghosts or psychic matters; our discussions were entirely topical and of mundane matters, in which Dr. Dilke, who seemed to have recovered his spirits, took his part with ability and agreeableness. When it was time to break up I asked him, half in jest, about his mysterious chill, and he looked at me with some surprise and appeared to have forgotten that he had ever said he had got such a thing; the impression, whatever it was, which he had received in the church, had evidently been effaced from his mind. I wish to make that quite clear.

"The next morning Dr. Dilke appeared very late at the breakfast table, and when he did so his looks were matter for hints and comment; he was pale, distracted, troubled, untidy in his dress, absent in his manner, and I, at least, instantly recalled what he had said yesterday, and feared he was sickening for some illness.

"On Mrs. Janey putting to him some direct question as to his looks and manner, so strange and so troubled, he replied rather sharply, 'Well, I don't know what you can expect from a fellow who's been up all night. I thought I came down here for a rest.'

"We all looked at him as he dropped into his place and began to drink his coffee with eager gusto; I noticed that he continually shivered. There was something about this astounding statement and his curious appearance which held us all discreetly silent. We waited for further developments before committing ourselves; even Mrs. Janey, whom I had never thought of as tactful, contrived to say casually:

" 'Up all night, doctor. Couldn't you sleep, then? I'm so sorry if your bed wasn't comfortable.'

" 'The bed was all right,' he answered, 'that made me the more sorry to leave it. Haven't you got a local doctor who can take the local cases?' he added.

" 'Why, of course we have; there's Dr. Armstrong and Dr. Fraser —I made sure about that before I came here.'

" 'Well, then,' demanded Dr. Dilke angrily, 'why on earth couldn't one of them have gone last night?'

"Mrs. Janey looked at me helplessly, and I, obeying her glance, took up the matter.

" 'What do you mean, doctor? Do you mean that you were called out of your bed last night to attend a case?' I asked deliberately.

" 'Of course I was—I only got back with the dawn.'

"Here Mrs. Janey could not forbear breaking in.

" 'But whoever could it have been? I know nobody about here yet, at least, only one or two people by name, and they would not be aware that you were here. And how did you get out of the house? It's locked every night.'

"Then the doctor gave his story in rather, I must confess, a confused fashion, and yet with an earnest conviction that he was speaking the simple truth. It was broken up a good deal by ejaculations and comments from the rest of us, but I give it you here shorn of all that and exactly as I put it down in my notebook afterward.

" 'I was awakened by a tap at the door. I was instantly wide-awake and I said, "Come in." I thought immediately that probably someone in the house was ill—a doctor, you know, is always ready for these emergencies. The door opened at once, and a man entered holding a small ordinary storm-lantern. I noticed nothing peculiar about the man. He had a dark greatcoat on, and appeared extremely anxious. "I am sorry to disturb you," he said at once, "but there is a young woman dangerously ill. I want you to come and see her." I, somehow, did not think of arguing or of suggesting that there were other medical men in the neighborhood, or of asking how it was he knew of my presence at Verrall. I dressed myself quickly and accompanied him out of the house. He opened the front door without any trouble, and it did not occur to me to ask him how it was he had obtained either admission or egress. There was a small carriage outside the door, such a one as you may still see in isolated country places, but such a one as I was certainly surprised to see here. I could not very well make out either the horse or the driver, for, though the moon was high in the heavens, it was frequently obscured by clouds. I got into the carriage and noticed, as I have often noticed before in these ancient vehicles, a most repulsive smell of decay and damp. My companion got in beside me. He did not speak a word during the whole of the journey, which was, I have the impression, extremely long. I had also the sense that he was in the greatest trouble, anguish, and almost despair; I do not know why I did not question him. I should tell you that he had drawn down the blinds of the carriage and we traveled in darkness, yet I was perfectly aware of his presence and seemed to see him in his heavy dark great-coat turned up round the chin, his black hair low on his forehead, and his anxious, furtive dark eyes. I think I may have gone to sleep in the carriage, I was tired and cold. I was aware, however, when it stopped, and of my companion opening the door and help-ing me out. We went through a garden, down some steps and past a fishpond; I could see by the moonlight the silver and gold shapes of fishes slipping in and out of the black water. We entered the house by a side door—I remember that very distinctly—and went up what seemed to be some secret or seldom-used stairs, and into a bedroom. I was, by now, quite alert, as one is when one gets into the presence of the patient, and said to myself, "What a fool I've been, I've brought nothing with me," and I tried to remember, but could not quite do so, whether or not I had brought anything with me—my cases and so on—to Verrall. The room was very badly lighted, but a certain illumination—I could not say whether it came from any artificial light within the room or merely from the moon-light through the open window, draped with mauve velvet curtains —fell on the bed, and there I saw my patient. She was a young woman, who, I surmised, would have been, when in health, of con-siderable though coarse charm. She was now in great suffering, twisted and contorted with agony, and in her struggles of anguish had pulled and torn the bedclothes into a heap. I noticed that she wore a dress of some light material spotted with small roses, and it occurred to me at once that she had been taken ill during the day-time and must have lain thus in great pain for many hours, and I turned with some reproach to the man who had fetched me and de-manded why help had not been sought sooner. For answer he wrung his hands—a gesture that I do not remember having noticed in any human being before; one hears a great deal of hands being wrung, but one does not so often see it. This man, I remember distinctly, wrung his hands, and muttered, "Do what you can for her—do what you can!" I feared that this would be very little. I endeavored to make an examination of the patient, but owing to her half-delirious struggles this was very difficult; she was, however, I thought, likely to die, and of what malady I could not determine. There was a table near by on which lay some papers—one I took to be a will—and a glass in which there had been milk. I do not remember seeing anything else in the room—the light was so bad. I endeavored to question the man, whom I took to be the husband, but without any success. He merely repeated his monotonous appeal for me to save her. Then I was aware of a sound outside the room—of a woman laughing, perpetually and shrilly laughing. "Pray stop that," I cried to the man; "who have you got in the house—a lunatic?" But he took no notice of my appeal, merely repeating his own hushed lamentations. The sick woman appeared to hear that demoniacal laughter outside, and raising herself on one elbow said, "You have destroyed me and you may well laugh."

" 'I sat down at the table on which were the papers and the glass half full of milk, and wrote a prescription on a sheet torn out of my notebook. The man snatched it eagerly. "I don't know when and where you can get that made up," I said, "but it's the only hope." At this he seemed wishful for me to depart, as wishful as he had been for me to come. "That's all I want," he said. He took me by the arm and led me out of the house by the same back stairs. As I descended I still heard those two dreadful sounds—the thin laughter of the woman I had not seen, and the groans, becoming every moment fainter, of the young woman whom I had seen. The carriage was waiting for me, and I was driven back by the same way I had come. When I reached the house and my room I saw the dawn just breaking. I rested till I heard the breakfast gong. I suppose some time had gone by since I returned to the house, but I wasn't quite aware of it; all through the night I had rather lost the sense of time.'

"When Dr. Dilke had finished his narrative, which I give here badly—but, I hope, to the point—we all glanced at each other rather uncomfortably, for who was to tell a man like Dr. Dilke that he had been suffering from a severe hallucination? It was, of course, quite impossible that he could have left the house and gone through the peculiar scenes he had described, and it seemed extraordinary that he could for a moment have believed that he had done so. What was even more remarkable was that so many points of his story agreed with what the medium, Mrs. Mahogany, had said in her trance. We recognized the frock with the roses, the mauve velvet curtains, the glass of milk, the man who had fetched Dr. Dilke sounded like the murderer, and the unfortunate woman writhing on the bed sounded like the victim; but how had the doctor got hold of these particulars? We all knew that he had not spoken to Mrs. Mahogany, and each suspected the other of having told him what the medium had said, and that this having wrought on his mind he had the dream, vision, or hallucination he had just described to us. I must add that this was found afterward to be wholly false; we were all reliable people and there was not a shadow of doubt we had all kept our counsel about Mrs. Mahogany. In fact, none of us had been alone with Dr. Dilke the previous day for more than a moment or so save myself, who had walked with him from the church, when we had certainly spoken of nothing except the black stone in the church and the chill which he had said emanated from it. . . . Well, to put the matter as briefly as possible, and to leave out a great deal of amazement and wonder, explanation, and so on, we will come to the point when Dr. Dilke was finally persuaded that he had not left Verrall all the night. When his story was taken to pieces and put before him, as it were, in the raw, he himself recognized many absurdities: How could the man have come straight to his bedroom? How could he have left the house?— the doors were locked every night, there was no doubt about that. Where did the carriage come from and where was the house to which he had been taken? And who could possibly have known of his presence in the neighborhood? Had not, too, the scene in the house to which he was taken all the resemblance of a nightmare? Who was it laughing in the other room? What was the mysterious illness that was destroying the young woman? Who was the black-browed man who had fetched him? And, in these days of telephone and motorcars, people didn't go out in the old-fashioned one-horse carriages to fetch doctors from miles away in the case of dangerous illness.

"Dr. Dilke was finally silenced, uneasy, but not convinced. I could see that he disliked intensely the idea that he had been the victim of a hallucination and that he equally intensely regretted the impulse which had made him relate his extraordinary adventure of the night. I could only conclude that he must have done so while still, to an extent, under the influence of his delusion, which had been so strong that never for a moment had he questioned the reality of it. Though he was forced at last to allow us to put the whole thing down as a most remarkable dream, I could see that he did not intend to let the matter rest there, and later in the day (out of good manners we had eventually ceased discussing the story) he asked me if I would accompany him on some investigation in the neighborhood.

" 'I think I should know the house,' he said, 'even though I saw it in the dark. I was impressed by the fishpond and the low doorway through which I had to stoop in order to pass without knocking my head.'

"I did not tell him that Mrs. Mahogany had also mentioned a fishpond and a low door.

"We made the excuse of some old brasses we wished to discover in a near-by church to take my car and go out that afternoon on an investigation of the neighborhood in the hope of discovering Dr. Dilke's dream house.

"We covered a good deal of distance and spent a good deal of time without any success at all, and the short day was already darkening when we came upon a row of almshouses in which, for no reason at all that I could discern, Dr. Dilke showed an interest and insisted on stopping before them. He pointed out an inscription cut in the center gable, which said that these had been built by a certain Richard Carwithen in memory of Philadelphia, his wife.

"'The people whose tablet you sat next in the church,' I remarked.

"'Yes,' murmured Dr. Dilke, 'when I felt the chill,' and he added, 'when I first felt the chill. You see, the date is 1830. That would be about right.'

"We stopped in the little village, which was a good many miles from Verrall, and after some tedious delays because everything was shut up for the holiday, we did discover an old man who was willing to tell us something about the almshouses, though there was nothing much to be said about them. They had been founded by a certain Mr. Richard Carwithen with his wife's fortune. He had been a poor man, a kind of adventurer, our informant thought, who had married a wealthy woman; they had not been at all happy. There had been quarrels and disputes, and a separation (at least, so the gossip went, as his father had told it to him); finally, the Carwithens had taken a house here in this village of Sunford—a large house it was and it still stood. The Carwithens weren't buried in this village though, but at Verrall; she had been a Verrall by birth—perhaps that's why they came to this neighborhood—it was the name of a great family in those days, you know. . . . There was another woman in the old story, as it went, and she got hold of Mr. Carwithen and was for making him put his wife aside; and so, perhaps, he would have done, but the poor lady died suddenly, and there was some talk about it, having the other woman in the house at the time, and it being so convenient for both of them. . . . But he didn't marry the other woman, because he died six months after his wife. . . . By his will he left all his wife's money to found these almshouses.

"Dr. Dilke asked if he could see the house where the Carwithens had lived.

"'It belongs to a London gentleman,' the old man said, 'who never comes here. It's going to be pulled down and the land sold in building lots; why, it's been locked up these ten years or more. I don't suppose it's been inhabited since—no, not for a hundred years.'

" 'Well, I'm looking for a house round about here. I don't mind spending a little money on repairs if that house is in the market.'

"The old man didn't know whether it was in the market or not, but kept repeating that the property was to be sold and broken up for building lots.

"I won't bother you with all our delays and arguments, but merely tell you that we did finally discover the lodgekeeper of the estate, who gave us the key. It was not such a very large estate, nothing to be compared to Verrall, but had been, in its time, of some pretension. Builders' boards had already been raised along the high road frontage. There were some fine old trees, black and bare, in a little park. As we turned in through the rusty gates and motored toward the house it was nearly dark, but we had our electric torches and the powerful head lamps of the car. Dr. Dilke made no comment on what we had found, but he reconstructed the story of the Carwithens whose names were on that black stone in Verrall church.

" 'They were quarreling over money, he was trying to get her to sign a will in his favor; she had some little sickness perhaps— brought on probably by rage—he had got the other woman in the house, remember; I expect he was no good. There was some sort of poison about—perhaps for a face wash, perhaps as a drug. He put it in the milk and gave it to her.'

"Here I interrupted: 'How do you know it was in the milk?'

"The doctor did not reply to this. I had now swung the car round to the front of the ancient mansion—a poor, pretentious place, sinister in the half-darkness.

" 'And then, when he had done it,' continued Dr. Dilke, mounting the steps of the house, 'he repented most horribly; he wanted to fly for a doctor to get some antidote for the poison with the idea in his head that if he could have got help he could have saved her himself. The other woman kept on laughing. He couldn't forgive her that—that she could laugh at a moment like that; he couldn't get help! He couldn't find a doctor. His wife died. No one suspected foul play—they seldom did in those days as long as the people were respectable; you must remember the state in which medical knowledge was in 1830. He couldn't marry the other woman, and he couldn't touch the money; he left it all to found the almshouses; then he died himself, six months afterward, leaving instructions that his name should be added to that black stone. I dare say he died by his own hand. Probably he loved her through it all, you know—it was only the money, that cursed money, a fortune just within his grasp, but which he couldn't take.'

" 'A pretty romance,' I suggested, as we entered the house; 'I am sure there is a three-volume novel in it of what Mrs. Janey would call "the good old-fashioned" sort.'

"To this Dr. Dilke answered: 'Suppose the miserable man can't rest? Supposing he is still searching for a doctor?'

"We passed from one room to another of the dismal, dusty, dismantled house. Dr. Dilke opened a damaged shutter which conccaled one of the windows at the back, and pointed out in the waning light a decayed garden with stone steps and a fishpond; and a low gateway to pass through which a man of his height would have had to stoop. We could just discern this in the twilight. He made no comment. We went upstairs."

Here Cuming paused dramatically to give us the full flavor of the final part of his story. He reminded us, rather unnecessarily, for somehow he had convinced us that this was all perfectly true.

"I am not romancing; I won't answer for what Dr. Dilke said or did, or his adventure of the night before, or the story of the Car-withens as he constructed it, but *this* is actually what happened. . . . We went upstairs by the wide main stairs. Dr. Dilke searched about for and found a door which opened on to the back stairs, and then he said: 'This must be the room.' It was entirely devoid of any furniture, and stained with damp, the walls stripped of paneling and cheaply covered with decayed paper, peeling, and in parts fallen.

" 'What's this?' said Dr. Dilke.

"He picked up a scrap of paper that showed vivid on the dusty floor and handed it to me. It was a prescription. He took out his notebook and showed me the page where this fitted in.

" 'This page I tore out last night when I wrote that prescription

434

in this room. The bed was just there, and there was the table on which were the papers and the glass of milk.'

" 'But you couldn't have been here last night,' I protested feebly, 'the locked doors—the whole thing! . . .'

"Dr. Dilke said nothing. After a while neither did I. 'Let's get out of this place,' I said. Then another thought struck me. 'What is your prescription?' I asked.

"He said: 'A very uncommon kind of prescription, a very desperate sort of prescription, one that I've never written before, nor I hope shall again — an antidote for severe arsenical poisoning.'

"I leave you," smiled Cuming, "to your various attitudes of incredulity or explanation."

E. F. BOZMAN

The White Road

"MILD weather for the time of year."

"Yes," I said; "not very seasonable."

I did not even trouble to turn round and look at the stranger who had addressed me. I remember a soft Sussex voice, strong and deep, and I have an impression of someone tall; but I had come in to have a glass of beer by myself and was not in the mood for chance conversation.

It was Christmas Eve, about nine o'clock in the evening, and the public bar at the Swan Inn was crowded. It was the first evening of my holidays and I had walked over from the farmhouse where I was staying with my mother, using the inn as my objective. I had just come down from London, and was in no need of company; on the contrary, I wanted solitude. However, the landlord recognized me from previous visits and passed the time of night.

"Staying down at the farm again?" he asked.

"Yes," I said.

"Well, we're glad to see you, I'm sure. Did you walk over?"

"Yes. I enjoy the walk. That's what I came out for."

"And for the drink?" he suggested.

"Well, it's good beer," I admitted, and paid for a glass for each of us. I felt rather than saw the stranger who had accosted me hovering behind me, but made no attempt to bring him in. I did not see why I should buy him a drink; and I wanted nothing from him.

"It must be pretty well three miles' walk down to where you are," the landlord said. "A tidy step."

"Yes," I said, "a good three. Two or two and a half down to Ingo Bridge, then another mile from where the lane turns off to West Chapter."

"Well, I suppose you know you've missed the last bus down. Must have been gone half an hour. There's only the one in from the Bridge, and that's the lot."

"Yes, I know," I said; "I don't mind."

Just then I heard the noise of the door latch followed by a creak as the door swung open, and half turned to see the tall stranger going out. I caught a glimpse of him before he shut the door behind him.

"Who was that?" I asked the landlord.

"I didn't notice him—he must have been a stranger to me. Funny thing, now you mention it, he didn't buy a drink."

"He seemed to be hanging round me. Cadging, I suppose."

"You get some funny customers at this time of year." The landlord was evidently not interested in the man. "It'll be dark tonight, along that road," he volunteered.

"Yes," I said. We finished our drinks, I said good night, and made my way to the door across the smoke-laden room.

It was pitch dark outside by contrast with the glow of the inn, and as I slammed the well-used wooden door behind me the shaft of light streaming from the parlor window seemed to be my last link with civilization. The air was extraordinarily mild for the time of year. My way lay by a short cut across the church fields which joined the road leading toward the sea; a difficult way to find a night had I not known it well; alternatively, I could have gone a longer way round, starting in the opposite direction, and making three sides of a square in the road which I was eventually to join by the short cut. I knew my ground and decided on the footpath without hesitation. By the time I reached the church fields I realized that the night was not really so dark as it had seemed to be at first, for I could see the black tower and belfry of the church looming against a background of lighter gray, and a glimmer of light in one corner of the church suggested eleventh-hour preparations for the great festival. Clouds were scudding across an unseen moon, full according to the calendar, discernible now only secondarily by a patch of faintly diffused light toward the south; knowing the lay of the land I could imagine the clouds swept away and the moon hanging in its winter glory over the cold English Channel a few miles away. Although the air was temporarily muggy with the presage of rain, there was a deep underlying chill in land and sea, the ingrained coldness of the short days.

The footpath across the fields was narrow and muddy, a single-file track. I stumbled and slithered my way along it until I reached a narrow wooden bridge with two handrails. Here I paused for a moment, looking at the dark swollen stream which was just visible, black and shining, below my feet.

I was now near the point where the path joined the road, and as I paused, my elbows leaning on the rail of the bridge, listening to the far-reaching silence, I heard in the distance the sound of footsteps along the road. In these days of heavy road-traffic this old-fashioned, unmistakable sound is a rarity, and I listened fascinated. The steady distant tread, gradually loudening, began to grow on me, and by the time I had made up my mind to move it was beating a rhythm in my brain. My path now led diagonally up a sloping bank to the road, and I crept up it silently, hearing and thinking of nothing but the approaching footsteps. The thought occurred to me that I must not let the walker catch me up, that something important, something connected with myself yet out of my own control, depended on the success of my efforts, and I began to hurry. I tried to dismiss the idea, but it would not be banished, and as I reached the swing gate leading out to the road the footsteps sounded unexpectedly near. They rang on the road, and I could hardly resist the temptation to run.

I compromised by stepping out briskly, swinging my arms. It was ludicrous, I argued with myself; there was nothing to be afraid of, and my own feet tried to reassure me by dimming the sound behind me. But the pursuing footsteps would not be drowned; they were implacable. I attempted to speed up, without allowing myself to hurry or panic, but I could not shake them off. They were gaining steadily on me, and as their loudness increased tingles of fear began to go down my spine. I could not turn round and look—could not, I realized, because I was afraid to.

The road at this point runs between high hedges and trees which shut out what little light was coming from the sky. Nothing could be seen except the dark shapes of the trees, and an occasional gleam from the black wet surface of the tarred road. There were some outlying farm buildings and barns immediately ahead, but no glimmer of light came from them. The overhanging elms dripped their moisture on me from leafless branches. No traffic was within earshot; the only sound was of footsteps, mine and my pursuer's.

Left right, left right, left right they went behind me. The walker had long legs. Left right, left right—the din increased alarmingly, and I realized that I must run.

"How far now to the bridge?"

A soft voice, almost in my ear, shocked me, and yet released the tension. I sweated suddenly and profusely.

I recognized the voice of the stranger who had addressed me in the Swan Inn. He had left just before me and must have walked round by the road, I realized, while I had taken the short cut across the fields. I could not immediately disguise my racing heart, but I managed to speak calmly, in a voice which must have sounded weak in contrast with the strong Sussex resonance of the stranger.

"About two miles," I said.

The stranger said nothing more for the moment, but fell into step

439

beside me, as if assuming that we were to walk together. It was not what I wanted, partly because I was ashamed of my panic of a few moments ago, and partly because I had been looking forward to walking the lonely stretch of road ahead by myself. I turned my head, but could see nothing of my companion except his tall dark form, vaguely outlined, and he must have been wearing a long coat which flapped below his knees. I was the next to break the silence.

"When we get past the farm buildings," I said, "and round the next corner we come to a long open stretch. It's a lovely bit of road, a special favorite of mine, absolutely deserted usually. On clear nights or days you can see the sea in the distance."

"There's a little hill about halfway along—by an S bend."

The stranger's remark surprised me. Why had he asked me about the way if he knew the district?

"So you know the road?" I asked querulously, as if I had been deceived.

The stranger muttered, "Years ago," and something else I could not catch. The detail he had remembered was a significant one. The open stretch ahead of us, nearly two miles in length, promised at first sight to run straight for the sea, where it joined the main coast road; but halfway along this section of the road there was a danger spot for speeding motorists, an unexpected S bend over a little mound. Just past the bend, as the road straightened itself out again and went down the far side of the little hill, heading between low hedges for the sea, there was a notable isolated thorn tree standing on the left of the road. Its trunk leaned toward the sea, while the twigs on top of the trunk were all swept in the opposite direction, like a mat of hair, blown by the prevailing wind. From the trunk two stumpy branches sprouted, each with its bunch of twigs held out like hands; these, too, were wind-swept. The trunk was not gnarled and sprang strongly from the ground—no dead post, driven into the earth from above, could have achieved that appearance of strength.

I was about to refer to this tree, which was a particular landmark of mine, when we heard the sound of a distant motor. My companion seemed to be unexpectedly nervous—I could feel his anxiety. The sound increased rapidly, so different a progress from approaching feet, and before we had rounded the sharp corner leading to the open stretch of road a Southdown bus flung itself round the bend and was almost on us. The headlights flooded us, gleaming on the stranger's face, making him look pale as a ghost, and lighting the road immediately in front of us to a brilliant white.

The stranger was so dazzled by the sudden brightness that he cowered into the hedge, shielding his eyes with his hand. In an instant the bus had charged past us and round another corner, taking its lighted interior and its warm passengers with it into the enveloping darkness of the countryside.

I heard my companion murmur: "The white road. The white road." Something in the way he said the words brought a picture of my youth to my eyes, of a time when this same lonely road was white and dusty, with flints, and I could see myself bicycling along it, in imminent danger of punctures, hurrying to the sea. I saw the white road, the white sea road, not the black and tarred contrivance of today, yet the same road with the same trees and banks. It has always been a lovely country road, and it still is.

We left the farm buildings behind us and entered the lonely stretch. It was too dark for us to see a glimmer of the sea ahead or anything behind the low banked hedges on either side. A light rain began to fall, driving in our faces.

"That was the last bus," I said; "we'll meet no more now."

The stranger ignored this remark, and his next words fitted in exactly with what had been in my mind when the bus distracted us.

"There's a thorn tree, isn't there?" he said, "just beside the road round the double corner." He spoke as if he knew the way by heart, yet obviously he did not remember it exactly. He had not even been sure enough of himself to take the short cut by the church fields.

"Yes," I said; "why do you ask?"

"You've noticed it yourself?" he inquired anxiously.

"Yes."

"And it's still there?"

"Yes, of course." I could not for the life of me imagine what he was driving at. Yet even as I spoke the words confidently I found myself in doubt. I remembered my mother saying something about workmen on the lonely road, how they were widening it at the bend and spoiling its appearance. Like me, she had an affection for it. I had passed the spot that very evening on my way to the inn, yet when I came to think of it I could not be sure whether I had seen the tree or not. I had been preoccupied, and had not looked for it specially. But surely I would have noticed, I thought, and said aloud: "At least it was there the last time I passed."

"When was that?" The stranger spoke very directly and forcibly.

I was about to say this very evening, but realizing my uncertainty, said instead: "About this time last year. I was down here for Christmas."

"There's a story told about that tree in these parts," he said.

"Oh," I said; "what do they say about it?"

"They say there was a suicide on that spot. A man from the village." The Sussex burr was soft and confidential.

"What happened?"

"He hanged himself on the tree."

"A man couldn't hang himself on that tree," I said, "it's too small."

"There's a seven-foot clearance from the fork," he said eagerly.

"Oh, well," I said, "it's a sturdy little tree. I've often noticed it, standing there all alone, holding out its branches like hands."

"Yes," he said, "that's right. Like hands. And have you seen the nails? Long and curved. They haven't been cut, any more than the hair. Have you seen the hair?" His voice was strained, and I felt that he must be looking at me. I turned to read his eyes, but it was too dark to see anything but the tall shape and the long coat beside me.

"That tree didn't grow in a day," I said.

"I don't know how old it is." The stranger spoke apologetically. "But it's an old story—maybe twenty, thirty, forty years old. I couldn't be sure."

The White Road

There was a pause for a few minutes. We must have covered half the mile between the farm and the tree before I spoke again.

"What's behind the story?" I asked. "What do they say?"

"They say there was a woman in it. A dark girl, one of the coast guard's daughters down at Ingo Bridge. He was a married man, you see."

I waited for him to go on. He spoke as if it mattered vitally to him.

"It had been going on a long time, they say. Then one night, one Christmas Eve, he left his home for good and went to the inn, and perhaps he had a drink or two there, though nobody knows that. He had made up his mind to take the girl. She was going to leave a light burning in her window, and he would see it from the distance, you see, when he turned the corner by the tree. That was to be the sign, if it was all right. Well, he left his home for good, to get that girl. But he never got her. His wife got him—by that tree."

"I thought you said it was suicide."

"Ah, yes, that's what they say. But it was his wife that got him."

"You mean she followed him?"

"No, I mean that she got him there."

We walked another two hundred yards before he added: "I mean that he saw her there, in his mind's eye. He couldn't take the girl then. He couldn't, however much he wanted to. He couldn't because he belonged to his wife. That's what I mean when I say his wife got him."

"It's a queer story," I said. "I've never heard it told before."

"Oh, you hear it among the older men. It's common knowledge," he said.

"It's a queer story," I said, "because who told it in the first place? Who was to know what was in the fellow's mind? Who was to know what actually happened?"

"He was dead, wasn't he?" The stranger spoke irritably. "A man doesn't die in these parts without talk about it. A lot of talk."

"But how did he die?" I insisted. "Did he hang himself or was he murdered?"

"He was murdered."

"What the devil do you mean?" I shouted angrily. "Murdered, by a tree?"

The stranger clutched me by the arm. "Have you seen the tree?" he whispered. "Have you seen it standing there year after year, leaning against the southwest wind, with the hair streaming and the hands outstretched, and the long nails growing——?"

I was suddenly aware of the loneliness of the road and of the darkness and desolation of the downs around me and the sea ahead. The stranger's next remark, though spoken in a low voice, seemed to shatter the darkness.

"By God! what's a man to do when a woman pulls at him? A dark girl. And what do men have daughters for, eh? I ask you that. Whose fault is that?" and then, as if brushing aside an imaginary criticism: "If I were to meet that coast guard's daughter down by the bridge tonight I'd tell her . . ."

His voice tailed off and I said nothing. The coast guards' cottages are still down by the bridge, true enough, but the coast guards have been disbanded years ago. Years ago. He must have known that.

We reached the little hill in the road, mounted it, and turned the first half of the S bend. The light rain had ceased and the clouds were thinning. We both of us knew that when we passed the next corner, the other half of the S, we should see the tree.

Just then the clouds broke suddenly and the full moon shone through. It whitened the black road, silvered the gleam of the sea ahead, and illuminated the low banks and hedges with the dark rising downs beyond. We turned the corner and both stared toward the thorn tree.

There was nothing to be seen. No tree. Nothing. The place where the tree stood was blatantly empty, and the moonlight seemed to emphasize the barrenness, showing it up like a sore, focusing the attention. I suppose I had been unconsciously visualizing the tree as I knew it, because I was more than surprised by its absence; I was shocked, profoundly shocked, and the recollection of that absence of tree, that nothingness, is more vivid to me than my memory of the tree itself. The clouds now scudded from the moon, leaving it cold and clear and agonizingly circular in an expanse of sky. In what seemed to be a blaze of light I put my head down and ran.

I ran toward the silver sea along a white road, a ribbon road of memory, and I could believe that the dust rose under my feet and powdered my boots; though with another part of me I knew that I was wearing shoes, not boots, and was pounding down a wet tarred road. In the moonlight that road seemed white and dusty and I pattered along it with the desperate urgency of a small boy who must deliver some message or run some errand of overwhelming yet not-understood importance. I ran and I ran, urgently and desperately, thinking no more of my strange companion, yet in some way intimately associated with him.

Along the white road I ran, past the signpost at the turning to the farm, knowing yet not knowing what I should see. The clouds had gathered again, a dark pillar over the sea, and the blaze of whiteness was already dimming. There was a light in the coast guard's cottage at Ingo Bridge. I headed straight for it but did not reach it, for a woman lay across the road, an elderly woman. She must have dropped her basket as she fell, and her parcels, little objects and toys that she had bought for her grandchildren perhaps, lay scattered around her. She might have been shopping for Christmas, I thought, and had missed the last bus at Ingo Bridge; then she had tried to walk home, but her strength had failed her, and she had fallen in the road.

I ran to her side and raised her head. She was too weak to stand on her feet, and I lifted her in my arms and carried her the few yards to the coast guard's cottage where the light was still burning. For those few steps the road was white and flinty—but then it is so now; it is only a little byroad—and I found myself speaking not to an old woman who had fainted or was dying, but to a young woman. And the words I spoke were not mine but someone else's; the words of the stranger who had accompanied me to the tree. They were framed without my help.

445

"That was no murder. That was no murder by the tree. I always belonged to you, all along, really. I see it all now."

The woman opened her eyes and there was an expression of love in them. I could not say whether it was I or my stranger who spoke the next words. They were said very gently and comfortably.

"There are things better left unsaid. Better left; you understand."

She nodded and closed her eyes, and then the stranger and the strangeness left me.

I knocked at the door of the cottage. A man opened it, then called to his wife, a gray-haired woman dressed in black, who must have been a beautiful dark girl in her time. I explained what had happened and they took my burden from me and laid her on their horsehair sofa. They knew who she was, of course, for she was from the village.

But I did not know. I could only guess. And as I walked back in the inky blackness of an oncoming rainstorm, back to my corner, then up the lane to the farmhouse where my mother was waiting up for me, I cast round in my mind for a missing fragment of knowledge, something I must know yet could not remember.

I discovered it at last accidentally, while in my mind's eye I could still see the thorn tree, standing there, holding out its branches, its mat of twigs all set toward the northeast, and from the fork a dark form hanging, twisting slowly in a long coat, a thing with a back to its head but no face, a dark thing twisting slowly beside a long white road which stretched in a dusty ribbon to the sea. I discovered the missing fragment of knowledge in the more exact recollection of my mother's remark, made only that very morning. "They are widening the white road at the bend," she had said—we always used to call it the white road between ourselves—"and this evening they are going to cut down that little old thorn tree."

Oh, What a Horrid Tale!

COME, friends, gather round the fireside, and listen to the sad but seasonable tale of Ernie the Actor.

Ernie was one of those actors who only find fame at Christmas. He could rule a Christmas pantomime like Robey or Little Tich, but between seasons he was lucky if he got a month's engagement with a concert-party. Sad, but true! However, he worked hard, lived soberly, and would doubtless have lasted to a ripe and insignificant old age, had not the course of his life been strangely altered by his marrying a Mrs. Tonks, a widow with four young children and an eye for the pay-packet.

Mrs. Tonks had booked a seat for *Cinderella*, to comfort herself for the recent death of her first husband. She liked a joke as well as the next woman, and she liked a good cry too. Ernie made her laugh so much that, being at once so happy and so sad, she fell in love with him. Ernie fell more in love with her four children than

447

with Mrs. Tonks; but nevertheless they got married. Now, Ernie took his work so seriously that he could hardly cease being funny, even when he was off the stage. His wife used to find his cross-talk and gags a great solace in her domestic worries; and the children were always happy when Ernie was at home, because his antics kept them laughing all the time.

As the years went by, however, the children needed more and more food, and more and more clothes, while Mrs. Ernie asked for more and more of Ernie's money. Ernie's engagements, on the other hand, became fewer and fewer, and he found it less and less easy to earn enough money to pay the larger and larger bills.

The strain of working too hard and always being anxious for the future told at last on Ernie's temper. He began to dislike returning home, after a tiring round of the managers' offices, only to be treated by his family as a joke. One day he brought his fist down on the breakfast table with a bang, and said: "I won't be a laughingstock any longer, I won't; I won't; I won't." And, putting his hat on his head, he announced that he was going to apply for a straight part, and act the clown no more.

It was not easy to persuade the managers that he meant what he said. Most of them laughed, offered him a cigarette, and exclaimed: "Jolly good joke, ha!" But one of them jestingly offered him the part of the Demon King in *Aladdin*, at a little second-rate theater in Staffs, for a salary which was half his former wage. Ernie accepted it.

"Well, you don't expect me to spend Christmas Day in the workhouse, do you?" said Mrs. Ernie, when he told her the news. And without more ado she departed with the children to stay at Chorlton-cum-Hardy with her married sister. But the pantomime ran for nine weeks, and the local dramatic critic wrote that "no more terrifying Demon King has ever walked the boards of the 'Alexandra.'" When the last performance was ended Ernie was paid a bonus. He packed his belongings and took the first train to Chorlton-cum-Hardy, that he might tell his wife of his success.

His welcome, however, was not so happy as he expected. When he put his head round the door he was greeted, not by cries of pleasure or yet of laughter, but by startled faces and a shriek of horror. Ernie pretended not to notice it; but in the weeks that followed it became clear that everyone was afraid of him. The children wept if he took them on his knee, and even Mrs. Ernie, who was so buxom and handy with a rolling pin, would shrink away when he approached.

Ernie was quite unable to account for this. It pained him more than any mockery could do, for he was naturally a gentle man. After some months he began to feel that his having played the Demon King had something to do with it. And now he often wished that he were Buttons or the Broker's Man once more, so that he could move them to laughter instead of fear.

When the time came for him to make his contract for the next year's pantomime, he decided that he would be Demon King no longer. He even refused the parts of the Giant in *Jack and the Beanstalk* and the Wicked Uncle in *Cinderella*, for which good and comfortable salaries were offered.

He no longer wished to frighten people.

The managers, very naturally, considered him daft to refuse good offers, and he would have gone without any engagement at all had not Puss in a touring company of *Dick Whittington and his Cat* fallen from the balustrade of the dress circle and lost its ninth (and last) life. Almost in despair, for there were only four days till the first performance, the manager offered the part to Ernie. Ernie accepted it.

He had never played an animal part before, but he very quickly learned what to do. He scratched, miaowed, and purred to a nicety.

It was very pleasant to feel once more the affection of an audience instead of its hatred. Before the season was finished Ernie had become a favorite with actors and public alike. But what made him happiest of all was that his own family's fear of him suddenly departed. Mrs. Ernie began to put her arms round his neck and caress him with every token of kindness, while the children no longer dreaded his touch, but climbed about him and played all sorts of loving games with him.

Ernie was affected almost to tears by this love and tenderness, and thereafter he lived very happily for several years, continuing to play the Puss at every Christmas pantomime. He only suffered two discomforts. One was that he was expected—and indeed compelled—to sit and sleep upon the mat, instead of an armchair or his bed. The other was that Mrs. Ernie forbade him to have a drop of beer or stout or whisky, but insisted that he should always drink milk.

After he had played Whittington's Cat or Puss-in-Boots at almost every reputable theater in the provinces, the time came when Ernie was no longer as supple in his limbs as a first-class cat should be. Giving long thought to the matter he finally made up his mind that he ought to take another part before people began to say: "Poor old Ernie isn't as nimble as he used to be." And after talking with his agent he contracted to play a part which entailed much less activity and effort than did that of Puss, namely the title role in *Mother Goose*.

Unfortunately Ernie's new salary was much less than that which he had earned before. Mrs. Ernie had some hard things to say when he told her about this, and blamed him very much for giving up his old part. But Ernie took a great pride in his calling, and informed her in no uncertain tones that there is more honor in competently laying a golden egg than in being but a lame companion to Dick Whittington. This difference of opinion led to the first dispute between husband and wife since the days of the Demon King.

The first rehearsals of *Mother Goose* went well—so well that Ernie begged his wife to come with the children to see the dress rehearsal, which was to take place on Christmas Day. But Mrs. Ernie refused, and when the day came Ernie left their lodgings to a volley of recrimination from his better-or-worse.

The performance went from start to finish without a hitch—a most unusual happening in a pantomime. As Ernie returned to the lodgings he felt that he had never given a better performance in his whole career, and he regretted more than ever that none of his family had been present to see his triumph.

Oh, What a Horrid Tale!

When he arrived he found that his wife and the children had gone to bed; so he sat down before the fire in the sitting room, as was his wont, and soon fell asleep.

Mrs. Ernie rose from her bed on the next morning in an evil temper. She was still furious about her husband's preference for Art over Money, and she was disappointed at having been unable to afford a turkey for the children's Christmas dinner.

She came downstairs and opened the door of the sitting room. To her surprise Ernie was not there. But in front of the fire, preening its feathers, was a fat, gray goose.

With a cry of delight Mrs. E. ran into the kitchen and fetched a carving-knife.

The children enjoyed their dinner that day more than on any other Boxing Day. And they all agreed that if there is one fowl more tender and delicious than a turkey it is a nice fat goose.

T. F. POWYS

A Christmas Gift

I T is a harmless wish to like a little notice to be taken of one's name, and a number of people, besides Mr. Balliboy, the Dodder carrier, like attention to be paid to their names when they are written down. Children will write their names upon a fair stretch of yellow sand, young men will carve their names upon an old oak in the forest, and even the most simple peasant will like to see his name printed in a newspaper.

For most of his life Mr. Balliboy was satisfied with having his name written upon the side of his van, and he was always pleased and interested when anyone paused in the street to read his name.

But Mr. Balliboy's pride in his name made him do more than one foolish thing.

Once he cut "Mr. Balliboy, Carrier," with his market knife upon one of the doors of Mr. Told's old barn, and again upon the right-

A Christmas Gift

hand post of the village pound. But, on his going to see how the names looked the next Sunday—and perhaps hoping that a stranger might be found regarding them—he discovered, to his sorrow, that the rude village boys had changed the first letters of his name into an unpleasant and ill-sounding word.

Mr. Balliboy was a lonely man, and a bachelor—for no young woman would ever look at his name twice and none had ever wished to have his name written beside hers in a church register.

One Christmas Mr. Balliboy journeyed, as was his wont, to Wey minster. His van was full of countrywomen, each one of whom thought herself to be of the highest quality, for each had put on the finest airs with her market clothes and, so dressed, could talk in a superior manner.

Mr. Balliboy had certainly one reason for happiness—other than the ordinary joyfulness of the merry season—which was that his rival, John Hawkins, had passed by with his van empty of customers, yet Mr. Balliboy was sad. His sadness came, strangely enough, only because he wished, for the first time in his life, to give a Christmas present.

It might have been only to give himself pleasure that he wished to do this. For whatever the present was that he should buy, he determined that a label should be tied on it, with his name written clearly upon it—"From Mr. Balliboy."

What the present would be, and to whom it should be given, Mr. Balliboy did not know. He decided to buy something that he fancied, and then allow destiny to decide to whom the gift should go.

When Mr. Balliboy reached the town he walked about the streets in order to see what could be bought for money. Many a shop window did he look into and many a time did he stand and scratch his head, wondering what he should buy.

There was one oddity that he fancied in a toyshop—a demon holding a fork in his hand, upon which he was raising a naked young woman. Mr. Balliboy thought the demon might do, but over the young woman he shook his head.

Mr. Balliboy moved to another window. Here at once, he saw

453

what pleased him—a little cross, made of cardboard and covered with tinsel, that shone and glistened before Mr. Balliboy's admiring eyes.

Mr. Balliboy purchased the cross for a shilling and attached a label to it, with his name written large. . . .

Sometimes a change comes over a scene, now so happy and gay but in one moment altered into a frown. As soon as Mr. Balliboy had buttoned the cross into his pocket the streets of Weyminster showed this changed look. The shoppers' merriment and joyful surprise at what they saw in the windows gave place to a sad and tired look. The great church that so many hurried by in order to reach their favorite tavern, appeared more dark and somber than a winter's day should ever have made it.

Even the warm drinks served out by black-haired Mabel at the "Rod and Lion" could not make the drinkers forget that care and trouble could cut a Christmas cake and sing a Christmas carol as well as they.

The general gloom of the town touched Mr. Balliboy, and had he not had the present hid in his coat, he might have entered an Inn, in order to drown the troubled feelings that moved about him, in a deep mug.

But, having bought the Christmas present, he had now the amusement of seeking the right person to give it to. And so, instead of walking along the street with downcast eyes, he walked along smiling.

While he was yet some way off his van, he could see that a figure was standing beside it, who seemed to be reading his name. And, whoever this was, Mr. Balliboy determined as he walked, that it should be the one to receive his Christmas gift.

As he drew nearer he saw that the figure was that of a young woman—wrapped in a thin cloak—who showed by her wan look and by her shape that she expected soon to be a mother.

At a little distance from his van Mr. Balliboy waited, pretending to admire a row of bottles in a wine merchant's shopwindow, but, at the same time, keeping an eye upon the woman.

A Christmas Gift

"Was she a thief—was she come there to steal?" A passing police-man, with a fine military strut, evidently thought so.

"Don't stand about here," he shouted. "Go along home with you!"

The policeman seized her roughly.

"I am doing no harm," the woman said, looking at the name again, "I am only waiting for Mr. Balliboy."

"Go along, you lying drab," grumbled the policeman.

He would have pushed her along, only Mr. Balliboy, who had heard his name mentioned, came nearer.

"Baint 'ee poor Mary," he asked, "who was to have married the carpenter at Shelton?"

The policeman winked twice at Mr. Balliboy, smiled and walked on.

"What was it," asked Mr. Balliboy, kindly, as soon as the police-man was out of hearing, "that made 'ee wish to study and remember the name of a poor carrier?"

"I wished to ask you," said the young woman, "whether you would take me as far as the 'Norbury Arms.' Here is my fare," and she handed Mr. Balliboy a shilling—the price of the cross.

Mr. Balliboy put the shilling into his pocket.

"Get up into van," he said, "and 'tis to be hoped they t'others won't mind 'ee."

That day the most respectable of the people of the village had come to town in Mr. Balliboy's van. There was even rich Mrs. Todd, clad in warm furs, whose own motorcar had met with an accident the day before. There were others too, as comfortably off—Mrs. Potten and Mrs. Biggs—and none of these, or even his lesser cus-tomers, did Mr. Balliboy wish to offend. He looked anxiously up the street and then into the van.

The young woman's clothes were rags, her toes peeped from her shoes, and she sighed woefully.

Mr. Balliboy gave her a rug to cover her. "Keep tight hold of 'en," he said, "for t'other women be grabbers."

The change in the town from joy to trouble had caused the

women who had journeyed with Mr. Balliboy that day to arrive at the van a little late, and in no very good tempers. And, when they did come, they were not best pleased to see a poor woman—worse clothed than a tramp—sitting in the best seat in the van, with her knees covered by Mr. Balliboy's rug.

" 'Tis only Mary," said Mr. Balliboy, hoping to put them at their ease. " 'Tis only thik poor toad."

"Mary, is it?" cried Mrs. Biggs angrily, "who did deceive Joseph with her wickedness. What lady would ride with her? Turn her out at once, Mr. Balliboy—the horrid wretch."

"Out with her!" cried Mrs. Todd. "Just look at her," and she whispered unpleasant words to Mrs. Potten.

Mr. Balliboy hesitated. He hardly knew what to do. He had more than once borrowed a little straw from Mrs. Todd's stackyard and now he did not want to offend her.

He had a mind to order Mary out, only—putting his hand under his coat to look at his watch—he felt the Christmas present that he had purchased—the cardboard cross.

"Thee needn't sit beside her," he said coaxingly to Mrs. Todd, "though she's skin be as white and clean as any lamb's."

"We won't have no lousy breeding beggar with we," shouted Mrs. Biggs, who had taken a little too much to drink at the tavern.

"Let she alone," said Mr. Balliboy, scratching his head and wondering what he had better do.

"Thrust her out," cried Mrs. Potten, and, climbing into the van, she spat at the woman.

"Out with her," screamed Mrs. Todd. "Away with her, away with her!" cried all the women.

Now, had it not been that Mr. Balliboy had taken Mary's shilling and so made her free of his van, with the right to be carried as far as the 'Norbury Arms,' he might have performed the commands of the drunken woman and thrown Mary into the street. But, as he had taken her shilling, Mr. Balliboy bethought him of what was his own.

The woman had read his name; he had taken her fare.

A Christmas Gift

"Let she alone," said Mr. Balliboy gruffly to Mrs. Biggs, who had laid hands upon the woman.

"We'll go to John Hawkins; he'll take us home," said Mrs. Todd angrily.

Mr. Balliboy winced. He knew how glad his rival would be to welcome all his company.

"Why, what evil has she done?" Mr. Balliboy asked in a milder tone.

With one accord the women shouted out Mary's sorrow.

"Away with her, away with her!" they called.

Mr. Balliboy put his hand into his coat, but it was not his watch that he felt for this time—it was his Christmas gift.

"Away with your own selves," he said stoutly. "Thik maiden be going wi' I, for 'tis me own van."

Mr. Balliboy took his seat angrily and the women left him. He knew that what had happened that afternoon was likely to have a lasting effect upon his future. Everyone in the village would side with the women with whom he had quarreled, and the story of his kindness to Mary would not lose in the telling.

But, before very long, an accident happened that troubled Mr. Balliboy even more than the loss of his customers. In the middle of a long and lonely road his van broke down.

Mr. Balliboy tried to start the car, but with no success. Other carriers passed him by, among whom was John Hawkins, and many were the taunts and unseemly jests shouted at him by the Christmas revelers who sat therein. But soon all was silence, and the road utterly deserted, for the time was near midnight.

For some while Mr. Balliboy busied himself with the aid of the car lamps, trying to start the engine. But, all at once and without any warning, the lamps went out.

Mr. Balliboy shivered. The weather was changed, a sharp frost had set in and the stars shone brightly. Someone groaned. Mary's pains had come upon her.

"I be going," said Mr. Balliboy, "to get some help for 'ee."

Mr. Balliboy had noticed a little cottage across the moor, with a light in the window. He hurried there, but before he reached the cottage the light had vanished, and, knock as he would at the door, no one replied.

"What be I to do?" cried Mr. Balliboy anxiously, and looked up at the sky. A large and brightly shining star appeared exactly above his van.

Mr. Balliboy looked at his van and rubbed his eyes. The van was lighted up and beams of strange light seemed to emanate from it.

" 'Taint on fire, I do hope," said Mr. Balliboy. He began to run and came quickly to the car.

Mary was now resting comfortably, while two shining creatures with white wings leaned over her. Upon her lap was her newborn babe, smiling happily.

Mr. Balliboy fumbled in his coat for his Christmas gift. He stepped into the van and held out the cross to the babe.

Mary looked proudly at her infant, and the babe, delighted with the shining toy, took hold of the cross.

The angels wept.

DAPHNE DU MAURIER
Happy Christmas

THE Lawrence family lived in a large house just outside town. Mr. Lawrence was a big heavy man, with a round face and a smile. He motored into town every day to his office, where he had a roll-top desk and three secretaries. During the day he used the telephone, and had a business lunch, and then used the telephone again. He made a lot of money.

Mrs. Lawrence had fair hair and china-blue eyes. Mr. Lawrence called her Kitten, but she was not helpless. She had a lovely figure and long fingernails, and she played bridge most afternoons. Bob Lawrence was ten. He was like Mr. Lawrence, only smaller. He was fond of electric trains, and his father had got some men to fix up a miniature railway in the garden. Marigold Lawrence was seven. She was like her mother, only rounder. She had fifteen dolls. She kept breaking them somehow.

459

If you met them anywhere you would not recognize the Lawrences as being different from any other family. Perhaps that was the trouble. They were just a bit too much like all the rest. Life was a comfortable and easy thing, which was, of course, very pleasant.

On Christmas Eve the Lawrence family did much the same as every other family. Mr. Lawrence came home early from town so that he could stand around and watch the household get ready for tomorrow. He smiled more than usual and put his hands in his pockets and shouted, "Look out, you damn fool!" when he tripped over the dog who was hiding behind some evergreen. Mrs. Lawrence had cut bridge for once and was threading lanterns across the drawing room. Actually it was the garden boy who threaded the lanterns, but Mrs. Lawrence stuck little frills of colored paper round them and handed them to him, and as she was smoking all the time the smoke got in the garden boy's eyes, but he was too polite to brush it away. Bob Lawrence and Marigold Lawrence kept running around the sofas and chairs and calling out, "What am I going to have tomorrow? Am I going to have a train? Am I going to have a doll?" until Mr. Lawrence got fed up and said, "If you don't stop that row you won't get anything," but he said it in a way that did not mean much, and the children were not deceived.

It was just before the children's bedtime that Mrs. Lawrence was called to the telephone. She said "Damn!" and some more smoke got into the garden boy's eyes. Mr. Lawrence picked up a piece of evergreen and stuck it behind a picture. He whistled cheerfully.

Mrs. Lawrence was away five minutes, and when she came back her blue eyes were full of sparks and her hair was rumpled. She looked like a kitten. The kind you pick up and say "Sweet Puss!" to and then quickly put down again.

"Oh, it's a bit thick, it really is," she said, and for a moment the children thought she was going to cry.

"What the hell's the matter?" asked Mr. Lawrence.

"It's that refugee officer for the district," said Mrs. Lawrence. "You know—I told you the place was swarming with refugees.

Well, like everybody else, I had to put our names down as receivers when the thing started, never thinking seriously that anything would happen. And now it has. We've got to take in a couple, here, tonight."

Mr. Lawrence stopped smiling. "Look here," he said, "the refugee officer can't do that sort of thing to people without proper warning. Why didn't you tell him to go to blazes?"

"I did," said Mrs. Lawrence indignantly, "and all he could say was that he was very sorry, but it was the same for everybody, and people in every house were having to do it, and he said something about a 'compulsory measure,' which I did not understand, but it sounded nasty."

"They can't do it," said Mr. Lawrence, sticking out his jaw. "I'll get on the phone to someone in authority. I'll see that officer is sacked, I'll go into town myself, I'll——"

"Oh, what's the use?" said Mrs. Lawrence. "Don't let's get ourselves all heated over it. You forget it's Christmas Eve and everyone's out of town by now. Anyway, the creatures are on their way, and we can't very well lock the doors. I suppose I shall have to break it to the servants."

"What will the refugees do?" clamored the children excitedly. "Will they want to take our things? Will they want our beds?"

"Of course not," said Mrs. Lawrence sharply. "Don't be such little idiots!"

"Where are we going to put them?" asked Mr. Lawrence. "We shall have every room full as it is with the Dalys and the Collinses coming over tomorrow. You surely don't suggest we put them off now?"

"No fear," said Mrs. Lawrence, her blue eyes sparkling. "That's one comfort, we can truthfully say the house *is* full. No, the refugees can have the room over the garage. It's been very dry up to now, so the damp won't have got through. There is a bed that we turned out of the house two months ago—the springs had gone. But there's nothing wrong with it. And I think the servants have an oil stove they don't use."

Mr. Lawrence smiled. "You've got it all taped, haven't you?" he said. "No one can get the better of you, Kitten. Oh well, as long as it doesn't hurt us, I don't care." He swooped down in sudden relief and picked up Marigold. "Anyway, we won't let it spoil our Christmas, will we, honey?" he said. And he tossed Marigold in the air, and she shrieked with laughter.

"It's not fair," said Bob Lawrence, his round face flushed. "Marigold is younger than me and she wants to hang up the same size stocking. I'm eldest, I ought to have the biggest, oughtn't I?"

Mr. Lawrence rumpled his son's hair. "Be a man, Bob," he said, "and don't tease your sister. I've got something for you tomorrow better than any toy you'll find in your stocking."

Bob stopped scowling. "Is it something for my railway?" he asked eagerly.

Mr. Lawrence winked and would not answer.

Bob began to jump up and down on his bed. "My present's going to be bigger than Marigold's," he shouted in triumph, "much, much bigger."

"It's not, it's not," cried Marigold tearfully. "Mine is just as nice, isn't it, Dad?"

Mr. Lawrence called to the nurse: "Come and quieten the kids, will you? I think they're getting too excited." He laughed and went down the stairs.

Mrs. Lawrence met him halfway. "They've arrived," she said. Her voice had a warning note.

"Well?" he asked.

She shrugged her shoulders and made a little face. "Jews," she said briefly—and went into the nursery.

Mr. Lawrence said something, and then he straightened his tie and put on an expression that he considered right for refugees. It was a mixture of sternness and bravado. He went round the drive to the garage and climbed the rickety stairs.

"Ha, good evening!" he said in loud, jovial tones as he entered the room. "Are you fixed up all right?"

The room was rather dim, for the one electric-light bulb had not been dusted for many months and it hung in one corner, away from the bed and the table and the stove. The two refugees stared for a moment without speaking. The woman was sitting at the table, unpacking a basket, from which she brought a loaf of bread and two cups. The man was spreading a blanket over the bed, and when Mr. Lawrence spoke he straightened his back and turned toward him.

"We are so grateful," he said, "so very grateful."

Mr. Lawrence coughed and half laughed. "Oh, that's all right," he said. "No trouble at all."

They were Jews and no mistake. The man's nose was enormous, and his skin that typical greasy yellow. The woman had large dark eyes, with shadows beneath them. She looked unhealthy.

"Er—anything else you want?" asked Mr. Lawrence.

The woman answered this time. She shook her head. "We want nothing," she said. "We are very tired."

"Everywhere was full," said the man. "No one could take us in. It is most generous of you."

"Not at all, not at all," said Mr. Lawrence, waving his hand. "Good thing we had this room empty. You must have had a stiff time where you've been."

They said nothing to this.

"Well," said Mr. Lawrence, "if there's nothing more I can do, I'll say good night. Don't forget to turn the stove down if it smokes. And—er—if you should need more food or blankets or anything, just give a knock on the back door and ask the servants. Good night."

"Good night," they echoed, and then the woman added, "A Happy Christmas to you."

Mr. Lawrence stared. "Oh yes," he said. "Yes, of course. Thanks very much."

He turned up the collar of his coat as he walked round to the front door. It was cold. There would be a sharp frost. The gong was just sounding for dinner as he went into the hall. The garden boy had finished stringing up the lanterns, and they fluttered from the ceiling with a jaunty air. Mrs. Lawrence was mixing a drink at the table by the fire.

"Hurry up," she called over her shoulder; "dinner will be spoiled, and if there's anything I loathe it's lukewarm duck."

"Kids asleep?" asked Mr. Lawrence.

"I shouldn't think so," said Mrs. Lawrence. "It's difficult to get them to settle on Christmas Eve. I gave them both some chocolate and told them to be quiet. Want a drink?"

Later, when they were undressing for the night, Mr. Lawrence poked his head round from the dressing room, a toothbrush in his hand.

"Funny thing," he said; "that woman wished me a Happy Christmas. I never knew the Jews kept Christmas before."

"I don't suppose she knows what it means," said Mrs. Lawrence, and she patted some skin food into her round smooth cheek.

One by one the lights in the house were extinguished. The Lawrence family slept. Outside the sky was bright with stars. And in the room over the garage there was one light burning.

"I say, gosh, just look at this, I've got an airplane as well as a new engine for my railway," shouted Bob. "Look, it works like a real one. Look at the propeller."

"Have I got two things from Dad as well?" asked Marigold, fumbling feverishly among the litter of paper on her bed, and she threw aside the large doll she had just unpacked. "Nurse," she shrieked, "where's my other present from Dad?" Her cheeks were hot and flushed.

"Serves you right for being so greedy," mocked Bob. "Look what I've got."

"I'll break your silly horrid plane," said Marigold, and tears began to fall down her cheeks.

"You mustn't quarrel on Christmas Day," said Nurse, and she drew a small box triumphantly from the heap of waste paper. "Look, Marigold, what's in here?"

Marigold tore aside the paper. Soon she held a glittering necklace in her hands. "I'm a princess!" she shouted. "I'm a princess!"

Bob threw her a glance of contempt. "It's not very big," he said.

Happy Christmas

Downstairs Mr. and Mrs. Lawrence were being served with their morning tea. The electric stove was lighted, the curtains drawn, and the room was flooded with sunlight. The letters and the parcels remained unopened, though, for both Mr. and Mrs. Lawrence listened aghast to the tale that Anna, the servant, had to tell.

"I can't believe it, it's preposterous," said Mr. Lawrence.

"I can. It's just typical of the sort of thing these people do," said Mrs. Lawrence.

"Won't I give that refugee officer hell!" said Mr. Lawrence.

"I don't suppose he knew," said Mrs. Lawrence. "They took jolly good care not to let on that anything might happen. Well, we can't keep them here now, that's certain. There's no one here to look after the woman."

"We must telephone for an ambulance and have them removed," said Mr. Lawrence. "I thought the woman had a bad color. She must be pretty tough to have stood it, all alone."

"Oh, those sort of people have babies very easily," said Mrs. Lawrence. "They scarcely feel it. Well, I'm very thankful they were in the garage room and not in the house. They can't have done much damage there. And, Anna," she called, as the maid was leaving the room, "be sure and tell Nurse that the children are not to go near the garage until the ambulance has been."

Then they settled down to the letters and parcels.

"We'll make everyone laugh at the story, anyway," said Mr. Lawrence. "It will go down well with the turkey and the plum pudding."

When they had breakfasted and had dressed, and the children had been in to tumble about on the beds and show their presents, Mr. and Mrs. Lawrence went round to the garage to see what could be done about the refugees. The children were sent up to the nursery to play with their new things, because, after all, what had happened was not very nice, as Nurse agreed with Mrs. Lawrence. And besides, you never knew.

When they came to the garage they found a little crowd of servants in the yard talking. There were the cook, and the parlor man, and one of the housemaids, and the chauffeur, and even the garden boy.

"What's going on?" asked Mr. Lawrence.

"They've cleared out," said the chauffeur.

"How do you mean, cleared out?"

"The fellow went off while we were having breakfast and got hold of a taxi," said the chauffeur. "He must have gone to the stand at the end of the road. Never a word to any of us."

"And we heard wheels by the back gate," chimed in the cook, "and he and the taxi driver were lifting the woman into the car."

"The fellow asked for the name of a hospital, and we told him there was a Jewish hospital just before you get into town," said the chauffeur. "He said he was very sorry to have given us all this trouble. Cool sort of customer, hadn't turned a hair."

"And the baby. We saw the baby," giggled the housemaid, and then she blushed furiously for no reason.

"Yes," said the cook, "a proper little Jew, the image of his father."

And then they all laughed and looked at one another rather foolishly.

"Well," said Mr. Lawrence, "there's nothing more any of us can do, I suppose."

The servants melted away. The excitement for the moment was over. There was the Christmas party to prepare for, and what with one thing and another they felt they had been run off their legs already, and it was only ten o'clock.

"We'd better have a look," said Mr. Lawrence, jerking his head at the garage. Mrs. Lawrence made a face and followed him.

They climbed the rickety stairs to the little dark room in the loft. There was no sign of disorder. The bed had been placed back against the wall, and the blanket was neatly folded at the foot. The chair and table were in the usual place. The window in the room had been opened to let in the fresh morning air. The stove had been turned out. Only one thing showed that the room had been used. On the floor, beside the bed, was a glass of cold water.

Mr. Lawrence did not say anything. Mrs. Lawrence did not say anything, either. They went back to the house and into the drawing room. Mr. Lawrence wandered to the window and looked out across the garden. He could see Bob's miniature railway at the far corner. Mrs. Lawrence opened a parcel she had not seen at breakfast. Overhead, shouts and yells told that the children were either enjoying themselves or not.

"What about your golf? Weren't you meeting the others at eleven?" asked Mrs. Lawrence.

Mr. Lawrence sat down on the window seat. "I don't feel very keen," he said.

Mrs. Lawrence put back the vanity case she had just drawn from sheet after sheet of tissue paper.

"Funny," she said, "I feel sort of flat too, not a bit Christmasy."

Through the open door they could see the table in the dining room being prepared for lunch. The decorations looked fine, with the little bunches of flowers amidst the silver. Round the center was a great heap of crackers.

"I really don't know what else we could have done," said Mrs. Lawrence suddenly.

Mr. Lawrence did not answer. He arose and began walking up and down the room. Mrs. Lawrence straightened the evergreen behind a picture.

"After all, they didn't ask for anything," said Mrs. Lawrence. "The man would have said," went on Mrs. Lawrence, "if the woman had been very ill, or the baby. I'm sure they were both all right. They are so tough, that race."

Mr. Lawrence took out a cigar from his waistcoat pocket and put it back again.

"They'll be much better off in the Jewish hospital than they would have been here," said Mrs. Lawrence, "—proper nursing and everything. We couldn't possibly have coped with it. Besides, going off in a hurry like that, so independent, we did not have a chance to suggest a thing."

Mr. Lawrence picked up a book and then shut it. Mrs. Lawrence kept twisting and untwisting the belt on her dress.

"Of course," she said hurriedly, "I shall go and inquire how they are, and take fruit and things, and perhaps some warm woollies, and ask if there is anything else they want. I'd go this morning, only I have to take the children to church. . . ."

And then the door opened and the children came into the room.

"I've got my new necklace on," said Marigold. "Bob hasn't anything new to wear." She pirouetted round on her toes. "Hurry up, Mummy, we shall be late, and we shall miss seeing all the people come in."

"I hope they sing 'Hark the Herald Angels,' " said Bob. "We learned the words in school and I shan't have to look at the book. Why was Jesus born in a stable, Dad?"

"There wasn't room for them at the inn," said Mr. Lawrence.

"Why, were they refugees?" said Marigold.

Nobody answered for a moment, and then Mrs. Lawrence got up and tied her hair in front of the looking glass.

"Don't ask such silly questions, darling," she said.

Mr. Lawrence threw open the window. Across the garden came the sound of the church bells. The sun shone on the clean white frost, turning it to silver. Mr. Lawrence had a funny, puzzled look on his face.

"I wish . . ." he began, "I wish . . ." But he never finished what he was going to say, because the two cars carrying the Daly family and the Collins family drove in at the gate and up the drive, and the children with shouts of delight were running out onto the steps and calling, "Happy Christmas, Happy Christmas!"

IV

Christmas Is Home

AMERICAN STORIES OF CHRISTMAS,
CHILDHOOD, THE OLD HOME, THE BIG SNOW
AND KINDRED THEMES

*Home and hearth—those words began to chime
in his brain. Losing them, one lost Christmas.*

WALTER PRICHARD EATON:
THE MAN WHO FOUND CHRISTMAS

LOUISA MAY ALCOTT

LOUISA MAY ALCOTT

Christmas at Orchard House

I

CHRISTMAS won't be Christmas without any presents," grumbled Jo, lying on the rug.

"It's so dreadful to be poor!" sighed Meg, looking down at her old dress.

"I don't think it's fair for some girls to have plenty of pretty things, and other girls nothing at all," added little Amy, with an injured sniff.

"We've got father and mother and each other," said Beth contentedly, from her corner.

The four young faces on which the firelight shone brightened at the cheerful words, but darkened again as Jo said sadly,—

"We haven't got father, and shall not have him for a long time."

She didn't say "perhaps never," but each silently added it, thinking of father far away, where the fighting was.

Nobody spoke for a minute; then Meg said in an altered tone, "You know the reason mother proposed not having any presents this Christmas was because it is going to be a hard winter for every one; and she thinks we ought not to spend money for pleasure, when our men are suffering so in the army. We can't do much, but we can make our little sacrifices, and ought to do it gladly. But I am afraid I don't." And Meg shook her head, as she thought regretfully of all the pretty things she wanted.

"But I don't think the little we should spend would do any good. We've each got a dollar, and the army wouldn't be much helped by our giving that. I agree not to expect anything from mother or you, but I do want to buy Undine and Sintram for myself; I've wanted to so long," said Jo, who was a bookworm.

"I planned to spend mine in new music," said Beth, with a little sigh, which no one heard but the hearth brush and kettle holder.

"I shall get a nice box of Faber's drawing-pencils; I really need them," said Amy decidedly.

"Mother didn't say anything about our money, and she won't wish us to give up everything. Let's each buy what we want, and have a little fun; I'm sure we work hard enough to earn it," cried Jo, examining the heels of her shoes in a gentlemanly manner.

"I know I do—teaching those tiresome children nearly all day, when I'm longing to enjoy myself at home," began Meg, in the complaining tone again.

"You don't have half such a hard time as I do," said Jo. "How would you like to be shut up for hours with a nervous, fussy old lady, who keeps you trotting, is never satisfied, and worries you till you're ready to fly out of the window or cry?"

"It's naughty to fret; but I do think washing dishes and keeping things tidy is the worst work in the world. It makes me cross; and my hands get so stiff, I can't practise well at all"; and Beth looked at her rough hands with a sigh that anyone could hear that time.

"I don't believe any of you suffer as I do," cried Amy; "for you don't have to go to school with impertinent girls, who plague you if you don't know your lessons, and laugh at your dresses, and label your father if he isn't rich, and insult you when your nose isn't nice."

"If you mean *libel*, I'd say so, and not talk about *labels*, as if papa was a pickle bottle," advised Jo, laughing.

"I know what I mean, and you needn't be *statirical* about it. It's proper to use good words, and improve your *vocabilary*," returned Amy, with dignity.

"Don't peck at one another, children. Don't you wish we had the money papa lost when we were little, Jo? Dear me! how happy and good we'd be, if we had no worries!" said Meg, who could remember better times.

"You said, the other day, you thought we were a deal happier than the King children, for they were fighting and fretting all the time, in spite of their money."

"So I did, Beth. Well, I think we are; for, though we do have to work, we make fun for ourselves, and are a pretty jolly set, as Jo would say."

"Jo does use such slang words!" observed Amy, with a reproving look at the long figure stretched on the rug. Jo immediately sat up, put her hands in her pockets, and began to whistle.

"Don't, Jo; it's so boyish!"

"That's why I do it."

"I detest rude, unladylike girls!"

"I hate affected, niminy-piminy chits!"

" 'Birds in their little nests agree,' " sang Beth, the peacemaker, with such a funny face that both sharp voices softened to a laugh, and the "pecking" ended for that time.

"Really, girls, you are both to be blamed," said Meg, beginning to lecture in her elder-sisterly fashion. "You are old enough to leave off boyish tricks, and to behave better, Josephine. It didn't matter so much when you were a little girl; but now you are so tall, and turn up your hair, you should remember that you are a young lady."

"I'm not! and if turning up my hair makes me one, I'll wear it in two tails till I'm twenty," cried Jo, pulling off her net, and shaking down a chestnut mane. "I hate to think I've got to grow up, and be Miss March, and wear long gowns, and look as prim as a China-aster! It's bad enough to be a girl, anyway, when I like boys' games and work and manners! I can't get over my disappointment in not being a boy; and it's worse than ever now, for I'm dying to go and fight with papa, and I can only stay at home and knit, like a poky old woman!" And Jo shook the blue army sock till the needles rattled like castanets, and her ball bounded across the room.

"Poor Jo! It's too bad, but it can't be helped; so you must try to be contented with making your name boyish, and playing brother to us girls," said Beth, stroking the rough head at her knee with a hand that all the dishwashing and dusting in the world could not make ungentle in its touch.

"As for you, Amy," continued Meg, "you are altogether too particular and prim. Your airs are funny now; but you'll grow up an affected little goose, if you don't take care. I like your nice manners and refined ways of speaking, when you don't try to be elegant; but your absurd words are as bad as Jo's slang."

"If Jo is a tomboy and Amy a goose, what am I, please?" asked Beth, ready to share the lecture.

"You're a dear, and nothing else," answered Meg warmly; and no one contradicted her, for the "Mouse" was the pet of the family.

As young readers like to know "how people look," we will take this moment to give them a little sketch of the four sisters, who sat knitting away in the twilight, while the December snow fell quietly without, and the fire crackled cheerfully within. It was a comfortable old room, though the carpet was faded and the furniture very plain; for a good picture or two hung on the walls, books filled the recesses, chrysanthemums and Christmas roses bloomed in the windows, and a pleasant atmosphere of home-peace pervaded it.

Margaret, the eldest of the four, was sixteen, and very pretty, being plump and fair, with large eyes, plenty of soft, brown hair, a sweet mouth, and white hands, of which she was rather vain. Fifteen-year-old Jo was very tall, thin, and brown, and reminded one of a colt; for she never seemed to know what to do with her long limbs,

474

which were very much in her way. She had a decided mouth, a comical nose, and sharp, gray eyes, which appeared to see everything, and were by turns fierce, funny, or thoughtful. Her long, thick hair was her one beauty; but it was usually bundled into a net, to be out of her way. Round shoulders had Jo, big hands and feet, a fly-away look to her clothes, and the uncomfortable appearance of a girl who was rapidly shooting up into a woman, and didn't like it. Elizabeth—or Beth, as everyone called her—was a rosy, smooth-haired, bright-eyed girl of thirteen, with a shy manner, a timid voice, and a peaceful expression, which was seldom disturbed. Her father called her "Little Tranquillity," and the name suited her excellently; for she seemed to live in a happy world of her own, only venturing out to meet the few whom she trusted and loved. Amy, though the youngest, was a most important person—in her own opinion at least. A regular snow-maiden, with blue eyes, and yellow hair, curling on her shoulders, pale and slender, and always carrying herself like a young lady mindful of her manners. What the characters of the four sisters were we will leave to be found out.

The clock struck six; and, having swept up the hearth, Beth put a pair of slippers down to warm. Somehow the sight of the old shoes had a good effect upon the girls; for mother was coming, and everyone brightened to welcome her. Meg stopped lecturing, and lighted the lamp. Amy got out of the easy chair without being asked, and Jo forgot how tired she was as she sat up to hold the slippers nearer to the blaze.

"They are quite worn out; Marmee must have a new pair."

"I thought I'd get her some with my dollar," said Beth.

"No, I shall!" cried Amy.

"I'm the oldest," began Meg, but Jo cut in with a decided—
"I'm the man of the family now papa is away, and I shall provide the slippers, for he told me to take special care of mother while he was gone."

"I .i tell you what we'll do," said Beth; "let's each get her something for Christmas, and not get anything for ourselves."

"That's like you, dear! What will we get?" exclaimed Jo.

Everyone thought soberly for a minute; then Meg announced, as if the idea was suggested by the sight of her own pretty hands, "I shall give her a nice pair of gloves."

"Army shoes, best to be had," cried Jo.

"Some handkerchiefs, all hemmed," said Beth.

"I'll get a little bottle of cologne; she likes it, and it won't cost much, so I'll have some left to buy my pencils," added Amy.

"How will we give the things?" asked Meg.

"Put them on the table, and bring her in and see her open the bundles. Don't you remember how we used to do on our birthdays?" answered Jo.

"I used to be so frightened when it was my turn to sit in the big chair with the crown on, and see you all come marching round to give the presents, with a kiss. I liked the things and the kisses, but it was dreadful to have you sit looking at me while I opened the bundles," said Beth, who was toasting her face and the bread for tea, at the same time.

"Let Marmee think we are getting things for ourselves, and then surprise her. We must go shopping tomorrow afternoon, Meg; there is so much to do about the play for Christmas night," said Jo, marching up and down, with her hands behind her back and her nose in the air.

"I don't mean to act any more after this time; I'm getting too old for such things," observed Meg, who was as much a child as ever about "dressing-up" frolics.

"You won't stop, I know, as long as you can trail round in a white gown with your hair down, and wear gold-paper jewelry. You are the best actress we've got, and there'll be an end of everything if you quit the boards," said Jo. "We ought to rehearse tonight. Come here, Amy, and do the fainting scene, for you are as stiff as a poker in that."

"I can't help it; I never saw anyone faint, and I don't choose to make myself all black and blue, tumbling flat as you do. Iı I can go down easily, I'll drop; if I can't, I shall fall into a chair and be graceful; I don't care if Hugo does come at me with a pistol," returned Amy, who was not gifted with dramatic power, but was chosen because she was small enough to be borne out shrieking by the villain of the piece.

"Do it this way; clasp your hands so, and stagger across the room, crying frantically, 'Roderigo! save me! save me!' " and away went Jo, with a melodramatic scream which was truly thrilling.

Amy followed, but she poked her hands out stiffly before her, and jerked herself along as if she went by machinery; and her "Ow!" was more suggestive of pins being run into her than of fear and anguish. Jo gave a despairing groan, and Meg laughed outright, while Beth let her bread burn as she watched the fun, with interest.

"It's no use! Do the best you can when the time comes, and if the audience laughs, don't blame me. Come on, Meg."

Then things went smoothly, for Don Pedro defied the world in a speech of two pages without a single break; Hagar, the witch, chanted an awful incantation over her kettleful of simmering toads, with weird effect; Roderigo rent his chains asunder manfully, and Hugo died in agonies of remorse and arsenic, with a wild "Ha! ha!"

"It's the best we've had yet," said Meg, as the dead villain sat up and rubbed his elbows.

"I don't see how you can write and act such splendid things, Jo. You're a regular Shakespeare!" exclaimed Beth, who firmly believed that her sisters were gifted with wonderful genius in all things.

"Not quite," replied Jo modestly. "I do think, 'The Witch's Curse, an Operatic Tragedy' is rather a nice thing; but I'd like to try 'Macbeth,' if we only had a trap door for Banquo. I always wanted to do the killing part. 'Is that a dagger that I see before me?' " muttered Jo, rolling her eyes and clutching at the air, as she had seen a famous tragedian do.

"No, it's the toasting fork, with mother's shoe on it instead of the bread. Beth's stage-struck!" cried Meg, and the rehearsal ended in a general burst of laughter.

II

Jo was the first to wake in the gray dawn of Christmas morning. No stockings hung at the fireplace, and for a moment she felt as much disappointed as she did long ago, when her little sock fell down because it was so crammed with goodies. Then she remembered her mother's promise, and, slipping her hand under her pillow, drew out a little crimson-covered book. She knew it very well, for it was that beautiful old story of the best life ever lived, and Jo felt that it was a true guidebook for any pilgrim going the long journey. She woke Meg with a "Merry Christmas," and bade her see what was under her pillow. A green-covered book appeared, with the same picture inside, and a few words written by their mother, which made their one present very precious in their eyes. Presently Beth and Amy woke, to rummage and find their little books also— one dove-colored, the other blue; and all sat looking at and talking about them, while the east grew rosy with the coming day. In spite of her small vanities, Margaret had a sweet and pious nature, which unconsciously influenced her sisters, especially Jo, who loved her very tenderly, and obeyed her because her advice was so gently given.

"Girls," said Meg seriously, looking from the tumbled head beside her to the two little night-capped ones in the room beyond, "mother wants us to read and love and mind these books, and we must begin at once. We used to be faithful about it; but since father went away, and all this war trouble unsettled us, we have neglected many things. You can do as you please; but I shall keep my book on the table here, and read a little every morning as soon as I wake, for I know it will do me good, and help me through the day."

Then she opened her new book and began to read. Jo put her arm round her, and, leaning cheek to cheek, read also, with the quiet expression so seldom seen on her restless face.

"How good Meg is! Come, Amy, let's do as they do. I'll help you with the hard words, and they'll explain things if we don't understand," whispered Beth, very much impressed by the pretty books and her sisters' example.

478

"I'm glad mine is blue," said Amy; and then the rooms were very still while the pages were softly turned, and the winter sunshine crept in to touch the bright heads and serious faces with a Christmas greeting.

"Where is mother?" asked Meg, as she and Jo ran down to thank her for their gifts, half an hour later.

"Goodness only knows. Some poor creeter come a-beggin', and your ma went straight off to see what was needed. There never was such a woman for givin' away vittles and drink, clothes and firin'," replied Hannah, who had lived with the family since Meg was born, and was considered by them all more as a friend than a servant.

"She will be back soon, I think; so fry your cakes, and have everything ready," said Meg, looking over the presents which were collected in a basket and kept under the sofa, ready to be produced at the proper time. "Why, where is Amy's bottle of cologne?" she added, as the little flask did not appear.

"She took it out a minute ago, and went off with it to put a ribbon on it, or some such notion," replied Jo, dancing about the room to take the first stiffness off the new army slippers.

"How nice my handkerchiefs look, don't they? Hannah washed and ironed them for me, and I marked them all myself," said Beth, looking proudly at the somewhat uneven letters which had cost her such labor.

"Bless the child! she's gone and put 'Mother' on them instead of 'M. March.' How funny!" cried Jo, taking up one.

"Isn't it right? I thought it was better to do it so, because Meg's initials are 'M.M.,' and I don't want anyone to use these but Marmee," said Beth, looking troubled.

"It's all right, dear, and a very pretty idea—quite sensible, too, for no one can ever mistake now. It will please her very much, I know," said Meg, with a frown for Jo and a smile for Beth.

"There's mother. Hide the basket, quick!" cried Jo, as a door slammed, and steps sounded in the hall.

Amy came in hastily, and looked rather abashed when she saw her sisters all waiting for her.

"Where have you been, and what are you hiding behind you?" asked Meg, surprised to see, by her hood and cloak, that lazy Amy had been out so early.

"Don't laugh at me, Jo! I didn't mean anyone should know till the time came. I only meant to change the little bottle for a big one, and I gave *all* my money to get it, and I'm truly trying not to be selfish any more."

As she spoke, Amy showed the handsome flask which replaced the cheap one; and looked so earnest and humble in her little effort to forget herself that Meg hugged her on the spot, and Jo pronounced her "a trump," while Beth ran to the window, and picked her finest rose to ornament the stately bottle.

"You see I felt ashamed of my present, after reading and talking about being good this morning, so I ran round the corner and changed it the minute I was up: and I'm *so* glad, for mine is the handsomest now."

Another bang of the street door sent the basket under the sofa, and the girls to the table, eager for breakfast.

"Merry Christmas, Marmee! Many of them! Thank you for our books; we read some, and mean to every day," they cried, in chorus.

"Merry Christmas, little daughters! I'm glad you began at once, and hope you will keep on. But I want to say one word before we sit down. Not far away from here lies a poor woman with a little newborn baby. Six children are huddled into one bed to keep from freezing, for they have no fire. There is nothing to eat over there; and the oldest boy came to tell me they were suffering hunger and cold. My girls, will you give them your breakfast as a Christmas present?"

They were all unusually hungry, having waited nearly an hour, and for a minute no one spoke; only a minute, for Jo exclaimed impetuously, "I'm so glad you came before we began!"

"May I go and help carry the things to the poor little children?" asked Beth eagerly.

"*I* shall take the cream and the muffins," added Amy, heroically giving up the articles she most liked.

Meg was already covering the buckwheats, and piling the bread into one big plate.

"I thought you'd do it," said Mrs. March, smiling as if satisfied. "You shall all go and help me, and when we come back we will have bread and milk for breakfast, and make it up at dinnertime."

They were soon ready, and the procession set out. Fortunately it was early, and they went through back streets, so few people saw them, and no one laughed at the queer party.

A poor, bare, miserable room it was, with broken windows, no fire, ragged bedclothes, a sick mother, wailing baby, and a group of pale, hungry children cuddled under one old quilt, trying to keep warm.

How the big eyes stared and the blue lips smiled as the girls went in!

"Ach, mein Gott! it is good angels come to us!" said the poor woman, crying for joy.

"Funny angels in hoods and mittens," said Jo, and set them laughing.

In a few minutes it really did seem as if kind spirits had been at work there. Hannah, who had carried wood, made a fire, and stopped up the broken panes with old hats and her own cloak. Mrs. March gave the mother tea and gruel, and comforted her with promises of help, while she dressed the little baby as tenderly as if it had been her own. The girls, meantime, spread the table, set the children round the fire, and fed them like so many hungry birds—laughing, talking, and trying to understand the funny broken English.

"Das ist gut!" "Die Engel-kinder!" cried the poor things, as they ate, and warmed their purple hands at the comfortable blaze.

The girls had never been called angel children before, and thought it very agreeable, especially Jo, who had been considered a "Sancho" ever since she was born. That was a very happy breakfast, though they didn't get any of it; and when they went away, leaving comfort behind, I think there were not in all the city four merrier people than the hungry little girls who gave away their breakfasts and contented themselves with bread and milk on Christmas morning.

"That's loving our neighbor better than ourselves, and I like it," said Meg, as they set out their presents, while their mother was upstairs collecting clothes for the poor Hummels.

Not a very splendid show, but there was a great deal of love done up in the few little bundles; and the tall vase of red roses, white chrysanthemums, and trailing vines, which stood in the middle, gave quite an elegant air to the table.

"She's coming! Strike up, Beth! Open the door, Amy! Three cheers for Marmee!" cried Jo, prancing about, while Meg went to conduct mother to the seat of honor.

Beth played her gayest march, Amy threw open the door, and Meg enacted escort with great dignity. Mrs. March was both surprised and touched; and smiled with her eyes full as she examined her presents, and read the little notes which accompanied them. The slippers went on at once, a new handkerchief was slipped into her pocket, well scented with Amy's cologne, the rose was fastened in her bosom, and the nice gloves were pronounced a "perfect fit."

There was a good deal of laughing and kissing and explaining, in the simple, loving fashion which makes these home-festivals so pleasant at the time, so sweet to remember long afterward, and then all fell to work.

The Birds' Christmas Carol

I: *A Little Snow Bird*

IT was very early Christmas morning, and in the stillness of the dawn, with the soft snow falling on the housetops, a little child was born in the Bird household. They had intended to name the baby Lucy, if it were a girl; but they had not expected her on Christmas morning, and a real Christmas baby was not to be lightly named—the whole family agreed in that.

They were consulting about it in the nursery. Mr. Bird said that he had assisted in naming the three boys, and that he should leave this matter entirely to Mrs. Bird; Donald wanted the child called "Dorothy," after a pretty, curly-haired girl who sat next him in school; Paul chose "Luella," for Luella was the nurse who had been with him during his whole babyhood, up to the time of his first trousers, and the name suggested all sorts of comfortable things. Uncle Jack said that the first girl should always be named for her mother, no matter how hideous the name happened to be.

Grandma said that she would prefer not to take any part in the discussion, and everybody suddenly remembered that Mrs. Bird had thought of naming the baby Lucy, for Grandma herself; and, while it would be indelicate for her to favor that name, it would be against human nature for her to suggest any other, under the circumstances.

Hugh, the "hitherto baby," if that is a possible term, sat in one corner and said nothing, but felt, in some mysterious way, that his nose was out of joint; for there was a newer baby now, a possibility he had never taken into consideration; and the "first girl," too — a still higher development of treason, which made him actually green with jealousy.

But it was too profound a subject to be settled then and there, on the spot; besides, Mamma had not been asked, and everybody felt it rather absurd, after all, to forestall a decree that was certain to be absolutely wise, just, and perfect.

The reason that the subject had been brought up at all so early in the day lay in the fact that Mrs. Bird never allowed her babies to go over night unnamed. She was a person of so great decision of character that she would have blushed at such a thing; she said that to let blessed babies go dangling and dawdling about without names, for months and months, was enough to ruin them for life. She also said that if one could not make up one's mind in twenty-four hours it was a sign that—— But I will not repeat the rest, as it might prejudice you against the most charming woman in the world.

So Donald took his new velocipede and went out to ride up and down the stone pavement and notch the shins of innocent people as they passed by, while Paul spun his musical top on the front steps.

But Hugh refused to leave the scene of action. He seated himself on the top stair in the hall, banged his head against the railing a few times, just by way of uncorking the vials of his wrath, and then subsided into gloomy silence, waiting to declare war if more "first girl babies" were thrust upon a family already surfeited with that unnecessary article.

Meanwhile dear Mrs. Bird lay in her room, weak, but safe and happy, with her sweet girl baby by her side and the heaven of motherhood opening again before her. Nurse was making gruel in the kitchen, and the room was dim and quiet. There was a cheerful open fire in the grate, but though the shutters were closed, the side windows that looked out on the Church of Our Saviour, next door, were a little open.

Suddenly a sound of music poured out into the bright air and drifted into the chamber. It was the boy choir singing Christmas anthems. Higher and higher rose the clear, fresh voices, full of hope and cheer, as children's voices always are. Fuller and fuller grew the burst of melody as one glad strain fell upon another in joyful harmony:

> "Carol, brothers, carol,
> Carol joyfully,
> Carol the good tidings,
> Carol merrily!
> And pray a gladsome Christmas
> For all your fellow-men:
> Carol, brothers, carol,
> Christmas Day again."

One verse followed another, always with the same sweet refrain:

> "And pray a gladsome Christmas
> For all your fellow-men:
> Carol, brothers, carol,
> Christmas Day again."

Mrs. Bird thought, as the music floated in upon her gentle sleep, that she had slipped into heaven with her new baby, and that the angels were bidding them welcome. But the tiny bundle by her

485

side stirred a little, and though it was scarcely more than the ruffling of a feather, she awoke; for the mother-ear is so close to the heart that it can hear the faintest whisper of a child.

She opened her eyes and drew the baby closer. It looked like a rose dipped in milk, she thought, this pink and white blossom of girlhood, or like a pink cherub, with its halo of pale yellow hair, finer than floss silk.

> *"Carol, brothers, carol,*
> *Carol joyfully,*
> *Carol the good tidings,*
> *Carol merrily!"*

The voices were brimming over with joy.

"Why, my baby," whispered Mrs. Bird in soft surprise, "I had forgotten what day it was. You are a little Christmas child, and we will name you 'Carol'—mother's Christmas Carol!"

"What!" said Mr. Bird, coming in softly and closing the door behind him.

"Why, Donald, don't you think 'Carol' is a sweet name for a Christmas baby? It came to me just a moment ago in the singing, as I was lying here half asleep and half awake."

"I think it is a charming name, dear heart, and sounds just like you, and I hope that, being a girl, this baby has some chance of being as lovely as her mother";—at which speech from the baby's papa, Mrs. Bird, though she was as weak and tired as she could be, blushed with happiness.

And so Carol came by her name.

Of course, it was thought foolish by many people, though Uncle Jack declared laughingly that it was very strange if a whole family of Birds could not be indulged in a single Carol; and Grandma, who adored the child, thought the name much more appropriate than Lucy, but was glad that people would probably think it short for Caroline.

Perhaps because she was born in holiday time, Carol was a very happy baby. Of course, she was too tiny to understand the joy of

486

Christmas-tide, but people say there is everything in a good beginning, and she may have breathed in unconsciously the fragrance of evergreens and holiday dinners; while the peals of sleigh-bells and the laughter of happy children may have fallen upon her baby ears and wakened in them a glad surprise at the merry world she had come to live in.

Her cheeks and lips were as red as holly-berries; her hair was for all the world the color of a Christmas candle-flame; her eyes were bright as stars; her laugh like a chime of Christmas-bells, and her tiny hands forever outstretched in giving.

Such a generous little creature you never saw! A spoonful of bread and milk had always to be taken by Mamma or nurse before Carol could enjoy her supper; whatever bit of cake or sweetmeat found its way into her pretty fingers was straightway broken in half to be shared with Donald, Paul, or Hugh; and when they made believe nibble the morsel with affected enjoyment, she would clap her hands and crow with delight.

"Why does she do it?" asked Donald thoughtfully. "None of us boys ever did."

"I hardly know," said Mamma, catching her darling to her heart, "except that she is a little Christmas child, and so she has a tiny share of the blessedest birthday the world ever knew!"

II: *Drooping Wings*

It was December, ten years later. Carol had seen nine Christmas trees lighted on her birthdays, one after another; nine times she had assisted in the holiday festivities of the household, though in her babyhood her share of the gayeties was somewhat limited.

For five years, certainly, she had hidden presents for Mamma and Papa in their own bureau drawers, and harbored a number of secrets sufficiently large to burst a baby brain, had it not been for the relief gained by whispering them all to Mamma, at night, when she was in her crib, a proceeding which did not in the least lessen the value of a secret in her innocent mind.

487

For five years she had heard "'Twas the night before Christmas," and hung up a scarlet stocking many sizes too large for her, and pinned a sprig of holly on her little white nightgown, to show Santa Claus that she was a "truly" Christmas child, and dreamed of fur-coated saints and toy-packs and reindeer, and wished everybody a "Merry Christmas" before it was light in the morning, and lent every one of her new toys to the neighbors' children before noon, and eaten turkey and plum-pudding, and gone to bed at night in a trance of happiness at the day's pleasures.

Donald was away at college now. Paul and Hugh were great manly fellows, taller than their mother. Papa Bird had gray hairs in his whiskers; and Grandma, God bless her, had been four Christmases in heaven.

But Christmas in the Birds' Nest was scarcely as merry now as it used to be in the bygone years, for the little child, that once brought such an added blessing to the day, lay month after month a patient, helpless invalid, in the room where she was born. She had never been very strong in body, and it was with a pang of terror her mother and father noticed, soon after she was five years old, that she began to limp, ever so slightly; to complain too often of weariness, and to nestle close to her mother, saying she "would rather not go out to play, please." The illness was slight at first, and hope was always stirring in Mrs. Bird's heart. "Carol would feel stronger in the summer-time"; or, "She would be better when she had spent a year in the country"; or, "She would outgrow it"; or, "They would try a new physician"; but by and by it came to be all too sure that no physician save One could make Carol strong again, and that no "summer-time" nor "country air," unless it were the everlasting summer-time in a heavenly country, could bring back the little girl to health.

The cheeks and lips that were once as red as holly-berries faded to faint pink; the star-like eyes grew softer, for they often gleamed through tears; and the gay child-laugh, that had been like a chime of Christmas bells, gave place to a smile so lovely, so touching, so tender and patient, that it filled every corner of the house with a gentle radiance that might have come from the face of the Christ-child himself.

Love could do nothing; and when we have said that we have said all, for it is stronger than anything else in the whole wide world. Mr. and Mrs. Bird were talking it over one evening, when all the children were asleep. A famous physician had visited them that day, and told them that some time, it might be in one year, it might be in more, Carol would slip quietly off into heaven, whence she came.

"It is no use to close our eyes to it any longer," said Mr. Bird, as he paced up and down the library floor; "Carol will never be well again. It almost seems as if I could not bear it when I think of that loveliest child doomed to lie there day after day, and, what is still more, to suffer pain that we are helpless to keep away from her. Merry Christmas, indeed; it gets to be the saddest day in the year to me!" and poor Mr. Bird sank into a chair by the table, and buried his face in his hands to keep his wife from seeing the tears that would come in spite of all his efforts.

"But, Donald, dear," said sweet Mrs. Bird, with trembling voice, "Christmas Day may not be so merry with us as it used, but it is very happy, and that is better, and very blessed, and that is better yet. I suffer chiefly for Carol's sake, but I have almost given up being sorrowful for my own. I am too happy in the child, and I see too clearly what she has done for us and the other children. Donald and Paul and Hugh were three strong, willful, boisterous boys, but now you seldom see such tenderness, devotion, thought for others, and self-denial in lads of their years. A quarrel or a hot word is almost unknown in this house, and why? Carol would hear it, and it would distress her, she is so full of love and goodness. The boys study with all their might and main. Why? Partly, at least, because they like to teach Carol, and amuse her by telling her what they read. When the seamstress comes, she likes to sew in Miss Carol's room, because there she forgets her own troubles, which, heaven knows, are sore enough! And as for me, Donald, I am a better woman every day for Carol's sake; I have to be her eyes, ears, feet, hands—her strength, her hope; and she, my own little child, is my example!"

"I was wrong, dear heart," said Mr. Bird more cheerfully; "we will try not to repine, but to rejoice instead, that we have an 'angel of the house.'"

"And as for her future," Mrs. Bird went on, "I think we need not be over-anxious. I feel as if she did not belong altogether to us, but that when she has done what God sent her for, He will take her back to Himself—and it may not be very long!" Here it was poor Mrs. Bird's turn to break down, and Mr. Bird's turn to comfort her.

III: The Birds' Nest

CAROL herself knew nothing of motherly tears and fatherly anxieties; she lived on peacefully in the room where she was born.

But you never would have known that room; for Mr. Bird had a great deal of money, and though he felt sometimes as if he wanted to throw it all in the sea, since it could not buy a strong body for his little girl, yet he was glad to make the place she lived in just as beautiful as it could be.

The room had been extended by the building of a large addition that hung out over the garden below, and was so filled with windows that it might have been a conservatory. The ones on the side were thus still nearer the Church of Our Saviour than they used to be; those in front looked out on the beautiful harbor, and those in the back commanded a view of nothing in particular but a narrow alley; nevertheless, they were pleasantest of all to Carol, for the Ruggles family lived in the alley, and the nine little, middle-sized, and big Ruggles children were a source of inexhaustible interest.

The shutters could all be opened and Carol could take a real sun-bath in this lovely glass house, or they could all be closed when the dear head ached or the dear eyes were tired. The carpet was of soft gray, with clusters of green bay and holly leaves. The furniture was of white wood, on which an artist had painted snow scenes and Christmas trees and groups of merry children ringing bells and singing carols.

The Birds' Christmas Carol

Donald had made a pretty, polished shelf, and screwed it on the outside of the foot-board, and the boys always kept this full of blooming plants, which they changed from time to time; the head-board, too, had a bracket on either side, where there were pots of maiden-hair ferns.

Love-birds and canaries hung in their golden houses in the windows, and they, poor caged things, could hop as far from their wooden perches as Carol could venture from her little white bed.

On one side of the room was a bookcase filled with hundreds — yes, I mean it — with hundreds and hundreds of books; books with gay-colored pictures, books without; books with black and white outline sketches, books with none at all; books with verses, books with stories; books that made children laugh, and some, only a few, that made them cry; books with words of one syllable for tiny boys and girls, and books with words of fearful length to puzzle wise ones.

This was Carol's "Circulating Library." Every Saturday she chose ten books, jotting their names down in a diary; into these she slipped cards that said:

> "Please keep this book two weeks and read it. With love,
> CAROL BIRD."

Then Mrs. Bird stepped into her carriage and took the ten books to the Children's Hospital, and brought home ten others that she had left there the fortnight before.

This was a source of great happiness; for some of the Hospital children that were old enough to print or write, and were strong enough to do it, wrote Carol sweet little letters about the books, and she answered them, and they grew to be friends. (It is very funny, but you do not always have to see people to love them. Just think about it, and tell me if it isn't so.)

There was a high wainscoting of wood about the room, and on top of this, in a narrow gilt framework, ran a row of illuminated pictures, illustrating fairy tales, all in dull blue and gold and scarlet and silver. From the door to the closet there was the story of "The Fair One with Golden Locks"; from closet to bookcase, ran "Puss in Boots"; from bookcase to fireplace, was "Jack the Giant-killer"; and on the other side of the room were "Hop o' my Thumb," "The Sleeping Beauty," and "Cinderella."

Then there was a great closet full of beautiful things to wear, but they were all dressing-gowns and slippers and shawls; and there were drawers full of toys and games, but they were such as you could play with on your lap. There were no ninepins, nor balls, nor bows and arrows, nor bean bags, nor tennis rackets; but, after all, other children needed these more than Carol Bird, for she was always happy and contented, whatever she had or whatever she lacked; and after the room had been made so lovely for her, on her eighth Christmas, she always called herself, in fun, a "Bird of Paradise."

On these particular December days she was happier than usual, for Uncle Jack was coming from England to spend the holidays. Dear, funny, jolly, loving, wise Uncle Jack, who came every two or three years, and brought so much joy with him that the world looked as black as a thunder-cloud for a week after he went away again.

The mail had brought this letter:

London, November 28, 188–.

Wish you merry Christmas, you dearest birdlings in America! Preen your feathers, and stretch the Birds' nest a trifle, if you please, and let Uncle Jack in for the holidays. I am coming with such a trunk full of treasures that you'll have to borrow the stockings of Barnum's Giant and Giantess; I am coming to squeeze a certain little lady-bird until she cries for mercy; I am coming to see if I can find a boy to take care of a black pony that I bought lately. It's the strangest thing I ever knew; I've hunted all over Europe, and can't find a boy to suit me! I'll tell you why. I've set my heart on finding one with a dimple in his chin, because this pony particularly likes dimples! ["Hurrah!" cried Hugh; "bless my dear dimple; I'll never be ashamed of it again."]

Please drop a note to the clerk of the weather, and have a good, rousing snow-storm — say on the twenty-second. None of your meek, gentle, nonsensical, shilly-shallying snow-storms; not the sort where the flakes float lazily down from the sky as if they didn't care whether they ever got here or not and then melt away as soon as they touch the earth, but a regular business-like whizzing, whirring, blurring, cutting snow-storm, warranted to freeze and stay on!

I should like rather a LARGE Christmas tree, if it's convenient: not one of those "sprigs," five or six feet high, that you used to have three or four years ago, when the birdlings were not fairly feathered out; but a tree of some size. Set it up in the garret, if necessary, and then we can cut a hole in the roof if the tree chances to be too high for the room.

Tell Bridget to begin to fatten a turkey. Tell her that by the twentieth of December that turkey must not be able to stand on its legs for fat, and then on the next three days she must allow it to recline easily on its side, and stuff it to bursting. (One ounce of stuffing beforehand is worth a pound afterwards.)

The pudding must be unusually huge, and darkly, deeply, lugubriously blue in color. It must be stuck so full of plums that the pudding itself will ooze out into the pan and not be brought on to the table at all. I expect to be there by the twentieth, to manage these little things myself—remembering it is the early Bird that catches the worm—but give you the instructions in case I should be delayed.

And Carol must decide on the size of the tree—she knows best, she was a Christmas child; and she must plead for the snow-storm—the "clerk of the weather" may pay some attention to her; and she must look up the boy with the dimple for me—she's likelier to find him than I am, this minute. She must advise about the turkey, and Bridget must bring the pudding to her bedside and let her drop every separate plum into it and stir it once for luck, or I'll not eat a single slice—for Carol is the dearest part of Christmas to Uncle Jack, and he'll have none of it without her. She is better than all the turkeys and puddings and apples and spare-ribs and wreaths and garlands and mistletoe and stockings and chimneys and sleigh-bells in Christendom! She is the very sweetest Christmas Carol that was ever written, said, sung, or chanted, and I am coming as fast as ships and railway trains can carry me, to tell her so.

Carol's joy knew no bounds. Mr. and Mrs. Bird laughed like children and kissed each other for sheer delight, and when the boys heard it they simply whooped like wild Indians; until the Ruggles family, whose back yard joined their garden, gathered at the door and wondered what was "up" in the big house.

IV: *"Birds of a Feather Flock Together"*

UNCLE JACK did really come on the twentieth. He was not detained by business, nor did he get left behind nor snowed up, as frequently happens in stories, and in real life too, I am afraid. The snowstorm came also; and the turkey nearly died a natural and premature death from overeating. Donald came, too; Donald, with a line of down upon his upper lip, and Greek and Latin on his tongue, and stores of knowledge in his handsome head, and stories—bless me, you couldn't turn over a chip without reminding Donald of something that happened "at College." One or the other was always at Carol's bedside, for they fancied her paler than she used to be, and they could not bear her out of sight. It was Uncle Jack, though, who sat beside her in the winter twilights. The room was quiet, and almost dark, save for the snow-light outside, and the flickering flame of the fire, that danced over the "Sleeping Beauty's" face and touched the Fair One's golden locks with ruddier glory. Carol's hand (all too thin and white these latter days) lay close clasped in Uncle Jack's, and they talked together quietly of many, many things.

"I want to tell you all about my plans for Christmas this year, Uncle Jack," said Carol, on the first evening of his visit, "because it will be the loveliest one I ever had. The boys laugh at me for caring so much about it; but it isn't altogether because it is Christmas, nor because it is my birthday; but long, long ago, when I first began to be ill, I used to think, the first thing when I waked on Christmas morning, 'Today is Christ's birthday—and mine!' I did not put the words close together, you know, because that made it seem too bold; but I first said, 'Christ's birthday,' out loud, and then, in a minute, softly to myself—'*and mine!*' 'Christ's birthday—*and mine!*' And so I do not quite feel about Christmas as other girls do. Mamma says she supposes that ever so many other children have been born on that day. I often wonder where they are, Uncle Jack, and whether it is a dear thought to them, too, or whether I am so much in bed, and so often alone, that it means more to me. Oh, I do hope that none of them are poor, or cold, or hungry; and I wish—I wish they were all as happy as I, because they are really my little brothers and sisters. Now, Uncle Jack dear, I am going to try and make somebody happy every single Christmas that I live, and this year it is to be the 'Ruggleses in the rear.' "

"That large and interesting brood of children in the little house at the end of the back garden?"

"Yes; isn't it nice to see so many together?—and, Uncle Jack, why do the big families always live in the small houses, and the small families in the big houses? We ought to call them the Ruggles children, of course; but Donald began talking of them as the 'Ruggleses in the rear,' and Papa and Mamma took it up, and now we cannot seem to help it. The house was built for Mr. Carter's coachman, but Mr. Carter lives in Europe, and the gentleman who rents his place for him doesn't care what happens to it, and so this poor family came to live there. When they first moved in, I used to sit in my window and watch them play in their back yard; they are so strong, and jolly, and good-natured—and then, one day, I had a terrible headache, and Donald asked them if they would please not scream quite so loud, and they explained that they were having a game of circus, but that they would change and play 'Deaf and Dumb Asylum' all the afternoon."

"Ha, ha, ha!" laughed Uncle Jack, "what an obliging family, to be sure!"

"Yes, we all thought it very funny, and I smiled at them from the window when I was well enough to be up again. Now, Sarah Maud comes to her door when the children come home from school, and if Mamma nods her head, 'Yes,' that means 'Carol is very well,' and then you ought to hear the little Ruggleses yell—I believe they try to see how much noise they can make; but if Mamma shakes her head, 'No,' they always play at quiet games. Then, one day, 'Cary,' my pet canary, flew out of her cage, and Peter Ruggles caught her and brought her back, and I had him up here in my room to thank him."

"Is Peter the oldest?"

"No; Sarah Maud is the oldest—she helps do the washing; and Peter is the next. He is a dressmaker's boy."

"And which is the pretty little red-haired girl?"

"That's Kitty."

"And the fat youngster?"

"Baby Larry."

"And that—most freckled one?"

"Now, don't laugh—that's Peoria."

"Carol, you are joking."

"No, really, Uncle dear. She was born in Peoria; that's all."

"And is the next boy Oshkosh?"

"No," laughed Carol, "the others are Susan, and Clement, and Eily, and Cornelius; they all look exactly alike, except that some of them have more freckles than the others."

"How did you ever learn all their names?"

"Why, I have what I call a 'window-school.' It is too cold now; but in warm weather I am wheeled out on my balcony, and the Ruggleses climb up and walk along our garden fence, and sit on the roof of our carriage-house. That brings them quite near, and I tell them stories. On Thanksgiving Day they came up for a few minutes —it was quite warm at eleven o'clock—and we told each other what we had to be thankful for; but they gave such queer answers that Papa had to run away for fear of laughing; and I couldn't understand them very well. Susan was thankful for 'trunks,' of all things in the world; Cornelius, for 'horse-cars'; Kitty, for 'pork steak'; while Clem, who is very quiet, brightened up when I came to him, and said he was thankful for 'his lame puppy.' Wasn't that pretty?"

"It might teach some of us a lesson, mightn't it, little girl?"

"That's what Mamma said. Now I'm going to give this whole Christmas to the Ruggleses; and, Uncle Jack, I earned part of the money myself."

"You, my bird; how?"

"Well, you see, it could not be my own, own Christmas if Papa gave me all the money, and I thought to really keep Christ's birthday I ought to do something of my very own; and so I talked with Mamma. Of course she thought of something lovely; she always does: Mamma's head is just brimming over with lovely thoughts— all I have to do is ask, and out pops the very one I want. This thought was to let her write down, just as I told her, a description of how a child lived in her own room for three years, and what she did to amuse herself; and we sent it to a magazine and got twenty-five dollars for it. Just think!"

"Well, well," cried Uncle Jack, "my little girl a real author! And what are you going to do with this wonderful 'own' money of yours?"

"I shall give the nine Ruggleses a grand Christmas dinner here in this very room—that will be Papa's contribution—and afterwards a beautiful Christmas tree, fairly blooming with presents— that will be my part; for I have another way of adding to my twenty-five dollars, so that I can buy nearly anything I choose. I should like it very much if you would sit at the head of the table, Uncle Jack, for nobody could ever be frightened of you, you dearest, dearest, dearest thing that ever was! Mamma is going to help us, but Papa and the boys are going to eat together downstairs for fear of making the little Ruggleses shy; and after we've had a merry time with the tree we can open my window and all listen together to the music at the evening church-service, if it comes before the children go. I have written a letter to the organist, and asked him if I might have the two songs I like best. Will you see if it is all right?"

Birds' Nest, December 21, 188–.

DEAR MR. WILKIE—I am the little girl who lives next door to the church, and, as I seldom go out, the music on practice days and Sundays is one of my greatest pleasures.

I want to know if you can have "Carol, brothers, carol," on Christmas night, and if the boy who sings "My ain countree" so beautifully may please sing that too. I think it is the loveliest thing in the world, but it always makes me cry; doesn't it you?

If it isn't too much trouble, I hope they can sing them both quite early, as after ten o'clock I may be asleep.

Yours respectfully,
Carol Bird.

P.S.—The reason I like "Carol, brothers, carol," is because the choir-boys sang it eleven years ago, the morning I was born, and put it into Mamma's head to call me Carol. She didn't remember then that my other name would be Bird, because she was half asleep, and could only think of one thing at a time. Donald says if I had been born on the Fourth of July they would have named me "Independence," or if on the twenty-second of February, "Georgina," or even "Cherry," like Cherry in "Martin Chuzzlewit"; but I like my own name and birthday best.

Yours truly,
Carol Bird.

Uncle Jack thought the letter quite right, and did not even smile at her telling the organist so many family items.

The days flew by as they always fly in holiday time, and it was Christmas Eve before anybody knew it. The family festival was quiet and very pleasant, but almost overshadowed by the grander preparations for the next day. Carol and Elfrida, her pretty German nurse, had ransacked books, and introduced so many plans, and plays, and customs, and merry-makings from Germany, and Holland, and England, and a dozen other countries, that you would scarcely have known how or where you were keeping Christmas. Even the dog and the cat had enjoyed their celebration under Carol's direction. Each had a tiny table with a lighted candle in the centre, and a bit of Bologna sausage placed very near it; and everybody laughed till the tears stood in their eyes to see Villikins and Dinah struggle to nibble the sausages, and at the same time to evade the candle flame. Villikins barked, and sniffed, and howled in impatience, and after many vain attempts succeeded in dragging off the prize, though he singed his nose in doing it. Dinah, meanwhile, watched him placidly, her delicate nostrils quivering with expectation, and, after all excitement had subsided, walked with dignity to the table, her beautiful gray satin trail sweeping behind her, and, calmly putting up one velvet paw, drew the sausage gently down, and walked out of the room without turning a hair, so to speak. Elfrida had scattered handfuls of seed over the snow in the garden, that the wild birds might have a comfortable breakfast next morning, and had stuffed bundles of dry grasses in the fireplaces, so that the reindeer of Santa Claus could refresh themselves after their long gallops across country. This was really only done for fun, but it pleased Carol.

And when, after dinner, the whole family had gone to the church to see the Christmas decorations, Carol limped out on her slender crutches, and with Elfrida's help, placed all the family boots in a row in the upper hall. That was to keep the dear ones from quarreling all through the year. There were Papa's stout top boots; Mamma's pretty buttoned shoes next; then Uncle Jack's, Donald's, Paul's, and Hugh's; and at the end of the line her own little white worsted slippers. Last, and sweetest of all, like the children in Austria, she put a lighted candle in her window to guide the dear Christ-child, lest he should stumble in the dark night as he passed up the deserted street. This done, she dropped into bed, a rather tired, but very happy Christmas fairy.

V : *Some Other Birds are Taught to Fly*

BEFORE the earliest Ruggles could wake and toot his five-cent tin horn, Mrs. Ruggles was up and stirring about the house, for it was a gala day in the family. Gala day! I should think so! Were not her nine "childern" invited to a dinner-party at the great house, and weren't they going to sit down free and equal with the mightiest in the land? She had been preparing for this grand occasion ever since the receipt of Carol Bird's invitation, which, by the way, had been speedily enshrined in an old photograph frame and hung under the looking-glass in the most prominent place in the kitchen, where it stared the occasional visitor directly in the eye, and made him livid with envy:

Birds' Nest, December 17, 188–.

DEAR MRS. RUGGLES—*I am going to have a dinner-party on Christmas Day, and would like to have all your children come. I want them every one, please, from Sarah Maud to Baby Larry. Mamma says dinner will be at half past five, and the Christmas tree at seven; so you may expect them home at nine o'clock. Wishing you a Merry Christmas and a Happy New Year, I am*

Yours truly,

CAROL BIRD.

Breakfast was on the table promptly at seven o'clock, and there was very little of it, too; for it was an excellent day for short rations, though Mrs. Ruggles heaved a sigh as she reflected that the boys, with their India-rubber stomachs, would be just as hungry the day after the dinner-party as if they had never had any at all.

As soon as the scanty meal was over, she announced the plan of the campaign: "Now, Susan, you an' Kitty wash up the dishes; an' Peter, can't yer spread up the beds, so 't I can git ter cuttin' out Larry's new suit? I ain't satisfied with his clo'es, an' I thought in the night of a way to make him a dress out o' my old red plaid shawl— kind o' Scotch style, yer know, with the fringe 't the bottom.—Eily, you go find the comb and take the snarls out the fringe, that's a lady! You little young ones clear out from under foot! Clem, you and Con hop into bed with Larry while I wash yer underflannins; 't won't take long to dry 'em.—Yes, I know it's bothersome, but yer can't go int' s'ciety 'thout takin' some trouble, 'n' anyhow I couldn't git round to 'em last night.—Sarah Maud, I think 't would be perfeckly han'som' if you ripped them brass buttons off yer uncle's policeman's coat 'n' sewed 'em in a row up the front o' yer green skirt. Susan, you must iron out yours 'n' Kitty's apurns; 'n' there, I come mighty near forgettin' Peory's stockin's! I counted the whole lot last night when I was washin' of 'em, 'n' there ain't but nineteen anyhow yer fix 'em, 'n' no nine pairs mates nohow; 'n' I ain't goin' ter have my childern wear odd stockin's to a dinner-comp'ny, fetched up as I was!—Eily, can't you run out and ask Mis' Cullen ter lend me a pair o' stockin's for Peory, 'n' tell her if she will, Peory'll give Jim half her candy when she gets home. Won't yer, Peory?"

Peoria was young and greedy, and thought the remedy so out of all proportion to the disease, that she set up a deafening howl at the projected bargain—a howl so rebellious and so entirely out of season that her mother started in her direction with flashing eye and uplifted hand; but she let it fall suddenly, saying, "No, I vow I won't lick ye Christmas Day, if yer drive me crazy; but speak up smart, now, 'n' say whether yer'd ruther give Jim Cullen half yer candy or go bare-legged ter the party?" The matter being put so plainly, Peoria collected her faculties, dried her tears, and chose the lesser evil, Clem having hastened the decision by an affectionate wink, that meant he'd go halves with her on his candy.

"That's a lady!" cried her mother. "Now, you young ones that ain't doin' nothin', play all yer want ter before noontime, for after ye git through eatin' at twelve o'clock me 'n' Sarah Maud's goin' ter give yer sech a washin' 'n' combin' 'n' dressin' as yer never had before 'n' never will agin likely, 'n' then I'm goin' to set yer down 'n' give yer two solid hours trainin' in manners; 'n' 't won't be no foolin' neither."

"All we've got ter do's go eat!" grumbled Peter.

"Well, that's enough," responded his mother; "there's more 'n one way of eatin', let me tell yer, 'n' you've got a heap ter learn about it, Peter Ruggles. Land sakes, I wish you childern could see the way I was fetched up to eat. I never took a meal o' vittles in the kitchen before I married Ruggles; but yer can't keep up that style with nine young ones 'n' yer Pa always off ter sea."

The big Ruggleses worked so well, and the little Ruggleses kept from "under foot" so successfully, that by one o'clock nine complete toilets were laid out in solemn grandeur on the beds. I say, "complete"; but I do not know whether they would be called so in the best society. The law of compensation had been well applied:

he that had necktie had no cuffs; she that had sash had no handkerchief, and *vice versa;* but they all had shoes and a certain amount of clothing, such as it was, the outside layer being in every case quite above criticism.

"Now, Sarah Maud," said Mrs. Ruggles, her face shining with excitement, "everything's red up an' we can begin. I've got a boiler 'n' a kettle 'n' a pot o' hot water. Peter, you go into the back bedroom, 'n' I'll take Susan, Kitty, Peory, 'n' Cornelius; 'n' Sarah Maud, you take Clem, 'n' Eily, 'n' Larry, one to a time. Scrub 'em 'n' rinse 'em, or 't any rate git's fur's yer can with 'em, and then I'll finish 'em off while you do yerself."

Sarah Maud couldn't have scrubbed with any more decision and force if she had been doing floors, and the little Ruggleses bore it bravely, not from natural heroism, but for the joy that was set before them. Not being satisfied, however, with the "tone" of their complexions, and feeling that the number of freckles to the square inch was too many to be tolerated in the highest social circles, she wound up operations by applying a little Bristol brick from the knife-board, which served as the proverbial "last straw," from under which the little Ruggleses issued rather red and raw and out of temper. When the clock struck four they were all clothed, and most of them in their right minds, ready for those last touches that always take the most time.

Kitty's red hair was curled in thirty-four ringlets, Sarah Maud's was braided in one pig-tail, and Susan's and Eily's in two braids apiece, while Peoria's resisted all advances in the shape of hair oils and stuck out straight on all sides, like that of the Circassian girl of the circus—so Clem said; and he was sent into the bedroom for it, too, from whence he was dragged out forgivingly, by Peoria herself, five minutes later. Then, exciting moment, came linen collars for some and neckties and bows for others—a magnificent green glass breastpin was sewed into Peter's purple necktie,—and Eureka! the Ruggleses were dressed, and Solomon in all his glory was not arrayed like one of these!

A row of seats was then formed directly through the middle of the kitchen. Of course, there were not quite chairs enough for ten, since the family had rarely wanted to sit down all at once, somebody always being out or in bed, or otherwise engaged, but the wood-box and the coal-hod finished out the line nicely, and nobody thought of grumbling. The children took their places according to age, Sarah Maud at the head and Larry on the coal-hod, and Mrs. Ruggles seated herself in front, surveying them proudly as she wiped the sweat of honest toil from her brow.

"Well," she exclaimed, "if I do say so as shouldn't, I never see a cleaner, more stylish mess o' childern in my life! I do wish Ruggles could look at ye for a minute! — Larry Ruggles, how many times have I got ter tell yer not ter keep pullin' at yer sash? Haven't I told yer if it comes ontied, yer waist 'n' skirt'll part comp'ny in the middle, 'n' then where'll yer be? — Now look me in the eye, all of yer! I've of'en told yer what kind of a family the McGrills was. I've got reason to be proud, goodness knows! Your uncle is on the police force o' New York City; you can take up the paper most any day an' see his name printed right out — James McGrill — 'n' I can't have my childern fetched up common, like some folks'; when they go out they've got to have clo'es, and learn to act decent! Now I want ter see how yer goin' to behave when yer git there to-night. 'Tain't so awful easy as you think 't is. Let's start in at the beginnin' 'n' act out the whole business. Pile into the bedroom, there, every last one o' ye, 'n' show me how yer goin' to go int' the parlor. This'll be the parlor, 'n' I'll be Mis' Bird."

The youngsters hustled into the next room in high glee, and Mrs. Ruggles drew herself up in the chair with an infinitely haughty and purse-proud expression that much better suited a descendant of the McGrills than modest Mrs. Bird.

The bedroom was small, and there presently ensued such a clatter that you would have thought a herd of wild cattle had broken loose. The door opened, and they straggled in, all the younger ones giggling, with Sarah Maud at the head, looking as if she had been caught in the act of stealing sheep; while Larry, being last in line, seemed to think the door a sort of gate of heaven which would be shut in his face if he didn't get there in time; accordingly he struggled ahead of his elders and disgraced himself by tumbling in head foremost.

Mrs. Ruggles looked severe. "There, I knew yer'd do it in some sech fool way! Now go in there and try it over again, every last one o' ye, 'n' if Larry can't come in on two legs he can stay ter home—d' yer hear?"

The matter began to assume a graver aspect; the little Ruggleses stopped giggling and backed into the bedroom, issuing presently with lock step, Indian file, a scared and hunted expression on every countenance.

"No, no, no!" cried Mrs. Ruggles, in despair. "That's worse yet; yer look for all the world like a gang o' pris'ners! There ain't no style ter that: spread out more, can't yer, 'n' act kind o' careless-like—nobody's goin' ter kill ye! That ain't what a dinner-party is!"

The third time brought deserved success, and the pupils took their seats in the row. "Now, yer know," said Mrs. Ruggles impressively, "there ain't enough decent hats to go round, 'n' if there was I don' know's I'd let yer wear 'em, for the boys would never think to take 'em off when they got inside, for they never do—but anyhow, there ain't enough good ones. Now, look me in the eye. You're only goin' jest round the corner; you needn't wear no hats, none of yer, 'n' when yer get int' the parlor, 'n' they ask yer ter lay off yer hats, Sarah Maud must speak up 'n' say it was sech a pleasant evenin' 'n' sech a short walk that yer left yer hats to home. Now, can yer remember?"

All the little Ruggleses shouted, "Yes, marm!" in chorus.

"What have you got ter do with it?" demanded their mother; "did I tell you to say it? Warn't I talkin' ter Sarah Maud?"

The little Ruggleses hung their diminished heads. "Yes, marm," they piped, more discreetly.

"Now we won't leave nothin' to chance; get up, all of ye, an' try it. Speak up, Sarah Maud."

Sarah Maud's tongue clove to the roof of her mouth.

"Quick!"

"Ma thought—it was—sech a pleasant hat that we'd—we'd better leave our short walk to home," recited Sarah Maud, in an agony of mental effort.

This was too much for the boys. An earthquake of suppressed giggles swept all along the line.

"Oh, whatever shall I do with yer?" moaned the unhappy mother. "I s'pose I've got to learn it to yer!"—which she did, word for word, until Sarah Maud thought she could stand on her head and say it backwards.

"Now, Cornelius, what are you goin' ter say ter make yerself good comp'ny?"

"Do? Me? Dunno!" said Cornelius, turning pale, with unexpected responsibility.

"Well, ye ain't goin' to set there like a bump on a log 'thout sayin' a word ter pay for yer vittles, air ye? Ask Mis' Bird how she's feelin' this evenin', or if Mr. Bird's hevin' a busy season, or how this kind o' weather agrees with him, or somethin' like that. Now we'll make b'lieve we've got ter the dinner—that won't be so hard, 'cause yer'll have somethin' to do—it's awful bothersome to stan' round an' act stylish. If they have napkins, Sarah Maud down to Peory may put 'em in their laps, 'n' the rest of ye can tuck 'em in yer necks. Don't eat with yer fingers—don't grab no vittles off one 'nother's plates; don't reach out for nothin', but wait till yer asked, 'n' if you never git asked don't git up and grab it.—Don't spill nothin' on the tablecloth, or like's not Mis' Bird'll send yer away from the table— 'n' I hope she will if yer do! (Susan! keep yer handkerchief in yer lap where Peory can borry it if she needs it, 'n' I hope she'll know when she does need it, though I don't expect it.) Now we'll try a few things ter see how they'll go! Mr. Clement, do you eat cramb'ry sarse?"

"Bet yer life!" cried Clem, who in the excitement of the moment had not taken in the idea exactly and had mistaken this for an ordinary bosom-of-the-family question.

"Clement McGrill Ruggles, do you mean to tell me that you'd say that to a dinner-party? I'll give ye one more chance. Mr. Clement, will you take some of the cramb'ry?"

"Yes, marm, thank ye kindly, if you happen ter have any handy."

"Very good, indeed! But they won't give yer two tries tonight—yer just remember that! Miss Peory, do you speak for white or dark meat?"

"I ain't perticler as ter color—anything that nobody else wants will suit me," answered Peory with her best air.

"First-rate! Nobody could speak more genteel than that. Miss Kitty, will you have hard or soft sarse with your pudden?"

"Hard or soft? Oh! A little of both, if you please, an' I'm much obliged," said Kitty, bowing with decided ease and grace; at which all the other Ruggleses pointed the finger of shame at her, and Peter grunted expressively, that their meaning might not be mistaken.

"You just stop your gruntin', Peter Ruggles; that warn't greedy, that was all right. I wish I could git it inter your heads that it ain't so much what yer say, as the way you say it. And don't keep starin' cross-eyed at your necktie pin, or I'll take it out 'n' sew it on to Clem or Cornelius: Sarah Maud'll keep her eye on it, 'n' if it turns broken side out she'll tell yer. Gracious! I shouldn't think you'd ever seen nor worn no jool'ry in your life. Eily, you an' Larry's too little to train, so you just look at the rest an' do's they do, 'n' the Lord have mercy on ye 'n' help ye to act decent! Now, is there anything more ye'd like to practice?"

"If yer tell me one more thing, I can't set up an' eat," said Peter gloomily; "I'm so cram full o' manners now I'm ready ter bust, 'thout no dinner at all."

"Me too," chimed in Cornelius.

"Well, I'm sorry for yer both," rejoined Mrs. Ruggles sarcastically; "if the 'mount o' manners yer've got on hand now troubles ye, you're dreadful easy hurt! Now, Sarah Maud, after dinner, about once in so often, you must git up 'n' say, 'I guess we'd better be goin''; 'n' if they say, 'Oh, no, set a while longer,' yer can set; but if they don't say nothin' you've got ter get up 'n' go. Now hev yer got that int' yer head?"

"*About once in so often!*" Could any words in the language be fraught with more terrible and wearing uncertainty?

"Well," answered Sarah Maud mournfully, "seems as if this whole dinner-party set right square on top o' me! Mebbe I could manage my own manners, but to manage nine mannerses is worse 'n staying to home!"

"Oh, don't fret," said her mother, good-naturedly, now that the lesson was over; "I guess you'll git along. I wouldn't mind if folks would only say, 'Oh, childern will be childern'; but they won't. They'll say, 'Land o' Goodness, who fetched them childern up?' It's quarter past five, 'n' yer can go now—remember 'bout the hats —don't all talk ter once—Susan, lend yer han'k'chief ter Peory— Peter, don't keep screwin' yer scarf-pin—Cornelius, hold yer head up straight—Sarah Maud, don't take yer eyes off o' Larry, 'n' Larry, you keep holt o' Sarah Maud 'n' do jest as she says—'n' whatever you do, all of yer, never forgit for one second that yer mother was a McGrill."

VI: *"When the Pie was opened, the Birds began to Sing!"*

THE children went out of the back door quietly, and were presently lost to sight, Sarah Maud slipping and stumbling along absent-mindedly, as she recited rapidly under her breath, "Itwassuchapleas-antevenin'n'suchashortwalk,thatwethoughtwe'dleaveourhatstohome —itwassuchapleasantevenin'n'suchashortwalk,thatwethoughtwe'd leaveourhatstohome."

Peter rang the doorbell, and presently a servant admitted them, and, whispering something in Sarah's ear, drew her downstairs into the kitchen. The other Ruggleses stood in horror-stricken groups as the door closed behind their commanding officer; but there was no time for reflection, for a voice from above was heard, saying, "Come right upstairs, please!"

> *"Theirs not to make reply,*
> *Theirs not to reason why,*
> *Theirs but to do or die."*

Accordingly they walked upstairs, and Elfrida, the nurse, ushered them into a room more splendid than anything they had ever seen.

But, oh woe! where was Sarah Maud! and was it Fate that Mrs. Bird should say, at once, "Did you lay your hats in the hall?" Peter felt himself elected by circumstance the head of the family, and, casting one imploring look at tongue-tied Susan, standing next him, said huskily, "It was so very pleasant—that—that——" "That we hadn't good hats enough to go 'round," put in little Susan, bravely, to help him out, and then froze with horror that the ill-fated words had slipped off her tongue.

However, Mrs. Bird said, pleasantly, "Of course you wouldn't wear hats such a short distance—I forgot when I asked. Now will you come right in to Miss Carol's room? She is so anxious to see you."

Just then Sarah Maud came up the back stairs, so radiant with joy from her secret interview with the cook that Peter could have pinched her with a clear conscience; and Carol gave them a joyful welcome. "But where is Baby Larry?" she cried, looking over the group with searching eye. "Didn't he come?"

"Larry! Larry!" Good gracious, where was Larry? They were all sure that he had come in with them, for Susan remembered scolding him for tripping over the door-mat. Uncle Jack went into convulsions of laughter. "Are you sure there were nine of you?" he asked, merrily.

"I think so, sir," said Peoria, timidly; "but anyhow, there was Larry." And she showed signs of weeping.

"Oh, well, cheer up!" cried Uncle Jack. "Probably he's not lost —only mislaid. I'll go and find him before you can say Jack Robinson!"

"I'll go, too, if you please, sir," said Sarah Maud, "for it was my place to mind him, an' if he's lost I can't relish my vittles!"

The other Ruggleses stood rooted to the floor. Was this a dinner-party, forsooth; and if so, why were such things ever spoken of as festive occasions?

Sarah Maud went out through the hall, calling, "Larry! Larry!" and without any interval of suspense a thin voice piped up from below, "Here I be!"

The Birds' Christmas Carol

The truth was that Larry, being deserted by his natural guardian, dropped behind the rest, and wriggled into the hat-tree to wait for her, having no notion of walking unprotected into the jaws of a fashionable entertainment. Finding that she did not come, he tried to crawl from his refuge and call somebody, when—dark and dreadful ending to a tragic day—he found that he was too much intertwined with umbrellas and canes to move a single step. He was afraid to yell (when I have said this of Larry Ruggles I have pictured a state of helpless terror that ought to wring tears from every eye); and the sound of Sarah Maud's beloved voice, some seconds later, was like a strain of angel music in his ears. Uncle Jack dried his tears, carried him upstairs, and soon had him in breathless fits of laughter, while Carol so made the other Ruggleses forget themselves that they were presently talking like accomplished diners-out.

Carol's bed had been moved into the farthest corner of the room, and she was lying on the outside, dressed in a wonderful dressing-gown that looked like a fleecy cloud. Her golden hair fell in fluffy curls over her white forehead and neck, her cheeks flushed delicately, her eyes beamed with joy, and the children told their mother, afterwards, that she looked as beautiful as the angels in the picture books.

There was a great bustle behind a huge screen in another part of the room, and at half past five this was taken away, and the Christmas dinner-table stood revealed. What a wonderful sight it was to the poor little Ruggles children, who ate their sometimes scanty meals on the kitchen table! It blazed with tall colored candles, it gleamed with glass and silver, it blushed with flowers, it groaned with good things to eat; so it was not strange that the Ruggleses, forgetting altogether that their mother was a McGrill, shrieked in admiration of the fairy spectacle. But Larry's behavior was the most disgraceful, for he stood not upon the order of his going, but went at once for a high chair that pointed unmistakably to him, climbed up like a squirrel, gave a comprehensive look at the turkey, clapped his hands in ecstasy, rested his fat arms on the table, and cried with joy, "I beat the hull lot o' yer!" Carol laughed until she cried, giving orders, meanwhile—"Uncle Jack, please sit at the head, Sarah Maud at the foot, and that will leave four on each side; Mamma is going to help Elfrida, so that the children need not look after each other, but just have a good time."

A sprig of holly lay by each plate, and nothing would do but each little Ruggles must leave his seat and have it pinned on by Carol, and as each course was served, one of them pleaded to take something to her. There was hurrying to and fro, I can assure you, for it is quite a difficult matter to serve a Christmas dinner on the third floor of a great city house; but if it had been necessary to carry every dish up a rope ladder the servants would gladly have done so. There were turkey and chicken, with delicious gravy and stuffing, and there were half a dozen vegetables, with cranberry jelly, and celery, and pickles; and as for the way these delicacies were served, the Ruggleses never forgot it as long as they lived.

Peter nudged Kitty, who sat next to him, and said, "Look, will yer, ev'ry feller's got his own partic'lar butter; I s'pose that's to show you can eat that 'n' no more. No, it ain't either, for that pig of a Peory's just gettin' another helpin'!"

"Yes," whispered Kitty, "an' the napkins is marked with big red letters! I wonder if that's so nobody 'll nip 'em; an' oh, Peter, look at the pictures stickin' right on ter the dishes! Did yer ever?"

"The plums is all took out o' my cramb'ry sarse an' it's friz to a stiff jell'!" whispered Peoria, in wild excitement.

"Hi—yah! I got a wish-bone!" sang Larry, regardless of Sarah Maud's frown; after which she asked to have his seat changed, giving as excuse that he "gen'ally set beside her, an' would feel strange"; the true reason being that she desired to kick him gently, under the table, whenever he passed what might be termed "the McGrill line."

"I declare to goodness," murmured Susan, on the other side, "there's so much to look at I can't scarcely eat nothin'!"

"Bet yer life I can!" said Peter, who had kept one servant busily employed ever since he sat down; for, luckily, no one was asked by Uncle Jack whether he would have a second helping, but the dishes were quietly passed under their noses, and not a single Ruggles refused anything that was offered him, even unto the seventh time.

Then, when Carol and Uncle Jack perceived that more turkey was a physical impossibility, the meats were taken off and the dessert was brought in—a dessert that would have frightened a strong man after such a dinner as had preceded it. Not so the Ruggleses—for a strong man is nothing to a small boy—and they kindled to the dessert as if the turkey had been a dream and the six vegetables an optical delusion. There were plum-pudding, mince-pie, and ice-cream; and there were nuts, and raisins, and oranges. Kitty chose ice-cream, explaining that she knew it "by sight, though she hadn't never tasted none;" but all the rest took the entire variety, without any regard to consequences.

"My dear child," whispered Uncle Jack, as he took Carol an orange, "there is no doubt about the necessity of this feast, but I do advise you after this to have them twice a year, or quarterly perhaps, for the way these children eat is positively dangerous; I assure you I tremble for that terrible Peoria. I'm going to run races with her after dinner."

"Never mind," laughed Carol; "let them have enough for once; it does my heart good to see them, and they shall come oftener next year."

The feast being over, the Ruggleses lay back in their chairs languidly, like little gorged boa-constrictors, and the table was cleared in a trice. Then a door was opened into the next room, and there, in a corner facing Carol's bed, which had been wheeled as close as possible, stood the brilliantly lighted Christmas tree, glittering with gilded walnuts and tiny silver balloons, and wreathed with snowy chains of pop-corn. The presents had been bought mostly with Carol's story-money, and were selected after long consultations with Mrs. Bird. Each girl had a blue knitted hood, and each boy a red crocheted comforter, all made by Mamma, Carol, and Elfrida ("Because if you buy everything, it doesn't show so much love," said Carol.) Then every girl had a pretty plaid dress of a different color, and every boy a warm coat of the right size. Here the useful presents stopped, and they were quite enough; but Carol had pleaded to give them something "for fun." "I know they need the clothes," she had said, when they were talking over the matter just after Thanksgiving, "but they don't care much for them, after all. Now, Papa, won't you *please* let me go without part of my presents this year, and give me the money they would cost, to buy something to amuse the Ruggleses?"

"You can have both," said Mr. Bird, promptly; "is there any need of my little girl's going without her own Christmas, I should like to know? Spend all the money you like."

"But that isn't the thing," objected Carol, nestling close to her father; "it wouldn't be mine. What is the use? Haven't I almost everything already, and am I not the happiest girl in the world this year, with Uncle Jack and Donald at home? You know very well it is more blessed to give than to receive; so why won't you let me do it? You never look half as happy when you are getting your presents as when you are giving us ours. Now, Papa, submit, or I shall have to be very firm and disagreeable with you!"

"Very well, your Highness, I surrender."

"That's a dear Papa! Now what were you going to give me? Confess!"

"A bronze figure of Santa Claus; and in the 'little round belly that shakes when he laughs like a bowlful of jelly,' is a wonderful clock—oh, you would never give it up if you could see it!"

"Nonsense," laughed Carol; "as I never have to get up to breakfast, nor go to bed, nor catch trains, I think my old clock will do very well! Now, Mamma, what were you going to give me?"

"Oh, I hadn't decided. A few more books, and a gold thimble, and a smelling-bottle, and a music-box, perhaps."

"Poor Carol," laughed the child, merrily, "she can afford to give up these lovely things, for there will still be left Uncle Jack, and Donald, and Paul, and Hugh, and Uncle Rob, and Aunt Elsie, and a dozen other people to fill her Christmas stocking!"

So Carol had her way, as she generally did; but it was usually a good way, which was fortunate, under the circumstances; and Sarah Maud had a set of Miss Alcott's books, and Peter a modest silver watch, Cornelius a tool-chest, Clement a dog-house for his lame puppy, Larry a magnificent Noah's ark, and each of the younger girls a beautiful doll.

You can well believe that everybody was very merry and very thankful. All the family, from Mr. Bird down to the cook, said that they had never seen so much happiness in the space of three hours; but it had to end, as all things do. The candles flickered and went out, the tree was left alone with its gilded ornaments, and Mrs. Bird sent the children downstairs at half past eight, thinking that Carol looked tired.

"Now, my darling, you have done quite enough for one day," said Mrs. Bird, getting Carol into her little nightgown. "I'm afraid you will feel worse tomorrow, and that would be a sad ending to such a charming evening."

"Oh, wasn't it a lovely, lovely time," sighed Carol. "From first to last, everything was just right. I shall never forget Larry's face when he looked at the turkey; nor Peter's when he saw his watch; nor that sweet, sweet Kitty's smile when she kissed her dolly; nor the tears in poor, dull Sarah Maud's eyes when she thanked me for her books; nor——"

"But we mustn't talk any longer about it to-night," said Mrs. Bird, anxiously; "you are too tired, dear."

"I am not so very tired, Mamma. I have felt well all day; not a bit of pain anywhere. Perhaps this has done me good."

"Perhaps; I hope so. There was no noise or confusion; it was just a merry time. Now, may I close the door and leave you alone, dear? Papa and I will steal in softly by and by to see if you are all right; but I think you need to be very quiet."

"Oh, I'm willing to stay by myself; but I am not sleepy yet, and I am going to hear the music, you know."

"Yes, I have opened the window a little, and put the screen in front of it, so that you won't feel the air."

"Can I have the shutters open? And won't you turn my bed, please? This morning I woke ever so early, and one bright, beautiful star shone in that eastern window. I never noticed it before, and I thought of the Star in the East, that guided the Wise Men to the place where the baby Jesus was. Good-night, Mamma. Such a happy, happy day!"

"Good-night, my precious Christmas Carol—mother's blessed Christmas child."

"Bend your head a minute, mother dear," whispered Carol, calling her mother back. "Mamma, dear, I do think that we have kept Christ's birthday this time just as He would like it. Don't you?"

"I am sure of it," said Mrs. Bird, softly.

VII: *The Birdling Flies Away*

The Ruggleses had finished a last romp in the library with Paul and Hugh, and Uncle Jack had taken them home and stayed awhile to chat with Mrs. Ruggles, who opened the door for them, her face all aglow with excitement and delight. When Kitty and Clem showed her the oranges and nuts that they had kept for her, she astonished them by saying that at six o'clock Mrs. Bird had sent her in the finest dinner she had ever seen in her life; and not only that, but a piece of dress-goods that must have cost a dollar a yard if it cost a cent.

As Uncle Jack went down the rickety steps he looked back into the window for a last glimpse of the family, as the children gathered about their mother, showing their beautiful presents again and again —and then upward to a window in the great house yonder. "A little child shall lead them," he thought. "Well, if—if anything ever happens to Carol, I will take the Ruggleses under my wing."

"Softly, Uncle Jack," whispered the boys, as he walked into the library awhile later. "We are listening to the music in the church. The choir has sung 'Carol, brothers, carol,' and now we think the organist is beginning to play 'My ain countree' for Carol."

"I hope she hears it," said Mrs. Bird; "but they are very late tonight, and I dare not speak to her lest she should be asleep. It is almost ten o'clock."

The boy soprano, clad in white surplice, stood in the organ loft.

514

The Birds' Christmas Carol

The light shone full upon his crown of fair hair, and his pale face, with its serious blue eyes, looked paler than usual. Perhaps it was something in the tender thrill of the voice, or in the sweet words, but there were tears in many eyes, both in the church and in the great house next door.

"I am far frae my hame,
I am weary aften whiles
For the langed-for hame-bringin',
An' my Faether's welcome smiles;
An' I'll ne'er be fu' content,
Until my e'en do see
The gowden gates o' heaven
In my ain countree.

"The earth is decked wi' flow'rs,
Mony tinted, fresh an' gay,
An' the birdies warble blythely,
For my Faether made them sae;
But these sights an' these soun's
Will as naething be to me,
When I hear the angels singin'
In my ain countree.

"Like a bairn to its mither,
A wee birdie to its nest,
I fain would be gangin' noo
Unto my Faether's breast;
For He gathers in His arms
Helpless, worthless lambs like me,
An' carries them Himsel'
To His ain countree."

There were tears in many eyes, but not in Carol's. The loving heart had quietly ceased to beat, and the "wee birdie" in the great house had flown to its "home nest." Carol had fallen asleep! But as to the song, I think perhaps, I cannot say, she heard it after all!

515

So sad an ending to a happy day! Perhaps—to those who were left; and yet Carol's mother, even in the freshness of her grief, was glad that her darling had slipped away on the loveliest day of her life, out of its glad content, into everlasting peace.

She was glad that she had gone as she had come, on the wings of song, when all the world was brimming over with joy; glad of every grateful smile, of every joyous burst of laughter, of every loving thought and word and deed the dear last day had brought.

Sadness reigned, it is true, in the little house behind the garden; and one day poor Sarah Maud, with a courage born of despair, threw on her hood and shawl, walked straight to a certain house a mile away, up the marble steps into good Dr. Bartol's office, falling at his feet as she cried, "Oh, sir, it was me an' our children that went to Miss Carol's last dinner-party, an' if we made her worse we can't never be happy again!" Then the kind old gentleman took her rough hand in his and told her to dry her tears, for neither she nor any of her flock had hastened Carol's flight; indeed, he said that had it not been for the strong hopes and wishes that filled her tired heart, she could not have stayed long enough to keep that last merry Christmas with her dear ones.

And so the old years, fraught with memories, die, one after another, and the new years, bright with hopes, are born to take their places; but Carol lives again in every chime of Christmas bells that peal glad tidings, and in every Christmas anthem sung by childish voices.

HOWARD PYLE

The Mysterious Chest

BEING A TRUE AND TEMPERATE NARRATIVE OF
THE EXTRAORDINARY ADVENTURES THAT BEFELL SEVERAL
CITIZENS OF THE TOWN OF NEW YORK ON THE EVE OF
CHRISTMAS DAY IN THE YEAR OF GRACE 1793

In Which the Mysterious Chest Is Claimed by an Owner

UPON the twenty-fourth of December in the year 1793 the
ship *Good Samaritan*, newly arrived from Brest in France
with a cargo of sundries consigned to Mr. Aminadab Peck,
Merchant, of the Town of New York, was warped into the dock adjoining the countinghouse of that worthy citizen at the foot of
Broad Street.

517

Upon the same day, and at about three o'clock in the afternoon, there being then a fine drift of snow spitting forth from a chill and leaden sky and it being unusually dusk for the time of day, there entered into the private office of the worthy merchant a stranger of a very singular and unusual appearance.

For the visitor, having disembarrassed himself of his muffler and opened his overcoat, exhibited a lean, cadaverous face with sunken eyes that shone very bright and alert beneath their overhanging brows, a head covered thickly over with a close crop of very black hair, a pair of extremely large ears standing out like wings upon either side of his head, and the thinnest person our merchant had ever beheld in all of his life.

"Sir, I see you do not know me," quoth the stranger. "But I have here a letter from your no doubt valued correspondents, MM. Valadon et Cie, of Paris, France, that will soon make us better acquainted. I am the owner (as you will discover by this note) of a certain cedar chest which is at this moment in the cabin of the *Good Samaritan* and under the very particular care of Captain Coffin. It is addressed to me under the name of 'Remo,' and it is further countersigned by a certain emblem which consists of two adjacent circles pierced by an arrow. Now I must, my good sir, have that chest immediately, for unless I can have it opened before eight o'clock tomorrow morning I shall regard it as being one of the great misfortunes of my life."

Meantime the stranger was speaking, the merchant had been examining the papers that had been delivered to him. They were in all ways perfectly clear and explicit, and there was no possible reason to doubt that the chest was certainly the property of the applicant. Accordingly he wrote an order to Captain Coffin to deliver the shipment, and having taken a receipt for the same the business was closed.

Captain Coffin of the *Good Samaritan* was sitting at a table in the great cabin when the skeletonlike stranger entered. He was very busy looking over his books and papers by the light of an oil lamp slung from the deck above, but he pushed his work aside and welcomed his visitor with gruff good nature, inviting him to join him in partaking of a stiff glass of the rum, hot water and sugar which he himself was enjoying with generous liberality.

But no sooner did he hear mention of the chest than his whole countenance changed; his good nature vanished in an instant, and he broke forth into such a torrent of execration as nearly to take away the breath of his hearer. He called the dominant powers of Heaven and Hell to witness that the sooner he was quit of the chest the better he would like it. He declared that ever since it had come into the ship it had brought with it nothing but ill luck and disaster. It had, he said, been sent aboard the vessel upon a Friday, and hardly had it been stowed in the cabin when a storm began to brew that followed the *Good Samaritan* with great violence for above a week. In the pitching of the ship the chest had broken loose from its moorings and had dashed into a locker across the cabin, smashing in not only the locker itself, but three cases of prime Hollands as well. Mr. Meigs, the third mate, in his efforts to catch the chest and lash it fast again, had had his shins so badly lacerated that he had been laid up for ten days or more. Three other storms of a like unusual sort had caught them upon this misfortunate voyage, and in each storm the chest had again broken loose from its moorings, always executing some disaster ere it was lashed fast again. From all these, and from various other circumstances which he particularized, the captain declared that it was his belief that the chest was certainly haunted.

"Haunted, did they say!" cried out the owner of the chest. "You would certainly say it was haunted if you could but see what is in it!"

These words were uttered with such a singular meaning that the captain was struck of a sudden very serious. "Well," said he, "I don't ask to see what is in it and I don't want to. But the sooner you get it out of my ship, the better I shall be pleased."

"And so shall I!" says the stranger, "and there we are of a like mind the one with the other."

The Mysterious Chest Begins Its Peregrinations

BUT now the question arose as to how the chest was to be taken away. For at that hour there was not a single soul about the dock except a watchman with a wooden leg. At this juncture the captain called to mind that the ship's carpenter was still aboard, completing some preparations for the opening of the hatches upon the morrow. He opined that if that worthy were paid well enough for his pains he would see to it that the chest was conveyed to its destination.

Accordingly, the carpenter was summoned, and after a great deal of contention a bargain was struck, at which the carpenter agreed to convey the chest to its destination upon the payment of a dollar down in hand and another dollar to be given when the box was safely delivered.

As the carpenter could no more read English than Greek or Sanskrit, he had to commit to memory both the name of the consignee and his address. In a little while, however, he had thoroughly mastered the fact that the name of the owner of the chest was Jedediah Stout; that the chest itself was to be delivered at a certain house on Van Cortlandt Street, the second from Broadway upon the right-hand side, and that the house might be further identified by the fact that it was painted white and had green shutters.

It was six o'clock and dark as pitch when the carpenter of the *Good Samaritan* with four stout fellows to help him got the chest out of the cabin and started it upon that terrific journey which brought such panic and terror into three quiet households. The snow was falling faster than ever, and the carpenter led the procession with a lanthorn to light the way through the obscurity. The chest itself was of the size and shape and very nearly of the weight of a loaded coffin, so that the cortège had much the appearance of a small funeral as it wended its way through the dark and deserted shed of the dock and so to the street beyond.

The Mysterious Chest

All went well until the bearers and their guide had reached the corner of Beaver Street and had come under the light of a lamp that overhung the doorway of a dramshop. Then, exactly at this place, the ill luck that seemed to have pursued the chest from the beginning of its peregrinations overtook those who now carried it. For one of the bearers happening to set his foot upon a sheet of ice hidden by two or three inches of snow, he slipped, and was precipitated violently forward. As his foothold slid away from beneath him he dropped his end of the chest, and as he fell his stomach struck so violently against the corner of the box that the breath was driven entirely out of his body, so that he could neither swear nor make any outcry whatever.

At first, terrified by his silence, the others of the party thought that the fellow had been fatally hurt; but he presently so far recovered himself that he was able to express, though in a feeble voice, his eternal condemnation of the sheet of ice that had caused his fall, of the chest, of its owner, and of everything concerning it. Nor would he consent to go a single step farther until he had been refreshed at the bar of the dramshop in front of which the late accident had overtaken him, and into which his companions now supported him with a ready alacrity.

Now the carpenter of the Good Samaritan had an excessive liking for strong waters. In the present instance he discovered the rum of the "Shovel and Tongs," as the pothouse was called, to be so uncommonly excellent that he could deny neither himself nor his fellows repeated libations of the same, made very stiff and hot. As a consequence, when the party left the rumshop and plunged once more into the snowy night, our carpenter found that he was not only not at all sure where Van Cortlandt Street was, but that he did not very greatly care.

Nevertheless, directed by a certain vague and obscure sense of duty, he plodded forward, swinging his lanthorn and followed by his laboring assistants, until, after a considerable while, he came to a broad highway crossed by another street which he opined must be the corner of Broadway and Van Cortlandt Street.

The bearers of the chest demurred that the one street was not Van Cortlandt Street at all, and that the other was not Broadway. But the carpenter was very positive that if these were not the streets to which he had been directed, they ought to be. He was further reassured in his conclusions by the extraordinary coincidence that there was a second house upon the right-hand side of the way, just as the owner of the chest had told him there would be; and though the house to which he called attention was a red-brick building, not a white house, such as his employer had described, it did not appear to him that the color could be a matter of importance, since one house was as good as another any day of the week. Moreover, the house upon which he had fixed as the proper destination of the chest had shutters which he opined might be green if seen by daylight.

All this being settled to his entire satisfaction, the carpenter ascended the stoop of the house he had chosen and beat a thunderous tattoo with the knocker upon the door.

How the Reverend Ebenezer Doolittle Received An Unexpected Christmas Box

THE Reverend Ebenezer Doolittle was a shy and retiring man of an anemic constitution and very subject to colds in damp weather. He had married a buxom and stirring wife, who shared neither his shyness and timidity nor his feeble health, but who was of a robustious build both mentally and physically. Indeed, it was a wonder to many of their friends how the reverend gentleman ever plucked up courage to pay his addresses to so bustling a lady. That he must have done so, however, was evident in itself, since she was now the companion of his bed and board.

Upon the particular evening of which this history has to deal our worthy divine was sitting in his study composing the latter sections of an extremely long and, to him, very interesting sermon of thanksgiving, which he proposed to deliver upon the morrow.

From a mood of profound analytical thought he was suddenly aroused by the tremendous detonations of the knocker beaten violently upon the front door.

Immediately after this he heard his wife pass along the hallway, then he heard her open the door, and then a man's voice, very gruff and hoarse, saying something concerning a certain chest or box.

Then there came the sound of shuffling and scuffling as of the feet of men carrying a burden, and then the thump as of a heavy weight deposited upon the floor of the entry.

By this time the reverend gentleman's curiosity had led him to quit his easy chair and his sermon, and he was now standing at the door, which he held ajar.

From where he stood he could hear that a loud altercation of voices was sounding in the hall below, and from the interlocution he could gather that a case or box of some sort had been brought thither by mistake; that his wife insisted that it should be taken away again, and that the chief of the bearers (who appeared to be in a condition of partial inebriety) protested that it belonged to the gentleman of the house, and that he, the bearer, had been promised a dollar for bringing it thither.

The lady assured the speaker that he was drunk, and that she would not give him a copper, and that she desired that the chest should be taken immediately away to the place where it belonged. To this the other voice responded with great exuberance of manner, calling upon his Maker to condemn him if he would move from the spot till he had got the dollar that had been promised him. Upon this the lady's voice rose to a sudden shrill and vituperative violence, and so vehement was her denunciation that her opponents were fairly beaten down before the tempest of her words; for our good divine could distinctly hear the sound of shuffling feet, followed by the banging of the door as it was clapped to behind the departing intruders.

Then succeeded a dead and ominous silence, broken only once by the violent concussion of a brickbat, which the carpenter had kicked out of the snow and had hurled against the front door as a parting salute ere he betook himself back to the pothouse where he had so enjoyed himself a short while since, and where he subsequently spent with inebriate generosity all that was left of the dollar that he had received at the beginning of his night's adventures.

The Terrific Experience
of the Reverend Ebenezer Doolittle in Connection
with the Mysterious Chest

AFTER tranquillity had fallen upon the house so lately the scene of so much noise and uproar, the Reverend Ebenezer became aware that his wife was calling upon him to come down and see what it was that had been left in the hallway.

Descending from his sanctum in reply to this demand, the reverend gentleman discovered a long coffinlike chest standing in the very midst of the floor and illuminated by a candle which his lady held in her hand.

"D'ye see," said she, "what the drunken wretches have left here?"

The reverend gentleman examined the box very carefully for a while, and finally, having reached a conclusion, opined that it must have been left there by mistake. To this the lady replied with considerable acerbity that she could have guessed that without being prompted. The Reverend Ebenezer then suggested that maybe the true owner of the chest could be discovered by means of the address upon the box, whereupon she replied that if he could make anything of the name on the lid he was a great deal more intelligent than she.

Upon this the reverend gentleman shook his head, for there was no other inscription than the one word "Remo," and a few unintelligible words in a foreign language. A surcharge representing two coadjacent circles pierced by an arrow conveyed no significance whatsoever to him.

He then suggested that if they should open the box they might learn from its contents where it belonged, and to this the lady acceded with great alacrity, her assent being stimulated by an absorbing curiosity to see what was in the box.

So a screwdriver was fetched and the parson set to work to remove the lid, his labors being illuminated by the candle which his wife held for him. In a little while the last screw was withdrawn, the lid was lifted, and below was seen a mass of soft white cotton wool. The wool had been padded into a thin sheet, and as the reverend gentleman lifted it a considerable portion of it was raised, immediately disclosing that which lay beneath.

The Reverend Ebenezer Doolittle stood as if turned into a stone! For directly beneath the pad which he now held suspended in his hand he beheld the calm white dead face of a head severed from the trunk to which it had once belonged, and which now lay in the coffin along with it. The dead countenance, illuminated by the light of the candle, was that of a portly gentleman—apparently a merchant of the better sort. The upper part of the body, disclosed by the lifted pad of cotton wool, showed that it was clad in decent black, and a close wig, powdered white, covered the head, from which it was slightly lifted so as to show the shaven crown beneath.

This the eyes of the reverend gentleman beheld as he gazed down upon the dreadful object directly beneath his fingers. For the instant, upon lifting the sheet of cotton wool, he knew not what it was that he saw. Question, doubt and then a dreadful and terrific certainty followed one another in such instantaneous succession that it was but a moment till a full realization burst upon him. And yet this certitude seemed a long time in arriving, and during its progressions a thousand thoughts flew like a swarm of flies through the hollow and ringing spaces of his brain. He had no power to move, but stood spellbound, like to an automaton, gazing upon that which his eyes beheld. It appeared to him that he no longer drew breath and that his heart had ceased its beating.

All this, as was said, occupied but a moment, and yet it appeared to him to be a portentously long time that he stood there looking upon the lifeless face that lay so close beneath the knuckles of his hand. Then he was suddenly and startlingly fetched to himself by a suppressed and smothered shriek from his wife, the clattering of the candlestick upon the floor, and an utter and perfect darkness as of oblivion as the flame was extinguished in the fall of the taper.

In this darkness the Reverend Ebenezer stood with shuddering and palsied limbs, his brain expanding like a bubble, and his eardrums singing as with a high and vibrating point of sound.

He heard, as though remotely, the babbling of his wife's voice beseeching him not to make any noise! Not to say a word! Not to let anybody know what had happened! "Be still, Ebenezer! Be still, and don't say a word!" she was saying. "We must cover it up! Cover it up! Don't let the servants hear anything!" Had the worthy gentleman been called upon to speak, he could no more have done so at the moment than he could have lifted himself up into the air. "Stay where you are!" babbled the lady. "Stay where you are, and I'll fetch a candle. We must put the lid back again, Ebenezer; we must put the lid back on the box again."

"For the love of Heaven!" cried the good dominie, in a hoarse and croaking voice, "don't leave me here alone."

"I must!" she said. "I must get a light. I will be but a moment, and I will be back again directly." And therewith she was gone, leaving him to face his terrors alone in the dark.

When she returned with the lighted candle they replaced the lid of the chest and screwed it down, the good parson using more muscular force than he had ever done in all his life, to make his work fast and secure. The sweat hung upon his brow in great beads, and, all the while he worked, his wife stood sunk in profound and silent thought.

Suddenly she aroused herself and smote her hand upon her hip. "My dear!" she cried, "I smoke it all! The thing must belong to Dr. Stagg next door. The wretches who fetched it hither must be body snatchers and have mistook our house for his, and so it has been left here instead of there."

"But, my dear," said the parson, "suppose it shouldn't be his any more than ours?"

The Mysterious Chest

"Well," said the lady, "we'll let that fly stick in the butter! In any case it is as likely to belong to him as to anybody else, and he knows more about disposing of such things than we do. It would make," said she, "a most excellent anatomy."

It was not twenty steps to the doctor's door, and by some means or other the parson and his wife made shift to drag and push the chest so far through the snow (which was now several inches deep), to tilt it up upon the door stoop, to knock upon the knocker, and then to go away and leave their burden where it was.

The Extraordinary Experiences
of a Physician and His Friends in Connection
with the Mysterious Chest

DR. ORPHEUS STAGG was a young physician not yet so settled in his life but that he was greatly addicted to little supper parties of his own sex, where exhilarating libations could be freely drunk, tobacco smoked, and amusing anecdotes recited without any of the disagreeable limitations to hilarity upon which the presence of the other and gentler sex is so apt to act as a check.

Upon the Christmas Eve of which this narrative treats, our medico had been indulging in such an evening of social pleasure as that just described, and now, about the hour of midnight, was betaking an uncertain way homeward with a party of three other gentlemen, all of whom were fully as elated as himself.

Being chilled by the bitter wind which encountered them, this merry party of cheerful wags were of a mind to take a last and parting cup ere they separated for the night, and with that intent they one and all entered the doctor's house together.

A candle burned dimly upon a console table at the end of the hall, but its feeble light was quite insufficient to enable our doctor in his present condition to see that a large and cumbrous object stood almost directly in the path of his footsteps.

Accordingly, upon leading the way into the house, his feet suddenly encountered so large and so unwieldy an object that he was precipitated upon the floor with great violence and with a prodigious noise and clatter of descent. "Angels of grace!" cries he (using, however, a very much more obstreperous objurgation which the author declines to repeat), "Angels of grace! What have we here?"

The night candle was brought from the console table, and by its light the four gentlemen discovered a large chest of cedar wood resembling a rude coffin. Upon the box was marked the name "Remo," and as a further mark there was surcharged upon it the representation of two adjacent circles pierced by an arrow.

"What is this?" says our physician. "And what is it doing here?"

"Doubtless," said one of his gay companions, "it is a Christmas box sent to you by one of your grateful patients whom you have dosed without fatal results. Perhaps it is full of Bordeaux or Hollands. Let us open it and see."

This suggestion appeared to the party to be so reasonable that a couple of case knives, sufficiently stout to serve as screw drivers, were presently fetched, and the four set to work so busily that in a very little while they had unscrewed and removed the lid.

"'Tis spread with wool," said one of the merry wags. "Let us see what lies beneath."

And thereupon our medico, holding the candle pretty steadily in one hand, lifted the mat of cotton wool with the other, and discovered to the eyes of all the white, motionless, lifeless lineaments that lay beneath—those lineaments set in the awful calmness of an immutable repose.

Our doctor was not unused to objects quite as horrific as that which his eyes now encountered, but so sudden and so violent was the shock upon his nerves at the unexpected unveiling of the dead face beneath the cotton wool that he was struck in the instant into a condition well-nigh as sober as ever he had been in all of his life.

If he were so affected, how much more dreadful must the spectacle have been to those who were altogether unused to such a sight! A silence utter and vast filled the entire space of hall for fully four or five seconds of time—a silence broken at last by the piping and tremulous outcry of one of the whilom revelers. At the sudden sound of a living voice the doctor let fall the cotton wool again, and the face was once more covered.

So dreadful was the shock that our revelers had received that it was small wonder that another of the party should presently have declared that he found himself to be taken violently unwell, and that unless he should presently have either a breath of fresh air or a glass of brandy to support him he should certainly swoon away altogether.

The suggestion of brandy met with such a hearty acceptance by all that they instantly adjourned in a body to the neighboring dining room, where they partook so freely of that exhilarating beverage that in a very short time they were not only raised to a fair level of mental equanimity, but were even elevated above it. They now found that they could discuss the adventure that had just befallen them with some degree of cheerfulness. Our doctor declared that he had no notion of how the chest had come into the house, and he repudiated, not without heat, the suggestion of one of the party that some friend had sent it to him by way of a Christmas gift. He proclaimed with fervor that he had not a single acquaintance who would act in such bad taste as to send him such a gift, and that, so far from its being to him a cheerful reminder of the season, it was not only altogether unwelcome to him, but that he would gladly dispose of it elsewhere if he knew how to do so.

At this point one of his friends suggested that inasmuch as the chest had come to him without his knowledge, it might easily be taken away and left in the same manner at somebody else's door.

This idea so pleased the party and fell so aptly into their then present mood of spirited elation that it was immediately seized upon, and after a good deal of serious discussion as to who should be its recipient it was at last decided that the box should be conveyed to the house of old Jacob Van Kleek, the moneylender, and should be left there for him to take care of.

This plan was no sooner determined upon than it was put into immediate execution. The lid was replaced and screwed into place, and half an hour later the four friends had conveyed the chest around the corner to the residence of the old usurer. Here they tilted it up against the door, and having beat with the knocker until the night-capped head of the old gentleman appeared at an upper window, they went their way, wishing him a merry Christmas and hoping that he might enjoy the box which they had left for him.

In Which Mr. Jacob Van Kleek Is Made Acquainted with the Contents of the Mysterious Chest

OLD Jacob Van Kleek's house was a tall, lean, ugly brick dwelling, so large that it might easily have held a considerable family with perfect convenience, but which contained only himself, a young and pretty niece who was his ward, and a half-grown starveling maid of all work.

Being awakened in the middle of the night by the obstreperous beating of the door knocker upon the door by our facetious medico and his companions, and having heard their message that a Christmas box had been fetched for him, he knew not what to think of it other than that some hoax was being played upon him.

In this conjecture, however, he could not rest entirely easy, for he could not but perceive that the late disturbers of his repose had left behind them in their departure something large and bulky that stood upon the door stoop beneath.

Feeling a considerable curiosity as to the nature of the object, which he could only dimly behold from the elevated station of his bedroom window, he withdrew his head, closed the window, lighted a candle, and, having clad himself in his breeches and stockings, issued forth with intent to satisfy himself as to what it was that had been thus mysteriously fetched to him in the dead of the night.

Upon the landing without he found his pretty niece, who had also been disturbed by the beating upon the door, and who, having heard the colloquy between her uncle and those beneath, was exceedingly curious to know what the midnight visitors had left behind them upon the door stoop. She eagerly volunteered to accompany her uncle downstairs to the front door; but to her offer the old gentleman replied very acidly, calling her attention to the fact that a patchwork bedquilt was so insufficient a costume for a modest young lady to wear even in the middle of the night, that she would better go back to her bed again. He added that if he had wanted her to help him manage his own affairs he would have called upon her without hesitation.

Having thus replied to her invitation to accompany him, he immediately descended alone to the hallway beneath. Having set his candle upon the floor, he proceeded with great caution and circumspection to open the door, proposing to hold it ajar until he had assured himself that no party of roisterers lurked without to welcome his advent with a shower of snowballs or of ribald jests.

His proposed precautions, however, were instantly frustrated by the accident of circumstances; for no sooner was the door released from its restraining bars and bolts than, impelled by some heavy weight that had been tilted against it upon the outside, it flew violently open, and a bulky object of great weight and momentum projected itself upon the moneylender so unexpectedly that both he and it were precipitated to the floor with a prodigious noise and uproar—his shins, in their common fall, being so barked that he could not put on his yarn stockings with any degree of comfort to himself for above a fortnight afterward.

A gust of icy wind and a cloud of snow burst in through the open portal, and in an instant the light of the candle was extinguished. So chill and biting was this blast that in spite of the smart of his hurts the old moneylender's first conscious performance was to arise and close the door.

He then sat himself down on the object that had caused his overthrow, and fell to feeling his injured extremities with a sort of tender violence, meanwhile addressing the door, the object upon which he sat, the extinguished candle, the frigid night, and even his own shins with a vehemence of language in which he rarely indulged himself. And when his niece called over the banisters to ask him if he was hurt, he assured her with great earnestness that it was his sincere belief that she was not only an utter fool, but a hopeless idiot as well. Having somewhat eased himself by these expressions of opinions concerning the various subjects of his discourse, he commanded his niece to fetch another candle, telling her that he thought that even her limited intelligence should have informed her that it was impossible for normal human eyes to see anything in total darkness.

When the young lady had descended with a fresh candle, the old gentleman turned a more particular attention on that which had caused his overthrow. It was a coffinlike chest superscribed with the word "Remo" and surcharged with an image of two contiguous circles pierced with an arrow.

The entire appearance of the chest was of so unusual a sort that he could in no wise conceive what it might contain. His niece suggested that perhaps it held a fat turkey and a bushel of apples sent as a propitiatory offering by some would-be borrower of money, but from this he dissented with immediate asperity, bidding her first of all to mind her own business, then to fetch him a screwdriver, and finally to go to her bed.

Being at last alone with the mysterious chest, the old money-lender addressed himself to the task of opening it with intent to master a knowledge of its contents. That the highest expectations of his curiosity were more than fulfilled the astute reader will no doubt concede with instant acquiescence.

It was fully ten minutes before the young lady heard him re-ascending the stairs with stealthy and laggard steps. Holding her bedroom door ajar, she immediately addressed him through the crack, desiring to hear what were the contents of the chest. For a moment or two he seemed disinclined to answer, but as with a second thought he replied in a tremulous and quaking voice that it was oakum.

"Oakum!" she cried, with a very natural surprise. "Why, what should they do to bring you a box of oakum at this time of night?" To this he answered that the box was not intended for him at all, but was meant for Gideon White, the ship chandler. Then feeling, perhaps, that his answer was not altogether adequate, he added that this particular kind of oakum came in a long case because it was what was called "long-cut oakum," being used for stopping cracks in main-masts when they became sun-dried, as they sometimes did, and split open with the heat.

In offering this explanation, he felt that his powers of invention had been stretched almost beyond the limits of credibility, but he was pleased to note that his story appeared to be quite acceptable to his niece, who, with many expressions of disappointment that the chest should have held nothing more interesting than oakum, closed her door and betook herself to bed.

How Mr. Augustus Beeker Finds an Unexpected Client

Mr. AUGUSTUS BEEKER was a young lawyer enjoying great expecta-tions but very little practice. He lived in a large and rather impos-ing house built in an old style of black and red brick. In this very genteel residence (which was directly next door to the abode of old Jacob Van Kleek) our young disciple of Solon dwelt with his mother, who was an elderly lady of corpulent build and great dignity of demeanor. She had in her unmarried years been the possessor of a considerable fortune, but having wedded a husband of a high social position but not possessed of very good morals, she had found her means so reduced at his death that there was hardly enough left to live upon with such a decent appearance of respectable gentility as became her and her son's quality.

Our young gentleman of the law was very much in love with the pretty niece of old Jacob Van Kleek, but as the guardian of the young lady set more value upon a bank account than he did upon high birth and personal merit, the suit of the enamored swain was by no means so prosperous as he and his charmer could have de-sired.

Our hero's inamorata was not at all averse to the addresses of her suitor, but so violent was the opposition of her uncle that there could be no possible hope for the realization of their mutual happiness for at least three years to come—at the end of which time (she being now eighteen years of age) she would become the mistress, in the eyes of the law, both of herself and of her father's fortune.

About two o'clock of the night upon which the events narrated in this history had transpired our young lawyer was awaked from a sound and refreshing slumber by the noise of a violent beating of the knocker upon the front door of the house. Upon opening his window and inquiring who it was that so disturbed the silence of the night, he learned, with astonishment, that the untimely intruder was none other than old Jacob Van Kleek, the uncle of his love.

To hurry into his clothes, to descend, to open the door to his astonishing visitor, occupied the space of not above a minute and a half.

By the light of the candle which he held our hero perceived that the countenance of his caller was disturbed by some unusual and very violent emotion, as of terror and amazement commingled.

The old moneylender made immediate demand that he should be instantly taken to some place where he could relieve an overburdened mind, and upon being introduced into the young attorney's private office he began without any delay to speak as follows:

"Sir, a terrible and astonishing misfortune has befallen me, and I am come to you to obtain your assistance. This I do, not only because I believe I can buy your advice cheaper than I could that of one who is older and more experienced, but also because you are no doubt so in need of a case that you will probably be willing to take up with one that an older man wouldn't touch. Besides this, I believe you are in love with my niece, and I have to propose to you that if you will bring me safe out of this affair I will not only withdraw my opposition to your suit, but will even further it in as far as I am able."

With this preface, so astounding that our young lawyer knew not whether his sense of hearing had not played him false, the old moneylender plunged at once into the depths of the business that brought him thither.

And to all that he said our young lawyer listened with ever growing amazement and equally increasing incredulity. He knew not what to think of that which he heard; he knew not whether to believe that his client had been hoaxed, or whether he himself was being made the subject of the old gentleman's wit; he knew not whether the moneylender had gone mad, or whether he was the victim of some unusual variety of intoxication. Yet none of these surmises could satisfy him, for, in spite of all his doubts and misgivings, he could not but perceive, from the distracted manner of the other, that something most amazing had certainly occurred to terrify him out of his usual dry and phlegmatic manner.

"Sir," said he, "'tis the most amazing story that I ever heard tell of. If you will wait till I dress myself I will go with you to your house to look more particularly into the business."

When our hero entered the old usurer's house he beheld at once the mysterious chest standing exactly where the old man had told him it had been left. A candlestick with its guttering candle stood near by upon the floor, and, taking it in his hand, our young lawyer began to examine the cedar chest with the greatest particularity.

"Remo," quoth he. "I can think of no such name."

"Nor can I," quoth the elder man.

"Two circles and a broad arrow," said our hero. "I cannot guess what that may signify."

"Nor can I," said the other.

"Stay!" said our hero, bending more closely over another and a smaller inscription that he observed to be upon the lid. "Do you read French, sir?"

"Not I," quoth the other. "'Tis a language I never bothered with."

"Nevertheless, 'tis sometimes an advantage to know that language," quoth our young lawyer. "That advantage I myself possess; therefore let us see what is written here." Thereupon, holding the flame of the candle close to the written inscription, he bent over and perused it with great particularity.

In a moment or two, and having made himself master of the

purport of the written words, he lifted his head and presented to the old usurer a countenance twisted and distorted as by some violent though suppressed emotion. Nor was he, for a considerable time, able to regain any mastery over that inner convulsion that so disturbed him, nor to articulate a single word.

At length, being able to speak, though in an unnatural and choking voice, he addressed the old moneylender as follows:

"Sir," said he, "have you, then, no suspicions of what it really is that hath so terrified you?"

"No," quoth the other, "except that it is a dead man with his head cut off."

"Know," said our hero, very solemnly, "that what you beheld was the lifeless form of a French gentleman of high and even royal blood, who was lately decapitated in Paris by the bloody and ferocious rabble of that city. All this I read here upon this coffin, and you yourself might also have read it had you but understood a little French."

"But why," cried out the unfortunate moneylender, "has this thing been fetched to me thus and at the dead of night? God knows I had nothing to do with the business and no concern in making away with his poor dead body."

"I well believe you," quoth the young attorney, "but it may be that some enemy hath sent it to you. However that may be, the thing is here, and now that it is here, it will, I fear, be not so easy a thing to convince others as you have convinced me of your innocence. Now I am prepared to assist you in ridding yourself of both this chest and its contents; but I will only undertake that commission upon such conditions as may be very unpalatable to you to fulfill."

At this the old usurer's face fell to a very melancholy length, for he foresaw a whacking fee that would bleed him deep. "What," said he, with a very dubitating voice, "is, then, your condition? I pray you, be as easy with me as you can."

"Sir," said the young lawyer, "it is well known to you that I have long loved that lady who is your niece and ward. If you will withdraw your opposition to my suit, and will permit us both to follow our inclinations, and if you will, from the day of our marriage and until she comes of age, pay her the interest upon her fortune, I shall be able, I doubt not, to help you out of all your embarrassment in this unfortunate business."

These conditions were so unexpectedly easy to the old money-lender that his face was instantly illuminated, almost as with an appearance of good humor. "Friend," cried he, with great alacrity, "if that be all you ask, I will grant it and give you my thanks into the bargain. For I shall regard you in the light of the best friend that ever I had in all of my life if you will but rid me of this horrific object, the very thought of which curdles my blood, I believe, to a jelly. For indeed if this dreadful thing is not taken away I shall go mad, or cut my throat with a razor, knowing that I have it about, and not knowing how I shall ease my house of so detestable a burden."

"Then," cried our hero, "we are both satisfied, and the next step in the business is to remove this coffin and its contents to my house. For, once there, I believe I shall have little or no difficulty in disposing of it."

"If that is all," cried out the old man, with extraordinary eagerness, "I myself will be very glad to help you to carry it thither."

Accordingly, half an hour later, the young lawyer and his new-found client lugged the mysterious chest through the snow to the former's house, and there deposited it in the back kitchen.

How the Mysterious Chest Found Its Proper Owner

UPON the day following this night of terror, there appeared in the window of a disused store upon Van Cortlandt Street near to Broadway a placard announcing the fact that Herr Zimmelberger, the famous living skeleton from Germany, would exhibit upon Christmas Day and two days thereafter, not only himself, but a perfect image in wax of the late unfortunate king of the French. The notice said that these two great curiosities were then upon their way to Philadelphia, but that they had stopped for three days in New York so that the people of that town might also enjoy a sight of two such unexcelled wonders. The advertisement added that the admission was but ten cents for adults and five cents for children, and it called upon the entire community to take advantage of an opportunity so rare that in all likelihood it would never be repeated.

In this otherwise empty store the living skeleton and the young lawyer stood side by side talking, whilst they considered the effigy of the late unhappy king of the French.

The figure lay upon a sort of bier, covered with black velvet and embellished with tinsel fleurs-de-lis. It was clad very respectably in black, and the colorless waxen hands were meekly laid the one upon the other as if in infinite repose. It was the figure that had brought so much terror into the three quiet households the preceding night. The living skeleton was Mr. Jedediah Stout, who had called at Mr. Peck's office the afternoon before.

"Well," said the living skeleton, " 'tis a beautiful figger, and if you had not brought it to me 'twould have been a great loss to me this day. Now what do I owe you for a fee?"

"Nothing at all," quoth our young lawyer. "Not a stiver! For your waxwork, it has already brought me, last night, the best stroke of luck that ever I had in my life! 'Twas a good thing I was able to read a little French, so as to know what it was in the chest and to whom it belonged."

Conclusion

IT is altogether likely that the thoughtless reader who follows this serious history will think but little of anything else than of the entertainment he can find in it. But the author has recounted the several events not that he might amuse the frivolous, but that he might supply food for thought to the more sober-minded. For how often doth it happen that the most innocent and harmless appearances will disturb the repose of mankind with terror and apprehension for which there is, only too often, no foundation whatsoever.

Yet to those who read in lighter vein it may be said that the young lawyer was married to the usurer's niece, with the grateful uncle's consent, in the following spring.

HAMLIN GARLAND

My First Christmas Tree

I WILL begin by saying that we never had a Christmas tree in our house in the Wisconsin coulée; indeed, my father never saw one in a family circle till he saw that which I set up for my own children last year. But we celebrated Christmas in those days, always, and I cannot remember a time when we did not all hang up our stockings for "Sandy Claws" to fill. As I look back upon those days it seems as if the snows were always deep, the night skies crystal clear, and the stars especially lustrous with frosty sparkles of blue and yellow fire—and probably this was so, for we lived in a Northern land where winter was usually stern and always long.

I recall one Christmas when "Sandy" brought me a sled, and a horse that stood on rollers—a wonderful tin horse which I very shortly split in two in order to see what his insides were. Father traded a cord of wood for the sled, and the horse cost twenty cents —but they made the day wonderful.

Another notable Christmas Day, as I stood in our front yard, mid-leg deep in snow, a neighbor drove by closely muffled in furs, while behind his seat his son, a lad of twelve or fifteen, stood beside a barrel of apples, and as he passed he hurled a glorious big red one at me. It missed me, but bored a deep, round hole in the soft snow. I thrill yet with the remembered joy of burrowing for that delicious bomb. Nothing will ever smell quite as good as that Wine Sap or Northern Spy or whatever it was. It was a wayward impulse on the part of the boy in the sleigh, but it warms my heart after more than forty years.

We had no chimney in our home, but the stocking-hanging was a ceremony nevertheless. My parents, and especially my mother, entered into it with the best of humor. They always put up their own stockings or permitted us to do it for them—and they always laughed next morning when they found potatoes or ears of corn in them. I can see now that my mother's laugh had a tear in it, for she loved pretty things and seldom got any during the years that we lived in the coulée.

When I was ten years old we moved to Mitchell County, an Iowa prairie land, and there we prospered in such wise that our stockings always held toys of some sort, and even my mother's stocking occasionally sagged with a simple piece of jewelry or a new comb or brush. But the thought of a family tree remained the luxury of millionaire city dwellers; indeed it was not till my fifteenth or sixteenth year that our Sunday school rose to the extravagance of a tree, and it is of this wondrous festival that I write.

The land about us was only partly cultivated at this time, and our district schoolhouse, a bare little box, was set bleakly on the prairie; but the Burr Oak schoolhouse was not only larger but it stood beneath great oaks as well and possessed the charm of a forest background through which a stream ran silently. It was our chief social center. There of a Sunday a regular preacher held "Divine service" with Sunday school as a sequence. At night—usually on Friday nights—the young people let in "ly-ceums," as we called them, to debate great questions or to "speak pieces" and read essays; and here it was that I saw my first Christmas tree.

I walked to that tree across four miles of moonlit snow. Snow? No, it was a floor of diamonds, a magical world, so beautiful that my heart still aches with the wonder of it and with the regret that it has all gone—gone with the keen eyes and the bounding pulses of the boy.

Our home at this time was a small frame house on the prairie almost directly west of the Burr Oak grove, and as it was too cold to take the horses out my brother and I, with our tall boots, our visored caps and our long woolen mufflers, started forth afoot defiant of the cold. We left the gate on the trot, bound for a sight of the glittering unknown. The snow was deep and we moved side by side in the grooves made by the hoofs of the horses, setting our feet in the shine left by the broad shoes of the wood sleighs whose going had smoothed the way for us.

Our breaths rose like smoke in the still air. It must have been ten below zero, but that did not trouble us in those days, and at last we came in sight of the lights, in sound of the singing, the laughter, the bells of the feast.

It was a poor little building without tower or bell and its low walls had but three windows on a side, and yet it seemed very imposing to me that night as I crossed the threshold and faced the strange people who packed it to the door. I say "strange people," for though I had seen most of them many times they all seemed somehow alien to me that night. I was an irregular attendant at Sunday school and did not expect a present, therefore I stood against the wall and gazed with open-eyed marveling at the shining pine which stood where the pulpit was wont to be. I was made to feel the more embarrassed by reason of the remark of a boy who accused me of having forgotten to comb my hair.

This was not true, but the cap I wore always matted my hair down over my brow, and then, when I lifted it off invariably disarranged it completely. Nevertheless I felt guilty—and hot. I don't suppose my hair was artistically barbered that night—I rather guess Mother had used the shears—and I can believe that I looked the half-wild colt that I was; but there was no call for that youth to direct attention to my unavoidable shagginess.

I don't think the tree had many candles, and I don't remember that it glittered with golden apples. But it was loaded with presents, and the girls coming and going clothed in bright garments made me forget my own looks—I think they made me forget to remove my overcoat, which was a sodden thing of poor cut and worse quality. I think I must have stood agape for nearly two hours listening to the songs, noting every motion of Adoniram Burtch and Asa Walker as they directed the ceremonies and prepared the way for the great event—that is to say, for the coming of Santa Claus himself.

A furious jingling of bells, a loud voice outside, the lifting of a window, the nearer clash of bells, and the dear old Saint appeared (in the person of Stephen Bartle) clothed in a red robe, a belt of sleigh bells, and a long white beard. The children cried out, "Oh!" The girls tittered and shrieked with excitement, and the boys laughed and clapped their hands. Then "Sandy" made a little speech about being glad to see us all, but as he had many other places to visit, and as there were a great many presents to distribute, he guessed he'd have to ask some of the many pretty girls to help him. So he called upon Betty Burtch and Hattie Knapp—and I for one admired his taste, for they were the most popular maids of the school.

They came up blushing, and a little bewildered by the blaze of publicity thus blown upon them. But their native dignity asserted itself, and the distribution of the presents began. I have a notion now that the fruit upon the tree was mostly bags of popcorn and "corny copias" of candy, but as my brother and I stood there that night and saw everybody, even the rowdiest boy, getting something we felt aggrieved and rebellious. We forgot that we had come from afar—we only knew that we were being left out.

But suddenly, in the midst of our gloom, my brother's name was called, and a lovely girl with a gentle smile handed him a bag of popcorn. My heart glowed with gratitude. Somebody had thought of us; and when she came to me, saying sweetly, "Here's something for you," I had not words to thank her. This happened nearly forty years ago, but her smile, her outstretched hand, her sympathetic eyes are vividly before me as I write. She was sorry for the shock-headed boy who stood against the wall, and her pity made the little box of candy a casket of pearls. The fact that I swallowed the jewels on the road home does not take from the reality of my adoration.

At last I had to take my final glimpse of that wondrous tree, and I well remember the walk home. My brother and I traveled in word-less companionship. The moon was sinking toward the west, and the snow crust gleamed with a million fairy lamps. The sentinel watchdogs barked from lonely farmhouses, and the wolves answered from the ridges. Now and then sleighs passed us with lovers sitting two and two, and the bells on their horses had the remote music of romance to us whose boots drummed like clogs of wood upon the icy road.

Our house was dark as we approached and entered it, but how deliciously warm it seemed after the pitiless wind! I confess we made straight for the cupboard for a mince pie, a doughnut and a bowl of milk!

As I write this there stands in my library a thick-branched, beautifully tapering fir tree covered with the gold and purple apples of Hesperides, together with crystal ice points, green and red and yellow candles, clusters of gilded grapes, wreaths of metallic frost, and glittering angels swinging in ecstasy; but I doubt if my children will ever know the keen pleasure (that is almost pain) which came to my brother and to me in those Christmas days when an orange was not a breakfast fruit, but a casket of incense and of spice, a message from the sunlands of the South.

That was our compensation—we brought to our Christmastime a keen appetite and empty hands. And the lesson of it all is, if we are seeking a lesson, that it is better to give to those who want than to those for whom "we ought to do something because they did something for us last year."

ZONA GALE

To Springvale for Christmas

"Her children arise up and call her blessed."

WHEN President Arthur Tilton of Briarcliff College,
who usually used a two-cent stamp, said, "Get me
Chicago, please," his secretary was impressed, looked
for vast educational problems to be in the making, and heard
instead:

"Ed? Well, Ed, you and Rick and Grace and I are going out to
Springvale for Christmas. . . . Yes, well, I've got a family too, you
recall. But mother was seventy last fall and—Do you realize that it's
eleven years since we all spent Christmas with her? Grace has been
every year. She's going this year. And so are we! And take her the
best Christmas she ever had, too. Ed, mother was *seventy* last
fall——"

544

To Springvale for Christmas

At dinner, he asked his wife what would be a suitable gift, a very special gift, for a woman of seventy. And she said: "Oh, your mother. Well, dear, I should think the material for a good wool dress would be right. I'll select it for you, if you like——" He said that he would see, and he did not reopen the subject.

In town on December twenty-fourth he timed his arrival to allow him an hour in a shop. There he bought a silver-gray silk of a fineness and a lightness which pleased him and at a price which made him comfortably guilty. And at the shop, Ed, who was Edward McKillop Tilton, head of a law firm, picked him up.

"Where's your present?" Arthur demanded.

Edward drew a case from his pocket and showed him a tiny gold wrist watch of decent manufacture and explained: "I expect you'll think I'm a fool, but you know that mother has told time for fifty years by the kitchen clock, or else the shield of the black-marble parlor angel who never goes—you get the idea?—and so I bought her this."

At the station was Grace, and the boy who bore her bag bore also a parcel of great dimensions.

"Mother already has a feather bed," Arthur reminded her.

"They won't let you take an automobile into the coach," Edward warned her.

"It's a rug for the parlor," Grace told them. "You know it *is* a parlor—one of the few left in the Mississippi Valley. And mother has had that ingrain down since before we left home——"

Grace's eyes were misted. Why would women always do that? This was no occasion for sentiment. This was a merry Christmas.

"Very nice. And Ricky'd better look sharp," said Edward dryly.

Ricky never did look sharp. About trains he was conspicuously ignorant. He had no occupation. Some said that he "wrote," but no one had ever seen anything that he had written. He lived in town—no one knew how—never accepted a cent from his brothers and was beloved of everyone, most of all of his mother.

"Ricky won't bring anything, of course," they said.

But when the train pulled out without him, observably, a porter came staggering through the cars carrying two great suitcases and following a perturbed man of forty-something who said, "Oh, here you are!" as if it were they who were missing, and squeezed himself and his suitcases among brothers and sister and rug. "I had only a minute to spare," he said regretfully. "If I'd had two, I could have snatched some flowers. I flung 'em my card and told 'em to send 'em."

"Why are you taking so many lugs?" they wanted to know.

Ricky focused on the suitcases. "Just necessities," he said. "Just the presents. I didn't have room to get in anything else."

"Presents! What?"

"Well," said Ricky, "I'm taking books. I know mother doesn't care much for books, but the bookstore's the only place I can get trusted."

They turned over his books: fiction, travels, biography, a new illustrated edition of the Bible—they were willing to admire his selection. And Grace said confusedly but appreciatively: "You know, the parlor bookcase has never had a thing in it excepting a green curtain over it!"

And they were all borne forward, well pleased.

Springvale has eight hundred inhabitants. As they drove through the principal street at six o'clock on that evening of December twenty-fourth, all that they expected to see abroad was the popcorn wagon and a cat or two. Instead they counted seven automobiles and estimated thirty souls, and no one paid the slightest attention to them as strangers. Springvale was becoming metropolitan. There was a new church on one corner and a store building bore the sign "Public Library." Even the little hotel had a rubber plant in the window and a strip of cretonne overhead.

The three men believed themselves to be a surprise. But, mindful of the panic to be occasioned by four appetites precipitated into a Springvale ménage, Grace had told. Therefore the parlor was lighted and heated, there was in the air of the passage an odor of brown gravy which, no butler's pantry ever having inhibited, seemed a permanent savory. By the happiest chance, Mrs. Tilton had not heard their arrival nor—the parlor angel being in her customary eclipse and the kitchen grandfather's clock wrong—had she begun to look for them. They slipped in, they followed Grace down the hall, they entered upon her in her gray gingham apron worn over her best blue serge, and they saw her first in profile, frosting a lemon pie. With some assistance from her, they all took her in their arms at once.

"Aren't you surprised?" cried Edward in amazement.

"I haven't got over being surprised," she said placidly, "since I first heard you were coming!"

She gazed at them tenderly, with flour on her chin, and then said: "There's something you won't like. We're going to have the Christmas dinner tonight."

Their clamor that they would entirely like that did not change her look.

"Our church couldn't pay the minister this winter," she said, "on account of the new church building. So the minister and his wife are boarding around with the congregation. Tomorrow's their day to come here for a week. It's a hard life and I didn't have the heart to change 'em."

Her family covered their regret as best they could and entered upon her little feast. At the head of her table, with her four "children" about her, and father's armchair left vacant, they perceived that she was not quite the figure they had been thinking her. In this interval they had grown to think of her as a pathetic figure. Not because their father had died, not because she insisted on Springvale as a residence, not because of her eyes. Just pathetic. Mothers of grown children, they might have given themselves the suggestion, were always pathetic. But here was mother, a definite person, with poise and with ideas, who might be proud of her offspring, but who, in her heart, never forgot that they were her offspring and that she was the parent stock.

"I wouldn't eat two pieces of that pie," she said to President Tilton; "it's pretty rich." And he answered humbly: "Very well, mother." And she took with composure Ricky's light chant:

"Now, you must remember, wherever you are,
That you are the jam, but your mother's the jar."

"Certainly, my children," she said. "And I'm about to tell you when you may have your Christmas presents. Not tonight. Christmas Eve is no proper time for presents. It's stealing a day outright! And you miss the fun of looking forward all night long. The only proper time for the presents is after breakfast on Christmas morning, after the dishes are washed. The minister and his wife may get here any time from nine on. That means we've got to get to bed early!"

President Arthur Tilton lay in his bed looking at the muslin curtain on which the street lamp threw the shadow of a bare elm which he remembered. He thought: "She's a pioneer spirit. She's the kind who used to go ahead anyway, even if they had missed the emigrant party, and who used to cross the plains alone. She's the backbone of the world. I wish I could megaphone that to the students at Briarcliff who think their mothers 'try to boss' them!"

"Don't leave your windows open too far," he heard from the hall. The wind's changed."

In the light of a snowy morning the home parlor showed the cluttered commonplace of a room whose furniture and ornaments were not believed to be beautiful and most of them known not to be useful. Yet when—after the dishes were washed—these five came to the leather chair which bore the gifts, the moment was intensely satisfactory. This in spite of the sense of haste with which the parcels were attacked—lest the minister and his wife arrive in their midst.

"That's one reason," Mrs. Tilton said, "why I want to leave part of my Christmas for you until I take you to the train tonight. Do you care?"

"I'll leave a present I know about until then too," said Ricky. "May I?"

"Come on now, though," said President Arthur Tilton. "I want to see mother get her dolls."

To Springvale for Christmas

It was well that they were not of an age to look for exclamations of delight from mother. To every gift her reaction was one of startled rebuke.

"Grace! How could you? All that money! Oh, it's beautiful! But the old one would have done me all my life. . . . Why, Edward! You extravagant boy! I never had a watch in my life. You ought not to have gone to all that expense. Arthur Tilton! A silk dress! What a firm piece of goods! I don't know what to say to you—you're all too good to me!"

At Ricky's books she stared and said: "My dear boy, you've been very reckless. Here are more books than I can ever read—now. Why, that's almost more than they've got to start the new library with. And you spent all that money on me!"

It dampened their complacence, but they understood her concealed delight and they forgave her an honest regret of their modest prodigality. For, when they opened her gifts for them, they felt the same reluctance to take the hours and hours of patient knitting for which these stood.

"Hush, and hurry," was her comment, "or the minister'll get us!"

The minister and his wife, however, were late. The second side of the turkey was ready and the mince pie hot when, toward noon, they came to the door—a faint little woman and a thin man with beautiful, exhausted eyes. They were both in some light glow of excitement and disregarded Mrs. Tilton's efforts to take their coats.

"No," said the minister's wife. "No. We do beg your pardon. But we find we have to go into the country this morning."

"It is absolutely necessary that we go into the country," said the minister earnestly. "This morning," he added impressively.

"Into the country! You're going to be here for dinner."

They were firm. They had to go into the country. They shook hands almost tenderly with these four guests. "We just heard about you in the post office," they said. "Merry Christmas—oh, Merry Christmas! We'll be back about dark."

They left their two shabby suitcases on the hall floor and went away.

"All the clothes they've got between them would hardly fill these up," said Mrs. Tilton mournfully. "Why on earth do you suppose they'd turn their back on a dinner that smells so good and go off into the country at noon on Christmas Day? They wouldn't do that for another invitation. Likely somebody's sick," she ended, her puzzled look denying her tone of finality.

"Well, thank the Lord for the call to the country," said Ricky shamelessly. "It saved our day."

They had their Christmas dinner; they had their afternoon — safe and happy and uninterrupted. Five commonplace-looking folk in a commonplace-looking house, but the eye of love knew that this was not all. In the wide sea of their routine they had found and taken for their own this island day, unforgettable.

"I thought it was going to be a gay day," said Ricky at its close, "but it hasn't. It's been heavenly! Mother, shall we give them the rest of their presents now, you and I?"

"Not yet," she told them. "Ricky, I want to whisper to you."

She looked so guilty that they all laughed at her. Ricky was laughing when he came back from that brief privacy. He was still laughing mysteriously when his mother turned from a telephone call.

"What do you think?" she cried. "That was the woman that brought me my turkey. She knew the minister and his wife were to be with me today. She wants to know why they've been eating a lunch in a cutter out that way. Do you suppose——"

They all looked at one another doubtfully, then in abrupt conviction. "They went because they wanted us to have the day to ourselves!"

"Arthur," said Mrs. Tilton with immense determination, "let me whisper to you, too." And from that moment's privacy he also returned smiling, but a bit ruefully.

"Mother ought to be the president of a university," he said.

"Mother ought to be the head of a law firm," said Edward.

"Mother ought to write a book about herself," said Ricky.

"Mother's mother," said Grace, "and that's enough. But you're all so mysterious, except me."

To Springvale for Christmas

"Grace," said Mrs. Tilton, "you remind me that I want to whisper to you."

Their train left in the late afternoon. Through the white streets they walked to the station, the somber little woman, the buoyant, capable daughter, the three big sons. She drew them to seclusion down by the baggage room and gave them four envelopes.

"Here's the rest of my Christmas for you," she said. "I'd rather you'd open it on the train. Now, Ricky, what's yours?"

She was firm to their protests. The train was whistling when Ricky owned up that the rest of his Christmas present for his mother was a brand-new daughter, to be acquired as soon as his new book was off the press. "We're going to marry on the advance royalty," he said importantly, "and live on——" The rest was lost in the roar of the express.

"Edward!" shouted Mrs. Tilton. "Come here. I want to whisper——"

She was obliged to shout it, whatever it was. But Edward heard, and nodded, and kissed her. There was time for her to slip something in Ricky's pocket and for the other good-bys, and then the train drew out. From the other platform they saw her brave, calm face against the background of the little town. A mother of "grown children" pathetic? She seemed to them at that moment the one supremely triumphant figure in life.

They opened their envelopes soberly and sat soberly over the contents. The note, scribbled to Grace, explained: Mother wanted to divide up now what she had had for them in her will. She would keep one house and live on the rent from the other one, and "here's all the rest." They laughed at her postscript:

"Don't argue. I ought to give the most—I'm the mother."

"And look at her," said Edward solemnly. "As soon as she heard about Ricky, there at the station, she whispered to me that she wanted to send Ricky's sweetheart the watch I'd just given her. Took it off her wrist then and there."

"That must be what she slipped in my pocket," said Ricky.

It was.

"She asked me," he said, "if I minded if she gave those books to the new Springvale Public Library."

"She asked me," said Grace, "if I cared if she gave the new rug to the new church that can't pay its minister."

President Arthur Tilton shouted with laughter.

"When we heard where the minister and his wife ate their Christmas dinner," he said, "she whispered to ask me whether she might give the silk dress to her when they get back tonight."

All this they knew by the time the train reached the crossing where they could look back on Springvale. On the slope of the hill lay the little cemetery, and Ricky said:

"And she told me that if my flowers got there before dark, she'd take them up to the cemetery for Christmas for father. By night she won't have even a flower left to tell her we've been there."

"Not even the second side of the turkey," said Grace, "and yet I think——"

"So do I," her brothers said.

ELSIE SINGMASTER

"I Gotta Idee!"

JUST before suppertime on Christmas Eve, Amelia Brodhead suffered a shock, the first of a series. She laid down her wooden spoon, covered her bread dough with a fragment of old table-cloth and a darned shawl, and stood the mixing bowl on a chair behind the stove. She was a short woman, thirty-five years old, with unnaturally large black eyes and the odd wrinkles of skin shrunk by a sudden falling away of flesh.

"Where are the children?" she asked impatiently.

Bill, the children's father, sat by the window staring at a steep hillside covered with snow. He, too, was small and thin; his large workman's hands, which were not brown and callused but white and soft, looked out of proportion to his body. He had long ago come from Pennsylvania to Colorado with other miners.

"Coasting," he said.

"They'll have the appetites of tigers," said Amelia. "It's their own fault if they go hungry to bed."

On the other side of the table Gran'ma Brodhead sat knitting stockings from Red Cross yarn. She was so small that she looked like an aged fairy. Unable to move from her chair, she knitted all day and all evening; sometimes Amelia heard her needles clicking at night. All the little children in Coaltown had been sweatered and stockinged by Gran'ma. She looked anxiously at her daughter-in-law—Amelia had a hard time.

"I have a little peppermint candy put away," she said. "That will help."

From his high chair the year-old baby, still unnamed, lifted his voice. His howls said: "I'm hungry, that's what I am! I'm starving!"

Amelia threw her apron over her head and stepped out the door and along the side of the house. It was like walking in a tunnel, the piled snow was so deep. To her right towered the mammoth breaker and a veritable mountain of mined coal for which there was no market. Black against an orange sky, where hung the new moon like a golden thread, and Venus like a glittering gem, stood a row of fifty frame houses, all alike.

Moved by the impulse which had moved Amelia, four women appeared on doorsteps and at gates. Next door stood tall Grace Tanger, in dark blue Red Cross cotton cloth, which she had cut stylishly without a pattern. She was the only woman in Coaltown with a claim to beauty. She looked not at the breaker at which she appeared to look, but through it at the grim hill in whose depths her husband had met his death. When the mine opened, if it ever opened, other women would have men to work for them, but Grace would have no one: moreover, her home would be taken from her. Farther down the row stood Gwenny Thomas, a Welsh woman, wrapped in a red shawl, Irish Mrs. O'Hara in black, and Mrs. Nuncio, part Mexican and part dear knows what, in dull orange.

"Where are the children?" asked Grace, in her clear, serious voice.

"The Lord knows," answered Mrs. O'Hara. "Not a sound do you hear."

"I Gotta Idee!"

"They're coastin'!" shouted O'Hara, from the end of the street. "Leave 'em play—what else can they do?"

Mothers' minds ran on the same track. "An' git appetites like houn' pups!" cried Mrs. O'Hara. "Go in, Grace Tanger, wid yer bare head!"

"Merry Chris'mass!" called a man's voice, and instantly Grace stood still and every other woman turned her head. In line with the row of dwellings and a little apart stood the Community House, a broad, squat building, some of its rooms on the street level, others running down the hill. Here under one roof were the store, the bunk rooms which accommodated forty men, the dining room where they ate, the lounging room where they played games and talked, the kitchen fitted with electric appliances run from the plant. The speaker was Michael Larson, a Swede, formerly cook. He stood on the step, a giant with long, pendant yellowish mustaches. His English, learned from Italian laborers, was the queerest English ever heard.

He was now an important person; the departing superintendent had put him in charge not of the property alone but of the ten families who stayed because they had no place to go. "They can at least keep warm. Let them have the coal they need. The Red Cross will give flour and the company will furnish a per capita allowance of food."

"If only the teacher could stay!" sighed Coaltown. But the teacher was invited to take a vacation without pay through December, January, and March. Hitherto a home missionary had preached in the schoolhouse on alternate Sundays; now even he failed to appear.

His greeting answered by silence, the Swede called "Merry Chris'mass," again, with exactly the same result. Then a shocking thing happened. This second blow Amelia gave to herself. Of all the dwellers in Coaltown she was most careful of her speech, most ambitious for her children; she had even dreamed of sending them thirty miles to high school. In her desperation she became suddenly another person. "Oh, yeah?" she said loudly, sarcastically and savagely.

" 'Chris'mass'!" mocked Mrs. O'Hara, quick to imitate. "What's that?"

" 'Chris'mass'!" scoffed black-browed Gwenny Thomas. "That's done for!"

Imperturbable, unaffected by jeers, stood the Swede. "Four o'clock tomorrow da treat," he called. "Eferybody promp'."

" 'Treat'!" mocked Gwenny. "A dry orange and a stick of stale candy!"

Horrified at herself, Amelia went into the house. "I'm ashamed," she thought. "The Evil One tempts me."

The six children came with a roar—Mary and Harry, Doris and Belle, Raymond and Melvin. Amelia gave them bread, spread thinly with apple butter, and large portions of mush spread with nothing, and Gran'ma gave each a peppermint drop. Gran'ma sat knitting and knitting; her clever hands seemed to fly. Amelia determined that she would keep all the children at home. They ought not to coast any more, nor ought they torture other mothers as frantic as she was. Sometimes they visited the Community House, but lately the Swede locked the doors and apparently went to bed early. "I could read them the Christmas story," she thought. "And Gran'ma could tell about Christmas back in Ohio."

As she ate supper, she changed her mind. "I can't stand the noise," she thought. Never had the children been so tantalizing. "Where are you going?" she asked when the oldest four put on their sweaters. "Coasting," they said, and were gone.

Bill went to play checkers in the engine house; she put Melvin and Raymond and the baby and Gran'ma to bed; then she lay down. "I go to no treat," she thought. "They don't dare for shame's sake let us die; that's all the responsibility they feel. Treat! They'll take whatever they give off the dole." When she heard the children laughing she meant to look at the clock, but she was too tired. "Idle," she thought. "No schooling, no trades."

Deep down in her heart she was not so despairing as she was on the surface. "Gran'ma'll have presents. She'll have little things put away, she'll have made something for each one."

She woke early, dressed quietly, and went down to the kitchen. The cold was bitter; the fires, two or three in each house, did not last through the long night. It used to be that the mine whistle wakened everyone; now there was no whistle. Let Bill sleep and forget. She avoided looking at the kitchen mantel—that was where Gran'ma, aided by Bill, placed her gifts. She laid kindling in the stove, lighted it, and tipped up the coal scuttle. It was not until she turned the dough out on the baking board that she lifted her eyes. For the third time, her heart stopped. There was nothing on the mantel but the clock! She drew in her breath. "She has nothing. Everything's gone. Gwenny's right—Christmas is done for. I'm glad I answered the Swede as I did. Not a step will I go to the treat. Treat!"

She served her family a late breakfast of boiled hominy. "Dinner at four," she announced grimly. "Two meals on Christmas."

With one voice Mary and Harry, Doris and Belle, Melvin and Raymond protested. "That's the time for the treat!" The baby added a howl.

"Well, you pack yourselves right back here after your treat."

"Ain't you goin', Mom?"

"No, I'm not."

Her fourth shock was that of awful fright. The day was clear as a bell, the bright cold still held, the hills were like glass. At half-past three she groaned, "What'll I feed 'em, Mother?"

Gran'ma's answer seemed almost insulting to a person of intelligence. "The Lord will provide."

"Oh, yeah?" Amelia lifted her shawl from the nail behind the door. "I'm going to walk out. The baby'll sleep till I get back."

Gran'ma said nothing; she always knew when to say nothing.

Amelia walked to the end of the street. "The Lord will provide —oh, yeah?" said she.

Presently the road turned away from the hill, and instantly she was in a drift to her knees. "No doubt he's awake and yelling," she thought without tenderness, and turned back. The snow was no longer a dead white; near buildings there were lavender and purple shadows, and in the open there were orange and yellow reflections. Soon the moon would hang like a golden thread and Venus would glitter like a gem. She saw men, women, and children hurrying toward the Community House. "Not me!" she thought. "The poor idiots!"

Opening her door, she stood terrified. For five years Gran'ma had not taken a step; she was tied to her chair as if by chains. On summer evenings Bill and Harry lifted her, chair and all, to the porch. Now, with the weather at zero, Gran'ma was gone. Moreover, the baby, able only to totter, was gone too. Amelia sank down in a chair. Before she caught her breath, fright gave place to anger. "They're at the treat!" Bill, no doubt, got help and took them; he was soft-hearted; he could never stand up for his rights. Of course the children would go, and of course everyone else in Coaltown would go. But not Gran'ma, risking her life! Or the baby! "I'll get *him* back in a jiffy!"

Excited as she was, she did not forget to put coal on the fire. She ran out the door and up the street. The shades at the Community House were raised and there were wreaths in the windows. She stepped into the lounging room and stood gasping.

First of all, she saw eyes—Gran'ma and Bill and Mary and Harry and Doris and Belle and Melvin and Raymond turned necks already stiff with turning. "There she is!" cried three or four of her children. The baby uttered a shriek. The lounging room was decked with boughs of blue spruce from the canyon five miles away, and packed with human beings. "She's here!" yelled a dozen voices. Gwenny Thomas' oldest boy leaped to the folding doors which shut off the dining room and pounded upon them. "She's here!" The big Swede opened the doors. "Merry Chris'mass!" he said. "Now slow! Gran'ma first, den laties an' babies."

"Ain't Gran'ma a lady?" demanded Mrs. O'Hara hysterically.

The Swede ignored this witticism. "Who pushes, gets gizzards."

"Gizzards!" mocked Coaltown.

"Gizzards," said the Swede, his mustaches quivering.

In the dining room was Grace Tanger, her fine body erect, her eyes smiling, and little dark Gwenny Thomas, who had declared that Christmas was done for. The turkeys were carved, the mashed potatoes and the corn and the stuffing and the onions were served. Adult hearts actually stopped beating; young hearts throbbed all the faster. "Wow!" shrieked some. "Lookit!" screamed others. "I've got a drumstick!"—"Get on to the white meat!"

"You pray, Gran'ma," ordered the Swede.

Gran'ma prayed earnestly and with appropriate brevity.

"Go slow," ordered the Swede. "Leetle bit bites. Chew mooch."

The Swede was now here, now there. Once he was out of the room a long time, but when the children called for him he was standing by the pantry door. He had made not only mince pie; he had made ice cream with condensed milk, the best Coaltown ever tasted. He directed everyone to stay in place until the tables were cleared; then he pushed the tables back against the wall and faced the chairs toward the lounging room. Standing on each side of the broad doors, Harry Brodhead and Millie Tanger rolled them back.

"Oh!" cried Amelia. Oh's, ah's, laughter—the confusion was greater than any which ever tortured Amelia's ears in her own house. There stood a blue spruce, pushed in on a low-wheeled platform. "We helped trim it! We helped get it!" shrieked forty adolescent voices. "I have a speech!" screamed a young Thomas. "I can sing a song!" yelled an O'Hara.

Under the tree lay at least forty pairs of stockings—Gran'ma knew whose feet were most nearly bare. The teacher, who was to have three months' vacation without pay and who had little enough at the best, sent a thick storybook, and her hand was to be discerned in much of the program.

When the children's speechmaking and the singing were over, the Swede stood up. The children had spoken of stockings, hanging in a row, of gifts, of sleigh rides, of Santa Claus; he spoke of the Christ child. "I vill sing a Chris'mass song. In Swedish." The song had only two stanzas, but he could scarcely reach the end.

"I know that in English!" said Gran'ma. " 'Away in a manger, no crib for His bed.' " "An' I! An' I," cried most of the men and women.

The Swede swallowed a few times. "I gotta make a speech for da Companee. Da Companee say, 'Michael, make a Chris'mass.' "

559

So I make a Chris'mass. Now Chris'mass bring da idee. I gotta lotta idee. No school for two mont'. I have school. I teacha young laties to cook. All here on my stove. No home folk need eat cooking." No comedian had ever a more instantaneous or hysterical response. "I gotta 'nother idee. Gran'ma teacha young laties to knit. Young laties knitta da sweater for beau."

"Ha, ha!" shrieked Coaltown. The women covered their mouths with their hands, men slapped each other on the back.

"I gotta idee. Mis' Tanger, she teacha young laties to sew. I gotta 'nother idee. Mis' Nuncio she teacha da laties da fancywork. She cut out da hole and sew in da spider and da crab." Again Coaltown shouted. "I gotta idee. Thomas, he teacha da boys to hammer an' saw. How about?"

"Fine," shouted Bill Brodhead, breaking his silence. His voice had an odd sound, as though he strove for but did not quite achieve cheerfulness. What of the men? he seemed to say.

The Swede took a folded paper from his pocket, handling it as though it were spun glass. "I gotta letter," he said. " 'Dear Larson,' it say. 'On January 1, we begin ship little coal. Approx' tree day a week work for each man in January. Estimate necessary repairs.' "

"Repairs on what?" asked Bill Brodhead quickly.

The Swede opened his arms in a wide gesture. "Breaker, engine house, everyt'ing. It say too, 'Merry Chris'mass!' "

Brodhead drew his sleeve across his eyes. "Ah!" sighed mothers and fathers.

Gran'ma traveled home as she had come—in the Swede's arms; rolled in three quilts, she made a great bundle. Bill carried the baby, and Melvin and Raymond trotted sleepily in the rear. Venus had vanished and the moon hung just above the horizon. Amelia stayed with Grace Tanger and Gwenny Thomas and the Mexican woman to do the dishes.

"You dirtied 'em, Swede," said Gwenny gaily. "We'll wash 'em." Again and again the dumb waiter creaked to the kitchen. Down the shaft with it came shouts, the patting of feet, and loud victrola music.

The shouts increased in intensity. "He's back—you can tell

that," said Amelia indulgently. The Swede came down the steps; suddenly she faced him and the women. "What is there about Christmas?" she asked, the tears running down her cheeks.

The Swede looked smilingly round the little room. "My, I lika see da work gittin' done! I gotta idee about Chris'mass. At Chris'mass everyt'ing start fresh. Leetle baby come, heart swells up, gets soft. Everyt'ing new, fresh. New heart, new hope. God say, 'Now try again!' Dat my idee."

"He says, 'Now try again, you poor boobs,' " said Gwenny, weeping.

The Swede shook his head. "He not dat rough. He say, 'Poor leetle babies!' "

The Swede walked home with his assistants. It was nine o'clock, the moon was gone, the star-filled sky had a greater glory. He dropped Gwenny at her door, Mrs. Nuncio at hers, Grace Tanger at hers, then he crossed the street with Amelia Brodhead.

"Bill would be glad to see you," said Amelia. "Come in."

The Swede ignored her invitation. "You smart woman," he said. "House clean, children clean, Gran'ma happy. Soon you get pretty again."

Amelia laughed. "Not very smart and often very cross and never pretty."

"I gotta 'nother idee," said the Swede. "Mis' Tanger all alone. Lotta children. Nice children. Eferybody but she got man to earn wages. I shy. You t'ink she take me?"

Amelia's brain seemed to spin like a wheel; now one recollection was uppermost, now another. She saw Grace's fine figure, her deep bright eyes. Her face had been flushed, she seemed a little excited. The Swede was handsome, he was kind, he was steady as could be. "I gotta idea she might," she gasped.

"Now da time?" asked the Swede. "New business for me."

"Now!" urged Amelia. "This very minute!"

"Good-by!" said the Swede, already halfway across the street. "Merry Chris'mass."

"Merry Christmas!" called Amelia, with all her heart.

ALICE VAN LEER CARRICK

Christmas in Our Town

DO you know, I have discovered an infallible test for old age, my old age, my *real* old age—when I shall be tottering, and worn by time, and ancient enough to welcome my last long home? It will come on that doleful day when I do not feel a little shiver of happiness at the fall of the first snow, or the joyful ringing of Christmas bells. Of course, I am all too well aware that the gladsome sensation is but fleeting; that, in mid-April, I shall be somewhat surfeited with the deep drifts high-piled beneath my parlor windows, and that, when the madding holidays are over, I shall croon to myself a sad little song of my own making:

> *Christmas comes but once a year;*
> *If it came any more I wouldn't be here!*

But the magic of the seasons blessedly will intervene; soon my tall syringas, dressed for bridal, are going to tap with slender fingers at the pane; green Summer, her train embroidered thick with flowers, again will walk in beauty over our North Country, and, to carry further my lyric analogies, I know that Autumn plans to ply her gaudy paint brushes, and once more lacquer the hillsides with gold and crimson. And then the quiet, bare-brown time when all the distances are luminously purple, and the naked trees outline the pattern of their branches against a November sky—why, that's a gentle prelude, played in a minor key, to softly falling snow, and I begin to listen for the "musical jangle of sleigh bells"—there's frost in every word of that phrase!—and, even, to feel a certain enthusiasm for the long and strong bands of a New England winter inevitably to be laid across my life. Somehow, cold weather has lost its fancied austerity and become wholly lovable.

I wish I remembered more about the Southern Christmases, but, you see, I was so little then, and now, in my mind, there is just a whirling kaleidoscope of windy weather and a gray river that rose and rose; of a huge turkey and a huger spiced round—a delicacy I have never forgotten—and the steaming fragrance of eggnog; of black little darkies shouting "Christmus' gif'!" and of firecrackers! Some of the Tennessee customs we brought North with us; that is, our toys were put in our stockings—stockings that, if you had been very naughty, might hold switches and ashes, or so my nurse said —but our Christmas goodies, the oranges and candy, were all piled on a big plate. (Do you know that this was a Pennsylvania Dutch custom, too?)

But we never had a tree, and I always wanted one, and, after I was four, I never had a Santa Claus! My brother, whose word was to me as the law and the gospel, told me that Kriss Kringle (another Southern term) was just our parents, and, for me, the bottom dropped out of the world then and there! So I made up my mind that our children should have trees forever, and Santa Claus as long as they wanted him. And they have! M——kept her faith till she was eight, when, one day, walking through the great pine woods where we pretended the giants went to cut their Christmas trees, she suddenly asked, "Mamma, is there a Santa Claus? Because, you see, the girls at school say there isn't, and when I grow up and get married and have little children of my own and I think there is one and don't fill their stockings, just 'magine how broken-hearted they will be!" Of course, I enlightened her, but neither of us regretted that the beautiful legend had been loved and believed. Moralists may say what they please, but I shall always be sorry for the child who has never had fairies in his life, or given his trust to this kindly saint.

J——, on the other hand, arrived at the truth by science, not sentiment, by his head, not his heart, remarking, when he was seven, that he didn't think it was possible for Santa to climb down every single chimney in one night, especially since he had to come all the way from the North Pole; and as for the Littlest Daughter, why, she was too polite to hurt my feelings by allowing me to dream that she harbored even the shadow of a doubt, a trust that grew into a delightful family festival. Her birthday falls in December, and for years we celebrated it on the sixth, on Nikolastag, the snowy eve when the good Bishop, the first real Santa Claus, comes back to earth, and admonishes the unworthy, and showers goodies upon the deserving; this last, by the way, a faraway echo from the fourth century when Nicholas of Myra gave purses of gold as dowry to the poor nobleman's three lovely daughters. I wish you could have seen our beneficently boisterous saint; in real life he is the head of the History Department, an authority on Calvin, and known as a stern disciplinarian; but with little children he is tenderness itself, and as a rollicking, racketing, jolly old elf, plump with pillows and merrily capering, I hold him to be without equal. Come back with me into the past, and picture, if you can, my long, low dining room: candlelight and firelight throwing shadows on the irregular ceiling, and twenty little children, gay as flowers, sitting in a ring. All waiting! Because, you see, the sandwiches and cocoa and ice cream and birthday cake have gone down the small red lanes, and every Saint Nicholas legend I know has been told, and my tiny guests are racked with impatience as they listen for the first jingle of the sleigh bells that will tell them Santa Claus is coming. And then the jingle comes, and grows louder, and a big, red, snowy-bearded man bounds into the room, and calls every boy and girl by name, and gives them each a toy, and rehearses the deadly sins of childhood: greediness, and teasing the pussycat, and not minding their dear parents, and being unkind to smaller sisters and brothers, and coming to the dinner table with very dirty hands! (Mothers, during the next month, will rise up and extol my name, for the morality chart of the small fry is to show a high upward curve in virtue!) Last of all, for a climax, and that Saint Nicholas may authentically vanish, a sheet is spread upon the floor, and on it he throws great handfuls of candy—all you can see is one wriggling mass of tangled arms and legs—and in the melee Professor F—— disappears to divest himself of his pomp and ancientry in my Hepplewhite bedroom. Mr.—— and J—— and the Littlest Daughter are grown too old for such fantasies now, but next year I really think I'll give another Nikolastag party, just because I so love the joy of little children and the beauty of old festivals.

How Our Three have always adored winter, white winter with Christmas as the core of its heart: wide, glistening fields and pine-trimmed hills; gardens tucked away safe until spring, but where, nonetheless, that magic rose of Noel might blossom; and all the little houses asleep under thick, smooth coverlets—coverlets made, you must understand, from the feathers that Frau Holde has shaken down out of the wonderful sky.

O—— says that Christmas always makes him think of tinkling bells, but to me it means long-ago legends and our children gathered about the friendly fireplace. One such memory comes to mind now; we were sitting in front of it popping corn, and we had been writing letters to Santa Claus. Do you remember how it is done? Well, this is the way: you write your letters very carefully, addressing them to Rock Candy Castle, Elfland—I've forgotten where we first got that idea, but we've always used it—and then you drop the notes into the embers. (If you are wise parents you will first leave doors open so that the draft may whisk the papers up the chimney, for that's how Santa gets his mail.) It was very warm and pleasant in there by the hearth, the walls painted by the firelight, and the witches cozily making tea out under the lilac bush, and all at once M—— looked at me with trustful, round blue eyes, and said, "I don't s'pose that any little children in the world are as happy as we are!" Oh, those blessed, bygone days when our bairns were wee things, and all their simple pleasures lay in our willing hands!

And here, too, we read aloud the Christmas stories. We began with the *Christmas Carol*, but, alas, we had to abandon it, for at Marley's ghost J—— wept with abject terror, an emotion I well understood, for when I was six and one of the little waits singing under Scrooge's windows in our Sunday-school play, I grew cold with fear when the powdered white-clad figure of Marley stalked upon the stage, clanking his chains, and this in spite of the fact that I perfectly well knew that he was our harmless librarian, the mildest-mannered man who ever handed out hymnals or recommended *The Daisy Chain* to inquiring scholars. So we gave up Dickens, and turned to *The Night Before Christmas* and *The Tale of the Tailor of Gloucester*, that beloved whimsy of the good little mice and the bad, big Simpkin, and the Mayor's coat which must be finished by Christmas Day in the morning!

Now, as I look back at those beginning years, I wonder that we ever could have thought them hard. No, our difficulties were to come later! Of course, being the first grandchild, M—— was showered with gifts; O——'s study became a huge unpacking establishment full of delightful, inappropriate things like trains and rocking horses and elaborate walking and talking dolls with which her enthralled parents played most of the evening. And then, in our ambition, we had bought too large a tree and the bottom had to be sawed off, and the branches lopped away, and it wabbled appallingly every time we tried to put it up. And when at last, tired to the bones of our souls, we had just drowsed off, well-meaning students, caroling under our bedroom windows to the effect that they "were all dead-broke, or they wouldn't be staying here, so here's to a Happy New Year" shattered our dearly bought repose.

No, our real troubles lay yet ahead of us, when M—— was seven, and J—— was four, and the Littlest Daughter very much indeed the Littlest Daughter, for those two big bad ones developed the ears of a lynx and the eyes of Argus, and although they theoretically went to sleep straight after supper, at eight and nine and ten, small voices called down and insisted that Santa Claus had come; that they had heard his sleigh bells, and his reindeer on the roof, and that they wanted to see their presents! We didn't dare stir any more than the little mouse in the poem, and the college bell had struck eleven before we ventured to trim the tree and fill the stockings. At two o'clock I dragged wearily off to bed (ah, yes, we also, have heard the chimes at midnight, Master Shallow!) and O—— remained alone, a drowsy modern squire, to shake down the furnace, and wind up the clock, and lay the fires for the morning— it can be shiveringly cold of a winter's dawn in our North Country —and at five the children awoke! Permanently! And not to be gainsaid! We began to realize how fearfully and wonderfully young parents had to be made.

Somehow, in those early days, I never remember being able to get to church; I had to content myself with the octave. For, if I had a maid, she either demanded a holiday, or, more solicitous of her own soul's welfare than of mine, insisted on going to service herself. And if I didn't have one—well, that supposition answers itself. Eight-o'clock celebration was out of the question; I was far too busy seeing that the children didn't eat too many Christmas goodies, or dash out, improperly clad, to try their new flexible fliers or their shiny skis. And there was the big pewter platter to burnish, the platter that invariably held our Thanksgiving and Christmas turkeys —somehow, in the hurry, it was always forgotten until the last moment—and then that same turkey to cook. And what a busy social whirl the morning was: our tree to be displayed, other trees to be visited—for we are still a simple-minded folk, and neighborly; a community where each depends upon the other—last, belated presents to be given and received, and a thousand, thousand cards to range on my tip-table.

Ah, well, perhaps it's not so different now! For we are creatures of beautiful habit, and Christmas is always a blessed bother and bustle: wreaths to put in all the windows, and lovely, trailing greens —a big box comes to me from a gracious Friend-in-Collecting 'way down in Texas—to drape along the tall white mantels, and to place over every picture. The mistletoe hangs on the cottage wall, sing heigh-ho, the mistletoe bough, and all my dear silhouettes have sprigs of holly so that they won't feel homesick and neglected. There's always a last-moment rush, too; already we have bought *miles* of crimson ribbon, enough, apparently, to girdle the globe, but we are sure to need some final bit, and M——, nimble-footed and willing, dashes down just before the Big Store, our local Marshall Field's, closes, and buys *miles* more. And next we must trim our candles and set them in our small-paned windows, welcoming lights to guide the wandering steps of the little Christ child. Everywhere up and down the elm-arched, curving street, tapers are twinkling, and although we know just how it is going to look, we needs must walk down to the end of the flagged pathway to enjoy it afresh, and to say again as we have said so many years, that our little cottage, dreaming under the soft coverlet that good Frau Holde has woven, is the very loveliest of all.

Then come the stockings to be hung with care, not just by the chimney, but according to an odd family custom of our own, on chairs in front of the friendly fireplace, each pair pinned together with stout safety pins, and I must admit that our plight is as poor Mr. Gissing's; we have used multitudes, and always we are searching for these elusive necessities. The Littlest Daughter still brings down the tiny old slatback, grown far too small for her now, but, oh, how different the stockings are; no longer small, warm, woolly things, but cobwebby chiffon silk for the girls, and for J—— those resplendent hose that emblazon the windows of our college shops. (However, to be strictly truthful, O——'s and my modest gear remains much the same.) Another minor difference is that the children no longer wake us in the gray dawn. No, *we wake them! At nine o'clock!* But, just as when they were very small, we still circle 'round the tall fir, glittering with tinsel, and gay with bobbing glass balls and dangling icicles, and sing, "There's a Wonderful Tree, a Wonderful Tree." Thank Heaven, we have always been together at Christmas, that magic time when the years fall away, and Our Three are once more little children.

Truly, I don't believe people can ever love Christmas in the city as we do in the country; it must be less human, more impersonal. Another joy of ours, a holy joy, is the Mystery we give every year in Our Town, a festival that belongs to us all. In the strangest setting! For the Mystery might have come straight down from the Middle Ages—at least, it is a lineal descendant of the Church—and yet it is held in the old white eighteenth-century meetinghouse, a fine, cold piece of architecture, calmly severe in its classic lines, and utterly aloof from the ardent religious glow that comes from jeweled windows and the Gothic tradition. But on that one marvelous night it grows wonderfully gentle and warm, blazing with a myriad candles, and garlanded with green laurel; I suppose Judge Samuel Sewall, rigorous dissenter and outspoken detester of Christmas as a Popish celebration, would turn in his narrow grave if he could see it. For, always we choose the loveliest of our girls for the Madonna; sometimes Rossetti might have painted her, seated among tall lilies; and, again, with her long and lustrous brown eyes and dark, smoothly banded hair, she could have stepped straight from an Italian canvas of the early Renaissance. And the Angels are young, too, and fair; akin to the Lady Mary's handmaidens whose names are like sweet symphonies. (In Our Town every little lass grows up in the hope of sometime being an Angel, just as the little lads plan to be Shepherds.)

If ever you are in Hanover at Christmastide, come with me to the Mystery. I know you will love it just as I do: the thronged church, yellow candle flames illumining the shadows, a distant harmony of clear voices, and then the Angels, bearing great waxen tapers, and chanting "Silent Night, Holy Night" as they pass in reverent processional down the long aisles. They are just the girls I have known all their days in Hanover, and their robes are only white cheesecloth trimmed with gilt paper, their crowns of glory twisted tinsel, but to all of us it is a hallowed and gracious vision, and when they kneel before the Madonna and the little Manger, and sing, "What Child is this that's laid to rest?" my heart literally skips a beat with sheer happiness. And next come the Shepherds —they, too, are my familiar friends—praising that first Noel; and, last of all, the Wise Men, offering their gifts of gold and frankincense and myrrh, and gorgeous with every Oriental robe and scarf that we can beg or borrow. Next year we mean to have a Moorish king— wasn't he Balthasar?—with a turban like a blossoming almond tree; and cherubim with gilded hands and faces; and Raphael's Holy Family. Ah, if only I might invite old Samuel Sewall; he'd come, of course, to thunder denunciations, but maybe he would remain to pray. For what does our Christmas Mystery mean but peace on earth and good will to men?

ARCHIBALD RUTLEDGE

A Plantation Christmas

WHEN to the mystical glamour that naturally belongs
to the Christmas season one can add the romance that
belongs to the South—especially the old-time South—
nothing short of enchantment is the result. I do not think that even
in the England of Cavalier days was Christmas more picturesquely
celebrated than it is today on those great plantations of the South
which have managed to preserve the integrity of their beauty and
their charm. But descriptions in general terms are never very interesting or impressive. Instead, I shall give certain vivid impressions
that Christmas on the plantation have afforded me, hoping thereby
to convey at least a little of the charm with which, in the Southland,
this ancient festival is invested.

At home I have never seen snow at Christmastime. True, it sometimes falls there, but never seriously. Instead, we have a green Christmas, made so by the prevalence of pine, holly, myrtle, sweet bay and smilax that over the top of many a tree weaves emerald crowns. Always, when I go home for Christmas (and this has been an unbroken habit for twenty-five years), what first impresses me is the freshness of the forest—the apparent livingness of the trees, the vernal balminess of the air. And next to the green of the woods, what heartens me most is the singing of the birds. A plantation Christmas is one of wildwood fragrances and wildwood lyrics, as well as one of roaring open fires and festive boards and ancient carols, consecrated as only the centuries can hallow.

I remember getting a Christmas tree that may be considered typical of the plantation variety. A Negro and I hitched an ox to a cart. In the spirit of the occasion the ox apparently did not share. His aspect was lowering, and motions were physically mournful. Nevertheless, he took us into the plantation pine forest, where dulcet odors were abroad, where the huge pines were choiring dimly, where the mellow sunshine was steeping the coverts in the mute rapture of deep-hearted peace. It was "holly year" that year—that is, the crop of holly berries was unusually good. Under a shadowy canopy of live oaks we came to a holly tree some thirty feet high, heavy-foliaged, perfect in symmetry, cone-shaped, and ruddily agleam with berries. Its clean bole shone like silver. Out of this tree we flushed a horde of robins that had been feasting on the berries. The scarlet of their breasts blended with the brightness of the berries. The birds were not frightened. Many of them, alighting on the immense limbs of the oaks, at once broke into trills of delicate song, of the sort that we hear in the North in early-April twilights.

We cut our Christmas tree and the ox bore it homeward for us. In the old ballroom of the house—a room that, running up two stories, has a prodigious height of ceiling—we set it, directly in front of the vast fireplace, which will accommodate logs seven feet long. There stood the regal tree, all jade and silver and scarlet, dewy and tremulous. It needed no decorations. We didn't have to make a Christmas tree—we just brought one in. I felt sorry to have cut so lovely a thing, but Christmas deserves such a tribute. For decorations of a minor sort we use the red partridge berry, mistletoe, smilax, cedar, pine. He who cares to investigate the druidical history of the mistletoe will discover that it is a symbol of the plighting of love's troth. As such, nothing could be more appropriate at this festival of joy and human affection.

In the South, as perhaps is the case nowhere else in the world, there are many superstitions associated with Christmas. No doubt this fact is due to the Negroes, without whom no plantation can be exactly natural or picturesque. One of their superstitions, which amounts to a genuine belief, is that "Christmas *falls*." Possibly long ago some slave heard his master say, "Christmas falls on Friday this year." But whatever the origin of the expression, plantation Negroes firmly believe that the coming of this great day is heralded by some mighty convulsion of Nature. This belief really has an august source; for we find it in Milton. He describes with what tumult and dismay the powers of darkness fled at the birth of Christ.

On the plantation I used, as a boy, to sit up until midnight on Christmas Eve to hear Christmas "fall." It always fell, somehow or other. True, I never heard it; but the faithful always did. Ears that are attuned to hear something supernatural usually hear it. My hearing was too gross; but I used to be immensely impressed by the spiritual advancement of those of my dusky comrades who declared that they distinctly heard the mystic far-off detonation.

Another superstition that I also used firmly to believe—and it has a poetic beauty that the other lacks—is that on the stroke of twelve on Christmas Eve every living thing of the bird and animal world goes down on its knees in adoration of the newborn Master. Convinced that what the Negroes were telling me was true, and not a little impressed by the grandeur of the phenomenon as it was described, I went one Christmas Eve to the stable yard, and there sat drowsily with my Negro comrade Prince, while the stars blazed, and the pines grieved, and the distant surf roared softly on the sea-island beaches. As midnight approached we became restless, and our nervousness was communicated to the various creatures in the ample old barnyard. The roosters crowed with uncommon vigor and assurance, the hogs grunted with unwonted enthusiasm, and the sheep bleated with strange pathos. After a time, clearly in the moonlight we saw an old ox heave himself for a rise. For a moment he assumed a most singular position: his hind quarters were up, but his head was quite low—he was actually kneeling. Prince pointed him out in awed triumph. Nor did I raise any question; for deep faith in another human being, even though you may consider it merest superstition, is ever an impressive thing, having about it also a certain sacredness that the heart with unreflecting wisdom and generosity willingly pays obeisance to.

Yes, on a plantation, Christmas *falls*; and likewise, every living thing goes down on its knees in the dust before its Maker.

Awaking one Christmas morning, I remember what a pleasure I experienced from hearing, just outside the window, a Carolina wren caroling like mad. Of course, this bird is not a great singer, but for sheer joyousness and abandonment to gladness I do not know his equal. His ringing call, without a trace of wariness or doubt, carries farther than the note of any other bird of the same size. I have heard it full three hundred yards across a river. Now I heard it coming through my window, the curtains of which were gently stirred by a faint breeze out of the aromatic pinelands. Climbing a pillar under my window was a yellow jasmine vine, and in a festive mood to suit the season it had put forth a few delicious blossoms—golden bells to ring for Christmas, saffron trumpets to sound the Day's welcome. Beyond the window I could see the mighty live oaks, with their pendulous streamers of moss, waving gently like my white curtains; then the imperial pines, towering momentously. Christmas morning, with birds and sunshine and scented sea winds! Going to the window, I looked out. All the dim sweet plantation was steeped in faërie light. The far reaches of bowed and brown cotton field; the golden broom sedge fringing the fields; the misty river rolling softly; the sleeping trees, jeweled with dew; the uncertain pearly sky—all these had a magical look. A silvery silence held the world divinely, in virginal beauty.

But soon the stillness was broken, and by no gentle sound. It did not surprise me, but not many Americans other than plantation dwellers would have expected it. Firecrackers! "What is home without a mother?" queries the old saw. Why, it's like Christmas to the plantation pickaninnies without firecrackers! The Puritan Christmas of New England has something exceedingly snowy and austere about it. In the South it is a day for frolic—at least, on the plantation it is not associated in any way with church services. Nor do I think it less a genuine festival of the hearth and the home because all the little Negroes shoot fireworks, all the plantation belles hang mistletoe (and strangely linger near it), and all the plantation men go deer hunting.

The Negroes do not stay long in the colored settlement, but with a promptness that is hardly a racial characteristic they repair to the Great House, thronging gleefully across the fields, shouting and singing and exercising that extraordinary power for social affability among themselves that is truly a racial characteristic. They help to make Christmas what it is on the plantation. They are friendly, affectionate, simple-hearted folk, faithful and grateful. In no way do they resemble the curious caricatures that are presented to us in the popular magazines. These people are dusky peasants—dull, perhaps, in some ways, but exceedingly acute in others. For example, as a judge of human character, motive and behavior, a plantation Negro is, I believe, an expert. He is capable of acute observations on life and manners; and his criticism is sometimes delicately veiled. Now they are gathering for a share in the plantation's Christmas festival.

I find the yard thronged with them when I take a little stroll before breakfast. Here I see Ahasuerus, the overseer; then Gabriel, a hunter of renown; then Blossom and Dollie, swarthy twins; then old Sambo, who remembers the days of slavery, which he has often told me, he enjoyed far more than the days of desolate freedom that followed; then a score of meek-eyed patient women, and twice as many frolicking little blacks. They are human, lovable people, these plantation Negroes. And I have found them trustworthy in the highest sense. I remember that, when I took my bride to the plantation for a visit, our trunk had to be brought the last ten miles by cart. For the precious trunk containing all sorts of bridal apparel I sent an old Negro named Will Alston, impressing on him the importance of his guarding the trunk with his life.

Twilight of that day fell, and Will did not arrive. Moreover, a rain had set in, and I did not see how, if he had started from the steamer's wharf with the trunk, he could have escaped disaster. Donning a long raincoat, I mounted a horse and rode through the lonely pinelands to meet Will. About three miles from home I saw his cart standing in the middle of the road. Upon it a lively shower was roaring. The driver was not in sight. Dismayed, I rode up quickly, to see a sight I shall remember as long as I live. The trunk was in the road under the cart; on the cart's bottom, just above the trunk, Will was sprawled, taking all the rain that came, and shunting it away from the precious treasure he was guarding. I was considerably touched by this display of his humble but genuine fealty, yet he appeared to think nothing of it.

"I couldn't let the trunk get wet," he said simply. He was driving an ox, which was, of course, perfectly willing to stand, plantation oxen being somewhat expert in that particular.

Before breakfast we distribute to the Negroes whatever we have for them in the way of Christmas cheer. . . . Then the family gathers for breakfast. I love to think of it; the ample room from the walls of which gaze down faded portraits of the plantation owners of an earlier generation; there gaze down, too, a whole fringe of deer horns, festooned with Spanish moss. A plantation home without its collection of staghorns is hardly to be found; and in passing I may say that some of the collections, dating back almost to the time of the Revolution, are of remarkable interest. I know of one such collection that contains upward of a thousand racks of the whitetail, every one having been taken on that particular plantation. In some families, there is a custom, rigorously adhered to, that no deer horns must ever leave the place; so that the horns of every buck killed find their way into the home's collection. Such a frieze in a dining room seems to fill the place with woodland memories, and serves in its own way to recall the hunts and the hunters and the hunted of long ago. Here on the same wall hang the portrait of a famous sportsman and the antlers of many a stag he took in the old days. Gone now are they all. We have only the dim picture and the ancient antlers.

Christmas breakfast on the plantation makes one think of a wedding breakfast. The table is gay with sprigs of holly, with graceful ropes of smilax. A huge bunch of mistletoe, large enough to warrant the most ardent kissings of whole communities, stands upright in the center of the table, its pale, cold berries mysteriously agleam. Then Martha and Sue bring in the breakfast—wholesome, smiling Negroes they are, devoted to the family, and endeared to it by nearly fifty years of continuous, loving service. Here the breakfaster may regale himself on plantation fare: snowy hominy, cold wild turkey, brown crumbly corn breads, venison sausages, beaten biscuits, steaming coffee, homemade orange marmalade. Unless my observation be at fault, the making of coffee on a plantation is a solemn rite not to be trusted to anyone save the mistress of the house. She loves to make it herself before the ruddy fire in the dining room, its intriguing aroma mingling with the fresh fragrances from the greenery hung about the walls. She loves to carry coffee making to the point of a fine art, and to serve it out of a massive silver coffeepot—the same used when a gentleman named General George Washington visited this home during his Southern tour in those last years of the eighteenth century.

While we are at breakfast, we have evidence that the day is not to be spent in languorous and ignoble ease, for from the yard we can hear the Negro huntsmen tuning up their hunting horns; and in response to the faint mellow blasts we hear the joyous yowling of staghounds. Some of these come to the dining-room door, and there stand, ranged in the order of their temerity, fixing us with melancholy great eyes—more eager, I really think, to have us finish our repast and join them in the woods than envious of us for our festive feast.

On the plantations that I know deer hunting on Christmas Day is as natural as a Christmas tree, or kissing one's sweetheart under the mistletoe.

After breakfast, we gather on the plantation porch, and I smell the yellow jasmine that is tossing her saffron showers up the tall white columns. In the flower garden two red roses are blooming. In the wild orange trees beside the house myriads of robins, cedar wax-wings, and a few wood thrushes are having their Christmas break-fast. A hale, dewy wind breathes from the mighty pine forest. The whole landscape, though bathed in sunshine, is still fresh with the beauty of the morning. Now the Negro hunters come round the side of the house, leading our horses, and followed by a pack of hounds. A rather motley crew they are, I think, for few plantations can boast of full-blooded staghounds; but they know their business. What they lack in appearance they supply in sagacity.

There is, I suppose, no grander sport in the whole world than riding to hounds after deer; and this is a sport typical of a planta-tion Christmas. It is almost a religious rite, and it never fails to supply the most thrilling entertainment for visitors. Indeed, I do not know exactly what the rural South would do without deer hunt-ing as a diversion. Even in the cities, when distinguished guests ar-rive, the primary entertainment always provided is a stag hunt. Nor is such a matter at all difficult to arrange. A city like Charleston is full of experts in this fascinating lore; and these nimrods are ever ready to leave all else to follow the deer. During the Great War, when many notable officials were in Charleston, they were exceed-ingly diverted by this practice of deer hunting. It seemed to take them centuries back, to the time when the cavaliers of Shakespeare's time rode to hounds in the New Forest, in Sherwood and in Windsor. In the coastal country deer are, and have always been, plentiful; and I believe that they are so used to being hunted that they are inured to the surprise and the rigor of it.

Soon we are astride our mounts, turning them down the live-oak avenue toward the deep pinelands. As we ride down the sandy road, we are on the lookout for deer tracks; and these are seen crossing and recrossing the damp road. The Negro hunters who have charge of the pack have to use all their powers of elocution to persuade the hounds not to make a break after certain hot trails. The horses seem to know and to enjoy this sport as well as the men and the dogs do. No horse can be started more quickly or stopped more abruptly than one trained to hunt in the woods.

We start a stag in the Crippled Oak Drive, and for miles we race him: now straight through the glimmering pinelands, sun-dappled and still; now through the eerie fringes of the "Ocean," an inviolate sanctuary, made so by the riotous tangle of greenery; now he heads for the river, and we race down the broad road to cut him off—down the very same stretch of road that in Revolutionary days the planters of the neighborhood used as a race track. There is a stretch of three miles, perfectly straight and level, broad and lying a little high. Down this we course. But the crafty buck doubles and heads northward for the sparkleberry thickets of the plantation. I race forward to a certain stand, and just as I get there, he almost jumps over me! The dogs are far behind; and the stag gives the appearance of enjoying the race. Away he sails, his stiffly erect, snowy tail flashing high above the bay bushes. I await the arrival of the dogs, and soon they come clamoring along. I slip from my horse and lead him into the bushes. I love to watch running hounds when they do not observe me. They always run with more native zest and sagacity when they are going it alone. A rather common dog, of a highly doubtful lineage, is in the lead. The aristocrats come last. I am always amused over the manner in which full-blooded hounds perform the rite of trailing. This business is a religion with them. They do not bark, or do anything else so banal and bour-geois; they make deep-chested music, often pausing in the heat of a great race to throw their heads heavenward and vent toward the sky perfect music. Their running is never pell-mell. A good hound is a curious combination of the powers of genius: he is Sherlock Holmes in that he works out infallibly the mazy trail; he is Lord Chesterfield in that he does all things in a manner becoming a gentleman; and he is a grand opera star, full of amazing music. I get a never-failing thrill out of listening to hounds and out of watching them at close hand. To me it appears that the music they make depends much upon their environment for its timbre. And as they course over hills and dip into hollows, as they ramble through bosky water-courses or trail down roads, as the leafy canopies over them deepen or thin, their chorus hushes and swells, affording all the "notes with many a winding bout" that the best melody offers.

Our stalwart buck makes almost a complete circle, outwits us, enters the mysterious depths of the "Ocean," and is lost. But per-haps—at any rate, on Christmas Day—for us to lose his life is better than for him to lose it. Yet his escape by no means ends our sport. We start two stags next, and they lead us a mad race toward Wambaw Creek. I catch a far-off glimpse of white tails and glinting horns. We horsemen, taking our lives in our hands, essay to race the two bucks to the water. We manage to overtake the hounds but not the deer. Indeed, after almost a lifetime of following deer, I may truthfully say that I have seldom, in our country, seen deer in dis-tress before hounds. Unless wounded, or unless very fat (as they are in September), or unless cornered against wire, deer play before dogs. They pretend that they are going to run spectacularly; but after a show of gorgeous jumping and running, they skulk in deep thickets, dodge craftily, cross water, and in other ways rest them-selves and baffle their pursuers. When the hounds do approach them again, the deer are as fresh as ever.

After a few more chases, we return to the plantation house; and if there is a sport that whets the appetite more keenly than deer hunting, I do not know it. To the ancient home we return, to the patriarch live oaks watching before it, to the red roses, to the yellow jasmine; and within, to the ruddy fires, the rooms festooned with fragrant greenery. As we enter the dining room almost everyone begins to smile in a most understanding fashion; for on either side of the huge bunch of mistletoe in the center of the table are two decanters—and they are full!

A Plantation Christmas

I remember what an old Negro said to my father when he was describing to the old servitor a certain kind of liquor. The Negro, in such matters, had an almost painful imagination. This description was just a little more than he could stand. "Oh, please, boss," he said, "don't tell me about that if you don't have none along with you." His was a sentiment with which I can heartily sympathize. I hate, for example, to describe a plantation Christmas dinner if I cannot offer my readers the dinner itself. And yet I cannot think of it without recalling the snowy pyramids of rice, the brown sweet potatoes with the sugar oozing out of their jackets, the roasted rice-fed mallards, the wild turkey, the venison, the tenderloin of pork fattened on live-oak acorns, the pilau, the cardinal pudding!

And this is a dinner by candlelight, even though the daylight lingers outside. Twilight falls as we come to the nuts and raisins. Then we form a great semicircle before the fire, and we rehunt the chases of that day, and of many of the long ago. One or two of the older hounds have the privilege of the dining room, and their presence on the firelit rug adds reality to our stories. I often think that, had they the power of speech, what they could tell us would be well worth the hearing.

It is late ere our stories are ended. It has been a glorious day. I wander out now on the front porch. The risen moon is casting a silvery glamour over the world. Certain great stars blaze in the velvet void of heaven. Far off I can hear the Negroes singing their spirituals of Christmas—the sweetest melody, I think, of which the human voice is capable. The live oaks shimmer softly in the moonshine. I hear flights of wild ducks speeding overhead, hastening toward their feeding grounds far down the river. The magic of the night is abroad; now, I know, the deer are coming out of their coverts delicately to roam the dim country of the darkness. Over the old plantation the serenity of joyous peace descends—the peace of human hearts at Christmastime. Beauty and love and home—these are of peace, these make that peace on earth that Christmas in the heart alone can bring.

VINCENT STARRETT
Snow for Christmas

I

FEARS had been expressed that there would be no snow for Christmas, but three days before the world's holiday it began to fall. Quietly it came, like a thief in the night, and in the morning it lay thickly in the streets, soft, feathery and glistening. During the day it fell again, and by nightfall it covered everything within view. The roofs and gables of the neighborhood were heavy with snow, and the bare branches of the trees seemed to droop with its weight.

To David Thursk, for all the white loveliness of the scene, it brought its inevitable sorrow. Standing at the upstairs front windows of his home, as evening set in, he watched the street lamps become globes of pale light in the chill dusk, and his heart was heavy with the thought of his father. The old-fashioned stone block beside the curb across the way was suddenly a grave of ice; the ancient dwelling at which he gazed seemed to lean and totter toward some dreadful revelation.

Tomorrow marked an anniversary, the first anniversary of his father's death. It would be a year on Christmas morning since John Thursk had come down those steps for the last time on the shoulders of his friends. He had loved the Christmas season. On a Christmas morning he had first seen the dawn make ribbons of light through those shutters, now closed perhaps forever; and on a Christmas morning he had been laid away beneath his final coverlet of earth. He had earned his repose, the good, kindly man.

But David Thursk still mourned for his dead father. Their pride had been great. No tears had run from David's eyes the day his father died. A man's tears are like diamonds at the core of a mountain. But in his heart a poignant hurt still throbbed and ached.

There had been nights when his agony had seemed more than he could bear. There came to him moments of seeming revelation when the full horror of what had happened brought him to a sitting position in his bed; when a sense of the finality of the separation was stark upon him. The terror and the mystery of death! Never again to see and know the man whose understanding had filled his heart, in whom he had seen himself ennobled and glorified. At such times he grasped desperately at the straws of religion that swam about him on the dark stream that was his mind. Alternately they tortured and comforted him. At other times he was rebellious at the injustice of death, the injustice of the shrouding mystery; times when, in a frenzy of hate, he wanted to tear the skies apart to unveil the sham and cruelty of whatever lay behind. It would be an act of defiance, of obscene insolence, an insult so gigantic as perhaps to lay the world in ruins.

What he really wished was simply proof of all that early he had been taught to believe; some shining presence with valiant voice unanswerably to declare the best news true; a miracle of comfort and illusion. For there had never been anyone quite like John Thursk, not even David's mother, long dead, a placid and peaceful memory.

Darkness had fallen over the city. A red glow, square and warm, sprang out of a neighboring window, and was reflected upon the snow field beneath. A second followed, and then a third. The shadows of the trees wavered in the oblique planes of light. With a sigh, David turned from his window. Belowstairs sounded a medley of pleasant noises; a rattle of pans and dishes, the closing of an oven door, and in the intervals a warming gust of voices in happy altercation. The evening meal was preparing, and the younger John was keeping persistently underfoot. Something of the heartiness of the occasion came to the lonely man on the stairs, and with a little smile he finished the descent and stood briskly rubbing his hands before the open fireplace.

"Dear old Dad!" he murmured, as happier memories began to crowd his mind. "How he would have loved to be with us tonight!"

When the dinner dishes had been cleared away, and his wife had gone upstairs with the younger John, he smoked a pipe before the fire, and the thought of his father no longer disturbed him. It was pleasant now to think of the fine old fellow. Not that he had been really old. Sixty! That was part of the tragedy and injustice of it. David could almost hear that deep, remembered laugh from the big chair on the other side of the grate. The flames danced fantastically on the hearth, unchanged as always, and by a little stretch of fancy David could see his father leaning forward to poke at the truant sparks and fags that endeavored to escape the holocaust.

His stick was there in the corner, where it had stood since his death; the stout staff he had cut and trimmed and varnished himself, companion of his strolls about the neighborhood. He had been a famous walker. How the squirrels had run to him at the familiar rattle of that old stick on the pavement! His books too were there, in the old bookcase that had been brought across the street with the books. Gallant stories of highhearted ladies and gentlemen of another day, punctuated at intervals by sober history and old-fashioned poetry. There was never such another man as John Thursk. There never could be such another.

"John Thursk just missed being a great man, by inches," some body had said of him, after his death. When the compliment had been relayed to his son, David had smiled and replied: "He was something better than that; he was a great human being. It is the hardest of all things to be. Great men are relatively common."

Now Christmas was at hand, and everything was going forward as in other years. Only John Thursk was absent from the familiar scene. For years he had been there, and now he was not there. He would never be there again. Everything else was as it had been, yet nothing was the same.

David Thursk heard his wife's step upon the stairs, and put aside his dreaming. She entered the room and placed a letter in his hand.

"I've been wild to give you this all evening," she told him, "but I was afraid John would catch me at it, and think I didn't understand. You mustn't let him know you have read it."

Her husband received the letter with a smile, which altered as he glanced at the superscription.

"Poor little chap!" he said quaintly and turned the envelope in his hands. Hideously smeared with ink as it was, and more than a little dirty, it was addressed quite plainly, albeit tortuously, to "Santa Claus, North Pole, Norway."

"Read it," said his wife, still proudly smiling; and awkwardly he inserted his fingers beneath the flap.

"It's almost a betrayal," he protested. "I really feel guilty, Nora!"

"Skittles!" she deprecated. "He'd be proud as a peacock if he thought you liked it. There's a clause in it relating to you; that's why he asked me not to show it to you."

With sensitive fingers David unfolded the paper and read his son's communication, a not particularly remarkable document filled with solemn injunctions and ecstatic promises. His eyes blurred for an instant, and were turned upon the leaping flames as he handed it back.

"Poor little chap!" he said again. "We must get him everything he wants, within reason. But, do you know, Nora, I seriously question the wisdom of allowing such letters to be written. They serve no purpose other than to disappoint the child, in some particular, and to perpetuate a lying legend that, later, if he has sense, he will not thank us for putting into his head."

He spoke with more vigor than he had intended, and his wife was shocked.

"Why, David!" she cried. "I thought you loved that old legend. You've always been so happy at Christmas—except, of course—last Christmas. I've heard you tell John about Santa Claus, yourself, and answer his questions about him. Your father loved it too. I remember you and your father helping John to write a letter to——"

She broke off suddenly, and her voice was anxious. "David, are you ill?"

He shook his head impatiently. "I know," he said; "I do love it, or I always thought I loved it. I loved it as a boy—although I still remember the agony I suffered when my mother told me it wasn't so. I believed for a long time," he added wistfully. "I must have been a pretty big boy when she told me; too old to be believing that sort of thing."

He stared hard into the flames.

"The fact is, Nora, we believe too many things. We're taught things that aren't so, because they are pleasant things to believe. And because they are pleasant, we go on believing them long after we ought to know better. We know they're not so, and still we go on believing them. We won't give them up. Life would be too terrible without them. We'd go crazy if we didn't believe *something*. And we clutch at straws to make things seem true that we know are only lies, told us by our parents to make us happy. *Happy!* We'd be happier if we were told nothing, and grew up believing nothing. Then we wouldn't expect things to happen that can't happen. It wouldn't hurt us so much when the unhappy things came. We'd have learned to expect them, and not to cry afterward."

He realized that he was becoming incoherent.

"I'm sorry, Nora, if I seemed to speak hotly. I didn't mean it that way. I do love it all—the whole Christmas season; everything it stands for. I only wish to God that I could believe it all again!

Snow for Christmas

That's what I meant. If I hadn't been taught all this—about Santa Claus—about God and heaven——"

He stopped again, and she laid a hand on his shoulder and another on his bent head. His body shook so that she was alarmed; but she concealed her apprehension and spoke without nervousness.

"You've been thinking about your father," she said slowly. "I know how you feel, and I'm sorrier than I can tell you. You know, I went through it all with you, and I miss him almost as much as you do. I've been thinking about him a lot today," she concluded on a note intended to comfort him. Immediately, she added more brightly: "I asked John today if he remembered how his grandfather used to help him write his letters to Santa Claus, and he said he wished Grandfather were here to help him, now."

Understanding the kindly intent of the anecdote, David smiled up at her. "Did he? Good little chap! It was nice of him to ask for a new desk for me, at the office. He must have heard me say I needed one."

Late that night, as he sat alone before the fire, David again noticed his son's letter. It lay face upward on the table, close to his hand, where his wife had dropped it. He took it up idly and began to finger it. Poor little chap! What disillusionments, he wondered, were ahead for John? What disappointments, and what overwhelming sorrows? And what a dreadful responsibility one undertook who brought children into the world!

And yet how jolly it had been in the old days. When his father had been with them, he—David—had been happy without believing, as had John Thursk. They had been happy in another's belief. Happy in encouraging that belief. Was it a vicious thing that they had done? They had sought to make John happy. Was it so evil a thing to make a child happy? Surely happiness was a thing to be taken wherever found. The trouble was, he—David—had been too happy—too happy all along the line. He had believed in everything too hard. Whatever was blissful and soothing, he had been taught, he had accepted without question, and he had fervently believed, until with mounting years and some modicum of intelligence, had come the doubts natural to all who think. Even then he had fought them back—or had put them out of his mind. His naïve agnosticism had been overwhelmed by avalanches of proof and reproach, and new delights had been added to the legend. Still the doubts had persisted, until alternately he had been torn between belief and unbelief, between bitter atheism and ardent acceptance of everything that was fantastic and comforting. In the end he had adopted the easy attitude of the many; perhaps it was so, perhaps it was not so; at any rate, there was nothing that he could do about it, nothing he could ascertain beyond question; and the happiest solution of the difficulty was not to think of it at all. And so he had not thought of it at all.

Now the death of his father had brought it all back with new and more terrible tortures for his soul. Now he had a profound and ghastly interest in the problem, a personal interest that, curiously, he had not felt when his mother died. For a time David believed, desperately, knowing that he was afraid not to, and knowing, deep underneath, that he did not believe.

To make a child happy! To make a man happy! To make a soul happy! And how jolly it all had been in the old days. If only he could believe again! That was what he wanted, and it could never be. He knew it. He knew that he could not even pretend any more.

He turned the letter over and over in his hands, while he stared into the fire. Yes, he would like to go back and believe it all again. The straggling characters on the envelope caught his eye, and he smiled. To write a letter to Santa Claus again! And believe that it would be answered! However, that was past—and rapidly, he thought, he was becoming a raving lunatic. Dear old Dad! Had he ever had doubts? Had he ever been tormented in this way? How quiet had been his philosophy! How fine his tolerance!

David's heart overflowed. He turned his chair to the table. Slowly he drew a sheet of paper toward him, and reached for a pen. The ink bottle was handy. One thing, at least, he could do with entire sincerity. He could set down his love for his father. Not that his father had not known; but no words had been spoken. Of course his father had known. But it would be a relief and a happiness to write it down; to say the foolish, sentimental, loving words that had lain so long unsaid in his heart.

A quaint idea came to him, sitting there; it had been with him, subconsciously, for some moments. He would write a letter to his father! Just as if he were still living and could read it. In it he would say all of the things that his reserve would never have permitted him to say aloud to his father's face, and that the reserve of John Thursk would never have permitted him to hear without embarrassment.

The idea pleased David enormously. He dipped his pen into the bottle. It was an idiotic thing, of course, although no more ridiculous than that in which he had encouraged his son. Self-consciousness began to steal over him, but he held fast to his idea and recaptured the mood. He would even seal the letter in an envelope, and address it, as the younger John had done.

But where?

He smiled happily. "John Thursk—Address Unknown." He would write the words on an envelope, and Dad—wherever he might be—would understand and know, at last. The younger John's letter would be dropped into the postbox tomorrow; but his own would be——Why, yes! it too would be mailed. It would be dropped into the fire. In a swift moment of fancy he saw the letter lying in the deep glow, at first white, then rapidly becoming a dull brown. The edges were curling, his father's name seemed to stand forth in letters of fire; the envelope was opening; then a little burst of flame, a heap of crumbling black, and the message was a red spark whirling up the chimney and into the outer air. Up . . . up . . . and out . . . a red spark mounting higher and higher into the night, toward . . . ?

"Dear old Dad," David wrote, and paused. Once more he dipped his pen into the ink bottle; and then his heart began to pour itself out across the sheet.

II

ON Christmas Eve, the barometer dropped starkly and an arctic storm broke over the city. The snow, which had fallen all day long, vanished on the wings of an icy blast out of the north. The wind roared in the streets and whined dismally in the chimneys. It plucked great armfuls of snow from the drifts and flung them across the night in swirling clouds and columns. The cold was bitter, and as the night advanced the cry of the storm rose higher. Few persons were abroad in the streets. The lights gleamed ghostily through the driving spray of ice and snow.

David Thursk sat before the open fire in the living room of his home and listened to the fury of the storm. The hour was late, and he was alone. An hour before, his wife had placed her final gift on the glittering tree, and climbed the stairs to her room. For a time he had heard her stirring in the room above; then silence had fallen on the place, a silence of which the background of storm had become a part. For many minutes he had not moved in his chair. He was thinking again of his dead father, and of a wind-swept grave. It was cold tonight out there on the hillside. John Thursk had loved a roaring fire on an open hearth. He had disliked the cold.

As they were affected by the gusts outside, the blue and yellow flames alternately flickered with low hissing and tongued roaring up the chimney. Leaning forward to apply another log, David fancied that again he saw his letter lying upon the fire, a square of white that swiftly became a black wafer, stamped with a glowing spark of red; and again he saw it swiftly mounting to the eternities, a valiant gleam lost in the dark immensity of space.

It had been a childish fancy and a childish performance, but it had been good to be a child again. Many times, in moments of cynical sanity, he had blushed about his folly; had seen in that leaping scarlet flame the counterfeit of his own illusions. For it is in the nature of fire and flame, he told himself, to turn to smoke and ashes. He rationalized his folly and again found comfort, only again to find himself floundering in the labyrinths of theology. Dimly he felt that it was all madness. Madness to believe, madness not to believe, madness to attempt to understand or explain. The greatest minds were as helpless before the mystery as his own. "To be or not to be" was not the question posited by death. The question had never been put. It was not as simple as that, and it had not only two horns. Yet he must accept wholly or wholly reject. He might not pick and choose. A religion subsisted by its dogmas only. Men did not become martyrs to a code of ethics, to that which was comprehensible and involved no passion. But his own emotion, he realized, was for his father; it had little to do with religious ecstasy.

Times without number he reproached himself for the pride that had sealed within his lips the expressions of affection that now lay so heavily on his heart. And times without number he comforted himself with the thought that all was well, that somewhere—somehow—his father knew. And yet—were it only possible to call back a single day, an hour, five minutes of that other time that now seemed to have been so incredibly happy, how he would employ the moments to make clear the deeps of his heart! Every syllable he had poured from the silences of his soul into that letter, gone forth into mystery, would find its duplicate on his tongue. Not the windy continent of rhetoric, but the simple story of a boy's long love for his father, in such words as he might have uttered in childhood.

Exactly a year ago this dreadful night, John Thursk lay dying in the old home across the street. Only by the pressure of his hand in David's hand, and of David's hand in his, had father and son spoken. Only a few hours now, and the clock hands would mark the moment of the solemn anniversary.

David's eyes were turned upon the clock. Midnight had struck some minutes before. The fire was falling into ash. Half-heartedly he stirred to replenish it. Outside, the storm had not abated; if anything, its fury had increased. At intervals a white smother flung itself against the panes, beyond the drawn blinds, and the cold fingers of a cedar tapped urgently against the wall of the house, beside the steps. A grim and deadly night, he thought. . . . Then heavy feet crunched upward on the steps, and David Thursk came upright from his chair as the shrill alarm of the doorbell sounded through the house.

With a curious feeling of apprehension he glanced again at the clock. Then his mind functioned automatically, and his lips formed the words, "A telegram!"

But from whom? And with what conceivable message on this night of riot?

For an instant his heart seemed to stop beating; then his feet moved of their own volition and he walked quickly into the corridor and opened the inner door. In the passage between door and door he wrestled for an instant with the latch. And then the storm whirled past him with savage eyes, and seemed to fill the entry.

On the porch, against the doorstep, stood a tall stranger wrapped in an overcoat. His great collar was turned up against the gale, and a huge muffler swathed his face almost to the eyes, which were protected by the peak of a high cap that descended at the sides and back.

"Special delivery," said the man gruffly, as the dim light from inside fell outward across the doorsill. "For David Thursk," he added.

"I am David Thursk," said David, accepting the envelope from the gloved fingers. "A bad night to be out," he continued with a little shiver. "Do you want me to sign for it? You'd better step inside for a minute. It will give you a chance to get warm." He drew his smoking jacket more closely around him.

The messenger hesitated; he had been groping in his pocket as if for a pencil. His eyes smiled and seemed to blur. Their gleam and the droop of his shoulders called sharply on David's sympathies.

"You are older than is usual with messengers," he added kindly, noting the man's hesitation. "If you care to come inside while I open this, I'll make some tea for us both. We might even have a pipe together, eh? You must be cold, and there is a good fire inside."

What strange vicissitudes, he wondered, had brought his visitor to such a pass. The man appeared to be quite elderly; not at all the sort of brisk lad ordinarily employed by the post office for such errands. A queer sense of the unreality of the episode came suddenly to David, even as his heart warmed to the derelict on his doorstep. His prompt hospitality, although born of an emotion not unusual in a lonely man, seemed all at once to be charged with a disturbing significance. For a moment even the midnight letter had been forgotten in an unexplainable desire to make this cheerless stranger happy before a fire, to ply him with tea and tobacco, and warm his heart with conversation.

A thin white avalanche flung itself up the steps with a roar; for an instant it filled the entry and obliterated the figure on the doorstep. Choking and coughing, brushing the snow from his garments, David turned his back and shoulders to the assault. When it had cleared the messenger had moved back from the door; he stood now at the head of the descending flight. His voice when David heard it again was low and gruff.

"Thank you, Mr. Thursk, but I guess not. I'd like to, very much— but not tonight. I must get back."

And suddenly the man's figure seemed to droop. He stood with tilted head, one shoulder lifted slightly above the level of the other; a peculiar mannerism. The gruff voice cleared.

"It's good of you to ask me. I'd like to have tea with you sometime—yes, and smoke a pipe too. Most of all, I'd like to talk with you. That would be great happiness for me. You asked me in because you thought I was cold and unhappy; but I'm not. You've warmed me and made me very happy. I'll see you again sometime, you know; when I have another message—out this way. You are very like your father, David Thursk!"

Then David's heart skipped a beat, and instantly ran faster than ever. Out of a little empty silence, he heard his voice whispering: "You knew my father?"

The storm-clad figure turned its eyes; and suddenly, in a blinding flash of revelation, David knew what manner of stranger this was that he had invited to enter his home. Shuddering, he shrank back into the doorway.

"You took my father!" he cried. "I know you now. You are . . ."

But the stranger smiled so kindly that there was no room for fear, and his voice, clear and high, struck through David's heart like a flight of bird notes.

"Thank you, David, for your invitation," he said. "When I come again, don't fear that I shall not accept. I shall be glad to warm myself before your fire. It was a kindly thought. And perhaps you will care to go with me for a distance, when I leave. I could ask no better company. . . . Good night, David!"

"Now!" cried David Thursk, eagerly. "Let me go with you now!"

But the messenger had turned away and was stamping down the steps through the long snow drifts. His deep laugh seemed to echo against the night.

"When I come again," called the memorable voice. "Farewell!"

His feet crunched on the walk; the tall figure straightened until it seemed to obscure the light, until it seemed to fill the street and the sky, until . . .

Somewhere above and behind a voice was calling anxiously, and David knew it was his wife's voice. "David!" she called; and vaguely he knew that in a minute she would come down to join him. Slowly he began to close the door.

Something inside was trying to tell him something; his mind was shredding itself against barricades of intervening bewilderment. Desperately he fought back toward comprehension. The messenger! That stranger at the door! What was it that was clamoring at his heart? A revelation was impending that would shake his reason. The droop of those familiar shoulders, the poise and tilt of that familiar head; the eyes that had compelled him to ask a midnight stranger to sit beside him at the fire. Even the voice, at first gruff and harsh, which at the last had struck through him like the sound of a distant bell. That final laugh, deep as an organ note. How could he have forgotten it!

He had almost closed the door, but suddenly he wrenched it open so that it crashed against the wall and splintered at the corner.

"Dad!"

Snow for Christmas

His cry of anguish rang above the storm. He flung himself down the steps and into the deserted street, calling the name. He screamed and sobbed; and the wind seized his words and flung them across the night, and up into the skies, and over the empty spaces of the world. He ran up and down the sidewalk in the deep snow, calling. He found the trail of footprints leading away from the steps, and saw them vanish into unbroken drifts before they reached the walk. From end to end the street lay bare and white under the lights, under the stars—and there was no footfall in all creation.

III

DAVID THURSK came back to consciousness slowly. Even when it was certain that he would recover, he asked no questions for some days, but lay quietly and thoughtfully in his bed, thinking thoughts as long and slow as had been his return to life. Then, very quietly, one day he turned to his wife and asked for the letter.

She was very much surprised, but she rose instantly from her chair.

"What letter do you mean, dear?" she asked brightly, preparing to seek out anything that he might care to see.

But when he had told her, her face was grave and her eyes became a little frightened. There was no one near, however, on whom she might call for advice, and so she answered as best she was able.

"David," she said, "you must try to understand what happened to you that night. I was asleep upstairs, with John, and I thought I heard the front door open. Then for a little while I heard nothing at all. I called to you, but you didn't answer. And then I heard you throw open the door and run out into the storm. I heard you calling. I found you out there in the snow. One of the neighbors helped me to get you into the house, and I telephoned for the doctor. You have been very ill ever since. There wasn't any letter, David. You frighten me when you tell me you had a letter from your father."

"I wrote to him," he replied gravely, "the night you showed me John's foolish, pathetic letter to the North Pole. I posted my letter in the fire. It sounds like madness, doesn't it? But you would think me madder still if I told you what occurred on Christmas Eve—and so I shall not tell you, Nora darling, and I shall never speak of it again."

When she had gone away he lay back gently on his pillow and watched the winter sunlight on the windowpane.

"Dear old Dad!" he said, half aloud, half smiling. "Shall I recognize you when you come again? And is it until next year, or for fifty years, that you would have me wait for you? No matter, I shall be ready when you ring; you shall not go away alone. We know each other now, you and I. I have been close to mystery, and I think that also I have been close to madness. It is not well to inquire too closely even into oneself. But I have understood your message. It is just to love—and to tell others that you love. You will come again in a solemn hour. If there be an awakening beyond that hour, it is because of love. And if there shall be no awakening, that too, I think, will be because of love."

He smiled.

"Meanwhile, it is well to live, and to find happiness in love. I have much to do."

For some minutes he lay thinking, then quietly dropped off to sleep. His wife, entering the room an instant later, listened for a moment to his peaceful breathing and tiptoed to her chair.

LANGSTON HUGHES

One Christmas Eve

STANDING over the hot stove cooking supper, the colored maid, Arcie, was very tired. Between meals today, she had cleaned the whole house for the white family she worked for, getting ready for Christmas tomorrow. Now her back ached and her head felt faint from sheer fatigue. Well, she would be off in a little while, if only the Missus and her children would come on home to dinner. They were out shopping for more things for the tree which stood all ready, tinsel-hung and lovely in the living-room, waiting for its candles to be lighted.

Arcie wished she could afford a tree for Joe. He'd never had one yet, and it's nice to have such things when you're little. Joe was five, going on six. Arcie, looking at the roast in the white folks' oven,

Reprinted from *The Ways of White Folks* by Langston Hughes, by permission of Alfred A. Knopf, Inc. Copyright, 1934, by Alfred A. Knopf, Inc.

wondered how much she could afford to spend tonight on toys. She only got seven dollars a week, and four of that went for her room and the landlady's daily looking after Joe while Arcie was at work.

"Lord, it's more'n a notion raisin' a child," she thought.

She looked at the clock on the kitchen table. After seven. What made white folks so darned inconsiderate? Why didn't they come on home here to supper? They knew she wanted to get off before all the stores closed. She wouldn't have time to buy Joe nothin' if they didn't hurry. And her landlady probably wanting to go out and shop, too, and not be bothered with little Joe.

"Dog gone it!" Arcie said to herself. "If I just had my money, I might leave the supper on the stove for 'em. I just got to get to the stores fo' they close." But she hadn't been paid for the week yet. The Missus had promised to pay her Christmas Eve, a day or so ahead of time.

Arcie heard a door slam and talking and laughter in the front of the house. She went in and saw the Missus and her kids shaking snow off their coats.

"Umm-mm! It's swell for Christmas Eve," one of the kids said to Arcie. "It's snowin' like the deuce, and mother came near driving through a stop light. Can't hardly see for the snow. It's swell!"

"Supper's ready," Arcie said. She was thinking how her shoes weren't very good for walking in snow.

It seemed like the white folks took as long as they could to eat that evening. While Arcie was washing dishes, the Missus came out with her money.

"Arcie," the Missus said, "I'm so sorry, but would you mind if I just gave you five dollars tonight? The children have made me run short of change, buying presents and all."

"I'd like to have seven," Arcie said. "I needs it."

"Well, I just haven't got seven," the Missus said. "I didn't know you'd want all your money before the end of the week, anyhow. I just haven't got it to spare."

Arcie took five. Coming out of the hot kitchen, she wrapped up as well as she could and hurried by the house where she roomed to get little Joe. At least he could look at the Christmas trees in the windows downtown.

The landlady, a big light yellow woman, was in a bad humor. She said to Arcie, "I thought you was comin' home early and get this child. I guess you know I want to go out, too, once in awhile."

Arcie didn't say anything for, if she had, she knew the landlady would probably throw it up to her that she wasn't getting paid to look after a child both night and day.

"Come on, Joe," Arcie said to her son, "let's us go in the street."

"I hears they got a Santa Claus down town," Joe said, wriggling into his worn little coat. "I wants to see him."

"Don't know 'bout that," his mother said, "but hurry up and get your rubbers on. Stores'll all be closed directly."

It was six or eight blocks downtown. They trudged along through the falling snow, both of them a little cold. But the snow was pretty!

The main street was hung with bright red and blue lights. In front of the City Hall there was a Christmas tree—but it didn't have no presents on it, only lights. In the store windows there were lots of toys—for sale.

Joe kept on saying, "Mama, I want . . ."

But mama kept walking ahead. It was nearly ten, when the stores were due to close, and Arcie wanted to get Joe some cheap gloves and something to keep him warm, as well as a toy or two. She thought she might come across a rummage sale where they had children's clothes. And in the ten-cent store, she could get some toys.

"O-oo! Lookee . . . ," little Joe kept saying, and pointing at things in the windows. How warm and pretty the lights were, and the shops, and the electric signs through the snow.

It took Arcie more than a dollar to get Joe's mittens and things he needed. In the A. & P. Arcie bought a big box of hard candies for 49c. And then she guided Joe through the crowd on the street until they came to the dime store. Near the ten-cent store they passed a moving picture theatre. Joe said he wanted to go in and see the movies.

Arcie said, "Ump-un! No, child! This ain't Baltimore where they have shows for colored, too. In these here small towns, they don't let colored folks in. We can't go in there."

"Oh," said little Joe.

In the ten-cent store, there was an awful crowd. Arcie told Joe to stand outside and wait for her. Keeping hold of him in the crowded store would be a job. Besides she didn't want him to see what toys she was buying. They were to be a surprise from Santa Claus tomorrow.

Little Joe stood outside the ten-cent store in the light, and the snow, and people passing. Gee, Christmas was pretty. All tinsel and stars and cotton. And Santa Claus a-coming from somewhere, dropping things in stockings. And all the people in the streets were carrying things, and the kids looked happy.

But Joe soon got tired of just standing and thinking and waiting in front of the ten-cent store. There were so many things to look at in the other windows. He moved along up the block a little, and then a little more, walking and looking. In fact, he moved until he came to the white folks' picture show.

In the lobby of the moving picture show, behind the plate glass doors, it was all warm and glowing and awful pretty. Joe stood looking in, and as he looked his eyes began to make out, in there blazing beneath holly and colored streamers and the electric stars of the lobby, a marvellous Christmas tree. A group of children and grown-ups, white, of course, were standing around a big jovial man in red beside the tree. Or was it a man? Little Joe's eyes opened wide. No, it was not a man at all. It was Santa Claus!

Little Joe pushed open one of the glass doors and ran into the lobby of the white moving picture show. Little Joe went right through the crowd and up to where he could get a good look at Santa Claus. And Santa Claus was giving away gifts, little presents for children, little boxes of animal crackers and stick-candy canes. And behind him on the tree was a big sign (which little Joe didn't know how to read). It said, to those who understood, MERRY XMAS FROM SANTA CLAUS TO OUR YOUNG PATRONS.

One Christmas Eve

Around the lobby, other signs said, WHEN YOU COME OUT OF THE SHOW STOP WITH YOUR CHILDREN AND SEE OUR SANTA CLAUS. And another announced, GEM THEATRE MAKES ITS CUSTOMERS HAPPY— SEE OUR SANTA.

And there was Santa Claus in a red suit and a white beard all sprinkled with tinsel snow. Around him were rattles and drums and rocking horses which he was not giving away. But the signs on them said (could little Joe have read) that they would be presented from the stage on Christmas Day to the holders of the lucky numbers. To-night, Santa Claus was only giving away candy, and stick-candy canes, and animal crackers to the kids.

Joe would have liked terribly to have a stick-candy cane. He came a little closer to Santa Claus, until he was right in the front of the crowd. And then Santa Claus saw Joe.

Why is it that lots of white people always grin when they see a Negro child? Santa Claus grinned. Everybody else grinned, too, looking at little black Joe—who had no business in the lobby of a white theatre. Then Santa Claus stooped down and slyly picked up one of his lucky number rattles, a great big loud tin-pan rattle such as they use in cabarets. And he shook it fiercely right at Joe. That was funny. The white people laughed, kids and all. But little Joe didn't laugh. He was scared. To the shaking of the big rattle, he turned and fled out of the warm lobby of the theatre, out into the street where the snow was and the people. Frightened by laughter, he had begun to cry. He went looking for his mama. In his heart he never thought Santa Claus shook great rattles at children like that —and then laughed.

In the crowd on the street he went the wrong way. He couldn't find the ten-cent store or his mother. There were too many people, all white people, moving like white shadows in the snow, a world of white people.

It seemed to Joe an awfully long time till he suddenly saw Arcie, dark and worried-looking, cut across the side-walk through the pass-ing crowd and grab him. Although her arms were full of packages, she still managed with one free hand to shake him until his teeth rattled.

"Why didn't you stand where I left you?" Arcie demanded loudly. "Tired as I am, I got to run all over the streets in the night lookin' for you. I'm a great mind to wear you out."

When little Joe got his breath back, on the way home, he told his mama he had been in the moving picture show.

"But Santa Claus didn't give me nothin'," Joe said tearfully. "He made a big noise at me and I runned out."

"Serves you right," said Arcie, trudging through the snow. "You had no business in there. I told you to stay where I left you."

"But I seed Santa Claus in there," little Joe said, "so I went in."

"Huh! That wasn't no Santa Claus," Arcie explained. "If it was, he wouldn't a-treated you like that. That's a theatre for white folks —I told you once—and he's just a old white man."

"Oh . . . ," said little Joe.

MARGARET CARPENTER

The Pasteboard Star

GREGORY curled himself in as small a space as possible and pulled the bedclothes over his head. His breath made a safe, warm little cave under the covers, which shut out the larger darkness around him, and made him forget that he was afraid. It was the way he had gone to sleep ever since Aunt Martha had taken him out of the nursery and given him a room to himself, because he was big enough to begin to grow up. The cave made it all right—made it so that he didn't mind not being able to hear Christopher talking to himself, or Alan singing tunes under his breath that were not tunes at all. At first he made believe he was a lion or a bear going to sleep out of doors, but soon he began telling himself stories. They were not word stories, like the ones in books, but picture stories—pictures of things happening, and sometimes, when they were very good, not even pictures, but the things themselves. Always, when they were done, he felt warm and tingly and happy, and it seemed as if there were a light in the cave, and as if his mother were there, nodding and smiling at him because he had done something brave and beautiful, and then he was asleep.

Tonight it was different. It was Christmas Eve, but that was not what made the difference. He had something very important to do —something that he simply had to do before he could go to sleep. It had begun at supper. He still had supper with Christopher and Alan, because his father almost never came home for dinner, almost never came home before he went to bed, in fact. It was because his father was a doctor, and sick people couldn't wait, but children could. Tonight they had hoped perhaps he might get home, and they had been waiting, and Aunt Martha was cross because she had had too much to do. He didn't really mind much about Aunt Martha. She was like the weather. You had to take her as she was and just not listen. Maybe she'd be better tomorrow.

Christopher had started it. Aunt Martha had gone out of the room on business of her own, and they were alone. He had pushed his chair back, because the nursery table hurt his knees. Christopher was spilling milk down his sweater as usual, and Alan was making islands out of his oatmeal.

"Listen, Greg, do you really remember her?" It was funny how Christopher seemed to know sometimes just what people were thinking about.

"Sure I do," he had answered.

"Tell me something."

"Well, she wore a white dress, and she carried a baby."

"You?"

"No, I guess it was Alan."

"I made two islands," said Alan, who never paid any attention to anything except what he himself was doing.

"It couldn't have been Alan. I heard Aunt Martha telling Sadie about how she died before Alan was born."

"Silly, how could she? Isn't she Alan's mother too?"

"Well, anyway she never saw Alan, because she died in a horse pital and never came home."

"Not 'horsepital'—hospital."

"Maybe it was me she carried."

"All right, it was you."

"Go on. Tell something else."

"Well . . . she wore a white dress."

Then Christopher had said that awful thing. "You mean like the picture in the dining room?"

It was like the picture in the dining room, and it must have been that the fear had shown in his face, because Christopher had shouted: "You're making it up. You don't remember any more than I do. You're making it up out of the picture."

"I'm not making it up! I'm not! I'm *not!*" He had said it fiercely, because of the queer feeling in his stomach. "I see her in—in——" He had been going to say the cave, but had pulled himself up in time. It was a secret promise that he would never tell anyone about the cave, because it was queer that when you told about things like that they never seemed so real afterward. That was why he ought not to have talked about his mother, for now it seemed, all of a sudden, as if she were not real at all.

"I see her in—in—the dark," he finished lamely, "and she has on a white dress—and she smiles at me—and——"

"You are making it up."

"I'm not. . . ."

Just then Aunt Martha had come in.

"Boys, boys, can't you stop quarreling even on Christmas Eve?"

"He's telling stories again," said Christopher. "He says he sees her in the dark, and she has on a white dress——"

"Gregory!"

He had tried to look back at her, but her eyes frightened him. If he looked at them, they would take away the realness of his mother altogether, and then everything would be spoiled, for it was that feeling about his mother that made him able to grow up, to be more like his father and sleep by himself and not mind about Aunt Martha being cross. Christopher and Alan were babies—they didn't remember, but he did. And now they were trying to take his remembering away from him, and he was afraid.

"Where's Daddy?" asked Alan brightly, just as if nothing had happened. "I want him to draw a boat."

"I'm sure I don't know where your father is," Aunt Martha's voice was high the way it got when she was tired, "but we can't wait any longer. You will hang up your stockings and go to bed." When she sounded like that, it was no use hoping about anything any more, and here he was, all curled up in the cave, and he didn't care whether it was Christmas Eve or not, because he had to remember, he simply had to remember, before he could go to sleep.

Downstairs there were people moving about and a faint murmur of voices. His father had come home and they were trimming the tree. Every Christmas Daddy and Aunt Martha trimmed the tree. He knew that, but Christopher and Alan didn't. Santy Claus was a game Aunt Martha played, and he wouldn't spoil it, not for anything. He liked to play it, only why didn't Aunt Martha ever like to play his games? He screwed up his eyes tight. He wasn't getting anywhere. He was thinking as if his mother's realness was a game, and it wasn't. It was really real, not just a pretend, like Santy Claus, and he must remember something that even Aunt Martha would know was real, before he could go to sleep. He tried to make his mind very still and empty, so that he could remember the very first thing.

"No, you must tie your shoes yourself. You are a big boy now. . . ." He remembered that—sunlight in a room, and someone kneeling in front of him. Was it his mother? Someone in a white dress? But it sounded like Aunt Martha's voice. "Now you are a big boy, you must sleep in a room by yourself. . . ." No, it was Aunt Martha, always Aunt Martha. The cave was dark and there was no one there but Aunt Martha. Supposing they were right, and he didn't remember? He popped his head out from under the bedclothes. For the first time he was afraid in the cave, and the room was so very dark that he was afraid there too. He must not call, because that would wake up Christopher and Alan. Only he was so much afraid that he would have to do something about it quickly.

He jumped out of bed and very carefully opened the door. Perhaps, if he could hear his father's voice, it would make everything all right again. It was dark in the hall, but just at the foot of the stairs a warm, lovely glow streamed out from the library door. They were in there, trimming the tree. He sat down on the top step of the stairs, curling and uncurling his toes against the carpet.

"They are frightfully tarnished, and the tinsel is all matted. I'll get new ones next year." That was Aunt Martha. Then his father answered, only it wasn't exactly an answer, which was the way his father often did. "I had a hard time finding candleholders. Everybody uses electricity apparently."

"Of course, it is much safer."

"I like real candles."

"Will you hand me one of those angels, please?"

He knew he ought not to listen, but he moved down a few steps. It wasn't as if they were saying anything important. All he wanted was to hear his father's voice, not what he said. It was beginning to make him feel safe again. In a minute now he would go back to bed, and be able to remember quite easily.

"I want," said Aunt Martha again, "to talk with you about Gregory."

He held his breath. All the safeness was gone, splintered into bits. There was a faint rustle of tissue paper.

"Oh, but the wings are broken!"

"Never mind," said his father; "hang it just the same."

Perhaps his father hadn't heard. He was like that sometimes—you had to say a thing two or three times before he answered. He dug his toes into the carpet and waited.

"What was it about Gregory?" His father's voice sounded so gentle, as if he thought he were going to hear something pleasant.

"I'm having a difficult time with him. He is turning into a regular little liar, and I can't seem to get hold of him at all. He simply doesn't seem to distinguish truth from fiction."

Silence again. Gregory sat very still, only his heart was pounding so terribly, it seemed as if they must hear it.

"What sort of lies?"

"He tells the children the most impossible stories—tells them he killed a tiger on the stairs, and how he stopped a runaway on the way back from school."

"That's not exactly lying, is it?"

"Not lying? Well, there wasn't any tiger, and he certainly did not stop a runaway."

"No, but if there had been a tiger, he would have wanted to kill it, and if he had seen a runaway, he would have imagined himself stopping it, just as you or I would."

"Well, whatever you call it, it has got to stop. It is giving Alan nightmares, and now—now he has begun on something else."

There was the sound of a match. His father was lighting his pipe.

"He has begun," said Aunt Martha, "to tell stories about his mother."

There was a long, long silence. Gregory pressed up close against the banisters. He had a horrid feeling. It was just as if he were a rag doll, and they had him in there, passing him about and poking him and pulling him, and he could not make a sound.

"What sort of stories?"

"Well, tonight he said he saw her in the dark."

Gregory stood up. He could not stay, and he could not go, and something was going to happen.

"Perhaps," said his father slowly, "he wishes she were there in the dark."

"That is very different from telling the children that he sees her. It's not wholesome. Will you hand me the top piece to the tree, please?" Aunt Martha's voice was a little high. There was the tissue paper sound again.

"No—no—not that. That's nothing but a pasteboard star. It looks like a kindergarten toy. I mean that tall spike for the top."

Gregory closed his eyes. Something very queer was happening inside himself. He felt as if he were going to be sick.

"Try the star," said his father.

"But look, the silver paper is peeling off, and one of the point is——"

Afterward Gregory could remember nothing except that one minute he had been holding on to the banisters and feeling as if he were going to be sick, and the next he had been standing right there between them and shouting at them.

"I remember! I do remember. I made that star, and my mother cut it out, and we pasted the paper on it, and I sucked a red ribbon so it would go through the hole and she lifted me up so I could hang it, and you got to hang it. . . . You got to hang it. . . ."

Aunt Martha was standing on a chair staring down at him, and her mouth was open, and suddenly he had pointed his finger at her.

"I do remember and you're a liar, and you get out of here! . . . This is my tree and my mother's tree and you get out—get out. . . ."

"Hush, Greg," said his father very quietly, and laid his hand on his shoulder. Everything seemed to be swimming a little, as if he were in the middle of a soap bubble and it was going to burst.

"I never in my life heard a child speak so to an older person," said Aunt Martha in a shaky voice.

"I'll handle this," said his father. He was helping her off the chair.

Gregory stood alone by the tree. It was very beautiful. It moved a little as if it were in a wind. He heard the door close, and his father was beside him. He was going to tell him what a dreadful boy he had been. He was going to handle it himself, and that had never happened before. His father was picking up something from the floor. He was putting it into his hands. It was the pasteboard star.

"Here, Greg," he said, "here, you hang it. You climb up and hang it yourself."

He climbed on the chair and hung it as high as he could. It was pretty high—one of the little branches next the top. It twisted slowly around on its red ribbon. It made him dizzy to watch it, so that he put out his hand to his father's shoulder. Suddenly their arms were about each other and, because he was on the chair and so very tall, it made him seem as if he were grown up, and his father the little boy. He laid his cheek against his father's head, so that he could hear what he was saying.

"Greg—Greg—I didn't know about your remembering. . . . I didn't know! We'll never either of us have to be alone again!"

MARGERY WILLIAMS BIANCO

The Little Guest

EVERY year, at about Christmastime, the holy child came on a visit to the nuns. He came with his mother and Saint Joseph and the shepherds and all the pet animals, and they all stayed together in the little house that the nuns fixed up for them.

The house stood on a table, in the entry just outside the chapel. First there was a white cloth over the table, with lace edges hanging down. On this stood the house. It had only a roof and one wall, at the back, so that you could see right inside it. Behind were the mountains that Sister Gertrude had made, of brown paper covered with sparkly snow, and there were evergreens all round, and ivy, and two real little pine trees growing by themselves in pots.

The holy child seemed to like his little house. He lay just inside it, smiling, on a bed of straw, with a little white shirt on. He didn't seem to mind about its only having one wall, or that the nuns hadn't thought about putting any furniture in it. He lay there and smiled, with his arms stretched out. His mother and Saint Joseph knelt, one on each side, and behind them knelt two angels. That made five people, and the little house wouldn't hold any more, so the shepherds had to stand outside, as close as they could get, and near them stood the animals, the cow and the gray donkey and the three white lambs, two lying down and one standing up. The standing-up one was a little bigger than the others, and had a red collar on. When all the candles were lighted it looked just like a party, with the holy child in the middle.

Twice a day, going to chapel and coming out, the file of little blue-pinafored girls passed the table where the holy child lived; fourteen heads, two by two, brown and yellow and mouse-colored under their thin starched veils, bobbing by sedately, with wrinkled, kindly Sister Elizabeth in her black robes walking behind. Going to and from chapel there was no time to pause, because all the older girls walked behind and one had to keep moving; one had only a glimpse in passing of the little house with all the family gathered round it, bright and dazzling in the light of the wax candles. But every evening at Christmastime, instead of going up the two long straight flights of stairs to the landing outside the dormitory, where the little girls usually said their prayers, Sister Elizabeth would take them the long way round, down the hall and up the back staircase and through a door by the linen room to the chapel entry.

To Louisa, spending her first Christmas with the nuns, there was something very exciting in this detour. The back stairway was rather dark; the boards creaked underfoot and it had a queer cupboardy smell. There were shadowy corners in it, and the most shadowy place of all was just by the linen-room door. Here you had to stand still and wait, and not make any noise because this was the nuns' part of the house and next door to the chapel. You had to stand very quietly while Sister Elizabeth's feet in their flat shoes came creak, creak along the passage, past all the little girls in turn, till she reached the door and turned the handle.

And then, when the door swung open, there were the candles

shining, and the Christmasy smell of evergreens and hot melting wax, and in the middle of all this sudden brightness was the little holy child on his straw bed.

Kneeling on the hard boards that always made her shift and wriggle long before Sister Elizabeth's measured voice reached the last "Amen," Louisa had a good view of the little house and every thing about it. The mountains looked just like real, the snow glit tered on the evergreen branches and on the white cotton batting, where the shepherds stood. It was as if you could walk right up be tween the pine trees, past the gray donkey and the lambs, straight into the little room where the holy child lay. It was all very beautiful.

And yet there was something about it not quite right.

Privately, Louisa had her own opinion of how the nuns treated the holy child.

The snow was lovely, and so were Sister Gertrude's mountain, and the little pine trees, but something better could have been done about the house. There was no furniture, there were no curtains, there wasn't even a rug. It was true that the holy child stayed in bed, but he couldn't be very comfortable even there. It was made of straw and it looked prickly, and the holy child had only a small shirt on. There should certainly have been a pillow, and as long as the nuns sewed so well they could have made sheets and a quilt and a little blanket too. Louisa supposed that they just hadn't thought about it, which was funny, because they had known for days and days that the holy child was coming. It was no way to treat a guest, and the holy child was a guest; Sister Elizabeth had said so.

Nuns, Louisa thought, were very curious people.

It was unusually cold that Christmas. When you went outdoors, even for a moment, your toes pinched and the wind stung your face. Indoors the little girls had to wear their sweaters going to chapel and along the corridors, and when they got up in the morning their fingers were pink and stiff. Because the big register in the floor, for some reason or other, was not giving all the heat it should, Sister Elizabeth brought an oil heater and stood it on the dormitory floor, and the children dressed around that.

There came the frostiest day of all.

Tucked in bed that evening, her toes drawn up under her nightgown to keep them from touching the chilly sheets, Louisa thought about the holy child. He must be terribly cold down there. The nuns, evidently, were doing nothing about it. They didn't even seem worried. They wouldn't mind if the holy child froze!

The oil heater, turned low, glowed like a red eye in the middle of the dormitory floor. Through the looped-up curtains of her bed Louisa could see the long shadows it threw across the floor and up the walls. From the other beds came occasional rustlings and the small breathing sounds of sleep. Louisa tried to sleep too. But every time she shut her eyes she saw the holy child, with only his little shirt on, lying there on the straw bed as she had seen him that evening.

Presently she heard, far off and hollow, the three tolls of the gateway bell, and after what seemed a very long time, the slow, tired steps of Sister Saint Ann, the portress, making her last round. She came along the lower corridor, up the stairway, carrying her lantern, and then Louisa could hear the clink as she set it down finally at the head of the dormitory stairs, where it would burn until morning.

For a little while longer Louisa lay still, the blanket dragged up to her chin. Then very cautiously she pushed back the covers, slid first one leg, then the other, out of bed. It was chilly on the floor. Louisa felt for her slippers, pulled on her dressing gown. Edging her way past the other beds with their humped, sleeping mounds, she reached the doorway and the open landing.

There were two stairways. One, where the lantern stood, was that which the children always used. The other, narrower and steeper, led down through the nuns' part of the house to the chapel entry. Little girls had no business here alone, especially at night.

Holding her breath, Louisa began to creep down, praying that the boards would not creak. The first landing at the bottom was easy; one turned to the right. There was a big room to cross, lined with closets; then came a corridor, another little flight of steps, and then one reached the chapel entry.

The Little Guest

There was nothing to be afraid of in the dark; Louisa knew that. All the same there were shadows. They reached out after you. They closed in behind, so you did not dare turn your head. And the corridor was long, much longer than it ever seemed by daylight. It stretched and stretched. It seemed as if you would never get to the end.

The entry door was closed. Louisa tugged at it. It did not stir. She tugged again and it gave suddenly, with a creak that seemed to echo through the whole house.

She was in the chapel entry. There were no candles burning. Everything was dim and mysterious. Only a faint, uncertain flicker came from the little red swinging lamp overhead, shining down on the pine trees, the tiny house and the small waxen figure of the holy child.

For a moment, in that dim, pinkish glow, Louisa stood uncertain, her heart beating very fast. Then she moved closer, nearer still, till her fingers touched the white tablecloth. Resolutely she reached out her hand, snatched the holy child from his straw bed, and thrusting him into the warm folds of her dressing gown, turned and ran.

In the morning Louisa woke early. She pushed her hand under her pillow, where she had put the holy child to sleep the night before, wrapped up in a handkerchief to keep him warm.

Something very awful had happened to the holy child. No one would have recognized him. His limbs had lost their shape; his face was flattened and stuck fast to the handkerchief. He was nothing but a horrible messy lump of softened wax.

It was a judgment. She had been a wicked little girl. Hastily, too conscience-stricken even for tears, she folded the handkerchief back over what had been the holy child. But somehow through her misery a sense of injustice struggled. She hadn't wanted to be wicked; she had wanted to be good. She wanted to make the holy child warm and comfortable. She thought he would understand, and he hadn't understood. He had melted.

What could be done? She couldn't leave him there. She couldn't put him back into the chapel. Had there only been an earthquake, then and there, if it could have buried her and the whole school and the holy child all together so that nobody, nobody would ever know what had happened. . . . But earthquakes didn't come like that. And the dressing bell was ringing. . . .

The Ancient Mariner, with the dead albatross hung about his neck, suffered nothing in comparison with Louisa that morning. He at least did not have to carry his burden secretly. He was not in terror every moment that someone would say, "What's that lump inside your frock?"

Louisa seemed to hold herself rather queerly all morning. At recess she showed an inclination to sit alone and sniff. The young nun who was in charge of the children called her over.

"Why aren't you playing with the others, dear?"

"I—d'know. I think I got a cold."

"You shouldn't sniff like that. Where's your handkerchief?"

"I—haven't got one."

Louisa flushed guiltily. It was a lie. She knew where her handkerchief was. Even as she said it she could feel something slipping . . . slipping . . . right down by her waistband. If only the elastic would hold!

"Then I think you had better go and fetch one. Go quietly up and quietly back, and if you meet anyone on the stairs you can say that Sister sent you."

No sign from a relenting heaven could have been more welcome.

Clutching her waistband, treading with every precaution till she was once outside the door, Louisa went. Once she reached the corridor she flew, still gripping her garments tightly to her. All the morning she had prayed for just this chance. When she reached the dormitory landing she turned neither to left nor right but went straight on to the bathroom.

This particular bath had been put in when the school was remodeled. It was a high, old-fashioned tub, and underneath it, where the pipes went down, there was a piece of floor board missing. Louisa knew this, for she had once lost a big glass bead down there. It had rolled under the bath and she couldn't get it out. What she was going to do was wicked, but it couldn't make things any worse than they were already.

She groped, shook herself; something fell with a little thud to the linoleum. She picked up the holy child, handkerchief and all, and lying down flat on her stomach she poked him through the hole and as far in under the floor boards as she could reach.

She had done with taking care of him. She had done with trying to be kind to people, ever again, as long as she lived.

Four o'clock came. Two by two the little girls went into chapel. As they passed the holy child's house, with the candles blazing before it, Louisa never turned her head. Invisible strings were pulling her, but she dared not look.

Nothing had been said all day. Perhaps in chapel they were going to speak about it. Perhaps, when they all stood up to go out, someone would step out into the aisle . . .

But still nothing happened. The little girls rose, filed one by one out of the straight pews and joined their ranks, just as usual.

Louisa looked straight ahead. She crossed the mat by the chapel door. Now she could smell the evergreens and the hot wax; the warm breath from the candles was right in her face. She had to turn.

There was a little house, just as usual. There were Sister Gertrude's mountains, all shiny, and the pine trees and the shepherds and the gray donkey. And there, just where he always had been, was the holy child. He seemed to have grown a little, that was all. The candlelight shone on his yellow tight little curls and his waxen arms, stretched out. He smiled at Louisa as if nothing had happened at all.

CHRISTOPHER MORLEY
The Worst Christmas Story

WE had been down to an East Side settlement house on Christmas afternoon. I had watched my friend Dove Dulcet, in moth-riddled scarlet and cotton wool trimmings, play Santa Claus for several hundred adoring urchins and their parents. He had done this for many years, but I had never before seen him insist on the amiable eccentricity of returning uptown still wearing the regalia of the genial saint. But Dove is always unusual, and I thought—as did the others who saw him, in the subway and elsewhere—it was a rather kindly and innocent concession to the hilarity of the day.

When we had got back to his snug apartment he beamed at me through his snowy fringes of false whisker, and began rummaging in the tall leather boots of his costume. From each one he drew a bottle of chianti.

From *Letters of Askance*, copyright, 1939, by Christopher Morley, published by J. B. Lippincott Company.

The Worst Christmas Story

"From a grateful parent on Mulberry Street," he said. "My favorite bootlegger lives down that way, and I've been playing Santa to his innumerable children for a number of years. The garb attributed—quite inaccurately, I expect—to Saint Nicholas of Bari, has its uses. Even the keenest revenue agent would hardly think of holding up poor old Santa."

He threw off his trappings, piled some logs on the fire, and we sat down for our annual celebration. Dove and I have got into the habit of spending Christmas together. We are both old bachelors, with no close family ties, and we greatly enjoy the occasion. It isn't wholly selfish, either, for we usually manage to spice our fun with a little unexpected charity in some of the less fortunate quarters of the town.

As my friend uncorked the wicker-bound bottles I noticed a great pile of Christmas mail on his table.

"Dove, you odd fish," I said. "Why don't you open your letters? I should have thought that part of the fun of Christmas is hurrying to look through the greetings from friends. Or do you leave them to the last, to give them greater savor?"

He glanced at the heap, with a curious expression on his face.

"The Christmas cards?" he said. "I postpone them as long as I possibly can. It's part of my penance."

"What on earth do you mean?"

He filled two glasses, passed one to me, and sat down beside the cheerful blaze.

"Here's luck, old man!" he said. "Merry Christmas."

I drank with him, but something evasive in his manner impelled me to repeat my question.

"What a ferret you are, Ben!" he said. "Yes, I put off looking at the Christmas cards as long as I dare. I suppose I'll have to tell you. It's one of the few skeletons in my anatomy of melancholy that you haven't exhumed. It's a queer kind of Christmas story."

He reached over to the table, took up a number of the envelopes, and studied their handwritings. He tore them open one after another, and read the enclosed cards.

"As I expected," he said. "Look here, it's no use your trying to make copy out of this yarn. No editor would look at it. It runs counter to all the good old Christmas tradition."

"My dear Dove," I said, "if you've got a Christmas story that's 'different,' you've got something that editors will pay double for."

"Judge for yourself," he said. From the cards in his lap he chose four and gave them to me. "Begin by reading those."

Completely mystified, I did so.

The first showed a blue bird perched on a spray of holly. The verse read:

> *Our greeting is "Merry Christmas!"*
> *None better could we find,*
> *And tho' you are now out of sight,*
> *You're ever in our mind.*

The second card said, below a snow scene of mid-Victorian characters alighting from a stage coach at the hospitable door of a country mansion:

> *Should you or your folk ever call at our door*
> *You'll be welcome, we promise you—nobody more;*
> *We wish you the best of the Joy and Cheer*
> *That can come with Christmas and last through the year!*

The third, with a bright picture of three stout old gentlemen in scarlet waistcoats, tippling before an open fire:

> *Jolly old Yule, Oh the jolly old Yule*
> *Blesses rich man and poor man and wise man and fool—*
> *Be merry, old friend, in this bright winter weather,*
> *And you'll Yule and I'll Yule, we'll all Yule together!*

The fourth—an extremely ornate vellum leaflet, gilded with Oriental designs and magi on camels—ran thus:

> *I pray the prayer the Easterners do;*
> *May the Peace of Allah abide with you—*
> *Through days of labor and nights of rest*
> *May the love of Allah make you blest.*

The Worst Christmas Story

"Well," I said, "of course I wouldn't call them great poetry, but the sentiments are generous enough. Surely it's the spirit in which they're sent that counts. It doesn't seem like you to make fun—"

Dulcet leaned forward. "Make fun?" he said. "Heavens, I'm not making fun of them. The ghastly thing is, I wrote those myself."

There was nothing to say, so I held my peace.

"You didn't know, I trust, that at one time I was regarded as the snappiest writer of greeting sentiments (so the trade calls them) in the business? That was long ago, but the sentiments themselves, and innumerable imitations of them, go merrily on. You see, out of the first ten cards that I picked up, four are my own composition. Can you imagine the horror of receiving, every Christmas, every New Year, every Easter, every birthday, every Halloween, every Thanksgiving, cards most of which were written by yourself? And when I think of the honest affection with which those cards were chosen for me by my unsuspecting friends, and contrast their loving simplicity with—"

He broke off, and refilled the glasses.

"I told you," he said, "that this was the worst Christmas story in the world! But I must try to tell it a little better, at any rate. Well, it has some of the traditional ingredients.

"You remember the winter of the Great Panic—1906, wasn't it? I had a job in an office downtown, and was laid off. I applied everywhere for work—nothing doing. I had been writing a little on the side, verses and skits for the newspapers, but I couldn't make enough that way to live on. I had an attic in an old lodging house on Gay Street. (The Village was still genuine then, no hokum about it.) I used to reflect on the irony of that name, Gay Street, when I was walking about trying not to see the restaurants, they made me feel so hungry. I still get a queer feeling in the pit of my stomach when I pass by Gonfarone's—there was a fine thick savor of spaghetti and lentil soup that used to float out from the basement as I went along Eighth Street.

"There was a girl in it too, of course. You'll smile when I tell you who she was. Peggy Cassell, who does the magazine covers.

Yes, she's prosperous enough now—so are we all. But those were the days!

"It's the old bachelors who are the real sentimentalists, hey? But by Jove, how I adored that girl! She was fresh from upstate somewhere, studying at the League, and doing small illustrating jobs to make ends approach. I was as green and tender as she. I was only twenty-five, you know. To go up to what Peggy called her studio— which was only a bleak bedroom she shared with another girl—and smoke cigarettes and see her wearing a smock and watch her daub away at a thing she intended to be a 'portrait' of me, was my idea of high tide on the seacoast of Bohemia. Peggy would brew cocoa in a chafing dish and then the other girl would tactfully think of some errand, and we'd sit, timidly and uncomfortably, with our arms around each other, and talk about getting married some day, and prove by Cupid's grand old logarithms that two can live cheaper than one. I used to recite to her that ripping old song 'My Peggy is a young thing, And I'm not very auld,' and it would knock us both cold.

"The worst of it was, poor Peggy was almost as hard up as I was. In fact, we were both so hard up that I'm amazed we didn't get married, which is what people usually do when they have absolutely no prospects. But with all her sweet sentiment Peggy had a streak of sound caution. And as a matter of fact, I think she was better off than I was, because she did get a small allowance from home. Anyway, I was nearly desperate, tearing my heart out over the thought of this brave little creature facing the world for the sake of her art, and so on. She complained of the cold, and I remember taking her my steamer rug off my own bed, telling her I was too warm. After that I used to shingle myself over with newspapers when I went to bed. It was bitter on Gay Street that winter.

"But I said this was a Christmas Story. So it is. It began like this. About Hallowe'en I had a little poem in Life—nothing of any account, but a great event to me, my first appearance in Big Time journalism. Well, one day I got a letter from a publisher in Chicago asking permission to reprint it on a card. He said also that my verses had just the right touch which was needed in such things, and that I could probably do some 'holiday greetings' for him. He would be glad to see some Christmas 'sentiments,' he said, and would pay one dollar each for any he could use.

"You can imagine that it didn't take me long to begin tearing off sentiments though I stipulated, as a last concession to my honor, that my name should not be used. There was no time to lose: it was now along in November, and these things—to be sold to the public for Christmas a year later—must be submitted as soon as possible so that they could be illustrated and ready for the salesmen to take on the road in January.

"Picture, then, the young author of genial greeting cards, sitting ironically in the chilliest attic on Gay Street—a dim and draughty little elbow of the city—and attempting to ignite his wits with praise of the glowing hearth and the brandied pudding. The room was heated only by a small gas stove, one burner of which had been scientifically sealed by the landlady; an apparatus, moreover, in which asphyxia was the partner of warmth. When that sickly sweetish gust became too overpotent, see the author throw up the window and retire to bed, meditating under a mountain of news-print further applause of wintry joy and fellowship. I remember one sentiment— very likely it is among the pile on the table here: it is a great favorite—which went:

> *May blazing log and steaming bowl*
> *And wreaths of mistletoe and holly*
> *Remind you of a kindred soul*
> *Whose love for you is warm and jolly!*

"My, how cold it was the night I wrote that."

Dove paused, prodded the logs to a brighter flame, and leaned closer to the chimney as though feeling a reminiscent chill.

"Well, as Christmas itself drew nearer, I became more and more agitated. I had sent in dozens of these compositions; each batch was duly acknowledged, and highly praised. The publisher was pleased to say that I had a remarkable aptitude for 'greetings';

623

my Christmas line, particularly, he applauded as being full of the robust and hearty spirit of the old-fashioned Yule. My Easter touch, he felt, was a little thin and tepid by comparison. So I redoubled my metrical cheer. I piled the logs higher and higher upon my imaginary hearth; I bore in cups of steaming wassail; blizzards drummed at my baronial window panes; stage coaches were halted by drifts axle-deep; but within the circle of my mid-Victorian halloo, all was mirth: beauty crowded beneath the pale mistletoe; candles threw a tawny shine; the goose was carved and the port wine sparkled. And all the while, if you please, it was December of the panic winter; no check had yet arrived from the delighted publisher; I had laid aside other projects to pursue this golden phantom; I ate once a day, and sometimes kept warm by writing my mellow outbursts of gladness in the steam-heated lobbies of hotels.

"I had said nothing to Peggy about this professional assumption of Christmas heartiness. For one thing, I had talked to her so much, and with such youthful ardor, of my literary ambitions and ideals, that I feared her ridicule; for another, my most eager hope was to surprise her with an opulent Christmas present. She, poor dear, was growing a trifle threadbare too; she had spoken, now and then, of some sort of fur neckpiece she had seen in shop windows; this, no less, was my secret ambition. And so, as the streets grew brighter with the approach of the day, and still the publisher delayed his remittance, I wrote him a masterly letter. It was couched in the form of a Christmas greeting from me to him; it acknowledged the validity of his contention that he had postponed a settlement because I was still submitting more and more masterpieces and he planned to settle en bloc; but it pointed out the supreme and tragic irony of my having to pass a Christmas in starvation and misery because I had spent so much time dispersing altruistic and factitious good will.

"As I waited anxiously for a reply, I was further disquieted by distressing behavior on Peggy's part. She had been rather strange with me for some time, which I attributed partly to my own shabby appearance and wretched preoccupation with my gruesome task.

She had rallied me—some time before—on my mysterious mien, and I may have been clumsy in my retorts. Who can always know just the right accent with which to chaff a woman? At any rate, she had—with some suddenly assumed excuse of propriety—forbidden me the hospitality of her bedroom studio; even my portrait (which we had so blithely imagined as a national triumph in future years when we both stood at the crest of our arts) had been discontinued. We wandered the streets together, quarrelsome and unhappy; we could agree about nothing. In spite of this, I nourished my hopeful secret, still believing that when my check came, and enabled me to mark the Day of Days with the coveted fur, all would be happier than ever.

"It was two days before Christmas, and you may elaborate the picture with all the traditional tints of Dickens pathos. It was cold and snowy and I was hungry, worried, and forlorn. I was walking along Eighth Street wondering whether I could borrow enough money to telegraph to Chicago. Just by the Brevoort I met Peggy, and to my chagrin and despair she was wearing a beautiful new fur neckpiece—a tippet, I think they used to call them in those days. She looked a different girl: her face was pink, her small chin nestled adorably into the fur collar, her eyes were bright and merry. Well, I was only human, and I guess I must have shown my wretched disappointment. Of course she hadn't known that I hoped to surprise her in just that way, and when I blurted out something to that effect, she spoke tartly.

" 'You!' she cried. 'How could you buy me anything like that? I suppose you'd like me to tramp around in the snow all winter and catch my death of cold!'

"In spite of all the Christmas homilies I had written about good will and charity and what not, I lost my temper.

" 'Ah,' I said bitterly, 'I see it all now! I wasn't prosperous enough, so you've found someone else who can afford to buy furs for you. That's why you've kept me away from the studio, eh? You've got some other chap on the string.'

"I can still see her little flushed face, rosy with wind and snow, looking ridiculously stricken as she stood on that wintry corner. She began to say something, but I was hot with the absurd rage of youth. All my weeks of degradation on Gay Street suddenly boiled up in my mind. I was grotesquely melodramatic and absurd.

" 'A rich lover!' I sneered. 'Go ahead and take him! I'll stick to poverty and my ideals. You can have the furs and fleshpots!'

"Well, you never know how a woman will take things. To my utter amazement, instead of flaming up with anger, she burst into tears. But I was too proud and troubled to comfort her.

" 'Yes, you're right,' she sobbed. 'I had such fine dreams, but I couldn't stick it out. I'm not worthy of your ideals. I guess I've sold myself.' She turned and ran away down the slippery street, leaving me flabbergasted.

"I walked around and around Washington Square, not knowing what to do. She had as good as admitted that she had thrown me over for some richer man. And yet I didn't feel like giving her up without a struggle. Perhaps it all sounds silly now, but it was terribly real then.

"At last I went back to Gay Street. On the hall table was a letter from the publisher, with a check for fifty dollars. He had accepted fifty of the hundred or so pieces I had sent, and said if I would consider going to Chicago he would give me a position on his staff as Assistant Greeting Editor. 'Get into a good sound business,' he wrote. 'There will never be a panic in the Greeting line.'

"When I read that letter I was too elated to worry about anything. I would be able to fix things with Peggy somehow. I would say to her, in a melting voice, 'My Peggy is a young thing,' and she would tumble. She must love me still, or she wouldn't have cried. I rushed round to her lodging house, and went right upstairs without giving her a chance to deny me. I knocked, and when she came to the door she looked frightened and ill. She tried to stop me, but I burst in and waved the letter in front of her.

" 'Look at this, Peggy darling!' I shouted. 'We're going to be rich and infamous. I didn't tell you what I was doing, because I was afraid you'd be ashamed of me, after all my talk about high ideals.

But anything is better than starving and freezing on Gay Street, or doing without the furs that pretty girls need.'

"She read the letter, and looked up at me with the queerest face.

" 'Now no more nonsense about the other man,' I said. 'I'll buy you a fur for Christmas that'll put his among camphor balls. Who is he, anyway?'

"She surprised me again, for this time she began to laugh.

" 'It's the same one,' she said. 'I mean, the same publisher—your friend in Chicago. Oh Dove, I've been doing drawings for Christmas cards, and I think they must be yours.'

"It was true. Her poor little cold studio was littered with sketches for Christmas drawings—blazing fires and ruddy Georgian squires with tankards of hissing ale and girls in sprigged muslin being coy under the mistletoe. And when she showed me the typewritten verses the publisher had sent her to illustrate, they were mine, sure enough. She had had her check a day sooner than I, and had rushed off to buy herself the fur her heart yearned for.

" 'I was so ashamed of doing the work,' she said—with her head on my waistcoat—'that I didn't dare tell you.' "

Dove sighed, and leaned back in his chair. A drizzle of rain and sleet tinkled on the window pane, but the fire was a core of rosy light.

"Not much of a Christmas story, eh?" he said. "Do you wonder, now, that I hesitate to look back at the cards I wrote and Peggy illustrated?"

"But what happened?" I asked. "It seems a nice enough story as far as you've gone."

"Peggy was a naughty little hypocrite," he said. "I found out that she wasn't really ashamed of illustrating my Greetings at all. She thought they were lovely. She honestly did. And presently she told me she simply couldn't marry a man who would capitalize Christmas. She said it was too sacred."

JAKE FALSTAFF

Merry Christmas

THE school was to have a Christmas tree, and a Christmas doings. On the last day before the vacation there were no classes. Instead, all the scholars helped to trim the tree.

They made chains of colored paper and festoons of strung popcorn. They unpacked a big box of brittle ornaments, and hung up those that weren't broken. In the afternoon, some of the women of the neighborhood came in and helped, and later some men came in too, and built a flight of seats on the rostrum.

They left the desks to the visitors. The schoolhouse was crowded at seven o'clock when the doings began. Every desk held at least two adults, and there were dozens standing up around the sides of the room. Babies were hushed.

On the blackboard, in colored chalk, was the masterpiece of Albert Smeed, the penman. It was a very elaborate bird, drawn all in one line and over it in old English letters, "Merry Christmas."

The scholars and the grown people sang the first song together: "Silent Night, Holy Night." Then the teacher called on old Solomon Preavy, who was a Civil War veteran, a bailiff in the courthouse, and an ordained preacher. In a quaking voice, the old man asked a Christmas blessing.

The children sang: "Up on the house, no delay, no pause, clatter the steeds of Santa Claus. Down through the chimney with loads of toys. Ho for the little ones' Christmas joys!" A pale, tall, beautiful girl played "Star of the East" on a violin, and two very bashful little girls sang "Beside a Manger Lowly." A sixth-grade boy recited, "Father calls me William, sister calls me Will, mother calls me Willie, but the fellers call me Bill."

A small boy, called up to recite " 'Twas the Night Before Christmas," got overcome with embarrassment along about the tenth line and ran bawling to the desk where his mother sat.

After some more speaking, the teacher began to distribute the presents which had been laid under the tree. Lemuel was astonished to hear his name called. He got five presents—one from the teacher (*Pickwick Papers*), and four from other scholars. One of them was a hand-painted plate from the little girl with pigtails who told him to mind his own beeswax on the first day he went to Maple Valley School.

He was terribly embarrassed because he had not brought any presents for anybody.

There was some excitement in the back of the room. Some of the big boys of the township, considering themselves too old to go to the schoolhouse doings, were trying to climb up the schoolhouse with the apparent intention of stopping the chimney.

Stern fathers went out to attend to them.

When the formal services were over, Lemuel ran to Barbara. "I never gave any of them anything," he said.

Barbara patted his head. "Yes, you did," she said. "I found out who was giving you things, and put things under the tree for them. I forged your name to the cards."

Ora and Barbara took Lemuel along over to Uncle Simon's on Christmas Eve. He supposed that it meant some kind of celebration. They hadn't told him anything, but he knew that they were taking the set of puzzles and parlor tricks he was giving Clyde and that they had some other packages along.

Lemuel was in the sitting room, and had taken a good quick look into the kitchen and downstairs bedroom before he would admit to himself that Uncle Simon's didn't have a Christmas tree! He could barely conceal his surprise.

It was a fact that Clyde was nearly fifteen years old, and also that the family would be going over to Ora's (where there was a tree) for Christmas dinner. Still it seemed strange to Lemuel.

Although everybody looked a little more slicked up than usual, and Aunt Jen was wearing a gay pink apron, there was hardly any other variation from the routine. However, something smelled a good deal like newly baked cookies.

It was odd to a boy who had always spent Christmas Eve with his mother and father, the three sitting together around a brightly lighted little tree.

That was one evening when they never had any company. The ritual of present opening was always exactly the same, and even Lemuel's father, though he seemed almost as absent-minded and sober as usual, took Christmas Eve seriously.

Mrs. Hayden always passed out the gifts, calling off the name on each one with a little air of surprise. When a package was opened by one of them, the other two always watched with close attention. Lemuel's father would nod approval and nearly always comment, "Very fine; very fine indeed."

If his wife gave him a pair of black socks with a gray thread running through, Perry Hayden received them with an air of conviction from which one would have thought that he had been thinking intently of his need for black socks with a gray thread ever since July. When he got a present from Lemuel, he would nod solemnly and say, "Very thoughtful, very thoughtful."

So Lemuel felt a little chilled when he heard that the commotion out in the side yard meant that Cousin Dellie Graf and her young man, Homer Henty, had been invited over. As usual with people he had never met, he was pretty sure that he was going to feel strange.

This feeling left him as soon as Cousin Dellie came bursting in, pulling at a black curl which hung loose down on her forehead. She was a merry, curvaceous girl in an elegant stiff cocoa-taffeta dress. Her young man wore a swallow-tailed coat and a ready-made four-in-hand tie. He was redheaded, and even more inclined to merriment than Dellie.

The young farmer started telling about the flashlight pictures he was going to take of the group.

He was on the way to being a professional photographer, it developed. He said that as soon as he sold his lower Thirty, and made some further arrangements with Old Man Snell, the photographer at Creston, he was set to take over the business there.

When Ora and Clyde asked him questions about starting out as a photographer, he maintained that it wasn't much of a chore, the way he figured it. There was a lot of business where a fellow didn't exactly have to be an expert to make good. That was because of the great numbers of new Swiss and Hungarian and Bosnian immigrants who came in for pictures as soon as they got their bearings in this country.

The newcomers would settle near Akron and work in the celery ground on farms owned by relatives who had already got a start. For their first pictures to send back to wherever they came from, they were likely to want to be rigged out in cowboy or baseball suits or something like that, and possibly equipped with guns or fencing foils.

About six months later they were likely to go in for something more sentimental. They would sit on a big crescent moon bearing large signs such as WANT SOMEONE TO LOVE YOU? Mr. Snell even knew how to oblige with a picture taken so that a young man could seem to be pasting a soul-kiss to the lips of a gorgeous actress.

Homer said he had never realized how much trouble a man could have with the English language until he had got friendly with some of the greenhorns who came into Snell's. He had helped explain some puzzling things to them.

There was one smart young fellow, with an ambition to be a rich farmer, who wanted to know the meaning of the sign, POST NO BILLS. He thought it could mean that in this enlightened country no man might dun another by mail. Yet he thought it might also mean dollar bills or ten-dollar bills.

Then there was the young cousin of the Rahmis who couldn't understand the sign in the telegraph office at Kerriston, DON'T WRITE —TELEGRAPH. All he could get out of it was that there was something wrong with the word "telegraph." Maybe the company preferred "telegram," but it seemed senseless to spend so much effort to correct a word.

Aunt Jen brought in a plate of cookies and Uncle Simon passed around elderberry-blossom wine. This caused Homer and Dellie to do a lot of joking which sounded as if what they were about to drink was a powerful intoxicant. Homer offered her a glass with exaggerated politeness, saying, "Would you care to take your drink garbled, or do you just make it a habit to swill it down straight?"

Dellie said he shouldn't behave like that, not in the merry holiday tide. Then Dellie said that Homer ought to play or sing something, even if he didn't have the rest of his quartet with him. This was a "string quartet" composed of four young men who played at many functions. Two played potato-bug mandolins and the others played guitars. Homer said he didn't like to try alone, but if they would all sing loud enough to drown him out he would try something like "Over the Waves." He had brought his guitar along, although he said it didn't sound like much alone.

After three or four numbers, which were chiefly duets by the visitors, they insisted on everybody's really joining in for "In the Shade of the Old Apple Tree." Clyde and Homer got to letting themselves out, booming and dragging the words toward the end of each verse. When they found that this made Dellie and even Barbara giggle, they also threw in some unexpected high and low notes near the end of the refrain.

Merry Christmas

About ten o'clock it seemed to be time for the flashlight pictures. Lemuel was surprised to hear that these were to be taken upstairs in the spare bedroom, which was the only place large enough to be suitable, or something.

They trooped up into the upstairs hall and then Aunt Jen flung open the door to the great spare bedroom.

"My goodness, gracious, gumption, Annabelle!" said Homer Henty. The others all cried out.

Though no lamp was lit in the room, it was gleaming brilliantly from candlelights on a great Christmas tree in one far corner, while in the opposite one the rectangle-shaped box stove shone with the coals with which it had been secretly fired until everything glowed with warmth.

For some reason the room seemed even more festive than the places where such events are customarily held. Perhaps the great four-poster bed, covered with its bright pink, lavender and white Wedding Ring quilt, and the gaudy rag rug with a Saint Bernard woven in the center (surrounded by a wreath of red roses) had something to do with the Christmasy look. The room was also festooned with brightly colored paper chains linking the tops of the ancestral pictures.

The tree was not decorated like any that Lemuel had ever seen. It had candles and popcorn and cranberry strands and gilded walnuts, but it had some stranger ornaments. The most surprising were the red-beet slices which hung on separate strings like precious tokens. He learned that this was one of the customs that had come from Switzerland with Grandpa and Grandma Nadeli, and that the beet slices would last very well for several days. There were also many fancy cookies, in shapes of everything from angels to camels. On a close inspection Lemuel saw that, though it was the prettiest tree he had ever beheld, it did not have a single store-bought trimming. At first people stood and stared, crowding at the door, until Uncle Simon had to remind them that Christmas trees don't bite. Then three huge lamps were lit and the presents were passed out.

Lemuel couldn't remember nearly all of the gifts, but he noticed that there were certain things which it was pretty much of a custom to give. From various absent female cousins and aunts to Aunt Jen and Barbara there were hand-painted dishes or handkerchiefs or corset covers. Younger people, too, seemed to give each other presents of dishes.

The dishes were usually hand-painted by the donor and might be decorated with yellow roses or enormous blackberries. The corset covers were pretty sure to have wide pink silk ribbon strung through them. Homer joked about trying one of these on, but Dellie got it away from him before he could carry out the threat.

When Aunt Jen got her present from Barbara, she looked a little tearful. It was a white hand-crocheted nightgown yoke with the word MOTHER in great solid white letters. She was also given a gold watch with a butterfly-shaped pin from Uncle Simon. Barbara received a beautiful tall glass pitcher from Clyde, and her mother had added twelve tall, heavy tumblers to match it.

Last Homer Henty took the flashlight pictures.

At first it was hard work to get started on picture taking because everybody made remarks to undo each other's composure. Homer begged them to remember to keep their eyes wide open while the flash lasted.

For one picture he stood Clyde and Lemuel up together in front of the tree and finally got everybody so quiet that the boys felt pretty serious. In the picture that resulted they both had terribly solemn, bug-eyed expressions. As Uncle Simon expressed it, "Those boys sure stared terrible for Homer Henty's pictures."

On some of the pictures it was noted with interest later that the hour on the clock was just eleven. As such a late hour was synonymous with midnight in their minds, it became their habit, whenever they spoke of those pictures, to refer to them as the Midnight Pictures.

Grandpa Nadeli woke on Christmas morning while it was still dark. Ever since a few weeks after the stroke had paralyzed his right side, he always thought when he first woke that he was a boy.

It seemed to him that his father had called him twice, and that if he didn't hurry his father would be coming in with a whip. So he always woke scrabbling at the covers, only his right hand wouldn't scrabble. It was the realization that only the ghost of his right hand was moving that reminded Grandpa Nadeli that he was an old man.

The realization came on Christmas morning without any sting or sorrow.

"Ach, ja," Grandpa Nadeli murmured to himself. "I am an old man. Half awake and half asleep, I thought I had a whipping to take and work to do that I hated.

"But I am safe from any man's blows, and there is no more work for me. If only for peace and ease, it is good to be an old man."

Faint light in the eastern sky made a silhouette of the wreath at the window, and he remembered that it was Christmas. A warm happiness flowed into his soul as he thought of this. It reminded him that he was a patriarch; the head of a family. He thought of the strong, stalwart comely men he had begotten and the fine women they had married; he thought of his grandchildren.

He thought of the son who had not turned out so well; the willful, errant boy who had married a woman of no account to spite his father, and had suffered the miseries of her company. Even Ben, he reflected, would be welcome today, and it might be that if he came, this would be the day on which they two could learn to see into each other's hearts, and heal what was amiss there.

He thought of his own youth; of the spring days when he went, with the goats and cows, up the mountain for the long stay; of his mother leaning over a kettle in the fireplace (a picture he often remembered); of his army years, when he swaggered and drank and fought; of his courtship (mostly he remembered a hillside deep in daisies and a girl in her Old World holiday dress).

He thought of the terror-stricken weeks of the sea voyage which brought him to the New World and of the lean years that came after that. Tears rolled down his cheeks as he thought of the day he loaded his weeping children into the wagon and drove away from the farm (but it was Simon's farm now) which the sheriff had taken from him.

But these thoughts were brief, as his ill fortune was brief in the stretch of his life.

Contentment made Grandpa Nadeli stretch his good leg and his good arm. Cool, the sheets refreshed them. He groaned with the pleasure of that pain. Today he would sit at the head of a table where two generations sprung from himself ate of an abundance in which he had an interest. Gently, he began to sing a peaceful, beautiful song.

Grandma Nadeli, coming in from her chores with Schelm, heard his voice: "*Stille Nacht, heilige Nacht . . .*"

She stood quite still a moment in the middle of the kitchen floor, joining in the song.

About nine o'clock Grandpa and Grandma Nadeli drove in at Ora's in a cutter, covered with a black bearhide. Old Schelm was very lively. Grandma Nadeli thought it was because of the cold and the winter resting. But Grandpa Nadeli said he thought it was because of the bells that jingled on the thills.

"He thinks he is young," Grandpa said. "If I had bells ringing beside my legs, maybe I could dance."

Because of the snow Ora carried Grandpa into the house. Grandma stomped through the drifts, and spent a great deal of time on the back porch shaking the snow out of her numerous skirts. She wiped her boots on the broom. Uncle Simon's, who had kept Lemuel overnight, arrived just as she finished.

It was very gay inside. For Lemuel it was really the second half of a double Christmas. The first thing he noticed was how greatly the sitting room had been transformed since just the night before. Even the kitchen was in a decorated state.

The dainty tree was set up, and underneath it there was a tiny, elaborate farmyard that had been carved in Switzerland by Grandma's brother, the one called Uncle Geometer because of his profession. The tree was heavily covered with gauds, including a whole regiment of little toy Santa Clauses.

Lemuel was immediately invited out to peer at the browning

ducks, stuffed with sauerkraut and knoepfle, and the wide dish of escalloped oysters.

When Uncle Valentine's arrived it was decided that they should open all the Christmas presents which were still to be exchanged.

First were brought out the black alpaca dress goods, from Simon's, for Grandma Nadeli, and the dark gray suit for Grandpa Nadeli from Simon's and Valentine's. He said that now he would be fine enough to run for county recorder. His what-whats and *ei-jahs* made the gift seem like an incredible goodness of Providence.

Grandma Nadeli handed to Clyde and Barbara and Lemuel the gift which she was presenting to all her grandchildren. These were quaintly bound little German Testaments.

Lemuel was amazed when Clyde began reading aloud in his Testament. His voice went up and down in deep tones, a little like Grandpa Nadeli's grace-saying voice, which still reminded the older members of the family of his pulpit days. Aunt Jen told Lemuel that Clyde's ability probably didn't indicate any natural smartness because he had had to learn the Swiss-German dialect of the Nadelis when he was younger. Uncle Simon's had refused to answer their children if addressed in English, and Uncle Simon spoke to them only in Swiss, while Aunt Jen spoke only in the Pennsylvania Dutch of her people. Both the children "took the Swiss." They had to pick up their knowledge of English from hearing their parents speak to each other.

"Isn't Pennsylvania Dutch more like English than Swiss is?" asked Lemuel. Well, yes, it was closer to English, Aunt Jen admitted, but there was something about the soft Swiss dialect that was easier to catch on to.

Besides the mufflers and socks and more dishes and hankies and corset covers, and some long Amish-style aprons from Grandma Nadeli, there was a shiny new phonograph from Ora to Barbara. It did not have disks but flat records. Uncle Val had brought a new and sparkling candy jar for Grandpa Nadeli; and Ora's presented the old man with a beautiful new edition of Tolstoy's works. This made him so emotional that everybody else felt pretty much the same way. Most exciting to Lemuel were the tubular skates which Uncle Valentine's had brought for Clyde and him.

When Lemuel said, "Gee whiz, Uncle Valentine, you shouldn't give me such a wonderful pair of skates," his uncle snorted.

He said: "Oh, that's all right, boys. Of course I kind of hated to have to mortgage the farm, but still I'd do it for nephews of mine. No, I got too much pride to see a nephew of mine do without."

Murdie had taken the things out of the oven, and Aunt Jen and Barbara were fussing with other items of the coming feast.

"Yes," drawled Uncle Valentine, "I doubt anybody's eating higher this Christmas season than the Nadelis, unless maybe it was Dave Gunder."

"Why, I heard they arrested Dave for stealing a calf," Ora said.

"That's just the point," Uncle Val said. "It wasn't just any old calf he stole. I run into the sheriff last night and he told me all about it.

"When he was taking Dave into Kerriston," Uncle Val went on, "the sheriff told him that it was for stealing Lambright's prize calf and he said he guessed Dave had taken Amos Yingling's harness, too. Dave didn't deny it.

"So the sheriff asked him about the calf. 'Dave,' he said, 'what in the world did you do with Old Lambright's calf?'

" 'If you want to know,' Dave said, 'I vealed it and ate it.'

" 'My gravy!' the sheriff said. 'What in Sam Hill would you go to do a thing like that for?'

" 'Well,' Dave told him, 'I wanted to know what three-thousand-dollar veal tasted like.' "

Barbara had laid the table, now lengthened by the introduction of all its leaves, with the very blue dishes, from Ora's family, which had come to them at their marriage and were only for ceremonial occasions.

When they sat down to dinner Grandpa Nadeli took off his looking spectacles and put on the reading spectacles. He opened the dark book from the top of the organ and read:

"Go thy way, eat thy bread with joy, and drink thy wine with a merry heart.

"Let thy garments be always white; and let thy head lack no ointment.

"Live joyfully.

"Whatsoever thy hand findeth to do, do it with thy might; for there is no work, nor device, nor knowledge, nor wisdom in the grave, whither thou goest."

This reminder of death did not dismay them. It was like a curtain hung at the window to make the festive lamps glow brighter.

Grandpa Nadeli laid down the book and gave thanks.

He offered thanks for the joy it was to an old man to have his family at the table with him. Suddenly, in the midst of that, tears began to run down his face. He choked in the middle of a sentence, and after swallowing a few times, he said "Amen."

The rest all looked at each other with pitying and loving expressions.

From the oven Barbara and Murdie brought the duck and the two roast chickens. There were escalloped oysters, and cranberries and dried corn, and the side table was laden with salads—including a magnificent fruit salad with sections of apples and bananas and oranges and marshmallows—and all manner of cakes and pies, pumpkin, mince and Grandma Nadeli's famed onion custard.

Ora picked up the carving knife and looked at the duck. There was a knock at the door, and Clyde rose to answer it. In a moment he came back.

"It's a tramp," he said.

"Tell him to come in," Ora said. At the same time, Grandpa Nadeli was saying, "Let him in, for he may be Jesus."

The tramp was a tall, gaunt man with deep eyes. He came in with his hat in his hand. In a voice thick with gutturals of another language he said, "God's blessing on you."

He washed his hands at the sink in the corner of the kitchen, and sat down at the place that was made for him between Clyde and Uncle Valentine. Uncle Valentine told him the names of all who were there. The wanderer said his name was Peterson.

"I am a sailor," he said, "but I was trying to get to my sister's home for Christmas. It takes me longer to go by land than I had thought."

He was very grave and silent, but after a while the rest became merry and noisy. To show that he approved of this, the man named Peterson smiled solemnly now and then, and nodded encouragingly to someone who had shouted a witticism.

When the meal was over, and they pushed back their chairs from the table and drank warm spiced wine, Peterson went to the wood-box and chose a sleek, round piece of greenish limb. With a gigantic knife he took from his pocket, he began to carve. Lemuel and Clyde went and watched him. He stood by the woodbox, being care-ful that the chips should fall into it. When one fell on the floor he immediately picked it up.

He carved a picture of Grandpa Nadeli, as accurate as a photo-graph. Everyone exclaimed over it. It became a family treasure.

BILL ADAMS

God Rest You, Merry Gentlemen

I

THE carrier's cart was drawn by two very slow old white horses. Only now and again, where the road was not too slippery with ice, did the carrier urge them to a heavy trot. There was a stout canvas cover over the cart, in which, besides myself, were five old village women. Young women walked to and from town on market day, saving tuppence each way. The carrier, who'd been paid tuppence to bring me from the little market town three miles away, whither I'd come by train, set me down where Bowers lane leaves the highroad at the edge of Peterstow village. I'd my clothes in a brown paper parcel. I'd been traveling since nine in the morning, and had come about a hundred miles.

It was very cold. There was snow on the ground. I had mittens on my hands, and a thick muffler round my neck. The tip of my nose felt frozen, and so did my feet. The old women each side of me helped keep me warm while I was in the carrier's cart; but when I was put down I set my parcel on the snow, stamped my feet, and beat my hands on my sides before starting down Bowers lane.

It was maybe three-quarters of a mile from the highroad to Bowers. The lane was steep, narrow, and full of curves. It had high banks on the top of which were tall leafless hawthorn hedges. The oaks and elms that stood here and there in the hedgerows were leafless too. Everything was bleak and bare and cold, except for the holly trees, which were covered with bright red berries.

Because I stopped to make snowballs, and to slide where there was smooth ice in the wheel ruts, it took a long time to reach Bowers farm. My paper parcel burst open, and I had to stop to tie it up. I didn't tie it very well, and it kept bursting open. By the time I came to Bowers a pair of my stockings, my toothbrush, and some handkerchiefs were missing. Garge Gwilliam found them, and brought them to Bowers next day. But this has little to do with what I'm writing about. I'm grown-up now, and have a good deal of gray in my hair and a great many wrinkles. My socks, toothbrush and handkerchiefs are in their right places. Yet it was on this same pair of feet that I first went to Bowers, and with this same heart pulsing. I'm still me.

It's Christmas night, and Bowers farm is very far away in that quiet valley through which the little silvery river flows westward to the wide Atlantic. Very long ago it is; yet also it is very near, and only yesterday. Things do not change unless you let them—not the things that count, the lovely things. The stars are bright tonight, and all is still, save for the echo of an echo on the silent air.

My wife and our two daughters—Apple Dumpling, aged thirteen, and Honey Bee, aged six—are in bed and asleep. Ellison, our grown son, and Helen, his wife, are gone home an hour or more ago. It is late. The floor is strewn with toys. I have just turned out the lights upon the Christmas tree—electric lights of many colors which one turns on and off by one switch. Artificial icicles that are quite safe hang from the tree, which is covered with artificial snow that is quite safe. When the lights are turned on, ice and snow glimmer and gleam. The sole gleam now is from a big red candle that stands in the window, its light shining out into the darkness of the night. By the gleam of the big red candle I am writing this.

I had not thought of Bowers farm for many years till yesterday, when we were all trimming the Christmas tree and hanging our stockings in a row along the wide mantel above the sunken open fireplace.

II

I⊤ was getting dark when at last I came to the door of Bowers farmhouse. As I approached it, I heard shouting and laughter. When it opened at my rap, a wave of warm air streamed out, as though to cheer all the cold world outside. It was the night before Christmas Eve, and what happened that night from the time the door opened I have no memory of. But the two following nights I can see very plainly, and can hear very plainly their sounds.

Bowers farm was owned and managed by a widow with four young daughters and a son of my own age. An old Welsh servant named Mary Llewelyn lived in the house, and two nephews and a niece of the widow were visiting. On Christmas Eve, John Thomas the wagoner, who lived in a cottage across the lane from the farmhouse, came with his wife and their fourteen children. Bill Weevin the shepherd, and the girl he was going to marry in the spring, came too, and Jack Evans the cowman, who was going with Thomas' eldest girl Annie. Last came old Garge Gwilliam, the gardener, with his old deaf wife and their grown half-witted daughter Jane. Everyone gathered in the stone-floored kitchen, from the whitewashed ceiling of which hung sides of bacon, and hams, and great bunches of herbs. There was a huge plum cake on the table, and there were loaves of fresh bread, with cheese, and ale and cider. For Mrs. Thomas, because she was nursing a baby, there was stout.

For the children there were pitchers of milk. Mistletoe hung from the oaken beams of the ceiling. There were red-berried holly wreaths on the whitewashed walls, and in the windows.

We played "Here we go gathering nuts in May," and "London bridge is falling down," and "Oranges and lemons said the bells of St. Clemens." Everyone but Garge Gwilliam's old deaf wife, and their grown half-witted daughter Jane, danced the quadrille, the lancers and the Sir Roger de Coverley, to the tune of old Garge's fiddle. The kitchen was lighted by one big bright oil lamp and several cow-horn lanterns. In the large window was a big thick candle burning to show the Christ child the way to Bowers farm.

While we were dancing the Sir Roger de Coverley there was a rap on the door. Mary Llewelyn opened to the bell ringers. They came in, sat just within the door, and rang their bells. Then they ate bread and cheese and drank ale, and went on to the next farm: Weir End, a mile away through the snow.

The bell ringers were but a little while gone when we heard voices without. Mary opened the door and there, in the snow, one of them carrying a cow-horn lantern, were six village children, necks muffled up, woolly caps drawn down on their foreheads, snow thick upon their ragged clothes. They sang "O come, all ye faithful," and "Hark! the herald angels," and about "peace on earth and mercy mild." And when they had sung:

> *The roads are very dirty,*
> *My shoes are very thin,*
> *I've got a little pocket*
> *To put a penny in . . .*

they were brought into the warm kitchen, and ate plum cake and drank milk and were given pennies by the widow. Then they went on their way to Weir End farm, and were gone but a little while when more carol singers came. Lads and lasses of round eighteen and twenty, they too sang, "O come, all ye faithful" and "Hark! the herald angels," and about "peace on earth and mercy mild," singing with strong voices in which was lightheartedness, and a note as of challenge. With flushed faces and sparkling eyes, they came jesting into the warm kitchen and ate bread and cheese and plum cake. Lifting mugs of ale and of cider, they drank to the health and the happiness of the widow and all our company, and went merrily off into the snow on their way to Weir End.

And not long had they been gone when again we heard voices and, opening the great oaken door, looked out upon a company of men and women of and beyond middle age. First they sang "O come, all ye faithful," and then one carol after another, singing as though for the joy and delight of it, all unconscious of the snow and the cold. Not till they had been bidden several times did they enter the snug kitchen, and eat and drink. In their wrinkled faces and steady eyes was a strong and a merry contentment. Yet also they resembled in a manner children, because of the frankness of their countenances. When, lifting their mugs, they wished us happiness —why, then it seemed that happiness must of a certainty be, so honest, so stolidly determined, were the tones of their friendly voices.

These, when they went, left behind them a great sense of peace in Bowers kitchen, yet also a something of regret, a sort of rue, because they had not stayed longer. But that sense of regret swiftly ceased; for of a sudden we heard their upraised voices again, and opened the great oak door and looked out after them. They had stopped at the end of the driveway, and stood in a ring in the snow singing "God rest you, merry gentlemen, Let nothing you dismay," singing for their own joy, with the light of the cow-horn lantern shining in their smiling faces.

A little after the last carol singers were gone the widow took down a lantern from its hook, wrapped a shawl about her head and shoulders, and went forth from the snug kitchen into the thickly falling snow. John Thomas, Bill Weevin, Jack Evans, and old Garge Gwilliam each took a horn lantern and followed. Her son and her daughters, her niece and her nephew; John Thomas' wife, carrying at her breast her last infant; the girl Bill Weevin was going to marry in the spring; old Garge Gwilliam's old deaf wife and their grown half-witted daughter Jane, and all the children, went out from the snug kitchen into the thickly falling snow, with Bill Weevin's two sheep dogs following after them. Last from the kitchen, old Mary Llewelyn shut the great oak door, then, holding tight to my hand, followed after Bill Weevin's dogs.

Down the long drive we walked, the light of the lanterns shining on the snow laurels, lilacs and red-berried holly trees that bordered it. Through the old iron gate we went, and across the lane, and through the high five-barred gate opposite, into the great fold upon which opened the stables and cow houses and sheep pens.

There was a jingle of halter chains, and a shifting of hoofs, as we entered the stable. Boxer and Dobbin, Prince and old Tom, Taffy and Merlin, looked round at us from questioning eyes.

"There be good 'ay in h'every manger, missis," said John Thomas.

"That's right, John," replied the widow, and, having handed to him her lantern, went to one after another of her horses and laid her hand upon it gently, speaking a few soft words.

From the stable we passed to the cow house, where Molly and Creamcup, Hilda and Bess, lying soft in deep straw, looked up at us with big round eyes. Beyond the milch cows the long row of great red oxen with white faces gazed at us from warm straw-strewn stalls.

"Good dry beddin' an' a manger full for each on 'em, missis," said Jack Evans.

"That's as it should be, Jack," replied the widow, and, having spoken a few low words to her milch cows, passed slowly down the long narrow passage in front of the white faces of the great red oxen that gazed at her placidly.

We looked into the pen folds where lay the quiet sheep, and into the small pen where by himself the horned ram dwelt. Silent, they gazed at us, expectant-eyed. The night was far advanced when we went from the fold through the big five-barred gate back to the lane. Sleepily holding to old Mary's hand, I heard Jack Evans say, "Midnight be a-comin', John!"

"Aye, Jack, lad! Soon they'uns'll be a-talkin' same as you an' me," replied John Thomas.

646

"Mary, who'll be talking?" I asked.

"The be-asts," replied old Mary Llewelyn.

"But, Mary, animals can't talk!" I argued.

"It be Christmas Eve, little lad," she answered me.

And then John Thomas and Jack Evans and Bill Weevin, old Garge and the women and sleepy children, were calling "Good night" and "Merry Christmas," and disappearing toward their cottages through the thickly falling snow.

We came back to the warm kitchen. The widow put out her lantern. Mary lighted tallow candles and handed them round for us to go to bed by. With the bright oil lamp extinguished, and our candles in our hands, we went from the kitchen into the hallway. Only the tortoise-shell cat was left in the kitchen, curled in her box by the stove. On the window sill the big candle still burned clear and steady, gleaming out into the snow, to show the Christ child the way to Bowers farm.

On our way to bed we were allowed to peep into the drawing room, in which, all along the wide mantel, hung a row of empty stockings high above the bright fire.

"Mary, how can Santa Claus come with a fire burning?" I fearfully asked.

"Doant 'ee be a-frettin', little lad! Just 'ee wait!" replied old Mary.

III

ALL I know of the rest of that night is that Santa came. I didn't see him, but my stocking was full next morning—as were those of all the other children. There was no question about his having been, for in those days there was no cynical child. In those days when you heard the carol singers' "O come, all ye faithful," that "ye" meant yourself. Without question you accepted the invitation. If ever a child wondered why the Christ child did not see the candle in the window and come to Bowers farm, the explanation was simple. We didn't fret about His coming. We waited. There were so many other farms for Him to go to. In time He'd come!

We opened our stockings in the drawing room, where was also the Christmas tree. The Christmas tree was covered with tiny wax candles of many colors, and every candle had to be lighted with a match. On the branches of the tree, to represent snow, was cotton wool. In those days a Christmas tree was not alone a thing of beauty and of joy. It was a thing of danger, too—a thing for small children not to come too close to.

Though we scattered paper and string everywhere, the widow didn't mind at all. The drawing room was a very special room, used only on very special occasions, such as weddings and funerals, and when the rector came to call, and at Christmas. On one wall was a photograph of the widow as a bride, and her husband. They had been married in the drawing room, and he had been buried from it. On the opposite wall hung the widow's "marriage lines" in a gilt frame. On another wall was a picture of Queen Victoria and the Prince Consort; and opposite them, on the remaining wall, one of a champion cow and bull together. The chairs and sofas were covered with antimacassars.

The widow always swept and dusted the drawing room herself, and no one else was permitted to enter it on ordinary days. But today we were allowed to play in it as though it were just like any other room. The widow, busy helping old Mary in the kitchen, came to look in on us now and then. Once when I chanced to look up I saw old Mary in the door watching us. There were tears in her eyes. I jumped up, ran to her, pulled her under the mistletoe that hung from the chandelier in the center of the ceiling, drew her head down, and kissed her withered cheek. "Oh, God bless 'ee, little lad!" she cried.

Old Mary was alone in the world. She had been engaged for twenty-two years before she married David Llewelyn, who was killed by a white-faced bull one evening eight months later while he was taking a short cut through a meadow, being in a hurry to get home because Mary wasn't very well. Her son, who was born a month later, grew up to take the Queen's shilling on market day, and was killed a little while afterward at Tell el-Kebir, in the Sudan.

God Rest You, Merry Gentlemen

I don't recall anything else very definitely of that day till evening. I see wrapping paper and string, toys and books and sweets, all over the house. I see turkey and goose, turnips and carrots, parsnips and baked potatoes, onions and cabbage and pickles; shiny apples, red, yellow, and green; big juicy deep-green winter pears; walnuts, hazelnuts, cobnuts, and filberts; and, from lands beyond the sea, oranges, figs, dates, raisins, prunes, coconuts, tangerines wrapped in tinfoil, and almonds and Brazil nuts. There was a sprig of red-berried holly stuck in the top of the Christmas pudding. The widow poured brandy over the pudding, set fire to it, cut it up, and passed it round while it was blazing. There was a dish of blazing snapdragon, too. I see it all in a sort of happy haze, and hear a continuous murmur of talk, with laughter rising and falling, young feet running to and fro, and young and old faces shining.

And I see old Mary come to the drawing room from the kitchen, where she has just finished washing the dishes. She says something in a low voice to the widow, who replies, "You stay here now, Mary. I'll go see to him."

The widow went to the kitchen. I followed, curious.

He stood with his back to the great oak door, his battered hat in his thin fingers. Bare knees showed through holes in his ragged trousers. A jacket with frayed sleeves and holes at the elbows, its collar missing, hung loosely from his sharp shoulders. His face was pale. He was shivering, at his feet a little pool of water from the snow that had melted and run from him.

The widow set a plate heaped with food on the table, and bade him sit down to it. About it she set other plates, with fruits and pudding and nuts, and a tankard of ale. Then, without having noticed me, she went back to the drawing room.

He didn't seem able to eat. He nibbled a bite of this and of that. The tortoise-shell cat leaped to a chair beside him and regarded him solemnly. He reached out a hand and stroked her soft warm fur. Having eaten scarce anything, he leaned wearily back in his chair. The oil lamp went out. Mary must have forgotten to fill it that morning. The only light in the kitchen was that of the big candle burning in the window to show the Christ child the way to Bowers farm. He gazed at it, his eyes full of longing. There wasn't a sound. By the light of the candle I could see beyond the windowpane the big flakes falling. He rose, picked his hat up from the floor, and looked uncertainly about the dimly lighted kitchen. Something told me that he wanted to say "Thank you" before he went away.

I was just starting to the drawing room to call the widow when he became aware of my presence. Without a word, reading my mind, he shook his head. Had he said aloud, "Don't disturb anyone any more on my account," his meaning could have been no plainer. Next moment he was gone through the great oak door out to the cold snowy night. Left alone in the dim kitchen, I was suddenly very frightened. Of just what I was afraid I could not have said. Old Mary Llewelyn appeared, closing the kitchen door behind her, shutting away the sounds of merriment in the drawing room. Unaware of me, she sat down in the just-vacated chair, longing eyes fixed upon the big red candle that burned on the window sill, her aspect one of utter loneliness. I ran to her and buried my face upon her flat breast.

"Doant 'ee be a-frettin', little lad! Yonder's the candle burnin'. Just 'ee wait!" said old Mary, stroking my head.

IV

Now, as I say, Bowers farm had been forgotten till yesterday, when my wife, Apple Dumpling, Honey Bee, Helen and Ellison, and I were trimming the Christmas tree and hanging our stockings along the wide mantel above the sunken fireplace, in which a bright fire burned.

I paused and looked from a window out to the starry dark. Faintly I could hear the murmur of the creek that, a short distance away, flows westward to the wide Pacific. Dim in the starshine I could see the trees that border our drive, the branches of the great oak that spread over our roof. On a hill a little to the north of the drive's end an air-mail beacon flashed alternate red and white rays across the sky. From high above our roof came the drone of a passenger plane. Round a curve in the paved highway that passes between the drive's end and the beacon hill came the lights of a transcontinental auto stage. It was at that instant that Honey Bee spoke.

"Daddy, how can Santa Claus come down the chimney with a fire burning?" asked Honey Bee. And spark touched spark. Memory's embers were fanned to flame, and I heard old Mary Llewelyn answering that same question asked by me so long ago when I was Honey Bee's age. And I wondered if in stage or plane was some small boy on his way to spend Christmas many hundreds of miles, perhaps a thousand miles, away. "How different it all is to when I was a child," I thought.

On our little farm, so little that it scarce can be called a farm, is neither wagoner, cowman, shepherd, gardener nor serving woman. It is but a few months since we moved here from the city, twenty miles away, where live many friends. Distance precludes neighborliness. Now, on Christmas Eve, no one would be dropping in upon us to wish us good cheer and to share for a space the warmth of our hearth. A sort of sadness came over me, a longing. There was too much haste, too much noise, in this modern world where all was so changed.

The trimming of our tree was finished. The stockings were hung in a row on the mantel. The many-colored lights on the tree twinkled and gleamed, the fire blazed bright, and in a window, on the window sill, a big red candle burned, as long ago a big red candle had burned at Bowers farm.

I took a powerful flashlight, opened the French door, and stepped out to the starry dark, my wife at my side, the children old and young following, and the two little terriers that keep the rats from our outbuildings and the gophers from our two acres following them. Under the branches of the great oak we went, past the pomegranate, oleander, deodar and redwood trees; beneath the sky in which, now far away, the lights of the passenger plane still winked, along which the beacon sent its constant ray, under which, along the paved highway, countless hurrying cars sped.

There was the jingle of a halter chain, and a shifting of hoofs, as we looked into the little barn where Moby the saddle horse, and Molly the cow, and Honey Bee's pet lamb, lay bedded in deep dry straw. They looked at us expectant-eyed. Honey Bee wanted to stay, to hear them talk. "They'd not talk with people about," I assured her. We looked in at my wife's turkeys, geese, chickens, ducks and pigeons. There was a rustle of feathers, and a low cooing from the gloom. When we went back to the porch Dumpling suggested that, since the night was not cold, we might leave the door open, and so overhear the beasts talking. When I negatived that, she said that she didn't believe animals talked on Christmas Eve, and asked if I had ever heard them.

"If I'd been near enough to overhear, they'd not have talked," I told her.

When the others went in, she lingered on the porch. I stayed with her. The ridges of the near hills were distinct in the starshine. The canyons were black gashes. In them, when spring came, the buckeye would flower, the madroña, and the wild mountain lilac. On hill and in canyon, in place of the red-berried holly of Bowers lane, were the no less bright red berries of the toyon. To match the memories of my boyhood, there was beauty for beauty. Home was very sweet. And yet upon me there was still that longing.

"Ah, if only the carol singers would come! If I could just hear carol singers again!" thought I, and thought also, "There was neighborliness in the lanes in the old days."

Dumpling went in. I followed. We all sat on the step of the sunken fireplace, with the firelight in our faces; behind us the lights of the tree, on each wall wreaths of red-berried toyon and of evergreen, and in the window, burning with a clear unwavering flame, the big red candle to show the Christ child the way to Oakcroft farm.

We had but sat down when there was a step on our porch. Our little lane is a blind lane. Sometimes someone from the paved highway near by mistakenly takes it and comes to ask directions. This would be someone from the hurrying mob. I rose and opened the door.

" 'Appee Kreesmas!" cried Tony Giammona. " 'Appy Kreesmas!"

cried Mrs. Giammona. "Happy Christmas!" came a chorus from the eight Giammona children.

Tony and his wife are from Sicily; the children were born in America. Mrs. Giammona has done our washing a few times. Dumpling takes it, the eldest Giammona child brings it back. My wife and I had scarce set eyes on Mr. or Mrs. Giammona.

Tony was dressed in his best suit, from a mail-order house. He can't write English, but his eldest girl goes to high school and writes his orders for him. Mrs. Giammona was dressed in an old silk dress worn long ago in Palermo and used on only the most special occasions. The girls were all in brightly colored new silk dresses from the mail-order house. Very lovely they were, with their black shoe-button eyes and olive faces. The boys were in gay, green, new sweaters, and new trousers.

"Dees not hurt you, my vren! You dreenk whole bottle, eet not hurt you!" cried Tony Giammona, handing me a bottle of his home-made wine. "I breeng eet you for 'appee Kreesmas!"

"I make two doz' loafs today. Dey not last long, I tell you! I vants you try my bread, for 'appee Kreesmas!" cried Mrs. Giammona, handing my wife two big loaves fresh from her oven.

While the little Giammonas laughed and talked with Dumpling and Honey Bee, Tony and his wife sat down and gazed round the big room. "Dees verra nice 'ome," said Tony. Mrs. Giammona said, "You sure got nice 'ome, you folks!" Their dwelling has some windows missing, and is devoid of carpets; in places wallpaper hangs in shreds. Tony prunes fruit trees for a living, but for a long time has not been well enough to work. Mrs. Giammona takes in washing. They "make out."

"We 'ave to go. We got forty peoples come tomorrow," said Tony presently. He has five brothers, each married and with a family. "We wants you folks to come. We goin' to dance old countree dances!" he added.

"Sure, we wants you folks to come! We goin' to barbecue a goat. Maybe two, t'ree goats!" cried Mrs. Giammona. We might have been her own kin.

Having allowed Dumpling to accept the invitation, being unable to do so ourselves because of other plans, we promised to come next time the Giammonas had a party. We loaded the children with oranges and candy and saw them away. As they disappeared in the darkness, Tony's voice came back to us. "Dose ees nice peoples. I 'opes zey 'ave 'appee Kreesmas!"

So here again was beauty for beauty. In place of John Thomas' honest friendship, that of Tony Giammona.

V

"AH, if only the carol singers would come!" thought I. But that would not be. A memory of the tramp came to me. There was something very pleasant in the memory. The tramp had, in a sort of way, helped to make Christmas. There had been no need for him to go off as he did. He could have stayed the night, and have gone forth in the morning warm and dry. I remembered how the widow had made up for him a big bundle of her dead husband's clothes. But he had gone away out of pride, and an unwillingness to intrude his poverty. I wondered if, perhaps, some poor wanderer would come to our door tonight. But no one would come, of course. No longer were there any tramps. A thing called "relief," coming in many forms and under many subtitles, had destroyed pride and made willing beggars out of people. The tramp had not been a beggar. Had there been work for him, he'd have worked eagerly. Today no one who can avoid it works; save for such Old World people as the Giammonas, who, despite poverty, manage to "make out" and would utterly scorn "relief."

I sat down on the step of the sunken fireplace, where all the others save Dumpling were seated. Dumpling sat on the couch in the far corner. Close by her burned the big red candle. From above our roof came the noise of another plane. Flying low, it passed with a roar of motors. From the paved highway came the insistent honk of another transcontinental auto stage demanding the right of way.

I glanced toward Dumpling, and I shuddered. A thoroughgoing

radio fan, she knows all the programs, and the special time for each. Her finger was on the button. In a moment she would turn it, and flood the room with something about "gang busters," or "phantom pilots," or with jazz or buffoonery.

"Dumpling, it's time for bed!" I called.

"Let me stay a little while. There's something I like coming on," pleaded Dumpling. And what could I say? Could a man with gray hair have his child think him an old crab, upon Christmas Eve? What could my child know or understand of the longing that was in me? If all was changed since I was a child, that was none of her doing.

There was silence now, no sound from sky or highway. In silence I sat thinking, waiting with dread the noise that Dumpling all too soon would turn loose.

"The lights of a plane, seen amongst stars, are beautiful," I thought. And I thought too, "So is a plane beautiful when the sun shines on it." And the beacon on the hill, its constant ray was beautiful, I admitted. Even the modern carrier's cart, speeding along concrete roads and honking for the right of way, had its own peculiar beauty. I was willing to admit all that. It was admitted not without some effort, true; and not without a distinct feeling of magnanimity. And besides, one could always forget these things by going into one's house. In one's home, in the sanctity of one's rooftree, one could shut modernity away and be at rest. But as for this thing upon which Dumpling had her finger, this thing I loathed. There was no escape from it. It was the very essence of all that was banal in modernity. And now, beneath the roof of home, on Christmas Eve, with my heart hungry for rest and for beauty, I must submit to its blatant banality.

I bowed my head. With my eyes on those same feet on which, so long ago, I walked down Bowers lane, I thought of Bowers farm. I said to myself, "I'll just keep thinking of when I was a child at Bowers, and of the carol singers. If I just keep thinking, it will drown out the horror of modernity."

There was a faint click as Dumpling turned the button.

And then, in a moment, my wife and our grown son and his wife, and our two small daughters, were singing, their voices joining with the air-borne chorus of many singers far away—singing, all of them, as though for the joy and the delight of it.

"O come, all ye faithful," they sang, and "Hark! the herald angels," and of peace on earth. And last they sang:

> God rest you, merry gentlemen,
> Let nothing you dismay . . .
> For Jesus Christ, our Saviour,
> Was born on Christmas Day!

While they were singing that last carol there came again from above our rooftree the drone of a plane, and a transcontinental auto stage upon the paved highway honked for the right of way. With my eyes uplifted, I saw the beacon's ray across the sky. Upon our window sill the big red candle burned, with faithful flame unwavering. And of a sudden it was as though nothing were changed—as though all were as it had been so long ago at Bowers farm. Bowers farm and Oakcroft were become one. And I said to myself, "Things do not change unless you let them change—not the things that count, the lovely things."

R. A. HALL SCHOOL LIBRARY
Beeville, Texas

Acknowledgments

The editor wishes to express his gratitude to the following authors, their representatives, and the publishing houses indicated, for their courtesy in permitting him to reprint the following material:

"Even Unto Bethlehem," by Henry van Dyke: copyright 1927, 1928, by Charles Scribner's Sons; used by permission of the publishers.

"The Other Wise Man," by Henry van Dyke. Reprinted by permission of Harper and Brothers.

"The Man at the Gate of the World," by W. E. Cule. Reprinted by permission of Ralph T. Hale and Company.

"The Husband of Mary," by Elizabeth Hart. Copyright, 1935, by Elizabeth Hart. Reprinted by permission of the author.

"Strange Story of a Traveler to Bethlehem," from *I Beheld His Glory*, by John Evans (Willett, Clark and Company, Chicago, 1945). Reprinted by permission of the publishers.

"The Little Hunchback Zia," by Frances Hodgson Burnett. Reprinted by permission of Ann Watkins, Inc., agents for the Burnett Estate.

"The Second Christmas," by F. K. Foraandh. Reprinted from *Fellowship*, by permission of the author and the Fellowship of Reconciliation.

"How Come Christmas?" by Roark Bradford. Reprinted by permission of the author.

"The True Story of Santy Claus," by John Macy. Reprinted from *The Bookman*, by permission of the Estate of the late John Macy and Mr. Seward B. Collins, owner of The Bookman Company.

"When Father Christmas Was Young," by Coningsby Dawson. Reprinted by permission of the author.

"The Realm of Midnight," from *The Doctor's Christmas Eve*, by James Lane Allen. Reprinted by permission of The Macmillan Company, publishers.

657

ACKNOWLEDGMENTS

"A Marchpane for Christmas," by Katharine Lee Bates. Reprinted from the *Virginia Quarterly Review*, by permission of Mrs. George S. Burgess and the *Virginia Quarterly Review*.

"The First Christmas Tree:" copyright 1897 by Charles Scribner's Sons, 1925 by Henry van Dyke; used by permission of the publishers.

Santa Claus: A Psychograph," by Gamaliel Bradford. Reprinted from *The Bookman*, by permission of Mrs. Gamaliel Bradford and Mr. Seward B. Collins, owner of The Bookman Company.

"The Almond Tree," by Walter de la Mare. Reprinted by permission of Leland Hayward, Inc.

"The Prescription," from *The Last Bouquet*, by Marjorie Bowen. Reprinted by permission of Mrs. Arthur L. Long and John Lane The Bodley Head, Ltd.

"The White Road," by E. F. Bozman. Taken from *The Christmas Companion*, edited by John Hadfield, published and copyrighted by E. P. Dutton and Company, Inc., New York. Reprinted by permission of E. P. Dutton and Co., Inc., and J. M. Dent and Sons, Ltd.

"Oh, What a Horrid Tale!" by P. S. Taken from *The Christmas Companion*, edited by John Hadfield, published and copyrighted by E. P. Dutton and Company, Inc., New York. Reprinted by permission of E. P. Dutton and Co., Inc., and J. M. Dent and Sons, Ltd.

"A Christmas Gift," by T. F. Powys, from *An Anthology of Christmas Prose and Verse*, edited by D. L. Kelleher. Reprinted by permission of The Cresset Press Limited.

"Happy Christmas," by Daphne du Maurier. Copyright, 1940, by Daphne du Maurier Browning. Reprinted by permission of the author.

"The Mysterious Chest," by Howard Pyle. Reprinted from *Harper's Magazine*, by permission of the children of Howard Pyle: Mrs. Roberts W. Brokaw, Mrs. Willard G. Crichton, Wilfrid Pyle, Howard Pyle, Theodore Pyle and Godfrey Pyle.

"My First Christmas Tree," by Hamlin Garland. Reprinted by permission of Isabelle Garland Lord and Constance Garland Doyle, and by special permission from *The Ladies' Home Journal*. Copyright, 1911, The Curtis Publishing Company.

ACKNOWLEDGMENTS

"To Springvale for Christmas," by Zona Gale. Reprinted by permission of William Ll. Breese.

"I Gotta Idee!" from *Stories to Read at Christmas*, by Elsie Singmaster. Reprinted by permission of the author.

"Christmas in Our Town," by Alice Van Leer Carrick. From *An Old Fashioned Christmas*, by Reginald T. Townsend, copyright, 1902, 1905, 1906, 1912, 1919, 1925, 1926, 1927, by Doubleday, Doran and Company, Inc. Reprinted by permission of the author and the publishers.

"A Plantation Christmas," by Archibald Rutledge. From *An Old Fashioned Christmas*, by Reginald T. Townsend, copyright, 1902, 1905, 1906, 1912, 1919, 1925, 1926, 1927, by Doubleday, Doran and Company, Inc. Reprinted by permission of the author and the publishers.

"Snow for Christmas," by Vincent Starrett. Reprinted by permission of the author.

"One Christmas Eve," reprinted from *The Ways of White Folks*, by Langston Hughes, by permission of Alfred A. Knopf, Inc. Copyright, 1934, by Alfred A. Knopf, Inc.

"The Pasteboard Star," by Margaret Carpenter. Reprinted by permission of Ann Watkins, Inc.

"The Little Guest," by Margery Williams Bianco. Reprinted by permission of Francesco Bianco.

"The Worst Christmas Story," from *Letters of Askance*, by Christopher Morley. Copyright, 1939, by Christopher Morley, published by J. B. Lippincott Company. Reprinted by permission of the publishers.

"Merry Christmas," from *The Big Snow*, by Jake Falstaff. Reprinted by permission of Houghton Mifflin Company.

"God Rest You, Merry Gentlemen," by Bill Adams. Reprinted from *The Atlantic Monthly*, by permission of the author.

The quotation from *This Way to Christmas*, by Ruth Sawyer, is reproduced by permission of Harper and Brothers.

The quotation from *The Man Who Found Christmas*, by Walter Prichard Eaton, is reproduced by permission of Robert M. McBride Company and W. A. Wilde Company.

R. A. HALL SCHOOL LIBRARY
Beeville, Texas